Jam

ICE

U700

CHURCHILL'S GOLD

This edition published by Arrow in 2004
an imprint of The Random Group,
20 Vauxhall Bridge Road, London SW1V 2SA

Papers used by Random House UK Ltd are natural recyclable products made from wood grown in sustainable forests. The manufacturing processes conform to the environmental regulations of the country of origin.

A catalogue record for this book is available from the British Library

Printed and bound in Great Britain by
Bookmarque Ltd, Croydon, Surrey

ISBN 0 09 190136 7

ICE

For Joanna and Richard
and anyone prepared to Think Big

The definitions at the beginning of some chapters are from the NATO Glossary of ABC (American/British/Canadian) Standardized Terminology.

Quotations from the bulletins of the International Ice Patrol are reproduced by kind permission of the Commandant, United States Coast Guard, Washington DC.

CONTENTS

PROLOGUE

The ice moved.

It moved slowly.

One yard. . . . Two yards. . . . Twenty yards. . . .

The long, lonely scream of the white wilderness lasted for one week as the twenty thousand square mile delta lurched towards the sea. The stupendous roar of freedom circled the earth in thirty hours. Creatures grazing in the primeval coal forests on the far side of the planet raised inquiring nostrils to the reverberating thunder that echoed from the south against the sullen skies.

The ice moved.

And the ice stopped.

The mountains that reared into the ice-cap, with their roots firmly imbedded in the jaw of the earth's mantle, arrested the great slide to the ocean. Stresses heaved and pulsed through the attenuated rocks, probing the hidden valleys and undulating strata for weaknesses, and found none. The fractured ice-cap tested its inexorable mass against the unyielding mountains, and the mountains held. They were far older than the life that stirred on the planet; they had been thrown up in the turmoil of the creation; they would not be moved.

The searching stresses simmered and weakened. The cycle of tremors that had dealt repeated hammer blows to the planet faded into tranquillity.

The ice fell silent.

The imprisoned mountains, deflected by the remorseless movement, settled to their eternal task of stemming the march of the ice to the sea.

The ice was patient.

The exposed peaks of the mountains, thrusting through the ice-cap, were eventually buried by the unceasing blizzards.

After five million years, the ice was ready to challenge the mountains.

PART ONE
Cold War

I

There was something in the room.

Julia Hammond woke and lay very still in the darkness, hardly daring to breathe. The strange noise and her imagination joined together to edge icicles of fear down her spine.

Her nerves screamed back at the insidious moaning of the Antarctic wind outside the steel shutters and the thick glass. But it wasn't the wind – there was something in the room. Something singing: a barely perceptible hum like the distant music of a tuning fork in an empty tomb.

She walked frightened fingers along the wall behind her bed until they gratefully found the light switch. The sudden explosion of brilliance chased away the nightmares.

There was nothing in the room.

She wanted to laugh but the strange noise hadn't been frightened away by the light. It continued. Soft and low.

Julia swung her feet on to the floor, keeping them away from the bed, and tracked down the strange sound to her cabinet that contained several hundred plankton specimen slides. The top drawer was open. Two of the glass slivers were occupying the same groove. They were vibrating against each other. She touched them and the singing stopped. It started again when she took her finger away. She re-positioned the slides, pushed the drawer shut and listened. The soft, musical note had stopped but her fingers, resting on the top of the cabinet, registered a mute vibration that seemed to reach up through the floor

She chided herself for her over-active imagination and went back to bed. Such was her relief that it didn't occur to her to ponder the cause of the delicate vibration. She switched out the light and was soon asleep.

She didn't wake.

Even though the gentle music had returned.

2

SUBMISS
When a submarine has failed to report at a scheduled time.

There was a silence.

A silence that was noted by a Honeywell computer. It digested the silence for fifteen minutes to allow for human frailty then flashed a terse message on the night duty officer's screen:

UNIT 7 // IDENT SCHEDULED 23+00 NOT RECEIVED // TIME NOW 23+15 // MESSAGE ENDS +

Frank Knight remained engrossed in his paperback novel. The Honeywell patiently waited another two minutes then sounded a muted warning buzzer. Knight looked up at the screen in the centre of the console. Somewhere in the world an embassy communications officer was late reporting. A common occurrence: especially around Christmas time when the embassy party season was in full swing. Knight returned to his book.

At 23:20 the buzzer sounded again. Knight swore softly to himself. The trouble with the computer was that it hadn't been programmed to accept wide deviations. His coffee was cold. He was about to cross the deserted communications room to the hot drink vending machine when he noticed that the message on the screen had lengthened by three words:

REACTION STATUS URGENT

Knight forgot the coffee machine. He sat down and reached for the blue standing orders manual. He flipped through the pages until he came to the instructions relating to Unit Seven. Unit Seven?

Knight frowned. He had never heard of Unit Seven. Yet the Honeywell had. According to the manual, Unit Seven, whatever it was, identified itself once every twenty hours. Until now.

The instructions were simple enough: all Knight had to do was call a London number by landline and tell them that their precious Unit Seven had lost its voice.

Knight picked up his phone and dialled the nine-digit number. It was answered immediately.

'Yes?'

Feeling slightly foolish, Knight said: 'This is the night duty officer at the Government Communications Headquarters, Cheltenham. Unit Seven is nearly twenty-five minutes late reporting.'

'What's Unit Seven?' asked the London voice.

Knight felt aggrieved. 'How should I know? It says here that I've got to tell you.'

Knight checked with the voice that he had the right number.

'Okay,' said the voice, 'I'll check this end.'

The line went dead.

3

SUBSMASH
Organization for the urgent rescue of a submarine and her company.

Lieutenant James Abbott RN stared at the phone he had just replaced.

What was Unit Seven? And why should GCHQ, who were responsible for the Diplomatic Wireless Service, call up Admiral Howe's night number? Why were they involved if Unit Seven was a naval matter?

Abbott turned the pages of the duty book. There was nothing under 'Seven'. He leafed through the alpha section. Nothing under 'U' either. A slip of paper caught his eye. It was a handwritten note stapled to one of the stencilled pages. Admiral Howe's handwriting.

'Notify me immediately upon receipt of any signals that relate to Unit Seven. Howe.'

Big Ben chimed the half hour.

'Notify me immediately. . . .'

Abbott decided to wake the old man in person rather than startle him with the telephone. He entered the corridor and made his way up to the admiral's flat on the top floor. The building gave the impression of being deserted but most of the upper offices contained duty officers boredly reading within reach of telephones. The admiral's sitting-room was a mess; Admiral Howe was one of the untidiest men Abbott had ever known. Abbott supposed that the old man's only bad habit was caused by his never having had a wife to snap at his heels.

He went into the bedroom and gently shook the frail shoulder. The admiral was awake immediately – an ability he had acquired as a convoy escort commander during the war.

'What is it, James?'

'A message from GCHQ, sir. Unit Seven hasn't reported on schedule. There's a note you've written in the duty book to notify you immediately.'

But Admiral Howe wasn't listening. He pushed his bony feet into his slippers and pulled on a dressing-gown.

'When did they call?'

Abbott followed the admiral into the sitting-room and out into the corridor. The old man could move surprisingly fast.

'Five minutes ago, sir.'

Admiral Howe looked anxiously at his watch without slackening his pace. 'Why have they left it so long?' he demanded. 'Didn't they give at least some sort of explanation?'

The white-haired old sailor's concern was infectious; Abbott looked extremely worried when he replied that they hadn't.

No, thought Admiral Howe – they wouldn't. No one other than himself and those members of the Admiralty Board who had a 'need to know' knew anything about Unit Seven and its mission. The Soviets knew of course. But they didn't know they were supposed to know.

Admiral Howe lowered himself into his chair and gazed at his aide.

Abbot sensed that this wasn't the right moment to speak. In truth he was shocked by the change in the old man. The driving vitality that was always present, no matter what the time of day or night, had gone. The good-humoured sparkle in the eyes was no longer there; the weathered face was now pale and drawn.

Admiral Howe was experiencing the once familiar crawling sensation at the base of his spine; the wedge of fear that had warned him of a U-boat's proximity before his ASDIC operator had detected it. The enemy no longer flew the swastika – but the sensation was the same.

Wearily Admiral Howe said to Abbott: 'Get me the Subsmash operational directives.'

It was then that Lieutenant Abbott began to have an inkling of what Unit Seven was.

4

SATSCAN
An operation specially mounted to listen for radio signals relayed from a communication satellite.

On the plains of San Augustin near Socorro in New Mexico stands the VLA (Very Large Array) of the world's largest steerable radio telescope, owned and operated by the United States Radio Astronomy Observatory. The twenty-seven dishes, each with an area of five hundred square yards, are capable of functioning as one dish twenty miles in diameter.

At 09:00 hours local time, after a series of exchanges between the observatory's director and the Ministry of Defence (Navy) in London, the mighty radio telescope was doing just that. But instead of listening to the electronic uproar from 50,000 light years away at the centre of the galaxy, the twenty-seven antennae were locked on to the United Kingdom's Skynet III military communications satellite poised in geostationary orbit 22,000 miles above the equator.

Apart from the position of the satellite and a channel frequency, the astronomers were given no information; if signals were heard, they wouldn't be able to decode them – all they were required to do was listen. So they obligingly tuned their sensitive receivers, and listened.

Silence.

Similar scenes were repeated throughout the southern hemisphere; South Africa, Australia and New Zealand listened intently for even the faintest electronic scratching from the ether and heard nothing. Even the US Navy's modest tracking facilities on remote islands in the South Pacific were required to listen and to report. Like all the others, they heard nothing.

The 'thank you' signals poured out from London.

The largest and least publicized Satscan operation ever mounted had been an abysmal failure.

5

HOSTILE ICE

Ice over two metres thick with no ice skylights thus preventing a missile-carrying submarine from using communication system or deploying weapons.

It was twenty-four hours since the submarine, *Asteria*, otherwise known as Unit Seven, had failed to report.

Apart from the abortive 'Satscan' operation, nothing had happened. Lieutenant James Abbott was baffled. Why hadn't a search and rescue operation been launched? Why hadn't the various NATO commands been alerted? And above all, why had Admiral Howe automatically assumed the worst from the moment the submarine had failed to report? There hadn't been a panic the time when the *Sovereign* had been late with a report; everyone had rightly guessed that the submarine had failed to find a skylight during the North Polar hostile ice season. News of the *Sovereign*'s overdue transmission had even been released to the press. But in this instance, before Admiral Howe left for Signals Command, he had given Lieutenant Abbott strict instructions that nothing about the *Asteria* was to be disclosed to anyone. 'Not even if the Prime Minister himself demands to be told', had been the admiral's exact words.

And so Lieutenant Abbott had spent an embarrassing day issuing a continuous stream of telephone excuses for the absence of his chief from various meetings. One permanent under-secretary had threatened to take the matter higher when confronted by the lieutenant's stubborn refusal to be more forthcoming.

Admiral Howe walked into the office as Big Ben was striking midnight, wearily dropped a bundle of bulging manilla files on Abbott's desk, and sank gracefully into his deep, leather armchair. Abbott stared at him in concern; he had never seen the old admiral looking so exhausted.

'Can I get you anything, sir?'

Howe shook his head slowly and closed his eyes. 'I'll be all right in a few minutes, James. Just a rather wearing day.'

'Have you had anything to eat?'

'They gave me lunch in the officers' mess at Stanmore.'

'I thought you said you were going to Signals Command, sir?'

'Well I've been to Stanmore as well.'

The admiral's tone did not encourage further conversation. Abbott's eyes dropped to the files that had been dropped on his desk. The top one was entitled 'Commander V. S. Sinclair-Holmes'. The record of amendments columns printed on the cover showed that the file had not been altered for a year.

'He's the *Asteria*'s commanding officer.'

Abbott looked up quickly. The intense blue eyes were watching him from the depths of the armchair.

'I'm sorry, sir,' said Abbott hastily. 'I thought you wanted me to look at them.'

'Of course I want you to look at them,' said Admiral Howe testily. 'Why else would I dump them on you?'

Abbott said nothing.

'There are thirty-one files there,' the admiral continued. 'One for each member of the *Asteria*'s company.'

Abbott was astonished. 'Only thirty-one, sir? You mean officers *and* men?'

Admiral Howe suppressed an angry reply; Abbott was entitled to be surprised. He rose from the armchair and sat on the hard chair in front of Abbott's desk. He rested his chin on his hands, fixed his uncomfortable eyes on the lieutenant and said softly: 'Thirty-one men, James. And I want you to become those thirty-one men for the next five hundred days.'

Abbott gaped. 'I beg your pardon, sir?'

Admiral Howe nodded to the files. 'You'll find a microfiche in each file that contains all the correspondence between each man and his family and friends – plus a few enemies in some cases. For example, Mechanician Fisher has been fighting a two-year legal battle with his brother over a house his mother left him. You're to become Mechanician Fisher and you're to continue the battle.'

Admiral Howe leaned across the desk and picked up the files one by one. 'I want you to become Commander Sinclair-Holmes; I want you to become second officer Lieutenant Bryan Finch whose wife has a twelve-month-old baby that he's never seen; I want you to become ERA Wall who's getting a divorce from a wife he's hardly ever seen. In short, I want you to become thirty-one men by perpetuating their correspondence with home for the next fourteen months. Until now, all letters for the men have been sent to a Signals Command box number. In future they'll come to you first. Letters from the *Asteria*'s crew, the letters that you'll now be writing, have been beamed to this country via Skynet and then telexed in the normal way – so you won't have handwriting problems. Just make sure that you get the style right. I've arranged for a microfiche viewer to be installed in here so that you can go over all the previous letters.'

Abbott swallowed. 'When do I start, sir?'

'Now.'

'Why me, sir?'

'Because I can trust you to keep your mouth shut, James. I can also trust you not to begin a love letter with "Dear Sir or Madam" which is probably what would happen if I were to give the job to a Main Building scribe.'

The admiral moved to the door.

'Wake me at ten please, James.'

'Why not report the *Asteria* as missing, sir?'

Admiral Howe didn't appear to have heard the question. 'Wake me at ten,' he repeated.

'Sir,' said Abbott firmly. 'If you want me to do this, you have to tell me why the *Asteria* isn't being reported as missing.'

Admiral Howe considered. Perhaps it might be wise to let Abbott have half the story. He sat down.

'The *Asteria* is not a properly commissioned submarine. She was built by Vickers for the Israeli Navy. Just before she was due to be launched, HMG stepped in and stopped the order and paid Vickers full compensation. So, the government ended up owning a submarine for which it had no real use. Then someone, not me thank God, had the bright idea of using the *Asteria* to carry out an experimental thousand-day submarine patrol.'

Abbott's eyes opened wide. 'A thousand days!' he echoed. 'I thought it was generally agreed that such a thing was impossible? There'd be psychological collapse of the crew after five hundred days.'

'That's exactly what I said at the time. I said that the thousand-day patrol is a naval strategist's pipe-dream and will always be so. But they said: no, we've got a sub, let's give it a try. Hand-picked crew – specially screened for stamina and emotional stability and that sort of thing. I said it would fail but they wouldn't listen.' Admiral Howe paused. 'It looks like I was right.'

Abbott nodded. 'No harm in trying, I suppose. So why not admit that the experiment was a failure?'

'We can't,' replied Admiral Howe. 'We've deliberately leaked information to the Soviets saying that the thousand-day patrol is possible and that this is our second. . . . That's why you're going to become the *Asteria*'s ghost for the next fourteen months. At the end of that period we'll announce that the *Asteria* is overdue. We'll give an Atlantic position – somewhere exceptionally deep.'

'What was her real position, sir?' Abbott's face was impassive as he waited for an answer.

There was a long pause before Admiral Howe replied. 'She was tucked up in our Antarctic depot where she was supposed to be safe.'

'Our what?' Abbott was so surprised that he omitted the 'sir'.

'I didn't like the idea at first,' said the old sailor, staring down at the floor. 'But they had an answer ready to counter every objection. They had found an ice shelf in the British Antarctic territory that was stable – it wasn't calving icebergs: honeycombed with deep water caverns hollowed out by summer melt water; easy to convert into a comfortable submarine depot with plenty of room for repair workshops and entertainment facilities.'

Lieutenant Abbott gazed at the admiral in astonishment. 'But there's a treaty – Antarctica can't be used for military purposes.'

Admiral Howe laughed bitterly. 'Exactly what I said. But national security outweighed an obscure treaty. I also said that there would be victualling problems but they had an answer for that as well: a phoney research base a few miles inland staffed with genuine scientists working on genuine projects to provide the cover, but administer it with service personnel – selected personnel – Royal Marines.'

'Perfidious Albion,' Abbott muttered. 'So what's happened to *Asteria*, sir, if the ice is safe?'

'They thought it was safe,' Admiral Howe replied. 'Seems like they thought there was something called glacial blockage – buried mountains preventing the ice from moving.'

'And now it's moved?'

Admiral Howe nodded. 'Several thousand cubic miles, according to the satellite pictures at Stanmore.'

Lieutenant Abbott looked disbelieving. 'Several thousand cubic *miles*, sir?' he echoed.

'I didn't believe it myself until I saw the pictures – there's now a bay in the coast that wasn't there on the last satellite survey.'

'So we're going to mount a subsmash, sir?'

There was a long pause. Admiral Howe shook his head slowly. 'It's not that simple, James. The ice has vanished.'

Abbott stared at the admiral. 'What?!'

'Normally I detest clichés but this time one is appropriate: the ice – all eight thousand cubic miles of it – has vanished. Vanished into thin air.'

6

ICE CORE
Ice sample removed from a glacier or ice-cap.

'Well, I think it's madness,' said Glyn Sherwood when the white-coated steward had poured their coffee.

Julia Hammond caught Oaf's eye and suppressed a smile. After three years with the Rosenthal Antarctic Survey team she knew enough about Sherwood to know that he disliked changes in his routine. Routine in a place like Antarctica, with either continuous darkness or continuous daylight and the struggle to remember whether the next meal would be breakfast or dinner, was essential if you didn't want to go quietly mad. But now, with the luxury liner *Orion* seventy-two hours out from Sydney and bound for Cape Town, normal periods of day and night had returned.

Oaf gave a booming laugh that caused other passengers at neighbouring tables to look up at the giant Norwegian with a mixture of distaste and alarm. He clapped Sherwood on the back. 'Still worried about those goddamn core samples, heh, Sherwood?'

The geologist shook his head. 'No. I dare say the refrigeration equipment on this nuclear-powered gin palace can cope. I just think record-breaking attempts by ocean liners are irrelevant today.'

Julia glanced round the opulent restaurant. There was a noisy gathering of wealthy industrialists and their wives enjoying a joke at the captain's table.

'Maybe they are irrelevant,' said Julia shrewdly. 'But still a good idea from the owner's point of view if you're way behind schedule and you've got a charter fleet of aircraft laid on at Heathrow to fly everyone home.'

Oaf produced a wicked-looking flensing knife with a long curved blade. He was about to probe his teeth with the point when Julia said in a mild voice: 'How many times have I told you about that, Oaf? You're not on one of your wretched whaling ships now.'

The huge Norwegian looked incongruously crestfallen. He sighed and slid the knife back into its sheath. Julia Hammond was a very forthright young woman and it was best not to antagonize her. He saw Sherwood grinning at him and gave a rich, deep chuckle.

'Sherwood's in no hurry to get back to Southampton. Heh, Sherwood?'

The geologist's grin disappeared. Julia looked interested. 'Oh? Why's that?'

Sherwood glared across the table at the amiable, bear-like Norwegian.

'Are you married, Glyn?' Julia's tone suggested that she was annoyed at her failure to acquire information about Sherwood earlier. She didn't like mysteries.

'He's married okay,' said Oaf, baring his rows of formidable teeth in a broad smile. 'He once tell me all about it.'

'I *was* married,' Sherwood corrected. 'Can we change the subject?'

Julia studied Sherwood speculatively. The geologist was uncomfortably aware of her grey eyes fixed on him. 'You signed on for three years with Rosenthal in Antarctica to forget?' she asked sarcastically.

Sherwood laughed. 'Hell no. I signed on for the same reason we all did – because it was a job and it was well paid. Now that I've confessed all my secrets perhaps we can change the subject.'

'Pity they didn't renew our contracts,' said Julia pensively.

Sherwood looked at her in surprise. 'Who's always going on about how nice it'll be to go shopping in London again?'

Julia shrugged. 'There's not that many jobs for marine biologists going.'

'Lot of phonies,' Oaf mumbled while exploring one of his tombstone teeth with a forefinger that was as thick as a broomstick.

Julia fastened her inquisitive eyes on the giant. 'Who? And leave your teeth alone.'

'Rosenthal,' said Oaf. 'Big phonies.'

Sherwood and Julia exchanged baffled glances. 'Oaf,' said Julia. 'Will you please stop poking at your teeth and tell me what you're talking about?'

Oaf stopped poking at his teeth. 'Rosenthal lab technicians.'

'What about them?'

'All over Sherwood's height. No glasses. All with good eyesight.'

Sherwood frowned.

'Don't be stupid,' said Julia with irritation. 'Of course they all had good eyesight – they had to pass medicals.'

'For height?' Sherwood queried thoughtfully.

Julia hesitated. 'Well . . . I suppose. . . .'

'Phonies,' Oaf repeated. 'And Brill the biggest phoney of them all.'

Julia had always found the chief executive at Rosenthal to be considerate and well-behaved. She was quick to strenuously defend him.

Sherwood winked at Oaf and said teasingly to Julia. 'Yeah. Everyone on the base noticed your play for him.'

Julia controlled her temper. 'Brill was the only gentleman on the base among a gang of sex-starved, uncouth so-called scientists whose idea on research didn't extend much beyond trying to find out what I wore in bed at night.'

'Don't blame me for your sensitivity over your flannel pyjamas,' said Sherwood mischievously.

'God give me patience.'

'An *officer* and a gentleman,' said Oaf abruptly.

There was a sudden silence round the table.

'English idiom I learn once,' said Oaf in response to Julia's and Sherwood's blank expressions. 'Brill an officer. Navy officer.' The Norwegian tapped the side of his nose. 'I smell 'em. Officers.' He would have spat in contempt but sensed that Julia would not have approved. 'I tell you something else,' he continued. 'You ever see in the stores building? No. You know why? Packing crates had marks on them. That's why the lab technicians never let anyone go in there.'

'What sort of marks?' asked Julia.

Oaf made a sketch on a napkin of the short broad arrow that denoted HM Government property. 'I see it once when tarpaulin get blown off,' the Norwegian explained.

Sherwood leaned forward. 'That's interesting. Remember how all of the extreme weather clothing we were issued with had had the labels removed?'

'So what?' said Julia. 'Rosenthal purchased government surplus stock. What's wrong with that?'

'Then why try to hide the fact?' Sherwood countered.

Julia turned to Oaf. 'So what are you trying to say? That Rosenthal is some sort of military base?'

'No,' said Sherwood before the Norwegian could answer. 'That would be a violation of the Antarctic Treaty. There's a clause that forbids military exploitation of Antarctica. For all their faults, the British government don't break international treaties.'

'Exactly,' Julia agreed. 'And even if they did, what possible military value could Antarctica have to anyone?'

Oaf remained silent.

Sherwood was unable to sleep that night. The atmosphere in the tiny cabin, buried deep in the bowels of the liner, was unbearably oppressive.

He lay in the dark, wondering why it was that a technological breakthrough in efficient air-conditioning, even on a new ship like the *Orion*, had yet to be achieved.

He switched the light on and tried to read a paperback. After five pages he realized that his brain was absorbing nothing of the story. The words were a meaningless blur. He tossed the book on to the dresser and knocked the brochure on the *Orion* to the floor. He reached down to pick it up. Inside was a hastily printed leaflet which outlined details of the proposed record-breaking run. Upon rounding Cape Horn, the *Orion* would be increasing her speed to nearly forty knots and, weather permitting, would maintain that speed for seven days so that the liner would arrive at Southampton on schedule.

Sherwood re-read the sentence. Thirty-seven knots for a week! It seemed an incredible figure. He turned to the brochure and read the information on the *Orion* that was included for 'the technically minded'. Four nuclear reactors. . . . Four turbines. . . . Maximum speed forty-two knots. Sherwood wondered if the liner had ever been tested at her top speed. He wasn't an engineer but it seemed to him that it was crazy to even consider pushing a largely untried ship to its limits.

He idly leafed through the rest of the brochure and came to a diagram of the ship's decks. It wasn't surprising that he couldn't sleep – 'G' deck was twenty feet below the waterline and immediately above the reactor rooms. He dropped the booklet on the floor, switched the light off and made another attempt to sleep.

Twenty feet below the waterline. . . .

Trust Rosenthal to book the cheapest cabins. . . .

Twenty feet below the waterline. . . .

Sherwood did a mental calculation and worked out that every square foot of hull plate by his head was having to withstand a water pressure of one ton.

7

It had taken Lieutenant James Abbott seven months to overcome his distaste at having to be a husband to twenty-three wives, a lover to six women and a father of thirty-one children.

The whole business was now a smooth-running operation aided by a giant wall chart that listed birthdays, anniversaries, children's names and ages, together with a mass of detailed information on likes and dislikes. Although Abbott was now familiar with the private lives of every member of the *Asteria*'s crew and could write letters without referring to the chart and a card index, he made a point of always checking his facts first. A mistake, such as the time when he had confused the first names of two wives, could be disastrous.

It was the fifteenth of the month. Mechanician Robertson had always written five hundred words of sleazy syntax on the fifteenth of every month.

Lieutenant Abbott sighed and reached for his notepad.

8

General Nikolai Zadkin of the Intelligence Secretariat placed his huge hands flat on Admiral Turgenev's desk and said in a dangerously mild voice: 'So where's that British submarine now, admiral?'

Admiral Turgenev, Commander-in-Chief of the Soviet Black Sea fleet, met the cold, Slavonic stare without flinching. He wasn't frightened of thugs like Zadkin. 'General. No one seriously believes that the thousand-day submarine patrol is possible. Either your department has made a mistake or you've got hold of some fake intelligence.'

'Where's that submarine!'

'The AGI ship lost track of it in the Southern Ocean. It's virtually impossible to use sonar from the surface in such cold water. Inversion layers bend the beam. The only way to successfully track a submarine without thermal wake satellite monitoring facilities such as the Americans have, is to use another submarine.'

'Locating and monitoring that sub,' said General Zadkin icily, 'is a number one priority. It is essential that we find out if the British really have solved the problems of sending men on a three-year patrol or if the crew are relaxing on a depot ship in the South Atlantic.'

'That's almost certainly what they are doing,' said Admiral Turgenev irritably.

'I need proof!' Zadkin thundered, crashing his fist down on the desk. 'Not the opinions of desk-bound sailors!'

The last words of Zadkin's insult were drowned by the thunderous roar of eight MiG 25s from the nearby Yevpatoriya airbase.

General Zadkin crossed to the window and shaded his eyes against the brilliant sunlight sparkling on the Black Sea. The fighters wheeled tightly over the Sevastopol naval dockyard and climbed fast, heading south across the Black Sea towards Turkey. The nerve-shattering howl from the sixteen Tumanski engines faded with astonishing speed to a muted thunder as the dwindling jets bored into the distant haze.

General Zadkin watched the shrinking black specks with pride; the Americans had nothing that could match the MiG 25 for speed, rate of climb and operating ceiling. It had started breaking world records in 1970 and had been breaking them ever since.

He spun quickly round to face Turgenev. 'If a submarine is the best thing to use for hunting another submarine in total secrecy, then that's what we'll use.'

'We'll need at least twenty to scour the South Atlantic,' said Turgenev impatiently. 'We can't spare that many.'

Zadkin smiled. 'Who said anything about using fleet or nuclear submarines, admiral? We'll use the prototype Delta Two.'

Turgenev shook his head. 'That's the maddest idea I've heard in a long time, general.'

'Remember who you are talking to,' said Zadkin mildly.

Turgenev snorted. 'I don't care. It's lunacy to even contemplate sending the Delta Two into the South Atlantic. You know their size of course? Eighteen thousand tons. They're designed to cover North American targets from home waters.'

'They have the best passive sonar equipment in the entire navy – correct?'

'Yes. But – '

'And they're fitted with SOSUS foxers?'

'Yes,' said Turgenev desperately. 'But if the Delta Two was detected in the South Atlantic the Americans would regard it as a gross provocation.'

'It will be under strict instructions to remain continuously submerged and to keep its SOSUS jammers operational at all times.'

'It'll be detected by thermal wake satellites,' said Turgenev irritably. 'And another thing – the Delta Two's inertials aren't suitable for position fixing in the South Atlantic.'

'Use the Omega system,' Zadkin replied smoothly. 'I understand that the American and British navies have no scruples about using it in their own submarines, even though it is a civilian system. The very low frequency signals generated by the Omega shore beacons penetrate the water to a depth of six metres do they not? It should not be beyond the abilities of your technicians to equip the Delta with a towed wire antenna so that it can obtain continuous position updating without the need to surface.'

'Please listen to me, general,' said Admiral Turgenev resolutely. 'We need much more oceanographic research before we can risk an eighteen thousand-ton submarine in unknown waters. If the Delta were to run into a sudden layer of cold water, it would lose trim and shoot to the surface. There's still much – '

'Admiral Turgenev,' said Zadkin dangerously. 'You will send the Delta Two into the South Atlantic with recordings of the *Asteria*'s signature. *I want that submarine found!*'

9

Julia stared wistfully at the shimmering peak of Table Mountain for some seconds before handing the binoculars to Sherwood.

'It's a bloody shame,' she muttered. 'I was looking forward to shopping in Cape Town.'

Sherwood rested his elbows on the mahogany-capped weather deck rail and focused the binoculars on the distant peak. 'You had three hours in Sydney,' he pointed out.

Julia gave a sarcastic laugh. She was about to launch into a tirade about not having had a chance to do some proper shopping for three years when she noticed that Sherwood was smiling.

'Are you mocking me again?'

Sherwood lowered the binoculars. His eyes were round and innocent. 'Me, Miss Hammond? Now why would I want to do a thing like that?'

Julia's retort was interrupted by a steward. He was very polite: 'I'm sorry to disturb you, but we're about to close this deck.'

Julia glanced along the deck. Similar requests were being made to the other passengers.

Sherwood took Julia's arm. 'Come on. I'll give you a game of electronic tennis. They'll probably close all the open decks once they start this crazy attempt on the record.'

'The after deck will remain open,' said the steward apologetically. 'It'll be out of the slipstream. There'll be extra films and the entertainment officer is organizing special events.'

'Ladies and gentlemen,' boomed a nearby public address speaker. 'We are about to increase our speed to thirty-seven knots. The *Orion* is well stabilized – indeed you may find that the ship is much more steady when running at high speed. . . .'

Sherwood snorted.

' . . . Weather reports are favourable so it looks as if we will be entering Southampton Water in exactly one week from today. We hope you all enjoy your participation in this memorable event.'

The speaker clicked off.

'Memorable event,' Sherwood repeated sourly.

'It'll be fun,' said Julia as Sherwood steered her through the sliding doors and into the glass-enclosed promenade.

'It'll be bloody dangerous.'

'Who says?'

'Oaf. He's a good engineer. He said machinery should never have to work flat-out if it wasn't essential.'

Julia stopped. 'I do believe you're scared, Mr Sherwood.'

The geologist looked annoyed. 'Of course I'm not scared.'

Sherwood was lying; he was scared of the twenty feet that his cabin was below the waterline. He knew it was an irrational fear and that the *Orion*'s owners and captain wouldn't allow the attempt unless they were satisfied that it was safe.

They reached the forward promenade deck overlooking the *Orion*'s bows surging through the white-flecked swell. Julia was about to point out a flock of Cape pigeons wheeling towards the mainland when they both heard the hitherto unobtrusive whine of the *Orion*'s turbines sharpen so that it could be heard above the incessant piped music. The deck quickened underfoot.

'Sounds like they're turning up the wick,' Julia commented cheerfully.

The *Orion* buried her bows in the swell and sent plumes of

wind-whipped spray lashing across the foredeck. Excited, chattering passengers gathered along the rail. The next mountainous swell seemed to cause the liner to hesitate. Passengers instinctively recoiled as a maelstrom of spindrift hurled against the glass.

Julia allowed herself to be taken below to the harsh clatter of fruit machines in the amusement centre. She noticed that Sherwood's hand was trembling slightly as he fed a coin into a slot.

'What the hell's the matter?' she asked.

Sherwood watched the moving spot of light on the screen for some seconds. 'There's a door leading off from "G" deck marked "Private – Staff only". Have you noticed it?'

'Yes,' said Julia, puzzled.

'It leads to a flight of stairs that comes out on the weather deck.'

'So?'

'It might be useful in an emergency.'

The next heavy swell caused the entire ship to lurch.

10

The Delta Two class SSBN, the *Podorny*, rolled. It was a gentle roll but it was enough for Commander Igor Leachinski to dive from his bunk and out into the companionway leading to the control room.

Submarines cruising at a depth of three hundred metres do not roll.

'What the hell was that?' Leachinski demanded as he burst into the control room.

The officer of the watch was baffled. 'I don't know, captain,' he began and the *Podorny* rolled again. The helmsman just saved himself from slipping out of his chair. There was a sound of breaking crockery from the wardroom. Leachinski was about to order the chief engineer to reduce speed when his blood ran cold: the control-room floor was tilting – the *Podorny* was losing trim. Even before the chief engineer reached the switches that operated the ballast pumps, the *Podorny* suddenly lurched violently and rolled over on to her side. Leachinski tried to save himself by grabbing hold of the back of the sonar technician's chair. His senses reeled, refusing to accept that the familiar control room was turning through ninety degrees. Objects were crashing around him. Men were yelling. There was a smell of burning, and then the lights were flickering.

'Emergency lights!' Leachinski yelled.

'You're sitting on the control panel!' shouted a voice.

The automatic breakers closed with soft clicks – the lights burned steadily. For some seconds there was silence; the turbines continued to hum, driving the *Podorny* along on her beam ends. For the silent, sweating men in the submarine, those seconds seemed to drag on for eternity. There was nothing to do but pray. In the recreation room thirty men lay entangled on a bulkhead that had been the side of the submarine; they prayed amid the smashed remains of the movie projector. In the galley the two cooks, badly hurt by falling against the cooker burners, prayed. Throughout the length of the *Podorny* men prayed while they waited for something to happen.

The two thousand tons of lead poured into the *Podorny's* bilge spaces began to assert itself. Slowly, the mighty submarine turned about her axis. Men slid down the bulkheads as the floor regained its rightful position. Their training took over: damage reports flowed along the submarine's fibre optic communication system to the control room.

'Missile control centre. All systems okay. Category Three damage only.'

'Reactor room. Category Three damage. One rating with a suspected broken arm.'

'Turbine room. Category Two damage: a fractured HP pipe which we're shutting off now.'

Ten similar reports were relayed over the control room's loudspeaker. Leachinski heaved a sigh of relief. There had been no Category One reports – none of the submarine's major systems were damaged. There was no need to order the *Podorny* to the surface. He stared at his white-faced chief engineer.

'What in the name of the Mother of God caused that, chief?'

The chief engineer didn't answer. He pointed dumbly at the depth gauges. Leachinski followed his finger. The depth gauges were reading zero and the pointers on the external light meters were off the scale, hard against the maximum reading stops.

The *Podorny* was on the surface.

Leachinski swore and switched the fin TV camera on. A distant horizon and a blue sky filled the screen. The horizon tilted gently. The motion was repeated underfoot as the *Podorny* responded to the swell.

'Down a hundred!' Leachinski yelled.

'Can't, captain,' said the sonar operator.

Leachinski rounded on him. 'Why not?'

'Only fifty metres of water under our keel.'

Leachinski glared at the sonar operator. 'We're in the middle of the South Atlantic, you idiot!'

'See for yourself, captain.'

The sonar operator was right: all three of the *Podorny*'s independent echo-sounders were indicating a depth of fifty metres when they should be showing five *kilometres*.

Leachinski gaped in disbelief.

'Hard echo too,' said the sonar operator. 'No sub-bottom penetration so it looks like we're over rock.'

For a moment Leachinski's mind raced.

'Stop engines,' he ordered.

The submarine had lost way by the time Leachinski stepped out of the fin lift and on to the bridge. The *Podorny*'s hemispherical whale bow, ideal for running at speed when submerged, gave her bad handling characteristics on the surface, and now, her cylindrical hull, without the stabilizing influence of the hydroplanes now that she was lying stopped, caused her to roll sickeningly through a thirty-degree arc. Leachinski pulled on an interphone headset and plugged the communication jack into one of the pressure-proof sockets. He heard the sonar operator say:

'Depth, forty metres.'

Leachinski swept the horizon with his binoculars. There was no sign of land. He listened to the voices from the radio room as the first and second navigation officers went about the business of obtaining a position fix from a satellite and shore stations.

From his position high above the surface, perched on the slender fin, Leachinski peered down at the sea as if hoping to spot a clue that accounted for the shallow water.

'Control room – bridge,' said the chief engineer's voice in

the headphones. 'I don't know if this means anything, but external water temperature is only two degrees above freezing.'

Leachinski frowned. If the *Podorny*'s position was correct, the submarine was riding northwards on the Benguela Current five hundred miles off the west coast of South Africa. The Benguela, which was an offshoot of the Antarctic West Wind Drift Current, was a cold current. But not that cold. Not thirty degrees south of the equator.

'We've got a fix on two South African Broadcasting Corporation transmitters,' said a voice in Leachinski's headphones. 'It looks like the SINS is okay.'

Leachinski gave the order to proceed at a cautious three knots.

'Depth steady at forty-eight metres,' said the sonar operator.

Leachinski told him to use the forward sonar scan so that the submarine had advance warning of depth variations ahead.

'It's a steady forty-eight metres for three kilometres, sir, and then it shelves away to seventy metres for as far as the beam will reach. Side scan is the same.'

Leachinski grunted. Something was seriously wrong with the charts for the South Atlantic. Was it possible that a recent earthquake could have gone undetected? He dismissed the thought: no subterranean upheaval could force the floor of the ocean from a depth of five kilometres to within fifty metres of the surface and not be detected.

'Radar room – bridge.'

'Bridge,' said Leachinski.

'We're getting a nine-tenths radar map from *Aerios Eight*.'

Aerios Eight was a satellite that provided an 'over horizon' radar display for Soviet shipping in the Atlantic. It overcame the problem of radar being unable to see beyond the horizon. Nine-tenths meant that reception was extremely good.

'Anything of interest near us?' Leachinski inquired.

'Nothing ahead, captain. The American nuclear-powered liner, the *Orion*, is six hundred kilometres astern of us. She's just rounded Cape Horn.'

Something was wrong with the sea. Leachinski stared down. He heard his voice say: 'I thought she was putting into Cape Town?'

'No, captain. She's still with us.'

But Leachinski didn't hear the reply. He was gazing down at the sea in shocked disbelief, hardly able to credit his senses.

'Depth steady at forty-eight metres,' intoned the sonar operator's voice.

The fin swayed. Leachinski stared in horror down at the water as it swelled towards him. His throat went dry. His knuckles were white as he involuntarily tightened his grip on the rail. Some spray lashed his face but he didn't notice it. Nor did he hear the warning from the radar room concerning a light aircraft on the *Podorny*'s quarter. One thought dominated Leachinski's bewildered mind.

The sea was turning to honey.

11

'Why's the sea the colour of shit?' demanded the CBS News cameraman.

The pilot of the Cessna Skymaster looked down at the sea and shrugged.

'Sand in suspension maybe,' he replied in his Afrikaans accent.

'No way.'

'So why worry about the sea? You want to film the *Orion*. I take you to the *Orion*. But I don't answer questions about the sea.'

The cameraman gazed down through the Cessna's plexiglas windows. 'Sure is odd though.'

'An optical illusion,' commented the pilot.

The cameraman screwed a long-focus lens on to his movie camera and looked down at the sea through the viewfinder. The telephoto effect made the sea appear to be a mere fifty feet beneath the aircraft. 'It's still the colour of shit,' he announced.

'So what do you want me to do? Drop a dye-marker on it maybe?'

The cameraman said nothing but continued to peer through his viewfinder. He slowly tilted the camera up to the horizon. He stiffened.

'Jesus.'

'What?'

The cameraman kept his camera trained at the horizon and

made a fine adjustment to the focusing bezel. Without taking his eye from the rubber eyepiece, he said: 'There's an enormous submarine about ten miles ahead.'

The pilot followed the direction in which the camera was pointing. His trained eyes picked out the white flash of swell breaking where it shouldn't break. He kept his eyes on the target and groped for his binoculars.

'See it?' said the cameraman.

'Yeah, I see it.'

The two men stared in fascination at the massive, whale-like hull. The discoloured swell seemed to be surging in slow motion across the featureless, grey flanks as the submarine punched effortlessly through the heavy seas. The cameraman was familiar with most of the various submarine classes of the world's navies but he had never seen anything like the monstrous apparition that he was now holding in his viewfinder. Unlike most submarines, the slender sail fin was located well forward – almost on top of the rounded bows. A heavy sea slammed into the sail and dissolved: the spray seemed to hang in the air before falling back.

'Get over to it,' breathed the cameraman.

'What about the *Orion*?'

'Forget it. If that baby doesn't dive, I'm going to run all my footage on her.'

The pilot made a slight alteration of course.

The cameraman loaded his camera and whirred the leader through the gate while the pilot tried to call Cape Town to tell them about the submarine. He cursed in Afrikaans as he spun the tuning dial.

'What's the matter?'

'Radio loused up proper,' answered the pilot in disgust. 'Noise right across the band.' He pushed the headphones away from his ears.

'Maybe that's deliberate,' said the cameraman thoughtfully.

'You mean that thing's jamming us?'

'We live in a world of sophisticated electronic countermeasures,' said the cameraman, raising his camera to his eye.

The pilot muttered an oath. 'I thought maybe it was an American job.'

'No way.'

The giant submarine was now less than a mile away. The two men in the Cessna could see the head and shoulders of a man on the top of the fin. The cameraman swore to himself as he used the height of the man to gauge the size of the submarine.

'Goddamnit – she must be all of five hundred feet long. Please, God, don't let her dive. Take her down lower – I want an oblique.' His sentences were a continuous, excited stream.

The Cessna approached the submarine from astern, flying above the curious, double wake that is a characteristic of cigar-shaped vessels moving on the surface.

The Cessna pilot had never seen a nuclear submarine before so he was not as awed by the *Podorny*'s size as the cameraman. Even so, there was something frightening about the arrogant way the monster smashed her snub bows through the ponderous swell.

The movie camera whirred.

'Circle right round and come up behind her again!' shouted the cameraman as he twisted round in his seat to hold the mighty submarine in the centre of his viewfinder.

The Cessna flashed over the *Podorny* at five hundred feet and banked steeply. The cameraman swung round and aimed across the pilot.

'Look, will you get that thing out of my ear!'

'Right round and come behind her as low and as slow as possible. Jesus – she doesn't seem to give a damn about us!'

It was the most inaccurate statement the cameraman had ever made in his life; Commander Leachinski cared very much about the presence of the little single-engine, twin-boom aircraft and was giving orders to do something about it as it approached from astern for its second pass.

'Lower!' yelled the cameraman, aiming through the windscreen. 'Good grief – you can see her missile tubes!'

The pilot presumed the cameraman was referring to the double row of twenty circular marks aft of the submarine's fin.

'Slower!'

The Cessna's stall-warning alarm chirruped merrily.

'If I go any slower, we fall off the goddam sky!' the pilot snarled.

The aircraft swept over the submarine for the second time. The cameraman frantically changed lenses.

'What a stupid time to take your goddam camera to bits,' the pilot complained.

'Wide-angle. Hell – I've crossed the thread. Do you have to fling her about like that?'

Another man had appeared on the bridge. They kept their faces turned towards the Cessna.

'Here's looking at you, baby,' said the cameraman as the film whirred through the gate. 'Keep her steady and we might get some usable stills.'

The Cessna flashed over the *Podorny* for the third time and banked so steeply that it came close to stalling.

The cameraman spun the wide-angle lens off the camera body and screwed on a zoom lens.

'Okay – now approach her on her beam. Slow as you can. Trail your wheels in the water or something.'

'If I do that, we end up on the water, on our back,' growled the pilot, but he throttled back and pulled the Cessna's nose up until the aircraft was barely maintaining flying speed.

'Beautiful . . . Beautiful,' breathed the cameraman as the huge Soviet submarine swelled in his viewfinder. He zoomed in on the two men. One of them was holding something on his shoulder: something the cameraman had seen before. What the hell was it? He was too excited by his scoop to think properly.

'What's that guy got?' demanded the pilot.

The Cessna was approaching the *Podorny* at an angle to minimize closing speed. The cameraman rotated the zoom lens to keep the submarine's apparent size constant. He watched the man point the tube. An alarm jangled at the back of the cameraman's mind: Egyptian soldiers during the '73 Arab-Israeli War!

There was a bright flash from the submarine's bridge. The pilot saw it.

'What was that?'

The cameraman didn't answer. He was a professional photographer; his world was the world he saw through his viewfinder. And like a professional – he kept filming it until it fell apart.

12

At twenty minutes past midnight, the *Orion*'s wake disappeared.

Sherwood was dozing in a deckchair on the darkened and virtually deserted after deck, sheltered from the slipstream of the *Orion*'s forty-mile-an-hour charge by the ship's superstructure. Four hundred miles to his left was the coast of South West Africa and four yards to his right an unseen couple were giggling. He opened his eyes and looked up at the moon. It was for some, he supposed, a romantic situation: a luxury liner, a tropical night, and the moon sparkling on the swell, adding its luminescence to the ship's glittering phosphorescent wake.

Except that the wake had disappeared.

He leaned forward in his deckchair, puzzled. The *Orion*'s phenomenal speed had created a spectacular wake – a trail of luminous turbulence stretching across the sea to the horizon. Now there was nothing but a curious, muddy-coloured pattern of disturbed water that hardly reflected the moonlight. He crossed the after deck to the rail and looked down into one of the howling eddies created round the *Orion* by its incredible speed. It was then that he noticed the smell – the wet, indescribable smell that he had come to know so well in three years. It was the flesh-crawling smell that Oaf had said could even permeate the stink of blood and blubber from a gutted whale on a factory ship's flensing deck.

'Ice,' said a deep voice at his side.

Sherwood jumped, then relaxed. The big Norwegian could move like a cat.

'I thought my nose was playing tricks,' muttered Sherwood, angry at having been startled.

Oaf shook his grizzled mane and leaned on the rail. Both men stared across the water at the yellow wake, their backs to the *Orion*'s bows.

'No tricks, Sherwood. That's ice okay. I leave Julia and I go forward. Clear night. No ice. Not in this part of ocean. But I smell it good. I look for you. Your cabin's empty so I reckon you're up here.'

Oaf flashed his Stonehenge teeth.

'I reckon right, heh, Sherwood?'

'How long ago was it when you first smelt the ice then?'

'Fifteen minutes. Maybe more.'

Sherwood looked up in surprise at the impossible hulk towering over him. 'Fifteen minutes? You've been able to smell it all that time?'

'I smell good,' Oaf replied simply. 'And now wake stop shining. That's bad, Sherwood. Very bad.'

Sherwood was about to ask Oaf what he meant when the deck suddenly heaved. There was a tremendous crash from forward followed by a series of thunderous concussions that seemed to rip through the ship with the speed of an express train. The force of the *Orion*'s deceleration would have thrown Sherwood back against the superstructure had not Oaf's huge arm quickly circled his waist and held him in a vice-like grip. The rail Oaf was gripping with his other hand bent under the load as the *Orion* ground to a shuddering halt. The pulverizing shockwaves that slammed through the length of the ship merged into one sustained explosion that seemed to last for ever. People were screaming. The air was filled with flying deckchairs, lengths of rope – everything that hadn't been secured. Numb with shock and unable to comprehend what was happening to his orderly world, Sherwood saw the two lovers tumble from their hiding place as the deck became the side of an erupting volcano. The man went through the rails and must have fallen to the weather deck. The girl managed to grab a stanchion for an instant but the force of her fall and the steepening deck angle broke her grip. She fell into the yellow sea that seemed to be racing up towards Sherwood. Oaf was yelling something, his arm holding Sherwood in an anaconda grip so that he could barely breathe. There was a heavy crump of more explosions mingling with hideous screams echoing from an air-conditioning duct. The deck heaved again.

'Got to get to the lifeboats!' Oaf yelled above the cacophony of tearing metal that seemed to come from below. 'You hear me, Sherwood? Lifeboats!'

Sherwood nodded dumbly. He felt curiously detached from the pandemonium around him.

Oaf grabbed Sherwood's hands and wrapped the fingers round the rail.

'You get good hold before I let go!'

Sherwood nodded and tightened his hold on the rail. He felt Oaf's grip on his waist relax and nearly panicked when he saw the sickly yellow sea at the end of the slope that had been the deck. His fear drew on unsuspected reserves of strength as he clung in terror to the rail.

'You okay?' shouted Oaf.

Sherwood heard himself croak: 'I'm okay.'

'I find rope and good lifeboat. I come back.'

The moon went behind a cloud. Sherwood, holding on to a rail he couldn't see, cried out in fear.

But Oaf had gone. He was completely alone save for the anguished cries from the air-conditioning duct. Then there was a man's faint voice from the passenger address speakers – as if the amplifiers weren't receiving full power. His ankles twisted painfully as he tried to keep his body upright on the remorselessly canting deck. He could hear the struggles and desperate cries of those who had been swept overboard.

The deck gave another shudder. Someone nearby was shouting through a loudhailer but he couldn't make out what was being said. Something about lifeboats.

The moon reappeared. Sherwood was again seized by panic when he saw how steep the deck had become. Something hit him. He shrank back in fear. It was a rope.

'You pass it under rail and throw back to me,' called out Oaf's reassuring voice from the shadows of the companionway that led down to the aft weather deck.

Sherwood groped blindly with one hand for the end of the rope. He gathered it clumsily into a coil and tossed it in the direction of the Norwegian's voice. He felt the rope tighten.

'Okay,' said Oaf. 'Now you come down rope like monkey.'

Sherwood's feet slipped from under him when he transferred his hold from the rail to the rope. He half-fell, half-slid along the rope until he felt Oaf's huge fingers close on his forearm and haul him to his feet.

A flare arched high into the black sky and exploded into a dazzling light suspended from a drifting parachute. Four more flares sailed up. The night became day beneath the brilliant magnesium suns.

'That's better,' Oaf growled. 'Follow me, Sherwood. I've found a raft.'

Sherwood stumbled down the steps behind the Norwegian. He found himself walking on the ridges of stairs that were now virtually horizontal.

'Bloody queer, eh?' said Oaf over his shoulder.

Sherwood slipped again. Oaf cursed in Norwegian and picked Sherwood up as though he were a rag doll. He reached the end of the steps and turned towards the port weather deck that seemed to be towering over the two men, so steeply was the *Orion* listing to starboard. Oaf set Sherwood down and pointed up. He saw Sherwood's bewildered expression, cupped his hands against the geologist's ear and shouted above the uproar of screaming passengers and bellowing loudhailers from the starboard side.

'We gotta go up,' Oaf yelled. 'Come on, Sherwood. We move pretty damn quick!'

Sherwood followed Oaf's finger to the edge of the deck where the bulwarks were etched against the moonlit clouds.

'That's the wrong way!' Sherwood screamed. 'All the lifeboats will be jammed up there!'

'Raft!' Oaf shouted back. 'Easy to launch down side of ship. And no big crowds going crazy. Come on!'

The *Orion* gave a sudden lurch. There was renewed screaming from the far side of the ship. Sherwood shut the noise out and concentrated on climbing up the weather deck. The ascent was made easier by many teak deck planks that had been forced from their seams by the enormous twist that had been induced throughout the length of the liner's hull. He reached a lifeboat davit and pulled himself to his feet. The seemingly endless climb had left him exhausted. Oaf had one leg over the bulwark and was hauling on a rope that disappeared into the shadows.

'Need help, Sherwood. You pull as well.'

Hardly knowing what he was doing, Sherwood braced himself against the davit and tried to grasp the rope. His arms were jerked back by the force of the Norwegian's pulls.

'Heave, damn you,' Oaf growled.

More flares lifted gracefully into the sky and exploded into light. Sherwood's arms were aching from the climb up the deck but he pulled as hard as he could. There was a bulky life-raft pack attached to the end of the rope.

'Got to get it over side, Sherwood. Come on.'

'Christ, Oaf. For God's sake let's rest a minute.'

'Plenty of time to rest in raft.'

The two men lifted the heavy canvas pack on to the bulwark and balanced it there while Oaf felt for its inflation lanyard.

'Okay, Sherwood. Now we heave smart on three. One. . . . Two. . . . Three. . . .'

The pack tumbled down the side of the *Orion*'s hull, trailing the lanyard. Sherwood felt sick as he looked down the *Orion*'s sloping flank at the evil yellow sea. The pack hit the surface with a splash that couldn't be heard. Oaf jerked the lanyard. The floating bundle swelled and burst its specially weakened fasteners. Bright orange fabric appeared. It spread out into a disc some twenty feet in diameter and then the rim of the disc began to inflate until two-foot-high sides to the raft were formed.

Oaf lashed a length of rope to the lifeboat davit and tossed it down to the raft.

Sherwood shook his head. 'I couldn't do it, Oaf. You go without me.'

Oaf pushed the rope into Sherwood's hands. 'You bloody climb down or I throw you down!'

Sherwood was desperate. 'Oaf, I can't do it!'

The giant Norwegian moved menacingly towards Sherwood. 'You go first. Bloody now! You go backwards and you don't look down!'

Sherwood took the rope and reluctantly swung his legs over the bulwark. He did as the Norwegian said and was surprised to discover that the descent wasn't as difficult as it looked. He paid the rope out mountaineer-fashion as he walked backwards down the long slope to the waiting yellow sea. He had one bad moment when mounting air pressure inside the hull blew a port-hole glass out of its mounting right beside him with explosive force.

After two minutes his feet had crossed the waterline and he found himself walking on the coppery anti-fouling paint that had been exposed by the *Orion*'s heavy list. The rope vibrated. He looked up. The huge bulk of Oaf was swaying down towards him. He could now hear the dull boom of the swell hurtling itself against the steel hull. The life-raft lifted and fell away. Sherwood timed the next heave and allowed himself to drop the last six feet into the water.

The intense cold was like a thunderbolt. It jarred the breath from his body. He lashed out in panic, terrified that the sudden shock was going to make him faint.

Oaf succeeded in dropping straight into the life-raft. It was a credit to its makers that his 280-pound bulk didn't go through the fabric floor. He grabbed Sherwood by his collar and waist-band and rolled him inboard. The geologist lay on the floor of the raft coughing up the freezing sea water he had swallowed while Oaf pounded his back with rib-shattering, sledgehammer blows.

'For Christ's sake, Oaf,' Sherwood spluttered. 'You'll kill me.'

Sherwood pulled himself into a sitting position. He had been in the water for less than thirty seconds but he was shivering uncontrollably and his teeth were clattering like clockwork cast-anets. Oaf held up the arm he had plunged into the water to grab Sherwood.

'Pretty bloody cold, eh, Sherwood? Three minutes kill a man.'

Sherwood shook his head. If someone made a statement he disagreed with, he would dispute it, no matter what state he was in. 'You'll argue on your deathbed,' his mother used to say.

'Benguela Current, Oaf. Cold – but not that cold.'

'Current don't matter a damn,' Oaf muttered. 'If it's cold like that – it kills. Pretty damn quick too.'

'Now look,' Sherwood disputed. 'If I say –'

'I say I throw you back,' Oaf growled. 'Too damn small.'

Sherwood stared uneasily at the giant. Oaf flashed his row of monolithic teeth in a broad grin. The geologist forgot the agony of the cold and laughed.

'Thank you for everything you did, Oaf.'

Oaf made no reply but stared up at the canting bulk of the *Orion*.

'Hadn't we better get the raft away?' asked Sherwood.

'Pity about woman,' said Oaf. 'She damn good. Not enough in world.'

'You mean Miss Hammond?'

Oaf nodded. A flare burned a trail into the sky. The liner's mass reminded Sherwood of a huge Celtic burial mound.

'Good at what?' inquired Sherwood, half-guessing what the Norwegian's answer would be.

Oaf's answer was a broad, knowing grin.

Sherwood heard some faint screams. He looked up the mountainous incline. The life-raft had drifted fifty yards from the liner. It no longer looked such an impossible climb. He turned to Oaf.

'We were all on "G" deck on this side, weren't we?'

'Sure. Two decks below waterline.'

Sherwood pointed to the *Orion*'s exposed waterline. 'But above the waterline now, Oaf. Is there a torch in that pack?'

Oaf opened the life-raft's survival pack. He pulled out the raft's insulated roof and its tubular aluminium support, two folding paddles, water containers and packs of food. There was even some fishing tackle. The torch was sealed into a watertight bag that Sherwood ripped open.

'Come on, Oaf. Paddle back to the side.'

The two men assembled the paddles and steered the life-raft back to the *Orion*. Sherwood shone the torch beam on the porthole that had been blown out by air pressure. The rope they had used to descend the liner's side lay alongside it.

'What are you thinking of, Sherwood?'

'I'm small enough to squeeze through that porthole to check her cabin. What was its number?'

'G12. Sherwood, you're crazy. Maybe she's in a lifeboat.'

'And maybe she isn't.' Sherwood jammed the torch into his pocket.

Oaf shook his head and paddled the life-raft cautiously into the water seething against the liner's hull. Sherwood clutched the life-raft's inflated sides, watching for an opportunity to grab the rope.

The swell lifted the life-raft. Sherwood tensed and jumped. His fingers closed thankfully round the rope. He pulled himself up the *Orion*'s side while Oaf watched anxiously, fending the raft away from the stricken hull with a paddle. Two minutes later Sherwood had wriggled through the opening and had disappeared.

Sherwood was surprised by the silence in the ship. He switched the torch on and walked downhill into the passageway. 'E' deck was deserted. He found the stewards' companionway and picked his way carefully down the crazily inclined stairs – walking half on the corners of each tread and half on the bulkhead.

'G' deck, two deck levels below 'E' deck, was a different story; there were terrible moanings from within the cabins. They heard Sherwood trip over something. Suddenly the trapped passengers were screaming and beating on their doors. Sherwood tried to open one but it was firmly jammed in its surround by the *Orion*'s distortion.

He walked along the tilted passageway, steadying himself with one hand and flashing the torch on the cabin numbers.

G20 . . . G19 . . . Seven more doors to G12.

His feet splashed through water. Warm water. He flashed the torch ahead. The passageway was sloping down. G12 was at the end of the passageway with the water up to its door handle. Why the hell was it warm when the water outside had been freezing?

Then he remembered the nuclear reactors.

The water was up to his waist outside G12. Supposing it was radioactive? If it was, it was too late. He tried the door. It was either jammed or locked. He banged on it.

'Julia?'

He could hear her crying.

'Julia! Is the door unlocked?'

A distraught voice answered: 'No. It's stuck. I can't get it open.'

'Hold the handle down!' Sherwood called.

There was a movement inside the cabin. The handle twisted down.

'Like that?' There was hope in her voice.

Sherwood threw his weight ineffectually against the door. It was useless – the water absorbed most of his effort and the *Orion*'s heavy list meant that he had to exert upwards. Maybe a drop-kick. . . .

He braced his spine against the opposite bulkhead and lashed out at the door with both feet. The shock jarred his whole body. The door splintered inwards. Julia winced with pain as she helped drag the door open; her fingernails were torn and bleeding from her desperate hammering and clawing at the unyielding door. She collapsed into Sherwood's arms.

'I thought no one would come,' she croaked, her voice hoarse from shouting.

The *Orion* trembled. The list was getting worse. Sherwood grabbed Julia's hand and dragged her into the passageway. He didn't notice her grimace in pain as his fingers closed on her lacerated nails. 'Come on! We've got to move fast!'

Ten minutes later they were at the open porthole. Sherwood peered out. Oaf had rigged the life-raft's cover. He had it open and was looking up. He grinned with relief when he saw Sherwood's head.

'Can you climb down this rope?' Sherwood asked Julia.

She looked down and saw the heaving yellow seas crashing against the liner's flank. Her voice didn't betray her terror. 'Yes I think so.'

'You sure?'

His tone annoyed her but she said nothing and allowed him to help her squeeze through the porthole. The breaking seas drowned her cry of pain as she grasped the rope. Her hands were slippery with blood and she would have lost her grip had Sherwood not seen her hands and grabbed her.

'You'll have to hang on to me!' he yelled.

'I'll be okay!' she shouted back defiantly.

'You won't. Let me do the climbing – you hang on to me!' He put an arm round Julia's waist and did his best to emulate Oaf's vice-like clasp while hanging on to the rope with his other hand. 'I've got you,' he panted. 'You take some of the weight if you can, but I've got you.'

Julia decided not to argue. Despite her torn hands she felt certain that she could climb down the rope unaided. Naturally, she was grateful to Sherwood for coming back for her but resented his automatic assumption that she was a helpless female.

Inch by painful inch, Sherwood began the nerve-wracking backwards walk down the rope while supporting Julia's weight. He was half way down when both of them were swamped by a freezing sea breaking against the hull. The impact swept Sherwood's feet from under him. In terror, he felt his hold on Julia's waist slacken. At the precise moment he tried to renew his grip, another wave roared up the side of the hull and slammed into them. Sherwood gave a scream as Julia was torn away. For a wild moment he thought she would fall into the madly spinning life-raft. Oaf's mighty arms plunged towards her. But it was too late; her helpless body tumbled head first into the foaming cauldron of yellow water.

Sherwood let the last few yards of rope burn through his fingers. Oaf was screaming obscenities at him. He landed on top of the giant Norwegian just as he was swinging the life-raft round to where Julia had hit the water and disappeared.

Oaf swore bitterly at Sherwood and tossed him contemptuously across the life-raft. 'Stupid bastard, Sherwood!' he snarled.

'I couldn't help it! I swear I couldn't help it!' Sherwood pleaded in desperation.

But Oaf wasn't listening. He was staring at the honey-coloured water – searching for Julia – calling her name. He saw something and started paddling frantically with his hands while roundly cursing Sherwood in a mixture of Norwegian and English.

'Come on, Sherwood! You help!'

Sherwood snatched up a paddle but Oaf tore it out of his hands and threw it down.

'You push wreckage out of the way!'

For five minutes they searched – Oaf sometimes churning the freezing water to foam whenever something caught his eye and Sherwood fending away the debris that was haemorrhaging into the sea from the hidden wound in the doomed liner's hull.

Oaf pointed suddenly. 'Hey, Sherwood! We both paddle like stink!'

There was no time to hunt for the paddle; Sherwood plunged both hands into the water and followed Oaf's example. The cold was an agonizing thunderbolt. His numbed hands felt as if they had been amputated. The wind had risen to a shriek. It whipped spray off the broken sea that lashed his face with bull-whip ferocity. He paddled blindly, obeying Oaf's bellowed orders like an android.

The Norwegian lunged his great bear-frame forward. There was a sudden flurry of violent movement.

'Okay, Sherwood. You stop paddling. Get cover shut fast.'

Sherwood opened his eyes. Julia was lying in the bottom of

the raft. Her face was the same ghastly pallor that he had seen once before when a Rosenthal laboratory technician was brought back to base three days after his sno-cat had broken down. He stared guiltily down at the pathetic body. She was lying very still.

'Is she dead, Oaf?'

'What the hell do you care, Sherwood?' the Norwegian growled. 'Just get cover fixed good. Keep out wind.'

Sherwood zipped the cover closed and extended the centre tube to provide more headroom. He hung the torch from a clip.

Oaf was cradling Julia's head in the crook of his great arm. He gently prised her jaw open. 'You push down on her chest every time I stop blowing,' he commanded.

He forced her lips into a pout and covered her mouth with his own. He blew steadily into her lungs for three seconds then raised his huge head. Sherwood pressed down on her sternum.

'Both hands!' roared Oaf. 'And hard! You won't hurt her!'

Oaf blew again and Sherwood pressed down with both hands spread across Julia's breasts. Her body felt like ice through the thin material of her blouse. There was a faint sound of air rushing past her frozen lips.

Oaf blew and Sherwood bore down on her chest again.

The two men settled to a steady rhythm. Blow . . . press. Blow . . . press. . . .

Fifteen minutes passed. The gale worsened. They tried to ignore the life-raft's crazy motion.

Blow . . . press. Blow . . . press. . . .

Two more agonizing minutes slipped by.

Sherwood felt a flicker of life beneath his aching fingers. He looked up at Oaf in exaltation. 'She's alive, Oaf! She's alive! I felt her heart beat!'

Oaf grunted. 'Heart going all the time. First time it start going stronger.'

Sherwood's misery was forgotten. He grinned happily at the Norwegian. 'She's going to be all right, isn't she? She's going to live!'

'Maybe. Maybe not,' was the laconic reply as Oaf started unbuttoning Julia's blouse.

'What the hell are you doing?' Sherwood demanded angrily.

'You get jeans off, Sherwood.' Oaf looked up at the geologist. 'Come on! You want her to die?'

Oaf leaned Julia forward and peeled her blouse off while Sherwood struggled with the zip on her saturated jeans. Oaf swore with impatience. Sherwood grasped both sides of the material and ripped the fly open. Oaf held Julia off the bottom of the life-raft while Sherwood rolled the jeans down to her knees. Her face was fixed in a mask of death. There was a lace-work of raw-looking veins visible beneath her transparent skin. He pulled the jeans clear of her feet.

Oaf tore the wrappings off the survival-pack blankets and spread one out on the life-raft's floor. He pulled his sweater and shirt off and started to wriggle out of his trousers.

'Get undressed, Sherwood. Everything off.'

'Why?'

'Just do it! Got to get her warm. Only hope.'

Sherwood struggled out of his clothes while Oaf pulled Julia against himself. The giant Norwegian's body was a mass of thick, tangled hair from chest to groin. He grinned at Sherwood as he arranged the blankets.

'Come on, Sherwood. We make a sandwich with this little one in the middle, heh?'

Sherwood suddenly understood. He knew from the brief survival course he had attended before leaving for Antarctica that warmth was the best immediate treatment for exposure although no mention had been made of Oaf's method.

Oaf reached up a gorilla-like arm and switched off the torch. Sherwood eased himself up against Julia. She was facing him, folded like a child into the matted curve of Oaf's hard body. He shivered as the frozen nakedness of her thighs and breasts greedily sucked the warmth from his body.

He lay still in the darkness, listening to the sounds of the storm and Oaf's stentorian breathing. A reassuring ghost of air from Julia's lungs brushed against his shoulder. He put his hand on her waist. Julia's presence reminded him of his wife. He wondered what Clare was doing; whether there had been a letter waiting in Cape Town; whether he would survive. . . . Whether Clare would care. . . .

Very soon he slept.

13

SACLANT (Supreme Allied Commander Atlantic (NATO))
The wartime task of SACLANT is to ensure the security of the whole Atlantic area and to deny its use to an enemy.

The matter was sufficiently urgent for Admiral Brandon Pearson, SACLANT, to be flown in his Hustler bomber direct from his headquarters in Norfolk, Virginia, to the Anti-Submarine Warfare Research Center at La Spezia in north-west Italy.

He and his aide, Captain Rolf Hagan of the Marine Corps, were taken straight to the submarine 'signature' library and played a sonar recording that had been made by the US Navy oceanographic research ship USS *Eureka* at a range of seven hundred miles. Computer analysis showed that the 'signature' – the sound fingerprint – of the mysterious submarine matched recordings that had been made in the Soviet Navy's trials area in the White Sea. It was conclusive proof that one of the Russian's monster 18,000-ton Delta Two class nuclear submarines was loose in the South Atlantic.

Pearson chewed on a cigar as he listened to the various experts arguing about Soviet reasons for sending their latest piece of largely untested nastiness into his patch of ocean. He was a broad, powerful man in his late fifties with a relaxed, easy-going air that inspired confidence. He was tough, resourceful and efficient. Apart from his qualities of leadership, he had an uncanny insight into the Soviet mind acquired when he was a junior liaison officer in Moscow during the closing stages of the Second World War. He could also speak fluent Russian.

He was worried. He couldn't think of one good reason for the Russians to send a Delta Two into the Atlantic. What was the point when its SS–N–8 missiles had the range to wipe out every North American city without the submarine having to stray from home waters? Why risk an untried weapon such as the Delta Two where it was far from help if an emergency arose?

Hagan read his thoughts. It was something the captain was getting good at. 'Maybe it's a provocation probe, sir?'

Pearson shook his head. 'They use their old Novembers for that so that they alarm the press and not the Pentagon.'

Something else was worrying him: the submarine had been heard in the same area that the *Orion* had gone down in. He bit on his cigar and summed up with a six-word sentence that made up in conciseness what it lacked in finesse: 'Those bastards are up to something.'

14

SARAH (Search And Rescue And Homing)

A buoyant, self-righting, automatic radio transmitter that broadcasts a continuous homing signal on the international distress frequency 2182. Standard equipment in lifeboats, life-rafts and the like.

Pale daylight was filtering through the life-raft's cover when Sherwood woke. There was no sensation in his body; he was paralysed with the murderous cold that had clawed its way through the insulated floor and was now gnawing into his vitals.

He could feel nothing except that the raft was now still.

The danger point is reached when you no longer feel the cold.

He fought his protesting brain into full wakefulness.

Julia's face was the colour of death. Her mouth was open but she wasn't breathing.

'She die soon,' said Oaf's voice.

Julia's deathly appearance frightened Sherwood badly.

He eased his body away from her and placed his hand on the now grey skin beneath her breasts. There was an almost imperceptible movement as her lungs gradually filled.

Sherwood gently lifted an eyelid. The grey, lustreless eye stared at him accusingly.

You killed me. You let me fall because of your stupid masculine ego and you killed me.

Oaf was dressed. He knelt beside Julia. 'She die soon,' he repeated. 'Big pity, Sherwood. Kid good screw.'

Rage welled up inside Sherwood at the Norwegian's words. He looked up into the deep-set blue eyes under their shaggy brows and was about to say something scathing, but Oaf sensed his anger and said quickly: 'I only screw her, Sherwood. You dropped her.'

Sherwood said nothing. He tucked the blankets round Julia's cold body and got dressed.

'How long have I been asleep?'

'Three hours, Sherwood.'

'For God's sake, Oaf, there must be something we can do for her. We can't just sit and watch her die.'

Oaf shrugged. 'No heat. She need heat bad.'

'Well, Christ – we could burn some wreckage or something!'

'No wreckage,' said Oaf simply.

'The sun, you idiot!'

'No sun.'

Sherwood reached up to the roof zip.

'You let heat escape,' Oaf commented.

Sherwood ignored him, pulled the zip open and stood up.

Oaf was right: there was no sun. Only a thick, cloying fog. So thick that it didn't even swirl. Visibility was less than four yards. The honey-coloured water was strangely still and silent.

There's always an ocean swell.

'What the hell are we going to do, Oaf?' asked Sherwood despairingly.

'I've set the SARAH,' said Oaf. He stood beside Sherwood and pointed to the little floating radio transmitter that was tethered to the life-raft by a cord. 'Like goddam fools we forget it. Someone hear it soon maybe.'

'I wonder how far we are from the *Orion*?'

'We come a good way north in the storm,' said Oaf.

'Nothing makes sense,' said Sherwood, staring down at the water. 'The water temperature; this yellow stuff whatever it is. And now fog and no swell.'

Oaf spat. 'Men make rules for the sea, Sherwood. And sea always breaking them, heh?'

There was a strange noise from the depths of the fog. A whistling sound like the breathing of an unimaginable sea monster. Sherwood felt the hair prickling on the back of his scalp.

'What the hell's that?'

The noise was repeated: a flesh-crawling, half-moaning, half-sighing that made Sherwood's chilled blood run even colder. Then there was a series of heavy splashes that seemed to get louder – as if some malignant creature of the depths was swimming towards them with long, purposeful strokes. Ripples were spreading out of the freezing fog from the direction of the terrifying sound. The life-raft began to rock with a rhythm that quickened with Sherwood's heartbeat. Oaf's razor-sharp whaler's knife had appeared in his gnarled, ham-like fist.

But Sherwood knew that it would be useless against the thing that was coming for them from the fog.

15

TAT 12 (Transatlantic Telephone cable)
4000 channel voice highway linking South Africa and the United States. Same cable pattern as used in the United States – France TAT 6.

The *New York Times* sub-editor watched the story unfolding on the teleprinter.

. . . . FOG STILL MAKING IT IMPOSSIBLE FOR HELICOPTER CRUISER SPRINGBOK TO OPERATE ITS WASP HELICOPTERS IN THE SEARCH FOR ORION SURVIVORS. SOUTH AFRICAN WEATHER EXPERTS BAFFLED BY THE PERSISTENCE AND DENSITY OF THE FOG WHICH IS NOW COVERING 10,000 – REPEAT – TEN THOUSAND SQUARE MILES OF OCEAN IN THE DISASTER AREA. SOUTH AFRICAN PREMIER TODAY DESCRIBED ORION LOSS AS WORST PEACETIME MARITIME DISASTER SINCE TITANIC. A SPOKESMAN FOR THE

The teleprinter stopped abruptly in mid-sentence.

At the same time, all over the United States, all telephone conversations with South Africa were cut without warning leaving thousands of angry subscribers on both sides of the Atlantic shouting uselessly into their phones.

Ten minutes later, the telegraph cable was also cut.

Frantic engineers in Cape Town and New York carried out

resistance tests on their respective ends of both cables and established that the breaks had inexplicably occurred in the three-mile-deep Cape Basin off South West Africa. It was baffling because oceanic cables are usually safe lying in dark tranquillity on the abyssal floors of the oceans. Only where they are exposed to trawls and the tides in the shallow coastal waters over the continental shelves are they likely to suffer damage.

Even more extraordinary was the fact that the cables had been cut in approximately the same position from which the *Orion* had broadcast her distress calls.

16

'Shut up, Sherwood!' Oaf hissed. 'You shut up so I listen!'

Sherwood fell silent. He felt a bitter resentment for the way the big Norwegian had automatically assumed command.

Oaf listened intently to the deadened, eerie noises coming out of the fog. He swore suddenly, jammed the long whaler's knife back into its sheath and thrust one of the folding paddles at his companion.

'Come on, Sherwood! We paddle like stink!'

It was an order Sherwood was more than willing to obey. He snatched the paddle from Oaf and drove it into the water. Fear gave him strength. He spun the life-raft round.

'That way!' yelled Oaf, jabbing a huge finger in the direction of the sound and arresting the life-raft's motion with his own paddle.

Sherwood stared at him. 'Are you crazy?'

Oaf ignored him, swung his paddle into the water and propelled the life-raft through the water with effortless sweeps. 'Come on, you lazy shit, Sherwood! Paddle like stink!' He suddenly grabbed Sherwood by the shoulder and held his paddle up in a threatening gesture. 'You paddle like stink or I kill you!'

Sherwood did as he was told and started paddling, letting Oaf do the steering.

The hideous noise drew nearer.

A minute of arm-breaking effort passed. Oaf signalled to

Sherwood to stop paddling. The big Norwegian strained his sensitive ears into the fog, turning his head to the left and right to get a bearing. The noises were louder and the ripples had become small waves.

'How far?' whispered Sherwood. How far to what?

'Fog play tricks,' answered Oaf. 'But pretty near maybe. Paddle.'

Sherwood paddled. He glanced down at Julia. Her face was changing from its deathly white to an ashen grey. He was certain that she was now dead.

The terrifying breathing noise was less than twenty yards away. Then there was a sudden explosive hiss that sounded like super-heated steam escaping from a safety valve. It was followed by the sound of rain. Warm spray blew in Sherwood's face. He paddled without thinking. He was reaching the point where he no longer cared very much what happened to him.

There was a tremendous splash. A second later the life-raft was nearly turned over in the maddened turmoil of enraged water.

Sherwood was thrown across Julia's body. He heard Oaf screaming: 'Paddle back! Paddle back!'

The life-raft span round as Oaf frantically back-paddled.

Then Sherwood saw it: a ghastly double-headed spectre of childhood nightmares rearing into the fog. For a terrifying second it was poised high against the fog-diffused daylight. Despite his fear, Sherwood's scientific instincts asserted themselves: he estimated that the two heads spanned at least sixteen feet. Oaf was yelling at the top of his voice but Sherwood was too transfixed by the apparition to heed what the Norwegian was saying.

There was a savage hissing. The two heads swooped down and smashed into the water. As Sherwood fought to remain in the bucking life-raft, he suddenly realized what the apparition was.

The twin flukes of a blue whale's tail.

'We get down the side of him!' Oaf was shouting.

The life-raft circled clear of the giant mammal's tail as Oaf drove his paddle through the water.

'Why get near the bloody thing at all!' Sherwood shouted.

Oaf didn't answer. He steered the life-raft alongside the

creature's fluted flank. Sherwood was convinced that the Norwegian was crazy. He knew that Oaf had seen many whales close-to during his days as a whale-catcher and lemmer so why risk going near this animal when it might sound at any monemt?

'Him near dead,' said Oaf as if he was reading Sherwood's thoughts.

The tail rose again. The motion was sluggish.

'How do you know?'

'He's beached,' said Oaf. 'His own weight crushing him so he can't breathe properly.'

'You mean, we're in shallow water?' asked Sherwood incredulously.

Oaf pointed at the whale's curving hulk that looked like an overturned ship. 'Lot of him out of the water. He's beached okay.'

Air blasted out of the creature's blow-hole. Sherwood felt an eddy of warm, fetid air on his face. The smell was appalling. He was nearly sick.

'How the hell can we be in shallow water?'

Oaf shrugged. 'You're the scientist, Sherwood.' The Norwegian jerked the aluminium roof support tube out of its mountings and examined it critically, flexing it to test its strength.

The life-raft drifted near the creature's absurdly small eye, which was gazing uninterestedly at Sherwood. Oaf steadied himself by resting one hand on the whale's side while gripping the aluminium tube with the other hand. With one swift movement, he drove the makeshift harpoon into the whale's eye. He then placed his palm on the end of the tube and rammed the entire five-foot length deep into the creature's body and held it there.

Nothing happened for some seconds; perhaps the whale was already on the point of death. Then, with graceful slowness, the tail lifted high into the fog, and instead of slamming down on the water, gently lowered itself so that there was scarcely a ripple.

'Dead now,' said Oaf unnecessarily. Without waiting for an answer, he jumped on to the whale's back, produced his flensing knife and started to work the blade into the thick blubber.

Sherwood watched, transfixed.

'Do you think you'll be able to eat it all, Oaf?'

'Tie raft to harpoon,' the Norwegian grunted.

Sherwood did so. 'Now what?'

'Get girl up here bloody quick.'

'Why, for Christ's sake?'

Oaf didn't pause in his work. He pushed a hand deep into the mountainous corpse. 'Do it.'

Sherwood tried to be gentle as he dragged Julia's lifeless body to the side of the raft and propped her up. The blanket fell away. He tried to push it back into place.

'Don't need blanket,' said Oaf. He reached down with one blood-covered hand and grasped Julia under the armpit.

The two men lifted her frozen, naked body on to the whale's back.

'Need paddles and a lifejacket,' said Oaf, pointing into the life-raft.

Sherwood passed them up. Oaf took them and held out his hand. 'Need help,' he said.

Sherwood grasped the hand that was slippery with whale blood and allowed himself to be hauled on to the whale's back beside Julia.

Oaf went back to work on the two-foot-square section of blubber he was hacking off the corpse. Sherwood watched in fascination as the Norwegian's swift knife strokes sliced through the tissue. Oaf gestured.

'Get hold and pull.'

Sherwood helped tear the section of thick blubber clear. The underside felt pleasantly warm in his frozen fingers. He began to understand what Oaf was planning. The knife went down into the flesh, releasing a strong, sickly odour and clouds of steam as the cold fog combined with the warm air rising from the wound. Oaf made a long cut and wedged it open with one of the paddles. Sherwood did the same with the other paddle. Life-giving heat poured out from the interior of the dead whale through the gaping incision in its body.

Oaf took a deep breath and pushed himself head first into the whale, holding his knife above his head. There was a heavy gurgling noise. Oaf wriggled backwards out of the hole. The upper half of his body was covered in the hot, thick blood from the severed artery that was filling the gaping wound like a cistern.

The Norwegian wiped the blood away from his eyes and pointed at the lifejacket.

'So she don't slip down too deep. Fix it round her tits.'

Sherwood tied the lifejacket round Julia's chest and the two men lowered her body feet first into the bath of hot, steaming blood until she was immersed to her neck. Oaf eased the paddles out so that the sides of the incision closed on Julia and held her firmly.

'Many years ago,' said Oaf as he splashed the blood out of his hair with icy sea water, 'a man try walking on grease ice and he go through. We fish him out half-dead like girl. We shoot a sea elephant, slit belly open and put man inside.' Oaf grinned. 'Two hours later he was walking about again but he stink terrible for weeks.'

Sherwood sat down on the whale's back. He hadn't realized until now just how exhausted he was.

'You ought to take over the Rosenthal survival course, Oaf.'

Oaf spat into the sea. 'Them old women never been outside London.'

Sherwood watched Julia's face. It was serene. 'Will she live?'

'We know in an hour. Maybe more. Maybe less.'

It was less.

To the delight of the two men, colour was returning to Julia's face after thirty minutes.

Fifty minutes after she had been placed in the whale, with the strengthening sun dispersing the fog, Sherwood realized that Julia's eyes were open. She was watching him with a quizzical expression. The lifejacket under her chin restricted her vision; all she could see was the sky. Her voice when she spoke was sweet music: 'Hallo, Mr Sherwood. Where am I?'

Sherwood stared at her. 'Oaf!' he yelled. 'Oaf!'

The Norwegian scrambled out of the life-raft on to the whale's back and knelt beside Julia. He kissed her, placing his huge arm around her head. Sherwood turned away, leaving them to talk. He wondered how Oaf would tell her about the whale. Jealousy was an emotion he had no experience of. He climbed back into the life-raft. Oaf had been cleaning the aluminium tube he had used as a harpoon. Sherwood reached down into the water with it. The end of the tube struck the sea bed before the icy water had reached his shoulder. He forgot his jealousy for the moment as he pondered the phenomenon of such shallow water in the Cape Basin. Although the bottom felt like rock through the aluminium tube, he twisted it back and forth in the hope of obtaining a sample.

There was the distant beat of an engine. Oaf started dancing up and down on the whale's back, waving the bright yellow folding paddles like semaphore flags.

Sherwood looked up. The fog was clearing rapidly. Silhouetted against the pale sky, with its absurd undercarriage resembling the wheels of a tea trolley, was an anti-submarine Wasp helicopter with Royal Navy markings. It was losing height as it homed in on the automatic radio signals from the life-raft's SARAH beacon.

It was within two hundred yards when Sherwood remembered to look at the end of the tube he had ground into the sea bed. His breath was melting the curious, off-white powdery substance. He stared at it. Several seconds passed before he realized what it was.

Ice.

17

The ITN news presenter adopted a grave expression as he replaced his phone.

'We've just heard,' he told the television camera and fifteen million people throughout the United Kingdom, 'that three more survivors from the *Orion* have been found today by a helicopter from the British frigate *Snow Tiger* that is helping the South African navy in the search and rescue operation. . . .'

Admiral Howe dozed in front of his television. The news presenter's voice washed over him. He was exhausted after a long day in his Whitehall office. The room was its usual mess.

'. . . . the three – Julia Hammond, a marine biologist from South London, Glyn Sherwood, a geologist from Kingston-upon-Thames and Oluf Johansen, a Norwegian engineer – were returning to Southampton after a three-year tour of duty with the Rosenthal survey team in Antarctica. . . .'

Admiral Howe was suddenly awake at the mention of the Rosenthal Base and paying close attention to the rest of the news presenter's words. Mention of Rosenthal by the media always made him nervous.

'The extremely high death toll is due to the exceptionally low temperature of the water. South African oceanographers have admitted to being baffled by the icy sea which is only one degree above freezing. . . .'

The last sentence stunned the old sailor. It's not possible, he reasoned. Not after seven months.

Then he remembered just how much ice was missing. His arthritic hand shook as he dialled Lieutenant Abbott's number.

'And now for the rest of the news. . . .'

But Admiral Howe wasn't interested in the rest of the news.

18

George Fielding, a normally easy-going retired bank president from Houston, was beginning to get irritated by the South African naval officer questioning him politely in the *Springbok*'s sickbay as the cruiser headed for Simonstown.

'Look,' said Fielding. 'Let's take it from the top again. Shortly after midnight I went up on the weather deck for air. It was closed to passengers but I stepped over the rope.'

'Wasn't it cold, sir? The *Orion* was doing thirty-seven knots.'

'Chilly,' said Fielding. 'But I didn't pay it no mind.'

'And you saw this white track in the water at thirty minutes after midnight?'

'Torpedo track,' Fielding corrected.

The naval officer sighed.

'Just before the ship was blown apart,' Fielding finished.

'Sir,' said the naval officer earnestly. 'I want you to think very carefully. Are you absolutely certain it was a torpedo track you saw?'

'Yes,' said Fielding without hesitation. He had said the first time that he had seen a torpedo track and he wasn't a man to change his mind once he had made it up. Maybe the white pattern that had flashed on the surface for a few seconds had been irregular but he had read somewhere that modern torpedoes didn't have to run straight – they weaved about as they homed in on their target. *Time* magazine had run an article on them: that was good enough for George Fielding.

'Did you see bubbles from this . . . this torpedo track, sir?'

The banker stared at the naval officer. 'Hell, no. Since when did modern torpedoes use compressed air?'

It was the naval officer's turn to stare. He looked at Fielding in surprise.

'I know what a cavitation track looks like,' Fielding stated stubbornly. 'I was on the old *Nevada* in Pearl Harbor.'

The naval officer was desperate. It was vital to convince the elderly businessman that he could be wrong. In twenty hours the *Springbok* would be docking. Simonstown was swarming with journalists from all over the world, eager to interview the *Orion*'s survivors.

'Look, Mr Fielding, you *must* be mistaken. Why would anyone want to torpedo the *Orion*?'

'I saw a tinfish,' Fielding insisted. 'And if it wasn't a torpedo exploding outside the *Orion*'s hull, how is it that that pod of whales were thrashing about half-stunned on the surface smashing up all the lifeboats except ours?'

The naval officer was writing up his report an hour later in the wardroom when his commanding officer walked in and sank wearily into a chair. He looked across at the officer.

'I've just been talking to that Japanese shirt manufacturer. He was on the port weather deck at the time. You'll never guess what his crazy theory is about the sinking.'

'That the *Orion* was torpedoed?' ventured the officer.

The captain gaped at his subordinate.

'Yours said the same?'

The officer nodded unhappily.

'Hell,' breathed the commanding officer.

19

It was the first time that the press officer had a written statement to read to the sweating journalists packed into the suffocating conference room at Simonstown. Hitherto, the press conferences had been informal question and answer sessions.

He held a sheet of paper in his hand and waited for the snap of camera shutters to die away. He had never bothered before. The room quietened. There was only the soft whirr of movie cameras as he spoke.

'It was decided at ten this morning to extend the search and rescue operation by another seventy-two hours – until the same time on Wednesday. The number of survivors still stands at twenty-three. Twenty on the *Springbok* and three on the British frigate *Snow Tiger*. Both ships have excellent hospital facilities so that the survivors can remain aboard until the search is called off.'

There was a loud groan from all the journalists.

'Does that mean we won't be able to see them for three days?' demanded a Canadian.

'Yes,' said the press officer.

'Supposing we charter a helicopter? Will we be able to land on the *Springbok* or the *Snow Tiger*?'

The press officer smiled self-effacingly. 'I'm very sorry, ladies and gentlemen, but the helicopter handling facilities on both ships are fully committed to their own machines during the search.'

The answer was too glib. Journalists always get suspicious when they think they're being frozen off a story.

Ralph Kroll of CBS News had a question:

'What search, Mr Stevasson?'

The press officer looked surprised. 'I don't understand your question, Mr Kroll.'

The cameras swung towards Kroll.

'Forgive me, Mr Stevasson,' said Kroll, pinning his victim down with thirty years' experience in dealing with officials, 'but I was under the impression that no actual searching was involved – that your choppers had only to home in on the lifeboat beacons.'

The press officer hesitated. His mind raced. 'There might be people in the water,' he pointed out.

Kroll nodded. 'Dead from exposure like the seven hundred bodies that you've recovered so far?'

The press officer smiled. 'And there's the possibility that

there's a lifeboat somewhere whose occupants haven't switched on their beacon because they don't know what it is.'

'There is that possibility, of course,' Kroll admitted. 'Even if the operating instructions are etched on each beacon in eight languages, including Chinese and Japanese.'

'We can't take chances with people's lives,' said the press officer evenly.

Kroll made a note and then looked up at the press officer with a puzzled expression.

'Is there any connection between the loss of the *Orion* and the arrival of the NATO Supreme Allied Commander Atlantic here in Simonstown?'

There was a stir in the room. The journalists looked gratefully at Kroll.

'I have no information,' said the press officer, glancing at his watch.

Kroll's innocent blue eyes opened wide.

'Maybe I can enlighten you then, Mr Stevasson; his Hustler is right here on the Simonstown airbase. I recognized its tail markings. Everywhere that Hustler goes, Admiral Brandon Pearson goes too. Perhaps you'd be good enough to tell us why he's here – save all these ladies and gentlemen having to file home a lot of speculative copy.'

The press officer's reply was tinged with hostility.

'I have no information.'

The sleepy blue eyes remained fixed on him. 'And I guess that goes for news about my colleague whose plane has disappeared?'

'I'm sorry. I have no information.'

Kroll maintained his innocent expression. 'Would you care to comment on the rumour that a helicopter of the South African Navy spotted the wreckage of a light airplane on the water and recovered a body? A body clutching a movie camera?'

'I have no information,' the press officer repeated doggedly.

No one in the room believed him.

20

The tourists were pressed six deep against the railings of Buckingham Palace, watching the changing of the guard. Lieutenant

Abbott accelerated past a laden coach. Admiral Howe was deep in thought at his side, paying little attention to Abbott's conversation.

'I keep thinking of this seven-month period between the loss of the submarine and the sinking of the *Orion*,' said Abbott. 'I don't see how the ice could've been the cause. It just doesn't seem possible.'

'You heard those experts,' muttered Howe, rousing himself.

'But they wouldn't commit themselves, sir.'

'Do they ever?'

The two men fell silent. Abbott concentrated on his driving. Admiral Howe spoke first.

'It's lucky those three Rosenthal survivors are on one of our ships.'

Abbott turned his head. 'What does it matter what ship they're on, sir? They don't know anything about the depot.'

'No. They don't know anything. But I don't like the idea of Rosenthal personnel being subjected to press probing and publicity.'

'But none of the survivors have seen anything unusual, sir.'

'We've only the South Africans' word for that. Our three survivors are trained observers and one of them, the girl, is an oceanographer. I don't want them talking to the press – not newshounds of the calibre that the agencies have sent to Simonstown.'

'Then how do you propose to stop them, sir?'

'We need time on this operation, James.'

'But how can we stop them talking to the press?' Abbott persisted.

Admiral Howe considered for some moments. 'We'll have to think of something, James.'

21

Pearson and Hagan recognized the face of the dead CBS News cameraman as soon as the cover was pulled back.

'Yes, I know him,' said Pearson. 'I know most of them by sight. You didn't drag me here just to identify a body, Mr Differing?'

'No, admiral.' The South African Defence Minister waited for the naval doctor to move away. 'You know, this guy was hanging on to his camera so tight that the doctors who examined his body had to break two of his fingers. Now we know why. Film was ruined by sea water getting into the magazine through the core but there's four metres at the end which maybe will make your flight worthwhile.'

The South African spoke quickly. Hard, Cape Town vowels. He ushered his visitors to the door. 'They've shown me how to use the projector in the lecture hall.'

'Holy cow,' Pearson muttered to himself in the darkness.

'My sentiments exactly,' said Differing.

There was an 18,000-ton Soviet Delta on the screen. The picture was so vivid, so compelling, that Pearson had no difficulty in imagining the surging roar of breaking water as the mighty submarine drove its massive, bullet-shaped bow contemptuously through the heaving yellow sea. Its sheer physical presence breathed icy life into the time-worn, half-forgotten phrases coined during the uneasy fifties and sixties: Megadeath. . . . Over-kill. . . . Flash zone. . . . Primary fire zone. . . .

The picture zoomed in on two men on the slender fin. One was pointing a tubular device up at the approaching camera.

'A Soviet Grail shoulder launched anti-aircraft missile,' said Differing. 'Watch carefully.'

There was a bright flash from the two men standing on the submarine's fin. Differing slowed the projector down. A series of clicks punctuated each frame change. A pencil-slim, flaring rocket jerked up towards the camera. The screen went blank.

Pearson broke the silence that followed when Differing had restored the lights. 'Why in hell didn't it dive before the airplane got close? They've got over-horizon radar facilities.'

'Simple,' said the South African. 'Our guess is that it was towing several thousand metres of hawser with a telephone cable cutter on the end.'

Pearson lit a cigar. 'And they'd use their latest and largest submarine?'

'Sure. Six miles of hawser takes up space.'

'It's a pity that the clip didn't show the sub's stern,' said Pearson pointedly.

Differing smiled thinly. 'You can have the original film back, admiral. Your own experts will confirm that it was damaged by sea water. The only thing we can't account for is the unusual colour of the sea. It's not a colour processing fault. We were careful.'

Pearson thought for a few moments. 'You've interviewed *all* the *Orion* survivors?'

'Except three scientists returning from Antarctica. The British frigate *Snow Tiger* picked them up. They'll be in Simonstown tomorrow.'

'I want to talk to *all* the *Orion* survivors before drawing conclusions such as you've drawn, Mr Differing.'

Differing looked pained. 'We're going on the eye-witness accounts of two reliable people, admiral. One of them is a fellow citizen of yours who knows all about being torpedoed. And the survivors who didn't see the torpedo tracks will tell you all about the pod of whales that were struggling on the surface, smashing up lifeboats. It's obvious that the explosion occurred outside the *Orion*'s hull.'

'What about the freezing water, Mr Differing? You have a neat theory for that as well?'

The South African shrugged. 'Freak conditions, admiral.'

Pearson inhaled deeply on his cigar, carefully choosing his words. 'Assuming the Soviets did sink the *Orion*, have you asked yourself why they should do such a senseless thing?'

'There was the sinking of the *Athenia* on the first day of the last war,' said Differing. He paused before adding in an expressionless voice: 'It seems to be the modern way of starting them these days.'

22

Reduced to unparaphrased plaintext, the signal printed out on the British frigate's secure channel data link line-printer read:

ACQ LONDON TO COMMANDER LEYSDOWN, SNOW TIGER. CONGRATULATIONS YOUR RESCUE ROSENTHAL PERSONNEL. IMPORTANT THEY HAVE NO CONTACT PRESS OR PUBLIC. DO

NOT RETURN SIMONSTOWN. LT JAMES ABBOTT ON WAY TO YOU TO ADVISE. REMAIN ON PICKET.

23

'Ice?' exclaimed Julia. She would have laughed but Sherwood was serious. 'Are you sure?'

'I know what ice looks like,' Sherwood answered.

'Even inside a roof support tube?'

Sherwood refused to reply. Julia didn't blame him. As a scientist, Sherwood wouldn't make claims unless he was sure of his facts. She gazed pensively down at wake foaming out from under the *Snow Tiger*'s transom, carefully studying the frigate's dancing shadow on the broken water. She apologized but Sherwood quickly brushed it aside.

'I want to say sorry to you,' he said.

'What for?'

'For dropping you into the water. It was childish of me not letting you try to climb down that rope.'

Julia laughed to ease his embarrassment. 'Forget it. I've been dropped by men before. I don't suppose it'll be the last time. And no permanent damage has been done. As a matter of fact, the ship's surgeon paid me a dubious compliment by saying that I'm as strong as a horse.'

Sherwood laughed. 'Some horse.'

Julia didn't seem to hear him; she was screwing up her eyes to look at the sun. 'Have you told anyone else about the ice?' she asked.

'No.'

She returned her attention to Sherwood. 'Why not?'

'I didn't think anyone would believe me.'

'Then why tell me?'

'I thought that you might be able to offer some sort of explanation. I'm damned if I can come up with one.'

Julia thought for a few seconds, then glanced up at the sun again. '*If* it was ice, it doesn't make sense. Maybe it was ice from the *Orion*? Wait a minute – what about your core samples in the liner's refrigeration hold? They ran into several tonnes of ice didn't they?'

'Yes, but –'

'There's your answer – some submerged wreckage from the *Orion* with some of your ice cores must've drifted with the life-raft and you stuck the life-raft's roof support tube in one of them. Simple. Say thank you.'

'I suppose that is a possible explanation,' Sherwood conceded.

'You should be grateful to me for setting your mind at rest,' said Julia, grinning.

'But it doesn't explain the unusual colour of the sea or its near freezing temperature.'

'I'll give you a real mystery to ponder on,' said Julia. 'Ask yourself why this remnant of our once glorious navy turns a few degrees to port every thirty minutes so that we're steaming in a huge circle.'

Puzzled, Sherwood looked up at the sun.

It was in the wrong place.

24

NORAD – North American Air Defence Command
Joint US–Canadian organization to defend the North American continent against surprise attack from over the polar regions.

Admiral Brandon Pearson was furious. Captain Hagan was the nearest to receive his wrath. It was virtually unheard-of for a NATO country to invoke the 'urgent national business' clause to pull out a ship without prior notification.

'No explanation?' he barked.

'No, sir.'

'You told Northwood that I want to talk to those three survivors they've got on the *Snow Tiger*?'

'Yes, sir. They said that they're very sorry, but the *Snow Tiger* is unable to return to South Africa at the moment.'

Pearson grunted. 'Trouble from their goddam Left I suppose, Okay. Fix me a chopper – I'll fly out to the *Snow Tiger* myself.'

Hagan hesitated. 'Before you do, sir, I think you ought to look at this signal from the *Johnson*.' He held out a buff signal envelope. 'The carrier has reported that ten bottom-fixed sonobuoys in the South Atlantic Seaguard barrier have ceased functioning. They suggest using one of NORAD's magnetic anomaly detector 707s to plug the gap until new sonobuoys can be dropped into position.'

Pearson spun round quickly, his face shocked. '*Ten* buoys?'

Hagan nodded. 'That's what I thought. Maybe the Soviet sub wasn't just cutting telephone cables.'

Pearson thought quickly. The Soviets *were* cooking something. Something big. Something that made his flesh crawl. Ten buoys! That meant there was a gap in the barrier that the entire Soviet Navy could sail through undetected. He started firing orders.

'I'm going straight out to the *Johnson* now. Tell them I want their strike command combat control centre in a go condition by the time I arrive and the conference-secure satellite channels to Washington, Norfolk, Mons and Northwood checked out and cleared for immediate operational use. I also want all SSBNs set to AQ readiness. After that, you're to fly out to the *Snow Tiger* and talk to those three *Orion* survivors – you know the sort of questions I want asked. That is all.'

Hagan was dismissed. He saluted and left.

Outside the office he collected his reeling thoughts. In sounding general stations throughout his command, the admiral was calling an Alert.

A low-key, unendorsed Alert maybe.

But still an Alert.

25

SILENT RUNNING

A condition aboard a submerged submarine in which engine noise and crew movement is kept to a minimum to avoid detection by passive sonar.

The *Podorny* was running blind at a depth of three hundred metres when she collided with the frozen cliff beneath the sea.

There was no warning; her forward scan sonar had been

switched off to reduce noise. Her off-watch crew, under severe movement restriction, were watching a movie in the forward missile room and listening to the sound-track through headphones.

They died immediately – crushed into instant oblivion by the cataclysmic inrush of the Atlantic as the *Podorny*'s unstoppable 18,000-ton momentum split the submarine like a self-opening sardine can.

At the moment of impact, Commander Igor Leachinski was radioing the *Podorny*'s position to Sevastopol through a surface-trailed antennae wire. The sudden deceleration threw him against the communications room bulkhead. And then the countless tons of water were upon him, driving the breath from his lungs and the life from his body in one devastating blow that swept through the length of the submarine in less than three seconds.

The concertina'd remains of the *Podorny* hovered for timeless, silent moments against the edifice that had completely destroyed it. Then, with seemingly infinite care, they grated down the face of the submerged cliff on the first stage of their three-mile last voyage to the abyssal floor of the Angolan Basin in the South Atlantic.

Thousands of irregular headstones of every conceivable size came bobbing to the surface, marking the *Podorny*'s grave. They twisted and jostled in the long, easy swell.

Then they began to melt.

Ice.

26

The British frigate *Snow Tiger* made another of her imperceptible alterations of course as Julia sat in the vacant chair between Oaf and Sherwood. Oaf was sound asleep and snoring. The afternoon sun was warm and agreeable. Sherwood looked inquiringly at Julia as she made herself comfortable.

'Did you see the captain?' he asked.

'Yes. He said that they're searching for an *Orion* life-raft that's been seen in this area by a scheduled SAA flight. I asked him why none of the men on watch were using binoculars and he said that their radar was more sensitive. He's not certain when we'll get to Simonstown.'

Sherwood glanced at the *Snow Tiger*'s deserted helicopter deck. 'Is that what the Wasp is doing – out searching?'

Julia shrugged. 'How should I know?'

'It's odd.'

'What?'

'That helicopter's been gone since this morning – at least twelve hours. As its duration is 2½ hours it must've landed somewhere. Why didn't it take us with it?'

Julia shaded her eyes and stared at the horizon. 'Talk of the devil. . . .' she murmured.

They watched the distant black dot that was swelling against the blue background.

'I know what caused your yellow sea,' said Julia casually.

'Oh?'

'Ostracods.'

'Now why didn't I think of that? What are they?'

The dot became the unweildy shape of a Wasp helicopter.

'They're microscopic organisms that live at depths of two to three thousand metres. A sudden change in the sea temperature kills them and they come to the surface in their countless millions and turn the sea a muddy yellow colour. I remember reading about a nine-day press wonder when the liner *Corinthic* steamed for several days through a sea of honey. It must have been ostracods.'

The Wasp approached the *Snow Tiger* from astern.

'What sort of temperature change?' Sherwood persisted. An increase or a decrease?'

'Either.' Julia had to raise her voice to make herself heard above the uproar from the helicopter turbines.

Oaf stirred in his sleep but amazingly failed to wake.

Sherwood was too preoccupied to pay any attention to the Wasp as it lowered itself on to the helicopter platform.

He was thinking about ice.

27

From: Minister of Defence, Chairman of Military Council.
To: All First Deputy and Deputy Ministers of Defence.
Subject: The loss of the submarine *Podorny*.

Instructions are to be issued to Admiral Turgenev, Commander-in-Chief, Black Sea Fleet, that the recovery of the *Podorny* is *absolutely vital* irrespective of cost or the undoubted difficulty. There must be no repetition of the *Glomar Explorer** incident we experienced when Howard Hughes and his CIA minions stole one of our submarines. The Black Sea Fleet has the deep ocean recovery vessels and the necessary heavy surface units to establish a significant naval presence in the area where the *Podorny* went down. Such a presence will be essential to deter over-inquisitiveness by American-controlled NATO forces who consider the Atlantic their own territory.

Once the recovery task force is in position, the Americans will guess immediately what has happened and will watch carefully for a chance to recover the submarine themselves. For that reason, the salvage vessels *must* be provided with *continuous* protection and logistic support.

Admiral Turgenev is to be provided with all the facilities necessary to execute the recovery of the *Podorny*, including the authority to release our new Kiev-class carriers to assist in the provision of air cover.

Admiral Turgenev heaved a sigh of relief when he read his instructions – no blame for the use of the Delta submarine had been steered his way. Thank God he'd ensured a wide distribution of his memo to General Zadkin in which he had deplored the assignment of a Delta to the unknown waters of the South Atlantic.

With any luck, General Zadkin's star should now be on the wane in Moscow.

* Project Jennifer: the recovery by the CIA in June 1974 of a lost Soviet Golf-class submarine that had sunk in the Pacific.

28

Lieutenant James Abbott was wearing a civilian suit and an apologetic smile that he hadn't allowed to slacken for an instant since he had landed on the *Snow Tiger* an hour earlier. He was surprising himself with his acting ability. He introduced himself to Julia, Sherwood and Oaf as the Rosenthal Foundation's new scientific establishment officer and quickly explained the purpose of his visit. As expected, the three survivors were incredulous.

'You want us to go back to Antarctica?' echoed Julia.

'That's right,' said Abbott, smiling easily at all three in turn. 'But only for a year. Until your replacements get the feel of your work. I was appalled when I discovered how inexperienced they were. A complete admin foul-up the whole thing. They didn't even hire an engineer to replace Mr Johansen.' Abbott smiled at Oaf. 'At least, not an engineer with your experience of working in polar conditions, Mr Johansen.'

Oaf grunted.

'So we'd be extremely grateful if you'd return on the supply flight that'll be refuelling in the Azores. The navy have agreed to fly you there from the *Ark Royal*.'

'When?' asked Sherwood. His voice didn't betray his excitement at the prospect of returning to Antarctica.

'Now,' said Abbott, maintaining the smooth, friendly smile. 'Naturally we'll increase your pay. Will thirty percent be okay? Should be a tidy sum on your accounts when you get back to England.'

'I don't think I'll ever see a shop again,' said Julia forlornly.

Captain Rolf Hagan's helicopter touched down on the *Snow Tiger* late that afternoon and was told that the three *Orion* survivors had left for the *Ark Royal*. He was also told that his helicopter couldn't be refuelled because the supply pump to the platform deck had broken down and that repairs wouldn't be completed until the following day.

'Okay,' said Hagan to the *Snow Tiger*'s first officer. 'Maybe you'd refuel her with cans? I've got to get to the *Ark Royal* and then return to the *Johnson.*'

The first officer was extremely apologetic. 'I'm terribly sorry, old boy, but the captain's a fearful stickler over the rules about loose fuel on the platform.' His tone became consolatory. 'But he sends his compliments and says he'd be delighted if you'll be our guest of honour for the night. Unlike American ships, we do carry an excellent selection of liquid refreshment.'

The offer appealed to Hagan's Irish instincts.

'We'll explain the situation to the *Johnson,*' concluded the British officer with a dazzling smile.

Hagan had no alternative but to accept.

29

The President of the United States listened, grim-faced and silent, as the Defense Secretary summed up the growing list of Soviet provocations while his advisors sitting down each side of the conference table made notes.

'Item one – definite,' said the Defense Secretary. 'The Soviets move a flotilla of Delta Two SSBNs into the Atlantic.'

The Defense Secretary paused to polish his gold-rimmed spectacles. 'Incidentally, Mr President, those SSBNs now account for eighty-five percent of all submarine-borne ballistic missiles at sea.'

No one commented. The Defense Secretary went back to his list.

'Item two – definite. They kill an American citizen – a CBS cameraman – with a surface-to-air missile. Item three – probable. They sink the United States–United Kingdom liner, the *Orion.* Item four – definite. They destroy a major section of the South Atlantic sonobuoy barrier. Item five – definite. They cut the United States to South Africa transatlantic telephone cable. And as we've just heard, four more telegraph and telephone cables linking us with the African continent have also been cut in succession. And finally, item six – definite. The Soviets are working round the clock bringing their entire Black Sea fleet and auxiliary supply fleet to a condition of strike-readiness.'

'Including their new Kiev carriers,' added the President.

'Yes, Mr President.'

Everyone was silent. They had all said their piece. It now remained for the President to make his decision.

'Admiral Pearson will be in Washington within the hour,' the President stated. 'Are we all in agreement with Professor Galland that the admiral is the best man for this task?'

There was a murmur of assent.

The President considered for a few moments before speaking again.

'Very well, gentlemen. We will adopt the professor's suggestion to first give the Soviets the chance to back down without losing face. There will be no issuing of dramatic statements to the press or appearances before the nation. Let us pray to Almighty God that the Soviets seize the opportunity we are offering. If they don't, and they continue with their present senseless course, then they will learn that the consequence of extreme and persistent provocation is that the time inevitably comes when we are provoked.'

30

It was spring in Antarctica.

Sherwood sat at the rear of the RAF Hercules' un-soundproofed freight cabin staring down at the hummocked and rafted pack ice of the unending Weddell Sea. Julia and Oaf were playing their twentieth card game; there hadn't been much else to do during the long flight from Graham Land.

The low, returning sun cast long distorted shadows across the ridged ice field that never melted. So clear was the pollution-free atmosphere that it was impossible to judge whether the distant ice cliffs rising out of the sea ahead of the Hercules were five miles or fifty miles away.

'Beautiful, isn't it?'

Sherwood looked up, startled. Julia was sitting in the seat opposite.

'Glad to be back?' she asked.

'I don't know. I suppose so.'

'Will your wife mind? You being away for another year?'

'No.'

'I would – I'd probably divorce you.'

'She has.'

They both lapsed into silence and gazed out of the window. The Hercules was nearer the soaring ice cliffs and taking a straight line across a vast bay. The bleak edges of the cliffs captured the northern sun and stood out with razored sharpness against the cold, blue sky. Immediately below the freighter the pack ice was disintegrating – honeycombing into regular slabs like the baked mud of a dried-up river-bed.

'Rotten ice,' commented Julia. 'Bit early in the year for the pack ice to be breaking up, I would've thought.'

Baffled, Sherwood could only nod as he stared down at the frozen sea.

Oaf joined them. 'What do you make of that, heh, Sherwood? Field rotting early.'

'Maybe it's a freak warm current?' said Sherwood.

Julia was sceptical. 'This far inside the convergence?'

'Excuse me a minute.' Sherwood rose and threaded his way through the narrow passage created through the crates of supplies destined for the Rosenthal Base. He opened the door leading to the flight deck.

Squadron Leader Merrick, the Hercules' captain, turned round in his seat and genially welcomed Sherwood to the 'front office'. The atmosphere on the flight deck was stifling – all the crew seemed to be smoking foul-smelling pipes.

'Top of descent checks start in thirty minutes if you're after a progress report,' said Merrick, exhaling a cloud of smoke. He nodded to his co-pilot. 'Paddy's been on to Rosenthal. They say the landing strip's in good condition so we should have a reasonable landing – no skidding half way to the South Pole this time.'

Sherwood laughed. 'I've come to beg a small favour. We're flying over a large bay. Do you know if it's shown on your charts?'

'Our charts were drawn up for Captain Scott,' said Merrick shortly. 'They're pretty useless. We don't need them. Mike navigates with his inertials. Just as well really. He couldn't read a chart to save his life.'

Mike was absorbed in an instrument check and refused to be baited.

'Could you draw me a radar map of the bay please? Nothing too elaborate – just an outline of the coast will be fine.'

'No problem,' said Mike, flipping switches below the radar screen on the navigator's panel.

The sparkling cliffs Sherwood could see ahead were reproduced as a glowing, irregular line on the radar screen.

'Intermediate range ought to do it,' said Mike.

He twisted a knob and the entire bay appeared on the screen It was a simple matter to place a piece of thin paper over the display and trace the coastline with a pencil.

'There you are,' said Mike, handing the sheet of paper to Sherwood. 'One map of the bay. It's roughly a hundred and eighty miles across by ninety miles deep. Isn't modern technology marvellous?'

Sherwood thanked the navigator and agreed that it was.

Merrick jabbed the stem of his pipe down at the approaching cliffs. 'Something odd down there. Lots of sno-cat tracks. Looks like it's been busier than Hyde Park Corner.'

Sherwood followed the direction in which Merrick was pointing. The plateau along the top of the cliffs was scarred with the parallel herring-bone marks that sno-cat grousers made.

'That's odd,' said Sherwood. 'We were never issued with enough fuel to reach the coast. Brill had strict rules.'

'Don't blame him,' Merrick commented as he tapped out his pipe. 'Sorry, old boy. Got to throw you out now. Top of descent in a few minutes.'

Sherwood thanked the squadron leader and left the flight deck. He closed the door behind him and studied the map of the bay. It was triangular-shaped . . . one hundred and eighty miles by ninety miles . . . eight thousand square miles of melting pack ice that had no right to be melting. The theory that he had been pushing to the back of his mind ever since the *Orion* disaster, because it was such a crazy half-baked notion, began to assert itself again. Sherwood was annoyed with himself for even considering it. It was the sort of theory that could result in his reputation being laughed into oblivion.

And yet, in a way that was almost too terrifying to contemplate without a sensation of sickness in the pit of his stomach, it was one of those improbable theories that fitted the equally improbable facts.

31

The two men met for a discreet lunch in the Rib Room of the Mayflower Hotel in Washington DC. They spent the three courses reminiscing in Russian about their wartime experiences. They also enjoyed the meal.

Admiral Pearson offered his guest a cigar after their coffee had been served and said: 'How do you like Washington, Max?'

The other man sensed that his host was about to come to the point. 'Anna likes it,' he replied cautiously.

Admiral Pearson inhaled on his cigar as he considered his words. 'Would it surprise you, Max, if I tell you that this meeting is at the request of the President?'

The Soviet official's face remained impassive. 'Possibly,' he conceded.

Pearson grinned at the understatement. 'I want to talk to you about the Black Sea fleet build-up at Sevastopol, Max. I don't suppose you know anything about it, so I'll do the talking.'

'Wait a minute,' interrupted the Russian, his voice losing its friendliness. 'I had to get the ambassador's permission to have this lunch with you.'

'Of course,' said Pearson.

'I was told not to discuss political or current military matters.'

'You don't have to,' Pearson replied. 'What did your ambassador say about listening?'

The Russian shrugged.

Pearson stirred his coffee. 'This is an informal meeting, Max, so that views can be informally exchanged.'

Max smiled and shook his head. 'What you really mean, Brandon, is so that the United States can make its own views known without having to commit itself in public. Correct?'

Pearson came straight to the point. 'We have evidence that the cruise liner *Orion* was sunk by a Soviet submarine.'

The Russian nearly choked. He stared at the admiral for a few seconds and then laughed. 'No wonder you don't want to commit yourself in public if those are the sort of accusations you're throwing about.'

'Furthermore,' said Pearson, 'we have irrefutable proof that one of your SSBNs, operating in the South Atlantic, shot down a light aircraft and killed an American citizen.' Pearson reached into his jacket pocket and slid a package across the table. 'You can keep that, Max. It's a film of the incident, and the last few frames show the launching of one of your Grail missiles at the airplane the film was shot from.'

The Russian opened his mouth to protest but Pearson silenced him by holding up his hand.

'Just hear me out, Max,' said Pearson. He pointed to the package. 'You'd better put that away.'

Max pocketed the film and remained silent, waiting patiently while Pearson relit his cigar.

'There are a number of other provocative actions your country has carried out,' said Pearson, dropping his match in the ashtray, 'which I'm not prepared to discuss just yet.'

'I've no idea what you're talking about,' the Russian said sulkily.

Pearson smiled. 'Sure you don't, Max. I'll list some of them for you: you're operating a fleet of Delta Twos in the Pacific and the South Atlantic; you're drafting in a lot of surface units into Sevastopol and bringing them to operational readiness, and fast.'

'Maybe they're getting ready for an exercise,' said Max, leaning back in his chair and regarding Admiral Pearson with hostility.

'You've recently unloaded in the region of six hundred thousand tons of war material at the deep-water ports of Maputo, Beira and Porto Amelia in Mozambique,' continued Pearson. 'Plus another half a million tons at Luanda in Angola. You've also built an airstrip outside Luanda which is long enough to handle your long-range Antonov transports which you're already using for a squadron of Yak 28 interceptors.'

Max shrugged but said nothing.

'We're not arguing about your presence in Africa,' said Pearson. 'If we did, you would say that you are there at the invitation of the Angolan and Mozambique governments.' Pearson bit down on his cigar and clasped both hands together on the table. He leaned towards his guest. 'What we're concerned about, Max, are those Kiev carriers at Sevastopol.'

The Soviet official looked contemptuous. 'Those *cruisers* are part of the planned strength of our Black Sea fleet, admiral. We've made no secret –'

'I don't give a shit what they are, Max,' Pearson interrupted. 'I'm telling you this – if one of those carriers, or any aircraft carrier for that matter, passes through the Bosphorus Straits and pokes its bow into the Sea of Marmara, we'll sink it.'

The Russian's face went white. He carefully replaced his coffee cup on the saucer and stared at Pearson.

'You'll what?'

Admiral Pearson repeated his statement and sat back, watching his guest carefully. The Soviet official opened his mouth to speak, and shut it again. Pearson waited patiently for him to collect his thoughts. The Russian recovered quickly. He toyed idly with his napkin and said flatly: 'As you well know, admiral, the Black Sea is land-locked and we have a right of access to the Mediterranean through the Bosphorus.'

'Bullshit,' Pearson observed drily in English.

Max stood up. 'Thank you for the lunch, admiral. It's a pity it's been spoilt for me by your after-dinner conversation.'

'Sit down, Max,' said Pearson crisply. 'I'm not through. And I don't suppose for one minute that your ambassador will thank you if you go running back to him with half the story.'

'If your government has anything to say,' the Russian replied harshly, 'he can always be summoned to the State Department.'

'They'll deny everything. That's why you'd better sit down and hear me out.'

The Russian hesitated. He met the shrewd blue eyes and subsided back into his chair with an air of arrogant resignation.

'Nothing you say can change the fact that we have a right of access through to the Mediterranean.'

Admiral Pearson smiled amiably. Sure you have, Max – the 1936 Montreux Convention. It must be one of the oldest arms control agreements still in force.'

Max folded his arms. He was back on safe ground. 'I'd forgotten its name but I remember that it grants our warships unhindered passage through the Bosphorus.'

'Except aircraft carriers,' said Pearson.

'That's nonsense.'

Pearson eased the ash off his cigar. 'I've spent this morning going over the approved translations of the Montreux Treaty with a team of State Department linguists. It's there in several languages, Max – English, Russian, French, Turkish and German. No aircraft carriers may pass through the Bosphorus Straits. And your country is a signatory to that treaty.' Pearson grinned at the Russian's bewildered expression. 'None of the translations define an aircraft carrier but our lawyers are of the opinion that any warship that carries aircraft or is capable of carrying aircraft, is a definition that will stand up in any international court.'

Max shook his head. 'You're forgetting something, admiral – the Soviet navy does not possess aircraft carriers.'

Pearson snorted.

'Listen,' said the Russian angrily. 'The Kiev-class ships are submarine-intercepting cruisers.'

'Sure. Sure. That's what you told the world when you sent your first Kiev through the Bosphorus. We didn't kick up a fuss then but we are now. As far as NATO is concerned any warship in the Soviet navy that can deploy aircraft – whether fixed-wing or rotary-wing – is an aircraft carrier.'

'Including helicopters?' asked the Russian coldly.

'I said, rotary-wing.'

'Helicopters hadn't been invented at the time the treaty was signed,' said the Russian angrily. 'So how can it possibly be interpreted as including them?'

'Well now,' said Pearson easily. 'We thought you might throw that one at us so we've done a little scratching around in the Library of Congress. A Frenchman, Paul Cornu, flew a helicopter in November 1907. And before that, Leonardo da Vinci sketched the idea for one in 1488. Even earlier is the unknown artist who painted a Madonna and Child in 1460; the Christ Child is shown holding a toy helicopter.' Pearson grinned. 'Take a trip to the museum at Le Mans if you don't believe me. Of course, the father of the modern helicopter was a countryman of yours – Igor Sikorsky. He was designing and building helicopters in Russia before the First World War so you can't say that in 1936 you knew nothing about them.'

The Russian said nothing.

Admiral Pearson hunched his shoulders over the table. So you go back to your ambassador, Max, and tell him that if any

Soviet carrier, and that includes destroyers fitted with a helicopter platform, as much as shows its nose in the Marmara – we'll sink it.'

The Russian's scalp went back. 'This isn't 1962, Brandon. The Soviet navy is now the most powerful fighting force in the world. And how do you think the rest of the world will react to the news that the Americans are once again reverting to imperialist blackmail?'

Pearson shrugged. 'The same way that the world will react to the news that the Soviet Union flouts international agreements. Maybe a few African countries might have second thoughts before they enter into treaties with you. And besides, this is going to be a NATO action – every country in the organization has agreed to it.'

'Do you think we'll accept a situation in which a third of our navy is bottled up in the Black Sea?' the Russian demanded.

'Two-thirds,' Pearson amended.

'Well?'

'You should've thought of that before you started embarking on a violation of international agreements,' Pearson replied cheerfully. 'Cheer up, Max. They don't still shoot the bearers of bad news, do they?'

Two hours later an Aeroflot jet left Washington with one passenger on board – the Soviet Ambassador to the United States. He had told newsmen at the airport that his sister had been taken ill. Fourteen hours later, after a refuelling stop at Shannon Airport in the Republic of Ireland, the Tupolov touched down at Moscow Airport. There were no customs formalities; a black, chauffeur-driven Zim drove the ambassador direct to the Kremlin.

All through the long flight, the ambassador had been too preoccupied to alter his watch from Eastern Standard Time.

32

Angus Brill, chief executive at the Rosenthal Base, nearly had a heart attack when Sherwood had first shown him the sketch map of the bay. Studying it carefully for a few minutes while

Sherwood made his request gave him time to recover from his initial shock. His voice was its normal cheerfulness when he managed to speak.

'Of course you saw sno-cat tracks, Glyn. I authorized an expedition there about two months ago.'

Sherwood looked puzzled. 'But from the number of tracks, it looked like more than just one expedition – it looked as if there had been regular trips back and forth.'

Brill's heart nearly stopped beating. He prayed that his voice sounded annoyed when he said: 'I hope those young devils haven't been wasting fuel again. You scientists are all the same – you've no idea how much a gallon of diesel is worth once it's been flown out here.'

'But you'll let me go out to the bay?'

Brill thought for a moment. 'I agree that if the pack ice is melting prematurely, then it ought to be investigated. But I really need you to work on the replacement of those ice cores that went down with the *Orion*. Did you know that we all prayed for you when we heard the news? Dreadful business. Dreadful. I can't tell you how pleased I am to have you, Julia and Oaf back with us – even if it is for only a few months.'

Sherwood had tried to interrupt but Brill had taken him gently by the arm and was leading him to the door as he spoke.

'Look,' said Sherwood. 'I could do the trip with just one cat. . . .'

'But it's still a round trip of six hundred miles, Glyn. I honestly can't spare the fuel – even for one cat.' Brill paused. 'Maybe later on during the summer if consumption between now and then doesn't get out of hand as it did last season.'

'But it might be too late then,' Sherwood protested.

'I promise to see what can be done as soon as possible,' said Brill sincerely.

Sherwood sighed. 'Can you answer me one thing, Angus?'

'If I can.'

'Why don't we get our supplies from Australia or New Zealand? Wouldn't it be cheaper than having the RAF fly the stuff all the way from England?'

Brill chuckled as he opened his office door. 'You know, Glyn – that's exactly the same question I asked headquarters when I first took up this job. Apparently it's some mutual back-scratching they've fixed up with the Ministry of Defence – we need the supplies and they need the training flights.' Brill pumped Sherwood's hand for the second time and guided him into the corridor. 'Anyway, it's really nice having you back. I only hope that you don't find having to go back over your old work too much of a bore.'

Sherwood was alone in the corridor before he could open his mouth to reply.

Brill returned to his desk and sat down. God, what a mess. But at least he could congratulate himself on his smooth handling of a potentially explosive situation. He stared down at his desk top deep in thought; then suddenly realized to his anger that Sherwood had taken the sketch map of the bay with him.

33

ICE WISE

A modification of reinforced bows and protected propellers that enables a ship to operate in low-density ice fields.

The United States Navy oceanographic survey ship *Eureka* drove her 10,000-ton bulk through the decaying pack ice of the Southern Ocean and into the teeth of a freezing 120-mile-an-hour gale that blew with the ferocity of ten thousand demented breadknives. The crazed ice floes splintered and ground along the length of the hull as if seeking a weakness so that they could tear the ship's side out. The screaming wind whipped spray off the broken sea and flung it across the *Eureka*'s superstructure. The steel drained the spring warmth from the water and froze it into a steadily thickening layer of sea ice that clung to masts, radio and radar antennae, and lifeboats. The steel shrouds that supported the satellite tracking dish were four times their normal thickness and severely weakened by the cold and the strain thrown on them by the research ship's sickening eighty-degree roll.

To Captain Rolf Hagan, hanging on to a deckhead safety strap in the heated wheelhouse, it seemed inconceivable that any ship could take such punishment for two unrelenting weeks as the *Eureka* had done on this vital mission into Antarctic waters.

Deke Sutherland, the commanding officer, turned to Hagan after a brief conference with the deck officer. He seemed to have made up his mind about something.

'We can make another fifty miles but no more. Not in this weather. And this ice field is getting worse.'

'How near does that get me to Rosenthal Base?' asked Hagan.

'Three hundred miles.'

'That's no goddam good,' Hagan replied shortly.

'Don't blame me for the weather.'

Hagan bridled. 'You said you would get me within helicopter range of Rosenthal, captain.'

The *Eureka* shook as an ice floe, forced on to its edge by the plough-like action of the bows, cartwheeled slowly along the ship's flank before falling back to the sea. For the thousandth time in two weeks, Sutherland wondered why it was so important that Hagan got to see the three *Orion* survivors.

'No,' said Sutherland. 'I said I'd get you within range of Rosenthal, weather permitting.' He jabbed a thumb at one of the spinning glass discs that afforded a clear view through the wheelhouse windows. 'Even if I got you to within two hundred miles of Rosenthal, you wouldn't be able to fly off your chopper in this shit.'

The *Eureka* corkscrewed into a trough separating two mountainous seas and splintered an ice floe. Spicules raked the wheelhouse windows like grapeshot.

'Jesus Christ,' Hagan muttered. 'How much longer can this last?'

Sutherland shrugged.

'What's the weather forecast, for God's sake?'

'There isn't one,' said Sutherland. 'Not in these latitudes. And the satellite-tracking antenna can't be moved until we get a steam hose on it – it's frozen up.'

'To think this is spring,' Hagan muttered.

'Sure it's spring,' Sutherland replied. 'And it'll be summer in a few weeks. But this weather is manufactured at the South Pole where it's winter all the year round.'

The bridge interphone shrilled. The deck officer lifted the handset off its hook.

Hagan thought for a moment. 'Okay. We ride this out until it eases up.'

Sutherland stared at him. 'Are you crazy? This could blow for another month. Two months. You'll louse up our schedules.'

'We ride it out,' Hagan repeated.

Sutherland pointed at Hagan's helicopter lashed to the platform. The machine was encrusted with ice. Long stalactites were forming on the drooping rotors, dragging them even lower. The rotors flexed and twisted in harmony with the *Eureka*'s savage motion.

'What state will that chopper be in after a few more days of that sort of treatment, Captain Hagan?' Sutherland demanded.

'My orders are to interview those survivors,' Hagan said doggedly. 'And your orders are to obey my orders.'

The deck officer approached the two men. He saluted Sutherland with one hand and hung on to a safety strap with the other.

'Ensign Katz reports that he's raised Rosenthal, sir. Their radio operator says that he misunderstood our earlier signals and has stated that the three *Orion* survivors are *not* at the base.'

Hagan nearly let go of his strap in his anger. 'How the hell did that misunderstanding arise?'

'Because Glyn Sherwood, Julia Hammond and Oluf Johansen used to be members of the Rosenthal team,' the deck officer explained. He paused and glanced from his captain to Hagan. 'Rosenthal's chief executive sends his sincere apologies and hopes that we haven't been too inconvenienced.'

Sutherland began to laugh. He turned to Hagan. 'So what are your orders now, Captain Hagan?'

34

Julia opened her shutter. A laboratory technician was checking the double doors on the sno-cat building to ensure that they were locked. She watched him leaning against the gale force wind as he trudged back to the accommodation block.

'Well I think it's you two who are being unreasonable,' she said. 'You're forgetting that Brill has overall responsibility for the success of every project and can't possibly authorize the release of fuel just so individuals can go off on trips to satisfy their curiosity.'

Oaf pared a huge thumbnail with his flensing knife. 'That's why everyone's in Antarctica, heh? Curiosity.'

'Oaf's right,' said Sherwood. 'An extraordinary phenomenon has been reported that's within range of this base, therefore Brill ought to allow a visit.'

'How can he if there's not enough fuel?'

'Plenty of fuel,' Oaf said without looking up.

Sherwood nodded to the double-glazed window. 'Trouble approaches.'

The laboratory technician had altered course and was walking towards Julia's unshuttered window. He stopped, pushed up his goggles and pointed to his watch. Julia sighed and closed the steel shutter. One of the base's standing orders during the continuous daylight months was that all shutters were to be closed by 10:00 pm. It was Brill's conviction that health on the base was improved by observation of normal periods of night and day.

'How do you know there's plenty of fuel?' asked Sherwood.

'Once I go into the sno-cat shed. Drums of diesel to the roof.'

'Weren't you caught?' Julia inquired.

Oaf bared his gleaming teeth. It was supposed to be a smile. 'No. Like Sherwood – I was curious.'

'How much diesel was there?' asked Sherwood, trying not to sound excited.

Oaf thought for a moment. 'How far to that bay? Three hundred miles? Six hundred miles the round trip?'

'About that.'

Oaf considered. If the going was easy the sno-cats could average five miles per gallon fuel consumption. He toyed with his knife and murmured: 'They won't miss a hundred and fifty gallons – fifteen drums.'

Sherwood warmed to the big Norwegian. Oaf could always be relied on to make a decision without a lot of argument.

'And how about you, Julia? Fancy a trip to the beach?'

'It won't be a picnic. You're both crazy.'

Sherwood nodded. 'That's right, love. No doubt Brill will skin us alive when we get back.'

'We'll take sixteen drums,' said Julia firmly. 'One for luck.

We'll need it. And food and extreme cold weather clothing. And climbing gear in case we can't find a way for the sno-cat down those cliffs.'

Oaf gave a mischievous grin. 'No trouble.'

Brill thoughtfully removed his headphones and lifted the arm off the record. An unexpected visitor would have automatically assumed that the chief executive was listening to his beloved Chopin.

Brill remained deep in thought for some minutes. The conversation between Sherwood, Miss Hammond and Oaf was, he felt, one of those events that he would have to report to London.

35

Admiral Howe was sitting on his favourite bench in St James's Park when Lieutenant Abbott tracked him down and sat beside him. He gave the admiral an internal post envelope.

'Sorry to disturb you during lunchtime, sir, but this has just arrived from GCHQ.'

Admiral Howe broke the nylon seal and unfolded the message: a typical Cheltenham plaintext print-out – a yard of paper for a hundred-word message.

He read it quickly, then a second time slowly. Abbott was bursting with curiosity. Let him. This was something that he couldn't be told.

By the time Admiral Howe had reached his office, he had mentally composed a reply to Brill. It would be a message that Admiral Howe knew he would be ashamed of for the rest of his life, but it had to be sent. He half-hoped that Brill would disobey orders but it was unlikely. Brill was an officer who didn't disobey orders. Which was why he had been given the job in the first place.

36

AWACS (Airborne Warning and Control System)

A continuously airborne fleet of battle management centres

with a primary function of providing advance 'over-horizon' warning on the movements of enemy aircraft and surface ships.

The AWACS was flying at 55,000 feet in 'friendly' Turkish air space but its radar beams were slanting down through 'unfriendly' air space to the Soviet naval base at Sevastopol on the land-locked Black Sea.

It was 03:00 hours local time when the long-expected event happened: five of the AWACS's radar plots indicated that a blip had detached itself from the Crimean peninsula and was heading south-west with incredible slowness.

The AWACS's precision radar beams narrowed – increasing their intensity and eliminating the background 'clutter' from dockyard buildings and cranes. There was little sound within the Boeing's air-conditioned, soft-lit interior as the crew set the computers to work to analyse the flood of incoming data. There wasn't even the click of key-switches; the glowing control panels responded to the touch of the human finger and not the pressure.

The beams probed the Soviet ship, evaluating its length, its beam and hull profile, and even its bow wave.

The electronic interrogation proceeded at the speed of light. Line by line, the results materialized in silence on the AWACS's cathode ray tubes and simultaneously on the screens before Admiral Pearson in the *Johnson*'s strike command combat control centre:

0300
TARGET + KIEV CLASS CARRIER
POSITION + ZONE BS GRID SQUARE 8900
COURSE + 326 DEGREES
SPEED + 2 KNOTS
SECONDARY OBSERVATIONS + NO FIXED OR ROTARY WING AIRPLANE DEPLOYMENT ON FLIGHT DECK
ETA BOSPHORUS AT PRESENT COURSE AND SPEED + 100 HOURS

The carrier was creeping across the Black Sea, just as Admiral Pearson had predicted it would. The Russians weren't accepting the situation but they were creating a hundred-hour lead time.

Four days.

Time enough for a lot of talking to be done.

37

Julia, Oaf and Sherwood were singing above the roar of the diesel as the sno-cat raced across the plateau at twenty miles an hour.

They were now a hundred miles from Rosenthal. Stealing the five-ton bright yellow vehicle had been unexpectedly easy – no laboratory technicians had been around when they had opened the double doors of the motor transport hut. Oaf had set the sno-cat's inertial navigation instruments while Sherwood and Julia filled the fuel tanks to capacity. Ten sealed drums of diesel fuel were stacked conveniently near the sno-cat. These would be needed for the return journey. Oaf had helped lift them into the sno-cat's stowage bay.

No one had come to investigate when the Perkins diesel engine coughed into life – the eternal winds that shrieked round the cluster of low buildings effectively cloaked the roar of the engine and the sound of the track grousers as they crunched into the hard snow.

Oaf had steered the sno-cat away from Rosenthal, keeping the transport hut between the vehicle and the accommodation buildings. Only when they were four hundred yards away did he open the throttle and circle round until they were heading on the correct course for the mysterious bay in the coastal ice shelf.

'I don't think I can sing any more,' announced Julia.

'I know some Norwegian whaling songs,' said Oaf.

He was voted down.

The sno-cat thundered on across the flat, white wilderness. The upper snow layers were frozen into a hard pan that made easy going for the track-laying vehicle. The warmth and humidity in the cab caused Oaf's snow goggles to keep misting up. He gave up trying to wipe them and pushed them up on his forehead, squinting against the glare caused by the low sun reflecting off the ice.

'What about crevasses?' asked Julia.

'I've drilled this area for three years,' said Sherwood. 'The ice-cap's as solid and stable as Gibraltar. We'll have to start taking it easy when we're within a hundred miles of the coast.'

'Why's that, Sherwood?' demanded Oaf.

'Two reasons,' said Sherwood. 'Firstly, I was never allowed enough fuel to survey near the coast; and secondly, without the self-buttressing effect of ice, there are more likely to be crevasses in the coastal area.'

The vivid yellow machine charged on over the featureless frozen landscape.

The three escapers eventually tired of trying to make themselves heard above sustained reverberation of the engine in the enclosed cab and fell silent.

An hour of seemingly unending monotony passed.

Julia was about to suggest that they stop to stretch their legs and eat, when the ice suddenly opened up beneath the sno-cat. She was thrown forward against the windscreen. She screamed as the cab tilted down. Oaf threw the tracks into reverse and slammed the throttle open. The diesel's note rose to a howl – the frenzied grousers ground the snow to powder as they bit down deep into the edge of the three-mile-deep chasm. But it was too late: the remnants of the snow bridge collapsed under the sno-cat's five-ton mass and its momentum carried it over the brink. Julia had been catapulted against the instrument panel. The headlights sprayed parallel beams of quartz iodine light into the awesome fissure in the ice-cap. As the sno-cat plunged down, Julia realized, foolishly, that she was staring at a ribbon of exposed Antarctic continent.

38

The Lucas grapnel's jaws closed round the silent transatlantic telephone cable and held it securely. Three miles above, a switch was thrown on the cable-laying and repair ship. An electrically operated blade on the complex grapnel sheared through the cable on one side of the jaws. A power winch began turning, lifting the cable from the abyssal darkness of the Angolian Basin.

An hour later, engineers began collecting round the winch, watching the lifting hawser climbing out of the water and waiting for the cable to appear. Many of them were the same engineers that had helped lay the cable three years previously. TAT 12 was their baby.

It was 3:25 pm when the grapnel broke the surface. The cable end was passed round a capstan and the cable carefully coiled in one of the ship's circular holds as it came aboard.

The first repeater appeared an hour later. Externally, it was nothing more than a bulge in the cable; internally, the four-thousand-channel voice amplifier represented the most advanced technology in the world. There were over a hundred and fifty repeaters in the cable, strung out like beads across the ocean floor. They were built with painstaking care and were designed to last a hundred years without attention. Failure of one of the $150,000 repeaters would put the entire cable out of action.

The second repeater appeared the following morning at breakfast time. The winch operator stopped lifting and sounded the alarm. Engineers abandoned their meals and poured on to the deck to investigate.

The senior engineer stared speechless at the suspended repeater. Its armour sheathing had been ripped open and its components, more carefully selected than the gems in the crown jewels, were hanging out. Some of the delicate solid-state circuits had been torn completely away, and the cable seals, which were capable of resisting a water pressure of several tons per square inch, had been savagely torn from their housings. It was a similar story with the visible length of cable hanging from the sheaves; the heavy insulation was lacerated as if it had been flailed in a giant threshing machine. So deep were some of the cuts that the teredo tapes had been sliced right through to expose the reinforcing jute yarn.

The senior engineer gave the order to re-start the winch. During that day, eighty miles of wrecked cable and two more disembowelled repeaters were coiled down into the cable ship's hold.

Lifting continued throughout the night under the glare of floodlights. The damage to the fifty-million-dollar voice highway got progressively worse. At one point the two-inch diameter cable was virtually sliced right through.

It was 4:00 am when the senior engineer was woken and told that the winch strain gauges were indicating that the severed end of the cable had finally been reached and was now being lifted off the floor of the South Atlantic.

With over a hundred miles of mutilated cable in the hold, the senior engineer was certain of one thing.

The damage could not possibly have been caused by a human agency.

39

'Keep still,' said Oaf through clenched teeth. 'You both keep pretty damn still.'

Julia and Sherwood remained frozen in the positions they had fallen into. Sherwood's arm was trapped painfully against the side of the cab. The sno-cat had plunged twenty feet into the narrowing chasm. The roof had gouged deep into the ice and spun the vehicle round so that it was now facing upwards towards the band of grey sky.

'We move one at a time,' said Oaf. 'But we don't even breathe.'

It took the three an hour to shift their positions. Miraculously, none of the windows had been broken in the fall; it was the slender aluminium window surrounds supporting the roof panel that were preventing the vehicle from crashing down into the depths of the crevasse.

They arranged themselves on the seat, staring upwards like three Apollo astronauts waiting for lift-off.

Moving with infinite care, Sherwood reached for the radio-telephone handset.

'Won't be any good,' said Julia. 'Even if the aerial's not been torn off, you won't get a signal out down here.'

'Maybe,' Oaf muttered. 'But it's worth a try.'

The radiotelephone was dead.

'So what do we do now?' Sherwood demanded.

'I go out,' said Oaf. 'I climb round back and open stowage bay – release oil drums to lighten her. We have to do that first.'

Julia thought of the bottomless gulf she had seen for an instant when the sno-cat had gone over the edge.

'You'll have to let me do it,' she said.

'Don't talk crazy,' said Sherwood.

'I weigh the least,' Julia pointed out. My weight moving about isn't so likely to dislodge anything.'

Sherwood started to argue but Oaf cut him short.

'She's right, Sherwood.'

Julia groped cautiously under the seat for her extreme cold weather mittens and pulled them on. She stood very slowly while Oaf released the windscreen catches.

'We better all put cold weather clothing on before I open this,' said Oaf.

Two minutes later, Oaf pushed the windscreen open inch by inch until the opening was wide enough for Julia to ease herself through. Freezing air knifed into the cab.

'Close it again.' Julia ordered when she had climbed out.

To Sherwood, such an action would seem like abandoning her.

'No!' he shouted hoarsely.

'For Christ's sake, shut it!' Julia repeated as she gingerly tested her weight on the upturned track guards.

Oaf was about to pull the windscreen down when Sherwood reached up to stop him.

'No! Leave it open!'

The sudden movement caused the sno-cat to rock. There was a harsh scream of metal slicing into ice. A side window cracked like a pistol being fired. The report echoed along the crevasse. Julia threw herself flat across the sno-cat's snub radiator grille and clung to the power winch. The side window exploded to granules of glass that rattled down the side of the hanging vehicle and fell into the black void. Julia heard them clattering into the echoing darkness. Hypnotized, Sherwood and Oaf stared at the slowly buckling roof pillar. Another side window disintegrated. Julia could see where the track grousers were pressing into the ice wall – they were slipping – forcing up ridges of ice.

The sno-cat fell.

Oaf pushed Sherwood against the floor. The roof caved in and all the remaining windows, including the windscreen panels, shattered. The sides of the chasm seemed to close in on Julia like the jaws of a gargantuan vice. Then there was silence. The inverted sno-cat had stopped its mad, backwards plunge.

Julia opened her eyes and stared in horror at the flattened

cab. She could have reached out and touched the frozen sides of the abyss. She called out in panic: 'Glyn! Oaf!'

'Don't move, Sherwood,' Julia heard Oaf's voice growl from the depths of the mangled cab. She cried out in relief.

'Can you hear me, Oaf?'

'I can see you,' the Norwegian replied.

Julia realized that a shaggy face was watching her through a tear in the folded metal.

'Are you hurt?' she asked.

The face moved away. The sno-cat swayed.

'Hey, Sherwood,' said Oaf's voice. 'You hurt?'

'No. . . . I don't think so.'

Julia forgot her own predicament and offered a silent prayer of thanks. Moving with extreme care, she turned round until she could peer into the yawning fissure down one side of the crushed cab. The crumpled remains of the door were rammed deep into the scored ediface. It was obvious that the other side would be the same. The sno-cat swayed again. One of the trapped men was trying to open a door. There was a grinding sound. At that moment Julia saw with horrifying clarity the perilously narrow ice-ledge that was barely supporting the stricken sno-cat.

'NO!' she screamed with an anguish that sprang uninhibited from her soul. 'NO! NO! NO! Don't move! Whatever you do, *don't move*!'

The starved acoustics in the ice-maw seized her voice and snatched it into the depths, hurling it gleefully from wall to wall as they drained its strength.

Julia took five minutes over lifting herself on to one knee. She steadied herself against the power winch and turned her head up. The razor edge of the chasm sliced the sunlight into its component colours. She estimated that the sno-cat had fallen fifty feet.

'Listen, Oaf. I've got an idea.'

Oaf's puzzled face appeared at the opening.

'You'll have to shift your weight to the right-hand side of the cab,' Julia said. 'That's *your* left. The cat should be more stable. But for God's sake do it slowly.'

There was no reply. Julia felt the vehicle give a slight tremble. Two minutes later, Oaf's voice said: 'Okay. What now?'

'Can you reach the climbing gear?'

There was a pause. Another tremble. Then: 'Yes.'

'Pass them out to me one at a time. The rope, the pitons and ice-axes – everything.'

'What are you thinking of doing?' asked Sherwood's voice.

Julia told him. Sherwood started protesting. Oaf told him to shut up. One by one, the items of mountaineering equipment were passed through the opening to Julia.

'And the spades.'

Oaf eased the sharp-pointed ice spades through the narrow gap. Julia carefully spread all the items out so she could pick them up one at a time without making unnecessary movements. It took her ten minutes to prepare for the climb. She was forced to remove the heavy mittens so that she could adjust and secure the harness. She had forgotten the cold until she saw a strip of skin from the ball of her finger adhering to one of the metal quick-release fasteners. With the harness in place and trailing two ropes from the small of her back, she was ready. She stood, held a piton against the ice-face, braced herself, and swung the hammer.

For the rest of her life, Julia was to have great difficulty in remembering details from that gruelling, fifty-minute climb. Occasional subliminal scenes would come back to her: hanging by the safety harness from a single piton while swinging the hammer above her head; transferring her weight to an ice-axe and straightening her legs to gain another six inches. But she retained a clear impression of the searing cold that seeped continuously through her protective clothing. The cold was part of lying utterly exhausted on the ice near the lip of the crevasse.

She closed her eyes and rolled on to her back. Maybe the extreme cold weather parka had thicker insulation in its back panels, for the cold didn't feel quite so bad. Even the bright sun on her face felt warmer. She pulled off a mitten and let the warm shingle of the Dawlish beach trickle through her fingers. Her parents took her to Dawlish every year despite Dad's grumbling about the railway track that ran along the top of the beach. She could hear a train coming – the wail of twin-tone air horns getting louder – rising to a frenzied shrieking that seemed to blast from the bowels of the earth.

Then she remembered. Freezing water was dripping from her

hand. She opened her eyes. There was no sign of the beach – only the white desolation. But the howling siren continued. She rolled on to her stomach and peered over the brink of the crevasse. Her brain reeled as she stared down at the sno-cat's headlights; she felt as if she were clinging helplessly to the edge of a cliff with the strange vehicle charging towards her – its horn blaring for the final yards of its headlong suicide rush. Then she saw the two ropes snaking down from her safety harness. One of them was tied to the two long-handled ice spades. She waved feebly and began hauling the spades up.

She removed the harness, anchored it with a piton and began digging a trench in the ice with one of the spades, first loosening the ice with the axe. It took her thirty minutes to complete the task. The finished trench, thirty yards from and parallel to the chasm, measured five feet long, six inches wide, and three feet deep.

The simplest part of the operation was cutting a slit with the ice-pick from the centre of the trench to that part of the brink immediately above the trapped sno-cat.

She grasped the second rope leading down to the vehicle and called out: 'I'm ready to haul up now! Release the clutch on the winch!'

The cable drum on the sno-cat's power winch turned slowly as she hauled the cable up. She used the ice-pick to imbed the cable into the groove. The free end that emerged into the trench was tied firmly around the hafts of two spades. The spades were then laid in the trench and buttressed hard against the trench side.

Julia stood back and studied her handiwork. There seemed no reason why the makeshift T-shaped snow anchor couldn't take the sno-cat's five-ton weight – the hafts on the steel spades, now lying in the trench, were thicker than the ten-ton breaking strain winch hawser.

She crawled to the edge of the brink and looked down. She thought she could see Oaf's eyes through the opening in the torn metal.

'Ready, Oaf. But there's about six feet of slack that you'll have to take up first.'

There was a movement inside the crushed cab. The sno-cat rocked slightly.

'Okay,' Oaf's voice answered. 'If this bastard will start. Pretty crazy angle, heh?'

'Pretty crazy,' Julia agreed, her voice tight.

The Perkins diesel fired on the third attempt. The vibration dislodged ice that rattled hollowly down into the abyss. Julia screamed in horror as the sno-cat fell. The winch hawser gave a sharp musical note as it snapped taut.

'Start the winch!' Julia screamed and then she almost sobbed with relief when she heard the crunch of the gearbox and saw the winch drum start turning. Without stopping to see if the sno-cat was climbing the cable, she raced back to the trench. The two spades, with the lifting cable lashed round their hafts, were pulled up hard against the side of the trench. Everything about the T-anchor looked right – the sno-cat couldn't possibly drag the spades through the thirty yards of ice between the trench and the brink.

There was an echoing crash from the crevasse. Julia ran near to the brink, threw herself down flat on her stomach and looked over the edge. The diesel's roar was sweet music.

There was another crash and the sound of tearing metal. The sno-cat was pulling itself clear of the frozen jaws!

Even as Julia stared down, she could see that the machine was inching towards her – inexorably winding the cable round the drum and climbing – like a giant yellow spider hauling itself up a strand of silken web.

Powdered ice jetted from under the grousers as the sno-cat's tracks scored into the side of the chasm. The hawser had pulled itself firmly into the ice like a wire cheese slicer.

She went back to the trench. Her heart nearly stopped when she saw the two spades. The knot tied around the hafts was slowly flattening them and the spades were distorting into a vee-shape with the apex driving into the side of the trench. As she stared aghast, she realized that the spade hafts were tubular and not solid as she had supposed.

The sno-cat's power winch appeared above the edge of the crevasse. Above the roar of the diesel was the sharp twanging noise made by the rigid hawser as the changing angle jerked it out of the ice. The tracked vehicle seemed to be climbing into the air. Julia threw herself down and began frantically packing loose ice around the spades that were grating up the side of the trench and slowly closing like dividers. She even tried jumping on the spades to force them down, but it was useless – her weight was no match for the five-ton force being exerted by the sno-cat's bulk. The sides of the trench crumbled as the now wedge-shaped spade hafts drove into the ice. Julia cried with despair and frustration. She tore off the mittens and used her fists to beat the ice down. Then she transferred her blows to the slowly buckling spades, heedless of the intense pain as the cold welded her skin to the metal and tore it away in strips.

There was a crash from behind her. Turning round was her last conscious action. The spades jerked free – flailing the icy air as the tension in the hawser was unleashed. A flying handle struck her on the temple.

Then there was a black nothingness.

40

The President of the United States regarded the Defense Secretary thoughtfully and said: 'If the Chairman is not offering anything, John, why should I speak to him?'

'He's on the line now, begging you to see reason.'

The President pointed to the sheaf of papers and cables lying on his desk. 'Tell him that his country will have to appeal to virtually every member of the NATO alliance. How long before that carrier reaches the Bosphorus?'

'Fifty-two hours.'

The President nodded. 'Tell him that it is his country that has to see reason. That it is *his* country that is about to violate an international agreement.'

The Defense Secretary moved to the door.

'I see no reason to withdraw the orders issued to Admiral Pearson,' the President concluded.

41

MIRVOS (Multiple Independently-Targeted Re-entry Vehicle Orientation Satellite)
Active satellites which provide mid-course guidance for multiple warhead intercontinental ballistic missiles.

With forty hours to a major East–West confrontation, four unmanned rockets were launched from Andrews Air Force Base at intervals of ten minutes.

The first one jettisoned its spent main booster at an altitude of a hundred miles and continued climbing on its second-stage rocket until it reached a hundred and eighty miles. Its target was a Soyuz satellite which had been launched, unannounced, eighteen months previously.

The orbital injection manœuvre was successfully completed; the ground controllers' computers and instruments told them that their rocket, moving at 18,000 miles per hour, was closing on the Soyuz satellite at five miles per hour on a matching orbit.

After five minutes of precision jockeying with retro-rockets, the US rocket was within three feet of the Soviet satellite.

A panel set into the nose of the rocket slid open and the payload, millions of copper dipoles, the size and shape of darning needles, were slowly ejected so that they clung in a dense cloud around the satellite, effectively screening all incoming and outgoing command signals.

There would be no permanent damage to the satellite. But for two hundred hours, until the million-mile-an-hour solar wind eventually swept most of the dipoles away, the Soviet MIRVOS would be useless.

During the next two hours, the other three Soviet MIRVOS satellites were similarly disabled.

42

There were two reasons why Admiral Pearson had selected the British Leander-class frigate HMS *Swiftfire* for the task of disabling the Soviet aircraft carrier should it try to enter the Sea of Marmara from the Bosphorus. Firstly, the small warship workhorse had been on a visit to Turkey and was already in the Marmara when the crisis erupted. Secondly, the *Swiftfire* had an ideal weapon – a single anti-submarine Wasp helicopter. The use of such a small torpedo-carrying machine launched from one of the smallest ships in the NATO force gave the West a propaganda advantage if the attack on the Kiev carrier was eventually carried out – the Soviets would be made to look foolish if they started screaming about imperialist bullying.

With twenty-five hours to confrontation, the *Swiftfire* was operating in a 'closed down' condition; her decks were deserted. All hatches and doors were closed and sealed, and the windows of the enclosed bridge heavily shuttered. The *Swiftfire* was a ghost ship. Even her long-range warning radar antenna was still; all the information the *Swiftfire* needed was pouring into her electronic warfare office from the Boeing AWACS which was maintaining a continuous watching patrol in Turkish airspace to the east. Her Seacat surface-to-air missiles mounted on top of the helicopter hanger were poised for action.

The *Swiftfire*'s principal warfare officer was now in overall command of the warship's weapon systems and had the authority to issue 'requests' to the captain. He, like all the technicians and ratings manning the consoles in the darkened computer room and electronic warfare room, was wearing a white one-piece Nuclear-Biological-Chemical protective suit complete with hood and tinted nuclear flash visor. The air supply throughout the ship was provided from an independent system so that the ship could continue to fight at maximum efficiency even if her combat zone became saturated with intense radioactive fallout.

'PWO, *Swiftfire* to *Johnson*,' said the principal warfare officer.

Admiral Pearson glanced at the voice-print screen. It had taken the computer a thousandth of a second to analyse the British officer's voice, compare its inflexion and tonal qualities, and display on the screen:

PRINCIPAL WARFARE OFFICER – HMS SWIFTFIRE – LT GERALD C HOLMAN.

'Go ahead, *Swiftfire*.'

'Phase Four achieved, sir.'

'Very good, *Swiftfire*. Continue to the ten-hour threshold.'

The PWO acknowledged and cleared the circuit. Admiral Pearson spun his swivel chair round and studied the floor-to-deckhead glass map of the North and South Atlantic that dominated the *Johnson*'s combat control centre. At the foot of the map, in Antarctic waters, was the marker for the research ship *Eureka* that Hagan was aboard. He wished Hagan was with him and cursed the continuing weather conditions that had prevented his aide's return. Interviewing the *Orion* survivors now seemed an unimportant and fruitless ènterprise. Admiral Pearson turned his chair back to face his control console and leaned towards the microphone. He pressed the key that connected him with the *Johnson*'s meteorological officer.

'Any change in the conditions in the *Eureka*'s area?'

'Checking now, sir.'

There was a pause while the met officer checked the latest satellite weather pictures.

'Yes, sir. Looks like a significant improvement. The gale has moderated to Force Seven and is getting better all the time.'

Pearson grunted and called up the communications room.

'Keep trying to raise the *Eureka*. When you do, tell Captain Hagan that I want him back on the *Johnson* as soon as possible.'

Pearson next spoke to the *Johnson*'s logistics officer who confirmed that with in-flight refuelling and a fast transport from the USS *Guam*, Hagan could be back on the *Johnson* within ten hours.

Admiral Pearson's next task on Washington's orders was to upgrade the alert status of the United States' nuclear submarines. It was an order which, until then, he had given only during exercises. He said a simple but heartfelt prayer to himself, and said into the microphone: 'All SSBNs designated in combat radial Charlie-Hotel-Foxtrot to set condition ISQ readiness.'

Translated from the jargon the order was: 'All missile-carrying nuclear submarines get ready for war.'

43

'Hey, Sherwood! She's awake!'

Sherwood abandoned the sno-cat's radio that he had been attempting to repair and crawled into the tent beside Oaf. Julia's hands and head had been expertly bandaged by Oaf. She was sitting in the sleeping bag and staring wide-eyed at Sherwood.

'Now I believe it,' she said to Oaf.

'Believe what?' asked Sherwood.

'That we're not all dead. What happened?'

Sherwood caught Oaf's eye. The Norwegian shook his head. 'I've not told her, Sherwood.'

'Told me what? Speak,'

'You hit your head.'

'I guessed. Where are we? How far are we from the base?'

'Three hundred miles.' said Sherwood apologetically.

'Now listen,' said Julia reasonably. 'How can we be that distance from Rosenthal? That was the distance to the coast.'

The two men looked at each other for mutual support. Before they could move to stop her, Julia ripped back the tent flap and gaped in astonishment at the pack ice some fifty yards from where the tent was pitched on the shale-strewn beach. She groaned.

'The coast,' was Sherwood's unnecessary explanation.

Julia made no reply. She turned her head to gaze at the sno-cat parked a few yards away under the soaring ice cliffs. The vehicle's wrecked cab had been cut away. She could see twin grouser tracks down a plunging fold in the ice-cap.

'And we managed to find a safe route down,' said Oaf triumphantly.

Julia closed her eyes and muttered something that sounded like a request to God to give her patience. She opened her eyes and, carefully choosing her words, said: 'Why is it, knowing the mess we were in, that you two idiots – or rather imbeciles – *didn't turn back to base*!'

Sherwood nodded vigorously. 'A good question. There's a good answer – you climbed up the wrong side of the crevasse. Not that we're complaining mind,' Sherwood added hastily. 'We think you did very well to do what you did, don't we, Oaf?'

'Better than a man,' agreed Oaf.

Julia was in no mood for flattery. 'Have you found out why that pack ice is melting?'

'Yes,' said Sherwood. 'You won't believe this but –'

'Good. I feel fit enough to travel, so we'll break camp right now and start back.'

'We can't. . . .'

'We damn well will. We might have to make a long detour to avoid that crevasse.' Julia started to struggle out of her sleeping bag but Sherwood restrained her.

'Julia. It's no use. You might as well rest.'

She angrily shook Sherwood's hand off her arm.

'You tell her, Oaf.'

'Not enough diesel for return,' said Oaf simply. 'Enough for fifty mile – maybe more but not much. I've just found out that spare drums are full of petrol – no good in a diesel engine. Wrong markings on the drums.'

Julia sat back suddenly and stared at Oaf. 'Are you sure?'

Oaf nodded unhappily.

'And the radio's bust,' said Sherwood. 'It can receive but not transmit.'

There was a long silence.

'So we start walking,' said Julia dully.

'When you've rested.'

Another silence.

'So what's causing the pack ice to melt?'

'It's not melting,' said Sherwood. 'But it is breaking up. Quite fast too.'

'Why?'

'The entire beach and sea bed in the bay is lifting.'

'*What!*'

'The same sort of thing is happening in some parts of Norway and Scotland but much more slowly. The land is still recovering after having been compressed by the weight of the ice-cap and glaciers during the last ice age.'

Julia frowned. 'But why is it happening here?'

Sherwood pointed to the sweeping curve of razor-sharp ice cliffs that bordered the bay. 'Those cliffs are unweathered. New. This bay wasn't here until quite recently – last Christmas or thereabouts.' He paused. This camp and that ice field is where eight or nine thousand cubic miles of ice was standing. And now it's gone.'

44

While crowds gathered along the shores of Istanbul's Golden Horn peninsula and lined the great bridge that linked Europe and Asia to watch the Kiev's stately progress through the Bosphorus, a hundred miles away on the Sea of Marmara the

British frigate HMS *Swiftfire* began her final preparations to cripple the Soviet warship.

Shortly after midday, the frigate's hangar door was opened and two men wheeled the Wasp helicopter out on to the *Swiftfire*'s tiny helicopter deck. They quickly unfurled the rotors and swung the folding tail into the open position.

There was a small torpedo hanging beneath the Wasp. Its warhead had been set to detonate at a depth of sixty feet beneath the Kiev's stern. A depth calculated to stop the carrier by wrecking her stern gear without causing injury or loss of life to her crew.

45

'Sabotage,' announced Julia.

Oaf and Sherwood peered at the printed circuit board that Julia had removed from the sno-cat's radiotelephone.

'If you look closely you can see where someone has snipped three wires to remove a component. Probably a transistor. We should've tested the set before leaving.'

'There wasn't that much time,' commented Sherwood drily.

All three stared down at the tiny board that was smothered with electronic components.

'Well,' said Julia at length. 'If we had a soldering iron I suppose we could try a transistor from the receiver board.'

Sherwood shook his head. 'Even if we could repair it, who would hear us? We'd never get a signal out over those cliffs.'

'Twelve-volt soldering iron in the toolbox,' remarked Oaf.

'And wire cutters?'

'Sure.'

'But it's useless,' said Sherwood. 'No one will hear us.'

46

The oceanographic research ship USS *Eureka* heard them.

An ensign caught up with Captain Hagan as he was about to

board his helicopter on the first stage of the long flight back to Admiral Pearson on the *Johnson*.

'Captain Hagan!'

Hagan had one foot on the helicopter's boarding steps. His pilot was holding the door open. Hagan turned. The breathless ensign was clutching a piece of paper. He saluted clumsily.

'A message from Captain Sutherland, sir. We've just picked up a distress call. Very weak. Three members of the Rosenthal survey team are stranded on the Coats Land coast and we can't hear anyone answering them. . . .'

'So?'

The junior officer held out the piece of paper. 'Their names and position, sir.'

Hagan glanced at the message. He sat down abruptly on the helicopter steps and gave the ensign a suspicious look. 'Is this your captain's idea of a joke?'

'No, sir.'

Hagan handed the paper to his pilot. 'Can we make that position if this hole in the weather holds?'

The pilot disappeared into the helicopter and reappeared with a chart. He looked doubtful. 'It's a seven-hundred-mile round trip, sir.'

'Okay,' said Hagan impatiently. 'So it's a long way. Can we make it?'

'Just about, sir. If you stay behind.'

'Okay,' said Hagan wearily. 'Go get them.'

47

BUS

The final stage of a submarine-borne Trident missile which carries a set of MIRV nuclear fusion warheads up to targeting height.

The scene being enacted on the USS *Virgil Grissom* was being duplicated on all the Trident nuclear submarines. It was a scene that was enacted once a week but this time there were illuminated signs displayed in the nuclear submarine's various control centres; signs that flashed on and off at one-second intervals – a frequency calculated to create a sense of urgency without causing irritation:

THIS IS NOT A DRILL. . . . THIS IS NOT A DRILL. . . . THIS IS NOT A DRILL. . . .

The weapons officer placed his face against the soft rubber visor and rotated the unmarked combination wheel. One by one, the glowing digits appeared: his wife's birthday in reverse prefixed by the first two numbers of his home address ZIP code. He cleared the display and pulled the safe's outer door open. Next, the executive officer pressed his eyes to the visor and spun his combination. The two men did not know each other's combination.

THIS IS NOT A DRILL. . . . THIS IS NOT A DRILL. . . .

The executive officer opened the inner safe and removed the two identical keys. He gave one to the weapons officer. The two men returned to their respective stations: the executive officer to the command centre and the weapons officer to the missile control centre three decks below the command centre. They moved through the carpeted, air-conditioned passageways in total silence.

THIS IS NOT A DRILL. . . . THIS IS NOT A DRILL. . . .

Once in his control centre, the weapons officer opened his safe. Inside were two triggers similar to a Colt 45's. One red, one black. The black trigger was for drills. The weapons officer selected the red trigger. He closed the safe and surveyed the row of technicians hunched over their consoles, saying nothing. The usual ebb and flow of good-natured banter had died when the submarine had been set to an ISQ condition and the signs had started flashing:

THIS IS NOT A DRILL. . . . THIS IS NOT A DRILL. . . .

'Assign Missile One,' the weapons officer ordered the weapons supervisor.

'Assign Missile One,' the supervisor repeated woodenly for the benefit of the weapons centre voice recorder. He pressed the button that started a computer check-out of Trident Missile One's control systems. Targets were automatically assigned to each MIRV depending on the submarine's position; the BUS's orbital trajectory was planned so that it could sprinkle its warheads to maximum effect.

The weapons officer inserted the firing key in the fire control box and turned it. He then screwed the red trigger into place. For psychological reasons the missile fire control mechanism had been designed to resemble the stock of a hand gun. It was felt that yet another button did not convey sufficient emotional regard for the control's significance.

Without turning round as he always did on the weekly drill, the weapons supervisor said: 'Missile One assignment initiated.'

The weapons officer flipped the intercom switch to the captain in the submarine's command centre. 'Missile assignment programme initiated, sir.'

The captain acknowledged and stared at the first of the many target lists that were appearing on a screen: names of cities, large towns, small towns. Some names that he recognized, some that he did not – spelt out in phonetic English with the Cyrillic version indented underneath. His firing key was in his left-hand pocket. It would remain there until the President's scrambled voice was received on four separate radio frequencies, reassembled by the submarine's computers and submitted for voice-print identification. Until the President had given the order and the captain had inserted his firing key, none of the Tridents could be fired. In the meantime, there was little to do but wait and try to ignore the flashing signs that repeated:

THIS IS NOT A DRILL. . . . THIS IS NOT A DRILL. . . . THIS IS NOT A DRILL. . . .

48

The President of the United States was sitting in a sound-proof glass booth, feeling like a contestant in a TV quiz show except that the stakes were the lives of a sixth of the world's population.

His mouth was dry. He poured another glass of water from the carafe and sipped, watching the soundless activities on the other side of the glass. The vast room was filled with senior officers from all the services. There were at least twenty phone conversations in progress but the President could see only lips moving. The wall map, showing the positions of the NATO and Warsaw Pact forces, was for the benefit of the humans in the room: the computers didn't need wall maps – the information on it was out of date by the potentially disastrous margin of five seconds.

His mouth was dry.

There was a marker that indicated the Kiev carrier crawling through the Bosphorus. Another marker in the Sea of Marmara that was the British frigate tensely lying in wait for it.

His mouth was dry. He poured some more water. An army general was watching him. He managed to keep his hand steady.

A flashing light appeared on the wall map. Another Soviet Yankee-class nuclear submarine had been pinpointed, two hundred miles off Long Island. Anti-submarine helicopters would be tracking it with dipping sonar. The President had been a helicopter pilot and had once tracked a submerged Yankee for three hours. During that time the Russian captain had done everything within his command except perform underwater somersaults in his frantic efforts to shake off his remorseless pursuer. After three hours of twisting, abrupt changes of depth and course, sometimes stopping dead then making off at thirty-five knots, the Russian had managed to escape by plunging beneath a layer of cold water that had bent the beam of the dipping sonar through twenty degrees. After that there had been another two hours fruitless casting about over five hundred square miles of ocean – but the Russian sub had vanished.

Damn Yankees.

His mouth was dry.

Another glass of water.

'*Your voice must sound quite natural when you give the order, Mr President.*'

How the hell could anyone be expected to make their voice sound 'quite natural' when giving such an order?

He bumped the microphone with the carafe. A dozen pairs of eyes turned towards the booth.

His mouth was still dry.

Damn Yankees.

49

The Kiev-class carrier moved through the late afternoon haze like a grey ghost. The most formidable ghost ever to move on the surface of the Marmara. It was the Soviet Navy's first aircraft carrier – the result of thousands of hours spent by intelligence-gathering trawlers in the vicinity of American and British carriers; photographing them, measuring flight-deck lengths, height above the water, underwater hull form. One had even passed suicidally under the bows of the *Ark Royal* to see how quickly the British warship could manœuvre.

Admiral Turgenev had transferred his flag to the Kiev. He knew about the British frigate and that it was still in the Marmara long after its Turkish visit was supposed to be over. It wasn't hard to guess why. For a week, as the Kiev had made its way across the Black Sea, the admiral had prayed that the politicians would see sense and would order him back to Sevastopol. Now, as he leaned on the bridge rail and studied the *Swiftfire* through his binoculars, it seemed too late. No one was going to yield.

He estimated that the British frigate was twenty kilometres away – straight ahead. The frigate's Wasp helicopter appeared to have been wheeled out of the aft hanger. The haze made it impossible to determine what was happening on the frigate's decks. They'd know in the radar room – at that range they'd be able to pick up even the slightest movement of the Seacat missile launchers.

A junior officer approached and saluted. 'The captain sends his respects, sir. The helicopter on the frigate has started its motor. The chief radar officer has reported that its rotors are turning.'

Turgenev returned the salute. His reply was drowned by the shrill clamour of the general quarters alarms sounding throughout the aircraft carrier.

He raised his binoculars. The Wasp was lifting away from the British warship. Slung between the machine's four oversize wheels was the unmistakable cigar shape of a torpedo.

50

The *Eureka*'s doctor bandaged Julia's hands in the research ship's sick bay while Captain Hagan fired questions at Oaf and Sherwood. The geologist's answer to his last question had staggered him.

'The *Orion* was what?'

'It's possible that it was sunk by a submerged iceberg,' Sherwood repeated.

Hagan seemed unable to speak for a moment. 'Do you seriously expect me to believe that?'

'I'm certain it was an iceberg,' said Sherwood stubbornly. He wished he had kept quiet but Julia had insisted that he should make his suspicions known.

'A submerged iceberg?' said Hagan sarcastically.

Sherwood glanced at Julia but she avoided his eye. 'It's up to you to stand up for yourself. No one else can believe in something for you,' she had told him.

'It's submerged because there's a mountain in it – perhaps several. They were sheared away when they could no longer resist the ice-cap loading.' Sherwood paused. It wasn't easy to talk with Hagan glaring at him with undisguised hostility. 'At calving it would've measured about a hundred and eighty miles by ninety miles – triangular-shaped. Around eight thousand cubic miles of ice if it stayed in one piece.'

Hagan had a glazed look. 'I've a mind,' he said hoarsely, 'to fly the three of you back to where we found you.'

Sherwood decided that it would be easier to back down and said: 'It is only a theory, captain. I'm not saying that – '

'No!' said Julia angrily. 'It's not. There are too many facts that fit: the freezing water where the *Orion* went down; the colour of the sea – everything!'

Hagan remembered the curious hue in the CBS film. He frowned. Then there was the mystery of the freezing water that had killed so many after they had escaped from the liner. 'What about the fog? Can your iceberg explain that too?'

'Warm air – cold sea,' said Oaf, speaking for the first time.

Hagan was beginning to feel uncomfortable. Every time one of these three spoke they touched a sensitive nerve. 'Okay,' he said. 'So where's this berg now?'

Sherwood thought. 'This is where guesswork creeps in, but going on when the *Orion* sunk and the slowness of the current, I'd say that it's moving in the general direction of the Cape Verde Islands.'

'Drifting below the surface?'

'Yes. It must be. Until it drops the mountains, of course – then it'll surface. But even submerged it shouldn't be too difficult to locate. All you've got to do is base a team on the Cape Verde Islands with a helicopter so that they can systematically block-search the ocean for the iceberg's trail of low salinity sea water – it'll be shedding millions of tons of freshwater each day.'

Hagan decided that Sherwood was mad.

'I've just thought of something,' said Julia.

So's she, thought Hagan.

Julia looked thoughtfully at Sherwood and said: 'Is the ice-berg touching the ocean floor as it moves?'

'It's possible,' Sherwood admitted. 'But there may not be any seismic indication because there's a layer of sediment on the ocean floor that's several hundred metres thick.'

'But the sediment is dense enough to support the weight of telephone cables, isn't it?'

'Yes,' Sherwood agreed, wondering what Julia was leading up to.

'There you are then,' said Julia triumphantly. She turned to Hagan. 'If Glyn is right, sooner or later his iceberg is going to cut a transatlantic cable.'

Julia's words had an immediate effect on Hagan. The colour drained from his face and he stood abruptly. With a curt 'wait here' he moved quickly to the door and was gone.

51

'It's a report from Western Electric,' said the Secretary of State's voice over the booth's speaker. 'They say that their repeaters in the TAT 12 United States–South Africa transatlantic telephone cable could not have been damaged to the extent that they were by a human agency. They cite the damage to repeater 133 as a typical example – '

'I'm not interested in details,' interrupted the President curtly. 'I want to know if we have sufficient grounds to call off this operation.'

'There's something else, Mr President. Western Electric say the mysterious cutting of cables has happened before. On 18 November 1929, most of the telegraph cables between America and Europe were cut one by one. A similar event happened even earlier in 1888 when several cables to Australia were cut. That led to Australia mobilizing her navy. In both cases the cause was never discovered.'

The President watched the activities in the room for some seconds before replying. The latest development was a polar patrol of twenty long-range Tupolev 95 bombers flying dangerously close to US territory. NORAD were preparing to deal with them if their courses became Alaskan intrusive.

'The operation continues,' he said.

52

Admiral Pearson acted on his own initiative in ordering that a ship-to-ship communication link between the American and Russian aircraft carriers be opened when he heard that the Russian ship was flying Admiral Turgenev's pennant.

Silence fell in the *Johnson*'s combat control centre when Admiral Pearson picked up his phone.

'Good afternoon, Admiral Turgenev,' he said in Russian. 'This is Admiral Brandon Pearson speaking.'

'Good afternoon,' said the Russian politely.

'I'm sorry that you have not heeded our warnings and that you've gone ahead and violated the Montreux Convention.'

'I'm not at liberty to discuss the matter,' said the Russian coolly.

'If you turn back –'

'That is out of the question,' said Admiral Turgenev. 'The Soviet navy has merely exercised its right of passage through the Bosphorus.'

Admiral Pearson listened patiently as the Russian outlined the background to the Montreux Convention.

'Have you requested permission to turn back?' Admiral Pearson asked, not expecting his opposite number to reply to the question.

He was surprised when the Russian said: 'Yes. Just before we entered the Bosphorus.'

'Can you see a British Wasp helicopter near you?'

'Yes. It is hovering six kilometres on our starboard quarter. We are watching it carefully.' The Russian officer's tone was flat. Disinterested.

'It's waiting for my order to attack you,' said Pearson simply.

A signals ensign, holding a sealed envelope, tried to approach Admiral Pearson but was intercepted by a lieutenant.

'It's from the admiral's aide on the *Eureka*,' the ensign explained. 'Captain Hagan. He says it's important.'

'What did it say?'

'I don't know, sir. As it was classified, I sealed it as it came off the printer without reading it.'

'Where is the *Eureka*?'

'In the South Atlantic. Its exact position is given in the header code.'

The lieutenant took the envelope from the ensign. He considered it unlikely that a message from a research ship several thousand miles away could be of sufficient importance to warrant disturbing the admiral at this critical stage of the operation.

'Okay,' the lieutenant said to the ensign. 'I'll see the admiral gets it when he's free.'

The ensign saluted and withdrew. The lieutenant dropped the envelope on a nearby console's working surface and promptly forgot it.

Admiral Pearson transferred the phone to his right ear. The Russian had made no reply to his previous statement. 'Do you hear me, admiral?'

'I heard you,' said Admiral Turgenev after a long pause. 'If you do behave in such an aggressive manner, we have been instructed not to retaliate. But I very much doubt if similar instructions have been issued to the rest of our armed forces.'

'Listen,' said Pearson earnestly. 'I'm prepared to avert this clash by cancelling the operation and resigning my job if you're prepared to do the same by ordering your carrier to turn back.'

'Resign my job?' the Russian echoed incredulously.

'Does it matter what happens to us?' said Pearson doggedly. 'What the hell does it matter what happens to us just so long as our actions give everyone some breathing space?'

'We train our officers to obey orders,' said Turgenev.

'Bullshit. You train them to use their initiative – just as we do.'

'You obey your orders,' said the Russian, 'and I'll obey mine.' There was a click and a hiss of carrier wave in Pearson's handset.

Pearson muttered to himself and dropped the phone back on its cradle. He ignored the 'no smoking' signs and lit a cigar. He looked up and met the eyes of the control officer who was regarding him speculatively.

'Nothing from Washington?' asked Pearson.

'Nothing, sir.'

Pearson inhaled on his cigar. He suddenly felt very old. For the first time in his life he regretted his choice of career. He looked at the digital clock and said: 'This order timed at nineteen-zero-ten Zulu Time. Initiate the attack.'

53

The words spoken by the Wasp pilot as he gave a running commentary on his attack approach were heard in every major command centre throughout the NATO alliance. Every head of state was listening; every general, admiral and air marshal. The crisp, even tones of the British pilot gave no indication that he was aware of his distinguished audience.

'Ten thousand yards,' he said into his microphone.

He maintained a constant fifty feet above the sea without referring to the Wasp's ground proximity radar.

'ASI indicating six-zero knots. . . . Reducing to four-zero now.'

The pilot kept his eyes fixed on his objective. If the Soviet carrier, now looming larger with every passing second, made the slightest alteration to her speed or course, he was to break off the attack immediately and await further instructions. At two thousand yards, he was to drop the homing torpedo.

'Eight thousand yards. I have excellent visual contact.'

The President sipped from the glass of water.

'Six thousand yards,' said the speaker in the glass booth.

Strange that my pulse should be normal, thought the President.

'Five thousand yards,' said the speakers in the *Johnson*'s combat control centre. 'No sign of any flight-deck activity. It looks deserted.'

Admiral Pearson beckoned to the lieutenant he had seen take the envelope from a signals ensign while he was talking to the Soviet admiral.

'Four thousand yards,' intoned the speakers.

'Sir?'

'What was the message?'

The lieutenant looked blank.

'You chased an ensign away just now.'

The lieutenant's face cleared. 'Oh yes, sir. That's right – there's a message for you from Captain Hagan.'

'Three thousand yards,' said the Wasp pilot. There was a perceptible quiver in his voice. There was something surrealistically beautiful about the serene carrier nosing its way gracefully through the clear, blue water.

His hand went to the torpedo release control. He knew exactly where it was – there was no need for his eyes to flicker from his magnificent target.

At two thousand five hundred yards he released the safety catch.

At two thousand three hundred yards he made the final course correction so that the torpedo would run true even if its acoustic homing controls failed.

The water was a blur beneath the Wasp. The pilot was aiming his machine so that the carrier's stern gear and the torpedo's warhead would be occupying the same place at the same time.

A red light flickered and then glowed steadily: the torpedo's detonator was already sensing the magnetic anomaly of the carrier's 45,000-ton presence.

'Positive gauss indication,' said the pilot. 'Two thousand one hundred yards. Dropping now.'

He was about to operate the torpedo release control when a voice crashed urgently in his headphones: 'Abort! Abort! Abort!'

The pilot hesitated. The Kiev's towering bulk swelled towards him. 'Codeword!' he shouted, his fingers tensed on the release.

But before he had finished the word, the voice was urgently repeating: 'Icarus! Icarus! Icarus!'

The pilot sheered away from the Soviet warship.

54

The tension between East and West slackened as quickly as it had began. Neither side offered nor expected apologies. Servicemen and women throughout the Warsaw Pact and NATO alliance countries whose leave had been suspended were allowed to go home. Bombers were recalled, submarines returned to their billets and border infantry movements halted.

It had been the thirteenth major alert since 24 August 1949 – the day the North Atlantic Treaty had come into force.

There was a final touch of irony: five hours after the British Wasp helicopter had abandoned its attack on the Kiev, the Soviet aircraft carrier developed a serious steering-gear fault and was forced to turn back to Sevastopol.

PART TWO
Menace

I

CAPE VERDE ISLANDS

Group of fifteen mid-Atlantic volcanic islands off north-west coast of Africa. Part of the central Atlantic intrusive ridge that stretches from Iceland to Tristan da Cunha. Portuguese. Sugar, fruit and tourism. Pop: 300,000. Formerly a listening centre for a 'Seaguard' array.

The ice moved.

It moved slowly northwards; an unseen, undetected harbinger of death.

Julia picked her way past the sunshades that speckled the beach like acne and sat on the sand beside Sherwood. He opened an eye.

'Well?'

'We start work tomorrow. The instrument package has arrived. You lower it into the water for five seconds and get an instant reading.'

Sherwood said nothing. Lying on a hot beach was something he had dreamed about in Antarctica. Julia made herself comfortable. It was two hours to sunset and still blindingly hot on the west-facing beach.

'Where's Oaf?'

'Swimming somewhere.'

Julia shaded her eyes. She had to look virtually directly into the sun but she could pick out Oaf swimming with long, easy strokes some twenty yards from the surf that was indifferently demolishing shrieking children's sandcastles. There were about a hundred people in the water.

'Have you drawn up the search schedule?' asked Julia.

Sherwood yawned and sat up. 'I'll do it tomorrow morning. Never do today what you can put off till tomorrow.'

A zephyr rustled the lunch wrappers of a nearby English family. The sudden breeze started a newspaper and sent it scudding for cover under an outcrop of rocks.

'Hey, Sherwood!' Oaf bellowed from the water. 'Come and swim, you lazy bastard!'

'His manners are impossible,' said Julia, noticing the disapproving look from the English mother.

The breeze strengthened slightly. Sherwood pulled a towel round his shoulders and watched Oaf swimming. 'I've not noticed you complaining.'

'Oaf's great advantage is that he is totally devoid of complications,' said Julia with an impish smile.

Oaf trod water and swore loudly at some children who were splashing him.

Julia shivered. 'There's a mist coming in. Look.'

A bank of grey cloud, looking strangely out of place against the blue sea and sky, was seeping from the south across the water and dissolving the horizon.

Julia shivered again. 'It's gone a bit chilly.'

'Sunset soon.'

'Yes, but it didn't do this the same time yesterday.'

A dog was running along the tideline, chasing after pieces of driftwood thrown by its owner. It suddenly sat down in the surf, lifted its head to the darkening sky and bayed mournfully. Nearby children squealed in delight.

Julia heard one of the English children say: 'Daddy, look! The sea's changing colour!'

'That's because the sun's going down.'

Julia was about to comment on the mist that had completely obliterated the horizon, when the dog's baying became a continuous, blood-curdling howl of fear.

'You don't know if there's rabies in these islands, do you?' said Sherwood, apprehensively eyeing the terrified creature that was dragging its hindlegs through the surf and ignoring the soothing noises its frantic owner was making.

Julia felt her scalp crawl. She and the dog had sensed that something was terribly wrong.

Then the child was yelling excitedly. 'Daddy! Mummy! Look! Look! The sea's burning to blood!'

The ice struck.

A hundred yards out to sea several dolphins leapt high into the air, their tails thrashing wildly. They fell back and flailed the water white. Men, women and children in the water were suddenly screaming in terror and jerking their arms and legs convulsively. People ran down the beach and plunged into the sea to rescue their children but were immediately seized by the same hideous paroxysms as soon as their bodies were immersed.

Julia and Sherwood stood and stared aghast at the terrible scene, knowing instinctively that there was nothing they could do.

A maddened dolphin bored blindly through the ferment of screaming, struggling people. Its sharp snout, moving at forty miles per hour, rammed into the small of a man's back with the full force of the creature's four-hundred-pound mass. The man's spine snapped like a piece of dry spaghetti. He died instantly but the nerve cells in his disrupted brain kept firing repeatedly, causing his dead arms to continue their savage spasms. He moved slowly through the seething mass of the dead and the dying. In death he had acquired an ability that had eluded him in life: he could swim.

Oaf's deep, guttural bellows carried across the blood-red water. The bodies of the children who had splashed him were floating face down within reach of his mighty, pounding fists.

Sherwood took a blind step forward. Julia reached for his arm. Without taking her eyes off the nightmare before her, she said quietly: 'There's nothing we can do, is there?'

They stood motionless, side by side, letting the sight and sound of the horror before them etch deeply into their memories.

2

The dead man gave the Portuguese army truck a friendly wave.

The motor convoy stopped. Six pairs of headlights lanced along the silent beach littered with the glistening corpses of dead fish. A searchlight on the leading truck probed the dead man. He waved again, moving a huge, hairy arm with a curious jerking motion.

Four men jumped down from the leading vehicle's tailboard: two soldiers carrying a folding stretcher, an army doctor and a black-gowned priest. The sea whispered mockingly at the group as they approached the dead man. They stepped over a tunny fish and carefully skirted a hammerhead shark that was lying on its side, its crescent jaw gaping and a pectoral fin twitching.

The soldiers set the stretcher down beside the giant dead man, staring apprehensively at the body while the doctor listened to his chest. The corpse lifted an arm which became entangled in the doctor's stethoscope. The doctor pinned the arm down with his knee and nodded to one of the soldiers.

The priest faltered in his droning recital of the last rites. He licked his lips nervously and continued reading, holding his book at an angle to trap the light shining from the trucks. The soldiers reluctantly passed a leather strap around the shaggy corpse and fastened the buckle securely.

The doctor completed his examination and straightened up. Without being ordered, the soldiers lifted the heavy body on to the stretcher and carried it back to the waiting convoy.

Oaf's body was the sixty-third recovered from the Cape Verde beaches that night. Few of them had required so much effort to carry.

They were mostly children.

3

Admiral Howe absently tossed pieces of bread to a squabble of London starlings as he listened to Abbott making his report. It was amazing that those three had turned up on the Cape Verde Islands but he was confident that they knew nothing about the missing submarine *Asteria*. If Brill was certain then that was good enough.

'But my big worry,' Abbott concluded, 'is that sooner or later I'm going to make a serious mistake in the crew's correspondence.'

Admiral Howe threw the last piece of bread. 'You're coping admirably, James.'

'There have been minor errors, sir,' Abbott confessed. 'Luckily I've always managed to explain them away in subsequent letters.'

The starlings moved aggressively in on a St James's Park drake who had a whole slice of bread to himself. Admiral Howe watched their antics with amusement.

'Well you won't have to worry for much longer, James. It's been decided to abandon the operation. The *Asteria* will be posted as missing as soon as a favourable opportunity arises.'

4

Sherwood looked on as Julia drew a column of the red-tinted sea water into a pipette and carefully smeared a few drops on to a clean slide. The nuns who ran the hospital on Cape Verde had agreed to let her use their tiny laboratory.

She placed the fresh slide under the microscope and indicated that Sherwood should look. She had hardly spoken since morning when she had stood by Oaf's coffin during the mass burial service.

Sherwood peered through the eyepieces at the thousands of magnified creatures that resembled delicate, transparent bells.

'Are they the ostracods you told me about?' he asked.

'No.'

'What then?'

'They're a dinoflagellate – *Cymnodinium breve*. A sudden drop in sea temperature kills them and they release a mild nerve toxin into the water. Quite common in the Gulf of Mexico where they cause the so-called red tides.' Julia's voice was expressionless.

'And they caused . . .?'

'Fish swimming through the red bloom are killed as their nerve axons start firing – their entire nervous systems are disrupted.'

Sherwood straightened up and eyed the flask of sea water. 'Is that stuff still dangerous?'

'No. The toxin decays rapidly in sunlight.'

'But if they release a mild toxin, then surely –'

'Take another look,' said Julia. 'I've never seen such a concentration of them.'

Sherwood looked through the microscope again at the myriads of bell-like organisms.

He found it impossible to believe that they could turn the sea into a deadly nerve gas.

5

Supreme Allied Commander Atlantic, Admiral Brandon Pearson was a better listener than talker. He sat very still in his cabin on the aircraft carrier *Johnson*, asked only the occasional question and nodded his head from time to time to encourage Sherwood to keep talking. Nothing in his face betrayed his reactions to the geologist's theory concerning a gigantic, submerged iceberg. Just once, when Sherwood repeated his figure of eight thousand cubic miles of ice, did Pearson catch Hagan's eye. That was the only lapse. The Marines captain was sitting on a chair near the door making notes. Julia had said her piece and was silent.

Pearson held up a hand. 'Wait a minute, Mr Sherwood. Tell me how your berg reached the Cape Verde Islands from Antarctica.'

'My belief is that it was carried on the West Wind Drift Current in the Southern Ocean, then picked up by the Benguela Current that flows northwards up the coast of South West Africa, and is now being pushed north-west across the Atlantic towards the Eastern Seaboard of America by the North Equatorial Current.'

A tap at the door broke the silence that followed. Hagan answered it and returned to his seat reading two signals.

Pearson tipped his chair back and steepled his fingers. 'And what's your estimate of your berg's present size?' He had used the expression 'your berg' in all the questions put to Sherwood.

'I'm not sure, sir,' Sherwood answered after a moment's thought. 'We've no information on the behaviour of submerged icebergs and virtually none on the temperature or direction of sub-surface ocean currents. I've based my guesswork – and that's just about what it is – on the known movements of surface currents.'

Pearson stood. 'Thank you for seeing me, Miss Hammond – Mr Sherwood. I'd appreciate it if you would agree to remaining a while on the *Eureka* until we've investigated further.'

The interview was over.

. . . . .

'And you believe them?' Pearson fired at Hagan a minute later, when Julia and Sherwood had left.

'Yes, sir. That's why I sent them to Cape Verde in the first place.'

'My God, I've been asked to swallow some things in my time,' Pearson muttered. 'Did you get down everything Sherwood said?'

'Yes, sir.' Hagan passed the two signals to Admiral Pearson. 'These came while you were talking to him.' Hagan gave a ghost of a smile as he spoke.

The SACLANT read the first one. It was from the Scripps Institution of Oceanography. They had completed their own tests on the Cape Verde sea water sample and confirmed Julia Hammond's findings. In addition, they cited the incident at Miami Beach in February 1969 in which several bathers had suffered dinoflagellate brain damage.

The second signal was from the Naval Space-Surveillance Center at Dahlgren, Virginia:

YOUR REQUEST INFORMATION LARGE ICEBERGS. LARGEST SEEN PHOTOGRAPHED BY ESSA-3 SATELLITE DURING 1967/1968. BERG REMAINED IN WEDDELL SEA. FIRST SEEN ORBIT 4699 ON OCTOBER 11 1967. LAST SEEN ORBIT 6408 ON FEBRUARY 27 1968. SIZE 175 KILOMETERS BY 111 KILOMETERS. BERG DESIGNATION – GIANT TABULAR. . . .

Pearson broke off reading. His eyes met Hagan's.

'Only a few kilometres smaller than Sherwood's iceberg,' said Hagan, reading Pearson's thoughts.

6

FLIP
Floating Instrument Package

From: Walter J. Krantz
Department of Transportation
US Coast Guard (3rd Coast Guard District)
International Ice Patrol Headquarters
Governors Island
New York, NY 10004

To: Admiral Brandon Pearson, SACLANT, USS *Johnson*.

Dear Admiral,

Reference: Conversation transcript – yourself/G. Sherwood/ J. Hammond.

We have read. We have considered. And we are sceptical. Our experience of icebergs is limited to Greenland bergs, in particular those bergs calved in Baffin Bay and swept into the North Atlantic shipping lanes by the Labrador Current. These are the icebergs that concern us. Occasionally a large berg drifts as far south as Boston and we've heard from contacts in South Africa of an Antarctic berg that was sighted off Cape Town in 1955, so there's no doubt that icebergs can and do drift exceptionally long distances. But it is impossible for any iceberg, Arctic or Antarctic, to survive long enough to cross the equator. We are astonished that Mr Sherwood (whom we recall served with us for a period as an IIP observer) should believe that such an unprecedented event has taken place. Ask Mr Sherwood why the calving of eight thousand cubic miles of ice did not leave a seismic fingerprint and why the inevitable wave disturbance was not registered by FLIPS owned by Scripps and the British IOS.

A detailed analysis of all Mr Sherwood's points will be with you within twenty-four hours. We are not qualified to comment on Miss Hammond's remarks concerning ocean toxin level increases caused by the death of plankton.

Sincerely,

(Signed)

Walter J. Krantz

Deputy Vice-Commander, International Ice Patrol.

7

'Sit down, Mr Sherwood,' said Admiral Pearson affably as the geologist was shown into his cabin.

Sherwood sat in the indicated chair. His original awe at meeting the Supreme Allied Commander had faded. He now felt irritated at being shuttled back and forth by helicopter between the *Eureka* and the *Johnson*.

'There's a flaw in your theory about your giant iceberg,' said Pearson. 'A serious flaw.'

'I'm surprised you've found only one,' said Sherwood evenly. 'Personally, I don't care if you find a thousand and one flaws.'

Pearson ignored the comment. 'Experts on icebergs say that eight thousand cubic miles of ice taking to the water would cause a seismic disturbance. They've been going over the records. There's been no significant earthquake activity in Antarctica for several years.' He unwrapped a cigar while waiting for Sherwood to answer. 'Well, Mr Sherwood?'

'The iceberg more than likely rode on a lubricating cushion of water melted by friction as it broke away from the ice-cap,' Sherwood answered. 'I never said that it moved quickly. It's possible that it took as long as a month to slide into the sea. But however slowly it moved, it would've had more than enough momentum to carry it over the continental shelf and into deep water.'

Pearson lit his cigar. He was beginning to revise his opinions about Sherwood.

'So where's that iceberg now, Mr Sherwood?'

Sherwood noticed that for once Admiral Pearson didn't say 'your berg'. 'Have you kept up the search for it, admiral?'

'I called it off. So where is it now?'

'I can only make a rough guess.'

'Right now, Mr Sherwood, your guesswork is all we've got to go on.'

Sherwood looked up into the expressionless eyes. It was Admiral Pearson's first admission, though indirect, that he believed in the iceberg's existence. 'Approximately half way between the Cape Verde Islands and Puerto Rico, admiral. But please understand that that is a very rough guess indeed.'

Pearson nodded. 'That's understood.'

'May I make a suggestion please?'

'Sure.'

'My estimate could be miles out. It might be a good idea if you broadcast a request to all shipping to report to the *Johnson* or the *Eureka* any unusual phenomenon – no matter how minor it may seem. Slight changes in the colour of the sea – anything.'

Two hours after the request was issued a US Coast Guard cutter called up the *Johnson* and said that they had spotted an apparently abandoned schooner, the *Bermuda Witch*, sailing by itself under a full spread of canvas, and were proposing to board it.

8

The ice moved.

Each day the embracing warmth of the Atlantic depths destroyed a hundred million tons of its titantic bulk – an infinitesimal percentage. But the mass of the mountains locked in the five-million-year-old grip of the ice remained unchanged. Gradually, they dragged the ice deeper and deeper into the thick primeval sediment that covered the floor of the ocean.

The moment came when the ice stopped.

Once again the mountains had triumphed.

9

The black-headed gulls screamed raucous insults at the coast guardsman as he stood unsteadily on the low roof of the cutter's motor launch. He tensed his thigh muscles and jumped. His fingers closed thankfully round one of the schooner's deck stanchions. The sudden movement raised an angry, swirling storm of screaming gulls from the sailing ship's rigging. A second later he had swung over the rail and was safely aboard the seemingly abandoned *Bermuda Witch*. The motor launch sheered away and paced the big schooner on her quarter.

The wheeling gulls settled on rigging and coamings and stared malevolently at the guardsman with hard, gimlet eyes. A thousand vicious beaks and a thousand pairs of bead-like, unblinking eyes followed him as he moved aft. The ship was heeling under a full spread of canvas. The guardsman slid his hand along the rail to support himself, for the teak deck was slippery with fresh guano. A gull refused to move even though the guardsman's hand had moved to within a yard of its perch. Its dazzling white plumage was flecked with crimson. There was something in its stiletto beak – something red that dripped red on to the deck. The bird gulped and a bulge moved down through the feathers that covered the creature's throat. The guardsman felt his heart beating faster. He glanced up into the rigging. Blue sky. Bright sun. And the birds. Thousands of birds. Watching him speculatively.

And all of them had crimson-flecked plumage.

The guardsman reached for the two-way radio clipped to his belt. The movement startled the bird. It rose up suddenly – its three-foot span flashing white and red – and lunged at the guardsman. He saw the beak darting for his eyes and threw up his arm. The screaming bird lifted effortlessly into the rigging. The guardsman lowered his arm. There was a long gash above the wrist.

Then he saw the young man. He was sitting under an awning near the wheelhouse. A black-headed gull was perched unconcerned like a pet on the young man's lap. The guardsman crept fearfully forward. His eyes open wide in horror and disbelief. He jerked the radio to his mouth and pressed the transmit button with a trembling finger. He moved his lips in terror but could make no sound.

The young man was dead but he had been helping the black-headed gulls to live.

The guardsman dropped the radio, staggered to the rail and was violently sick.

10

The ice lay still.

It was weighed down by the mountains and partially covered by the thousand-feet-deep layer of sediment that covered the ocean floor.

There was no daylight. There never had been daylight at this depth and never would be.

There was movement; the continuous luminescent flurry of grotesque bottom-feeding fish shying away from the sudden increase in the density of the sea water caused by the intense cold.

There were sounds; splintering and groaning noises from deep within the ice. The tensions and forces that had gripped the mountains for five million years were being prised loose by the ocean's tenuous warmth.

The moment of freedom for the ice was at hand.

11

GLORIA (Geophysic Long Range Inclined Asdic) A streamlined, towed sonar instrument package with an angled scan that enables three-dimensional pictures of the ocean floor to be constructed.

'Tuna fish,' were Admiral Pearson's first accusing words as he stepped out of his helicopter that had landed on the *Eureka*'s platform. 'How in the world could a freshly caught tuna kill everyone aboard that schooner?'

Before Sutherland, the *Eureka*'s captain, could reply, Admiral Pearson had turned round and was giving Hagan orders. 'Take this chopper back to the *Johnson* and round up my things. Bring them straight here. If Captain Sutherland has a suitable cabin, I'm staying here. Okay with you, captain?'

Sutherland recovered his composure quickly. 'You're very welcome, admiral. We have a spare cabin that I can move in to –'

'Anywhere will do, captain,' Pearson interrupted. He caught sight of Sherwood and Julia watching him and gave them a cursory nod. 'Now what's all this about tuna fish?'

Sutherland opened the *Bermuda Witch*'s log and pointed to one of the last entries.

09:44 Extraordinary behaviour by several fish. Dolphins and porpoises charging about on the surface as if demented. A good-sized tuna stunned itself by ramming us amidships; enough for generous portions for everyone tonight. Sea an unusual reddish colour.

'And your biologists have examined the tuna?' inquired Admiral Pearson when he had finished reading.

'The remains were in the schooner's freezer,' said Sutherland. 'It was suffering from an inflammation of the brain and there were large quantities of toxic neural cells in its flesh – probably released from the creature's bloodstream.'

'And they're tasteless?'

'Presumably, yes.'

Pearson lit a cigar. 'What do you think of Sherwood's theory?'

'It's the only one we've got. All scientific theories are in essence torture chambers for the facts. If one of my team comes up with another theory, then we'll put it to the test.'

Pearson inhaled. 'Has that happened?'

'A Scripps member who's with us suggested a leaking can of nerve gas on the ocean floor. Sherwood's theory was the one that survived.'

'Well, he's persuasive – I'll give him that,' Pearson commented.

Sutherland smiled. 'That's because he doesn't give a damn whether or not you're persuaded.'

'And you've come across nothing to disprove him? Absolutely nothing?'

'Absolutely nothing.'

'And it's not worrying him?'

Sutherland shook his head. 'Not until the *Bermuda Witch* came along. Now he seems to think that we might be in with a chance of getting evidence.'

'How's that?'

Sutherland indicated the *Bermuda Witch*'s log that was lying open. 'We know the exact time and date when that schooner ran into trouble, admiral. . . . *And* we know the exact position.'

Pearson looked faintly amused. 'I wouldn't put too much faith in the positions obtained by a weekend sailor.'

'It's not like that,' said Sutherland. 'The *Bermuda Witch* had some good equipment. Namely Decca Navigator. The recorder was running when the coast guard found her.'

Pearson was immediately very interested. 'The hell it was?'

'We're going to swing our GLORIA out in about an hour. Towing it will mean a speed reduction, but we should be scanning the ocean floor where the *Bermuda Witch* picked up that poisoned tuna fish in approximately ten hours.'

12

Twelve men, including Captain Sutherland, Sherwood and Admiral Pearson were crowded into the *Eureka*'s GLORIA control cabin, watching the sonograph scanning head draw a fresh picture of the ocean floor three miles below the research ship. There was a meandering groove in the sediment.

'There it is,' said Sherwood. 'An iceberg plough mark.'

'A what?' asked Pearson.

'An iceberg plough mark,' Sherwood repeated. 'About twelve miles wide by a mile deep. Fairly common in the North Atlantic. They're caused by icebergs cutting a furrow in the sediment. Most of them date from the last ice age and have been virtually obliterated by subsequent sediment deposits.'

'It's the biggest one I've ever seen,' said one of the sonar technicians.

Sherwood pointed to the sonograph. 'You can see where it crosses much older plough marks.'

Admiral Pearson stared at the groove. Even his untrained eye could see that the edges of the giant plough mark were fresh. Twelve miles wide! Sherwood answered his next question before it was asked.

'Unless we're heading the wrong way along that plough mark, it looks like only a matter of time before we. . . .'

Pearson didn't hear the rest of the sentence. He nodded to Sutherland and Hagan, and gestured to the door. Once outside in the passageway, Pearson said to Sutherland: 'I want you to maintain a twenty-four-hour watch with GLORIA.'

'We never tow at night in case something goes wrong,' Sutherland protested. 'GLORIA cost over two million dollars.'

'I'll take the responsibility,' said Pearson crisply. He turned to Hagan. 'Tell the *Johnson* to get here fast. It doesn't matter if there are Soviet AGIs around that might learn her top speed.'

'But what will be the point in having that CVB under our feet, admiral?' Sutherland asked.

Pearson ignored the 'no smoking' sign and lit a cigar. 'Because I'm developing a healthy respect for Sherwood's opinions and I'd feel a lot happier having her around. And happier still if it turns out that she won't be needed.'

13

The plough mark had vanished.

Sherwood dropped wearily into the chair beside the sonar technician and watched the picture emerging under the GLORIA scanning head. 'When did it disappear?'

'It hasn't,' said the technician. 'Watch.'

The technician operated a control that swung the questing sonic beam to the left of the *Eureka*'s heading. A new image of the ocean floor appeared under the scanning head. This time the sonograph showed a steep precipice that swept up one side of the recording paper.

'Seven thousand feet high,' said the technician uneasily. 'The plough mark's still there – it's just that it's too wide to be displayed on the paper. That's the edge of it.'

'How wide?'

The technician swallowed. 'Would you believe . . . forty-five miles . . . right on maximum range of this thing?'

Sherwood kept his voice steady. 'You've checked the transducer array?'

'And the back-up. Same result.'

The two men watched the sonograph in silence.

'Have you called anyone else?' asked Sherwood when the scanning head started filling in a new sonograph.

'No.' The technician looked unhappy. 'You know something? I've been five years on this ship and I've tracked plough marks in the south that must've been made by the grandfathers of all icebergs, but I've never seen anything like that before.'

But Sherwood wasn't listening. He had noticed something about the sonograph that was turning his bowels to water.

14

It was 5:30 am. A clear sky over the Atlantic held the promise of another warm day. But the weather did nothing for Admiral Brandon Pearson's temper. Usually it improved as the day lengthened. At 5:30 am it was dangerously short. He resented being woken and made his resentment abundantly clear to Hagan.

'Sherwood requests your presence in the control cabin, sir,' said Hagan smoothly, handing his superior a cup of hot, black coffee. 'I didn't want to disturb you but Sherwood does seem very agitated about something.'

Pearson punctuated his sips of the scalding drink with biting remarks about civilians.

Any second now he'll notice that the ship's stopped, thought Hagan.

'Why's the ship stopped?'

'I don't know, sir.'

Ten minutes later Pearson was venting his temper on Sherwood in the confined space of the GLORIA control cabin.

'Why have the engines stopped, Mr Sherwood?'

'So that we can hear properly,' said Sherwood, plugging in a pair of headphones. 'If you would kindly sit here, sir.'

Pearson allowed himself to be sat in one of the swivel chairs facing the console. Sherwood gave him the headphones.

'And *I* need to sleep properly, Mr Sherwood.'

'Would you put them on please, sir.'

'It had better be something soothing,' Pearson growled, settling the headphones over his ears. The geologist's anxious expression had a calming effect on his temper. 'What am I supposed to hear?'

'Increase the volume,' Sherwood said to the technician.

The technician increased the volume.

Pearson frowned. 'Well?'

'Can you hear anything?'

'No.'

'We're using the GLORIA's receiver as a passive listening device,' explained Sherwood. 'And we're sweeping through three hundred and twenty degrees. . . .'

Pearson opened his mouth to blast Sherwood but the words froze on his lips as the silence in the headphones penetrated his sleep-hazed judgement.

The sea is never silent! Never!

Sherwood noticed that Pearson had almost imperceptibly stiffened with shock. He correctly guessed that the shrewd old sailor knew all about the continuous background uproar in the ocean caused by the interminable clicking and chirruping noises made by dolphins and porpoises. Their high-pitched sonar was known to have a range of many miles.

Sherwood said slowly: 'There are probably more dolphins and porpoises on this planet than there are people. So where have they all gone?'

Pearson made no reply. He listened, his face taut with concentration.

'Nor is there a trace of any fish on the sonograph,' Sherwood continued. 'Nothing. It's as if all marine life has been wiped out. . . . Or frightened away.'

'So what does it prove?' asked Pearson. He pulled one of the padded headphones away from his ear so that he could hear Sherwood properly. 'Strange things happen at sea, as they say.'

'This is even stranger,' Sherwood replied while operating a control on the console. 'I'm angling the receiver up so that it's picking up noises generated on the surface. Have a listen. Sounds like a heavy ship is going all out for breaking records. Getting stronger too. It's about a hundred miles away.'

Pearson listened to the heavy beat of powerful screws turning at high speed. He could even hear the unmistakable whine of steam turbines.

'That's probably the *Johnson*,' said Pearson, now getting angry again. 'Have you got me up at this ungodly hour to listen to –'

'No,' said Sherwood sharply. 'We got you up to listen to this.'

Sherwood spun the inclination control. The sound of the *Johnson* was replaced by a noise that was like no noise that Pearson had ever heard before. His expression changed to one of astonishment and he clamped both headphones more firmly over his ears. There were echoing reports that sounded like underwater explosions and a demonic shrieking rising to a crescendo with undertones of distant thunder. The hideous cacophony of the deep boomed like a malignant, unimaginable being that was devouring the bowels of the earth. Pearson was unable to hear his own voice when he said: 'What the hell is it?'

'Ice,' said Sherwood simply.

The admiral seemed to be hypnotized by the terrible sounds

in his headphones. He listened for some seconds, then removed the headphones and laid them on the console without speaking.

'The receivers are picking up those noises from the ocean floor,' said Sherwood quietly. 'About seventy miles away and in the *Johnson*'s path. It sounds as if the carrier's moving at high speed.'

Pearson nodded and stared at the headphones. The whispering, ethereal sounds were clearly audible. 'I told it to get here as fast as possible.'

'Then surely she'll hear those noises and alter course?'

Pearson looked at Sherwood with lustreless eyes. 'No. . . . She won't hear anything. She has to retract her underwater listening gear into the hull when moving at speeds above thirty knots.'

Suddenly the noises in the headphones stopped. Sherwood snatched them up and clamped them over his ears. He turned the amplifier up to maximum gain and listened intently. His eyes widened with shock.

'Admiral,' he said, keeping his voice under tight control. 'We've got to get out of this area as fast as possible.'

PART THREE
Destruction

1

The ice moved.

It moved with infinite slowness – testing its new-found buoyancy now that it had finally torn itself free from the mountains it had dragged half way across the world.

The ponderous, multi-billion-ton mass moved uncertainly in the sluggish bottom current.

The ice lifted.

One hundred feet. . . . Five hundred feet. . . .

A small mountain, whose jagged escarpments had held it in place, was finally dislodged. It fell slowly into the layer of primeval ooze that carpeted the ocean floor.

The ascent of the ice quickened. It gently, but inexorably, shouldered aside the millions of tons of sea water of its own displacement.

Suddenly the movement of the colossus became an accelerating, exultant surge of freedom.

2

Lieutenant Jack Klein, flying a Skywarrior from the USS *Johnson,* was the only witness.

He was at fifteen thousand feet when he spotted the sudden discoloration of the sea. He estimated that the bloom covered an area twenty-five miles by forty miles – a thousand square miles of ocean turning to blood.

He dived while maintaining a running commentary to the *Johnson* that was a hundred and fifty miles to the east and cramming on every knot to get away from the scene of the impending diaster.

Then it happened.

Klein levelled out at five thousand feet and stared aghast at the surface. It was lifting and changing from its red hue to a maddened welter of white foam as if the sea was boiling.

It continued to heave upwards – swelling into a mighty hump like a gargantuan cancer on the face of the ocean.

The ice erupted into the dawn sunlight. Sparkling crystal cliffs rounded by the erosion of the warm water; hills, valleys; a curious mountain in the centre that was shaped like an up-ended anvil; and even rapidly forming rivers of cascading sea water that cut deep ravines as Klein numbly watched.

It was a country. A floating country. In ice. Millions upon millions of tons of ice.

Klein forgot the commentary as he circled the glistening continent. His hands on the controls moved automatically. The querulous voice of the *Johnson* is his flying helmet was forgotten. He gazed down over the rim of the Skywarrior's canopy, hypnotized by the dreadful beauty of the largest moving object on the planet.

A remote corner of his stupefied brain clung grimly to its powers of reason. And even that was dominated by one thought: *There's nine-tenths of it below the surface.*

Huge cataracts continued to roar into the broken sea, adding incalculable energies to the encircling tidal wave that was racing outwards from the scene of the terrible renaissance.

3

The tidal wave was three miles away and roaring towards the *Eureka* at the speed of an express train.

Sutherland was the only man on the bridge – on his orders. He spun the helm so that the research ship's ice-wise bows would meet the charging mountain of water head on.

The *Eureka* and her company had had ten hours to prepare mentally and physically for the catastrophic, inescapable event that was now virtually upon them. Every hatch was battened down. The huge space track antennae, which could have punched right through the decks if they were dislodged, were now dismantled and stowed below. All heavy equipment had been secured, watertight doors closed, and buoyancy chambers tested. The harnesses on the ship's scuba breathing sets had been cannibalized so that everyone could lash himself into his bunk with his hands resting on the quick-release buckles.

Admiral Pearson had refused to leave in his helicopter on the grounds that no sailor would dream of quitting a ship that was in trouble. And besides – they were out of range of land so where could the helicopter go to?

When Sherwood had checked Julia's harness, she had thrown an arm round his neck and given him a kiss.

In their respective cabins, Hagan and Pearson lay silent. Hagan had adjusted the older man's buckles to ensure that they were not too tight and had left without speaking. They had shaken hands. Nothing more than that was necessary.

Forty-nine men and one woman prayed to their individual gods as they listened to the approaching thunder that heralded the end.

Sutherland viewed his own end with equanimity as he watched the roaring wall of water hurtling towards him. There was a certain peace of mind derived from knowing that there was nothing he could do; neither his skill nor the *Eureka*'s reinforced hull could save it. The ship, although designed to survive the worst weather the planet could throw at it, would be slammed on to her side and crushed within seconds.

An ironic thought crossed his mind that made him smile: as a keen surf rider, he had dreamed of meeting the mythical, unbroken giant roller that went on for ever. It was also his wish that when he died – it would be at sea.

Both those ambitions were about to be realized.

4

The USS *Johnson* survived.

Just.

She was saved from certain annihilation by her hundred-mile head start and her third-of-a-million horsepower that gave her a top speed of forty-two knots.

The tidal wave, diminishing in mass and velocity, finally caught up with her after an eastwards trans-oceanic charge that had covered a thousand miles in just under twenty-four hours. The *Johnson* broke records but there were no celebrations aboard as she swung her bows to meet the tidal wave when it was within three miles. Five minutes later it was upon her. The angled flight deck disappeared under the rolling mountain. Those aircraft for which there was no room on the hangar deck or which couldn't be flown off were swept over the side like confetti in a wind tunnel.

For a few seconds that stretched into eternity only her towering island was visible above the seething maelstrom. To her aircrews circling above the stricken flat top it seemed inevitable that she would flounder, leaving them air-stranded. For agonizing moments the mighty pride of the US Navy teetered on the brink of destruction, her flight deck level with the boiling sea in the tidal wave's wake.

Slowly, the prayed-for miracle happened; the carrier's huge reserves of buoyancy fought back. The blunt bows lifted, shedding countless tons of her impossible burden. The sea roared through her scuppers like the discharge valves at the base of a dam.

And so the *Johnson* survived. The damage she had sustained would cost several million dollars to repair. But she still had her flight deck, she still had her aircrews and most of her aircraft.

She was still a warship and was still capable of fighting.

5

London.

A gloomy day for the Lloyd's underwriters as the Lutine bell clanged mournfully through the steadily lengthening list of those ships that had been lost between the Bermudas and Barbados.

The great bell (formerly the ship's bell of HMS *La Lutine* which had sunk off the Dutch coast in 1799), was rung once when a ship was reported missing and twice when an overdue ship was reported safe.

Only solitary chimes were heard that day.

The *Plaistow*, the *Cobra*, the *Esso Cumbria*, the *Eureka*. . . . The names rattled out unceasingly on the teleprinters.

Then the first unconfirmed reports began to trickle out of New York. . . . Hispaniola – severe flooding; the Virgin Islands – hit by freak tidal wave; Puerto Rico – disastrous flooding; Haiti and the Dominican Republic – extensive flooding of coastal areas caused by freak tidal wave. . . .

Then the names of more ships and radio reports relayed to

London that spoke of a freak tidal wave. Baffled huddles of underwriters discussed the mystery.

At 4:00 pm the satellite pictures arrived and the stunned world learned about White Atlantis. The named was coined by a journalist holidaying in Miami where only minor effects of the exhausted tidal wave were felt.

As usual with natural disasters, it was the poor countries that suffered the most.

6

The hot Indian summer that was dominating the weather systems of the northern hemisphere was encouraging the tourists to linger in London. St James's Park was unusually crowded.

Admiral Howe sat down beside Lieutenant Abbott and stretched out his legs.

'How did the meeting go, sir?'

'You can forget your letter writing now, James. It was decided to add the *Asteria*'s name to the list of missing ships. The submarine's loss will be announced tomorrow.'

Abbott looked immensely relieved. 'Thank you, sir. I don't think I could've kept up the charade much longer.'

Admiral Howe frowned. Abbott's labelling of the operation as a charade irritated him. But he said nothing. There was no point – the whole wretched business was over and tomorrow the submarine *Asteria* would be officially 'dead'.

Or so he thought.

7

The President was in no mood for half measures.

'Now listen,' he said bluntly to his aide. 'There's a million people on those islands who need help, and need it badly. Medical attention, food, shelter and clothing – in that order. We don't hold discussions with local government officials – that's how relief supplies end up on the market. We fly supplies right in to where they're needed and we rely on the helicopter aircrews to do the decision making. What do we know about that iceberg? Who is taking responsibility for it?'

'The Coast Guard.'

'Why?'

'They run the International Ice Patrol.'

'How big is it?'

'No one knows.'

The President looked annoyed. 'Why not?'

'It's covered in fog. The Coast Guard have been using their slant radar on it from a C-130. They say that ice plays hell with returns. They won't commit themselves on its size.'

The aide was used to being grilled; his answers were fired back as quickly as the questions were asked.

The President considered. 'Presumably, all available surface ships are involved with relief operations?'

'That's right.'

The two men were close friends. There was no need for the aide to use the formal 'Mr President' when they were alone.

A telephone rang. The aide picked it up and listened. 'Yeah . . . I'm with him now.' His faced paled with shock. 'She's what?'

The President raised inquiring eyebrows.

'Yes . . . I'll tell him. . . . Yes. Thank you.'

The aide slowly replaced the receiver and stared at it for some seconds.

'This is going to take some believing. The *Eureka*'s safe. No casualties – no injuries. She's only just fixed up her radio antenna and got a signal out.'

'Pearson's alive?' The President looked delighted.

'And well. But the *Eureka*'s a long way out of the tidal wave's primary destruction zone.'

'Wait a minute. She was right in the middle of it yesterday before she disappeared. How the hell did she escape?'

'That's the bit that you won't believe.'

8

Deke Sutherland grinned broadly at the TV interviewer's incredulous reaction to the answer he had given him.

The interviewer tightened his grip on his microphone and looked desperately around the *Eureka*'s helicopter platform that he and his film crew had landed on. The research ship had stopped to allow the machine to land and had resumed its steady ten knots. Everything about the ship was in perfect working order. There was no damage – nothing for the carrion movie camera, perched one-eyed and disappointed on its operator's shoulder, to feed on.

'Would you repeat that please, Captain Sutherland.'

'We rode the wave,' said Sutherland, ignoring the interviewer's pre-take admonishment not to look at the camera.

It panned away briefly to eye Julia up and down.

'You surfed a ten-thousand-ton ship on a tidal wave?'

'In front of it,' Sutherland corrected. 'Would you like me to explain?'

'Please.'

'Well, the *Eureka*'s got a vee underwater hull form that enables her to ride up if she's ever trapped in pack ice. Pretty unusual. It also enables her to go into areas where episodic waves are known to occur. Five years ago we found one just inside the hundred fathom line off South East Africa. The way the *Eureka* rode that wave made me wonder if she would do the same for the tidal wave.' Sutherland looked sheepish. 'I only thought of it just before the wave was upon us. I put the helm over so that the *Eureka* was running at an angle to it when it reached us. . . . Except that it didn't get to us until we'd reached ten degrees north and the wave was down to a reasonable size.' Sutherland went on to outline some of the finer points of surfing until the interviewer cut him short.

Then it was Admiral Pearson's turn before the eye. He praised Captain Sutherland's seamanship and concluded: 'He gave us a ride that we'll never forget.'

'But there are definitely no casualties?'

'None,' said Pearson.

'And no damage?'

'There is some.'

The interviewer looked hopeful.

'About three thousand dollars for new scuba harnesses,' said Pearson.

9

ICE BLINK

The white glare visible on the underside of low clouds from ice that is below the horizon.

'I owe you a sincere apology, Mr Sherwood,' said Admiral Pearson, studying the strange sunlight flickering on the horizon.

Sherwood said nothing. Pearson offered his binoculars. The geologist stared at the enigmatic shape of the Anvil Mountain that was edging slowly into the sky above the low, clinging cloud that shrouded the mystery of White Atlantis.

'Looks like we'll be there in three hours,' commented Pearson.

Julia joined the two men leaning on the *Eureka*'s rail. 'The sea temperature's falling fast,' she announced. 'It's now seven degrees below what it should be.'

Pearson shrugged. 'So? What's seven degrees? Well within normal variations I would have thought,'

'Centigrade,' said Julia, remembering that Americans still clung to the elephantine fahrenheit scale.

Pearson did a mental calculation. It was a hell of a drop. He turned his attention back to the glittering ice blink. 'The *Johnson* and what's left of her escorts will be back tomorrow,' he said. 'We'll be able to talk to the flier who saw it surface.'

Sherwood made no comment. He had argued with Pearson over Lieutenant Klein's report and the admiral had flatly refused to accept that the iceberg could be as large as twenty-five miles by forty miles. Pearson was convinced that Klein must have made an understandable mistake. He pointed out that it was Klein who had once claimed seeing four flying saucers in formation over Florida. No one else had reported them. 'We all make genuine mistakes,' Pearson had said.

Julia interrupted Sherwood's thoughts. 'Why the *Johnson*?' she asked.

'I've pulled her out of her strike force,' said Pearson. 'She's lost too many of her escorts. But she's still a fine floating airbase. Her job's going to be to keep the rubbernecks away from that thing until we know more about it.'

Sherwood smiled. 'Until it melts, admiral?'

'Yes.'

'Then she's got a long job ahead.'

'The IIP say that it'll melt fast once it reaches the Florida Current,' said Pearson.

Sherwood nodded. The Florida Current flowed northwards along the Eastern Seaboard of the United States before being deflected eastwards by Long Island and becoming the Gulf Stream surging across the Atlantic to northern Europe.

'As I've already pointed out,' said Sherwood, 'with all due respect to the International Ice Patrol, their experience and terms of reference are geared to the Greenland bergs moving southwards.' Sherwood pointed to the ice blink where the sparkling peak of the Anvil Mountain was now visible to the naked eye. 'That's not an iceberg in the true sense of the word – it's a fragment of Antarctic ice-cap. None of the rules relating to icebergs apply. It's big enough to make up its own and to break all ours – which it's already done.'

Pearson remained silent. His increasing respect for the British geologist's views was tempered by two indisputable facts: ice was ice and warm sea was warm sea, and the two didn't go together.

'Okay, Mr Sherwood. How long will it take to melt?'

'Let's find out how big it is first,' was Sherwood's irritating reply.

10

The ice moved.

The great white shroud of the enveloping fogbank moved with it over the eerily calm sea.

It moved at two knots – fifty miles each day. A slow but unremitting speed that steadily consumed the miles.

After twenty-five days afloat it was passing between the South Carolina seaport of Charleston, where the Civil War had started, and the Bermudas.

Its cautious escort followed at a distance – a fast motor launch from the *Eureka* or the *Johnson* occasionally chasing away over-curious cruisers from the countless marinas dotted along the coast between Wilmington and Jacksonville.

An enterprising airline operator organized flights out to White Atlantis, but the passengers returned with little to show for their thousand-mile round trip apart from a brief glimpse of the Anvil Mountain's crystal spike thrusting up out of the fog like a ghostly dagger rammed through a sheet.

No one, apart from Lieutenant Klein, had seen White Atlantis. It was as if the mighty iceberg was seeking to preserve its aura of mystery until the warm waters of the Atlantic ultimately destroyed it.

It was Sherwood who correctly guessed that it was creating a surrounding sub-climate that would enable it to survive.

He was keeping the knowledge to himself until he was certain.

II

The air was so incredibly still that Sherwood didn't have to hold the map that Admiral Pearson had dropped on to his lap.

'Looks like you were right all along,' said Admiral Pearson, sinking into the deckchair beside Sherwood. 'A map of White Atlantis built up from the radar survey. Thirty miles by twenty miles. Sure is one helluva chunk of ice.'

Sherwood concentrated on the map with great interest. The sudden gathering of the contour lines into tight, concentric lines like the rings of a tree marked the soaring Anvil Mountain. In other places the lines were incomplete.

'Too much clutter,' said Pearson in answer to Sherwood's query. 'Angels on the PPI plots. Even the *Johnson*'s radar team can't eliminate them without the carrier getting in close. And I'm not taking that risk.'

'What really matters is the nine-tenths below the surface,' said Sherwood. 'How's the sonar team making out?'

'They've still no map. They're complaining that the cold water is playing hell with their beams – bending them.'

A dull roar reached the *Eureka* from the distant fogbank. A small iceberg drifted out of the mist and rolled slowly over, spewing plumes of spray that climbed gracefully into the air.

'Third growler today,' Pearson remarked. 'God damn that fog. This weather's got everyone baffled. Why the hell is it so still?'

Another growler rumbled and crept out of the fog.

'Anyway,' Pearson muttered, 'at least it's decaying fast.'

'Not as fast as I thought it would, though,' said Sherwood. 'What was her distance made good yesterday? About forty-eight miles?'

'Forty-seven point seven.'

Sherwood made a rough calculation on the back of the map. 'Assuming an average thickness of one and a half miles, White Atlantis still has a respectable volume – about a thousand cubic miles.'

'So what's your estimate of its melt rate?'

'A cubic mile a day – a thousand million tons.'

Pearson lit a cigar. 'Remember Walter Krantz of the International Ice Patrol? He remembers you.'

'Yes.'

'His melt rate figure is a hundred times your value. He reckons that White Atlantis will be gone in under a week.'

'You wired him a copy of this map?'

Pearson nodded. 'So how do you account for the wide variation between your figure and his?'

'Walter knows everything there is to know about the Greenland bergs. He might be basing his calculations on an assumption that White Atlantis is hollow or crescent-shaped – that's the shape the Greenland bergs usually weather themselves into.'

'So he could be right?' Pearson was discovering that scientists could be very frustrating people to get straight answers from.

'Yes – if White Atlantis is hollow.'

'And so could you be right?'

'If it's solid.'

Pearson groaned.

Sherwood grinned at the American officer's annoyance. 'I tell you what, admiral. Why don't you let Miss Hammond and me take a close look at White Atlantis?'

12

The sensation of terror returned with the indescribable smell of the ice.

It was the same fear Sherwood had experienced when the *Orion* had struck the hidden iceberg off the coast of South West Africa; the same gut-gnawing premonition.

He resisted the impulse to swing the motor launch round and head back towards the *Eureka*. The research ship and the *Johnson* were in their usual positions, standing five miles away from the fogbank. Julia was sitting unconcerned on the foredeck winding in her water sampler and transferring the contents to labelled test tubes. Sherwood looked up at the leaning spike of the Anvil Mountain rearing a thousand feet out of the cloying fog. It shone like a dazzling beacon in the clear, still morning air. He noticed that the lean of the towering edifice had become more pronounced during the week and guessed that it was due to the corrosive effect of the sun on its southern flanks.

'Now steer a degree to your right,' said the voice in his earphone. It was one of the radar technicians on the *Johnson*; Sherwood was guiding the boat along a narrow radar beam from the aircraft carrier that would take the launch through the impenetrable wall of the fogbank and between the arms of the crescent-shaped ice lagoon where, hopefully, there would be calm water to enable a safe icefall to be made.

Sherwood altered course.

'Okay. Fine. Hold that heading.'

The awesome presence of the approaching fog wall affected Julia, for she stopped filling her test tubes and gazed ahead.

'Listen,' she said.

Sherwood throttled the outboard back until he too could hear the creaking of the invisible ice.

'What the hell is it?' breathed Julia.

'All icebergs are noisy. It's caused by the relaxation of stresses as it melts. Haven't you ever heard the same noise when you've held a frozen-up icecube tray under a running tap?'

'You'd better switch your echo sounder on,' said the *Johnson*. 'You're doing fine.'

Sherwood switched on the instrument. The glowing neon settled on the hundred-foot mark. The ice was beneath t[illegible]

'We'd better get into the suits now,' said Julia.

They helped zip each other into the one-piece extreme cold weather garments.

The launch was within a hundred yards of the fog wall when the voice from the *Johnson* instructed Sherwood to make another minor course correction.

There was a new sound as the fogbank loomed nearer: the dull boom of the restless Atlantic swell heaving itself impotently against the impregnable ice.

Julia shivered, despite the insulated suit, as the first icy fingers of the strangely still mist touched her face.

'It's one of the reasons why the ice is surviving so long,' said Sherwood, seeing her reaction. 'The fog is reflecting ninety per-cent of the solar energy that would otherwise reach the ice.'

'And the cushion of cold water that's surrounded it is pre-venting the Atlantic from doing its work,' added Julia. 'Correct?'

'Yes.'

'Have you told the admiral?'

'He wouldn't believe me.'

The launch entered the fog. The sudden dive in the air tem-perature stopped their conversation. It was as if they had walked through the open door of a deep-freeze storage room. Floating ice frazils crunched under the boat's bow. Sherwood checked the echo sounder. Twenty feet. He wondered what would happen if the mighty iceberg decided to tip over to assume a more stable attitude. Once, while on a flight in an International Ice Patrol C–130, he had seen the incredible sight of a giant, horseshoe-shaped Greenland iceberg perform a slow somersault.

'Hold it!' said the *Johnson* sharply. 'We're losing you against the clutter. Cut your motor and await instructions.'

Sherwood flipped the Mercury outboard's ignition switch and explained the reason to Julia.

'God, what a creepy place,' said Julia, peering into the fog and pulling her hood against her face.

Visibility was less than ten yards. All around was the in-sidious creaking of the ice and a slow dripping sound that set their teeth on edge.

'Run the thing in neutral,' Julia urged. 'Let's have some noise, for God's sake.'

'Best to save fuel.'

The creaking stopped. The sudden silence seemed worse.

Julia clapped her hands. A dispirited echo answered from the depths of the fog – evidence of the sombre menace of the unseen cliffs lurking nearby.

'The echo seemed to come from all round,' said Julia, talking to keep her spirits up.

'We're in the lagoon,' said Sherwood.

Julia shivered again. She was beginning to realize that Sherwood's theory that the ice had wrapped itself in winter to protect itself was substantially correct. 'What the hell is the *Johnson* doing?' she demanded.

Five minutes of the oppressive silence passed.

'Why has the creaking stopped?'

'It comes and goes,' was Sherwood's unhelpful answer.

The *Johnson* asked Sherwood if he was reading them. The voice in the earphone was stronger although Sherwood had not touched the volume control on the radio receiver.

'We've moved in closer,' said the voice when Sherwood had replied. 'You're now clearly fixed on our plot.'

Julia sighed with relief as Sherwood started the Mercury and began steering the boat through the fog in answer to the *Johnson*'s commands. But the welcome purr of the outboard did not dispel her irrational fear that the ice, which had killed so many and had inflicted so much misery, was planning something new.

13

The keel of the boat touched ice.

Sherwood jumped on to the ice shelf that formed a false beach and pulled the boat's bows firmly into the yielding slush. He helped Julia out. She held the mooring spike while he drove it deep into a firm outcrop.

'I thought it would be cleaner,' she said, pointing at the mud-rimed beach.

Sherwood didn't answer. He had seized a handful of the grey

slush and was examining it closely, allowing it to trickle through his mittened fingers as if searching for diamonds.

'Well?' asked Julia.

Sherwood lifted the recorder out of the boat. 'It looks easy to walk on – let's find some high ground.'

'High ice,' corrected Julia as she broke the seal on a dye-marker aerosol that she would use to mark their route.

The mist was slightly clearer at five hundred feet above sea level. Julia released the snap-fastener on her pack and allowed it to slip to the crumbling, powdery ice. She sat down.

'Let's rest, Glyn.'

Sherwood glanced round. They were on a level area of ice that was surrounded by rounded, forbidding hillocks. The icy mist seemed to percolate through the protective suit now that he had stopped climbing. Julia pulled off her spiked overshoes and rubbed a frozen foot.

'My God, it's like being back at Rosenthal. And impossible to believe that we're four hundred miles off North Carolina.'

'I could take the first recording here,' said Sherwood, as he started to unpack the machine.

Julia marked their position on the map while Sherwood positioned the microphone and switched on the machine. He planned to make a series of recordings of the sounds occurring from deep within the ice in the hope that the creakings and groanings of the massive iceberg might provide yet another clue as to its melt rate.

There was a sudden freezing breath of the long-awaited wind.

'The fog's lifting!' shouted Julia. 'Look, Glyn! It's dispersing! There's a wind! Feel!'

The breeze hesitated then returned with renewed strength. Sherwood looked up. Clouds of mist were swirling past the hillocks. A freshly cut water gully appeared less than a hundred yards away.

'Look!' Julia's voice was a cry of undisguised fear.

Sherwood followed her finger to the evil splendour of the Anvil Mountain's shining dagger that was emerging from the fog. Clouds were streaming off the dazzling stiletto like the gushing albino blood of a wounded sky.

Sherwood and Julia stood rooted; hypnotized by the awesome

spectacle of the rampant crystal tower that seemed to be lifting into the heavens as the enveloping fogbank that had hidden the white continent was swept away by the wind.

Timeless seconds became minutes. And the minutes, during those moments of the terrifying revelation, fled like seconds. The contour lines on the map conveyed nothing of the Anvil Mountain's disfiguring twist that made it lean towards the sea from which it had escaped.

Sherwood tore his eyes away from the frozen Matterhorn and gazed in wonder at the materializing icescape of White Atlantis. The undulating hills, deep ravines and crazy profusion of iridescent crags blazing white fire in the startled sunlight seemed to stretch away to the horizon. It was then, as he looked down on the metallic bulk of the *Johnson* standing less than half a mile from the iceberg's tortuous cliffs, that Sherwood began to appreciate the titantic proportions of the grotesquely beautiful monster the Antarctic ice-cap had spawned.

Julia's terrified grip was digging deep into his forearm. There was a new sound from above. She gave a cry of despair and pointed.

The five-hundred-foot-high ice buttresses of the Anvil Mountain were breaking away and falling outwards. A huge fissure began to open in the base of the crystal mountain just as the first rumblings of the impending icequake quickened beneath their feet.

14

The first shockwave that slammed through the ice catapulted Sherwood and Julia face down into the powdery ice, when they still had twenty yards to go before reaching the supposed safety of the ice mass that was between them and the lower slopes of the disintegrating mountain.

Julia risked a quick glance up the dazzling incline. Half a mile away huge irregular ice boulders, some the size of a three-storey house, were dementedly charging towards them.

They scrambled to their feet and were about to start running when the second shockwave struck with the pent-up force of an unleashed steam-hammer concealed beneath the ice. Sherwood gave a loud cry of intense agony and collapsed. Both his ankles had been savagely twisted by the shockwave's vicious, bone-pulverizing blow.

'Come on!' screamed Julia, tugging with blind strength at his arm.

Sherwood tried to struggle to his feet. His face twisted in pain and he sank down. 'I can't,' he whimpered.

'You've got to!' Julia saw that the first wave of shattered, avalanching boulders was less than a hundred yards away and was hurtling straight at them. Weeping with fear, she grabbed hold of Sherwood under the armpits and ignoring his protests, began to drag him backwards towards the shelter of the icecrop.

15

Walter Krantz of the International Ice Patrol arrived aboard the *Eureka*; a slightly built man in his late forties with a creased, worried expression. He shook hands with Admiral Pearson and asked after Sherwood. The answer that he was on the iceberg seemed to increase his anxiety. He was about to protest that no one should be on White Atlantis but was interrupted by a sudden flurry of excitement: the fogbank was lifting from the iceberg.

Pearson and Krantz watched without speaking as the freshening wind shredded White Atlantis's shroud. The *Eureka* was six miles from the colossus – a distance that in no way diminished the majesty of the unfolding continent that was dominated by the shining, weather-honed pinnacle of the leaning Anvil Mountain. Against the sparkling, emerging cliffs was the diminutive outline of the *Johnson* – its 100,000-ton bulk reduced to toy-like proportions by its nearness to the titanic White Atlantis.

'That flat top shouldn't be so near,' said Krantz worriedly.

There was a sudden stir among the scientists and crew lining the rail. Someone swore.

'The mountain's falling apart!'

Pearson forgot Krantz at his side and stared in horrified fascination at the Anvil Mountain. A dark band was appearing at the base. It was some seconds before he realized that it was a huge crack, which was slowly lengthening and widening. Then the mountain was changing its shape as if it was twisting. The needle-like peak began to slowly swing through an arc.

The sound of the appalling fracture reached the *Eureka*. It was the scream of thousands of tortured banshees shrieking for mercy.

The Anvil Mountain fell.

For a few seconds there was nothing to see but a charging plume of white smoke into which the mountain had disappeared. The noise steadily increased as the pale avalanche roared across the sea.

And the USS *Johnson*.

It was over in a fleeting moment, so brief that the expressions on the faces of the watchers on the *Eureka* did not have time to change: the million-ton dagger burst across the sea and smashed into the giant aircraft carrier. The ice didn't stop. Two huge curtains of spray erupting into the air marked its passage across the sea.

It slowed. The spray, which had defied gravity, began to settle.

There was no sign of the *Johnson*.

It was as if the aircraft carrier had been an image projected on a screen; an image composed of nothing more substantial than light and shade.

And then the projector had been abruptly switched off.

16

The President stared at the black flag on the wall display of the North Atlantic that marked the grave of the USS *Johnson*. He shook his head sadly.

'Two thousand five hundred men. . . .'

Pearson sat in silence, his fingers tracing the gold braid on his cap that he was holding in his hands.

'. . . There's at least five names on the list that I remember from my days in the navy.'

'We've not fixed the date for the memorial service,' said Pearson, 'in case you wish to attend, Mr President.'

'What are we going to do about that iceberg?'

'Krantz thinks it will be completely melted within the next few days, Mr President.'

The President studied one of the photographs of White Atlantis that was lying on his desk. 'It's going to have to do a helluva lot of melting then.'

Which was exactly what Pearson had been thinking all that morning during the flight to Washington. He said nothing and watched the younger man skim once more through the reports. He knew from the questions that had been fired at him that the President hadn't missed one key word or important sentence.

'These two British scientists – Hammond and Sherwood – they're survivors from the *Orion*?'

'Yes, Mr President.'

More reading. Pages turned. Then: 'J. Hammond. He was proved right about the cause of the Cape Verde Islands disaster?'

'Yes, sir.'

'And G. Sherwood's theories about the ice have been borne out by subsequent events?'

Pearson agreed that they had. 'There's a difference of opinion between him and Krantz.'

'Whom do you side with?'

It was an awkward question. 'Well,' said Pearson slowly. 'Sherwood and Hammond – Hammond is a woman – have first-hand experience of the iceberg. Firstly – when the *Orion* went down; secondly – they've been to the area it was calved from; thirdly – they were on the beach at Cape Verde when the sea was turned into nerve gas; and lastly – their narrow escape yesterday when the Anvil Mountain collapsed. . . . It all adds up to a lot of experience. On the other hand, it's possible that they're no longer objective. And their experience of icebergs is limited to White Atlantis –'

'Which is all we're interested in,' the President pointed out.

'But Krantz has experience of an average of a thousand icebergs a year.'

'And not one of them has done as much damage as that one,' said the President, holding up a photograph of White Atlantis. 'Will you be able to keep people away from it?'

'The combined resources of the navy and the Coast Guard –'

'How?' interrupted the President sharply. 'How the hell will you be able to cover every inch of the iceberg's coast?'

'With helicopters –' Pearson began.

'I once had the job of trying to keep boats a reasonable distance from the *Britannia* during a visit by Queen Elizabeth and Prince Philip. It was virtually impossible – as I chased one away, two more would dive in.'

'We've managed so far, Mr President.'

'Wait till the berg's off Cape Hatteras – you'll be inundated with pleasure craft.'

'But its course is keeping it over two hundred miles out!' Pearson protested.

'That won't stop them. My first yacht was a forty-foot Silver yet it had a cruising range of eight hundred miles on full tanks.'

'Technically,' said Pearson thoughtfully, 'we don't have a legal responsibility to stop people wanting to break their necks by climbing White Atlantis. It's in international waters – not even over our continental shelf.'

It was the kind of negative statement that the President heartily disliked. He fixed his blue eyes resolutely on Pearson and said firmly: 'If it's within our power to prevent people hurting themselves – no matter what their nationality – then we have a moral duty to exercise that power. I want that iceberg destroyed and I'll ensure that you are given all the resources and authority to see that my order is carried out.'

The President stood. The interview was over. He shook hands with Pearson and wished him good luck.

One thought occupied Pearson's mind as he flew back to the *Eureka*.

How the hell did one set about destroying an iceberg the size of a small country and weighing many billions of tons?

17

Krantz's expression was even more worried than usual. He and Sherwood were sitting in a laboratory on the *Eureka* listening to the recording Sherwood had made on White Atlantis before the Anvil Mountain had collapsed.

'Play it again, Glyn,' said Krantz when the recording reached the point where it had been obliterated by the icequake.

Sherwood spooled back and pressed the start key. Krantz

looked at his watch as the sharp tap . . . tap . . . tap . . . clicked out from the speaker. Each tap seemed to increase Krantz's worry.

'Far too regular to be caused by stresses,' said Sherwood emphatically. 'I've checked the exact timing – each tap's duration and the interval between each tap doesn't vary by much more than point zero one of a second. And you still say it's caused by released stresses?'

Krantz shook his head sadly. 'I'm not saying anything, Glyn – merely offering an explanation.'

'An unbelievable explanation.'

Krantz smiled suddenly. 'Our roles are reversed; I was the one who refused to believe you about White Atlantis.'

'I only half-believed myself.' Sherwood broke off and looked sharply at Krantz. 'Have you revised that crazy melt rate figure of yours?'

'What's the point, Glyn? After tomorrow –'

'After tomorrow, White Atlantis will still be there!'

Krantz looked extremely worried. 'Don't you think it will work?'

'No.'

'So *you* know what sort of bang exploding a thousand tons will make?'

Sherwood sensed that the IIP official was mocking him and began to get angry. 'No, Walter. Do you?'

Krantz nodded. 'It'll blow that iceberg into four quarters, Glyn.'

18

'White Atlantis is a fantastic sight from the helicopter,' enthused the radio reporter's voice. 'It's shining on the water like a priceless diamond. . . .'

Julia giggled as she placed the microfilm cassette in front of the viewer Sherwood was using. The two of them were searching the *Eureka*'s technical library for information that Sherwood was certain existed.

'. . . a diamond that will be destroyed in exactly one minute.'

It was Sherwood's turn to be amused.

'Pity we're too far away to see anything,' said Julia, sitting down at a vacant viewer and loading it with a film cassette.

'There won't be anything to see,' Sherwood muttered morosely. 'God damn it, this is going to take hours.'

'White Atlantis is now honeycombed with five hundred boreholes,' said the reporter. 'And each borehole is filled with two tons of TNT. This operation must compare with the blowing up of Heligoland in 1921 except that Heligoland didn't need a thousand tons of TNT to destroy it. . . . Thirty seconds now. . . .

Julia quickly read through a frame displayed on the viewer's screen. 'Antarctic Record, 1967. Number thirty – a report on giant icebergs in Lützow-Holm Bay. Any good?'

Sherwood shook his head. 'It's earlier than '67.'

'I was talking to Walter Krantz of the International Ice Patrol earlier today,' the reporter told his listeners. 'And he says breaking White Atlantis into four will increase the amount of ice in contact with the water and so speed up the rate at which it's melting. . . .'

Sherwood impatiently changed cassettes.

A voice cut across the radio reporter's to start the ten-second countdown.

'It's like using a firework to blow up Mount Everest,' said Sherwood.

'Five. . . .'

Sherwood gaped at the screen.

'Four. . . .'

'What's the matter?' asked Julia.

'Three. . . .'

Sherwood excitedly operated the foot control that spun the film through the viewer.

'Two. . . .'

'So what's the matter?' Julia repeated.

'One. . . .'

There was the sound of a dull explosion from the radio. Then the voice of the reporter – almost hysterical with excitement: 'Staggering! Fantastic! The biggest man-made explosion since the H-bomb tests stopped! There's a huge cloud of white debris shooting into the air along the entire length of White Atlantis! The iceberg has virtually disappeared but nothing – not even a thousand tons of TNT – can conceal this incredible, this magnificent monster of an island in ice!'

'I've found it,' said Sherwood, not taking his eyes off the printed page displayed on his screen. Julia joined him.

'Hey, wait a minute!' bawled the reporter's breathless voice. 'This can't be true! I don't believe it! The debris is settling. . . . White Atlantis is exactly the same as it was before the explosion! It's not even dented!'

'Well,' said Julia, reading the information on the screen. 'It looks as if you were right all along. Will you enjoy gloating?'

19

As no one was within earshot of the two men peering into the ice crater, Admiral Pearson's comments to Krantz tended to be scathing.

'It's worrying,' Krantz admitted when he managed to get a word in.

'You're goddam right it's worrying,' Pearson answered with feeling. 'Especially as you said –'

'I was about to say that I'm not completely surprised. Ice is a surprisingly resilient material.'

'So it seems.'

'Next time we use more explosive. How long would it take to have five thousand tons shipped out?'

Pearson pushed his snow goggles over his eyes. 'Let's take a look at the next hole.'

The two men trudged through the rotten ice. Since landing on White Atlantis, Pearson had been surprised to discover that close to it wasn't white but a pale grey. In some places, where the strata were cut through by surface water, the ice colouring varied from yellow to the pale green of iceberg lettuce.

The next borehole had filled with water. They moved on and paused to watch a sparkling waterfall cascading over the edge of a hundred-foot-high inland cliff. From the base of the cliff was a fast-flowing river carrying twisting miniature icebergs through a deep canyon that broadened into a slower-moving estuary where it met the sea.

'It's interesting,' said Krantz. 'What we're seeing – the

erosion – rivers cutting ravines – is exactly what happens on land except that an hour on this iceberg is the equivalent of a hundred million years on land.'

The third borehole was beginning to fill with melt water. Like the previous holes, the force of the explosion had widened it to a diameter of thirty feet at the brink from the original ten inches bored by the drill. But there was no sign of a major fault or crack in the ice that could have been caused by the explosion.

Krantz frowned anxiously into the cone-shaped hole. He could hear a faint, regular tapping noise similar to that recorded by Glyn Sherwood. Pearson heard it too.

'What in hell is that?'

Krantz went down on one knee and listened. 'Stresses in the ice. Most of this berg's been compressed under the weight of millions of tons of its own ice and now it's relaxing. This hole is acting as a giant amplifier – like the horn on an antique phonograph.'

Pearson wasn't entirely convinced; the tapping was too regular. But Krantz was the expert – his suggestion made some sense whereas Sherwood's ideas were too crazy to even contemplate. And yet. . . .'

Pearson's thoughts were interrupted by the whine of gas turbines. He raised his binoculars and focused them on the 378-foot Coast Guard cutter that he had assigned to guard this sector of White Atlantis. White water creamed past the diagonal hull stripes near the bow that were the distinctive marking of all US Coast Guard ships no matter what their size. The height of her bow wave increased. She was leaving. A minute later the relief cutter appeared – the *Jason* – operated by the Fifth Coast Guard District.

White Atlantis was still five hundred miles off the coast of the United States. But that coast, with the slow, unstoppable northwards drift, now belonged to the State of Virginia.

20

It was the first of what were to become routine morning conferences aboard the *Eureka*, presided over by Admiral Pearson.

Hagan made notes. Deke Sutherland looked bored. Walter Krantz, worried.

Sherwood could see the pale coastline of White Atlantis through the port windows. Sunlight flashing on the iceberg's rounded hills heliographed a continuous signal of contempt at the research ship.

Pearson got straight down to business. 'After yesterday's failure with a thousand tons of HE, Mr Krantz is now suggesting a similar operation with five thousand tons and deeper bore-holes.'

'Back-tapered and plugged with concrete,' Krantz added – his anxious eyes moving quickly round the gathering.

'Opinions anyone?' inquired Pearson.

'Yes,' said Sherwood. 'It won't work.'

Krantz blinked. 'Why not, Glyn?'

'Because the caps will be blown off and ninety percent of the explosive force will be lost. The same thing that happened yesterday only louder.'

Krantz looked hurt. 'Don't you at least think it's worth trying?'

'That depends on what five thousand tons of TNT is worth,' said Sherwood, grinning. 'But I'll tell you this much: nothing but the sea will destroy that iceberg – just as it eventually destroys all icebergs. The easiest way is to just wait and watch.'

'That's out of the question,' Pearson stated. 'There's a major political storm brewing over the loss of the *Johnson* and destroying that berg artificially is now a matter of national prestige.'

Krantz groaned. Sherwood shared his sentiment.

'There's more,' Pearson continued. 'If we project Mr Sherwood's melt rate figures, then we end up with a situation that I prefer not to think about: that White Atlantis gets into the North Atlantic shipping lanes which are, as Mr Krantz will tell you, the busiest in the world. Even with radar, there're still plenty of captains around who insist on ramming icebergs. The most recent being the Danish ship, the *Hans Hedtoft*, in which ninety-eight people died.'

'That won't happen,' said Krantz. 'And even if it did, the International Ice Patrol would –'

'What about that berg's growlers?' demanded Sutherland, speaking for the first time. 'We're getting more of them every day – most of them bigger than the bergs you sometimes get off Newfoundland – and they're not following the same drift pattern as Big Daddy. If you want my opinion, I'd say you can't count on anything with that thing.'

'I'd count on it breaking up with five thousand tons of TNT erupting in its belly,' said Krantz drily.

'All past attempts to destroy icebergs have failed,' said Sherwood. 'Including attempts using high explosive.'

Pearson looked interested. 'What attempts?'

Sherwood reached into his pocket and produced the documents copied from the microfilm in the *Eureka*'s library. 'This is a copy of Bulletin number forty-six issued by the International Ice Patrol back in 1960. It describes a series of experiments that were carried out by the IIP into ways and means of destroying icebergs.' Sherwood paused and looked at Pearson. 'Do you want to hear what it has to say, admiral?'

'I'm familiar with that bulletin,' said Krantz. 'It's very old and I doubt if its findings are relevant today.'

'Let's decide when we've heard it,' Pearson suggested. He nodded to Sherwood. 'Go ahead.'

Sherwood cleared his throat. 'A special detail from the IIP selected a typical Greenland iceberg for a series of experiments to see if it was possible for it to be destroyed. The first phase was the dropping on the iceberg of twenty thousand-pound bombs.' Sherwood held up a page bearing a photograph that showed an amphibious aircraft flying over a horseshoe-shaped iceberg. There was an explosion taking place at the base of the iceberg. 'Phase One failed,' said Sherwood. 'Nearly ten tons dropped on one small iceberg and they had no effect whatsoever. Phase Two was similar in concept to the operation yesterday: three men boarded the iceberg and buried a selection of different types of high explosive charges at strategic locations. I quote: "Figure 22b is the final burst which consisted of 560 pounds of thermite planted at the base of the pinnacle. Again a magnificent display took place as smoke and molten iron was hurled hundreds of feet into the air, but the berg remained virtually unchanged." Unquote.'

Sherwood glanced up at Krantz who pointedly ignored him by staring out of a window at the sea. Sherwood continued: 'The final phase was to cover six thousand square yards of the iceberg with carbon black to increase the iceberg's absorption of heat from the sun. Five hours later the iceberg began to break up but the test was inconclusive because the berg was about to break up anyway. I'll read you the report's conclusion: "Although some damage to the iceberg resulted, it must be admitted that all the means tried were unsuccessful in destroying icebergs." '

There was a brief silence when Sherwood finished speaking. It was broken by Admiral Pearson reaching out a hand for the papers the geologist was holding. 'I'd like to see that report please.'

Sherwood passed the papers across the table. Pearson examined them for some moments. He tossed them on to the table and felt in his pocket for a cigar.

'Well, gentlemen,' he said at length. 'It's beginning to look as if we've been wasting our time.' His voice was tired; drained of emotion.

21

Admiral Pearson and Sutherland looked on with intrigued expressions as Sherwood rested each end of the twelve-inch bar of ice on laboratory stands so that the ice formed a bridge above the bench. The horizontal frozen rod began a slow drip on to the working surface.

Sherwood smiled at his two-man audience. 'This is one of those experiments, like cutting glass underwater with scissors, that I've heard about but never carried out for myself.'

As he spoke, he looped a length of fine piano wire round the centre of the bar of ice, twisted the two ends together and hung a kilogram laboratory weight from the join so that it was suspended beneath the ice.

'Now watch,' said Sherwood.

Pearson and Sutherland watched. Nothing happened at first. Then, very slowly, the weight began dragging the loop through the ice like an old-fashioned wire cutter slicing a piece of cheese in half.

It took the weight five minutes to drag the wire loop right through the bar of ice and to clatter on to the bench. But instead of falling with the weight in two halves, the ice remained rigidly in place, resting on the laboratory stands.

'Well, isn't that the craziest thing?' said Pearson, staring at the intact bar of ice.

Sherwood lifted the ice off the stands and gave it to the two men to examine closely. 'The wire cuts through the ice easily enough but the ice welds itself back together again – almost as if it's healing itself. The phenomenon was discovered by Michael Faraday – one of his few useless discoveries. . . .' Sherwood hesitated and looked apologetically at Sutherland. 'That's why I'm afraid that your idea of hauling heated cables through the iceberg to cut it up just won't work, captain. Sorry.'

Sutherland shrugged. 'I never thought it would. It was just an idea.'

Pearson gave one of his rare smiles. 'Well I guess Faraday's discovery has come in useful after all; he's saved us a few million dollars.'

'This may seem a basic question and I'm probably making a fool of myself,' said Sutherland. 'But why is it that no one has come up with the idea of using heat to melt that iceberg?'

'There's a good reason,' Sherwood replied. 'You've used steam hoses to de-ice frozen-up superstructure and rigging haven't you, captain?'

Sutherland nodded. 'Sure.'

'Ever thought about the lousy return you get; having to use up a hell of a lot of energy just to melt a small quantity of ice?'

'Yeah. That's right.'

'A given quantity of ice needs nearly as much energy to melt it as it does to boil the resulting water. There's not enough available energy in the world to melt that iceberg – not even if we were to harness the output of every power station for a month.' Sherwood thought for a moment. 'Ice,' he said at length, 'is one of the strangest materials known to mankind.'

'That's exactly what I'm beginning to think,' agreed Pearson. 'Which leaves me with only one final possibility.'

22

'I've given it a lot of thought,' said the President, 'and the answer has to be no. So long as you guys in the navy and Coast Guard are managing to keep sightseers away until it's melted down to a safe size I see no point in agreeing to your request.'

Pearson said nothing. He hadn't risen to his present rank by arguing with presidents on every issue.

'Thank you for raising the matter with me,' said the President as he accompanied Pearson across the Camp David lawns to the helicopter landing pad. 'You were within your rights to have gone right ahead with that blanket authority I gave you. When is the goddam thing expected to melt by?'

'The experts are divided, Mr President,' said Pearson. 'Those who've been proved wrong on everything else up to now say it can't last two weeks – they were saying one week – and the experts who've been proved right so far don't know. All *I* know is that I'd sooner deal with the Russians than with icebergs any day – at least the Russians are predictable.'

The President treated Pearson to his vote-winning smile as he bade his visitor goodbye.

Pearson arrived back on the *Eureka* seven hours later to be greeted with the news that White Atlantis had altered course and was slowly swinging towards the Delaware coast.

23

Julia, like so many others, found it impossible to believe that White Atlantis was dying. It rode serenely under the warm sun of the early spring, a beautiful crystal creation, a virgin country with sparkling rolling hills, silent lagoons and noisy streams feeding swift-flowing rivers.

And yet it was inexorably dying. The evidence of its approaching death was all around: the growlers that roared down the towering cliffs and drifted away to become another headache for the hard-pressed International Ice Patrol; growlers that merely detached themselves from their parent and sat innocently on the water waiting for one of the vigilant circling IIP Hercules to spot them and radio their position to Governors Island where each one would be allocated a number and its likely course estimated by computer.

A helicopter, crammed to the rotors with press photographers, moved against the leaning cliffs like a fly on a whitewashed wall.

Julia became aware of Sutherland beside her at the rail. 'They've just finished the day plot,' he said.

'What's it down to now?'

Sutherland watched the weaving helicopter. 'Eight hundred and twenty square miles. Half the size of Long Island.'

'So it hasn't changed since yeaterday?'

'According to Krantz and Sherwood, the surface area is fairly static – it's losing most of its bulk below the surface.'

'That's what I thought must be happening,' said Julia. 'I helped with this morning's salinity tests in the lab. White Atlantis is surrounded by freshwater. You know, it's strange that it's reducing its draught faster than its surface area.'

Sutherland frowned. 'Why?'

'You'll laugh at me.'

'I promise not to laugh.'

'Well. . . . It's as if White Atlantis knows that there's shallower water closer to the coast.'

Sutherland kept his promise.

24

'There are several things that Mr Sherwood and I are agreed on,' said Krantz at the morning conference. 'Firstly –'

'Where is Sherwood?' asked Pearson. 'Sorry to interrupt Mr Krantz.'

'He's with Captain Sutherland in the plot room,' said Hagan. Krantz started again. 'Firstly, that the volume of White Atlantis is now down to five hundred cubic miles.'

Sherwood quietly entered the cabin and took his place at the table.

'How much does it weigh?' demanded Pearson.

'Its weight isn't important,' said Krantz with some irritation.

'Five hundred thousand million tons,' said Sherwood quickly, seeing Admiral Pearson about to explode.

Pearson calmed down but he looked far from happy.

'And secondly, Mr Sherwood and I are agreed that White Atlantis has altered course ten degrees east during the past twenty-four hours.'

'Fifteen degrees,' said Sherwood. 'I've just come down from the plot room. She swung through another five degrees a few minutes ago.'

Krantz's poise deserted him momentarily. 'Well. . . . That doesn't change our forecast regarding the eventual fate of White Atlantis.'

'I think it changes it significantly,' said Sherwood. 'I'll go further and say that we now don't have a forecast.'

'Yesterday,' said Krantz calmly, 'we both agreed that Atlantis would eventually be picked up by the Gulf Stream and pushed west – that it would most likely finally disintegrate in mid-Atlantic between forty and fifty degrees west.'

'That was yesterday.'

'A five-degree change of course doesn't change –'

'I think it changes everything, Walter,' said Sherwood mildly. 'The thing's now heading for New York.'

25

The President didn't miss a word of what Admiral Pearson was saying as he studied a map of the coastline between Atlantic City and the eastern extremity of Long Island. The coast formed a huge funnel-shaped bay with New York at the throat of the funnel.

'If it does get trapped in the bay,' Pearson was saying, 'and it breaks up there, it's going to be impossible to guarantee the safety of shipping unless all shipping movements are banned. In its final stages of disintegration, we won't be dealing with one berg but several thousand – each one with a mass of several million tons.'

The President said nothing. What Admiral Pearson was telling him was much the same as Coast Guard and IIP experts had told him during an emergency conference called earlier that day before Pearson had arrived in Washington from the *Eureka*.

'And there's the safety angle to consider if we act now while the iceberg is still two hundred miles off the coast,' Pearson continued. 'We've been enforcing a prohibited zone in the White Atlantis area for some days now, so that's no problem. All we need is for the FAA to do the same and intensive air force patrols will do the rest.' Pearson paused. There was no way of judging from the President's impassive expression the impact his words were having. 'There's something else, Mr President. I'm not an expert in such matters but I wouldn't even like to guess at the effect on New York's economy that a protracted ban on shipping would have – indeed on the economy of the whole nation.'

The President had the figures before him. They made for unpleasant reading. Shipping was supposed to be on the decline yet exports to Europe through New York still ran into millions of dollars each day.

'What sort of yield are you thinking in terms of?' asked the President.

The question gave Pearson hope. 'General Warren Floyd says that we should start with one megaton. A clean device – there won't be a danger of contamination.'

'How deep in the ice?'

'Six hundred feet. There's no question of a violation of the test ban treaty.' Pearson refrained from adding that drilling had already started in accordance with General Floyd's specifications in anticipation of the President giving his consent.

'It's over the hundred and twenty kiloton limit agreed for underground tests,' the President pointed out.

'The Russians would be inviting ridicule from the world if they start kicking up dust over one megaton,' Pearson retorted.

The President pushed the map to one side and read through the cryptic typed order that needed only his signature. He sighed and picked up his pen.

'Okay,' he said with finality, and signed the document.

It was the third time in history that an American president had authorized the use of a thermonuclear device against an enemy of the United States.

26

'We're down five hundred and fifty feet,' said General Warren Floyd, lowering his huge frame into a chair in Admiral Pearson's cabin. 'And we've stopped drilling.'

Pearson looked surprised. 'Why?'

'We've hit a problem.'

'What sort of problem?' Pearson was finding General Floyd's tendency to communicate in short, inconclusive sentences extremely frustrating. The general, he had learned, disliked volunteering information. It had to be wormed out of him question by question.

'A noise,' said General Floyd.

'What sort of noise?'

'I haven't heard it.'

Great, thought Pearson.

'But my boys have.'

'And what sort of noise do they say it is?'

General Floyd considered the implications of parting with this information. 'A regular tapping noise.'

Pearson groaned inwardly. 'Yes, we know about it, general. Mr Walter Krantz and others are of the opinion that it's caused by stresses within the ice.'

General Floyd seemed saddened to learn that his priceless information was common knowledge.

'So we carry on drilling?'

'Yes please, general.'

General Floyd made no move to leave the cabin. 'There's something else.'

Pearson waited. He was beginning to understand why it was that General Floyd was responsible for nuclear ordnance.

'The device arrives on this ship at 09:00 tomorrow.' The admission caused Floyd considerable pain but he stood the stress remarkably well.

'Yes.'

'A nuclear device.'

'Yes,' said Pearson, wondering when Floyd would get to the point.

'You have two non-US citizens aboard,' said Floyd, approaching the point with an accusing tone of voice.

'Julia Hammond and Glyn Sherwood,' said Pearson sharply, smelling trouble. 'And before you go any further, general, you ought to know that those two have been of incalculable value to me in dealing with White Atlantis.'

'Now I'm the one whose of incalculable value,' Floyd observed drily. 'I'm very sorry, admiral, but they can't be here tomorrow. Their work has finished so I suggest you send them to New York for a well-earned vacation.'

'But what's the point, general? It's no secret that we're going to use a nuclear device tomorrow. I've told the press and there'll be full TV coverage.'

'They've got to go,' said Floyd firmly. 'Sorry, admiral.'

27

The device was a terrorist's dream.

It measured less than twenty inches in diameter by forty inches long and was light enough to be carried by three men.

For safety, six men manhandled it from the helicopter to the shaft opening that plunged six hundred feet into the frozen heart of White Atlantis. They shackled it to the power winch that straddled the shaft, connected the control cable, tested the arming circuitry and, slowly and carefully, lowered the device down the shaft. Once it was in position bulldozers set to work to shovel tons of rotten ice down the shaft to seal it. It took two hours. The six men returned to assemble a small, prefabricated tower over the plugged shaft. On top of the twenty-foot-high structure was a photoelectric laser receiver. Radio control was considered too dangerous; New York's countless private and public radio transmitters were swamping a sizeable percentage of the radio spectrum, even two hundred miles out at sea.

By 3:00 pm, three hours before the blast, everything on White Atlantis was ready. Thirty miles to the east was the aircraft carrier USS *Saratoga*. The pilotless aircraft sitting on its catapult launcher was also ready.

28

Sherwood and Julia stopped talking when the television news presenter appeared on the screen to say that they were going straight over, live, to the *Eureka*.

Julia crossed the hotel room and turned up the volume. 'It's not fair,' she said, kneeling to one side of the screen and watching the reporter talking to Admiral Pearson. 'They kick us off and yet they let reporters on.'

'It wasn't the admiral's fault,' said Sherwood. 'Can we watch without your commentary?'

They watched in silence as Pearson explained that a pilotless, radio-controlled aircraft would fire a coded laser pulse at the tower on White Atlantis to trigger the nuclear device.

The picture cut to an aerial long-shot of the giant iceberg.

'The picture you're seeing is coming from a TV camera on board the pilotless aircraft,' explained Admiral Pearson's voice-over.

The reporter pressed him for a prediction on the outcome of the operation but Pearson remained noncommittal.

'*Will* it work?' asked Julia.

Sherwood shrugged. 'Lord knows. One-megaton bombs are a whole new ball game as they say.'

The digits of a lapsed time indicator appeared at the foot of the screen. Two minutes to go.

'Maybe this time it's like using a hand grenade to blow up Mount Everest?' said Julia teasingly.

Sherwood grinned. 'That's very good, Miss Hammond.'

The pilotless aircraft was circling the iceberg at a distance of three miles, its gnat-like shadow flitting erratically across the uneven surface of the silent, brooding cliffs.

'There's the tower!' said Julia suddenly.

The gleaming latticework of the laser target appeared briefly.

One minute.

The aircraft sheered away. There was nothing on the screen except the sea and the distant outlines of toy ships.

A drawling voice announced that the TND was now armed.

The camera on the *Eureka* caught the reporter and Admiral Pearson looking at an out-of-shot monitor.

'The airplane will circle round now to begin its approach,' explained Pearson.

The unending sea reappeared. It was swinging across the picture and steadied when the humped outline of White Atlantis materialized.

Forty-five seconds.

'The airplane is about ten miles from the target,' said Pearson's voice, 'and will fire the beam when it's within three miles.'

'What will happen to the airplane after the detonation, admiral?'

'Hopefully, it won't be hit by flying ice so it'll be able to land on the *Saratoga*. It's a mighty valuable piece of hardware.'

'But not as valuable as New York's shipping trade?'

Pearson's rich laugh boomed in the hotel bedroom. 'That's right.'

Thirty seconds.

The swelling outline of White Atlantis hardened rapidly and individual features of the jagged, crumbling icescape became progressively more distinct. Julia experienced a surge of emotion as she gazed at the doomed creation. It was too beautiful to be destroyed. Then she remembered the *Orion*, the coffins laid out in the tiny walled cemetery on the Cape Verde Islands, and Oaf. . . . Dear, kind, Oaf. . . .

'Ten seconds,' said the drawling voice from the television speaker.

Julia seized Sherwood's hand and held it tight, watching the growing monster that was still half the size of Long Island. The tower was in the centre of the screen, hurtling with incredible speed towards the camera.

'Five. . . .' intoned the drawling voice. 'Four. . . .'

Julia involuntarily tightened her grip on Sherwood's hand.

'Three. . . . Two. . . . One. . . .' The controller's drawl was devoid of expression.

A pencil beam of light flashed at the tower from one side of the picture.

'Firing initiated. We have detonation.'

Nothing happened. The cameraman on the *Eureka*, working by remote control, managed to keep White Atlantis centred as the pilotless aircraft banked away.

'Minus One. . . . Two. . . .' droned the voice. 'Pressure building. . . .'

A quarter of a square mile of ice, with the tower at its centre, bulged upwards. There was a hesitation as the two forces – the mass of the ice and the trapped energies of the nuclear inferno – pitted themselves against each other. The nuclear device won. There was a white eruption as countless tons of ice were blasted upwards at the speed of sound. It was an explosion that seemed to last for ever; ice, water and steam continued vomiting into the sky from a steadily widening crater.

'They've failed,' said Sherwood, staring woodenly at the television screen. 'My God! They've failed!'

The sound of the colossal eruption reached the microphone on the pilotless aircraft. The sudden roar was distorted by the audio equipment that couldn't handle the savage onslaught on its systems.

'They've failed,' Sherwood kept repeating.

'Why?' asked Julia, unable to tear her eyes away from the spectacle of the blizzard with house-size snowflakes that miraculously didn't crash into the pilotless aircraft.

'The iceberg should've split open – broken up. All that's happened is that they've blown a damn great hole in it.'

Julia continued to stare at the screen. 'But look at the size of the hole! Just look at it!'

The terrible wound in White Atlantis was at least two miles across – twice the diameter of the huge meteorite impact crater in the Arizona Desert. Sherwood shook his head sadly.

'Yes. . . . It's big. But I doubt if the ice they've blasted out of that hole amounts to much more ice than White Atlantis normally loses in a day anyway.'

29

The ice moved.

It had proved itself. It was unstoppable. Indestructible. It moved very slowly. Almost as if it was possessed of a blind but certain instinct.

And that instinct was to kill.

30

To Sherwood's disgust, Julia's insatiable appetite for New York and its shops continued unabated the following day. She insisted on dragging Sherwood with her on shopping and sight-seeing expeditions – two activities that Sherwood heartily detested.

They emerged from Macy's – Sherwood laden with parcels and Julia wearing her latest purchase. She gazed across Herald Square at the magnificent, towering building on 34th Street while Sherwood tried to hail a taxi and clutch the parcels at the same time.

'That's the Empire State Building, isn't it, Glyn?'

The bright yellow cabs in the tidal wave of traffic surging down Broadway weren't interested in Sherwood's business.

'Yes,' he snapped irritably, not bothering to check what Julia was looking at.

'Have you ever been up it?'

'No.'

'I'd like to go up it.'

'Later.'

'Now.'

'We have to confirm our flight back to London with the airline. Don't you want to go home? Besides, there's a haze – you won't see a thing.'

The sign in the Empire State Building's incomparable marbled lobby announced that the balcony visibility was unlimited. They went down to the concourse level where Sherwood, in bad grace, purchased two tickets. Once on the balcony he sulked in the cafeteria until Julia resolutely dragged him out to admire the view.

'I was hoping for dinner tonight at somewhere like the Four Seasons,' she said angrily. 'I want to wear some decent clothes for once. But if you find the idea of going out with me so repulsive, we'll settle for a hamburger!'

A tourist smiled at them. 'You two go right ahead if you want to fight.' He obligingly increased the volume of his portable radio. The news was about White Atlantis and had been about little else that day.

Julia leaned against the parapet and stared down in wonder at the ant-like bustle on the microscopic sidewalks eighty-six floors below. She looked at her pamphlet.

'Good God – we're a thousand and fifty feet up.'

Sherwood nodded. He was listening to the tourist's radio. White Atlantis was drifting slowly towards New York – a studio pundit was expounding a theory on the possible ecological effect the melting freshwater would have on marine life.

'Why is it that Manhattan can have such high buildings? Look – forget White Atlantis – it's not our problem now.'

Sherwood continued listening to the radio. Julia had to repeat her question.

'Sorry,' Sherwood apologized. 'What did you say?'

'Why is it that New York can go in for such vast skyscrapers?'

'Every school kid knows why; under Manhattan's glacial drift is high-density metamorphic rock – Manhattan Schist. It goes down several thousand feet – the finest building platform any engineer could wish for – although they curse it when they have to tunnel. . . .'

Sherwood's words died on his lips. Julia looked at him sharply The vitality was draining from his face. His body had gone rigid with shock.

'Glyn? What's the matter?'

His lips moved.

'What's the matter? You must tell me!' Julia was suddenly very scared. Sherwood's face was frozen into an expression of unspeakable terror.

'Glyn! What is it?'

Sherwood stared at Julia with wide, frightened eyes. His gaze went past her – to the distant Verrazano-Narrows suspension bridge and the open sea beyond. He suddenly grabbed her hand.

'Come on!' he yelled, his voice hoarse with fear. 'We've got to get in touch with Admiral Pearson!'

31

'Please,' Sherwood implored. 'It's a matter of life and death. I beg of you – call up the *Eureka* and tell them that Glyn Sherwood wants to speak to Admiral Pearson. He'll talk to me.'

The coast guardsman was apologetic. 'I'm sorry, but the admiral is busy. You've seen the news?'

Sherwood placed both hands on the guardsman's desk. 'Listen. I used to work here. I know where the communications room is. If you don't move, and move fast – I'm going straight through that door and I'll call him up myself!'

The guardsman stood. 'You ain't going anywhere, friend. Have you got means of identification?'

Julia tried to grab Sherwood to prevent him pushing past the guardsman. 'Don't be stupid, Glyn.'

The guardsman seized Sherwood's arm, spun him round and held him securely in a firm lock.

'You're just going to sit down,' said the guardsman easily, 'and you're going to tell me who you are and you're going to state your business in an orderly manner. Okay?'

Sherwood swore. Julia searched desperately in her bag. Their passports were at the hotel.

A familiar voice behind her said: 'Seems like you two have gotten yourselves into trouble again.'

32

Gus Maguire, mayor of New York City, was at a port authority meeting to discuss the catastrophic proposed ban on shipping movements in the New York approaches, when he received an urgent message to return to Gracie Mansion.

He was back in his office an hour later. There was no sign of his usual good-humoured expression as he stared down at the map of New York spread out on his desk while listening to Sherwood. Admiral Pearson had said his piece and was remaining silent.

'As Admiral Pearson has explained,' Sherwood was saying,

'White Atlantis has a mass of four hundred thousand million tons and it's moving towards the continental shelf off New York at a speed that varies between one and a half and two knots.'

'And then it goes aground,' said Maguire, 'and starts to break up. Right, admiral?'

Sherwood wondered how to get the point without having to contradict the city's chief executive. He hesitated. 'Well. . . . It's not as simple as that, Mr Mayor. . . . At least, I don't think it is. . . .'

Maguire waited patiently.

'It's this question of the huge mass that White Atlantis has and the colossal amount of kinetic energy that's stored in that mass.' Sherwood pointed to Manhattan Island. 'Most of New York consists of metamorphic rock – that's rock that's been subjected to change either by heat or pressure or both.' Sherwood wished that the mayor would shoot questions at him rather than leave him to struggle for words.

'All metamorphic rock – quartz and so forth – have one thing in common: they're extremely hard and dense. Manhattan Schist is one of the hardest.'

'Manhattan what?' interrupted Maguire.

'Manhattan Schist. It's a metamorphic rock that's fairly unique to this island and it extends right out under the glacial drift and Hudson silt to the continental shelf.'

'What's glacial drift?' asked Pearson, spotting Maguire's hardening frown.

Sherwood forgot his initial nervousness. 'It's the debris that was brought down from the mountains by the glaciers during the ice ages. It's a semi-metamorphic, homogeneous mass of boulder clay, sand, gravel and other glacial erratics that covers a good deal of Manhattan to a depth of up to ninety feet. It might help absorb some of the shockwaves, but I doubt it very much. . . .'

Maguire's eyes opened very wide. 'What shockwaves?'

'. . . All your skyscraper builders excavated through the drift so that they had bed-rock to build on –'

'What shockwaves?' Maguire thundered.

'High-density, unbroken strata transmit shockwaves over long distances with very little loss of energy,' said Sherwood. 'If White Atlantis holds its present course and speed, it will strike the continental shelf eleven days from today and release more seismic energy than the San Andreas Fault slipping ten yards. The entire city of New York will ring like a bell.'

33

The shockwave crashed through the foundations of the city at 4:00 am while the majority of its population was asleep.

The Woolworth building swayed drunkenly, showering masonry from its framework as it shook itself like a wet dog. The towers of the World Trade Center heeled like the masts of a schooner in the grip of a savage storm, and then collapsed. The man-made canyon of Wall Street steadily filled under a rain of coping stones and debris. The shockwave's expanding death blow swept through the city's five boroughs – a tidal wave of total destruction that decimated three hundred square miles in less than three seconds.

Silence fell. There was no movement. Then footsteps as the shaken men who had witnessed the simulated disaster gathered round the huge model: Sherwood and Admiral Pearson, Gus Maguire, Jonas Steele – Governor of the State of New York – and two US Government scientists from the US National Center for Earthquake Research at Menlo Park near San Francisco.

No one spoke as the two scientists examined the perforated strips of paper that their recording machines had spewed out during the three-second artificial earthquake. The men were in a large, disused warehouse on the West Side, two blocks from the Columbia Broadcasting System building on Tenth Avenue. It was CBS special effects technicians who had worked non-stop for twenty-four hours to build the huge model under the supervision of the two government scientists. It wasn't a complete model – that was impossible to achieve in the time – but all the streets and bridges were there together with a number of key buildings to represent every type of construction method used in New York. The buildings did not include fine details but their dimensions, as well as their strength, had been accurately to scale. Professor Gemell, the senior of the two scientists, had demonstrated the strength of the scale models before the simulated earthquake with an electric fan creating the equivalent of a hundred and fifty miles-per-hour gale; the buildings had swayed noticeably.

It was Professor Gemell who spoke first. 'Well, gentlemen, I can't give an exact figure until we've wired these recordings to Menlo Park for processing on our computer, but I can give an approximation.' He gestured to the boulder suspended from a gantry that had been used to generate the shockwave. 'When the iceberg strikes, we can expect a ground acceleration of one metre per second.'

'What does that mean?' asked Maguire testily.

'It means a severe earthquake,' said Sherwood.

Gemell smiled. 'Correct. But not only an earthquake. Mr Sherwood says that there's a possibility of the iceberg turning over.'

Maguire closed his eyes and groaned.

'If that happens,' Gemell continued. 'There's almost certain to be a tidal wave of significant amplitude.'

'A large tidal wave,' Sherwood translated.

'Manhattan and the other boroughs are low-lying, with the exception of some parts of Brooklyn perhaps. And then there's Kennedy, La Guardia and Coney Island.'

'All right,' growled Steele. 'We get the picture.'

'Jesus Christ,' Maguire muttered. 'Can't anyone stop the goddam thing?' There was a despairing note in his voice.

'We've tried everthing,' said Pearson. 'It's four hundred thousand million tons, Mr Mayor.'

It was the State Governor who finally put into words what everyone was thinking.

'We're going to have to evacuate New York, Gus.'

Maguire looked desperate. 'Surely, somewhere in this country, with its know-how and resources, some way can be found to stop a lump of ice?'

The silence answered his question.

Maguire lowered himself on to a packing case and stared at the devastated model. 'Evacuate New York. . . . Jesus Christ.'

Steele sat beside him. 'We've got ten days, Gus. I'll get the videos of this simulation to the Governor of New Jersey. With their state troopers and our state troopers, and your city police . . . we ought to be able to operate a phased programme.'

'Sure we can put something together,' said Maguire bitterly.

'I'm trying to grasp the scale of the operation . . . and . . . aw hell . . . I just don't seem able to think straight.'

'I thought Manhattan tended to evacuate itself every evening between four and six anyway,' Sherwood observed.

Maguire looked at the geologist in contempt. 'What kind of stupid remark is that? Shall I tell you something, Mr Sherwood? Manhattan covers twenty-one square miles and has a population of around two million. Brooklyn is double the size with a population of *three million*! The Bronx – forty-one square miles and another two million. Then there's Queens, Mr Sherwood. Know how big Queens is? I'll tell you – one hundred and eighteen square miles, Mr Sherwood. Population? I'll tell you that too – two million. Then there's Richmond. . . . Well I guess we can leave you to look after Richmond. Maybe you can manage quarter of a million people – you've done fine so far with a few hundred cubic miles of ice. Take the whole area and you've got over twelve million people. *People*, Mr Sherwood. People with homes, back yards, families, relatives, roots. And we're going to have to move them – five percent of the entire population of the USA!'

Steele put a hand on Maguire's arm. 'Okay, Gus. He didn't mean any harm.'

Maguire turned to Steele. 'Listen, Jonas. Even if we can move them, where in hell are we going to put them?'

'I'm sorry, Mr Mayor,' said Sherwood, inwardly cursing the inadequacy of the apology.

Maguire's shoulders had sagged. He had aged ten years. He shook his head slowly and disbelievingly as if the echoing warehouse, the model of a devastated New York and the silent people around him were terrifying figments of a ghastly dream clinging like leeches to his subconscious.

'What *are* we going to do?' he asked sorrowfully. 'What in the world are we going to do?'

34

'The State Governor is going to declare New York a disaster area and appeal for federal aid,' said Sherwood as he and Julia walked back to their hotel. The night had stolen all the taxis and had replaced them with slow-moving trucks that made rain.

'He's gone to see the Governor of New Jersey to work out a joint evacuation programme. There'll be announcements on radio and TV later this morning.'

They came to an all-night bar.

Julia stopped. 'I could do with a drink.'

Julia waited until the bartender had moved away. 'You told me once about the scheme to tow icebergs to the Middle East. Couldn't White Atlantis be stopped if you had enough ships?'

Sherwood sipped his drink as he uninterestedly watched the bartender polishing glasses. 'No force on earth can stop that momentum.'

Another customer drifted in and perched on a stool at the bar.

'I once read a book on karate,' said Julia. 'It told you how to take advantage of your opponent's superior weight. You know the sort of thing – when he pushes against you and you push back, you suddenly change your push to a pull and down he goes. That's the theory.'

The bartender took the new arrival's order.

'A one-megaton karate chop didn't make any impression on White Atlantis,' said Sherwood, watching the bartender struggling to free icecubes from a tray. He frowned and looked at Julia. 'What was that you said?'

'What?'

'About karate.'

'Oh that.' Julia repeated her recollection from the book she had read.

The icecubes clattered out of their tray. Sherwood stood up and took Julia's hand. He was oblivious of her protest that she hadn't finished.

'You know,' said Sherwood when they were back on the street, 'it's just possible that you and that bartender have solved the problem.'

35

The US Coast Guard helicopter swept over the three hundred square miles of White Atlantis for the third time. The survey was nearly over.

'Two more anchorage points there,' said Sherwood, marking the map.

Pearson watched him curiously. 'Well? What do you think?'

Sherwood pushed the snow goggles on to his forehead and rubbed his eyes. White Atlantis shone in the morning sun like a celestial beacon. 'I can't say for sure until we've got the latest sonographs of her underwater profiles.'

'For Chrissake, Sherwood – it's your crazy notion. You must have some idea if it'll work or not.'

'What does Krantz have to say?'

'He thinks it might. Heavy emphasis on "might".'

Sherwood nodded. 'For once Mr Krantz and I agree, admiral. It *might* just work. But we're going to have to move bloody fast.'

36

The State Department had been firmly opposed to the idea of a presidential appeal broadcast to the entire world. They had argued that they had the diplomatic machinery to approach individual governments, and that they had the right men in the right places to carry out such a mission. They had concluded by saying that such an appeal was undignified for a president of the United States to make.

The President dismissed their objections point by point. The appeal was to the people of the world. And if positive, constructive steps aimed at saving New York and the homes and livelihoods of several million American citizens meant seeming undignified, then so be it.

'And furthermore,' said the President. 'I've already drafted my speech and I've written notes saying how the appeal should be packaged.'

37

Sherwood and Julia watched the President's impressive broadcast in the *Eureka*'s crowded stateroom. The blinds had been lowered, shutting out the glaring picture of White Atlantis five miles away on the research ship's quarter.

The appeal opened with a long-shot aerial picture of Manhattan with a superimposed caption that proclaimed:

ICESTRIKE 200 HOURS 12 MINUTES.

There was no commentary, no sound effects, and no music. For once the loudspeakers of the nation's televisions were silent, and as such, the small screen was a compulsive focus of attention. The picture of Manhattan changed to a montage of the now familiar scenes that showed New York State troopers closing roads, marshalling traffic and arresting looters. There were pictures of the fleets of ambulances ferrying Bellevue patients across the Queensboro Bridge; steel cases containing bullion and securities being carried out of banks to waiting armoured cars guarded by alert lines of city police; families cramming their belongings into cars and trailers, and finally, helicopter shots of the huge up-state refugee camps spawling across thousands of hectares of commandeered farmland. All the sequences had been carefully edited so that there was no hint of the bitter gun battles that were erupting continuously on New York's streets between marauding gangs of ruthless looters plundering the deserted precincts and equally ruthless bands of vigilante lynch mobs. It was the nearest thing to civil war that the hard-pressed police and state troopers had to deal with; as soon as one incident was quelled with 'demotivation' gas grenades dropped from helicopters, so another flared up elsewhere.

The television pictures of the tented refugee camps were replaced by an animated film that showed White Atlantis striking the continental shelf. It was followed by scenes of the crumbling skyscrapers – the video recordings of the simulated disaster that had been created in the warehouse, realistically slowed down so that a cloud of dust clung to the city in the wake of the devastating shockwave.

A member of the *Eureka*'s scientific team who had once been mugged at knife point on Tenth Avenue commented: 'About the best thing that could happen to that place.'

The remark upset a New Yorker. Pearson was about to angrily intervene when everyone suddenly realized that the President was speaking. He was sitting at a desk, hands clasped lightly together. Relaxed. In command of the situation.

'A phased, orderly evacuation of New York and the threatened areas of New Jersey has been in operation since yesterday.'

He was looking straight at the camera and speaking without notes.

'By midnight tonight three quarters of a million of our endangered citizens will have been moved to safety; four million by midnight tomorrow, and a successful conclusion of the evacuation will be achieved by the day after tomorrow. During my visit to New York today, I spoke to many fellow Americans who have worked and lived all their lives in New York. People like Ab Shumann and his wife Martha who run a delicatessen on The Avenue of the Americas; Paul and Jean Macintyre who have built up a hardware business in Greenwich Village, and many many more. All of them hard-working citizens who've invested not just their money in New York, but their lives. They all wanted to know one thing: was it possible to save the city from destruction? To save their homes and livelihoods?'

The President paused. He had made his speech deliberately unsophisticated.

'The answer is, that the terrible menace of White Atlantis, despite its incredible size – *can be stopped.*'

The President paused again. He gave a very slight smile. 'I remember my Sunday school teacher used to tell me that faith can move mountains. That's something I still believe in. But this time we need it to stop the mountains.'

He raised his voice slightly and punched a balled fist firmly into his left palm to emphasize his point.

'And stop them we *will.*' Another pause. Then, quietly: 'But it is something that the United States cannot achieve by itself.' He looked down at the desk as he spoke, and then slowly raised his eyes to the camera again.

'There is a plan to defeat White Atlantis. A plan that is as bold in concept as it will be hazardous in execution. But it is a plan that, with the grace of God and the goodwill of the nations of the free world, can be made to work; the destruction of White Atlantis before it is ready to die of its own accord is within the bounds of Mankind's ingenuity and enterprise.'

This time the pause was longer.

'I say "Mankind" because the United States does not have the resources to carry out phase one of the plan unaided.'

That was the sentence the State Department had strenuously objected to. They held the view that it was better to admit to selling the Liberty Bell to the Russians rather than admit to something that the United States didn't have the resources to achieve. 'It happens to be the truth,' the President had argued, and the offending sentence had remained in the text.

The camera closed slowly on the tired face.

'Phase one sounds simple. Indeed it was proposed some days ago but I rejected it because there was no guarantee that White Atlantis would not endanger Canada and Newfoundland. Now I have that guarantee. Phase one of the destruction of White Atlantis involves the removal of the immediate danger facing New York. And that means the removal of White Atlantis. There's only one way that can be done in the time we have – and that is to physically tow it with ships. Not a hundred ships. Not two hundred ships, or even three hundred . . . But *three thousand* ships.'

The President allowed his words to sink in.

'Three thousand ships of not less than five thousand tons each. That is the magnitude of the power needed to deflect White Atlantis from its present course. The United States has such a quantity of ships in its merchant fleet, but they are scattered throughout the world. Only five hundred and fifty can reach New York in the time allotted to us.'

The President leaned forward. It was a slight movement but it imparted a confiding air to the rest of his speech.

'That is why I am appealing now to all the maritime nations of the North Atlantic to divert every suitable ship that you can spare that is capable of reaching New York Bay within the next six days. I am appealing to governments and shipowners on behalf of twelve million men, women and children whose homes, jobs, health, well-being and whole way of life are now in grave jeopardy. With your help and the help of Almighty God we can apply ourselves to averting the worst disaster in the history of this planet of ours. Thank you.'

The scene changed to an electronic display board in a busy television studio. Rows of attractive girls were sitting before telephones. A clock in the centre of the studio stated:

ICESTRIKE 199 HOURS 58 MINUTES.

'Aw, hell,' said a dismayed voice at the back of the *Eureka*'s stateroom. 'They're turning it into a telephon.'

'But it's working though,' said Pearson. 'Look at the board.'

The first pledge was being received. A girl was talking on a telephone while her fingers moved quickly over a keyboard.

Cunard were offering the *Queen Elizabeth* II providing her passengers could be disembarked at New York and moved to safety.

'This is when you find out who your friends really are,' the President commented to his aide. 'How many ships are promised now?'

'Seven hundred and eighty-five.'

The President nodded. It was better than he had expected. The appeal was an hour old.

'Well,' he said, stretching and yawning. 'Let's just hope that the crazy idea works.'

'The telephon or the towing scheme?'

'Both,' was the President's laconic answer.

38

The time was icestrike minus 173 hours when the first foreign arrival was spotted by the soldiers and marines swarming perilously on the decaying flanks of White Atlantis.

They stopped work on their mammoth task of sinking a forest of steel girders into the ice and wildly cheered the beautiful liner. She had been bound for Panama when she had received the diversion order from her owners. The passengers lined the rails and stared in amazement at the white continent slipping past eight miles off the ship's starboard quarter.

The *Queen Elizabeth* II had arrived.

'Make a right!' screamed the armed guard to the bus driver. More bullets smashed into the bus as it swerved into Forty-Sixth Street. Most of the shots ploughed into the backs of the seats, missing the terrified *Queen Elizabeth* II passengers by inches as they sprawled on the floor. The guard was yelling into his two-way radio when a chance shot tore into a rear tyre. The laden bus lurched across the sidewalk and spun its skidding rear into a shop front. The madly spinning tyres machine-gunned broken glass at the pursuing car as the bus driver frantically gunned his engine to keep the vehicle moving. Then he had to haul on the wheel to avoid two police cars with whooping sirens that howled down either side of the bus and braked to a standstill – blocking the looters' car. The sounds of the gun battle faded as the bus accelerated clear of the 'no-go' zone it had inadvertently strayed into while taking the passengers to hotels in Boston.

'Okay, folks,' said the guard wearily, 'we're now in a controlled area.'

But it had only become a controlled area an hour previously. And as the passengers saw to their horror when they looked up at the street lights – it was an area where the vigilantes had been busy.

By dusk the trickle of ships arriving in New York Bay and moving to anchorages as directed by the busy Coast Guard cutters had become a flood.

Tankers, liners, ore carriers, grain carriers, three whaling factory ships and over two hundred general-purpose cargo ships had converged on New York that day and rode at their anchors in line astern.

There was one unspoken prayer that was foremost in everyone's mind: Please, God, let the weather hold.

39

'My God,' said the newsman, clutching his microphone in one hand and clinging to a safety strap with the other to prevent himself from falling out of the helicopter. 'This is a fantastic sight. It must be the largest gathering of ships since D-Day. I've never seen anything like it in my life. No one has ever seen anything like it before. New York Bay has become a giant parking lot for what looks like every ship in the world! I can see the flags of virtually every nation in the world. There are hundreds of Union Jacks. Why are we for ever writing Britain off when she still possesses one of the largest merchant fleets in the world?

'And there's the *Eureka* which is the floating headquarters ship of Admiral Brandon Pearson who is co-ordinating the operation. . . . Over there is the Egyptian ship, the *Asyut*, which broke down three hundred miles off the Ambrose and had to be towed here by an Israeli grain ship. And on the horizon. . . . Can we have the camera up? . . . Maybe it doesn't show on your screens, but it's the pale light flickering against the sky of White Atlantis one hundred and seventy miles away and below the horizon. We understand from Admiral Pearson that the berg is ninety miles from the continental shelf and is approaching it at an angle, at a speed of one point five knots.'

The time was icestrike minus ninety hours.

40

Every one of the 2,070 seats in the General Assembly Hall of the United Nations was occupied by the masters of the ships riding at anchor in the bay. Another seven hundred uniformed men and women were crowded into the aisles. The magnificent blue, green and gold auditorium, hub of the most important meeting place in the world, was packed.

Nearly three thousand men and women listened in silence to Admiral Pearson standing at the speaker's rostrum in front of the President's and the Secretary-General's marble podium. Some listened on headphones to simultaneous translations while others studied the folder of instructions that had been issued to each of them.

'We can't stop White Atlantis,' concluded Admiral Pearson. 'But, with the grace of God, we can deflect if from its present course.'

There was a question and answer session and the briefing was over.

The time was icestrike minus sixty-three hours.

41

The forest of steel girders projecting out of a ten-mile-wide frontier of the iceberg's northern flank covered an area of six hundred acres and resembled a giant tank barrier, as if White Atlantis had been prepared to counter an invasion from the sea. The girders had been arranged in neat ranks and files on the rotting slopes so that each one had a clear sight-line to the sea.

Attached to the base of each girder, where steel met ice, was a slender wire cable with a breaking strain of fifty tons. These had been spliced together in groups of ten to form a cable as thick as a man's arm with a breaking strain of five hundred tons, and these intermediate cables were in turn also gathered into groups of ten to merge into the hundred primary towing hawsers. The Ohio plant that manufactured the titanium alloy cable was working non-stop to produce the required quantity within the specified time.

Sherwood and Julia crunched across the decaying icescape to the first row of girders and stood surveying the busy scene.

The men, members of the US Navy Construction Battalion, were working as a smooth, close-knit and efficient team.

Sherwood pointed to the nearest of the giant coils of towing hawser.

'There's six miles of cable in each of those coils. Just about enough to string out thirty towing ships along each one. Those Seabees look as if they're ready to start floating out the first one.'

Julia shaded her eyes. One of the coils, three times the height of the men standing beside it, was floating on a group of pontoons that had been lashed together. An outboard motor started. The pontoon raft began to rotate slowly as it paid out the massive hawser. Bright orange floats were fastened to the cable at intervals as it slipped into the sea. Little seemed to happen during the next hour apart from a group of civilians who moved among the sentinel-like girders, hanging numbered boards on each one so that they could be individually identified from the remote-controlled TV cameras if anything started to go wrong during the towing operation. At the end of the hour, the pontoon had dwindled into the distance.

A ship's siren blasted close to. Sherwood and Julia turned. A Canadian merchantman was rounding one of the glistening headlands and was heading towards the line of orange floats strung out like a string of gaudy beads across the surface of the sea in the same direction that White Atlantis was moving. Another ship appeared from the opposite direction. It cruised along the length of the floating towline, maintaining a parallel course with the first ship but with the towline between them.

With perfect timing, two more ships appeared; one from the left and one from the right. They too moved away from White

Atlantis on a parallel course with the floating towline between their hulls and defining their course in the wake of the first two ships. It was like a stately but grotesque square dance of the leviathans.

Julia rested her hand on one of the icy girders and stared in fascination as another pair of ill-matched partners accompanied each other along each side of the towline. A control helicopter appeared and fussed about above the ships like a midge supervising a procession of circus elephants.

Julia took her hand away from the girder, frowned, and put it back again.

'I can feel something. See if you can.'

'What?'

'A sort of tapping.'

Sherwood rested his fingertips on the girder. There was vague, very distant and regular vibration.

'Feel it?' inquired Julia.

'Probably the ice picking up the beat of the screws from one of those ships.'

'It sounds like that recording you made.'

Sherwood smiled. 'I shouldn't worry about it. Come on, we'd better get back to the *Eureka* before all the helicopters leave.'

From a thousand feet it was possible to see the herring-bone pattern that the ships formed along the length of towing hawser. There were fifteen ships on each side of the hawser to which each of the thirty ships had attached its respective towline. More ships were already detaching themselves from the main fleet and were swinging into position to form the second herring-bone. None of the vessels hitched to and moving ahead of White Atlantis were actually towing – not yet; they were merely idling their engines to maintain a constant slack.

'Ninety-nine towing groups to go,' commented Sherwood.

They arrived on the *Eureka* fifteen minutes later to be greeted by grim faces.

A gale was forecast for the Eastern Seaboard and would hit New York Bay within the next twenty hours.

The time was icestrike minus forty hours.

42

Television cameras were everywhere. There were at least two hundred in prominant places throughout New York; perched alone on high buildings, ready to snatch images of the city's death and toss them to a hungry world that was waiting, crouched and ready to pounce, before countless million TV sets.

There were several on the now deserted White Atlantis sending pictures of the rows of girders to the control room on the *Eureka*. On the central master screen before Admiral Pearson was the radar picture of White Atlantis that was being beamed down from an AWACS circling above at five thousand feet. Stretching ahead of the hard outline of the iceberg were the fingers of the hundred towing groups of ships – fanning out like fingers: 2,780 perfectly co-ordinated ships moving in front of and at the same speed as the 280 square miles of ice that they hoped to defeat.

Another screen provided a continuous computer assessment of the situation, listing atmospheric pressure, wind speed, wind direction, the direction and speed of the drift of White Atlantis and the predicted time and place of the icestrike. The atmospheric pressure was still falling and the wind speed climbing as the final 'all systems okay' was received from the last of the towing groups.

Some farewells and good luck messages were received from those departing ships that the naval engineers had not allowed to participate because their engines were not capable of standing up to the punishing ordeal of having to deliver full power for the anticipated twenty hours of the operation.

Pearson glanced at the master screen and looked at Sutherland sitting beside him. Sutherland gave a faint nod.

'Well, ladies and gentlemen,' said Pearson with finality. 'This is the moment.'

He picked up his microphone and said: '*Eureka* to all groups – ten percent power in ten seconds.'

Acknowledgements flooded into the control room. Someone on a ship held a transmit key open momentarily. There was the faint clang of an engine-room telegraph.

Julia was standing at Sherwood's side. He pointed at one of the TV monitors from a camera on White Atlantis that was trained on a group of the girders thrust into the ice.

The cables were tightening slightly.

Pearson sat impassively while the reports from the towing groups were being received. The run at ten percent power continued for half an hour to give the engineers on all the ships time to check strain gauges on the towlines and to ensure that everything was in order.

'*Eureka* to all groups,' said Admiral Pearson. 'Thirty percent power in ten seconds.'

A technician counted off the seconds.

Again the acknowledgements; again that faint clang from one of the ships.

2,300 towlines tightened; 2,300 anxiously watched strain gauge pointers started edging up.

Another thirty minutes to test the systems. The crews on all the ships apprehensively watched their respective towlines, ready in case a ship had to cut and run if anything went wrong.

The light was failing. The breeze steadily strengthened.

A British seaman swore more in fear than anger as a growler was suddenly spawned by White Atlantis from the midst of an exploding cloud of wind-blown ice splinters.

To the men on the ships it looked as if they were already towing the monstrous iceberg but it was an illusion created by the current and the poor light.

ICESTRIKE MINUS 30:49 read one of the cryptic lines of data on the computer display.

'We're two minutes behind schedule,' said Sutherland.

Pearson called for fifty percent power.

'Hey,' said Sutherland a minute later. 'Speed's up decimal one of a knot.'

Pearson's eyes went to the display. 'Wind increasing.'

Sutherland said nothing. Pearson was right; it was impossible to tell if the one-tenth of a knot increase in speed noted by the sensors left on the iceberg was due to the ships or the ominously changing wind that was relentlessly mustering its forces.

'*Empress of Oslo!*' said a Scandinavian accent urgently from the speaker. 'Group twenty-two. Hot bearing. We cut and run!'

A radar blip was pulling clear of one of the towing groups. A

US Coast Guard cutter announced that the ship looked as if she could pull ahead without assistance but they would stand by.

'Wind speed twenty-two decimal four,' said Sutherland. 'Admiral, don't you think the fifty percent power period should be reduced? The wind has gained three knots in fifteen minutes.'

'We stick to the schedule.'

Sutherland bit on his lower lip and eyed the data display. 'Admiral . . .' he began.

'We've got to give those ships plenty of time to make sure that their engines and steering gear can take what they're going to get during one hundred percent power,' said Pearson testily without looking at Sutherland. 'We stick to the schedule.'

A second ship, as if confirming the wisdom of Pearson's ruling, announced that she was about to cut and run.

'Charlie One to *Eureka*,' said the friendly voice from the circling AWACS. 'We've got the satpics on Hurricane Tricia. The high is still holding her east. Looks like you fellers will be tangling with her peripheral in eight hours twenty.'

'For God's sake, admiral,' Sutherland muttered. 'We've got to cut short and go for full power now.'

Pearson thought for a few moments, then pressed the transmit key on the base of his microphone. '*Eureka* – all groups. A change of plan. One hundred percent power required in ten minutes. Calls at five minutes, one minute, thirty seconds, and a ten-second countdown.'

Pearson released the key. 'Satisfied, Mr Sutherland?'

The computer said:

ICESTRIKE MINUS 30:50.

43

By midnight the ships had been delivering full power for six hours. One ship had been forced by impending mechanical failure to release her towline from the main hawser and abandon her position in the group by forging ahead of the convoy and veering to one side; a mad dash for safety like a small creature of the night scurrying out of the path of an advancing Panzer division.

White Atlantis had increased her speed by one knot and was

moving towards the continental shelf at two point five knots but it was still impossible to determine if this was due to the efforts of the straining ships or the moderate gale.

'It seems crazy,' Julia whispered to Sherwood.

'What does?'

'Trying to make it go faster.'

'Karate,' was Sherwood's cryptic reply.

There was an outburst of cheering. The radar display was showing another growler that had broken away from the northern end of its parent. The gap between mother and child was slowly widening – possible proof that the ships were exerting some influence on the monster's movement.

'That gale will be upon us in two hours, admiral,' said Sutherland.

'So?'

'If we wait for daylight before starting the turn, it may be too late.'

Pearson nodded. 'You're right of course, Mr Sutherland. And you expect me to give the order requiring a co-ordinated manœuvre by all those ships at night that will be difficult enough to perform in daylight?'

'You don't have any choice,' said Sutherland quietly.

'You're right again.'

The speaker clicked. '*Bonner* leading Group One to *Eureka*.'

'Go ahead, *Bonner*.'

'We've been listening to the weather reports, admiral, and I've been talking to the other ships in my group. We think it's feasible to allow my group to alter course now and for me to signal the leader of Group Two to carry out their course alteration when we've completed ours. And for Group Two to signal Group Three and so on along the line.'

'Thank you, *Bonner*. Hold.'

Pearson turned to Sutherland. 'What do you think?'

'Let's give it a try.'

'It means transferring control to the group leaders.'

Sutherland shrugged. 'They're the guys who're trying to stop the goddam thing.'

Pearson pressed his transmit key. 'Okay, *Bonner*. We'll issue new orders to the group leaders.'

There was a chuckle from the speaker. 'I've already done

that, admiral. We're altering course now.' The speaker went dead.

'A Texan,' said Sutherland, checking a list of the ships and their captains.

'That figures,' said Pearson sourly.

Julia nudged Sherwood. 'Look at the radar!'

The first group of towing ships was swinging to the right away from the main convoy. Then, one by one, like the questing tentacles of a sea anemone, all the groups began moving to the right.

'Good God Almighty,' breathed Sherwood in the darkness at the back of the control room. 'It's working! It's actually working!'

White Atlantis was slowly turning about her axis to keep what had been her northern flank pointing towards the struggling ships. It was irrefutable evidence that the huge convoy was establishing supremacy over the giant iceberg.

The computer processed the new information and predicted: ICESTRIKE MINUS 24:00.

Exactly one day left. But there was a glimmer of hope: the computer had made the same prophesy an hour previously.

44

The edge of the hurricane struck shortly after 2:00 am when the ships had managed to turn through 180 degrees and were pointing back in the direction they had steamed in.

The northern flank of White Atlantis was now facing south, presenting its disintegrating prow to the hundreds of battling ships, their screws madly churning the water to foam. The wind, blowing into the eye of the convoy, rose from the continuous moaning gusts that slammed through rigging and past derricks to a sustained, mocking howl of triumph. The sea became a rolling barrage of seething hatred that buried bows and contemptuously exposed propellers so that they spun impotently with nothing to bite on.

The watchers in the *Eureka*'s control room sat in silence – helpless witnesses of the ancient battle between man and the sea. The opposing forces were in a state of equilibrium; White

Atlantis was motionless. But the sea had endless reserves of colossal strength that it hadn't called upon while the pounding, shuddering engines of the two thousand embattled ships had none.

'We're not going to do it,' said Sherwood to Julia, his voice quietly despairing. 'It only needs one of those ships. . . .'

He didn't complete the sentence. One of the TV monitors showing the floodlit army of girders imbedded in the ice completed it for him: at least fifty of the steel cable anchors were slowly twisting and splitting the ice open.

45

'Groups Fourteen through Nineteen!' Pearson barked into his microphone. 'Blow! Blow! Blow!'

It was the pre-arranged signal for the group leaders to detonate the explosive charge wrapped round their respective main hawsers.

Seconds later the sound of six dull explosions in rapid succession reached the *Eureka*'s control room.

Pearson gazed at the radar plot that showed the glowing elongated blips that were the ships surging clear of the convoy like ants abandoning their colony.

'Those six groups amounted to a hundred and fifty ships,' said Sutherland dejectedly. 'A five to seven percent loss.'

Pearson made no reply. Like everyone else in the control room, he was intently watching the computer display. The wind and the tide were beginning to gain the upper hand; White Atlantis was on the move again. Northwards – slowly pulling the convoy backwards towards New York and the continental shelf.

ICESTRIKE MINUS 22:10 the computer predicted. It immediately revised the figure as White Atlantis picked up speed: ICESTRIKE MINUS 19:40.

46

The gale had moderated by dawn but the news did not dispel the atmosphere of despair and failure in the *Eureka*'s control room.

The flowing tide held White Atlantis in an unrelenting death grip and was ruthlessly pushing it north at an inexorable two knots that the puny efforts of the desperately struggling ships were powerless to halt or slacken.

Two more ships fell by the wayside through lack of fuel or mechanical failure. Of the 2,780 ships that had taken up towing at the outset of the operation, less than 1,900 were left grimly battling against the titan that was hauling them backwards like enraged, harnessed bulls destined for the slaughterhouse.

ICESTRIKE MINUS 10:03.

White Atlantis was twenty miles from the soaring submerged precipice of the continental shelf where the Atlantic stopped and America began.

Admiral Pearson stood stiffly and stretched. He sat down beside Julia and Sherwood. His face was lined with fatigue and worry.

'Well,' he said wearily. 'We tried. God how we tried.'

'When are you going to order the ships to abandon the tow?' asked Julia.

Pearson yawned. 'I guess we'll keep it up until just before icestrike. There's a chance that those guys out there are holding the speed of the drift down. Half a knot might help reduce the destruction. What do you think, son?'

Sherwood didn't think that half a knot would make that much difference but he hadn't the heart to say so. Instead he nodded and said: 'It might help.'

'It doesn't seem possible,' said Julia, shaking her head sadly. 'New York's nothing like as bad as the press try to make out back home. It doesn't deserve what's going to happen to it.'

'No city deserves what's going to happen to New York,' said Pearson shortly. 'So let's pray for a miracle.'

ICESTRIKE MINUS 9:55, said the computer display.

47

It was five hours to icestrike when a dull rumble heralded the beginning of the miracle.

The *Eureka*'s cafeteria rapidly emptied as personnel poured on to the decks to witness it.

Sherwood and Julia could think of nothing to say to each other, as they stared goggle-eyed at the spectacle five miles away.

The general stations alarms were sounding on nearby warships.

White Atlantis was splitting in two.

'I don't care if you haven't got enough data!' Pearson roared. 'Can't you guess? What sort of damage will that chunk of ice do by itself?! Come on! Think!'

Sherwood frantically tried to estimate the size of the giant iceberg that the radar display was showing as drifting away from the side of White Atlantis.

'It must be at least a third of the bulk of White Atlantis. But . . . but . . .' he stumbled over the words.

'Charlie One to *Eureka*,' said the speaker. 'Exact size of that breakaway berg is ten miles by ten miles – one hundred square miles – thirty percent of what's left.'

'So what damage will it do?' Pearson demanded again.

'Not much,' said Sherwood. 'Maybe a minor tremor – perhaps not even that.'

'*Eureka* to all groups,' said Pearson into his microphone, making no attempt to conceal his excitement. 'We've got the figures! The good Lord has relieved you of thirty percent of your burden! I want full power again in ten seconds!'

The ships threw themselves with fresh zeal into the renewed tug-of-war.

ICESTRIKE MINUS 4:40, announced the computer a few minutes later.

Five minutes passed by.

ICESTRIKE MINUS 4:35.

'Someone tell me why it's not stopping,' demanded Pearson.

'It's going to take time to kill its momentum before they can even start to pull it clear,' Sherwood pointed out.

'How long?'

'I'm sorry. I don't know.'

Two hours slipped by and still the decimated White Atlantis continued to drift towards the continental shelf. One of the computer prediction displays was even showing a map with the iceberg's anticipated course and the point of impact.

ICESTRIKE MINUS 2:00.

'Hell,' Pearson muttered moodily to himself, discovering that he had renewed his childhood habit of chewing his thumb and had drawn blood.

Julia was holding Sherwood's hand tightly and saying nothing.

ICESTRIKE MINUS 1:00.

'She's slowing decimal three of a knot,' said Sutherland. 'Come on you bastards – pull! Pull like hell.'

His exhortation to the ships went unheard; the transmit key was up.

ICESTRIKE MINUS 0:40.

Forty minutes, thought Sherwood. What was that in distance? Less than two thousand yards.

'We're getting a sonograph of the continental shelf,' commented Sutherland.

ICESTRIKE MINUS 0:30.

Julia's hand in Sherwood's was slippery with sweat. He tried to pull it away but she tightened her grip.

'Still slowing,' droned Sutherland's voice. 'Speed decimal nine of a knot.'

ICESTRIKE MINUS 0:20.

'Twenty minutes,' said Pearson bitterly. 'Why isn't the thing stopping?'

ICESTRIKE MINUS 0:10.

'She's down to decimal four of a knot.' Sutherland's voice cracked with excitement.

ICESTRIKE MINUS 0:05.

The outline of the rigid brink of the continental shelf was hard and clear on the sonograph.

'Decimal two of a knot!' shouted Sutherland. 'She's stopping! *She's stopping!*'

It won't stop, thought Sherwood.

ICESTRIKE MINUS 0:02.

'Decimal one.' This time Sutherland's voice was calm, as if he had suddenly remembered his position as captain.

ICESTRIKE MINUS 0:01.

Sherwood closed his eyes.

'Nothing,' said Sutherland. 'Nothing. Nothing.'

'What are you talking about?'

'It's stopped.'

Sherwood opened his eyes and looked up at the data display. ICESTRIKE MINUS 00:00.

He laughed. What was minus nothing supposed to mean?

White Atlantis had stopped and was resting its three hundred thousand million ton bulk against the edge of the plunging continental shelf.

ICESTRIKE . . . ICESTRIKE . . . ICESTRIKE . . . repeated the mindless computer but everyone was too busy laughing, cheering and crying to switch it off.

48

It took two weeks for the powerful jets of cold water from the monitors on the five oil platform fire-fighting ships to slice White Atlantis into manageable growlers for the relays of tugs and coasters to herd into the designated melt area that sprawled across New York Bay like a giant minefield.

The *Eureka* was at anchor within a mile of the nearest ship whose remote-controlled monitors were lancing eighty thousand gallons each second at the largest remaining piece of the once mighty iceberg.

Julia leaned thoughtfully on the *Eureka*'s rail and stared at the scene. 'You never told me why you didn't use hoses in the first place.'

'There wasn't time,' said Sherwood. 'Look how long it's taken. Even so, it doesn't excuse me for not thinking of it earlier. I should've realized much sooner that cold, running water melts ice faster than anything else when I saw how quickly those rivers on White Atlantis cut ravines, and not waited for a bartender to show me.'

The giant growler was cut in two by a rigid jet of water that sliced through the ice like a chain saw sinking into a balsa log.

Julia scanned the open channel for a sign of the launch bringing her parents from New York. They had arrived at the reopened Kennedy Airport the previous day.

New York was back to normal, much to the detriment of the US Coast Guard which had the difficult task of shooing away the swarms of small craft that had made the hazardous journey to marvel at the still dangerous ice field before it disappeared.

A growler near the *Eureka* and twice the ship's size suddenly split open of its own accord. Julia watched the unstable ice turn a slow somersault. After two weeks in the ice field the scene was losing its initial fascination. Something broke the surface for a few seconds near the shattered growler. It seemed to move quickly, leaving a vee-shaped pattern on the broken water. She pointed.

'Look. Over there. . . . Oh, too late – it's gone.'

Sherwood followed the direction of her finger. 'What has?'

Julia hesitated. 'You'll only laugh.'

'I promise not to laugh,' said Sherwood solemnly.

'Well. . . . Well it looked like a periscope.'

But Sherwood did laugh, and received a kick on the shin.

49

Frank Knight, the duty officer at the British Government Communications Headquarters near Cheltenham, dozed in front of his console. The paperback novel had slipped from his fingers.

At fifteen minutes past midnight, the Honeywell computer flashed a terse message on its screen:

URGENT UNSCHEDULED SIGNALS BEING RECEIVED CORRECTLY CODED ON GCHQ FREQUENCY FROM SOURCE IDENTIFYING ITSELF AS UNIT 7 // UNIT 7 INSTRUCTIONS NOW INVALID // PLEASE ADVISE // TIME 00:15 // MESSAGE ENDS +

The Honeywell patiently waited another two minutes then sounded a muted warning buzzer.

50

The riotous celebration party aboard the *Eureka* was into its third hour when Sherwood suddenly remembered to look in the marine specimen bucket that had the last bottle of champagne standing in it. He was just in time.

He found Julia laughing and joking with Admiral Pearson, and took her to one side.

'Hold your hand out and close your eyes. I've got a present for you.'

Puzzled, Julia did as he requested. Something gently stung the palm of her hand.

'Open your eyes.'

Julia looked down. A piece of ice, smaller than a sugar cube, was floating in the tiny pool of water in her palm. She raised questioning eyes to Sherwood.

He smiled. 'That's all that's left of it. Lucky I remembered in time.'

Julia looked down at her palm again.

But White Atlantis had vanished.

51

The continent was slowly lifting.

It was freed of the great weight it had borne for five million years. It was a gradual movement but a movement possessing the energies of the unremitting winters of fifty thousand centuries.

Cracks appeared in the ice-cap. They widened with a roar that seemed to fill the universe. The opening fissures became canyons.

And so. . . .

The ice moved.

U700

For my wife Christine

Part One

1

Death was lying in wait for the convoy straggler.

The grey, rust-streaked, silent hull lay stopped on the surface – water dripping from its periscope standards and jumping wire with the same regular rhythm as the heavy metallic throb of the approaching ship's engines. Inverted golden horseshoes gleamed on either side of the conning tower. Down below, the waiting men stood silently by the torpedo tube that contained the U-boat's next-to-last torpedo. The hydrophone operator in the control room, headphones clamped over his ears, gave the doomed merchantman's course, range, and speed to the inscrutable man standing behind him, answering the U-boat commander's questions in a steady voice and without turning around. If he was aware of the expressionless eyes boring into the small of his back, he gave no sign.

There was a sudden movement in the control room as the commander climbed the steel rungs that led up to the attack kiosk in the conning tower. The hydrophone operator sensed the sudden relaxing of tension. Someone even made a quick joke.

The four lookouts on the U-boat's bridge studiously kept their eyes pressed to their binoculars as they stared into the fog. They didn't need the pungent whiff of a cheroot to tell them that the new arrival on the bridge was their commander. One of them, bolder than his mates, risked a glance at the gaunt figure. The movement caused the lookout's oilskins to squeak. The commander scowled but said nothing. The four men sensed his displeasure and did their best to stand absolutely still. The sound of the engines faded. For some seconds all that could be heard was the gurgle made by the swell as it vented through the deck casing drains when the U-boat lifted.

All five men heard the music at the same time: a choir singing in the fog.

Silent night, holy night.

An old German Christmas carol that now belonged to the world.

All is calm, all is bright.

By one of those tricks that fog plays with sound, the beat of the ship's engines reached the U-boat after the sound of the record.

The commander lifted his specially engraved Zeiss binoculars and trained them in the direction of the singing. They had been presented to him by Admiral Karl Doenitz – a gift from a grateful commander-in-chief of the U-boat arm to his topscoring 'ace'.

Round yon Virgin, mother and child.

The commander lowered his binoculars and stared into the fog as if he were willing the invisible ship to materialize. He muttered an order into the voice pipe.

Driven now by its electric motors, a small wave crept up the shark-like bow as the U-boat slipped silently and purposefully through the water.

There was no warning.

In an instant the happy party scene aboard the *Walvis Bay*, with the children excitedly opening their Christmas presents, became a nightmare of devastation and death as the cabin floor heaved upward and burst open like a giant, ruptured diaphragm.

The ship gave a sickening lurch and began to list as it

lost way. The port engine was torn from its shattered mountings. It smashed through the side of the ship as if the steel plates had been stretched tissue paper.

The bewildered radio operator clung desperately to his table in the tilting darkness. His instinct had been to join the stampede past the door of his radio shack, but he managed to shut out the cries of the terrified children who were being shepherded onto the deck by the two army nurses. He set the radio to 'transmit' and tapped out on the antique morse key: 'SSSS . . . SSSS . . . SSSS . . .' Submarine! Submarine! Submarine!

He gave the *Walvis Bay*'s call sign and position several times, but there was no answer from the rest of the convoy fifty miles ahead. He tried to raise a Newfoundland station but without success; the antenna wire was trailing uselessly in the water astern of the rapidly sinking ship.

A spot of light moved on the surface of the oil-black water. The searchlight beam was filled with swirling fog. There was the soft purr of electric motors. Accusing exhibits of unrestricted U-boat warfare swam briefly into the spotlight and moved on like actors lining up and bowing after a macabre finale: a teddy bear, a half-opened present, a man's leg.

The boatman's mate manning the searchlight wanted to switch the light off and shut out the horror. But there was the even more frightening, icy presence of the U-boat commander at his side, staring down at the water – saying nothing.

There was the sound of a child crying in the fog. The commander tensed. He tuned his head to locate the direction of the sound and issued a curt order into the voice pipe.

A crewman emerged on the bridge. He moved aft to the railed wintergarten deck and swung the 20 millimetre anti-aircraft gun down so that it was pointing at the water.

The commander issued another order.

U99 altered course toward the sound of the crying child.

The captain of the *Walvis Bay*, still wearing a Father Christmas costume that was now sodden and caked with oil, stood up in the lifeboat and motioned the army nurse to keep the crying child quiet. She gathered the six-year-old boy into her arms and whispered gently to him. His tears began to subside. The older children sensed the approaching danger and remained silent while peering with wide, frightened eyes into the fog. There were fifteen people in the lifeboat: the captain, the army nurse, and thirteen children who were evacuees from the London bombing.

The muffled purr of the approaching U-boat's electric motors grew steadily louder.

The captain saw the searchlight hardening in the fog and swore bitterly. He shivered with despair as he tried to swing the lifeboat around so that it presented a smaller target. But he was too late; the long, lean hull was sliding past the crowded, open boat. A conning tower swayed out of the fog. The U-boat's motors were thrown into reverse.

U99 stopped beside the lifeboat and bathed its occupants with the glare from the searchlight.

A voice spoke. Perfect English with hardly a trace of German accent.

'What ship?'

The captain clutched the oar as though it were a club. He suddenly felt foolish in the remnants of his costume. He shaded his eyes and thought he could discern the ghostly outline of a man behind the blinding light.

'What ship?' the voice repeated. There was a hint of impatience.

'Walvis Bay.'

'Cargo?'

The reply was flat and unemotional. 'Children.'

The searchlight moved to the pinched, frozen faces and came to rest on the nurse. She sensed a pair of eyes taking in every detail of her Queen Alexandra's Nursing Corps uniform.

There was movement on the U-boat's deck. Something soft landed at the nurse's feet. A blanket. Then another. She realized that two U-boatmen were lowering a crate into the lifeboat. One of the crew was holding out a small wooden box to the captain. He took it reluctantly. An older child overcame her fear and put her hand into the crate. She held up a bottle of brandy and a carton of cigarettes and looked disappointed.

The searchlight clicked out. The voice on the bridge gave an order in German. There was a growl of hidden starter motors followed by the explosive roar of the U-boat's diesel engines bursting into life. The captain groped for the torch and flashed it on the conning tower. The two men's eyes met for a few seconds. It was a face the *Walvis Bay*'s captain had seen before in newspaper photographs – the humourless, forbidding eyes and sardonic features dominated by a prominent, hawk-like nose. It was a face that embodied the inherent menace of the eagle that was the emblem of the Third Reich.

There was a bump as the crewmen fended the lifeboat away from the moving U-boat. The captain steadied himself. His torch dipped and illuminated the gleaming, inverted golden horseshoe on the side of the receding U-boat's conning tower. But the captain already knew who his adversary was. He stared at the lone figure that was being absorbed into the fog – his emotions a mixture of awe and astonishment.

'My God,' he whispered. 'That was Otto Kretschmer.'

He stared after the disappearing U-boat for some

seconds before opening the wooden box that had been handed to him by one of the U-boat's crew. Inside he found a compass. Coincidentally, its needle was pointing to the precise point where the fog had swallowed *U99*.

On *U99*, the crewman who had manned the gun was about to close the hatch when he noticed a piece of paper wrapped around one of the stanchions. He carefully removed it and laid it flat on the deck casing. It was a stencilled list of the names of the children and nurses aboard the *Walvis Bay*. The reverse had been used to make a Christmas card. It bore a crayoned message written in a child's awkward hand: MERRY CHRISTMAS AND A HAPPY 1941.

2

The ancient Citroën taxi bounced across the rain-polished cobbles and grated to a standstill outside the gate that led to Lorient harbour's U-boat quays. A bored stabsfeldwebel, wearing the duty gorget and chain of the military police, approached the taxi and took the offered papers from the passenger.

Lieutenant Bernard Anders – the photograph matched the anxious face: fair hair, a pale complexion. He noted the long legs that were virtually drawn up to the occupant's chin in the taxi's cramped interior.

The stabsfeldwebel stood back and waved the taxi through the gate and returned to his guard box with its cracks stuffed with shredded newspapers to keep out the biting February wind that blew with toothache ferocity off the Atlantic and into a man's bone marrow.

He had just made himself comfortable when another

new arrival turned up in a taxi. Typical, he thought. Too full of self-esteem to even consider sharing a taxi.

Another officer, perhaps younger than the first one. He had an eager, confident air. His uniform was an essay in perfection: his collar was spotless, and his cap, which he was managing to wear in the taxi, was at the correct angle. Everything about Sub-Lieutenant Richard Stein was well-ordered neatness. Everything, that is, except the ugly sweep of a sabre scar on his left cheek.

Bernard Anders found Pier Six and gazed down at his new boat. It was at least double the size of the 'canoes' he had completed his Baltic training on. Two engineers were preparing the submarine for combat by removing the fore and aft safety rails. A third was checking the 88-millimetre gun that dominated the foredeck. Anders lost count of the minutes as he absorbed every detail of the U-boat that was to become his home. He was roused by a pleasant voice behind him.

'Good afternoon.'

Anders turned. It was the well-scrubbed, smartly turned-out U-boat officer he had noticed on the train.

'I'm Sub-Lieutenant Richard Stein.' The sabre scar crinkled as he smiled. The knife-edge creases in his trousers were two vertical lines of uninterrupted perfection. His travel bags had been packed so that they were outwardly symmetrical. Anders was uncomfortably aware of his own awkward frame, which had been the despair of his proud mother when she had tried to alter his uniform to fit properly. He shook the offered hand, noticing that Stein's nails had been manicured.

'Lieutenant Bernard Anders,' Anders said, returning Stein's smile.

Stein nodded to the U-boat and brushed an invisible speck from his sleeve. 'Your new boat?'

'Yes.' Anders resented Stein's air of casual confidence.

'Which one?'

'*U700.*'

'Bad luck,' Stein said, gazing critically down at his gleaming toecaps.

Anders bridled. 'Oh?'

Stein looked up. 'But you've heard, of course? There was a piece on *U700* in *Das Reich.*'

'My parents don't take that newspaper,' Anders said, immediately regretting the reply, for it made him sound arrogant, which he hadn't intended.

The smile vanished from Stein's face. He picked up his travel bags and said coldly, 'There was an accident during her trials at Trondheim. I can't remember the exact details, but there was something about a citation for presence of mind shown by her captain. He'd be the best one to tell you.'

'What boat are you joining?' Anders asked as Stein turned to leave. 'I didn't mean to sound rude.'

'*U99,*' Stein said unsmilingly. But a hint of pride was in his voice as he added, 'Kretschmer's boat. She's due back tomorrow.'

Anders made no reply. Stein regarded him for a moment and then gave a faint smile that barely creased the polished tissue of his sabre scar.

'Good luck with *U700*, Lieutenant Anders. Let us hope that she's not going to be an unlucky boat.'

Captain-Lieutenant Hans Weiner was a large capable man in his late forties who had ably commanded a Type II training U-boat on the Baltic up to the summer of 1939. He had resigned himself to spending the war training recruits because he suspected that his age was against his receiving a front-line command. He was therefore surprised and grateful when his flotilla commander informed him that he was to take delivery of *U700* from her builders. The accident that had deprived *U700* of nearly a quarter of her crew of forty men had happened during the second week of acceptance trials. After the necessary repairs had been completed, he had been ordered to sail for the newly captured port of Lorient in western France to await replacements. From his experiences on the Baltic with the large numbers of U-boatmen who failed to complete their training, he knew only too well that the chances of obtaining seasoned men to replace the nine men lost during the accident were slim.

He was sitting at his table adjoining the U-boat's wardroom, signing stores requisitions, when he heard someone descend the ladder into the control room. He drew aside his green curtain – the only concession to privacy that the commander of a Type VIIC U-boat was entitled to – and leaned into the companionway. An officer with an unfamiliar, loose-limbed build was peering through the sky periscope.

Weiner pulled his sweater straight and entered the control room. It was some moments before the new arrival noticed his presence. When he did, he straightened up from the periscope and smiled sheepishly.

'I didn't know anyone was aboard.'

Weiner studied the officer, noting the two gold rings on his sleeve. 'Are you Lieutenant Bernard Anders?'

'Yes. I have my papers.' Weiner took the sheaf of documents, glanced through them, and cursed inwardly. He had been promised an experienced first officer – one who had completed at least two war patrols – not a youngster hardly out of a cadet's uniform who had never poked his nose out of the Baltic's sheltered waters.

'Those papers are for Captain Weiner.'

'I'm Weiner.'

Anders' gangling frame came to immediate attention.

He saluted clumsily. I'm sorry, *kaleu*,' he said, using the customary abbreviation with which junior officers addressed a *Kapitanleutnant*.

Weiner waved the apology aside and gestured to the control room's interior. 'Well? What do you think of her?'

Anders smiled. He felt certain he was going to like Weiner. 'Impressive, kaleu. Bigger than the training boats.'

Weiner grunted. 'It will seem small enough after a few weeks on patrol.' He regarded Anders thoughtfully. 'So you're my new first watch officer?'

'I've served as an executive officer for three months, kaleu.'

Weiner grinned. 'On a Type II in the Baltic, eh?' He clapped Anders affably on the back. 'Come. I'll show you a real U-boat. Her teeth first.'

Weiner's powerful hand slapped one of the racked torpedoes affectionately. 'And this one is special, Mr Anders. Know what it is?'

Anders ducked his head under the overhead torpedo tube loading rails in the U-boat's bow torpedo room and peered at the long, black weapon. It looked the same as the other torpedoes except for the serial number suffix stencilled in neat white letters on the hemispherical warhead. He straightened up in surprise and nearly hit his head on the rails.

'A G7e warhead, kaleu.'

Weiner beamed. 'Right first time. But why the surprised expression?'

Anders stared at the sinister weapon gleaming dully in the light from the caged bulkhead lamps. Of its twenty-five-foot length, it was the jet-black warhead that held his attention; unlike the main body of the torpedo, the surface was smooth and highly-polished.

'I thought the magnetic warhead had been withdrawn from service, kaleu.'

'This is the Mark Two version,' Weiner replied, patting the warhead as if it were a dog. 'They say that all the bugs have been ironed out. Kretschmer, Schepke and Prien are sinking one ship per torpedo with these beauties.' Weiner's hand moved along the torpedo's curved flank to its propellers. 'And it's powered by electric motors instead of compressed air. No tell-tale bubble track.'

'The warhead appears to be made from a different type of metal, kaleu,' Anders said, unable to take his eyes off the gleaming hemisphere.

'It's a new type of "Wotan" steel developed by Krupp which allows the explosive in the warhead to build up to twice the pressure before it bursts. That way we get twice the explosive force for the same amount of explosive charge. But it's the fact that the warhead explodes underneath the target that does the real damage.'

Anders warmed to the older, almost fatherly man. Had Weiner been the kind of aloof senior officer he had experienced so far during his brief period in the *Kriegsmarine*, he would have lacked the courage to ask the question that was uppermost in his mind.

'What was the accident that happened to this boat, kaleu?'

Weiner spun around, the amiable expression gone. 'What accident?' he barked.

'I'm sorry, kaleu – I was told that during *U700*'s trials –'

'Oh that,' Weiner interrupted dismissively. He nodded to the group of four torpedo doors. 'Spot of trouble with Tube Three – faulty welding around the hinge.'

Anders understood exactly what that meant. 'You mean a door blew off?' he asked incredulously.

'Something like that,' Weiner said. 'But you don't want to be bothered with *U700*'s past misfortunes. It's her future successes that we're now concerned with.' He took Anders by the elbow. 'We'd better see about getting that uniform of yours sponged and pressed. Looks like you've slept in it. Can't have you meeting the admiral tonight looking like that.'

Anders froze. 'The admiral?'

'Why yes.'

'Admiral Doenitz?'

Weiner laughed. 'Of course. Unless Raeder has appointed a new U-boat Commander-in-Chief since this morning.'

A meeting with the legendary Karl Doenitz was the last thing Anders had bargained for. Weiner noticed his junior officer's alarmed expression and grinned broadly.

'If it's any comfort, I felt the same when I first met him at Wilhelmshaven some years ago. Tonight is *U700*'s precommissioning party. His Atlantic operations HQ is based here, so it's certain that he'll show up.'

3

The magnetic torpedo passed under the ore-laden ship and exploded directly beneath its keel.

Kretschmer and the other watchers on *U99*'s bridge saw a blinding sheet of flame leap high into the night sky. It had been *U99*'s last torpedo – fired from her stern tube.

The U-boat turned, bringing her main gun to bear so that the ship could be finished off with a mixture of incendiary and explosive shells. But the gun crew wasn't needed. As moonlight spilled across the sea through a gap in the cloud base, the astonished watchers saw the ore ship's masts tilt toward one another and slowly cross, like duellists' swords at the beginning of a contest. They could even see the twin rudders and propellers as the stern section lifted clear of the water. The bow also reared up to the sky and seemed to wait for timeless seconds.

'No time to break out even one lifeboat,' a lookout breathed.

Kretschmer remained silent.

There was a roar of water cascading into the stricken ship, and the two halves settled lower in the water – a swirl of black water and then nothing – not even wreckage. That would come later as the remains of the ship twisted and turned on their leisurely five-mile glide to the floor of the Atlantic Ocean.

Less than fifty seconds had elapsed between the torpedo explosion and the disappearance of the ship. None of *U99*'s crew had ever known a vessel to sink so quickly.

Chief Petty Officer Jupp Kassel, sitting below at the radio turned to the international distress frequency, with pencil poised to get the ship's name, heard nothing. It was conclusive proof that the magnetic torpedo, with its ability to break a ship's back, and Kretschmer's point-blank range surface attack tactics, made *U99* the most deadly weapon of war in the North Atlantic.

U99's devastating war patrol was over. There was little else she could do now but set course east for the U-boat quays of Lorient.

4

That night, in the lounge of the Hotel Beau Séjour, Sub-Lieutenant Richard Stein was struggling to the top of the unsteady pyramid of armchairs and settees. He warded off the giggling typist's cushion blows and grabbed her around the waist. In accordance with the rules, she submitted to a long, passionate kiss while the cheering U-boatmen chanted the seconds. After ten seconds she was entitled to push Stein off the pyramid. Two Waffen SS officers whom Stein had befriended that day during his first few hours in Lorient were pelting the embracing couple with paper streamers.

Weiner and Anders stood by the buffet table and watched as Stein pinioned the girl's arms and fumbled at her blouse buttons. Her protests were drowned in the general uproar.

'What do you think of our crew?' Weiner asked, splashing more wine into Anders' glass.

'They seem competent enough,' Anders replied. He was watching Stein and wondering how he managed to keep his hair and tie neat and straight while struggling with the girl.

Weiner gestured with his glass. 'Who the devil's. that fellow?'

'His name's Stein. He was on my train this morning.' As Anders answered, he realized how at ease he felt with Weiner. Here, at last, was someone prepared to treat him as an equal.

'Damned gatecrashers,' Weiner muttered into his glass.

'He says he's joining *U99*.'

Weiner gave a short, booming laugh. 'Kretschmer won't have him.'

Anders drained his glass. Normally he would have held onto one drink all evening, but now he was relaxed. He decided to enjoy the wine and savour the easy atmosphere between himself and the older man. 'Why not, kaleu?'

The girl suddenly screamed loudly. Stein had torn her blouse open. She clawed at Stein's face, and in retaliation he slapped her hard across the mouth, then caught hold of her hair and savagely jerked her head back. He used his other hand to tear away her bra. Brinkler, *U700*'s doctor and chief engineer, realized that Stein was going too far and tried to climb the pyramid to stop him, but he was dragged away by the two SS officers.

Weiner put down his glass and stared across the room at the frightened girl. Anders sensed what was coming.

'I'm not having that thug spoiling my party, Anders. Have him thrown out.'

Anders laughed uneasily, hoping that Weiner would treat the matter as a joke. But Weiner's face was deadly serious. One of the SS officers had joined Stein and was tugging at the typist's slip beneath her skirt. It was turning into an ugly scene, and some of the other girls were urging their escorts to intervene.

'For Christ's sake stop him,' Weiner said with quiet anger.

A Mercedes tourer drew up outside the hotel, and the driver jumped out to open the passenger door. Admiral Karl Doenitz stepped out and listened to the sounds of the party. He turned to John Kneller, his flag lieutenant, and smiled.

'There are times, John, when I devoutly wish I was still a U-boat commander.'

Doenitz, the commander-in-chief of the U-boat arm, was a shrewd, sharp-featured Prussian in his early fifties. His prematurely grey hair had led to his U-boat crews giving him the nickname 'The Grey Lion'. Doenitz didn't care. So long as his beloved U-boats sank plenty of ships, they could call him what they liked. After every patrol he would go carefully over the U-boat commander's report word by word and unmercifully castigate any officer who had shown the slightest weakness or hesitation in pressing home an attack. In return, Doenitz fiercely protected his

U-boatmen from the Berlin clique of string-pullers and propagandists. He tolerated a few SS in his headquarters, provided they concerned themselves with security and kept their noses out of U-boat affairs. There were many in Berlin who disliked him. They suspected that his organization of Prien's penetration of Scapa Flow to sink the *Royal Oak* at her anchorage in Scotland had been a stunt to win support from Hitler who had little patience or understanding of U-boat warfare. Goering heartily detested Doenitz because he had been forced to provide Doenitz with a squadron of long-range Kondor aircraft for convoy reconnaissance. Ever since, Goering had ceaselessly but unsuccessfully striven for the return of the Kondors so that his favourite expression 'everything that flies belongs to me' would once again have meaning.

As they entered the hotel, Doenitz said, 'You warned Weiner that I would put in an appearance at his party?'

'Yes, admiral.'

Doenitz didn't want his U-boatmen to feel that he was breathing down their necks even when they were relaxing.

Anders reluctantly put down his glass and pushed through the crowd clustered around the swaying pile of furniture. Stein and the SS officer had removed most of the terrified typist's clothes.

'That's enough, Stein. Leave her alone.'

The crowd fell silent. A restraining hand reached out for Anders' sleeve, but he shrugged it aside. Stein laughed drunkenly and poured the contents of a bottle of wine over the girl's stomach.

'She's enjoying it, Anders. Come and drink from her navel.'

Anders stepped closer and stared up at Stein. His face was level with Stein's gleaming toecap.

'I said that's enough!'

The girl struggled and whimpered as the SS officer started to force her legs apart.

'Try and stop us,' Stein sneered. He lashed out his foot at Anders' face – a move that Anders expected, for Stein found himself kicking at empty air. Then two powerful hands grasped his flailing ankle and twisted viciously. Stein's scream of pain was drowned in the uproar as the rickety pyramid collapsed in a confusion of scattered cushions and flailing arms and legs. There was an outburst of applause from the revellers. As Anders helped the sobbing girl to her feet he saw Doenitz enter the room. There was no mistaking the birdlike features beneath the high-peaked, gold-braided cap.

The dance band conductor had also spotted the admiral's uniform out of the corner of his eye and had launched his musicians into a fast dance number.

Stein failed to see the new arrival. Intent only on revenge, he spun Anders around and hit him unexpectedly in the ribs. It wasn't a hard punch because Stein's SS friends were pulling him away. Two women swooped on the distraught typist and helped her to a door. Brinkler and another member of *U700*'s crew held Anders steady for a few seconds until he had calmed down sufficiently to be allowed to make his way to the buffet where Weiner was pouring Admiral Doenitz a drink. Whitecoated stewards started moving the furniture back into place, and couples resumed dancing.

Weiner clapped Anders genially on the back and introduced him to Doenitz.

Doenitz turned to Anders with an amused smile and nodded to Stein who was scowling at the buffet from across the dance floor. 'Never take your eyes off the enemy for an instant during battle, Anders,' said Doenitz. 'But I like to see a determined attack.'

Anders took the drink Weiner offered and forced

himself to realize he was being addressed by the flag officer of every submarine in the *Kriegsmarine*.

'A momentary lapse, admiral,' Anders said uncertainly. But Doenitz wasn't listening – Kneller was whispering in his ear. The admiral placed his glass on the table, made a hurried apology to Weiner, and followed Kneller to the hotel lobby.

Weiner gloomily watched him leave. 'Well,' he said sadly, 'I suppose a brief visit is better than no visit at all.'

Anders turned and noticed Stein shrug aside the restraining hands of the two SS officers and stand up, his eyes fixed intently in Anders' direction. Somehow, Stein's appearance was still immaculate despite the recent mêlée.

'Trouble approaches,' Weiner said as Stein threaded an unsteady path across the lounge.

But Stein's anger seemed to have vanished. He smiled warmly at Anders. 'I see you're friendly with Uncle Karl,' he said, his speech slurred. 'If I were you, I'd exploit that friendship to get him to transfer you to a decent boat.'

Embarrassed, Anders said, 'This is Captain Hans Weiner – commanding officer of *U700*.'

Stein's smile broadened. He pretended to notice Weiner for the first time.

'Very sorry, kaleu. Just my little joke.'

'A pity to waste it,' Weiner observed coldly. 'Go and see if you can persuade your SS friends to laugh at it.'

Stein bowed mockingly and headed unsteadily back to his table.

'Cocky little bastard,' Weiner growled.

'Captain Weiner?'

Weiner turned. It was Kneller, all teeth and smiles. 'The admiral sends his apologies and regrets that he won't be able to return to the party for at least an hour.'

'Why not?'

'We received a message from the dockyard superintendent requesting permission to switch the Pier Three floodlights on. A U-boat is returning from a war patrol.'

'Which one?' Weiner growled, sensing a threat to his party.

'U99,' Kneller said, grinning even more broadly at Weiner's dismayed expression. 'Kretschmer's back.' He stepped on to a chair and clapped his hands for silence. '*U99* is about to enter the harbour,' he announced.

The news triggered a mass exodus.

There were nearly a hundred late-night revellers lined up along both jetties and the quayside that formed Pier Three. Some girls had even climbed on to *U700*'s bridge, and some crowded around the anti-aircraft gun on the raised wintergarten deck. Anders stood on the quayside beside Weiner. Doenitz, in his long greatcoat, was standing near a group of seamen who were ready with a wooden gangway. The only sound was the soft lap of water and the shivering of the less hardy girls in thin party dresses. Stein, his eyes alight with anticipation, stood between his two SS friends. Everyone was watching the navigation lights that were moving across the dark waters of the Scorff Estuary toward the oasis of Pier Three's floodlighting.

There was a film of night mist rising off the still, black water. For some seconds all that could be seen of the U-boat were the glowing navigation lights. Then Anders could discern the dark mass between the lights.

The crowd stirred at the sight of the motionless figure hunched over the bridge coaming. He seemed to be riding through the mist like the avenging spirit of the Rhine.

The shark-like bow slipped with sure precision under the pool of light that bathed the pier. The motors went astern, and the entire length of the secretive creature of the Atlantic night was exposed to view. Anders' attention was riveted on an object that gleamed on the side of the conning tower. It was part of a half-believed legend – something he thought the papers and newsreels had invented. And yet there it was – shining under the floodlights: a golden horseshoe.

'God,' Weiner muttered, craning his bull neck level with Anders' shoulder. 'Look at those pennants.'

A string of homemade flags drooped lifelessly from the periscope standards. Each one represented a ship sunk and was marked with a tonnage figure.

The U-boat's electric motors stopped.

The silence was suddenly broken when a girl began to clap. Another girl joined in. Then another. After a few moments the entire ensemble gathered around Pier Three was applauding and cheering. Even Doenitz joined in, but in keeping with his dignity, he did not cheer. Stein did both with great gusto – his eyes shining with pride as he looked on the boat that he was to join.

Eager, outstretched hands caught the mooring lines that were tossed ashore. *U99* was quickly made fast and the gangway run out to her foredeck. Kretschmer made no attempt to leave his boat until all forty-four members of his crew had filed ashore. He followed a man on a stretcher and shook hands with Doenitz who was waiting at the foot of the gangway.

The man on the stretcher was carried past Anders and Weiner. The blanket covering the wounded man was caked with congealed blood in the region of the man's stomach. It was Anders' first sight of blood drawn by the enemy and a reminder that the U-boats, despite the hysterical claims in the press, were not invincible. He felt a vicelike but reassuring grip on his arm.

'Come on,' Weiner muttered. 'Let's bring the commissioning party back to life.'

* * *

Less than 25 couples bothered to return to the party. Stein sat at a table between the two Waffen SS officers and wondered if befriending them had been a mistake. He looked at the group standing near the depleted buffet through a haze of drunken jealousy. Kretschmer, Weiner, Anders, Doenitz, and Weiner's bellowing laugh could be plainly heard above the band that was playing a slow waltz.

'God damn it,' Stein muttered into his beer tankard. 'Should've invited me over. Kretschmer's my CO now . . .'

The dance number came to an end. There was some desultory clapping. Most of the dancers drifted back to their tables. It was now 3:00 A.M.

Stein's hand went to his tie to make sure it was straight. He stood with the intention of walking over to the group but was pulled back onto his chair.

'Don't be a fool,' the SS officer growled.

Kretschmer was passing around a packet of his black cheroots.

Doenitz declined and said warningly to Anders who had accepted one of the cellophane-wrapped cigars:

'Treat it with great respect – they're more dangerous than his torpedoes.'

'Three failures,' Kretschmer said. 'They're getting better.'

Doenitz frowned. He hadn't had an opportunity to go over Kretschmer's war diary of the cruise. He made a brief apology to Weiner and Anders, and took Kretschmer to one side.

'Three failures?'

'Better than the last cruise,' Kretschmer said, 'but they're still not perfect. I lost three ships – one of them a tanker.'

Doenitz muttered an oath. The magnetic torpedo, though a brilliant concept, had been dogged by teething troubles since it had been introduced. So serious had been the failures in the early days that Doenitz once had declared that sailors had never before been sent to war with such a useless weapon. There had even been a court-martialling of the technicians responsible for the torpedo's development. But the German navy's production of a torpedo that didn't sink ships had been balanced by the British production of an anti-submarine bomb that didn't sink submarines, although there were disturbing intelligence reports that the RAF was perfecting an air-borne depth charge.

'At least three failures shows a marked improvement,' Doenitz said, 'but it's still three failures too many.' He paused. 'However, your new second watch officer has recently completed a familiarization course on the G7e warhead at Kiel and knows how to test their depth-keeping chambers before they're fired.'

Kretschmer looked interested. 'What's his name?'

'Sub-Lieutenant Richard Stein. That's him over there.'

Kretschmer's expressionless face studied Stein, who was unaware he was being watched. One of the SS made a joke. All three at the table laughed uproariously. Kretschmer carefully placed his glass down on the buffet and said, 'A small favour, admiral.'

Doenitz looked puzzled. 'Anything, Otto.'

'Find me someone else.'

'Reasons?'

Kretschmer permitted himself a rare ghost of a smile. 'Nothing I could put in writing.'

Stein seemed to sense he was being talked about; he stopped laughing and stared across at the two senior officers.

Doenitz nodded understandingly. '*U700* still isn't back to her full complement. I'll get Kneller to tell Stein in the morning.'

5

It was a cold, blustery, late February day in London as Commander Ian Lancaster Fleming RNVR, one-time journalist and stockbroker and now personal assistant to the Director of Naval Intelligence, studied. the three photographs before him. They were pictures of Germany's three U-boat aces: Otto Kretschmer of *U99*; Gunther Prien of *U47*; and Joachim Schepke of *U100*. He examined the photographs carefully, assimilating every detail of the three faces before him.

Suave, debonair, and frustratingly desk-bound, Fleming had more than a sneaking regard for the three U-boat aces, although he doubted if his regard for these men who were well on their way to sinking one and a half million tons of allied shipping would find much support in the carpeted and carbolic corridors of the admiralty.

The picture of Schepke showed a tall blond man surrounded by an adoring crowd of girls. Kretschmer's unsmiling, sardonic features had been captured by a studio photographer. The picture of the stocky Prien, grinning arrogantly at the camera, had been taken by a CBS News photographer shortly after the U-boat commander's destruction of the British battleship *Royal Oak* at its supposedly safe Scapa Flow anchorage in Scotland.

Fleming read an intelligence report on the three men and sighed: a character in a novel who was a combination of the swashbuckling Schepke, the arrogant Prien, and the ruthless, calculating Kretschmer would make an ideal hero in every respect.

Fleming pushed the photographs to the corner of his

desk and weighted them with a fragment of forged steel. The curved surface of the makeshift paperweight gleamed black and forbidding. He regarded it thoughtfully for a few moments before summoning a stenographer. He dictated rapidly to her for ten minutes.

The words came easily.

Admiral Godfrey, the Director of Naval Intelligence, read Fleming's report before the others because he knew it would be lively and spiced with picturesque phrases, a welcome change from the reams of turgid civil service prose that landed on his desk each day.

He read through the report once for enjoyment (he particularly liked the neat description of the three U-boat aces as 'the blunt instrument of Doenitz's carefully evolved U-boat strategy') and a second time to consider the implications of its conclusions. As was usual with Fleming's schemes, it was outlandish and imaginative but not impractical, although it did venture into the politically sensitive area that involved the neutral United States.

Fleming's closing words were, 'If we mice do manage, by some miracle, to catch ourselves a pussy cat, we ought to invite our cousins over to take a close look at its teeth and claws in exchange for some of their cheese.'

Admiral Godfrey chuckled to himself and scribbled 'agreed' at the foot of the page. He then sat back and read through the report for a third time.

Ian Fleming, he thought to himself, was an extraordinarily entertaining writer.

6

It was the morning after *U700*'s commissioning party.

Stein's face was a mask of unbridled fury as he stood rigidly at attention on the quayside at Lorient. With the other members of *U700*'s crew, he kept his arm and hand at the correct angle for the salute while the army band played the German national anthem. A rain-sodden sheet of music was snatched from a flute player by the biting East wind and wrapped around Stein's trouser leg, yet one more humiliation in a series that had started the previous evening and had culminated with him having to stand beside Anders and Weiner and the other members of *U700*'s crew.

The band finished playing, and Doenitz stepped forward to face *U700*'s officers and men. He cleared his throat and delivered a short, simple speech, expounding his favourite theme of the need for U-boats to press home the attack relentlessly when engaging a convoy.

Stein paid little attention, allowing his gaze to wander to the battle-scarred *U99* lying alongside *U700*. Kretschmer was standing on the veteran U-boat's deck casing in earnest conversation with his first watch officer. Stein wondered what the two men were talking about – probably discussing *U99*'s battle tactics on her next war patrol. His scowl deepened.

Doenitz finished his speech. Weiner stepped forward to accept *U700*'s logbook and pennant from the admiral, thanked him, and stepped back.

The simple ceremony was over; *U700* was now a fully commissioned, frontline U-boat. After the two shakedown cruises necessary to weld her crew into one close-knit fighting team, she would be ready for the bitter war being fought in the Atlantic.

7

Weiner tapped his pointer on the wall chart, described a circle around Iceland, and then turned his stocky frame to face *U700*'s crew. Anders sat in the front row, his long, loose-limbed legs stretched out across the polished floor. Apart from Stein's brooding presence, the atmosphere was relaxed and friendly. Stein was sitting alone at a window, gazing down at *U99*. The seasoned U-boat had been hastily refitted and repainted and now matched *U700* for smartness.

'I can't tell you our exact patrol position,' Weiner said, his rich voice booming in the large room, 'but I can tell you that it will be within range of RAF Coastal Command Catalinas and Hudsons operating from Iceland. Standing orders require four bridge lookouts and a continuous sky periscope watch. Remember, gentlemen – the aircraft is the U-boat's most mortal enemy.'

A band outside started playing the *Kretschmer March*, a piece specially composed by the bandmaster in honour of *U99*'s commander. Weiner noticed that Stein was tapping an immaculately polished shoe in time with the music. Two engine-room petty officers edged nearer the window and glanced down at the scene below. Members of a farewell party were waving to *U99* as it cast off.

'Shall we concentrate on *U700*, gentlemen?' Weiner asked, grinning wolfishly. 'I'm sure *U99* can look after herself.'

There was polite laughter. Weiner smiled and lifted into place a large picture that showed a torpedo exploding against the side of a ship.

'A conventional torpedo warhead detonates when its firing pistol strikes the side of a ship's hull – half the explosive force goes into the air doing no harm, and moreover, the side of the ship where the explosion takes place tells the convoy escort where the U-boat is to be found.'

Weiner lifted another picture into position. 'This, gentlemen, is what a magnetic warhead can do.'

Anders studied the picture with interest. It showed a torpedo exploding directly beneath a ship's keel. Weiner leaned on his pointer.

'You will be pleased to know that *U99* has been using the new version of the magnetic warhead and reports vastly improved reliability. As you can see, the explosive force, instead of going into the air as it does with a conventional warhead, is concentrated wholly on the ship's keel. And with the new Wotan steel used to encase the warhead to double the explosive force, one torpedo is sufficient to break a twenty-thousand tonner's back in two.'

Weiner had the attention of everyone in the room with the exception of Stein. 'Another advantage, gentlemen, is the lack of flash when the torpedo explodes. We know that *U47* was able to escape from Scapa Flow after sinking the *Royal Oak* because the British at first thought there had been an explosion in one of their precious battleship's magazines.

'You will also be pleased to know that *U700* has been supplied with one of the new warheads for her first patrol. By the time we leave for our second patrol, I'm sure there will be ample supplies for all fourteen torpedoes to be fitted with magnetic warheads. And that will enable us to adopt Lieutenant-Commander Kretschmer's favourite axiom.'

Weiner broke off and smiled frostily in Stein's direction. 'We are fortunate in having Sub-Lieutenant Richard Stein with us,' he continued. 'Not only has he completed a familiarization course on the new warhead, but he has also made a close study of *U99*'s battle tactics. Perhaps he would be kind enough to advise us of Lieutenant-Commander Kretschmer's axiom regarding the firing of torpedoes.'

Stein turned from the window and met Weiner's freezing smile with an innocent expression.

'Yes, kaleu?' he inquired politely.

Weiner's smile did not desert him.

'You know which axiom I am referring to?'

'Yes, kaleu.'

Weiner maintained the smile with some effort.

'We would like to hear it please, Mr Stein.'

'From whom, captain?'

Someone at the back of the room giggled.

'From you, lieutenant.'

Stein looked blank. 'When, captain?'

This time no one made a sound. Weiner took a pace toward Stein and stared down into the expressionless eyes. Yes, he thought, you'd like that wouldn't you? You'd like me to lose my temper in front of the entire crew.

'Stand up please, Mr Stein,' he said calmly.

Stein stood and made a minor adjustment to his tie.

'Don't worry about your tie, Mr Stein. As usual, your turnout is an example for us all. Please tell us now in a clear voice what *U99*'s battle tactics are regarding the economic expenditure of torpedoes.'

Stein gave a slow, deliberate smile. 'One ship,' he said, and paused for effect. *'One torpedo.'*

8

'One ship, one torpedo,' said Fleming gloomily. He tossed a file across his desk to Brice. 'Here's another – the *Convallaria* – sunk by one torpedo. And another – the *Beatus* – went down in less than a minute. Fifty ships altogether, and all sunk by one blasted torpedo each.'

Alan Brice read through the survivors' account. He was a careful man from the style of his dress to his unhurried Bostonian speech. As a scientist, one of the United States Navy's top torpedo designers, Brice was a disappointment to Fleming, who preferred his scientists to have characteristics that identified them as such: an eccentric nature, hair standing on end, egg on tie, and maybe a beautiful daughter thrown in for luck. The tall, blond American in his neat suit looked more like a product of Harvard than MIT. But he did have a beautiful daughter – he had shown Fleming her photograph – who was three.

Fleming cleared his throat.

'One thing all those reports have in common, Mr Brice, the survivors of nearly every ship talk about one explosion from *beneath* the ship, not the side. Also convoy escorts are complaining that there's no flash from the explosions to tell them where the U-boat's lurking. If your Newport Torpedo Station wants proof that the Germans have perfected the magnetic warhead idea, there it is.'

Brice returned the reports to Fleming's desk.

'It sure looks that way, commander. But I understand you're still losing ships by the old method – a fan of four contact torpedoes fired at one ship in daylight.'

Fleming smiled. Despite his measured speech, Brice was

no fool. 'We suspect that the new warheads are not yet in full production – that aces such as Kretschmer get priority.'

'The man with the golden horseshoe?'

You have done your homework, Fleming thought. He said, 'Kretschmer specializes in the surface night attack. He's been seen often enough – charging up and down the convoy lines, shooting his torpedoes at point-blank range.' Fleming's tone became morose. 'We think the wretched fellow's forgotten he's driving a submarine.'

'But it still needs one helluva bang for one torpedo to sink a ship – even a torpedo fitted with a magnetic warhead,' Brice said.

Fleming indicated a piece of metal that served as a paperweight. 'That and several other pieces of the same type of steel were found embedded in what was left of the *Royal Oak*'s keel after Prien had finished with her. It's a new type of Krupps Wotan armour with a tensile strength of one hundred tons per square inch. Our boffins – scientists,' Fleming quickly amended, seeing Brice's puzzled expression, 'are laying even money that Jerry's using his new steel to encase the magnetic warheads.'

Brice turned the piece of metal over in his fingers. 'I should say that that's a reasonably safe bet, commander. Is this a preliminary offer in exchange for information on our development work on torpedoes?'

Fleming smiled. He decided that he was going to enjoy dealing with the blond American. 'Consider it a down payment, old boy.'

Brice replaced the metal fragment on Fleming's desk. 'I suspect that my Admiral Swaffer will want something more substantial than this before he agrees to pooling information.'

Suddenly Fleming was serious. 'A general order has been issued which gives the capture of an *intact* German U-boat a number one priority. You tell your Admiral

Swaffer that we might be able to give you the chance of a close look at a Wotan warhead sooner than you think.'

After Brice had gone Fleming picked up the first of two reports that the pretty Wren writer had dropped in his tray. According to an observant Breton agent in Lorient, *U47*, *U100*, and *U99* had sailed that week. For the first time, the three aces – Prien, Schepke, and Kretschmer – were on patrol together.

The second report was more interesting. It confirmed that the new radar device fitted to a destroyer in one of the newly formed escort groups under the command of HMS *Walker* had been tested and found satisfactory. What little Fleming knew about precision radar was enough to convince him that it held the key to the eventual destruction of the U-boats. It was not the clumsy longwave equipment that the Germans had, but radio ranging using very short frequencies that yielded crisp echoes, which could be accurately plotted on a screen.

Fleming opened his private file on the three U-boat aces. Kretschmer's photograph was on top, and he gazed down at the handsome, unsmiling features.

'Soon, you bastard,' Fleming murmured to himself. 'Soon.'

9

At three minutes past midnight on February 26, 1941, U-boat operations room at Lorient received a signal from *U47* commanded by Gunther Prien saying that he had sighted a large convoy heading east.

Doenitz moved from his chair with its commanding view

of the giant plot table of the North Atlantic and beckoned to the operations room duty officer.

Five minutes later a signal was sent to Prien ordering him to shadow the convoy and send frequent reports on its course and speed so that other U-boats could be directed to the convoy for a mass surface attack. It was a technique that had been used with astonishing success against Convoy SC7 the previous October; of the 35 ships that left Nova Scotia, only half survived the U-boats to reach Liverpool. The surface night attack was Doenitz's own concept, based on his experiences as a U-boat commander during the Great War when he had discovered that the low profile of a surfaced U-boat was virtually impossible for the enemy to see no matter what detection equipment he used. Before the war Doenitz had even published a book, in which he had outlined the principles of the future of U-boat warfare. So far, those principles had been proved right; the Royal Navy's prized Asdic submarine detection equipment had proved virtually useless against a surfaced U-boat, and his commanders were learning not to fear it. And even if a U-boat was detected, it was not unknown for the commander to surface contemptuously within sight of an escorting sloop or corvette and use its superior surface speed to make an escape.

Kneller interrupted Doenitz's thoughts. '*U47* has been forced to break off shadowing, admiral.'

Doenitz's thin eyebrows went up. The stocky Prien, one of the few U-boat commanders who was a party member, was not the sort of man to give up; he would cling tenaciously to the convoy until ordered to attack.

'Did he say why?'

'He says that he was driven off by a destroyer that came straight at him,' Kneller replied.

'At night?' Doenitz asked incredulously.

Thirty minutes later Prien re-established contact with

the convoy but was again driven off by a 'destroyer that came straight at me.'

Prien was ordered to regain contact but was driven off for the third time. This time he managed to get the destroyer's number. OKM intelligence identified the warship as HMS *Walker*.

'It's as if the British can see in the dark,' was Kneller's gloomy comment on the night's proceedings.

Doenitz went to bed at 3:00 A.M. Kneller's comment triggered a nagging worry that kept him awake until dawn.

10

U700's first shakedown cruise was turning into a disaster. For the third time that day Bernard Anders jabbed a bony finger on the Klaxon button and screamed, 'Diving stations! Aircraft!' This time he had to bellow at the fumbling gun crew, 'Come on! Move!'

The diesel exhaust vent spewed a sudden cloud of black smoke. The Krupp steel beneath Anders' feet began pounding in harmony with the two MAN diesels as they opened up to full power. The gun crew centred the main gun and raced along the casing to the bridge. Below in the control room, Stein started his stopwatch at the exact moment the sirens started howling. Brinkler was roundly cursing his petty officer coxswain for being a fraction of a second late in spinning the hydroplane wheel. A lookout lost his footing on the ladder and tumbled into the control room. He sat on the floor dazed.

'Out! Out!' Stein screamed. He grabbed the lookout by the scruff of the neck and virtually threw him through the circular door that led aft. A sudden tangle of arms and legs in the control room caused by lookouts not moving out of the way quickly enough could spell disaster for a crash-diving submarine.

U700 tilted down as Anders followed the gun crew down the ladder. The boat was being driven under by the superior power of the diesels; Brinkler would wait until the last second before the hatches closed to switch over to the less powerful electric motors. Water was roaring into the ballast tanks as Anders reached up and slammed the hatch shut and spun the handwheel. He was about to shout down to the control room that the hatch was secure when there was a sudden explosion in his ears. It felt as if his skull had been blown apart. He gave a cry and tumbled through the attack kiosk into the control room. It was some seconds before he could hear the commotion around him – Brinkler was obviously in pain too as he roundly cursed the hydroplane coxswain for being too slow.

'Ears,' Stein mumbled, hanging onto a pipe and moving his hair-cream slicked head from side to side.

Anders climbed shakily to his feet. He forgot his lanky frame and struck his head on a manometer pipe. Weiner had disappeared, but his powerful voice could be heard from aft bellowing angrily. Moments later he propelled his bulk into the control room and looked at Anders and Stein in concern.

'Are you two all right?'

Anders, determined not to show weakness in front of his commanding officer, had come to attention. Stein had done the same and had given Anders the satisfaction of seeing a lock of hair fall out of place.

'Yes, kaleu,' Anders responded promptly.

'Damned diesel machinist didn't shut the engines off in time,' Weiner growled, his eyes fixed on the overhead depth gauge pointers that were edging down to the forty metre mark.

The two fifteen-hundred-horsepower diesels had been allowed to continue running for a fraction of a second after the hatches had been closed with the consequence that virtually all the air in the boat had been sucked into their cylinders.

'Forty metres,' Brinkler called out.

Stein's thumb automatically stopped the clicking stop-watch.

'Well?' Weiner demanded.

Stein pushed the offending lock of hair into place. 'One minute twenty, kaleu.'

Weiner muttered an oath under his breath. Anders could understand how he felt. The time to reach the required forty metres depth had taken twelve seconds more than the last dive.

Weiner leaned against the commander's chart table. 'Know how quickly Kretschmer can take *U99* down, Anders?'

Stein opened his mouth to answer.

'I'm asking Anders,' Weiner said curtly.

Stein closed his mouth and smiled sourly at Anders.

Suddenly the figure Anders knew by heart wasn't there.

'Well?' Weiner prompted.

'I'm sorry, kaleu,' Anders said, desperately searching his memory.

'Stein?'

'Thirty seconds,' Stein said smugly.

Weiner nodded. 'Thirty seconds,' he repeated sadly. 'And *U700* won't be allowed on patrol until she can get into the cellar in less than sixty seconds on ten successive dives. Did you know that, Anders?'

Anders shook his head. 'No, kaleu.' He avoided his commanding officer's eyes. He felt that he had failed Weiner – that *U700*'s poor performance was entirely his fault.

Weiner said nothing, sensing that Anders was assuming

responsibility for the U-boat's appalling showing. He was tempted to reassure Anders but decided against it. Goddamn it, he was Anders' commanding officer – not his father. If Anders felt he was to blame, that was his problem.

'Let's try again,' Weiner growled. 'Stand by to surface.' He swung up the ladder into the attack kiosk and sat at the periscope. As he watched the strengthening green light from the sun filtering down from the surface, he knew that his greatest problem was going to be Anders' lack of confidence and Stein's overconfidence.

He wondered how long it would be before *U700* would be ready for sea and whether there would be any enemy ships left for his U-boat when it was ready.

Kretschmer, Schepke, and Prien had already sunk well over a million tons between them.

11

On March 10, the British got their revenge on Prien for the *Royal Oak* and the 786 officers and men who perished with it.

Doenitz sat in his chair in the Lorient U-boat operations room for twelve hours, gazing down at U47's marker on a giant plot table. Waiting.

The cipher clerk set her machine to 'transmit' and tapped out for the tenth time that hour, '*DBU to U47. Report your position.*'

She set her machine to 'receive' and sat back. The keyboard remained silent.

Kneller set a cup of coffee down before his admiral but Doenitz allowed it to get cold. He found it impossible to believe that the British had finally caught up with the bumptious but cunning Nazi. Although Prien was probably the most heartily disliked commander in the U-boat arm, he was nevertheless a courageous officer and would be sorely missed.

There was worse to come, for during that March of 1941 the British escort group headed by HMS *Walker* had put to sea. They were the first submarine hunter-killer group to be equipped with what was later to prove the most decisive weapon in the struggle that Winston Churchill termed 'The Battle of the Atlantic'.

That weapon was radar.

12

March 17, St Patrick's Day, was ten minutes old when Patrick Gallagher left Toomley's pub through the open saloon window because it looked as if the fight was going to get out of hand. After the British, violence was Gallagher's biggest hate and the opening rumbles of a dispute, especially disputes in pubs, were the signal for him to head for the horizon. Ever since he had seen as a boy the despised Black and Tans at work in Dublin during the Troubles, violence of any kind had revolted him. His many friends and fellow telegraphers who manned the Valentia Bay trans-Atlantic cable station mistakenly considered Gallagher a coward. Rather than have to prove them wrong, Gallagher found it easier to agree with them cheerfully.

A cold wind was blowing in from the Atlantic across the bay. He pulled his collar up, crossed the road, and stood for some moments, drawing on a cigarette and listening to the sea fretting at the rocks. It would be a good night for a spot of sea fishing. There was a big conger eel he was after.

The sound of breaking glass from the bar broke in on his thoughts. A door burst open, spilling light and foul language into the night. It would be only a matter of time before the police arrived. Gallagher walked to his motorcycle. The machine and fishing were the only loves in his lonely life. He looked at the bike with pride. It was a magnificent flat-twin Douglas with an Ulster registration. As usual, the finely turned machine started on the first kick. A truck loaded to the roof with police screeched to a standstill outside the pub just as he was easing the machine on to the road. He was a hundred yards away and accelerating hard by the time the uniformed lads were making their first 1941 St Patrick's Day arrests. The icy wind wrenched his amiable features into a tight grimace.

Only when he was a comfortable mile from Toomley's pub did he ease up to the throttle. He was paid to stay out of trouble. And with the exchange rate of the German mark against the pound being what it was, he was paid very well indeed. He began humming a tune that he had learned from his German friends during his motorcycle fishing trips to the Black Forest in the late 1930s. He couldn't remember the original German words but the translated lyric was pleasant enough: *We're marching to war against England!*

13

While Patrick Gallagher was riding home, some 500 miles out in the Atlantic, Commander Joachim Schepke of *U100* and second to Kretschmer in the tonnage sunk league was dying a particularly unpleasant death. His U-boat had just been rammed by a destroyer that had come straight at him from out of the darkness as if the British, by some uncanny instinct, knew exactly where to find him. Schepke had stared in fascination at the destroyer's shuddering bow as it drove toward him like a charging cliff. He was confident that *U100* hadn't been seen, that the warship was racing to the aid of a glowing tanker on the horizon that Kretschmer had torpedoed half an hour previously. For a moment it had seemed that the destroyer would miss the stern of *U100* by centimetres. But at the last moment the monstrous bow made a sudden change of direction. The warning Schepke had been about to scream down the bridge voice pipe died on his lips. He stared aghast at the pounding, 30,000 horsepower apparition that was thundering straight at him behind a huge curtain of spray. He was unable to shout – unable to make the slightest move to save his life. There was a scream of metal on metal as the knife-edge bow sliced into the bridge coaming. Schepke was hurled against the torpedo aimer and felt a strange numbness in his legs. He lashed out in panic and grabbed hold of the attack periscope. There was a curious lightness in his body as he fought to prevent himself from going under, dimly aware of the destroyer's towering, flat-sided hull racing past. Something at the back of his reeling mind warned him about the danger from the warship's churning propellers. He clung desperately to the periscope standard that was now lying almost flat on the surface, or whatever it was he could judge was the surface in that seething maelstrom. It was when he tried to fend his body away from the British warship's rust-streaked side with his feet that he realized why it was that his body felt so light. His legs had been severed from his torso; there was nothing left to his body from the waist down.

U100 was sinking beneath him, dragging him down.

All he had to do was release his grip on the periscope standard and his oddly truncated body would bob to the surface.

But suddenly there didn't seem to be much point in letting go.

Kretschmer was unaware of Schepke's fate. He had expended all his torpedoes and sunk a total of five ships during the night's action. The remains of three targets were burning brightly in the distance. They had been a U-boat commander's most prized victims: tankers.

There was now nothing to do but set a course for Lorient, hand over to his first watch officer, and dine on coffee and sandwiches.

But the radar-equipped destroyer in HMS *Walker*'s hunter-killer escort group had detected *U99*'s presence on surface and was closing in fast on the unsuspecting U-boat.

14

At the exact moment that the pulverized remains of Kretschmer's *U99* sank for the last time, a light drizzle began to fall on Lorient, splattering against the blackout windows of the U-boat operations room.

Doenitz was sitting in his usual chair beside Kneller, saying nothing. Weiner, Anders, and Stein were in the gallery overlooking the giant map of the North Atlantic. *U700* had completed its shakedown cruise and had returned to Lorient. Doenitz liked his officers to familiarize themselves with the behind-the-scenes procedures, and the three men were sitting very still, leaning forward to catch the whispered exchanges between the controller and Doenitz.

A girl added the name of the *J B White* to the wall-mounted blackboard. It was the last ship to have been claimed as sunk that night. Her chalk squeaked noisily in the hushed room. An assistant flipped through Lloyd's and called out the *J B White*'s tonnage.

The cipher clerk stared down at the printing head of her silent machine. She had spent the last hour broadcasting repeated requests to *U99* and *U100* to report their positions. Each time, the reply from the Atlantic had been silence.

Anders touched Stein's sleeve and whispered, 'Maybe they've dived and can't use their radio.'

Stein shook his immaculate head. 'Kretschmer would never dive during an action. Nor would Schepke. You've read their standing orders to their crews: "Always remain on surface unless in dire peril."'

Anders fell silent. What Stein said made sense; a U-boat was essentially a craft designed to spend most of its time on the surface with the ability to dive to initiate a daylight attack or escape an air attack. Many U-boats were now returning from patrol without having dived once; a submerged U-boat under attack was a helpless U-boat, wholly dependent on the evasion skills of its captain.

The sudden click of the cipher machine interrupted Anders' thoughts. It was a noise he had come to recognize as the mechanical equivalent of a clearing of the throat. The cipher clerk and everyone else in the room looked expectantly at the machine. Its printing head rattled briefly across the paper and stopped. The girl tore the flimsy off the roll and passed it to an assistant who in turn handed it to the controller. He read it and looked across at Doenitz's sharp, inquiring features.

'It's from *U37*, admiral. She reports having broken off

the attack and has been unable to contact *U99* and *U100*.'

Anders met Weiner's eye and guessed what the admiral was thinking: first Prien a few days ago and now Schepke and Kretschmer in one night. It just didn't seem possible. And if the enemy could sweep such U-boats from the board, what of *U700* and her inexperienced crew?

Two long cues reached across the plot table and moved the markers for *U99* and *U100* to the 'overdue reporting' square at the edge of the plot. If nothing was heard from the U-boats for seventy-two hours the markers would be removed and Admiral Doenitz would have the task of signing letters to relatives that began: 'It is with deepest regret that I have to inform you . . .'

As Anders stared down at the giant map, it occurred to him that the plot table resembled a grotesque board game, a game with no rules, a game with an occasional victor – but many, many losers.

Stein remained seated as Weiner and Anders stood. He was gazing fixedly at the marker for *U99*. Anders touched his shoulder gently.

'It's late. We've got gunnery practice tomorrow.'

Stein nodded and rose to his feet. He gave one last look at the marker with its tiny, inverted golden horseshoe and then, by curious coincidence, said virtually the same thing as a British seaman on HMS *Walker* had said that night as *U99*, bathed in the beam of the destroyer's searchlight, had disappeared from view:

'His horseshoes were upside down. His luck was bound to run out.'

15

The sun was shining in London the next day, and Commander Ian Fleming was in a buoyant mood as he and Brice lunched at Scott's.

'I smell good news,' Brice said when the waiter had departed with their order.

'The best news ever,' Fleming said cheerfully. 'We sank two U-boats last night. And not just any old U-boats, but *U99* and *U100*. What do you think of that?'

'A capture would be good news,' Brice said pointedly.

Fleming looked crestfallen. 'I thought you'd be happy for us, Mr Brice. With Prien blown to glory a few days ago, that means our friends have lost their three aces in under a week. It ought to knock a hole in their morale that you could drive a bus through.'

'How did it happen?'

'Schepke's boat was rammed, and Kretschmer was forced to the surface. Unfortunately there was time for a member of his crew to set the scuttling charges. They blew the bottom out of *U99* and it went down like a brick.'

Brice smiled faintly. 'A pity, commander.'

'Please, old boy, call me Ian. *Walker*'s skipper had a boat lowered in the hope of getting a boarding party on to the U-boat, but it was too late. There was similar business in 1939 after *U39* loosed off a couple of torpedoes at the *Ark Royal*. Jerry would sooner scuttle before all the crew are safe than allow a ship to fall into enemy hands. They scuttled their entire grand fleet after the last war in accordance with their rigid tradition of never allowing the enemy to set foot on their warships.'

'Which is not going to make capturing an intact U-boat a . . .' Brice groped for an English expression, '. . . a cup of tea. Right, Ian?'

Fleming smiled. 'We live in hope, old boy.'

'In the meantime, I have to live nearly four thousand miles from my family.'

'You're not getting bored with London are you?' Fleming asked, looking mildly shocked.

'Frankly, yes. And don't go quoting Samuel Johnson at me.'

The waiter returned with their soup. Fleming tasted it cautiously and murmured when the waiter had gone, 'At least they're trying. How about a nice young lady to show you the sights? There's a suitable one in my address book.'

'I'll have you know that I'm a happily married man,' Brice said indignantly.

'You needn't worry about Clare,' Fleming said drily. 'She's a very proper young woman. I've never got anywhere with her, and I'm available.'

Brice laughed at Fleming's dead-pan expression.

16

Seven weeks later, on May 9, 1941, the British succeeded in capturing *U110*, commanded by Fritz Lemp, the man who, on the first day of the war, had mistaken the liner *Athenia* for a troopship and had torpedoed it in violation of the then prevailing Prize Ordinance Regulations.

The circumstances of the capture were kept a secret because the British didn't want to alert the Germans to the fact that they were intent on capturing a U-boat. Lemp's periscope had been spotted shortly after he had carried out a conventional submerged daylight attack against the lead ship in a westward bound convoy. Trapped in the escorts' Asdic beams and repeatedly pounded by accurate depth charge patterns, Lemp was forced to blow his tanks and surface.

HMS *Bulldog* was about to ram when the officer commanding the escort group decided that it might be worth trying to implement the admiralty order that urged the capture of an intact U-boat 'if humanly possible'. A boarding party from *Bulldog* succeeded in recovering a good deal of material from the U-boat including an Enigma cipher machine. But the boat was leaking badly, and they were unable to remove the one remaining magnetic torpedo. An attempt was made to tow the U-boat to Iceland, but the *Bulldog* was forced to slip the tow as the U-boat sank deeper in the water. That afternoon, watched by the disappointed boarding party now safely back on the *Bulldog, U110* rolled over and sank.

Fleming read Captain Baker-Cresswell's report on May 25 and decided that there was nothing to be gained in telling Brice about the failure.

A pity Lemp had drowned – it would have been interesting to find out exactly why he thought that the *Athenia* had been a troopship.

Fleming initialled the report and tossed it in his out tray. At least it was one U-boat less.

17

On August 23, 1941, after 18 weeks of intensive training, *U700* went to war.

Weiner's booming voice gave the order to cast off from

Pier Three at precisely twelve noon. He experienced a sensation of foreboding as he stared down from the bridge at the two lines of smartly turned-out men standing on the casing to take the salute.

Men? Dear God, they were little more than boys; nourished, loved and cared for by their parents for nineteen years each, for that was their average age. They had their entire lives to look forward to, and yet here they were riding an iron coffin as *wabo*, or 'depth charge fodder', for an Austrian corporal who cared as much for U-boatmen as he did for their type of warfare, which was little enough.

Weiner watched Anders out of the corner of his eye. The lean, awkward frame of the young officer was bent over the voice pipe issuing orders to the motor room. At least he no longer sought Weiner's confirmation of every course alteration. Three successful patrols by *U700* ought to see Anders with his own command.

A pretty girl detached herself from the small farewell crowd gathered on the quayside and trotted along the wharf to keep pace with the grey U-boat, waving to the impassive crew. Weiner recognized her as the HQ typist who had married boatsman's mate Bruch the week before. Bruch was standing near the main gun, staring straight ahead, feet the regulation distance apart, hands clasped firmly behind his back.

Wave to her, you idiot! Weiner willed. But the long weeks of training had left their mark – Bruch gave no sign that he had seen his bride. The girl stopped and lifted a handkerchief to her eyes as she stared after the departing U-boat.

It was the image of that lonely girl that hardened Weiner's resolve: he would bring *all* his crew back safely at the end of each patrol. He would sink enemy ships by tackling every one that presented itself as a likely target, but he'd make damn certain that the odds were a hundred and ten per cent in his favour first. He'd probably end up sinking more ships than the so-called aces and survive into the bargain. The decision helped to ease the recurring nightmare that had plagued him ever since *U700*'s accident on her trials.

He inhaled deeply. It was a beautiful summer's day. The shrill voices of the Breton fishwives cleaning the morning's catch carried clearly across the Scorff estuary. Anders was allowing the current to swing the U-boat's bows toward the sea. Weiner knew how much Anders enjoyed handling the boat and decided to leave him alone.

'Anders.'

'Yes, kaleu?'

'Take over, please. Dismiss the deck party and call me when the Isle de Groix is on our quarter.'

Anders saluted smartly and ordered the crew below.

'And Anders.'

'Yes, kaleu?'

Weiner pointed a stubby finger at the U-boat's bow. 'That jumping wire was damaged when the torpedoes were struck down. Have it repaired at the first opportunity.'

'I had noticed it, kaleu. One of the boatsman's mates is good at splicing wire. I've told him to carry out repairs on his next watch.'

Weiner gave a satisfied grunt and swung down the ladder leaving Anders alone on the bridge.

Anders opened the watertight box that contained the portable signal lamp and exchanged recognition signals with the minesweeper that was to escort *U700* clear of the estuary. He returned the lamp to its box and flipped open the voice pipe cover.

'Bridge – control room.'

'Control room,' Brinkler's voice answered.

'Bridge lookout party on the double, please.'

Anders then ordered a changeover from the electric

motors to the diesels before closing the voice pipe cover. The four lookouts emerged from the control room and took their positions while Anders hunched over the spray deflector and watched the white water surging past *U700*'s bulging saddle tanks. He felt confident of his ability to handle anything.

Twenty minutes later *U700* was clear of the French fishing harbour and was lifting its raked bow to the long, easy swell of the Atlantic Ocean.

18

Even as Anders yelled 'Aircraft!' and started the siren, Brinkler was flooding the tanks and roaring at his coxswain to spin the hydroplanes down for the fastest crash dive in *U700*'s short history.

One of the lookouts, who by now knew about Brinkler's dives, dropped Anders' binoculars, entangling the strap around the bridge hatch.

'It doesn't matter!' Anders shouted. He yanked the binoculars free and tossed them over the side. The forward deck casing was already awash and a huge wake was creaming past the main gun. Another ten seconds and tons of green Atlantic would be cascading down the U-boat's open hatch.

'For God's sake *move!*' Anders yelled at the last lookout who was half way through the hatch, groping for the ladder with his feet.

The amphibious biplane was less than two kilometres away, but the danger it represented was nothing compared with the danger of Brinkler taking *U700* down with the bridge hatch open. Cursing more in anger than fear,

Anders crashed his boot on the lookout's shoulder and shoved. Then he scrambled down after him and managed to slam the hatch shut just as the bridge was flooded, but too late to avoid being drenched by several litres of icy seawater.

Weiner was trying not to smile as Anders' undignified tangle of arms and legs tumbled angrily into the control room.

'What was it?' he inquired politely.

Anders' pale features were even paler as he climbed to his feet. 'Chief!' he snapped at Brinkler who was levelling out the boat at sixty metres. 'In future you will await confirmation that the hatches are closed and clipped before diving! Is that understood?'

Both Brinkler and Weiner were surprised at Anders' outburst.

You're learning, thought Weiner. There was nothing like a bad fright to put a man on his mettle.

'What was the time taken to get down?' Weiner asked.

'Twenty-nine seconds,' Brinkler answered, keeping his eyes firmly on his gauges.

Weiner nodded his bullet-like head. 'Pretty good, eh, Mr Anders?'

'Yes, kaleu. But the chief . . .'

Brinkler turned in his seat and adopted an injured expression. 'Mr Anders sounded the alarm and yelled "aircraft". From the way he yelled, I thought an entire squadron of Spitfires were on our tail. I decided not to waste time. I naturally thought that the bridge lookout wouldn't waste time either.'

'I'll enter it in the control room log,' said Anders, his face still white with anger.

'Enter the sighting,' Weiner suggested, smiling at the two antagonists. 'And that you dived in twenty-nine seconds.'

Annoyed at Weiner's refusal to discipline Brinkler, Anders turned on his commanding officer. 'There were four lookouts on the bridge plus myself, kaleu. We're not genies that can turn into a puff of smoke and vanish down the hatch whenever the chief decides to take the boat down like an elevator.'

'Let's discuss this in the wardroom,' Weiner said, moving aft. Anders and Brinkler followed him through the watertight door.

'Now then,' Weiner said, dropping onto the settee-berth. 'As far as I'm concerned you're both in the wrong for arguing in front of the crew.'

'*I* was not arguing with the chief,' Anders protested. 'The chief was arguing with me. He failed . . .'

Weiner held up a cautionary hand. 'He failed to do what, Mr Anders? He got the boat down in less than thirty seconds – the minimum possible time. So if anything, you were late in getting the hatch shut.'

Anders opened his mouth, but Weiner cut him short and turned to Brinkler. 'In future, chief, you will wait until you receive confirmation that the hatches are shut and clipped before taking the boat down.' Weiner regarded his first officer steadily. 'And you, Mr Anders, will train your lookouts to move faster. Now that's settled, and we're away from the weather. I trust you gentlemen will join me in a brandy after your watch.'

19

'What do you think you're doing in here, Helmann?' Anders demanded irritably.

The torpedoman, a nervous 19-year-old, hesitated, one

leg through the watertight door that led into the control room. His eyes were round and worried.

'Well?' Anders snapped.

Helmann mumbled an apology and withdrew, moving back to the safety of the bow torpedo room. He paused on the companionway outside the second officer's berth. Sub-Lieutenant Stein had rigged up a blanket as a curtain and Helmann could see the glow of a reading lamp through the thin material. Helmann was undecided. To him, petty officers were tyrants, and officers were worse. Suddenly the curtain whipped back.

'Yes?'

The low reading light caught Stein's sabre scar at a frightening angle. The youngster would have turned and fled, but Stein caught hold of his arm.

'Helmann isn't it? What's the matter?'

Helmann swallowed and tried to back away. 'Nothing, Mr Stein,' he stammered.

'Then why were you standing there like that? Planning something were you?'

Helmann bit his lower lip. 'It's Bruch, Mr Stein. I can't find him.'

Stein remembered that Helmann had been the best man at Bruch's wedding a few days before *U700* had sailed.

'Have you checked aft? If he's off watch he might be with those chess maniacs in the motor room.'

'I don't like to go through the control room,' Helmann said feebly.

Stein put his book down and swung his legs off his bunk. 'Have you checked Tube Six?'

'No, Mr Stein.'

'Wait here,' Stein said and walked toward the control room.

Anders ignored Stein as the second officer passed through.

A grim-faced Stein was back five minutes later. 'Is the captain asleep?'

Anders looked up from his clipboard. 'I don't think so. Why?'

Stein stepped through the watertight door and stopped outside Weiner's berth. 'I'm sorry to disturb you, kaleu,' he said loudly, 'but we have a man missing. Boatsman's Mate Bruch.'

Weiner's huge hand jerked back the green curtain. '*What?*' Alarm and disbelief spread across his usually good-humoured features. He leapt from his berth and dived into the control room where Anders was standing, white-faced, clutching his clipboard. Weiner's hand shook as he pulled the crew address microphone to his lips.

'Boatsman's Mate Bruch to report to the control room immediately. Boatsman's Mate Bruch to the control room at once.'

Weiner dropped the microphone and snapped his fingers for Anders' clipboard as Helmann appeared at the circular door. He seemed to have overcome his fear of officers for he said haltingly, 'He was good at splicing cables. He liked doing it, and he had been given the job of repairing the jumping wire. It had frayed by the first sheave, he said. A nice little job . . . Out in the open air . . . That's what he said . . .' Helmann's voice trailed off.

Silence in the control room. Weiner, his face haggard, took the clipboard from Anders' lifeless fingers and leafed through the documents, trying to read them with eyes that wanted to fill with tears as he thought of the girl running along the wharf, waving.

Anders managed to say, 'He was working on the forward casing.'

Weiner shook his head as if the nightmare would go away. 'Just before the crash dive?'

Anders nodded silently.

Brinkler turned from his dials and gauges. 'I'm sorry, kaleu. It was my fault. If I hadn't dived so quickly . . .'

'It wasn't your fault,' Stein said, brushing an invisible hair into place. 'Your job is to take the boat down quickly when the alarm sounds. The last man on the bridge should con the boat before closing the hatch.' Stein's cold eyes, staring hard at Anders, never wavered.

'I didn't ask for your opinion, Stein,' Weiner growled.

Stein turned. 'It's not an opinion, kaleu. I was quoting standing orders.'

Weiner's eyes glittered dangerously, but Anders spoke first.

'Do we turn back, kaleu? He might still be on the surface.'

'After six hours?' Stein asked sarcastically. 'I don't suppose he was wearing a life jacket?'

Weiner wheeled around to face Stein squarely. 'You're off watch, Mr Stein. Don't you need every minute of your free time to press your uniform?'

The insult drained the colour from Stein's face. He saluted Weiner stiffly and left the control room without speaking. Weiner looked at Anders. The younger officer had crumpled onto the chart stool and was staring at the floor, reminding Weiner of an abandoned marionette whose strings had been cut.

'Was he wearing his Drager?' Weiner asked, his voice soft.

Anders shook his head slowly.

'You know my regulations concerning men working on the deck casing,' Weiner snapped. 'Dragers *must* be worn at all times!'

There was another silence.

'Well,' Weiner said at length. 'It's for Flotilla HQ to decide whether or not we turn back.'

* * *

Weiner's request to be allowed to return and search the area where Bruch had been lost was refused by Lorient. If possible a minesweeper would be sent to the position, but *U700* was to continue to her patrol position south of Iceland.

That night *U700* lay stopped on the surface.

Anders, Stein, and the off-watch crew stood bare-headed while Weiner slowly recited a brief memorial service. The flowers scattered on the black, uncaring sea were made from tissue paper that had been dyed with coloured ink.

For Anders, that night marked the first of the many sleepless nights he would have to endure for the rest of his life.

20

By August 27, five days after she had left Lorient, *U700* neared her patrol position south of Iceland. The weather had been appalling for three days – days that with the steadily lengthening hours of daylight seemed to merge into a sustained hell of unremitting misery for every member of the crew.

Anders crawled into his bunk after four agonizing hours on watch, which he had spent lashed to the bridge with safety chains. There had been times during that watch when he thought it would be the easiest thing in the world to slip the quick-release catches and let the enraged seas take over his body and do what it liked with it.

His bunk was drenched with the condensation that ran down the bulkheads and was soaked up by his mattress like blotting paper. All his clothes were saturated with a foul-smelling mixture of urine, sweat, vomit, and condensation. He tried to sleep, but every time he closed his eyes his imagination painted a vivid picture of Boatsman's Mate Bruch clinging in panic and despair to the jumping wire as the boiling water rose higher and higher around his chest.

A violent roll heaved his limp body against the sodden bulkhead and sent his stomach surging into his throat. Just turn over and be sick, he thought. It wasn't worth the effort of trying to get up. But he turned the other way, taking care to keep his head on the same place on the pillow so that he wouldn't lose the carefully nurtured patch of wet warmth. At least he had his own bunk; not like the poor bastards forward and aft who had only one bunk between two men so that a man coming off watch had to crawl into the vomit-soaked blankets of the man going on watch. He tried to adjust the bunk's safety strap but his fingers wouldn't work as he wanted them to. He realized he was drifting off to sleep. He didn't want to sleep.

Sleep was where Bruch was waiting for him, crawling up the jumping wire from the swirling foam and reaching out with long, clutching fingers.

21

As exhaustion and seasickness dragged Anders into a fitful, nightmare-plagued sleep, 150 miles to the north at RAF Kaldadarnes in Iceland, Squadron Leader James Thompson of 269 Coastal Command squadron revved up the motors on his twin-engine Lockheed Hudson and taxied through the driving rain to the end of the desolate, levelled stretch of rock and lava that was jokingly referred to as an airstrip.

Slung against the Hudson's fuselage were a cluster of

the new air-borne depth charges that had replaced the 500 pound anti-submarine bomb – that unique weapon that was unable to sink submarines unless it was dropped down an open hatch. The only other armament the Hudson carried were nose and turret Browning 303 machine guns. The Hudson was a reasonably well-armed aircraft provided whatever it shot at didn't shoot back.

Five minutes later the twin-engined machine was airborne and heading south under a sullen cloud base on what Thompson and his three-man crew imagined would be one more protracted and infinitely boring anti-submarine patrol in an equally boring war.

22

While Thompson was levelling off at 300 feet over the North Atlantic, Alan Brice in London was fast running out of patience. He had been six months in England; six months of shortages of just about every commodity imaginable, six months of having to spend virtually every night in the hotel bomb shelter while Goering's Luftwaffe droned overhead. His work at Newport was falling steadily behind. And he very much missed his wife and daughter. The chances of the British capturing a U-boat now seemed very remote, and he felt that he would be achieving more if he spent his time working on the problems of the magnetic torpedo back at the research station in Rhode Island.

He was about to leave his hotel room to send a cable to his boss, Admiral Swaffer, when there was a gentle tap at his door. It was another of Fleming's seemingly inexhaustible supply of attractive, but very proper, Wren drivers determined to show him the sandbagged sights of London.

This particular one had been given the task of taking him to Hampton Court.

'All the paintings have been moved somewhere safe,' she explained. 'But it's still well worth a visit. They're opening it specially for you.'

Brice sighed. The British were determined to keep him in England.

23

The nightmare of being awake was only slightly more tolerable than the nightmare of being asleep.

Anders opened his eyes and tried to focus them on the reading lamp. The only bodily motion he was aware of was the pressure of the safety strap as *U700* rolled. He heard the sound of breaking china from the galley and was surprised that there was anything left aboard the U-boat to break.

He closed his eyes for a moment and tried to divorce his body from the U-boat's gut-churning motion. Then he looked blearily at his watch. In fifteen minutes he would be relieving Stein in the control room. He released the strap and forced his aching limbs to move. The effort of sitting up exhausted him, and the movement of his body inside his clothes reminded him how wet and cold he was. The indescribable stench in the U-boat hit him like a blow in the solar plexus. He opened a locker and groped for some dry clothing, but everything his hand encountered was saturated. He pulled out a sweater with the vague idea of wrapping it around an exhaust pipe in the engine to dry out. The sleeve disintegrated in his hands. The garment was rotten – covered with the same fungus that the cook complained grew on a loaf of bread within a few hours of the can being opened.

He stood unsteadily in the companionway and nearly lost his balance when his foot skidded where someone had vomited. Clinging to the wardroom curtain, he offered a fervent prayer to be conveyed quickly to hell or to anywhere in the universe that wasn't the interior of a U-boat.

As expected, Stein was immaculate – even at the end of his watch. His sweater was spotless, and his hair neatly brushed. He smiled warmly at the dishevelled apparition that shuffled into the control room like a reluctant ghost.

'Good morning, Anders,' came the bright greeting. 'You're a few minutes early.'

U700 suddenly heeled. Anders grabbed a pipe, but Stein merely reached out a languid hand and gripped a safety strap. He watched Anders with a self-assured expression. 'Everything's in order. No news about Bruch.' It was the subject he always mentioned when Anders went on watch.

The next roll sent Anders staggering through the circular door to avoid the shame of being sick on the control room floor.

Thirty minutes after Anders had relieved Stein, Weiner appeared in the control room, red-eyed and unshaven. His appearance restored some of Anders' self-confidence, for he looked as if he had suffered worse than most.

'We're going to have to dive until the weather clears,' Weiner said thickly.

'We'll be late reaching our patrol position,' Anders tactfully reminded the older man.

'I've just paid a visit to the bow torpedo room. Thirty minutes into the watch, and they're all too ill to know what they're doing. I'd rather be late with a fit crew than on time with a boat manned by sick men.'

* * *

It was pleasant at 50 metres.

The U-boat seemed to be motionless as Brinkler eased it along at two knots, a speed that made depth-keeping easy for the hydroplane operators without putting an undue load on the batteries.

It was two hours since *U700* had dived out of reach of the weather. Her interior had been cleaned and disinfected, and there was a smell of coffee from the galley. Anders felt human again and, above all, warm. Weiner had loaned him a dry sweater that he kept in an airtight biscuit tin; a sensible idea that Anders resolved to copy on his next patrol.

Weiner was sitting on a stool at the chart table. 'Feeling better?' he asked.

'I'm beginning to think I might survive, kaleu.'

Weiner laughed and glanced at the chronometer. 'We'll come down again if it's no better – I promise.'

Chuckling to himself, Weiner heaved himself up the ladder into the small attack kiosk in the conning tower while Anders gave orders to take the boat up to periscope depth. Weiner perched on the swivel saddle and placed his eyes against the periscope visor. There was nothing to see but blackness, which would gradually change to pea-green and then light green as *U700* neared the surface. Then there would be a champagne swirl of sparkling bubbles, followed by the shock of seeing waves as the periscope head broke the surface. It was a phenomenon that Weiner knew he would never tire of seeing.

As soon as the periscope was clear of the surface, he would quickly scan through 360 degrees in case there were ships near enough to spot a periscope. If there were none, he would carefully search the horizon for distant ships that might be able to see a U-boat blowing its tanks and surfacing. While this was going on, the petty officer on the hydrophones would carefully listen for the beat of ships' propellers, and Anders would search for aircraft on the sky periscope. Only when all three men were satisfied that all was clear would Weiner call down the order: 'Standby to surface!' That was the theory.

Squadron Leader Thompson suppressed a yawn. Three hundred feet below was the unending monotony of the grey, windswept North Atlantic – a continuous blur of bleak, uninspiring nothingness. They hadn't even seen a sea-bird. Just water, water, and more water. His navigator, sitting frozen in the tail, drew a line across his chart and calculated the distance the Hudson had flown since his last fix. Thompson's gunner was sitting disconsolately in his turret nursing a cold Thermos flask and thinking about nothing in particular. The flight-sergeant was below, trying to find some music on his two radio sets. None of the men had said much since they had taken off from Iceland. Being in RAF Coastal Command, the Cinderella service, they had long since resigned themselves to fighting a forgotten war.

'Twenty metres,' Brinkler called.

There was a slight roll, the first indication apart from the depth gauges that *U700* was nearing the surface. Anders tightened his grip on the sky periscope when he sensed Stein was standing behind him.

'I thought you were off watch, Stein.'

'I heard you were surfacing. I could do with a breath of fresh air.'

It was a simple enough statement, yet Stein managed to make it sound like an insult. Anders was about to reply, but Stein was climbing the ladder to join Weiner in the conning tower.

'Fifteen metres,' Brinkler said. He was taking the U-boat up carefully. It was his job to make sure the bows didn't break the surface before the hydroplane operator trimmed off to run at periscope depth.

Anders noticed the first glimmer of green, diffused daylight through his periscope.

'Ten metres,' Brinkler said.

The radio operator pulled his headphones on and arranged his papers. He had several messages to transmit to Lorient as soon as the antenna was out of the water.

'No hydrophone effects,' the hydrophone operator droned.

Like Anders, Weiner could see green daylight and was bracing himself to rotate the attack periscope the instant it broke the surface.

'Five metres,' Brinkler intoned.

Both periscope heads burst into daylight at the same time. Weiner's first sweep revealed nothing. Anders quickly checked the grey, depressing bowl of sky and saw nothing but low, scudding cloud. He was about to start the slow, meticulous sweep when the radio operator suddenly let out a loud exclamation.

'It's Bruch!' he shouted excitedly. 'He's okay! That British seaplane picked him up! He's a prisoner-of-war but he's okay!'

Anders took his eyes away from the sky periscope and stared at the radio operator in disbelief.

'Bloody hell!' Thompson yelled. He hauled back on the control column, opened the throttles wide, and yanked the Hudson up into the cloud. The navigator bobbed up beside him.

'What's up, skipper?'

'Something down there,' Thompson said laconically. 'A long way off, but it was something that shouldn't be there.'

* * *

Anders returned his eyes to the periscope and completed his slow sweep of the sky. He cursed the U-boat's rolling, which made it difficult to obtain a steady image.

'Sky clear, kaleu,' he called up to Weiner.

Stein had to press himself against the side of the attack kiosk as Weiner swung around with the attack periscope.

The sea was empty. 'All clear, chief,' Weiner called down to Brinkler. 'Surface!'

There was a hiss of compressed air blasting into *U700*'s ballast tanks, flushing out the water and making the U-boat buoyant. Stein reached up to the hatch, ready to spin the handwheel as soon as the roar of water draining off the bridge stopped.

'Jesus bloody Christ,' Thompson's navigator breathed.

Thompson had dived out of the cloudbase. Two miles away the impossible was happening: a U-boat was blowing its tanks and surfacing as if it owned the entire bloody ocean.

And it was dead ahead.

Confident that Anders would sound the alarms if anything appeared, Weiner climbed through the hatch and on to the bridge followed by Stein.

'He's ours!' the flight-sergeant shouted ecstatically. 'He's ours, skipper. By Christ, we've got the bastard cold.'

Thompson's hand was already gripping the depth charge release control. 'Please, God,' he whispered, 'don't let him see me.'

The U-boat was 500 yards away. Two men had appeared on the bridge.

Weiner was about to lift the binoculars to his eyes when he heard the sound of the Hudson's Pratt and Whitney engines. Stein heard them at the same time. Both men spun around and gazed numb with horror at the aircraft that was charging straight at them at a height of less than 300 feet. It was so close that Weiner could see someone in the turret sitting behind the twin machine-guns.

'Down!' Weiner screamed giving Stein a kick that sent him staggering against the torpedo aimer.

Four objects detached themselves from the side of the Hudson's fuselage. For an insane moment Weiner thought that the pilot had released the bombs or whatever they were too early. But then he realized that they possessed the Hudson's momentum and were arching down, following a graceful but invisible curve that would end alongside *U700*.

The hours of low-level practice that Thompson had spent dropping smoke bombs paid off: it was a perfect straddle. A depth charge fell on each side of the U-boat, a third bounced off the bow, and the fourth plunged into the water by the stern. Thompson could hear his crew yelling jubilant congratulations as he banked the Hudson sharply to see what was going to happen. What happened exceeded his wildest dreams. With a tremendous WHUMMMP from the half ton of Torpex high explosive, four columns of water were hurled high into the air from beside the U-boat, lifting it bodily out of the water as if a huge hand from the depths had thrust it into the air. As the U-boat disappeared from view, hidden by the tons of water erupting into the sky, it seemed to the four dumbfounded men in the Hudson that the submarine was rolling on to its side as it fell back into the hollow where the sea had been blown away from beneath it.

A terrifying thunderclap smashed against Weiner's ear-drums, driving the breath from his lungs and coherent thought from his mind. All that was left was a crude instinct to survive; an instinct that enabled him to struggle up and cling grimly to the periscope standard.

He was dimly aware of the heeling bridge being surrounded by a curtain of water that was climbing into the sky. His legs were jelly, but he embraced the periscope standard with a strength that threatened to crack his ribs. There was a distant sound of men screaming. Water surged across the bridge and cascaded down the open hatch. He felt someone trying to drag his body away from the periscope, but it was the force of gravity; for the U-boat, which had lain over, was now righting itself. He saw Stein struggling to grab hold of something. Another second and he would be swept into the maddened sea. Weiner reached down and grabbed Stein's arm. With a superhuman effort he managed to haul the second officer against the periscope and hang on to him.

The Hudson roared over the U-boat for a second time. The spray was falling back. Thompson was astonished to see that although the U-boat had taken a direct hit by four depth charges, it was still miraculously afloat.

'They build 'em well,' the navigator commented as if reading his captain's thoughts.

'I'll show them just how well we build machine guns if they go for that twenty-millimetre,' was Thompson's grim reply as he pulled the Hudson around in a tight turn.

'What now, skipper? I thought those depth charges were supposed to be an improvement on the anti-sub bomb?'

'Shoot him up if he tries to dive,' Thompson answered.

'With 303s?'

But Thompson didn't reply. He pulled the Hudson out of the turn and aimed it straight at the U-boat.

If I can't sink the bastard, he thought, I can at least frighten it to death.

* * *

'No!' Weiner croaked when he saw men crawling out of the forward hatch. 'They'll kill you! Get back! Get back!'

The men hesitated and looked up in bewilderment at the diving aircraft. Weiner had been about to give the order to dive, but in that moment he realized there was only one thing he could do if he was to keep his men from getting killed.

'I don't believe it,' Thompson said. 'Someone wake me up.'

The U-boat was showing a white flag.

'Looks like a shirt,' the navigator said.

A signal lamp started flashing from the submarine's bridge.

'Typical navy types,' Thompson grumbled. 'How do they expect us to read that speed? In German too.'

'Hang on,' said the navigator. 'I think it's in English. Yes! It must be! W . . . E . . . Stop. H . . . A . . . V . . . E . . . Stop. S . . . U . . . R . . . It must be *survived! We have survived!*'

'Damn cheek,' Thompson said indignantly. 'Let's plaster them.'

'Wait! It's "surrendered", skipper!' the navigator yelled. 'We have *surrendered!*'

Thompson still didn't believe it. 'Signal them to send again,' he ordered.

The light flashed again from the U-boat.

'We have surrendered,' the navigator repeated.

Thompson groaned. It was unheard of for a U-boat to surrender to an aircraft.

'Now what do I do?' he complained.

Stein stared transfixed at the shirt and then at Weiner. He tried to speak down the voice pipe, but Weiner snapped the cover down.

'We've got to dive,' Stein said hoarsely.

'It's too late, Stein.'

Stein shook his head disbelievingly. He looked up at the Hudson that was warily circling its prey. A wild look came into his eyes. Before Weiner could move, he dived on to the wintergarten deck and swung the anti-aircraft guns toward the Hudson.

Weiner started after him. 'No, Stein! For God's sake! They'll kill you. They'll kill us all!'

'Let them!' Stein snarled, his expression blazing contempt and hatred.

Weiner tried to pull him away from the gun but was sent staggering backward by a savage kick in the stomach.

Almost immediately, the Hudson's engines opened up and it came diving down toward the U-boat with tongues of fire dancing on its nose. A stream of miniature waterspouts raced across the water. Weiner threw himself down and saw a row of holes stitch themselves across the deck casing. The roar of the aircraft's engines as it swept over the U-boat at 150 feet completely drowned Stein's cry of agony. He fell away from the gun clutching his left arm.

Weiner was on his feet. He grabbed the tails of the shirt that had wound themselves around the periscope and spread the signal out so that it could be seen more clearly.

24

It was a hot and humid afternoon in Berlin on that fateful August 27.

At 3:30 P.M. an enciphered Iceland/C-in-C Western Approaches, Liverpool intercept was placed on Kurt Weill's desk. He looked at the neat columns of code numbers and wondered why anything Iceland had to say would be of interest to Sir Percy Noble.

Weill was one of the senior cryptanalysts with Doenitz's Observation Service Beobachtung-Dienst, the little-known but vital decoding organization that had started to break the British Naval codes at the beginning of the war and had been breaking them ever since. The 'B-Service' now provided Doenitz with a daily intelligence summary on convoy sailing times, escort rendezvous positions, courses, speeds, and even cargoes.

Weill studied the signal flimsy for some minutes. It was the straightforward two-part code that had been in use by the British for a year, a dangerously long time, but with a code having to contain upward of 10,000 code numbers to be useful, it was understandable that the British were reluctant to change it.

Weill picked up his pencil and wrote down the substitutions for the numbers he recognized immediately:

4556 meant 'patrol'; 3087 meant 'aircraft'; 9927 meant 'Coastal Command'; and 6294 – the most frequently used code number of all, one that Weill saw every day – meant 'U-boat'.

Ten minutes later Weill had fifty per cent of the signal reduced to plain text: a U-boat had become involved with a Coastal Command Hudson. The aircraft had dropped depth charges on the U-boat, and the U-boat had 2773.

2773?

Weill frowned. 2773 hadn't been cracked. It wasn't in his cross-index or the monthly supplement. Nor did it appear in the day file.

Obviously it was a verb but what verb? Sink? Dive? Scuttle? Escape? But all those words were already covered by known code numbers. So what else was there that a U-boat could do? It had to be something surprising for

Coastal Command to trouble Sir Percy Noble with the news.

Weill thought for a minute. There was a remote chance that 2773 had been used by the British in a previous signal that had not been completely decoded. He crossed the office and slid back the cover on the first bank of the giant rotary card index. He punched 2773 on the selection keyboard and watched the huge drum slowly turn, flipping through the cards like a giant fairground machine. It stopped. The claw was holding the cards open at one that stated:

'2773. Used 5/5/40. HMS *Seal*/British Admiralty. See file UB/5/6/40.'

Weill recalled reading a story about HMS *Seal* but couldn't remember the exact details. He picked up his phone and asked for the library.

'Walter, maybe you can help me. What does HMS *Seal* mean to you?'

'Hold on.' Weill could hear a muffled conversation at the other end. Papers were shuffled. Then: 'Yes. She's a British submarine. Or rather, was.'

Weill's pulse quickened. 'What happened to her?'

'She surrendered last year in the Baltic to a trawler after her motors had been smashed by depth charges.'

Weill slowly replaced the phone and gazed at it for some moments. No wonder the code number wasn't frequently used. He placed the signal flimsy in front of him and slowly, almost reluctantly, filled in the substitution for 2773.

The next thing was to put a scrambled call through to Lorient. He wondered how Doenitz would react when he heard the news.

25

The radio operator was smashing the U-boat's cipher machine with a hammer as Anders climbed down into the control room.

'I want to send a message to headquarters.'

'Can't,' the radio operator said insolently, not looking up at the tall, spare officer. He brought the heavy hammer down on the machine's keyboard.

'Why not?'

'Because it's smashed – that's why not.'

The man was insubordinate, but Anders didn't have the will to argue. Ducking his head, he moved through the wardroom where a human chain were passing weighted bags along the boat for ejection through a torpedo tube. The men were silent but openly hostile by gesture and expression. He stopped outside Stein's berth and pulled back the curtain.

Stein looked up and tidied his hair with his free hand.

'I've come to see if the dressing is okay,' Anders said uncertainly.

'It's fine,' Stein muttered. Beads of perspiration stood out on his forehead. Blood was seeping through the make-shift sling on his left arm. His cold eyes watched Anders carefully.

'If you'd like another shot of morphine . . .'

'I'm okay!' Stein snapped.

There was a sudden hiss of compressed air being released into the boat as the contents of a torpedo tube were expelled. Stein made room for Anders on the bunk.

Anders sat and drew his bony knees up to his chin and stared at the floor.

'What's the Hudson doing?' Stein asked after a few seconds silence.

'Still circling.'

'Weiner?'

'Watching it.'

Anders broke the embarrassed silence that followed. 'How about the torpedo in Tube Three?'

'Jammed,' Stein replied in disgust. 'They tried everything to shift it. The bomb must've warped the tube.' He paused. 'You know which torpedo it is in that tube?'

Anders nodded. The two men were silent for a moment. 'Were they bombs or depth charges?' Anders said at length.

'One lousy five-hundred-pound anti-submarine bomb,' Stein said bitterly. 'Useless unless it scores a direct hit, and the only anti-submarine armament those Hudsons carry.'

'There were men on the deck casing,' Anders said. 'They were unprotected. If Weiner hadn't surrendered, they'd be dead now, and so would we if that Hudson had more depth charges.'

'The RAF hasn't got an air-borne depth charge, as you should know.'

Anders remembered how he had taken his eyes away from the sky periscope at the crucial moment during the surfacing procedure. 'It wasn't Weiner's fault,' he said suddenly.

The scar on Stein's face gleamed in the light from the reading lamp. The cold eyes fixed on Anders were unblinking. 'What wasn't?'

Anders opened his mouth to tell Stein about the moment when the news that Bruch was safe had come through. But his eyes met Stein's icy stare, and he knew that Stein wouldn't understand.

'What wasn't Weiner's fault?' Stein prompted.

Anders hesitated. 'Surfacing so near an aircraft. I wouldn't like to try to calculate the odds against it happening.' His voice ended on a miserable note.

'The odds that we could still shoot that Hudson down are pretty good,' Stein observed drily.

Anders stared at him. 'What do you mean? We've surrendered.'

'We have not surrendered,' Stein said harshly. 'Only Weiner has surrendered.' He handed Anders a sheet of paper.

> We, the undersigned members of *U700* crew, deplore the surrender of our boat without a fight and urge Lieutenant Anders to arrest Captain Weiner and to countermand the surrender. We pledge Lieutenant Anders our total loyalty and will carry out whatever orders he issues to prevent this boat from falling into enemy hands.

Under the statement were some forty signatures arranged in a circle so that it was impossible to deduce who had signed first.

'Every member of the company has signed it,' Stein said.

'Everyone except me,' Anders said, eyeing the document with distaste.

'You don't have to sign it – just accept it.'

'Did they all sign willingly?'

'All that matters is that they signed.'

'Well I think it does matter,' Anders said evenly. 'Did you tell them when you twisted their arms that the captain did what he did to save their lives? That he didn't have any choice but to surrender? Brinkler had told him we couldn't dive because the depth charges had jammed the 'planes. Did you tell them that?'

'All that matters now,' Stein said softly, 'is that this boat must be prevented from falling into enemy hands. We have the guns . . .'

Anders snorted. 'They'd rake the casings with machine-gun fire before we could get near them.' He pointed to Stein's sling. 'Look what happened to you.'

'We put the best gunners in the middle of the party,' Stein said smoothly.

'What party?' Anders asked suspiciously.

'The party that rushes the guns.'

It was some seconds before Anders realized what Stein was suggesting. He stared at him with a mixture of loathing and contempt. For once the twisted scar didn't worry him. 'You're insane!'

'I'm prepared to be a member of the shielding party, Anders.' He paused and smiled. 'Are you? Or are you as big a coward as Weiner?'

'Weiner surrendered because he wanted to save lives, including yours,' Anders said angrily. 'If I were to arrest him and order us to fight after having surrendered, I'd be denying all of us the protection of the Geneva Convention. The British would have the right to hang the lot of us like common criminals.'

Stein opened his locker, placed a Luger on the table, and pushed it toward Anders. The two men's eyes met. Choosing his words carefully, Stein said in a matter-of-fact tone, 'If you allow this boat to fall into enemy hands by *not* arresting Weiner, then I shall see to it that after the war you hang anyway – for cowardice.'

Anders returned to his berth and placed the Luger on his table. He stared at it as he listened to the signalmen smashing equipment. Three minutes passed before he made up his mind as to what he had to do.

Thompson studied the lone figure standing on the U-boat's bridge, staring back at the Hudson through binoculars.

'Wonder what the poor sod's thinking,' the navigator pondered.

'The same as me,' Thompson replied. 'He's probably wondering what will happen when we run low on fuel and have to leave him.'

'Shall I signal him to muster all his men on deck so we can keep an eye on them? They might be destroying stuff below.'

'They're bound to be,' Thompson agreed. 'But we're stopping him from scuttling by keeping them below.'

The flight-sergeant entered the cockpit.

'So?' Thompson demanded.

'A couple of armed trawlers and a destroyer, the *Burwell*, are on their way.'

'When?'

'Twenty-two hundred.'

Thompson groaned loudly. 'We'll be out of fuel long before then. What the devil do they think we're flying? A Zeppelin?'

The flight-sergeant grinned. 'We've been ordered not to run out of fuel until a Catalina turns up to relieve us. And if we have to leave before the Cat shows up, we have to destroy the U-boat.' The flight-sergeant became serious. 'Without warning, sir.'

Thompson's face went white. He turned in his seat. 'Why, for Christ's sake?'

'In case it tries to dive and escape,' the flight-sergeant said, avoiding Thompson's eyes.

26

Admiral Karl Doenitz's chiselled features were devoid of expression as he contemplated the plot table in the U-boat operation room at Lorient. Kneller stood behind him, nervously twisting and untwisting his fingers, glaring at the operations controller as if he were to blame for the astonishing news that had just been received from the B-Service codebreaking agency in Berlin.

'They definitely haven't got the U-boat's number?' Doenitz fired at the controller.

'No, admiral. They don't think it's in the British signal, but they've promised to call as soon as the decoding is complete.'

Doenitz continued gazing down at the giant map of the North Atlantic. There were markers for at least six U-boats that were within range of Hudsons operating out of Iceland. He turned to Kneller, his face perplexed. 'It just doesn't make sense, John – a U-boat surrendering to an aircraft. It's unheard of.'

'We could call up all boats and ask for situation reports,' Kneller suggested.

Doenitz permitted himself a rare smile. 'The British are extremely clumsy. No U-boat *has* surrendered. If one has been damaged so that it couldn't dive, then the captain would obey the battle orders by scuttling.'

The controller looked baffled. 'Then why have the RAF in Iceland sent that signal to England?'

'Because the British are testing their code security,' Doenitz replied. 'All their monitoring stations are now tuned to forty-nine, ninety-five kilocycles – our main

U-boat frequency – to see if we suddenly start sending a flurry of signals to all boats.'

There was a relaxing of tension in the room; Doenitz's explanation made good sense.

'What the British signal won't include,' Doenitz continued, 'is the position of the U-boat. For the simple reason that the British don't know the position of any of our U-boats.'

The controller's phone rang. He picked it up. His face clouded with worry as he listened.

'Yes . . .' He scribbled rapidly on a pad.

There was a total silence in the room.

'Thank you for decoding it so quickly,' the controller said. 'Yes, he's with me now. I'll tell him.' He carefully replaced the phone and tore the sheet of paper off the pad.

Kneller took it from him and handed it to Doenitz who glanced at it and then impassively picked up one of the long cues. He rested the tip near London on the Greenwich Meridian.

'Thirty degrees west,' Doenitz said, reciting tonelessly.

The tip moved westward across England and stopped in mid-Atlantic.

'Sixty-one degrees north.'

The tip moved north toward Iceland. It came to rest pointing at the marker for a U-boat.

U700.

The long, stunned silence that followed was broken by Kneller.

'We've nothing that can reach it before dark,' he muttered. 'Even before dark at that latitude.'

27

There was an uncomfortable bulge in Anders' pocket as he climbed through the hatch onto *U700*'s bridge. Weiner was alone, hunched over the coaming, watching the Hudson. He looked around to see who the newcomer was and then returned to watching the aircraft. His good-humoured features were lined with anxiety. Anders was uncertain what to say and embarrassed by what he knew he had to do: place Weiner under arrest.

'It was a day like today,' Weiner said without turning around. 'Except there was thirty metres of water under *U700*'s keel instead of three thousand.' His voice was flat and unemotional, as if he were trying to relate the events without having to think about them. 'I'd joined *U700* the week before. A new command. Engineers were still working on her when I took her out for her first torpedo-firing trial. We trimmed off at periscope depth, and I gave the order to fire Tube Three. There was the usual popping in your ears caused by compressed air being released into the boat.'

Anders slowly eased the Luger from his pocket and released the safety catch.

Weiner paused for a moment, collecting his thoughts. 'Suddenly there were shouts and commotion from the forward torpedo room. Brinkler had compensated for loss of trim when the torpedo was fired, but he found that he couldn't hold her. She was going down by the bow. I rushed forward. Six men were trying to hold the broken torpedo door in place. Water was flooding into the boat. Then the pressure blew the door right off. The water was a raging torrent. In a few seconds the entire boat would be flooded.'

Weiner passed a hand over his face. Anders took a step toward Weiner and aimed the Luger at his captain's back. The steadiness of his hand surprised him.

'There was only one thing to do – close the watertight door as fast as possible. A torpedo hadn't been secured – it had rolled off the rack so that the men couldn't get to the door anyway. Something was stopping the door from closing. It looked like a piece of rag or something. I seized an axe and hacked at it. I hacked and hacked. Suddenly it came away, and the door closed.' Weiner stopped.

'What was it?' Anders asked, guessing the answer.

'A hand,' Weiner said flatly.

Anders could see sweat trickling down the older man's temple.

'We left through the aft hatch which was above water. Divers pumped the forward compartment out and *U700* continued with her trials a week later. Faulty welding around the torpedo door's hinge they said.'

'But you saved the boat and everyone else aboard,' Anders said quietly.

Weiner's laugh was hollow. 'That's what they said. They even gave me a medal. I threw it away. They wouldn't give a medal to those poor bastards trapped in the torpedo room because they said they hadn't done anything.' Weiner paused, adding sarcastically, 'Hadn't done anything. They only died, that's all.'

'What do you want to do now, kaleu?'

Weiner continued to stare at the Hudson. 'I'm not letting the British set foot on this boat. I'll go down and fire the scuttling charges as soon as everyone is safely off.'

'The British might not let you.'

'They will,' Weiner replied. 'They respect the tradition

of the captain being the last to leave. Except that I won't leave.'

Weiner turned and saw the Luger that Anders was holding levelled at his chest.

The navigator in the Hudson was puzzled. 'What are those two playing at down there?'

'What does it matter?' Thompson asked irritably. He pulled the Hudson out of the continuous circle it had been maintaining ahead of the U-boat and lined his machine up for the final approach. 'All I know is, no matter who wins this bloody awful war, no history book is going to have a kind word to say about us or the order we've been instructed to carry out this day.'

Thompson's hand went to the depth charge release control.

Weiner seemed saddened rather than surprised by the sight of the Luger.

'I'm sorry, kaleu,' Anders said.

'Why?'

'I have to place you under arrest.'

'Why be sorry if you're convinced you're doing the right thing? Or has Stein convinced you?'

'I have no choice.'

Weiner spread his stubbly fingers along the wind deflector and gazed up at the white shirt hanging from the periscope standard. 'That's the story of Germany, Anders – no choice. What do you plan doing?'

'Cancel the surrender and fight.' Then Anders was pleading with Weiner. 'Kaleu, if only you would do it. We could say that the surrender was a ruse of war. We could open fire on the Hudson. We could . . .' Anders' voice trailed into silence as Weiner shook his head.

Neither of the two men had noticed that the watchful

Hudson had stopped circling and was now approaching the U-boat.

'You're too late, Anders,' Weiner said, looking beyond the younger man's shoulder and smiling faintly. 'Too late.' Weiner pointed to the horizon.

'Hold it, skipper,' the Hudson's navigator called. 'What's he pointing at down there?'

Thompson's eyes went to the U-boat's bridge. One of the two Germans was pointing at something. Thompson craned his neck.

There was a smudge of smoke on the horizon. An armed trawler, the first of a small fleet of British warships converging on *U700*, had arrived.

28

At nine o'clock the following morning, August 28, Ian Fleming left his office at the Admiralty in London and took a taxi to Alan Brice's hotel. He found the American scientist eyeing a plate of kidneys.

'You won't believe this,' Fleming began.

'I've just tried the coffee,' Brice said. 'So I'm now in the sort of receptive mental state to believe anything.'

'We've captured a U-boat.'

'*Almost* anything,' Brice amended. 'Would you like my breakfast?'

'No thanks. I'm trying to live without American aid. It surrendered yesterday. South-west of Iceland.'

Brice put down his fork and stared at Fleming in surprise. 'You've finally done it.'

'It surrendered to Coastal Command,' Fleming said sadly.

'Is that so bad?'

'How would you feel if one of your lab cleaners won a Nobel prize for physics?'

Brice considered. 'I get your point. So what did they do to accomplish this amazing feat?'

'Nothing really. They just chucked a few depth charges at it. Coastal Command's policy of attacking anything afloat, friend or foe, has finally paid off. It'll be a long time before the navy forgives them.'

'Is it damaged?' Brice inquired.

'Our reputation?'

'The U-boat.'

'Slight damage to her hydroplanes so that she couldn't dive, but nothing that her crew couldn't've put right in a few minutes.'

Brice frowned. 'So why did she surrender?'

Fleming shrugged. 'Search me, old boy. Maybe the captain felt sorry for Coastal Command. No one on our side likes them.'

'Any torpedoes aboard?' Brice asked hopefully.

'That's the bad news. The boarding party have reported a spare warhead in the forward torpedo room. That's all.'

'Probably with an old contact firing pistol,' Brice said regretfully. 'They would've dumped it if it was a magnetic head.' The scientist looked up at Fleming. 'Even so, I'd sure like a chance to take a look at the sub. Will that be possible?'

Fleming looked uncertain.

'Look, Ian – I've seen enough castles and palaces. You haven't got a Wotan warhead but you have got a German U-boat which I'll happily settle for. After that I'd like to go home.'

'I thought you were enjoying yourself? All our girls are

throwing themselves at Americans. The night life . . .'

Brice gave a sour smile. 'How in hell can one enjoy the night life in a city that never gets dark?'

Fleming laughed at the reference to the double summer-time emergency wartime measure. In June there had been bright sunshine at 10:30 P.M.

'So about the sub?' Brice prodded.

'I'll see what I can do, old boy,' Fleming promised.

'What's happening to it now, or is that a secret?'

'It's a secret,' Fleming admitted. 'But I can tell you she's being towed to Iceland.'

29

'Iceland,' Doenitz said in disgust. He handed the decoded signal that had just been received from Paris back to Kneller and surveyed the plot table moodily.

'Well,' Kneller said with finality. 'There's nothing we can do about it there.'

Doenitz's expression became thoughtful. 'John, when we captured the HMS *Seal* last year what was the first thing we did with it?'

'We handed it over to the experts for them to look at.'

'And who were they?'

Kneller thought for a moment. 'I'm not sure, probably Blohm and Voss.'

'Exactly,' Doenitz said. 'Blohm and Voss, our largest submarine construction yard.' He seized a cue and jabbed the tip at Iceland. 'And the British equivalent of Blohm and Voss is . . .' Doenitz swept the cue eastward to the north-west coast of England, '. . . the Vickers submarine works at Barrow-in-Furness. Right on the edge of the Lake District.' He looked at Kneller in triumph, the light of battle shining in his eyes. 'And Barrow, John, *must* be within reach of a dive bomber fitted with long-range tanks!'

Kneller looked doubtful. He hated to disillusion the admiral, but it had to be said. 'With respect, admiral, the navy doesn't have a dive bomber, and Marshal Goering is the only man apart from the Fuehrer with the authority to loan us one. Personally, I don't think he will.'

Doenitz thought hard. 'We can't allow that U-boat to remain intact in enemy hands.'

'I appreciate that, admiral, but . . .'

'I shall fly to Karinhall and visit him,' Doenitz interrupted. 'God knows, I can't stand the man, but I have no choice.'

30

'Things are beginning to look interesting,' commented Ian Fleming as he and Brice strolled to the first hole on Coombe Hill golf course. 'A book found on *U700* has upset Franklin D. He was shown a copy yesterday.'

Brice was intrigued. 'What sort of book?'

'The crew destroyed just about every document on the U-boat except one. Perhaps they didn't think it important – probably because they never looked at it. It was a ship recognition guide – silhouettes – that sort of thing.'

Brice stopped walking. 'And that was considered important enough to show to the president?'

Fleming grinned. 'All the silhouettes were of the US Navy's capital ships with detailed information on the location of magazines and the best points along hulls to aim torpedoes at.'

Brice whistled.

'It's got Roosevelt hopping mad,' Fleming continued. 'Just the excuse he was looking for to step up the US Navy's belligerent neutral attitude to U-boats. From now on there's to be even closer co-operation between your navy and ours in the war against U-boats.'

The news astonished Brice. 'You're kidding. American warships are going to hunt and sink U-boats?'

'Good Lord no, old boy. But if one of your ships or aircraft spots one, they'll now fall all over themselves to tell us where it is.' Fleming paused and smiled. 'As soon as *U700* is brought to this country, you're to have unlimited access to it. Mr Churchill's orders.'

Brice was pleased. 'That's great. Hey, maybe I could talk to her crew? What about her torpedo officer?'

Fleming looked doubtful. 'Highly irregular, and besides, they're hardly talking to us. The interrogators are still beavering away at the captain, the second officer's in hospital with a shot up arm, and the first officer's on his way to a prisoner of war camp somewhere in England.'

Part Two

31

It was early September and already summer was losing its grip on the landscape as the first colours of autumn seeped into the trees that huddled in the valleys and stood alone on the high fells.

Anders had been awake for fifteen minutes, watching the passing scenery from the train window and wondering how far north they had come during the long night that had consisted of periods of fitful sleep disturbed by jerking shunts as locomotives were changed at an assortment of darkened stations.

Major Shulke, the dapper army officer who had been marched at gunpoint into his carriage after trying to escape the previous evening at Euston Station, was still sound asleep – watched by two resentful guards who sat at the far side of the reserved compartment with their hands resting on their rifles.

Anders caught a brief glimpse through the hills of sunlight burning on an expanse of water. A lake.

Shulke stirred and stretched. The two guards became more alert and tightened their grips on their rifles.

Shulke opened his eyes. 'Good morning, Bernard,' he said cheerfully.

'Good morning, Conrad. You slept well. I envy you.'

'Where are we?'

'I don't know. There's a huge lake over there.'

Shulke yawned and allowed the warm morning sun to

bathe his face. His hand dropped casually on to the window strap. The guards sat forward, watching him intently.

'You've upset them again,' Anders said.

Shulke smiled mischievously. 'I escaped again during the night while all three of you were snoring.'

Anders looked at the little major in astonishment.

'Hopped out through this window at a station,' Shulke said sleepily. 'The one with the long legs caught me at the end of the platform.' He winked at the taller of the two guards. Neither of them were amused. 'I wonder if they understand German?'

'Lucky you weren't shot,' Anders said chuckling.

'I zig-zagged.'

'Did you get the name of the station?'

'Of course,' Shulke said haughtily. 'Bovril.'

Anders and Shulke clutched the sides of the swaying army truck as it bumped along a narrow, rutted track through a dense forest of tall, depressing pines where the summer sunshine didn't reach. They had stopped talking as soon as the truck had turned off the main road. Both men were thinking the same thing: a truck with two prisoners driving deeper and deeper into a forest where shots would not be heard.

Shulke took a chance on the guards being unable to understand German. 'We make a break for it as soon as the truck stops. I'm not going to let these swine shoot me like a horse with a broken leg. I'd rather be shot while running.'

'They won't,' Anders said, pointing at the oppressive forest. 'Barbed wire if you look carefully. See?'

Shulke looked. Anders was right; where the bracken was dying down it was possible to discern the ugly gleam of skilfully positioned barbed wire entanglements threading through the trees.

'Why would they bother with barbed wire if they're going to shoot us?' Anders asked.

A shout and a gesture from one of the guards made it plain that the two prisoners were not to talk.

Shulke shivered. He noticed a tower rising above the gloomy pines.

'For fire watching,' Anders said quietly. 'But you can bet they've got searchlights and machine-guns up there.'

The truck stopped at a heavy, mesh-covered steel gate that stretched across the road. Two soldiers carefully checked the driver's documents before opening the gate and waving the vehicle through.

The trees thinned out and finally gave way to a pleasant, neatly trimmed hedge that lined each side of the track. The two prisoners experienced a sense of relief now that the truck was in the sun again.

'Looks like some sort of approach road,' Shulke said, half-standing to peer around the side of the truck.

Then came the shock: the army vehicle rounded a bend and drove down the side of a magnificent country mansion with an imposing gabled roof crouching protectively over ivy-covered walls. The truck boomed through an enclosed, cobbled stableyard where the walls of the mansion suddenly broke out in a rash of pipes and gutters that climbed the brickwork like varicose veins. Anders caught a glimpse of heavy bars and steel mesh covering upper windows. Then the truck was through an arch and into the sunlight again – and into another world.

The two prisoners could only stare in amazement, for it was a world of clipped lawns, gravelled paths, pleasant wooded slopes, and immaculate vegetable plots where an overall-clad army of gardeners were at work with hoes and rakes. At the foot of the wooded slopes was the spectacular sweep of a broad, hill-fringed lake.

The truck stopped. The guards jumped out and

motioned for the two prisoners to do likewise. Anders and Shulke climbed down from the tailboard and stood uncertainly, clutching the army-issue kitbags that contained their few possessions. The guards gave their charges a final scowl and jumped back on to the truck. First gear was crunched home, and the truck rumbled off through the stableyard.

'Now what happens?' Anders asked.

'Look!' Shulke said, pointing at a group of men who appeared to be inspecting the gardeners' handiwork.

'What?'

'Their uniforms!'

It was then that Anders realized why he hadn't seen anything that was so unusual about the men: they were wearing Luftwaffe, Wehrmacht, and Kriegsmarine uniforms. Common enough in Germany, not so common in England.

'You don't suppose that the British have made a mistake do you?' Shulke wondered as a whistling *korvettenkapitän* walked past pushing a wheelbarrow loaded with vegetables.

'Good morning,' a cheerful voice said.

The new arrivals turned. Coming down the broad flight of steps that led to the mansion's main entrance was a fresh-faced Luftwaffe lieutenant holding an official-looking clipboard.

Shulke and Anders regarded him solemnly.

'I shouldn't stand in the middle of the road,' the lieutenant warned. He consulted his clipboard. 'You must be Major Conrad Shulke and Lieutenant Bernard Anders?'

The two prisoners agreed that they were.

'Excellent,' the airman said. 'I'm Paul Faulk.'

He got no further for at that moment an ancient station wagon of indeterminate ancestry roared around the corner of the building from the direction of the stableyard. Its tyres scrabbled wildly on the loose gravel as the driver hauled the vehicle's heavy rear end straight with a neat handbrake turn. The engine opened up and the station wagon charged forward. Shulke and Anders grabbed their kitbags and jumped for safety in opposite directions as the vehicle braked to a standstill. Anders was surprised to see that the driver was a young woman aged between twenty and twenty-five, wearing what appeared to be a nurse's uniform.

'Lieutenant Faulk,' she said accusingly, ignoring the two prisoners she had nearly mown down. 'It's still not right. The brakes make a dreadful noise, and the engine still over-revs when I press the clutch.' Her German was slow but correct.

Faulk looked concerned. 'Well, we didn't promise to be able to cure it, nurse. But I'll get them to have another look.'

'Oh don't bother,' the woman said. 'Sorry I frightened you just then. New arrivals?'

'Yes, miss,' Shulke said.

The young woman smiled. She was brunette, poised and self-confident. 'Don't forget that we drive on the left in this country.'

Anders smiled. 'I don't suppose we'll get the chance to do much driving.'

'I was thinking of your curb drill,' the woman said briskly. She let out the clutch and drove toward a group of low buildings that were a hundred yards from the main building.

Faulk crossed to Anders and Shulke. 'Nurse Lillian Baxter,' he explained. 'She visits the hall several times a week from Barrow. She once told me that she opted for German rather than French at school, so watch what you say in front of her.'

'Her driving will ensure that she's never short of clients,' Shulke observed drily.

Faulk chuckled. 'She doesn't have to take a driving test – the British have scrapped them in order to make their country too dangerous to invade.'

The three men laughed. It was the first time in days that Anders felt the tension beginning to unwind.

'One small point,' Shulke said. 'Presumably this is a prisoner of war camp?'

Faulk was surprised. 'Yes, of course.' He pointed to the low buildings. 'You'd better report to Major Veitch's office while I see about your quarters.'

Sergeant Rogers of the Black Watch looked up from his desk. 'Shulke and Anders?'

'Yes,' Shulke replied.

Rogers tapped on a door marked 'Major J. R. Veitch' and entered. He emerged a few seconds later and held the door open. 'Your senior officer is with Major Veitch, but he'd like to see you now.'

Major James Reynolds Veitch of the Grenadier Guards was a tall, spare man in his mid-forties. He half rose from his chair as the two men were ushered into his office. Anders heard the door close softly behind him.

There was a high-backed chair facing Veitch's desk. All Anders could see of the chair's occupant were long, sensitive fingers holding a smoking cheroot and the cuff of a well-cut Kriegsmarine jacket.

Veitch briskly introduced himself and held his hand out to the man in the chair. 'And this is your senior officer . . .'

Anders didn't hear the rest of Veitch's sentence, for the man had stood and Anders found himself staring at a hawk-like nose and into a pair of compelling, unblinking eyes.

The senior German officer at Grizedale Hall was Otto Kretschmer.

32

'You've probably noticed,' Major Veitch said, 'that this is no ordinary prisoner of war camp. It's the first, the first of many most likely, that we've established for German officers. For non-National Socialist officers that is.' He selected his words carefully, keeping his eyes on Anders and Shulke to gauge the effect his words were having.

'And just in case you two have sympathies in that direction that weren't discovered when you were screened, let me say here and now that Nazi bullying is one thing that the commander and I will not tolerate under any circumstances. If there are incidents, those responsible will be sent to one of the camps that the Free Polish run, and we don't ask them too many questions on the way they choose to run their operation. So, if you want to stay here and be treated as officers, then it's up to you to behave like officers. You will find that you have reasonable freedom of movement inside the wire. Tunnelling is out of the question because Grizedale Hall is built on rock.'

Veitch paused and smiled faintly. 'My men look after perimeter security, and the commander is responsible for internal discipline among the prisoners. I've also heard that he's the chairman of the escape committee.'

Not a muscle in Kretschmer's face moved.

'Standard punishment for escape attempts is the maximum permitted under the Geneva Convention,' Veitch continued. 'Twenty-eight days in the punishment block. There's an army nurse on my staff who has her sick-bay on the ground floor of the hall. Finally, there's the hall itself – one of the finest in the country. After the war the army will have to restore it to its rightful owners in good condition, so if it's damaged in any way, the War Office will be only too pleased to rehouse you in huts. Any questions?'

Anders and Shulke had none. Anders had kept his eyes on the floor during Veitch's speech to avoid having to look at Kretschmer.

'Very good,' Kretschmer said, speaking for the first time. 'See Lieutenant Faulk about your quarters.' The unwavering eyes turned to Anders. 'Ask him to show you where my office is please, Anders. I'd like to see you in one hour precisely.'

33

While Anders was waiting for his interview with Otto Kretschmer, a Junkers 52 tri-motor transport aircraft took off from a small airfield near Lorient in western France and set a course for Germany.

The aircraft was the personal transport of Admiral Karl Doenitz. Accompanying him was his aide, John Kneller. The two men had arranged a meeting with the one person who could, if he wished, provide the navy with an aircraft that was capable of reaching and destroying *U700*.

34

'How is the admiral?' was Kretschmer's first question.

Anders glanced at the horseshoe fixed to the wall behind Kretschmer's gaunt head. It had been covered with gold chocolate paper and was the only decoration in the small, bare room that served as an office.

'He seemed well when I last saw him.' Anders could feel the dark eyes watching him dispassionately.

'What happened to your boat?'

The inevitable question, Anders thought. 'We were bombed by an aircraft.'

'Casualties?'

'One man was wounded in the arm.' Anders wondered if Kretschmer knew the truth about *U700*.

'Can you remember the last tonnage sunk figures?' Anders relaxed. Kretschmer apparently knew nothing. 'May and June was around six hundred thousand tons. July was very low – about a hundred thousand tons.'

'What about your boat?'

A pause.

'Well?' Kretschmer pressed.

'Nothing,' Anders said awkwardly.

Kretschmer's eyebrows went up. 'Nothing?'

'It was our first patrol.'

Kretschmer drummed his fingers on the desk, aware that the slender young officer was steadfastly refusing to meet his eyes. He opened a drawer and spread a British newspaper on his desk. Anders could see a pencil ring around a news item.

'We sometimes obtain newspapers from the guards in

exchange for Red Cross chocolate,' Kretschmer explained. 'Did the British hold you in the same interrogation centre as Captain-Lieutenant Weiner?'

The question surprised Anders. 'No.'

Kretschmer regarded him for some seconds and then tapped the newspaper. 'Can you read English?'

'With difficulty.'

'So you don't know about Weiner?'

Anders shook his head, suspecting that Kretschmer was playing with him.

'Weiner hanged himself,' Kretschmer said abruptly. 'Why do you think he did that? *U700* fought didn't it?'

Anders gaped at him in disbelief. It was a moment before he could collect his reeling thoughts. 'I – I don't know why. We fought . . . We used our anti-aircraft guns.'

'I'm sorry to be the one to tell you,' Kretschmer said sympathetically. 'The story merely says that U-boat commander Hans Weiner was found hanged in his cell.'

Anders stared miserably down at the floor, and Kretschmer realized little was to be gained by pressing the young man for more information. 'You've seen the nurse for medical inspection?'

Anders nodded.

'Very well,' Kretschmer said. 'First thing after breakfast tomorrow, you will report to Lieutenant Paul Faulk to be allocated a gardening schedule.'

Anders rose like a man in a trance.

'One thing more,' Kretschmer said. 'Was Richard Stein held at the same centre as you?'

'No, commander.'

'Well, I don't suppose the British will send him here.' Kretschmer dropped the newspaper in his drawer and slammed it shut. The interview was over.

Outside in the corridor, Anders leaned against the wall

and closed his eyes; his betrayal of Weiner was now irrevocable. His death had extinguished the spark of hope that one day, somehow, Anders would be able to confess, and that Weiner would understand.

35

The music stopped abruptly, and the girl froze in mid-dance step. Her chiffon veils continued to swirl about her body in the heat thrown out from the crackling log fire in the massive hearth that occupied one wall of the vast banqueting hall. She watched the SS captain pick up the bull-whip and advance slowly to the middle of the floor, which the Luftwaffe and SS officers had cleared for the entertainment. They were totally silent, sitting in a semi-circle, watching the girl intently.

The SS captain twisted his lips in a parody of a smile and slowly coiled the bull-whip's long, vicious leather thong around his fingers. The girl pushed her long, blonde hair away from her face and raised her eyes from the whip to those of the captain's as if seeking mercy. But there was none.

The SS captain flicked his wrist, and the tip of the whiplash landed lightly on the girl's bare foot. She flinched but kept her balance. The captain made a few deliberate movements to position the thong across the floor to his satisfaction. The girl watched it as though it were a snake – her face white, her eyes wide with terror. The only sound in the hall was the splutter and crackle of the huge log fire whose twisting flames silhouetted the girl's graceful body through her transparent veils.

The SS captain tensed. There was a sudden blur of

movement followed by a loud crack. A strip of the girl's chiffon fluttered to the floor exposing pale shoulders to the circle of greedy eyes. There was an outburst of wild applause. The music started, and the now smiling girl resumed her erotic dance.

Reichsmarshal Hermann Goering stopped clapping and poured a drink for his guest. 'What do you think of my magnificent Karinhall, admiral? Just the place for week-end houseparties, eh?'

Doenitz was sitting uncomfortably on the edge of his chair and making a poor attempt at concealing his disapproval at what was going on. He looked at the obese figure, resplendent in a white dress uniform, and smiled politely. 'A magnificent building, marshal,' he agreed.

The music stopped. The whip cracked, and another strip of chiffon fluttered to the floor. There was loud cheering as the music started again.

Goering watched the pirouetting girl with an amused smile. 'They're a husband and wife team you know. I saw their act in a Berlin night club. Clever don't you think?'

Doenitz remained silent.

Goering drained his glass and twirled the stem in his pudgy fingers. 'You still haven't told me why we have the pleasure of this visit, admiral.'

Doenitz hesitated and then decided to come straight to the point. 'I need the loan of a bomber together with an aircrew and ground crew for three days, marshal.'

The bull-whip cracked loudly, stripping more chiffon from the girl.

'What sort of bomber?' Goering inquired mildly as the girl began dancing again.

'A dive bomber. One capable of carrying a thousand-kilo bomb for two thousand kilometres, delivering it, and returning.'

Goering shook his head sadly. 'My dear admiral, I need

a thousand such bombers for my Luftwaffe – two thousand – three thousand!'

The bull-whip cracked twice – and the girl was suddenly naked. She covered her breasts with her arm, but the captain skilfully flicked the tip of the whip around her wrist and drew her hand to one side. He reversed the handle so that it was pointing at the girl and started pulling her toward him.

Goering turned his small, cunning eyes on Doenitz. 'Why a dive bomber, admiral?'

'For accuracy.'

'Ah. A small target?'

The girl stood motionless, legs slightly apart as the SS captain moved the bull-whip's handle toward her. She gave a little shudder as it lightly brushed against the side of her neck. And then it moved downward, between her breasts, across her stomach, and down the outside of her left thigh. Doenitz opened his mouth to speak, but Goering silenced him with a finger held to his moist lips. The bull-whip's handle began moving up the inside of the girl's thigh.

'A small target,' Doenitz agreed, irritated at having been silenced.

Goering smiled mischievously. 'About sixty metres by six metres, say?'

Doenitz looked up sharply. Goering seemed to be gently mocking him. 'About that size,' he said stiffly, wondering just how much the fat air marshal knew.

The bull-whip's handle completed its journey, and the girl began a writhing motion with a circular movement from her hips.

'Admiral,' Goering said spreading his hands like a magician trying to convince his audience of his honesty. 'If I had such an aircraft, I'd be only too delighted to lend it to you for as long as you needed it. But I haven't.'

The girl's hips were moving faster and she was making

low moaning noises from the back of her throat. She dropped backward onto her hands, but the SS captain kept the bull-whip's handle in position.

Goering smiled beguilingly. 'But if you have a special target in mind, then my Luftwaffe might be willing to consider a mass raid which would be certain to destroy this . . .' Goering smiled again, '. . . sixty metre target of yours.'

The girl let out a loud, gasping cry and slipped to the floor as her arms and legs lost the strength to support her weight. A light rash appeared on her chest under the glistening film of perspiration as the audience rose to their feet clapping and cheering.

'A remarkable climax to a brilliant act,' Goering said smugly, raising his voice above the uproar.

Doenitz put down the drink he hadn't touched and stood.

'You must excuse me, marshal, but I have to make an early start in the morning.'

Goering hauled himself to his feet. 'But my dear admiral, surely you'll stay for the morning hunt?'

'I'm extremely sorry, marshal,' Doenitz said politely. 'I am most grateful for your hospitality but I must return to France.'

The Ju52 took off from Goering's private airstrip at 9:00 the following morning and headed back to Lorient.

'One dive bomber,' Doenitz said bitterly as he stared down at the forest rolling past under the port wing. 'One dive bomber. My God, you'd think I'd asked him for a squadron on permanent loan.'

Kneller looked sympathetic. 'Did he come out with his favourite expression?'

'Everything that flies belongs to me,' Doenitz mimicked and lapsed into a brooding silence.

'He still hasn't forgiven you over those Kondors,' Kneller said.

'He suspects something,' Doenitz said.

Kneller was surprised. 'How?'

'I don't know. I'm certain he doesn't know all the details, but he will. It makes the destruction of *U700* even more urgent – before he goes crawling to Hitler with his own account of its surrender. One aircraft! One!'

Doenitz lapsed into a brooding silence staring pensively out of the window at the tri-motor's port engine. Then he turned and allowed his gaze to travel slowly around the aircraft's spacious interior. He stiffened and moved forward on to the edge of his seat. 'John,' he said thoughtfully. 'Tell Goder that I'd like a word with him.'

Lieutenant Hans Goder – one of the navy's few pilots – handed over control to his co-pilot Max Hartz and followed Kneller into the main cabin. The two men looked down in surprise at Admiral Doenitz who was on his knees examining the aircraft's floor.

'Ah, Goder,' Doenitz said, standing and kicking the carpet back into place, 'sit down.'

The admiral made himself comfortable.

'You and Hartz have been flying me around Europe for the best part of a year now. What's been our longest trip?'

'Berlin to Rome, admiral,' Goder said, wondering what this was leading up to.

It was Kneller who began to have an inkling of what was on his admiral's mind. He looked alarmed and was about to open his mouth, but Doenitz silenced him with a gesture.

'Mm, a Ju52,' Doenitz said. It was the work horse of Germany. One of the sturdiest, most reliable aircraft ever built. 'What's its maximum range?'

Goder considered. 'About two thousand kilometres with a low payload say, fifteen hundred kilos, admiral.'

Doenitz leaned forward in a confiding manner. 'I want

it to carry a payload of that weight but twice the distance. Would that be possible?'

'*Four thousand* kilometres?' Goder gaped at Doenitz in astonishment.

'Is it possible? Could it be lightened?'

It was Goder's turn to look around the cabin. 'Well,' he said doubtfully. 'I suppose it would be possible to reduce its weight drastically, admiral. Bulkheads could be taken out – extra tanks fitted. Yes, it might be possible.'

Doenitz looked delighted and even managed a smile, the first Kneller had seen since the *U700*'s surrender.

'What sort of payload have you in mind, admiral?' Goder asked tentatively.

'A torpedo,' Doenitz replied with satisfaction.

36

It was an hour since the night raid had started, and still the droning bombers were pounding London. After so many months in London, Alan Brice had learned to do what everyone else in the very opulent and very illegal private gambling club was doing: he ignored the distant crump of falling bombs and roar of anti-aircraft batteries and concentrated on the game before him. So far that night he had won a satisfying sum from Ian Fleming.

'Well,' Brice said smugly when Fleming started dealing for the third time, 'your Washington friends told me to avoid playing with you. Now I see it was to prevent me from becoming overconfident.'

'Careful, Mr Brice,' Fleming said coolly. 'You're in grave danger of tempting me to use a devastating technique

I tried on the Germans in Lisbon. The idea was to win staggering sums from their embassy staff in order to cripple the Nazi war machine.'

Brice smiled. 'Did it work?'

A much closer bomb dislodged some plaster from the ceiling.

'It's just possible,' Fleming said drily without looking up, 'that His Majesty's Government paid for that bomb.'

Brice laughed, and then noticed a man in evening dress signalling their table. 'Does he want you or me?' Brice asked.

Fleming turned around. 'Me, I fancy. Excuse me, old boy.'

Brice watched the two men hold a whispered conference in the corner of the room near the doorway. Fleming returned a minute later, sat down, and picked up his cards. He gazed at them for a few seconds while Brice waited patiently.

'*U700* has arrived at the Vickers submarine works at Barrow-in-Furness,' said Fleming quietly. 'Engineers have just finished giving her a preliminary once-over. You'll never guess what they've found jammed in one of her bow torpedo tubes.'

Brice suddenly forgot the game.

'Not a magnetic . . .'

'Right first time,' Fleming cut in.

Brice whistled softly. 'Complete?'

'Complete. The engineers have managed to draw it back into the boat. They'll leave it in place until you've had a chance to examine it.'

'When?' Brice asked eagerly.

'Whenever you like, old boy. I've been told to take you to Barrow to make sure you see everything you want to see and take plenty of photographs for the Newport Torpedo Station's photograph album.'

Brice grinned. 'About time. Another month in England, and my wife might file for a divorce.'

Fleming frowned at his cards. 'The question is, old boy,' he said, fanning out his cards on the green baize, 'will you be able to afford the film?'

37

The main feature of No. 1 Prisoner of War Camp, Grizedale Hall, was the hall itself. It had panelled walls and an ornate vaulted ceiling. Along one wall were a line of windows that afforded a panoramic view of Lake Windermere sparkling in the September sunlight. The hall served as a mess hall for meals and a prisoners' common room at other times. Even after a week, Anders still found it hard to accept that he was in a prison camp. The sense of unreality was heightened when he stood at a window and gazed down the uninterrupted slope to the lakeside, for the main barbed wire fence was concealed by a fold in the ground. Even the watchtowers had been constructed to look like firewatchers' lookouts.

It was lunchtime. Kretschmer was sitting at the head table with Paul Faulk and Willi Leymann, a jovial Bavarian lawyer who had joined the Luftwaffe, obtained a commission as a captain, and had been in the first aircraft to be brought down by a barrage balloon. Anders felt Kretschmer's eyes on him as he waited in the line at the serving table.

'It's only a five hour walk to Barrow-in-Furness,' Leymann was saying. 'So if Schumann and Kirk have a sound escape plan, I don't think we ought to stand in their way.'

Kretschmer's eyes went to one of the trestle tables at the side of the hall where Schumann and Kirk were watching him. They were two brutish gunnery officers who had been picked out of the sea when the *Bismarck* went down. Since then they had been inseparable. They were giants, both over six feet tall – and certain to attract attention if they broke out successfully.

'No,' Kretschmer said firmly.

'We'll have to give them a reason,' Leymann pointed out.

'What do you know about Barrow?' inquired Kretschmer.

The rotund lawyer smiled. 'Kirk says it's a large port. He's certain there'll be regular sailings to Southern Ireland that they could stow away on.'

'It's a large port,' Kretschmer agreed. 'But it also happens to be the home of the largest submarine construction yard in the country. There would be dockyard police *and* military police and customs – and perhaps civilian police as well. They wouldn't get within two-hundred metres of a ship.'

Anders collected his meal and started toward his table at the back of the hall where Conrad Shulke was sitting.

'As much as I'd like to see those two thugs out of here,' said Kretschmer, 'they'll have to come up with something better than that if they want to stay together . . . Anders!'

Anders nearly dropped his tray when the voice cracked out behind him. Kretschmer was beckoning him over.

'Yes, commander?'

'How are you settling in?' Kretschmer asked pleasantly.

'Very well, thank you.'

'You're not finding my gardening schedules too hard, I hope?'

'No, commander. I like gardening.'

'Excellent.' Kretschmer nodded his head dismissively.

Anders returned to his table and sat down. Shulke noticed that the young naval officer was shaken.

'What's the matter?'

'Nothing.'

'What did Kretschmer want?'

'Is it your business?'

Schulke looked hurt. 'Sorry.'

'He wanted to know how I was coping with the gardening. Sorry I was rude, Conrad. Do you want my dinner? I'm not hungry.'

Under any other circumstances Shulke would have understood why Anders wasn't hungry; the dish was what the British referred to by the disturbing name of shepherd's pie: mashed potato flecked with almost invisible specks of what everyone presumed and hoped was minced meat. But Anders' refusal to eat his meals was becoming a common occurrence.

'Do you want to talk about it?'

'Talk about what?'

Shulke shrugged. 'Not eating. Not sleeping.'

'Who said I wasn't sleeping?' Anders demanded irritably.

Shulke speared one of Anders' carrots and popped it in his mouth. 'There's two types of breathing at night: wide-awake breathing and sound-asleep breathing. Yours is wide-awake breathing.'

'What's it to you?'

'Curious.' He paused. 'No, I'm worried about you.'

'There's nothing to be worried about.'

'Fine. So eat.'

Anders spooned up some mashed potato and thrust it into his mouth. Shulke gave him an encouraging smile and was repaid with a scowl.

* * *

That night, when the prisoners in the dormitory were asleep and snoring, Shulke sensed that someone was standing by his bed. He groped for his matches and saw it was Anders, staring down at him. Shulke knew from the young U-boat officer's expression that something was desperately wrong. He let the match go out and said quietly, 'What's wrong, Bernard?'

There was a long silence. When Anders finally spoke, his voice was a distraught whisper in the darkness.

'I'm sorry to disturb you, Conrad.'

'Yes?' Shulke prompted, lifting himself on to an elbow.

There was a pause, then, 'You were shot down.'

'Yes,' Shulke said, baffled. 'A reconnaissance flight over the Channel. Did you wake me up to ask that?'

'Do you think the others will learn about *how* you were shot down?'

'What others?'

'Kretschmer. Faulk. The whole camp.'

'I don't understand what you mean,' Shulke said with poorly disguised annoyance. 'I've told everyone what happened.'

'I mean the exact details,' Anders persisted. 'Your position. The time. The type of boat that picked you up. Do you think they could ever find out that sort of thing?'

Shulke was puzzled. 'Well I suppose they could if they wanted to. Why?' There was no answer. 'Bernard?'

'Yes.'

'I'm a good listener if you want to talk.'

'No,' Anders said quietly. 'It doesn't matter. I'm sorry I woke you.'

Shulke reached a hand out into the darkness, but Anders had gone back to his bed.

38

Two days later at Lorient, Doenitz's Mercedes pulled up outside the hangar where the Junkers was kept. Doenitz and Kneller approached the door set into the main door and were, to Doenitz's delight, challenged by a military policeman. The admiral had ordered a strict security clamp down on the hangar and was pleased to discover that his instructions were being scrupulously obeyed.

A minute later they were inside the hangar surveying the trusty old Ju52. Mechanics were noisily stripping fittings from the aircraft's cabin and carrying them to Goder, who was weighing them on an industrial beam balance and transferring the figures to a blackboard.

It was some seconds before Goder noticed his visitors. He quickly gave Doenitz a clumsy salute, which Doenitz waved aside.

'Just so long as you're getting on with the job, Goder. That's all that matters. How is it coming along?'

'Better than I thought, admiral. It's amazing how much of this Iron Annie we can manage without.'

'How much weight has she shed?' Doenitz asked.

Goder turned to the blackboard. 'I haven't totalled it yet, admiral. But I would guess the best part of a ton of nonessential equipment.' The pilot grinned. 'Tomorrow we start on the essential equipment.'

Kneller frowned at Goder's temerity, but Doenitz merely smiled.

'The torpedo arrived an hour ago,' Goder said, pointing to a long, graceful weapon resting on a trolley. 'The dockyard has promised to have the release gear finished by Tuesday.'

Doenitz examined the torpedo with an expert eye. It was a Type G7e fitted with a magnetic warhead – the weapon that Doenitz was convinced would win the war for Germany if only the OKM would stop interfering in his management of the U-boat offensive. They had even refused to allow U-boat commanders to defend themselves against warships of the neutral United States, which were now harassing U-boats with ever increasing vigour.

'There is one thing, admiral,' Goder said. 'The torpedo is heavier than I thought.'

Doenitz nodded. 'This one has the Wotan armoured warhead, Goder. I'll tell the Torpedo Establishment to send you a G7a. They're a hundred kilos lighter. Not so powerful but powerful enough to destroy a U-boat.'

39

'Look out!' Shulke yelled.

Lillian's station wagon swerved violently, brakes screeching and tyres spewing gravel. Shulke grabbed Anders' sleeve and hauled him backward but he was too late. The vehicle's radiator clipped the garden rake Anders was carrying and spun him around. Before he could recover his balance, the station wagon's side mirror smacked into his ribs and threw him to the ground.

Lillian jumped from the driver's seat while the vehicle rolled to a standstill. 'Don't move him!' she called out to Shulke. But Anders had moved himself; he was sitting up and looking aggrieved by the time Lillian knelt beside him.

'I'm terribly sorry,' Lillian said. 'Those stupid brakes. It was my fault. Are you all right?'

A crowd of prisoners was gathering, offering suggestions.

'Yes, I think so,' Anders said, reaching a cautious hand behind his back. He winced in pain.

'I'd better have a look at him,' Lillian said. She noticed that Anders had allowed his eyes to linger on her legs and guessed that there was nothing seriously wrong with him. 'Help me get him to the sick bay.'

'Nothing to worry about,' Lillian said cheerfully to Anders who was stretched out naked on his stomach. 'Just a rather nasty bruise, which I'm terribly sorry about. Okay, you can get dressed.'

Anders climbed off the couch gingerly and self-consciously turned away from Lillian as he pulled up his trousers.

Lillian noticed how thin and pale he was. He was not merely thin – he was emaciated.

'The bruise is the same shape as my car mirror,' she said smiling.

'So?' Anders said as he pulled on his shirt.

'You've lost weight.'

'It's the food,' was Anders' noncommittal reply. He turned and noticed the newspaper lying on Lillian's desk. It was partly covered by a magazine, but the two-inch-high headlines were clearly visible.

The British press had been given the *U700* story.

Suddenly it was too much. The room began to spin madly. Anders felt as if his head had been wrenched from his body. Superheated steam was roaring in his ears.

And then there was a total and merciful silence.

* * *

At that moment Willi Leymann was about to check Paul Faulk's king with a rook.

But he never completed the move. A newspaper landed on the homemade chessboard, scattering the carefully carved pieces on the floor. The two players looked angrily up at Schumann and Kirk who were towering over them, grim-faced and silent.

'Read,' Kirk said economically, jabbing a huge finger at the newspaper.

There was no need for the chess players to ask which news item the giant gunnery officer was referring to. There was only one, and it was emblazoned across the frontpage in two-inch headlines: U-BOAT SURRENDERS WITHOUT FIGHT!

Lillian closed the sickbay window so that the work crew clipping the lawn could not hear what she had to say. She had long discovered that the prisoners had developed a taste for gossip. She turned from the window and looked thoughtfully at Anders who was sitting up and sipping from a glass of water. She picked up his medical card and tapped it against her teeth.

'Have you been passing blood, Lieutenant Anders?'

'Why?'

'I thought that you might have an ulcer.'

'Why should you think that?'

'Get on the scales please.'

'You weighed me less than a month ago – when I first arrived.'

'Well now I'm going to weigh you again,' Lillian answered irritably. 'On the scales please.'

Anders put the glass down and stepped on to the weighing machine.

'All right. Now show me your nails please.'

Anders held his hands out for inspection, catching a faint whiff of perfume.

Lillian regarded Anders steadily. 'Okay,' she said. 'Why aren't you eating your food?'

'How do you know I'm not?' Anders countered.

'Vitamin deficiency. You have every symptom plus an eleven pound weight loss since you arrived. I want to know why.'

'I don't like the food.'

Lillian flushed angrily. 'There's nothing wrong with the food here. You're getting fresh vegetables that a lot of people in this country would be glad to have. There's not much meat but that's something you can blame on your U-boat comrades. My medical cards are inspected by the Red Cross. Major Veitch would be very angry if they got the impression that we're ill-treating prisoners-of-war. So do you tell me why you're not eating properly, or do I recommend your transfer to another camp?'

From where Anders was sitting, he could see through the sickbay window. He noticed two men walking across the lawn. One was the unmistakable stocky figure of Leymann. The other looked like Faulk. They were both examining a newspaper.

'Maybe a transfer isn't such a bad idea,' Anders said dispiritedly.

Lillian was surprised. There had been no bullying incidents at the camp since Kretschmer had arrived, but Major Veitch had warned his staff to remain on the alert.

'Why?'

Anders saw Kretschmer join Leymann and Faulk.

'You wouldn't understand,' Anders said. 'What do you know about war?'

Lillian looked at him long and hard. 'I was among a party of army nurses evacuated from Dunkirk last year,' she said evenly. 'My sister was a nurse too. She was in charge of a group of officers' children being taken to

Canada last Christmas when her ship was torpedoed by a U-boat. She later died of exposure in the lifeboat.'

Anders pulled his eyes away from the three men in the garden.

Lillian forced a smile. 'I've never mentioned this to anyone in here. One of the little girls who survived said that the U-boat had a golden horseshoe on the conning tower.'

A prisoner who had helped carry Anders to the sickbay was pointing out his whereabouts to the three men on the lawn. It didn't need much imagination on Anders' part to guess what was being said.

'Have you told him?' he asked.

Lillian shook her head. 'What would be the point?' Anders noticed that Faulk was walking with long, purposeful strides toward the hall.

Lillian smiled. 'Well now I've told you my little secret . . .' She looked expectantly at Anders.

Faulk had disappeared from sight. He'd now be in the front hall, thought Anders. Turning left . . .

'I was the first officer on a new U-boat,' Anders began hesitantly.

'What was its number, or is that something you're not allowed to mention?'

Faulk would now be striding down the corridor toward the sickbay. Bernard thought he could hear footsteps approaching.

'It was U . . .'

He got no further. There was a loud, determined hammering on the door, and then it opened. Faulk stood in the doorway. A lock of hair had fallen across the clean-cut features.

'I'm terribly sorry to intrude, nurse, but we've just heard about the accident and we are all wondering if Lieutenant Anders is all right.'

Lillian noticed that he didn't look at Anders as he spoke.

'He'll be fine,' Lillian said. 'A nasty bruise, which is all my fault, but it'll clear up in a few days.'

Faulk gave a little bow. His courtly manners did much to dispel Lillian's initial annoyance at the way he had burst into her sickbay.

'We are all very concerned for him,' Faulk continued. 'The commander would be grateful to see Lieutenant Anders as soon as possible.'

'There's no reason why he shouldn't go now,' Lillian replied. She suddenly realized that they were talking about Anders as if he were not in the room.

Kretschmer lit another cheroot and tossed the matches on his desk. He drew on the slim cigar and watched Anders through the smoke. He noticed that the young naval officer's gaze was fixed on the pile of newspapers that Leymann had placed on his desk.

Kretschmer nodded to Leymann. The portly little Bavarian picked up the top paper and read aloud from the frontpage:

'Squadron Leader Thompson, the pilot of the Hudson which captured *U700*, said that the white surrender flag waved from the conning tower was the biggest shock of his life. "I expected the U-boat to dive or open fire with its anti-aircraft guns," he told reporters. "The last thing I expected it to do was surrender – especially as the U-boat appeared to be undamaged by the depth charges we had dropped."'

Anders was about to speak, but Kretschmer held up his finger for silence.

'An admiralty spokesman refused to comment on *U700*'s future,' Leymann continued, 'but said that the capture of an *intact* U-boat was of major importance and that the possibility of it serving under the White Ensign could not be ruled out.'

There was a long silence. It was even possible to hear Kretschmer's watch ticking.

'What about the other papers?' Kretschmer asked.

'They all carry the same story, commander. Virtually word for word.'

'And they all refer to an *intact* U-boat?'

'Yes, commander.'

'They're all lying!' Anders said suddenly. 'The depth charges caused extensive damage. The boat was thrown on its side. And we *did* open fire!'

Kretschmer addressed Anders for the first time. 'Why didn't you dive?'

'One of the hydroplanes was jammed.'

'Which one?' Kretschmer snapped. 'Bow? Stern? Port? Starboard?'

'I don't know,' Anders said miserably. 'But the boat *was* damaged. Commander Weiner saw the Hudson coming in for another attack. We were helpless. He had no choice but to surrender.'

'U-boats have scuttling charges, do they not, Anders?'

'Yes.'

'Why weren't they detonated?'

'I don't remember,' Anders said ineffectually. 'I think the wiring had been damaged by the depth charges.'

Kretschmer looked contemptuous. 'All right, Anders. Wait outside.'

'The boat *was* damaged,' Anders repeated defiantly.

'Wait outside.' Kretschmer's voice was emotionless.

Anders saluted and left the room. Kretschmer raised an inquiring eyebrow at Leymann.

'I think he's telling the truth,' the plump lawyer said.

'You're the expert,' Kretschmer said evenly.

'Meaning you don't believe him?'

Kretschmer thought for a moment. 'I'm not sure, Willi.'

'You've got to consider that the British might be putting out a false story to create unrest in the U-boat arm,' Leymann pointed out.

Kretschmer summoned Anders back into the office. 'I've decided to give you the benefit of the doubt, Anders.'

A weight seemed to be lifted from Anders' shoulders. 'Thank you, commander.'

'You may go.'

Anders turned to leave.

'One thing, Anders.' Kretschmer gestured to the newspapers. 'If those reports *are* telling the truth, you will most likely be hanged for cowardice after the war.'

Lillian returned Anders' medical card to the drawer and tidied up the sickbay. She decided to make herself a cup of tea, and while she was waiting for the kettle to boil, she picked up her paper and read the lead story on the front page.

40

That night, some 400 miles to the south-west in Southern Ireland, Patrick Gallagher was sitting in Toomley's drinking his third pint of the evening. He was careful with his money – to be seen out drinking every night would start gossip and speculation, and that would never do. On the other hand, he could buy the lads the occasional round because he was unmarried and his official job as a telegrapher was well-paid. It was all a matter of balance.

A man who was not a regular entered the bar and hoisted

himself onto one of the two stools that Toomley provided for those customers who didn't understand that bars should be leaned on and not sat at. Gallagher watched him out of the corner of his eye. He was about forty, short, and a little overweight. He was wearing a light blue suit. He ordered a whiskey and asked Toomley if he had any cigars. Toomley sold him the ancient Havana that had been in the sweet jar behind the bar for as long as Gallagher could remember.

The stranger lit the cigar, inhaled deeply, then looked suspiciously at the glowing tip. He caught Gallagher's eye, smiled, and raised his glass.

'Nice evening for fishing,' he said.

Gallagher was about to point out that it was pouring with rain when a warning bell jangled at the back of his mind. He lowered his tankard and stared at the stranger in the etched mirror at the back of the bar.

'Of course,' the stranger continued, 'I once tried fresh-water fishing, but I didn't like the taste of anything I caught. Now I stick to sea fishing.'

Gallagher turned. The stranger had been word-perfect. With a sinking heart Gallagher realized he was going to start earning all the money that had been paid into his Dublin account.

41

Five days later in Lorient, a truck drew up outside the hangar where Admiral Doenitz's Ju52 was being prepared for its mission.

Two fitters dragged back the tarpaulins and passed a heavy lifting chain around the torpedo. A mobile crane lifted the weapon onto a trolley. Five minutes later, with much armwaving and shouted instructions from Goder, the torpedo's centre-of-gravity marks were being positioned under the open claws of the makeshift release mechanism that had been attached to the underside of the Ju52's fuselage.

Satisfied that the torpedo was correctly positioned, Goder banged the side of the fuselage with his fist. Hartz, sitting in the copilot's seat, operated the lever that had been installed between the two seats.

The heavy steel claws snapped shut around the torpedo's fat body. Goder was delighted and signalled twice with his fist on the fuselage. The claws opened. Goder measured the distance across the open jaws of the clamps with a pair of large calipers and was about to make some adjustments to the setting screws, when he noticed two pairs of immaculately polished shoes and two pairs of faultlessly pressed trousers standing nearby.

'Good morning, Goder,' Doenitz said as the naval pilot scrambled out from under the fuselage. 'How's everything going?'

'Like a dream, admiral,' Goder said, wiping his hands on a rag. He pointed to the torpedo. 'It fits beautifully, but I think we'll have to rivet extra stiffeners to the outside of the fuselage around the mounting points to prevent flexing. That's in case we get buffeted by bad weather and can't get above it. She's not designed to have a ton weight hanging from her.'

Doenitz smiled. Goder was enjoying himself, and people who enjoyed their work invariably did it well.

'Will it fly properly?' Kneller asked.

Goder's expression became solemn. 'Fly – yes. Properly – no.'

Doenitz needed all his self-control to keep from laughing.

Kneller did not share Doenitz's amusement. 'So it won't be airworthy?'

Goder looked shocked. 'Good heavens, no. We've cut holes in the bulkheads so big they frighten me, but it will fly. There is one thing that's worrying Hartz and me. We've been going over the maps of the Barrow area until we know every inlet and creek. There's a thousand and one places the British could anchor the U-boat. We won't have the fuel for a long search. We're going to have to fly straight to it.'

'That problem has been anticipated,' Doenitz said. 'You'll be given *U700*'s exact position before you leave.'

Goder looked astonished. He knew no reconnaissance aircraft flew that far north, and even if they did, the Luftwaffe was not likely to provide the Kreigsmarine with information.

'How will you get the U-boat's position, admiral?'

Doenitz's expression hardened. 'You ask too many questions, Goder. Carry on with your work.'

Goder saluted and crawled back under the Ju52's fuselage.

'He's impertinent,' Kneller commented.

Doenitz gestured to the tangled pile of fixtures and fittings that had been removed from the Junkers' interior. There were seats, a chemical toilet, the folding steps, several crates of small items and large pieces of aluminum floor section with jagged edges where they had been hacked away from the fuselage. Each item was labelled with its weight.

'He's efficient, John. He does his job well, and that's all I ask. I've given the grand admiral a firm promise that *U700* will be destroyed – a promise that he's conveyed to Hitler.'

Kneller said nothing as they walked to the door. He had

heard that Hitler nearly had an apoplectic fit when he had learned about *U700*'s surrender.

'This observer the OKM are sending to Barrow,' Doenitz said. 'Is he ready yet?'

'He's on his way, admiral.'

Doenitz nodded with satisfaction. 'What was the hold up?'

'His radio transmitter. He wasn't happy about it. Barrow is virtually hemmed in by the Cumberland Fells, which means that it has to be extra-powerful to get a signal out. He also needs a thirty-metre-high antenna. It all makes for extra bulk, which the observer is most unhappy about.'

'What's his name?' Doenitz asked disinterestedly.
'Gallagher,' Kneller replied. 'Patrick Arthur Gallagher.'

42

'Patrick Arthur Gallagher,' he said in his best Belfast accent to the Liverpool Docks police officer.

'Your identity card please.'

'Sure thing.' Gallagher eased his motorcycle backward on to its stand. Two other policemen took over the inspection of passengers disembarking from the ship so that there wasn't a hold up.

The policeman carefully inspected Gallagher's identity card and seemed satisfied. There was no reason why he shouldn't be – the simple document, although a forger's delight, was genuine.

The policeman returned the card and looked curiously at Gallagher's Douglas. The panniers were crammed; there was a packed tent and sleeping bag lashed across the pillion and several fishing rod sleeves tied to the side of the machine.

'A fishing holiday,' Gallagher explained in response to the policeman's polite question.

A minute later he was wheeling his motorcycle toward the customs shed where the rest of the passengers from the ship were forming a line.

'Good morning, sir,' a voice said.

Gallagher stopped and turned. A senior customs officer was smiling pleasantly at him. He pointed to a pair of double doors at the rear of the customs shed. 'Perhaps you'd be kind enough to take your bike through those doors please, sir.'

Gallagher remained outwardly calm and smiling. He pointed at the line. 'Now I was thinking that that was the queue for customs.'

'It is, sir,' the uniformed officer said. 'But it's a little crowded in there. If you'd be good enough to follow me please . . .'

Gallagher's spirits fell even further as he pushed his machine into what could only be described as a workshop. There was a bench against a wall that was festooned with wrenches, pliers, and screwdrivers hanging from rusty nails. Near the double doors was a vehicle inspection pit equipped with two powerful swivelling lights. In the middle of the workshop was a low industrial table – the sort that an engine could be placed on for dismantling. Two men in overalls were sipping from chipped mugs. A third in uniform was warming his hands over an evil-smelling oil heater. He looked up and smiled as Gallagher entered.

'Ah, good morning, sir. Prop your bike against the table. Would you like a mug of cocoa while you're waiting?'

Gallagher noticed that he could talk and smile at the same time. Maybe he practised in front of a mirror. Gallagher showed him that he could do the same trick.

'Do you want to look in my suitcase then?'

The customs officer kept smiling. 'More than that, sir. More than that. Maybe you'd help us out a bit by unpacking everything and spreading it out on that table?'

'Even my tent and sleeping bag?'

'Everything, sir. Everything. Might as well be hanged for a sheep as for a lamb, eh?'

Gallagher bent over his motorcycle to unbuckle the pannier straps and wondered if the three men could hear his heart pounding.

43

The speedometer needle was hovering at the hundred mark as the grey, supercharged, 4½-litre 1930 Bentley coupé screamed north-west along the ten-mile straightaway on the A5 between Bletchley and Towcester.

Brice had a red-blooded American's love of speed, but there was something indecent about thrashing along at a hundred miles an hour in a huge, open-topped machine that was built like and looked like a customized tractor. At least Fleming seemed able to handle the monster. In fact, Brice admitted to himself, Fleming was an excellent driver; he was relaxed, sitting well back in the driver's seat, arms straight, hands on the wheel at the correct ten-minutes-to-two position.

'I didn't know you had roads as straight as this!' Brice yelled. Normal conversation was impossible: everything had to be shouted above the roar of the wind and the ear-splitting howl of the anguished supercharger.

'Roman,' Fleming answered. 'The only Europeans who knew how to build roads until the Germans came along.'

'When do we get to Barrow?'

'Late this afternoon, old boy. Fancy a spell of driving?'

'On the wrong side of the road? No thanks.'

Fleming laughed. 'The only reason I'm clipping along like this is to make you feel at home.'

Brice said nothing; the speedometer needle was edging up to a hundred and ten. He hoped that it wasn't a straight road all the way to Barrow-in-Furness. His nerves couldn't stand it.

44

Even Gallagher was surprised at just how much he had been able to pack into his motorcycle panniers. There was so much clothing, camping equipment and fishing tackle strewn across the table that it didn't seem possible it could all be restowed.

The three customs men had literally taken everything apart. They had even shined a torch inside his Primus stove and opened up all his tins containing sinkers and hooks.

The smiling customs officer picked up a reel and drew out a yard of line. He tried to break it and couldn't.

'Heavy line, sir.'

Gallagher grinned. 'I thought I might try for a spot of mackerel. Are you a fishing man, sir?'

The customs officer unscrewed the top of a jar of Brylcreem and probed the contents with a finger. 'No, sir. I thought you had good fishing in Ireland?'

'It is that,' Gallagher agreed. 'But when you've only a few days' holiday a year, you like to be spending it on a challenge.'

One of the overall-clad customs men was peering in

the motorcycle's petrol tank. He sniffed and seemed disappointed to discover that it contained petrol.

'You won't believe this,' Gallagher said cheerfully, 'but I once caught a fresh-water cod that long.' He spread out his hands.

The smiling customs officer entered into the spirit of the game. 'An Irish fresh-water cod was it, sir?'

'Well of course. Didn't it hop up on the bank beside me and guzzle me whole pot o' Guinness?'

The three customs men laughed.

An hour later Gallagher was riding through Liverpool. He was seething inwardly at his cavalier treatment by the customs men. The arrogant bastards hadn't even helped him repack his gear. Mother of God, how he loathed the British and everything they stood for.

There was one consolation he savoured as he rode through the dockland streets: at least the Luftwaffe had given the place a good plastering.

He began to sing his favourite tune. No one would hear it above the roar of the motorcycle engine: *'We're marching to war against England!'*

45

By late afternoon the grey Bentley coupé was north of Liverpool and skirting the breath-taking sweep of Morecambe Bay. The sea was a distant ribbon of light on the horizon.

'The tide comes in faster than a man can run,' Fleming said. 'The stagecoaches used to take short cuts across the sands to get to Barrow. Quite a number of people drowned over the years.'

Brice looked at the map. Another 45 minutes and they'd be in Barrow. The town was on the edge of the Lake District, and the scenery was incredibly beautiful. As he mentioned to Fleming, it was hard to believe that the north of England was fighting the same war as the south.

'We'll drive through Liverpool on the way back,' Fleming promised.

Brice forgot the map and relaxed to enjoy the last few miles of the long drive. He guessed that Fleming was tired; the Bentley was cruising at a steady forty, it's 4½-litre engine burbling contentedly under the eight feet of hood.

A horn suddenly blasted immediately behind Brice. He turned. A girl driving an ancient station wagon was sitting on Fleming's tail. She sounded her horn again and tried to pass the Bentley but was forced back by an oncoming truck. Brice smiled at her, but her face remained fixed in a frown of concentration. She was wearing what looked like a nurse's uniform. A pretty kid. She sounded her horn repeatedly.

'The most dangerous thing about living in London,' Fleming said as his foot went down on the throttle pedal, 'isn't the bombs but the ATS girls driving ambulances.'

Brice's laugh was snatched away by the wind as the giant car surged effortlessly into the eighties.

Gallagher was singing at the top of his voice as he bowled along at fifty miles an hour. The motorcycle's finely tuned engine was running like a sewing machine, the late evening sun felt pleasantly warm on his back, and all was right with the world. He was just thinking that it would soon be time to look for a suitable camp site when he thought he heard the distinctive whine of a supercharged engine. He glanced over his shoulder, and the two staring King of the Road Lucas headlamps on either side of a howling supercharger were suddenly upon him. He yanked the handlebars to the left and skidded the Douglas safely onto the shoulder, catching a glimpse of the driver before being blinded by the dense cloud of swirling dust in the charging monster's wake: wavy RNVR stripes on his sleeve, an English officer, relaxed, confident and uncaring – just like the bastard who, in September 1920 at Balbriggan, near Dublin, had ordered the despised Black and Tans to open fire on the crowd. Afterwards, Gallagher's father had been found bleeding slowly to death on the cobblestones.

Gallagher was about to restart the Douglas's engine when a station wagon driven by a nurse came hurtling past, missing him by inches. He sighed. He was beginning to realize that danger in the spying business could come from unexpected quarters.

46

It was sunset as Lillian drove through the stableyard and parked outside Grizedale Hall. The few prisoners strolling along the gravelled drive gave mock screams of terror when they saw her and made a great show of diving for safety. Lillian wasn't particularly amused. She was concerned about the station wagon's overheated engine; the straining radiator cap was blowing out enough steam to sterilize a hospital. Perhaps trying to chase the Bentley had been a mistake, but she couldn't stand men who drove as if they owned the road.

She looked quickly around to see if any prisoners were watching before clicking the hidden switch under the dashboard that isolated the vehicle's ignition. Her father had fitted it for her. It was less messy than removing the rotor arm every time she left the station wagon unattended. She locked the door and was about to enter the hall when she noticed Anders pushing a wheelbarrow.

'Good evening, Bernard. How's the bruise?'

Anders set his wheelbarrow down. 'It's fading I think.'

Lillian nodded and then looked anxiously at the steaming radiator cap. 'I've never known it to do that before. Do you suppose it's all right?'

She was about to touch the cap, but Anders stopped her. 'It's best to let it cool down first, then see if it needs more water.'

Lillian smiled. 'I know nothing about cars. So long as they go, the faster the better.'

'You like going fast?'

Lillian looked up quickly to see if the young naval officer was teasing her, but his eyes were serious. Anders, she suspected, did not have a strong sense of humour.

'If you like going fast,' Anders continued, 'it is important to have good brakes. Is your handbrake on?'

'Yes. Hard on.'

Anders gave the vehicle a gentle push. It rolled a yard.

'Perhaps your brakes need attention?' Anders suggested. 'Relining?'

'That's what the garage in Barrow said. But they can't look at them for a month. It's getting impossible to get anything done these days.'

An army truck passed the station wagon and pulled up twenty yards away, outside the front entrance to the hall.

'I could do them for you if you got the linings from the garage,' Anders offered.

Lillian chuckled. 'It's funny when you think about it. I nearly run you over, and so you offer to repair my brakes.' She watched the new arrival over Anders' shoulder. One of the guards was helping him down from the tailboard because his left arm was in a wrist sling.

'Will the commandant mind?' Anders asked.

'He didn't mind Lieutenant Faulk looking at them,' Lillian said. She was amazed that the new prisoner could look so smart after a ten-hour train journey. His naval uniform looked as if it had just been pressed and his collar was spotless. He waved aside the guard's offer of further help and swung his kitbag on to his shoulder with his free hand. As he straightened, Lillian noticed a bold scar that traversed his left cheek. 'New arrival,' she commented to Anders. 'Another navy type.'

Anders tuned around, and in that moment his legs felt as if they had suddenly dissolved. The new arrival was smiling at him. It was not a smile of friendship but one of triumph.

'My God,' Anders whispered. 'Stein.'

Thirty minutes later, Anders was waiting in the corridor outside Kretschmer's office. Stein hadn't wasted any time, he reflected bitterly. He could hear voices. Angry voices. The door opened, and Faulk beckoned.

'You can come in now.'

Stein was standing in front of Kretschmer's desk. Leymann was by the window, and Kretschmer was sitting with his chair tilted back, smoking a cheroot. Anders heard the door close softly behind him.

'Lieutenant Stein has made a very serious allegation about the loss of *U700*,' Kretschmer said without preamble. 'He says the newspapers are telling the truth – that it surrendered without a fight and that you played a significant role in its surrender. Is that true?'

'No,' Anders said. 'I wasn't even on the bridge when Weiner surrendered. But Stein was.'

Kretschmer's expressionless eyes turned to Stein. 'Is that true?'

'Yes,' Stein said. He indicated his wounded arm. 'I

got this offering the only resistance that *U700* put up. Immediately after I was taken below, I circulated a petition in which every member of the crew pledged support for Lieutenant Anders if he arrested Weiner and countermanded the surrender.'

'And I went on to the bridge to arrest the captain,' Anders protested. 'But it was too late because an armed trawler had arrived.'

'He had no intention of arresting Weiner,' Stein sneered. 'I don't suppose he even had the guts to take my Luger out of his pocket.'

'All right,' Kretschmer broke in before Anders had time to protest.

Anders and Stein remained silent while Kretschmer drew slowly on his cheroot. Then the U-boat ace fastened his hypnotic eyes on Anders. 'Weiner paddled across to the destroyer in one of the U-boat's dinghies?'

'Yes, commander,' Anders replied. 'He didn't want to. He wanted to be the last to leave the U-boat so that he could open the main vents and detonate the scuttling charges after the crew was safe.'

'He was ordered to paddle to the destroyer?'

'Yes. They said that they would sink us if he didn't.' Anders looked up, hoping for a flicker of understanding in Kretschmer's eyes, and found none.

'So you were left in command of the U-boat,' Kretschmer stated.

'No, commander.'

Kretschmer raised an eyebrow. 'You were *U700*'s first officer, were you not?'

'Yes,' said Anders. 'But as we had surrendered, command of the boat had been transferred to the captain of the British destroyer – even though he wasn't on board.'

Kretschmer's tone was suddenly icy. 'You were left in

command of *U700*, and you didn't order the boat to fight, and you didn't take the necessary steps to ensure the boat was scuttled?'

'I gave the order to scuttle the boat,' Stein said.

'And I cancelled it!' Anders retorted.

'Why?' Kretschmer demanded.

'Because we couldn't abandon the boat first,' Anders answered. 'The destroyer had threatened to open fire if any of the crew appeared on the deck before they could get a boarding party to us. I didn't want any needless killing.'

'Didn't it occur to you that the destroyer wanted to make sure that you didn't scuttle?' Kretschmer asked.

Anders made no reply.

'Commander,' Stein said, 'it's clearly stated in Battle Orders . . .'

'Thank you, Stein,' Kretschmer cut in sharply, 'but I do know what's in the Battle Orders.' He stared at the two naval officers for some seconds and stubbed out his cheroot in the cocoa tin lid that served as an ashtray. 'All right, you two – you can go. Show Stein his quarters please, Faulk.'

Stein looked surprised. 'But surely, commander, you're not going to let this little coward . . .'

'When I've decided what to do, Stein,' Kretschmer interrupted harshly, 'I'll let you know.'

Kretschmer waited until he and Leymann were alone before he lit another cheroot, blowing a thin cloud of smoke at the ceiling.

'What are you thinking, Willi?'

'I'm thinking that Stein is going to make trouble,' said the tubby lawyer. 'What little I've seen of him is enough. He's the sort to gravitate toward types like Schumann and Kirk, and when he does . . .' Leymann left the sentence unfinished.

'There will be no bullying in this camp,' Kretschmer said firmly.

'How will you stop it? As I see it, you're going to have to ask Major Veitch to have Anders transferred to another camp.'

'Pass the problem on to someone else?' Kretschmer sat forward. 'Listen, Willi. A U-boat has a crew of over forty. There's a good chance that there'd be one or two at any camp Anders is sent to. That's assuming that I ask Major Veitch to transfer him – which I won't.'

Leymann sighed. 'Which means that you're going to have to protect Anders, which means that some of the army and Luftwaffe types will be accusing you of favouritism toward a fellow U-boat officer. Which means that there will be trouble – real trouble – and we'll all end up at camps run by the Poles.'

Kretschmer inhaled deeply on his cigar. Leymann was right – protecting Anders from mob violence was going to be difficult. He had no sympathy for a coward – if indeed, Anders was guilty of cowardice. But that would be something for a court-martial to decide after the war. In the meantime, it was his duty to see that Anders came to no harm without alienating the respect that the POWs had for their senior officer. It was, Kretschmer reflected, a seemingly insurmountable problem. But there was a solution – a British solution – one that he remembered from his days as a student at Exeter. It was an unpleasant solution but it might work.

Kretschmer relit his cigar. 'There is a third course, Willi.'

47

It was dusk that evening when Gallagher found a suitable site on the Cumberland fells for his first transmission. It was a lonely spot by a stream that was sheltered by a tall, overhanging oak. The gasoline gauge on the motorcycle's instrument panel was indicating half full; that meant that he was over 600 feet above sea level. The gasoline gauge, like so much on the Douglas motorcycle, was not what it seemed.

Gallagher wheeled his machine to within three yards of the stream's bank and lifted it on to its stand. A minute later, he had unpacked all his fishing tackle and had the various tins and boxes spread out on the grass. He quickly assembled a fishing rod and loaded it with the reel containing the heavy line that the Liverpool customs officer had tried to break. A heavy lead sinker was attached to the free end of the line. He squinted up at the topmost branches of the oak tree and drew off about 100 feet of line from the reel. It was a good cast: the lead sinker, towing the line, which was in fact an insulated antenna wire, sailed up toward the top of the oak and became entangled in the upper branches.

The next stage of the operation was to get the transmitter-receiver working. Two grubby pieces of wire from the motorcycle's toolbox were quickly twisted around the two terminals intended for additional lighting when the machine was fitted with a sidecar. It was a simple matter for the other ends of the wires to be plugged into the tiny holes in one of the spare fishing line reels. Finally, Gallagher connected the end of the antenna wire to one of the spare terminals on the Douglas' magneto.

Everything was ready but there was still one minor, but important task to perform: he baited a real fishing line and cast it into the stream. He watched the float bob out into midstream.

He looked at his watch. It was five minutes to the hour.

At two minutes to the hour, he sat down on his folding stool beside the motorcycle, lifted the wired-up reel to his ear, and turned the Douglas' headlight switch to the left. Current started flowing from the machine's battery through the tiny radio valves sealed within the speedometer housing. It took a minute for them to warm up sufficiently to generate a gentle hum in the reel head phone that he held to his ear.

At thirty seconds to the hour, Gallagher rested his fingers lightly on the motorcycle's horn button. He stared at the second hand on his watch jerking toward the hour. When the hand reached '12' he rapidly tapped his call sign on the horn button. The impulses raced up the antenna wire and burst southward over England and across the Channel. They were picked up by receivers on the Eiffel Tower, re-amplified and beamed south-west to the receiving station at Lorient.

In the U-boat operations room, there was a sudden relaxing of tension as Gallagher's signals were decoded and clattered out on the cipher machine. Kneller gave a toothy smile; Admiral Doenitz remained impassive.

'Five-eight-one sent on four-eight decimal one,' the cipher clerk said, reading off the information that had appeared on the recording paper.

'That's him,' Kneller said. 'Acknowledge.'

Gallagher grinned to himself when he heard Lorient's faint bleeps in his headphone. His supple fingers went to the horn button again, and he began transmitting at high speed. He was so fast that the wire recorder had to be switched on at Lorient to be certain of receiving the complete message.

Fifty miles south of Gallagher's campsite, Corporal Anderson of the Royal Army Corps of Signals was half-dozing in a wireless truck while his captain boredly leafed through a book. One of the radio receivers in front of Corporal Anderson was automatically sweeping the section of the shortwave band that had been allocated to the wireless truck for that evening. One by one, in a pattern of unceasing monotony, the stations of Europe would rise to a crescendo in the corporal's headphones and gradually fade to be replaced by the next station.

Oslo – a news bulletin; London – someone yakking away in German; Cologne – Wagner, it was always Wagner; London again – this time in French. Another twenty stations and then the whole boring cycle was repeated: Oslo –

Corporal Anderson was suddenly alert. He cut the automatic bandsweep on the receiver and reached up to crank the handwheel that turned the direction-finder loop on the truck's roof.

'Something, sir,' he said crisply.

The captain dropped his book and plugged his headphones in to the console.

'Some joker on forty-eight point one – just below Oslo,' Anderson continued. He stopped cranking when the needle on the meter before him dipped. 'Bearing three-three one.'

Using a protractor, the captain marked off a thick black line on a map of northern England. 'What's his reciprocal, corporal?'

'North, sir. Christ, he's fast.' Anderson tried to scribble

Gallagher's morse down, but it was impossible to keep up with the rapid stream of bleeps in his headphones.

'Ground wave or sky wave?' the captain asked.

'Definitely ground wave, sir. He's on our doorstep. That's the lot – he's stopped.'

The captain looked disappointed. There hadn't been time to call up C for Charlie to get a triangulation fix. He looked at the line he had slashed across the map. It ran off the coast at Barrow-in-Furness. Whoever the mysterious radio operator was, he was somewhere on a fifty mile line between the wireless truck and Barrow. Next time he broadcast, they'd be ready for him. No matter how fast he was.

Gallagher packed quickly. The important thing now was to put distance between himself and his transmission site. He knew that the RACS' monitoring was good; speed and mobility were his only allies. He had just jerked the antenna wire down from the oak when the genuine fishing line he had cast into the stream suddenly started paying out with a loud scream from the reel. The unattended rod started slivering through the autumn leaves toward the stream.

With a loud yell of 'Be Jesus!' Gallagher dropped everything and dived for the disappearing rod.

The cipher clerk ripped the message off the roll and handed it to Kneller.

'He's in the Barrow area,' the aide said, 'and will start looking for the U-boat tomorrow.'

Doenitz held his hand out for the signal.

'Why has he signed himself "St Peter"?'

Kneller grinned. 'He's posing as a fisherman. Berlin did warn us that he's got a sense of humour.'

* * *

Gallagher wasn't usually keen on fresh-water fish, but the four-pound pike he had fried on his Primus had been delicious and was ample compensation for the inconvenience of having to pitch his tent in near darkness.

A cold wind was blowing across the desolate fells as he prepared for a well-earned night's sleep. He drained his mug of whiskey-laced cocoa and contemplated the evil-looking pike's head that he had jammed like a mascot under the motorcycle's headlamp. He patted it affectionately before crawling into his sleeping bag.

'May you bring me luck tomorrow, Fergus, me boy.'

48

Leymann had been right when he had guessed that Stein would make trouble. By lunchtime the following day every prisoner of war in Grizedale Hall had heard the sub-lieutenant's bleak version of *U700*'s surrender and the part played by Anders.

Anders was miserably aware of the changed atmosphere as he lined up for his meal. The clatter of cutlery on enamel plates was subdued, and there wasn't the usual clamour of mealtime conversation. He sensed that what little discussion there was concerned him and *U700*.

He picked a knife and fork out of the chipped basins and made his way to the table at the back of the hall, keeping to the wall so that he wouldn't have to walk between the rows of trestle tables. He was aware of 200 pairs of eyes following him – in particular Kretschmer's and Stein's and the two giant, ex-*Bismarck* gunnery officers who Stein hadn't wasted time in befriending.

Shulke was alone; the other officers who normally used

the table were sitting elsewhere. Anders sat opposite him and got straight on with the business of eating – bony elbows tucked in, head down, and looking neither to the left nor right. Shulke guessed that it would be better for the time being to say nothing.

There was a movement at the other end of the room. Shulke looked up and was alarmed to see that Stein, Schumann, and Kirk were carrying their trays toward their table. Without a word the three sat down: Stein dropped into the seat beside Shulke, and Kirk and Schumann – grinning broadly – sat on either side of Anders.

Stein began to tear pieces of bread off his regulation midday slice, chewing deliberately while keeping his eyes fixed on Anders.

'What do you want, Stein?' Shulke demanded.

Stein smiled and brushed imaginary crumbs from his spotless jacket before speaking. 'There's something that we'd like to learn from you, major.'

'Learn what?' Shulke was in no mood for guessing games.

'Something that will be very useful to all of us if we're stuck in this place for any length of time.'

'Learn what?' Shulke repeated irritably.

'How to eat with a coward.'

Shulke stiffened.

'You make it look so easy,' Stein continued, delicately placing another piece of bread between his gleaming teeth. 'Or is it a case of birds of a feather?'

Shulke started to grab Stein, but Anders quickly reached out a restraining hand. 'Don't, Conrad. It's what he wants.'

'Push off, Stein,' Shulke growled. 'And take your little friends with you.'

Stein continued to smile. 'Anders knows what I want. Shall I tell you?'

'The same sort of thing that your parents deserve for having you,' Shulke snapped.

Kirk's huge hand whipped across the table and seized Shulke by the collar. 'Do you know what a bosun's sabre is, major?' he asked, his voice a menacing rumble.

'I'm not in the slightest bit interested in naval affairs,' Shulke replied, disengaging his shirt from Kirk's powerful fingers.

Kirk thrust a massive thumb under Shulke's nose. '*That's* a bosun's sabre, major. Like to see what it can do?'

Kirk's left thumbnail was at least half an inch too long. The surplus nail had been carefully filed and honed to a razor edge along half its width. The other half consisted of serrations that appeared capable of slitting a man's jugular vein. It looked a deadly weapon when used by an expert, and Shulke had no doubt that Kirk was an expert.

There was a sudden rapping noise. Faulk was standing and banging for silence with a spoon. 'Gentlemen, Lieutenant-Commander Kretschmer has a statement to make.'

There was an immediate silence as Kretschmer rose, a silence that only the man who had caused more destruction than any other naval commander in world history could command.

'Lieutenant Bernard Anders,' said Kretschmer tonelessly. 'Will you stand up please.'

Anders stood like a man in a trance.

'As you all know,' said Kretschmer, 'Anders is here because his U-boat was bombed by the RAF, and as you also know, we treated British claims that *U700* surrendered without a fight as enemy propaganda. We now know that those reports are true.'

Kretschmer paused. He knew he didn't have to continue – he could merely deliver a speech that roundly castigated Anders. Then he noticed that Stein and the two *Bismarck* gunners were sitting at Anders' table, and he realized he had no choice.

'It has been decided that from now on, no officer will speak to, communicate, or attempt to communicate with Lieutenant Anders in any way whatsoever.' Kretschmer managed to catch Stein's eye. 'A serious view will be taken if anyone disobeys this order. I'm going to speak to Anders now, and I want it clearly understood that I shall be the last person to do so until further notice.' He paused. 'Lieutenant Anders, do you have anything to say?'

Unable to reply, Anders shook his head slowly.

'The British have an expression for your punishment, lieutenant,' Kretschmer said. 'It is called being sent to Coventry.'

Kretschmer sat. The whole wretched business had left a bad taste in his mouth, but he hoped to God the scheme worked.

Anders subsided into his chair. Shulke was too shocked for the full implication of Kretschmer's words to sink in. He opened his mouth to speak to Anders, but heard Stein say, 'One word to him, major. Just one word . . .'

Stein's smile was pleasant, but his voice was menacing.

Part Three

49

'Ten bob,' the boatman said sourly.

Gallagher looked askance at the rowboat. There were two inches of water in the bottom, and the thwarts were splattered with gull droppings. 'I said I wanted to hire it – not buy it,' he said.

The boatman spat over the harbour wall into the sea. 'Ten bob, and it's yours for the day.'

'You reckon it'll stay afloat for a day?'

The blast from a scruffy coaster heading toward the Meccano tangle of Barrow's dockland cranes drowned the boatman's reply. They eventually agreed on eight shillings for the day, and the boatman grudgingly helped load Gallagher's fishing tackle into the boat's stern sheets.

'Don't go beyond the *Falkus*,' the boatman warned as Gallagher cast off. 'Harbour master can get funny about people getting too near the submarine yard.'

By eleven o'clock the sun was pleasantly warm, and Gallagher had leisurely rowed nearly a mile along the broad reach toward Walney Island and the Vickers yard. The *Falkus* turned out to be an elderly rusting tramp that had hit a mine at the beginning of the war and was now kept afloat by its cargo of rotting pulp and old books.

Gallagher rowed languidly past the forlorn little coaster, up the narrowing estuary with its mud flats and screaming sea birds, which eventually gave way to the cranes and wharves of the ship and submarine construction yards. He had assembled a fishing rod and was trailing a line and float behind him in the water. He lay back against a rucksack, hands behind his head and cap pulled down over his eyes. Several pairs of binoculars had been trained on him at various times by various officials, and it had been decided that the dozing fisherman wasn't worth wasting patrol boat fuel to chase away.

But Gallagher wasn't dozing. He was wide awake and carefully examining every yard of the wharves, slipways and jetties that drifted by under the peak of his cap. There was such a confused mass of grey and camouflaged ships that Gallagher had some difficulty at first in discerning where one ship ended and another began. Eventually his brain created order out of the chaos, and he was able to detect the occasional low profile of a submarine. There were five 'S' class boats and even an old Holland. Then another on a slipway of a class that he didn't recognize, but it definitely wasn't a U-boat. After ten minutes he began to despair of ever finding *U700*. If it wasn't moored on the outside of the ships lining the basin where it could be hit by a torpedo, then he would have to tell Lorient that there was no point in the operation going ahead. It was puzzling; one thing that Gallagher had been taught about submarines was that they had delicate pressure hulls and that they were rarely moored between other ships. If *U700* was at Barrow, it ought to be visible from the water.

Gallagher was about to reel in his fishing line when he noticed a grey Bentley coupé driving along the quayside. He was certain that it was the same car that had nearly hit him the day before.

Brice was out of the car as soon as Fleming had applied the handbrake. He looked quickly around the wharf and was disappointed not to see the U-boat. Fleming showed their passes to a dockyard policeman who explained that they were welcome to go aboard and that the lights in the boat had been switched on.

Fleming gave the man a charming smile. 'Only one snag, old boy. Where exactly is the U-boat?'

The policeman pointed to a humped, tarpaulin-shrouded shape moored against the wharf. Brice had assumed from its small size that it was a refuelling pinnace. It was less than seventy yards long.

'That's it?' Fleming inquired incredulously.

'Nothing to 'em, is there, sir?' the policeman said. 'Was a shock for us all when it turned up. I'll give you a hand with the covers.'

It took less than five minutes for the policeman to unfasten the ropes and pull sufficient tarpaulin away from the central hump for Brice and Fleming to climb on to the bridge. The first thing Brice's engineer's eye noticed was the surplus metal that the welders had left when they had fixed the anti-spray lip around the outside rim of the conning tower. It was sound enough welding, but it hadn't been cleaned up: a sure sign of mass production and a shipyard working under pressure.

Fleming was first down the hatch. By the time Brice had climbed down into the control room, Fleming had the attack periscope out of the well and was eagerly peering through the eyepieces.

'Amazing,' he muttered. 'Absolutely amazing. Clear as a bell. Take a look at that.'

Brice looked through the eyepieces. Fleming had the periscope trained on an unsuspecting office girl who was sitting in the sun on a flight of steps eating sandwiches. Her skirt was hitched up around her thighs. It was an astonishingly clear picture.

'Zeiss optics,' Brice commented, 'the best.' There was

something fascinating about looking through a periscope, especially one that gave such a bright, clear image as this one. It turned easily too. Brice estimated that the lone fisherman sitting in the rowboat was at least half a mile away, and yet it was possible to see that man seemed to be sketching something on the flyleaf of a book.

Brice straightened up and looked curiously around the control room interior. There was nothing revolutionary about the design but the layout was good: all pipes and cables had been carefully routed so that they would be accessible in an emergency. The various depth and pressure gauges were large and sensibly located high so that they could be seen from any position in the control room and not be hidden by the operators when they were perched on their stools. The really amazing thing was the size of the U-boat's interior. It was incredibly small. Brice correctly guessed that dissent among the crew would invariably lead to trouble. And trouble in a submarine was as deadly as a depth charge exploding against the pressure hull.

'No wonder the devils are finding it easy to sink our ships if they show up on a periscope as clearly as this,' Fleming remarked, peering through the eyepieces again. He studied the lone angler and wondered if the fishing was worthwhile.

Brice examined the seals around the watertight door. 'What are you going to call it?'

Fleming didn't speak for a moment; he had swung the periscope head back to the girl. 'They're going to name it after the code name of the operation to bring it to Barrow. Graph, HMS *Graph*.'

Brice was examining a depth gauge. 'Hey, these things are calibrated to over two hundred metres – that's way over six hundred feet. Twice the depth our subs can dive to. And yours.'

Fleming shrugged. 'My Bentley can't do anything like the top speed marked on her speedo.'

'You don't design subs like cars,' Brice said. He paused and looked around the control room again. 'You know, I still can't believe I'm aboard a German U-boat.'

Fleming stepped through the watertight door. 'Come and have a look at the torpedo, old boy. See if you believe that.'

Brice carefully removed the inspection cover from the torpedo warhead and shined his torch inside. Fleming was stretched out on one of the drop-down bunks that lined each side of the U-boat's forward torpedo room, watching Brice anxiously.

'Sure it won't go off, old boy? Just the appearance of those things makes me nervous. I've never seen anything that was so obviously intended to go bang.'

Brice shook his head. 'It's not like a mine. There's no point in booby-trapping something that isn't likely to fall into enemy hands.' He fished a camera out of his bag and attached a flash gun.

'You scientists puzzle me,' Fleming said. 'You're not a bit like the chaps writers make you out to be. You have absolutely no scruples about pinching other peoples' ideas.'

Brice checked the camera's focus. 'I didn't invent the camera, but that doesn't prevent me using it,' he said. 'Why sweat to design something if it's already been done? You can then concentrate on trying to improve it.'

'Point taken,' Fleming agreed.

'My job,' the American continued, 'is to see that the US Navy has the best torpedo there is.'

'Do you know yet if that thing will help?'

'Ask me in a couple of weeks.'

Fleming hooked his hands together behind his head.

'You're a man of simple ambitions, old boy. Mine is even simpler – to make money.'

'You've done all right with me on that score,' Brice commented sourly.

Fleming chuckled. 'Not gambling, that's for fools. There are other ways though. And much more agreeable places to do them.'

'Such as?' Brice asked, aiming his camera at the warhead.

Fleming closed his eyes. 'For some reason the island of Jamaica always comes to mind.'

Brice fired the flash gun and then turned his attention to a spare warhead without a torpedo body that was resting on a wooden cradle. He tapped it with his foot. 'This spare is a conventional warhead fired by contact when the nose strikes the side of a ship. Seems you were right about the German's shortage of magnetic warheads.'

Fleming smiled. 'Maybe we'll soon be sending them a few of ours.'

Later that afternoon, by a stream on the high fells near Barrow, Gallagher carefully tore the flyleaf from his book on the Lake District and gently heated it over the Primus stove to activate the invisible ink. At the top of the page was the rough, freehand sketch he had made of the suspect submarine at Barrow. The centre of the page was blank.

Gallagher moved the paper in a circular motion above the flame watching the centre of the page intently. Soon, faint lines began to appear. The lines hardened, followed by a gradual emergence of fine detail to complete the picture: an accurate line drawing of a Type VIIC U-boat. Every detail matched the details in Gallagher's sketch. The submarine moored at Barrow was, beyond all doubt, a U-boat.

And the only U-boat at Barrow was *U700*.

He allowed the page to drop on the stove's hissing burner and grinned at the leering pike's head, still wedged under the motorcycle's headlight.

'Well, Fergus, my boy. Looks like you've brought me luck after all.' He patted the pike's head affectionately and looked up at the soaring elm for a suitable overhanging branch.

50

As had become usual, the swell of conversation was effectively silenced by Anders' appearance in the hall.

Not a head turned as he walked to the serving table and joined the line. Also, as usual, the line melted as those waiting for their lunch moved to vacant seats at the tables.

Anders collected his tray and cutlery and looked for somewhere to sit. There were plenty of spaces but nowhere where he could sit alone. He nervously approached a table occupied by six Luftwaffe officers at the back of the room where there were three vacant places on one of the long benches. As one, the six officers rose and silently dispersed themselves to various free places throughout the hall.

Anders sat at the empty table and began to eat.

At the head table, Kretschmer was angry at the way his instructions were being interpreted. Not talking to Anders did not mean treating him like a leper. He wondered how he could reword his order and then decided it wasn't possible.

'At least it's better than what might happen to him otherwise,' Leymann pointed out as if he had read Kretschmer's thoughts.

The one man in the hall who was bitterly ashamed of

what had been going on for the last six days was Conrad Shulke. He finally decided that to eat at the same table as Anders could not be construed as a disregard of Kretschmer's orders. He picked up his meal and crossed to Anders' table. With a defiant glance at Stein who was watching with unbridled hatred, he sat opposite Anders and proceeded to finish his meal.

'You've upset someone, major,' said Stein, watching Shulke lifting potatoes.

Shulke paused in his work. 'Who and why?'

Stein nodded to Kirk who was standing nearby. The giant gunnery officer gave Shulke a sickly smile. 'Kirk seems to think you're disobeying the commander's orders,' Stein observed, brushing an invisible speck from his wrist sling.

Shulke looked at the huge gunner with contempt and wondered how it was that such an obvious thug could become an officer. Kirk's hands looked capable of tying knots in lamp-posts.

'If your little friend thinks that,' said Shulke, resuming work, 'then I can only assume he is as stupid as he looks.'

Kirk stepped forward and carefully selected the largest of the potatoes that Shulke had dug up. He held the potato out at arm's length in fingers that resembled a bunch of bananas and began to squeeze. Shulke watched, fascinated; Kirk's knuckles went white. There was a cracking sound and water began to ooze between the straining fingers. Kirk slowly opened his hand exposing a mass of pulp that had once been a potato.

'Eat with Anders again,' Stein warned, 'and next time it won't be a potato.'

The little major watched the two men walk away and forced himself to face the unpleasant fact that he was scared.

* * *

Lillian Baxter was about to close the sickbay window when she noticed Anders. It was usual for two prisoners to work one plot, but Anders was working by himself planting winter cabbage seedlings. She realized she hadn't seen anyone working with him for several days.

As she watched, Kirk and Stein appeared from the far end of the plots and walked down one of the dividing paths. Kirk was pushing a wheelbarrow. The two men were laughing at a shared joke. Anders looked up at their approach. To Lillian's surprise, Kirk and Stein left the path and walked straight across Anders' careful handiwork. Not only that, they seemed to deliberately kick and trample on the freshly planted seedlings. What happened next was a series of events of an ugliness that was in no way diminished by its brevity: Anders grabbed a garden fork and lunged at Stein. Kirk knocked the fork to one side and swung a heavy blow at Anders that missed. Anders grabbed a handful of earth and flung it in Kirk's face. The giant gunner gave an enraged bellow and drove his fist into Anders' stomach. Other prisoners stopped work to watch but made no attempt to intervene. Anders' legs buckled under him. Stein hooked his right arm around Anders' throat from behind and hauled him to his feet. Shulke suddenly appeared with a rake, and he brought the back of it down on Kirk's shoulder just as the gunnery officer was aiming another blow at Anders' face.

By the time Lillian had reached the scene clutching her first aid box, six guards led by Sergeant Rogers had waded into the skirmish and had broken it up. Lillian saw another company of guards, rifles at the ready, fanning out along the wire fence that bordered the lake. The prisoners involved in the fight had melted away leaving Anders lying in the middle of his devastated vegetable plot.

'What was it all about?' Lillian asked Sergeant Rogers.

'A diversion,' the NCO replied. He pointed at the

soldiers checking the fence. 'That's why they're down there. Always look in the opposite direction when you see a diversion.'

'It didn't look like a diversion to me.'

'They're not supposed to.'

Lillian moved toward Anders. 'I'd better see if this one is okay.'

'Wouldn't bother,' Rogers said as he walked away. 'That's the one who's the troublemaker.'

Anders had climbed to his feet and was bending down to retrieve the few undamaged seedlings. Lillian stooped down and passed him a plant that had only one leaf broken off.

'I think this one might be all right.'

Anders took it and said nothing.

'*Was* it a diversion?' Lillian asked.

Anders did not look at her. 'Of course.'

Lillian realized it was useless.

'I've got the new brake bits for my car,' she said changing the subject. 'Major Veitch says it's okay for you to fit them if Lieutenant-Commander Kretschmer has no objections.'

Anders stared down at a seedling with torn roots.

Lillian stood up. 'Of course, you don't have to if you don't want to.'

Anders looked up at her. 'Yes,' he said uncertainly. Then he smiled. 'Yes, I would like to very much.'

51

At Lorient, a biting October wind was sweeping eastward across the desolate airfield, making mournful music in the untuned telegraph wires that skirted the perimeter fence near the hangers.

Doenitz examined the crack in the Junkers' undercarriage with a magnifying glass. The fuel that had been pumped into the aircraft was now draining back through the hoses into the storage tank.

'It's closing.'

Kneller and Goder stooped down to peer more closely at the crack that gradually became fainter as the Junkers shed the huge load that had been poured into its tanks.

Doenitz straightened up and thrust his hands into his greatcoat pockets. He stared at the cluster of iron bars that Goder had suspended between the Junkers' wheels to simulate the weight of a torpedo. 'Lucky you heard it crack before you started the taxi test.'

Goder nodded. He preferred not to think about what might have happened if the Junkers' undercarriage had collapsed with full tanks.

'Do you have a spare strut in stores?' Doenitz asked.

'Yes, admiral,' the pilot replied disconsolately. 'Fitting a new one is no problem. But there's nothing to stop it happening again.'

'Let's find someplace warm and discuss it over coffee,' Doenitz suggested.

Goder gratefully wrapped his numb fingers around the steaming mug and politely waited for Doenitz to speak first. Both Kneller and the admiral were studying the plans of the Junkers' drastically altered fuel system. It was some moments before Doenitz spoke.

'How much more fuel was to have been pumped aboard when you heard the crack?'

Goder put down his drink and pulled a clipboard toward him. 'Three hundred litres, admiral.'

Doenitz thoughtfully rubbed his chin. 'So presumably, cutting down your fuel load by six hundred litres would create a safety factor to prevent the Junkers being overloaded?'

Goder smiled wanly. 'Please don't think I'm being facetious, admiral, but it's crazy to talk about safety factors and that Iron Annie in the same breath.'

'You haven't answered my question,' said Doenitz acidly.

Goder thought for a moment. 'Cutting down our fuel load by six hundred litres will enable us to take off, and that's all. We need every drop of fuel we can carry to find that U-boat.'

'But you have its exact position now,' Kneller pointed out.

Goder jabbed his finger at a graph on the clipboard. 'I've worked out our fuel requirements to the nearest eggcupful. We'll need that six hundred litres for inflight course corrections.' There was a hint of annoyance in the pilot's voice. He opened a map and pointed to the route that had been drawn with a heavy pencil. It was a huge semicircle that swept north-west out into the Atlantic, skirted Ireland to the west before turning toward England north of Ulster to approach Barrow from the north-west. The thick black line on the map resembled a giant reversed question mark.

'It's the circular course, admiral. Two thousand kilometres. If we could take a straighter line . . .'

'No,' Doenitz said sharply. 'You'd be cut down by enemy fighters before you crossed the English coast. Flying around Ireland will enable you to stay clear of trouble.'

'But it's a difficult course, admiral,' said Goder. 'We'll be making constant corrections – we'll have to. Flying at night, no landmarks, and a good probability of early morning fog in the target area.'

Doenitz realized what a seemingly impossible task he was setting Goder; the young navy pilot had little night-flying experience and had certainly never flown a four-thousand-kilometre round trip. Moreover, he would have to fly a dangerously weakened and overloaded aircraft in the hope of accomplishing a mission it had never been designed for.

There was a long silence in the room. All three men looked down at the map.

'There is one thing,' Doenitz said. 'Suppose I could arrange for a radio signal to be transmitted from the vicinity of the U-boat at fifteen minute intervals for three hours before your estimated time of arrival.'

Kneller looked blank at first, but Goder was astonished by the suggestion.

'A homing beacon, admiral?'

'Would it make a difference?'

It was then that Kneller understood what Doenitz had in mind. He opened his mouth to speak but was silenced by a withering stare.

'Well,' Goder said slowly, wrestling with the implication of what the admiral had said, 'every fifteen minutes . . . three hours . . .' He sat back and chewed his thumbnail. 'Yes, admiral, it would make all the difference in the world. We could fly straight to the target area.'

'On a safe fuel load?'

'Yes. We could remove one of the extra tanks.'

'Thank you, Goder,' Doenitz said. 'Would you leave us for a few minutes please?'

Goder got up and left the room.

'Admiral,' Kneller began earnestly, 'you realize what . . .'

Doenitz cut in harshly, 'If Gallagher wasn't prepared to take risks, John, he wouldn't have taken on the job in the first place.'

'But not unnecessary risks, admiral,' Kneller protested. 'He can't alter his frequencies. Mobility is his only hope of escaping detection. To ask him to transmit for three hours at regular intervals from the same area would be the equivalent of signing his death warrant.'

'I want that U-boat destroyed before the British discover how deep it can dive and redesign their depth charges! The safety of my U-boat crews comes before anything else!'

Kneller said nothing.

'Gallagher's signals will not have to be so powerful to reach an aircraft in his vicinity,' Doenitz continued in a reasoning tone. 'He won't need a high aerial. It shouldn't be beyond his ingenuity to transmit while on his motorcycle.'

Kneller stared at the far wall and eventually nodded his head. 'He'll be sent his instructions this evening.'

Just before 4:00 P.M. on that same day, Gallagher rigged his transmitter-receiver by a stream on the high fells and sat on his folding stool with the headphone pressed to his ear. He hoped that this would be the last call. He was confident he had provided his employer with more than enough information. With luck, he would be able to spend the rest of the stay in England getting on with some serious fishing.

The pike's head grimaced fixedly at him as he waited.

At four o'clock precisely, Lorient started talking to him. Gallagher's hand went to the horn button, and he rattled out his call sign and an acknowledgement.

But Lorient kept talking: '555,' they said. Gallagher frowned. The three digit code meant 'long message to follow,' which also meant that he'd have to be ready with a pencil and paper. He began to feel uncomfortable; a long message could mean a long reply – long enough for the army's direction-finding trucks to get a fix on him. He found a pencil and paper and told Lorient he was ready. It took three minutes to broadcast the text of the signal. When Lorient started the repeat, Gallagher had virtually covered the entire paper with groups of numbers. He allowed them to continue while he substituted the numbers for letters extracted from his book on fishing sites. It was a simple but safe code that used the text of a book held by both parties. It was less dangerous than providing the agent with an incriminating one-time code pad.

Gallagher was on the third line when he began to realize what they were asking him to do. He stopped writing and stared down at the sheet of paper as an icy serpent of fear coiled around his spine. His hand began to shake as he completed taking down the message. The headphone fell silent. Gallagher's fingers went to the horn button and hesitated. He knew he hadn't made a mistake – the wording of the signal made deadly sense: '. . . remain in vicinity of U-boat . . . every fifteen minutes . . .'

The palms of his hands were sweating now. The headphone had fallen from his fingers and was lying on the grass, bleeping imperiously. He picked it up and placed it against his ear. Did he understand the message? Would he obey instructions? Please acknowledge. Please acknowledge.

Gallagher gazed with unseeing eyes at the dancing, sparkling stream for a long moment before he slowly reached for the horn button with fingers that continued to tremble.

The army direction-finding truck was twenty miles east of Gallagher. The captain replaced the radio-telephone handset and smiled broadly at Corporal Anderson.

'I have a co-ordinate for you, corporal: one-seven-zero on a northern reciprocal.'

Anderson opened an adjustable protractor, set the angle and tightened the knurled screw. He placed the instrument's base on the straight edge at the bottom of the chart and slid the protractor along until its angled side was touching the centre of the cross on the map that marked the position of the second direction-finding truck. He drew a line across the map using the angled edge of the protractor – a line that intersected an existing line.

The captain studied the intersection point and nodded with satisfaction. 'Search all farmhouses and cottages within a two mile radius of that point, corporal, and we might find a radio transmitter. What was the signal strength?'

'Seven, sir.'

The captain scratched his chin. 'That was Charlie One's reading too. Which means that our talkative little friend is using a high, undirectional aerial – up a chimney, I dare say. Shouldn't be too difficult to find.'

Corporal Anderson looked at the sheet of paper covered with numbers. 'What about this, sir?'

'I'll pass it on to Brigadier Scott, but I doubt if they'll be able to crack it. They'll be using a one-time code pad.' The captain smiled suddenly. 'We'll move Charlie One and ourselves closer to Barrow. Next time our friend starts squawking we ought to be able to pin him down to within ten yards.'

Gallagher stared at the pike's head. 'Fergus, me boy,' he said. 'You're looking at a dead man.'

His voice was filled with sorrow rather than fear.

52

Stein counted slowly. Seven seconds had passed before the blinding searchlight beam returned like a comet to fill Grizedale Hall's ground floor laundry room with light.

'Two seconds longer than an hour ago,' Schumann said. 'See? I told you those tommies get tired of twiddling their lights in proper sequence.'

Another blaze of light swamped the room and departed, leaving rainbows dancing on Stein's retinas like demented roman candles. 'They're crazy,' he muttered. 'Why don't the idiots use floodlighting?'

'They tried,' said Schumann with a chuckle. 'We kept stealing the cable. Nine seconds that time. What are we waiting for?'

Kirk rose silently from the floor where he had been sitting like a giant Buddha. He scooped up the roll of cloth. An object inside the roll rattled metallically. The huge gunnery officer flashed his teeth in the dark in a grin of eager anticipation.

The three men pulled black woollen hoods over their heads. Apart from eye slits, their faces were completely covered.

'Okay,' Stein said, carefully timing his release of the window catch. 'Let's go and fix the little coward once and for all.'

It was nine o'clock and dark when Anders finished relining the brake shoes on the offside rear wheel of Lillian's station wagon. He looked at his watch and decided that there wasn't time to start the tricky task of refitting the brake drum. He had to be back in the hall in thirty minutes. He wiped his hands and looked at his handiwork with pride.

Apart from mealtimes, which were still an agony, he liked being alone. It was a legacy of a brotherless and sisterless childhood. All his life his parents had spent long hours working in the family bakery and had little time to attend to the needs of the undemanding boy who seemed content with his life, provided he could spend it in the public library.

Anders had done extremely well at school but was handicapped by a lack of self-confidence. He regarded his academic successes only as an indication of low standards set by his schools rather than a mark of any real ability. As a result he set himself impossible targets and then suffered from the belief that others secretly ridiculed him when he failed to achieve them. It was fear of ridicule that always haunted him. He never joined in team games because he dreaded the possibility of letting his side down by doing something stupid. He played chess but only because he could memorize all the openings in solitude and familiarize himself with classic games before exposing himself to the risks of competition. He easily beat his first opponent – his headmaster – in fifteen moves and then quickly convinced himself that the teacher had deliberately let him win to spare his feelings. For Anders, victories were also crushing defeats.

His father had served in U-boats during the Great War and had fond recollections of the spirit of comradeship that had existed among their crews. With the onset of the war, he felt his sensitive son would be happier serving in the newly-formed U-boat arm rather than in the world of harsh disciplines and traditions that characterized service on the 'big ships'.

The letter ordering Anders to report to submarine training school at Kiel had come at a time when he was on the brink of establishing a close relationship with his father. But it came 14 years too late, and Anders' short periods of leave during his initial training were insufficient to sustain the delicate flower of trust and understanding that had flourished so briefly and so splendidly between them.

It was inevitable that the break with home, coming at such a crucial time, meant Anders would unconsciously turn to Weiner as a substitute for his father.

And now, alone, friendless and miserable, a prisoner in a strange land far from home, Anders lived with the agonizing knowledge that his carelessness, his stupid lapse of attention at *U700*'s sky periscope, had led to a betrayal of Weiner's trust. And after that, as if seeking to atone for his betrayal, he had taken a loaded Luger onto the bridge and had pointed it at Weiner. When Weiner turned and saw the gun, his eyes, revealing a strange expression of sorrow that time would never erase, mirrored Anders' innermost feelings about himself. He was a failure, a despicable coward and, worst of all, a Judas.

It was a few minutes past nine. Anders shivered as he dropped the wrenches into the toolbox. He dreaded the nights in the dormitory, having to be first into bed, curled into the foetal position with the blanket pulled over his head.

Kretschmer's orders had been obeyed to the letter; the only time anyone spoke to him was when the British NCO bawled out his name at morning and evening roll calls.

There was a faint sound from the loft, a sudden creaking of roof timber. The noise was repeated, louder this time. Anders crossed the floor to the steep flight of steps that led to the hay loft. A muffled thud was followed by a shuffling noise that didn't sound like the noise rats would make. Anders' pulse quickened.

'Is anyone there?'

Silence answered.

He was about to put his foot on the first step when there was a sudden swish of displaced air. The tip of a homemade sword hit the step level with his eyes with such force that it splintered through the timber.

Before Anders could react he was knocked to the ground by a huge shape. Nor could he cry out for a mighty hand, like a giant bat, clamped itself over his mouth. 'Make one sound,' rasped a harsh, guttural voice an inch from his ear, 'and I lay a vein open so that you bleed like a pig.' It was Kirk pressing his 'bosun's sabre' hard against the side of Bernard's neck. 'You understand?'

'Yes,' Anders managed to croak.

A powerful push sent him reeling backward against the station wagon's radiator. The three masked figures advanced slowly toward him. They were dressed entirely in black. The middle figure was shorter than the other two, and his left arm was in a wrist sling. He was holding two swords in his right hand. He tossed one of them onto the flagstones beside Anders.

'Pick it up.'

Anders shook his head. 'I'm not going to fight you, Stein.'

Stein moved forward and pressed the tip of his sword hard against Anders' temple. 'You're going to fight, Anders. Everything is in your favour.' Stein held up his sling. 'Just the sort of handicap that would appeal to a coward.'

Anders looked at Kirk and Schumann in contempt. The two gunners were standing on either side of the stable. They looked like two gorillas watching for an opportunity to tear him to shreds.

'You have seconds . . .' Anders managed to say.

Stein flicked his blade experimentally back and forth under Anders' chin. 'They won't interfere.'

'I'm not going to fight you,' Anders repeated defiantly. He put his hand on the flagstones to push himself up, and as he did so his fingers touched the sword's crude hilt.

It was a mistake – a challenge duel started the instant an opponent touched his sabre. Anders looked up and saw the steel tip of Stein's sword lunging toward his throat.

* * *

Lillian pursed her lips in the mirror propped against the medicine cabinet and decided that lipstick was too scarce for her to waste any more trying to get the twin arches of her Cupid's bow exactly right.

She looked at her watch. Ten minutes past nine. David, her fiancé, had promised to pick her up at quarter past to run her home to Barrow. It was a nuisance having the station wagon out of commission – it meant having to fight David off on weekdays as well as weekends. Oh well . . .

A last check to make sure her seams were straight – her last pair of civilian stockings – and then lock up. She could hear the faint strains of the choir rehearsing in the main hall. God, how the Germans could sing. Her high heels clomped hollowly on the scrubbed linoleum floor. It was dark outside. For a moment she wished that she had obeyed standing orders by asking for two guards to escort her to the main gate. But the prisoners had never been any trouble and had always treated her with respect. Sergeant Rogers had explained that German prisoners accepted a measure of discipline that no British soldier would tolerate where women were concerned.

Anders threw himself to one side and the tip of Stein's sword blazed a wake of sparks across the flagstones where he had been lying. He lashed out at Stein with his feet and, to his surprise, felt his shoes connect with Stein's shins.

Stein overbalanced and began to topple forward, suddenly realizing that the wrist sling was a greater handicap than he had anticipated. The point of his sword jammed in a cracked flagstone and the weapon, unable to support his weight, snapped off six inches from the end of the blade. His wounded arm collided with the station wagon's headlight. The pain that lanced his arm was so intense he thought he was going to faint. He recovered just fast enough to parry Anders' inexpert thrust at his side. The speed of Anders' recovery surprised Stein. Before he was properly on his feet and correctly balanced, he had to ward off two more thrusts. The missing six inches of blade was worrying; combined with Anders' long reach, it gave him a deadly advantage.

Stein drove forward for an opening, but Anders twisted sideways and deflected Stein's truncated blade. It was a neat move – one that would have meant the end for Stein had Anders been an expert. Nonetheless, it frightened Stein badly.

He sprang backward, moving lightly on his toes and feinting quickly to confuse Anders while he decided what to do. He noticed that Anders wasn't holding the hilt properly and realized it would be easy to disarm him. He feinted again, deliberately leaving himself open. Anders saw the opportunity and drove forward. Stein sidestepped adroitly and brought the flat of his blade down on Anders' sword with all his strength.

The shockwave raced up Anders' arm like a thousand volts and his sword clattered to the flagstones. He tried to grab the weapon but Stein, laughing, kicked it toward the station wagon. As Anders dived after it he tripped and fell heavily against the driver's door.

Stein pulled his mask off and smiled at Anders with thin, bloodless lips. He tossed his broken sword to Kirk, and picked up Anders' sword from the floor.

'Well now, Anders,' he said easily, 'you fight well for a coward.' He gestured to Kirk and Schumann. 'Now is the time, I think.'

The two bear-like gunnery officers removed their hoods. Grinning broadly Kirk walked slowly toward Anders, cracking his knuckles and flexing his broomstick fingers.

Anders climbed to his feet and backed away from the approaching giant. He didn't see Schumann edge around behind him until it was too late. Schumann seized his arms and pinioned them to his side.

'Over the hood,' Stein said curtly.

Kirk arched Anders backward until he was lying across the station wagon's hood with his back crushed against the radiator. Schumann hooked Anders' feet under the front bumper, his cry of pain stifled by Kirk's suffocating hand.

Stein stood over his victim and rested the tip of the sword on Anders' belt. 'Don't worry, Anders,' he said with a cold smile. 'I'm not going to kill you. But I am going to make sure you're the last of your cowardly line.'

With that he moved the sword's jagged tip downward.

Lillian was passing the stable when she heard a faint whimper. Frowning, she walked to the double doors. They were locked. She peered through a crack in the doors. It was some seconds before she could make out what was happening inside the stable and then she saw them: two men standing on either side of the car appeared to be holding something down on the hood. A third man had his back to her. He was holding a sword.

Suddenly Lillian was hammering on the double doors and screaming for help.

53

Major Veitch snatched the two swords up off his desk and held them angrily under Kretschmer's nose. The German officer did not flinch but kept his eyes fixed steadily on the British officer.

'What about these?' Veitch demanded. 'Have you felt their edge? Do you honestly expect me to believe . . .'

'Major Veitch,' Kretschmer interrupted calmly. 'This is an internal discipline problem, and I give you my solemn word that there is no Nazi bullying going on.'

Veitch tossed the swords contemptuously on his desk. 'One of those men could've been killed last night.'

'It was a duel. Nothing more.'

'A duel? Is that how civilized men behave in your country?'

Not a muscle moved in Kretschmer's face. He stared hard at the British major until Veitch was forced to drop his gaze. 'It's a tradition, major, in which, as we've seen, no one gets hurt.'

Veitch shook his head. 'Nurse Baxter is of the opinion that Anders would've been hurt if she hadn't raised the alarm.'

Kretschmer remained silent.

Veitch watched the German's face. 'Nurse Baxter is also of the opinion that Lieutenant Bernard Anders is being systematically bullied,' he stated flatly.

'If she has concrete evidence of that,' Kretschmer replied dispassionately, 'then I'd be most grateful if her evidence could be passed on to me so that I can deal with the culprits.'

It was the longest sentence that Veitch had ever heard from the aloof German officer. 'I sincerely hope you are able to stamp out this bullying without evidence from us,' Veitch said caustically. 'Because if you don't, the War Office most certainly will. I hope I make myself clear.' He stood. 'Good day, commander.'

Kretschmer returned Veitch's salute, turned on his heel and strode out of the office. Leymann was waiting outside. The tubby lawyer had to trot to keep up with Kretschmer as he walked angrily to the main hall.

'He's agreed to transfer Anders?' Leymann asked.

'No.'

Leymann was surprised. 'Why not?'

Kretschmer stopped to unwrap and light a cheroot. 'Because that's not what I asked for. I'm not going to unload the problem on another senior German officer at another camp.'

Leymann shrugged. 'So you let Anders stay. Stein or some other hothead will kill him, and it's no more than he deserves.'

'He deserves a fair trial,' Kretschmer said coldly.

'And what do we do in the meantime while we're waiting for the invasion of England?'

'You're to appoint bodyguards to keep a round-the-clock watch on Anders. Luftwaffe men would be best.'

'That won't cure the basic problem.'

Kretschmer blew out a thin cloud of smoke. 'I know, Willi. That's why we'll have to think of something that will solve the problem once and for all.'

54

Fleming parked his Bentley beside *U700*, trotted nimbly along the gangplank on the U-boat's deck casing, and disappeared down the hatch. Brice was too absorbed in his work to notice Fleming's arrival.

'Morning, Alan,' Fleming said breezily, hoisting himself on to a bunk. He pointed at a framed photograph hanging from a handwheel. 'Who's the charming lady? Your wife?'

Brice nodded and then yawned widely. 'I sent her a cable giving her my solemn word I'll be home in time for Thanksgiving.'

'You look all in,' Fleming commented sympathetically.

Brice smiled and reached for a Thermos bottle. 'The plant cafeteria has concocted a special brew for me to keep me awake. Like some?'

Fleming sniffed the flask's contents suspiciously. 'What does it taste of?'

'Acorns. They claim that it's coffee. It keeps me awake worrying what it's doing to me.'

'Thank you, no,' Fleming said. 'Actually, I'm going back to London, so unless you want a lift back, I've just dropped in to say cheerio.'

'Thanks, Ian, but I don't want to miss the test dive. A skeleton crew and two scientists are taking her out at daybreak next Tuesday.'

'How deep?'

'Two hundred feet to start with.'

Fleming's elegant features creased into a grimace. 'Rather you than me, old boy.'

Brice grinned. 'This baby's good for six hundred feet.'

'Bring it back in one piece,' Fleming said, jumping down from the bunk. 'There's a plan afoot to open it to the public for a few days. Oh well, I daresay our paths will cross in London.'

'They'd better,' Brice growled. 'I want to win some of my money back.'

Fleming laughed as he stepped through the watertight door. 'Not a chance.'

'Hold on, Ian,' Brice said, rummaging through the notes and diagrams that were strewn across the torpedo room floor. He straightened up and held out a paper bag. 'A small token of my appreciation. I'm very grateful for all you've done.'

Fleming accepted the bag, looked inside, and took out a book entitled *Birds of the West Indies*.

'You said you wanted to live in Jamaica after the war,'

Brice said quickly. 'I thought it might be useful. The girl in the shop said that James Bond was a world authority on birds.'

Fleming, touched by the gesture, shook Brice's hand warmly. 'That's jolly decent of you, Alān. Thanks very much indeed.' He paused and looked down at the partially dismantled torpedo. 'How's the scientific espionage progressing?'

'It's a fine torpedo,' Brice said. 'I've learned a helluva lot in the last few days.' He paused and then grinned broadly. 'Espionage, eh? Well, for all intents and purposes I guess I really am on His Majesty's Secret Service, aren't I?'

55

The mess hall had been converted for a Council of Honour, and the first thing Anders noticed when he walked in was the large, homemade Kreigsmarine flag, with its central black swastika, that was mounted on one wall.

'Council of Honour,' Shulke had scoffed the previous day. 'They're mounting a court-martial – an illegal court-martial at that.'

The double doors closed behind Anders, and the two Luftwaffe officers who had acted as his bodyguards since the incident in the workshop marched beside him through the rows of seated prisoners. Anders guessed that the entire camp was present.

Faulk was seated at a table directly beneath the flag. In front of him was a long table with Conrad Shulke sitting at one end and Willi Leymann at the other. The first row of chairs was occupied by Kretschmer – smartly turned out with the Knight's Cross gleaming at his throat – and Sub-Lieutenant Richard Stein.

Anders took his place beside Shulke. Faulk stood – the signal for everyone present to rise to their feet.

'Lieutenant Bernard Anders, Mr President,' one of the Luftwaffe officers announced.

'Thank you,' Faulk said.

The two Luftwaffe officers clicked their heels in unison, saluted, and marched back to the doors. They would remain within earshot of the alarm system that would alert them if and when the British approached.

Anders caught Shulke's eye. The whole business was turning out to be a more elaborate farce than either of them had anticipated.

'You will remain standing, Lieutenant Anders,' said Faulk, as he sat down, motioning everyone else to do likewise. 'There are two charges against you. One: as acting commander of a U-boat, you displayed cowardice in the face of the enemy. Two: that you failed to obey battle orders by scuttling your U-boat to prevent it from falling into enemy hands. How do you plead to these charges?'

Anders followed Shulke's instructions by remaining silent.

'How do you plead to these charges!' Faulk repeated.

Conrad Shulke stood. 'I've been studying the Geneva Convention, gentlemen. It's an interesting document. Not only does it lay down standards for the treatment of prisoners-of-war by their captors, but it also lists the responsibilities of the prisoners. The holding of courts-martial by prisoners is expressly forbidden.'

'If you are addressing me,' Faulk said, 'you will address me as Mr President. Otherwise I will nominate someone else to conduct Lieutenant Anders' defence.'

'Germany is a signatory of the Geneva Convention,' Shulke said tartly.

Leymann rose. Prison diet was improving his figure but not the fit of his uniform. 'Mr President, I have explained to Major Shulke that this is a Council of Honour and not a court-martial. It will hear the evidence that is available and *recommend* a sentence – not pass one. Afterward, Lieutenant Anders will be able to join in all normal camp activities and mention of, or reaction to in any form, the *U700* affair will be forbidden until we are liberated after the invasion.'

'If I'm to defend Lieutenant Anders,' Shulke said, 'it is my duty to challenge the legality of this council.'

Faulk nodded. 'Fine – you've challenged it. Now let's get on. How does your defendant plead to the charges?'

'Not guilty,' Shulke muttered and sat down.

Leymann hauled himself to his feet. The plump Bavarian lawyer was obviously enjoying himself. He read Anders' statement to the gathering and briefly outlined the circumstances that led to *U700*'s surrender. Then he turned to Faulk. 'For my first witness, Mr President, I wish to call Sub-Lieutenant Richard Stein.'

Stein stood very straight. He had gone to considerable pains over his appearance even by his standards; his blond hair had been carefully brushed and his shirt stiffened with starch obtained by boiling a potato. He answered Leymann's searching questions in a clear, resolute voice, without sparing Anders a single glance. The final questions dealt with the round robin – the document that Stein had circulated to the crew of *U700* before the armed trawlers and destroyer had arrived.

'Every member of the crew pledged their support for Lieutenant Anders if he were to arrest the captain and countermand the surrender?'

'Yes,' Stein replied. 'Everyone signed. There would have been no question of Anders having to cope with divided loyalty if he had arrested Weiner.'

Leymann lowered his bulk on to his chair. 'No more questions, Mr President.'

Shulke stood and referred to his notes. 'You said that the RAF do not possess an air-borne depth charge, Lieutenant Stein, but only an anti-submarine bomb that is useless unless it scores a direct hit. Correct?'

'Correct,' Stein said crisply.

Shulke smiled. 'Not all of us here are naval men so perhaps I had better enlarge. A bomb explodes on the surface of the water and has to hit a U-boat to be certain of harming it. A depth charge explodes beneath the surface and can cause severe damage to a U-boat even if it misses?'

'Correct,' Stein repeated. 'But the RAF do not have an air-borne depth charge.'

Shulke relaxed – Stein had walked into the trap. 'They most certainly do now. The three new arrivals this morning are survivors from a U-boat that was destroyed by depth charges dropped by a Sunderland flying boat. If necessary, I shall be calling them as witnesses.'

Stein remained silent, and Shulke began to feel more comfortable in his unfamiliar roll of inquisitor.

'Did you see this "bomb" fall?' he asked.

Stein hesitated momentarily. Then, 'No.'

'Why not?'

'I ducked. It's customary when a bomb falls – it helps you live longer.'

There was some laughter, which Faulk silenced with his homemade gavel.

Shulke remained outwardly unruffled. 'Did Captain Weiner duck?'

'I don't think so.'

'You don't think so,' Shulke's tone was scathing. 'So

you've no idea if the Hudson dropped a bomb or an infinitely more deadly pattern of depth charges. You ducked while Weiner bravely watched the Hudson all the time.'

'Bravely?' Stein echoed incredulously. 'He was paralysed with fear!'

'Did he wave his shirt after the Hudson dropped the depth charges?'

'Yes.'

'Immediately after? Before it had time to turn?'

'Yes. He tore it off in panic.'

Shulke frowned. 'But just now you said that Weiner was *paralysed* with fear! If Weiner was paralysed with fear and yet managed to get his jacket off, and tear off his shirt to wave at the Hudson, we can only conclude that you helped him!'

It was a wild guess yet it produced a reply that caused a murmur of surprise among the prisoners.

'I helped him off with his jacket and shirt because I thought he'd been injured by a bomb splinter.'

'Nevertheless, you helped Weiner and therefore played a significant part in *U700*'s surrender!'

Stein's face paled. 'That's a damned lie! I was the only one who fought that Hudson! Look!' He jerked back his sleeve revealing the bandage wrapped around his left forearm. 'This was caused by a round of 303 machine-gun fire from the Hudson's front turret.'

'Exactly, lieutenant!' Shulke barked. 'You were injured – you were carried unconscious to your berth, and you weren't in the control room after the attack. In view of this, how can you expect this council to believe you when you say, as you said in your evidence, that *U700* was undamaged after the attack and was capable of diving? And why, may I ask, should we take the word of a man who needs the support of a couple of thugs before creeping out of the hall at night to attack Lieutenant Anders as he worked alone in the stables!'

There was an outburst of jeering and catcalls directed at Shulke from the prisoners.

Leymann bobbed to his feet. 'Mr President, I feel that the council must instruct Major Shulke to stick to the issue and not resort to shouting abuse at the witness on irrelevant and unsubstantiated matters.'

'I have no more questions,' said Shulke, sitting down and folding his arms.

'In that case, I would like to call my next witness,' said Leymann. 'Lieutenant Bernard Anders please.'

Leymann looked smugly confident as Anders moved to the witness table and recited the oath. He carefully tidied his notes before addressing Anders.

'Were you paying close attention when Lieutenant Stein was giving his evidence?'

'Yes.'

'Excellent. Is there any part of his account that you wish to dispute or refute?'

'No,' Anders replied.

'Why didn't you relieve Weiner of command after the surrender?' Leymann asked, his tone mild. 'You knew that you had the support of the crew.'

'Because that would constitute a mutiny,' Anders replied resolutely.

'You went to training college?'

Anders sensed trouble. 'Yes.'

'Were you not taught the difference between mutiny and the justified relieving of command?'

'Yes.'

Leymann thrust his thumbs into his waistband and watched Anders carefully. 'Please tell the council the difference.'

'I can't remember the exact wording.'

'Then give us an inexact rendering.'

Anders thought for a moment. 'Mutiny is the refusal to obey the lawful commands of a senior officer. Justified relieving of command is . . .'

Leymann pounced the instant Anders faltered. 'Justified relieving of command is when the senior officer has demonstrated by his actions or inaction that he is no longer capable, either mentally or physically, of issuing lawful commands! Isn't that right?'

'Yes.'

'After the attack by the Hudson, you said in your statement that you went on to the bridge and found Weiner in a state of shock. A state of shock! Your own words! So why didn't you relieve him of command there and then?'

Anders stared at Leymann and wondered if he had the courage to blurt out the one thing that he had not mentioned in his statement: that at the crucial moment during the surfacing drill, he had taken his eyes away from the sky periscope.

But Leymann didn't wait for an answer. 'Didn't Lieutenant Stein *passionately* urge you to assume command?'

'I – I didn't trust him.'

'You didn't trust him,' Leymann repeated sarcastically. 'And yet every member of the crew signed that pledge. What was the matter, Anders? Wasn't that enough for you? Did you want their signatures in blood?'

Shulke half-rose to object but Leymann was relentlessly hounding his prey – determined to drive Anders into an inescapable corner. 'And still you refused to act! Nor did you act after Weiner abandoned the boat and paddled to the destroyer. You were left in command then!'

Anders looked up at his tormentor. 'No. The captain of the British destroyer was technically in command of the U-boat after the surrender.'

'You worried about legal niceties when there was a danger of your boat falling into enemy hands?'

'I was worried for the safety of the crew.'

Leymann ignored the answer. 'Why didn't you give the order to abandon ship so that you could scuttle the boat? There was plenty of time.'

'How could I when the British had threatened to open fire if I allowed the crew on deck?' Anders demanded.

'Didn't it occur to you that they wanted to prevent you scuttling?'

'I thought they were worried in case we tried to man the main gun.'

'And you refused Lieutenant Stein's offer to jump into the water to see if they were bluffing?'

'I was worried for the safety of the entire crew including Lieutenant Stein. In the heat of the moment I felt as Commander Weiner did – that the lives of the crew were more important than the capture of the boat.'

Leymann adopted a puzzled tone. 'Surely you realized that the secrets revealed to the enemy could lead to the deaths of countless sailors in the future? That the entire U-boat offensive could be endangered?'

'I've told you what my thoughts were,' said Anders. 'And besides – everything of value in the boat was destroyed.'

'Except the magnetic torpedo in one of the bow tubes!' Leymann roared. 'The one thing that the enemy wanted above all else!' Leymann regarded his victim with contempt. 'So you thought of nothing else but your own skin and the skin of the crew?'

Anders failed to see the inherent danger in the double-edged question and blundered into the lawyer's trap. 'Yes,' he began. 'But . . .'

'Yes!' Leymann thundered triumphantly. *'Yes!'* He

looked at the assembly as if seeking confirmation of Anders' guilt.

'Do you realize what your reply means?' he asked softly.

Anders shrugged. 'What does it matter what I say? You'll only twist it to mean something else.'

'Do you wish to reconsider?'

'I just want all this over. All I can say is that at the time I saw no point in needless killing and I had no wish to die myself. I saw nothing wrong in that. Now I don't care very much if I do die.'

Leymann gathered up his notes. 'I have no more questions for this coward.'

Faulk looked inquiringly at Shulke. 'Major Shulke?'

Shulke rose slowly to his feet and considered his words. 'My own definition of coward,' he said quietly, 'is someone who has the courage to show that he's not a hero.'

There was a silence that was broken by Faulk. 'Very well. The Council of Honour will now retire to consider its verdict.'

Everyone in the hall rose. Faulk, Kretschmer, Stein, Leymann, and Shulke left the hall by a side door. Shulke turned and gave Anders a brief smile as he turned to close the door behind him.

Anders sensed that another ordeal was about to begin. Before him was a sea of silent, expressionless faces. No one spoke. No one stirred. There was no overt movement or gesture from any individual that might set them apart from the other members of the mob. For that's exactly what they were. A mob. A controlled mob. A point-us-in-any-direction-and-we'll-fix-them mob.

Then someone started to hiss. It was, as is usual with mob behaviour, the signal for others to join in. The hissing spread, a venomous expression of hatred for something that they didn't understand and didn't want to understand.

A wad of newspaper smacked against Anders' cheek.

Another struck him on the forehead. Two more missed. A fifth hit his eye and produced tears.

The hissing stopped abruptly as the door opened and the members of the council filed back and took their places. They had been out of the room for less than three minutes. The prisoners waited for Faulk to sit, but he remained on his feet, grim-faced and silent.

Then he cleared his throat. 'Lieutenant Bernard Anders,' he said, 'you have been found guilty of failing to scuttle your ship to prevent it from falling into enemy hands. You have also been found guilty of displaying cowardice in the face of the enemy.' Faulk paused and referred to a piece of paper. 'With one dissension, the recommended sentence of the Council of Honour is that you be hanged at a convenient time and place as soon as this war is over.'

56

The next morning Lillian pushed the stable doors open and found Anders working on the last wheel of her station wagon.

'Good morning, Bernard,' she said cheerfully, kneeling beside him. 'How's it going?'

'Okay,' Anders replied without looking at her.

'I'm supposed to be meeting my fiancé tomorrow evening. I was wondering if you'll be finished in time.'

'It'll be ready tomorrow.'

Lillian smiled. 'You said that yesterday.'

'There was a holdup in the afternoon.'

Lillian became serious. 'I'm seeing Major Veitch later this morning to thank him for allowing you to repair the car. Is there anything you'd like me to mention to him for you?'

Anders fitted a wrench to the brake's cable adjustor. 'Such as?'

'Such as a transfer to another camp.'

'I'm okay here.'

Lillian frowned. 'I'm not blind, Bernard.'

'It was a duel. Friendly sword play. An old tradition.'

'I don't mean that,' said Lillian sharply. 'I'm talking about *U700*.'

Anders nearly dropped the wrench.

'The papers didn't give names of the crew,' she said, 'but it was your boat, wasn't it?'

'What if it was?'

'It surrendered. It was in all the papers. It doesn't need much intuition to guess that Kretschmer wouldn't look kindly upon someone involved in the surrender of a U-boat.'

Anders shrugged. 'Not if the surrender was unavoidable.'

Lillian began to get angry. 'Don't treat me as being completely stupid, Bernard. David, my fiancé, works at Barrow at Vickers. In two weeks time they'll be opening *U700* to the public. He said there was so little damage done to it that he couldn't understand why it surrendered.'

Anders spun the brake drum. 'I wasn't the captain. The surrender has nothing to do with me.'.

Lillian looked at him for a few moments and then sighed. 'I can't blame you if you don't want to talk. I am the enemy, I suppose.' She got to her feet and moved to the doors. 'But if you do need help, Bernard, please don't be afraid to ask.'

Anders stared at the brake drum after Lillian had left, thinking about what she had said. He remembered hearing a guard mention that he had a girl friend in Barrow. That meant that the town, or whatever it was, could not be far away.

The map of northern England was still in the station wagon's glove compartment. No doubt Major Veitch would burst a blood vessel if he knew about Lillian's carelessness. Anders spread it out on the floor and found Barrow almost immediately.

Amazingly, it was less than twenty miles from Grizedale Hall.

'Barrow?' Leymann echoed, his round, moon-like face sagging in amazement. 'Is he sure?'

Kretschmer nodded. 'It makes sense, Willi – a large submarine works with the expertise to assess the U-boat's capabilities. We should have guessed the British would send it there.'

Leymann looked down at the map. 'About twenty miles. What's that? Thirty kilometres?'

Kretschmer leaned back in his chair and lit a cheroot. 'A five hour walk across country for him, Willi.'

'You would send *him?'*

Kretschmer exhaled a cloud of smoke. 'It's his idea, Willi.'

'It's his fault the damned boat's there in the first place,' Leymann growled.

'That's why he ought to be given the chance to destroy it.'

'He wouldn't last five minutes out there,' Leymann protested. 'His English is barely passable.'

'Shulke has agreed to help him with it.'

Leymann stared at his senior officer. 'You really think Anders could do it?'

Kretschmer gave a ghost of a smile. 'If he survives the escape method that he's suggested. But he'll need a bomb – a substantial bomb – to blow that U-boat in half.'

57

Stein started counting as soon as the searchlight beam burst into the laundry room. He signalled to Anders and Kirk. The gunnery officer pushed his tools into his pockets and scooped up the roll of stair carpeting.

'Now!' Stein whispered as he pushed the window open.

Anders and Kirk dropped to the ground and dived for cover behind a group of shrubs. Kirk tightened his grip on the roll of narrow carpeting as a beam swept over their heads. Then the giant gunner was running, chasing the beam, with Anders close on his heels. They threw themselves flat as the beam completed its traverse of Grizedale Hall's facade and swung back in the opposite direction, passing above the two men. Kirk jabbed Anders in the ribs and ran toward the administration compound following an erratic route that utilized cover provided by the scattered trees. Anders, following close behind, was amazed at the gunner's ability to move like a cat despite his size.

They reached the high barbed-wire fence that surrounded the camp armoury. Kirk produced two pairs of stiff leather gloves. He and Anders stood on one end of the carpet roll and heaved it high into the air so that it dropped neatly over the fence near one of the concrete posts. When they went over the fence, using the carpet as protection against the needle-sharp barbs, their weight wouldn't leave a telltale sag in the wire. They pulled on their gloves and moments later were over the fence without difficulty. They disentangled the carpet and hid it under the autumn leaves for the return journey. Leaving it in place had been considered too risky.

The camp armoury was a substantial concrete hut protected by a heavy steel door and a massive padlock. Kirk examined the padlock by the light of a candle that Anders held cupped in his hands. Then he started to probe the interior of the lock with a variety of small tools and pieces of stout wire. The candle was beginning to burn Anders' hands.

'Come on,' he muttered impatiently.

Three minutes passed before Kirk grunted in satisfaction. There was a faint metallic click and the padlock fell open.

Anders followed Kirk into the armoury and pulled the door shut. He held the candle high and sucked in his breath in amazement. They were in an Aladdin's Cave of rifles, anti-riot equipment, small arms and ammunition. Kirk chuckled and held a hand grenade under Anders' astonished nose.

'No throwing stick,' said the giant gunner, grinning broadly. 'But I guess they still make a nice bang, eh? How many do you want?'

The events and planning of the past twenty-four hours had restored Anders' self-respect, giving him a degree of self-confidence he had never known before.

He set the box down on Kretschmer's desk and was able to meet the cold, watching eyes.

'You have everything?' Kretschmer demanded.

'Everything,' Anders said, reaching into the box and placing the items on Kretschmer's desk. 'Two kilos of wet clay, an alarm clock, a shoebox, string – and these.' Anders set six hand grenades in a neat row on the desktop, and Kretschmer picked one up and examined it curiously.

It was quite unlike the German grenade. Instead of a hollow throwing handle that contained the friction ignitor, there was a pin that passed through two diecast ears below the neck of the grenade. The pin held a curved, spring-loaded lever against the grenade's body.

'Pull that pin out,' Anders said, 'and the lever flies up and starts an eight-second fuse. They're not as good as ours because you can't carry several in your boots, but they're ideal for making a bomb.'

Kretschmer pushed the six hand grenades across to Anders. 'Show me,' he invited.

Anders pressed several handfuls of soft clay into the shoebox and picked up one of the grenades. He held the lever firmly and withdrew the pin. Still holding the lever in place, he gently pushed the grenade lever side down into the bed of clay in the shoebox and then packed more clay tightly around the grenade's body.

Anders smiled. 'This is the awkward part.'

Slowly, Anders removed his hand from the grenade. The clay held the lever safely in place. Anders dropped the pin on the desk.

Five minutes later there were five pins on Kretschmer's desk and five grenades packed into clay in the shoebox.

A large space at one end of the box comfortably accepted the alarm clock. The bells had been removed and a length of string had been tied to the key that wound the alarm. Anders tied the other end of the string to the pin on the sixth grenade and fitted it into the shoebox. The sixth grenade was the only one with its pin still in place.

'That's it,' Anders said, wiping the clay from his fingers. 'The alarm goes off, winds the string around the key as it turns and pulls the pin out of the priming grenade. It explodes, shatters the clay around the other five grenades, which all explode together eight seconds later.'

'Neat,' Kretschmer said. 'Are you sure the clock key develops enough power to pull the pin out of the grenade?'

'Plenty,' Anders said.

Kretschmer opened a drawer and placed a .38 Webley

revolver on the desk. 'Kirk took it from the armoury.' He slid it across to Anders. 'You'll need it to get aboard the U-boat.'

Anders shook his head. 'I don't think so, commander.'

'You'll take it!' Kretschmer rasped. 'Otherwise we send someone else.'

Anders stared at the gun. It was an agonizing reminder of the time he had pointed the Luger at Weiner on *U700*'s bridge. Then he picked it up and said, 'I've got nothing to lose, have I? If I'm caught before I plant the bomb, the British will hang me. If I'm caught afterward, they'll hang me anyway. And if I manage to escape to Ireland after destroying the boat, the navy will hang me after the war.'

'Very likely,' Kretschmer observed.

Anders smiled thinly. 'Well at least I know where I stand.' He paused. 'When do I break out?'

'Is the harness finished?'

'Yes, commander.'

Kretschmer drummed his fingers. 'We already have some papers and clothing, but not a great deal of money. On the other hand, I see no point in delaying the mission. We go tomorrow night.'

58

In Lorient, Admiral Doenitz had just completed his inspection of the modified Ju52. He stood back from the aircraft and gazed at it, an expression of satisfaction on his sharp features. He pointed to the torpedo that was slung between the Junkers' undercarriage legs.

'Is it safe to leave the torpedo in position?'

'Perfectly, admiral,' Goder said. 'We won't fuel her until thirty minutes before take-off. That way we'll keep the strain on the undercarriage to a minimum.'

Doenitz returned to his Mercedes and sat silently for some moments. Kneller knew better than to disturb his thoughts.

'Has there been a change in the weather forecast, John?'

'None, admiral.'

'Very well. See that Gallagher receives his final instructions today.' Doenitz tapped his driver on the shoulder and turned to Kneller as the car moved off. 'Goder and Hartz will be taking off for Barrow tomorrow night.'

59

The following day, after the evening roll call, Anders entered the stable. The station wagon was there. The major worry had been that Lillian might decide to leave before her usual schedule.

A few minutes after Anders entered the stable, a small party of prisoners armed with buckets, chamois and hand mops, appeared at the upper windows that overlooked the stableyard and its approaches and set to work to make the windows shine. Another man was weeding the lawn in front of Lillian's sickbay. His job was to walk whistling through the stableyard after Lillian had closed her windows preparing to leave her office.

Faulk and Shulke sauntered into the stableyard deep in conversation. One of the window-cleaning lookouts cracked his chamois twice. The two men raced into the stable and pulled the door shut.

Anders was struggling into a crude, homemade webbing

harness similar in design to a parachute harness. 'The hooks are in place,' he said as Shulke helped him. 'I haven't had time to test them, but they ought to hold if she doesn't drive too fast.'

'She will,' Faulk said.

'Sssh!' Shulke put a warning finger to his lips.

There were footsteps outside. The door opened, and Kretschmer entered. 'All set?' he asked.

'Nearly,' Anders said. 'The bomb and greatcoat are in position.'

Kretschmer went down on one knee and looked under the station wagon. The shoebox bomb had been hidden in a stolen British kitbag and was hanging from a clip secured to the station wagon's chassis. A greatcoat, rolled into a tight pack, was also hanging from the chassis.

'Excellent,' Kretschmer said, straightening up. 'Maps and papers?'

'Sewn into the greatcoat's lining,' Anders said, pulling the curious harness tight around his body. 'Okay. I'm ready.'

Kretschmer held out ten pounds in banknotes and loose change. The coins had been individually wrapped to prevent them jingling. Anders thrust the offering into his pocket.

'Everyone contributed something,' Kretschmer said. 'Including Lieutenant Stein. And don't forget, Anders, if you can't get aboard the U-boat, place the bomb under the deck casing.'

Anders nodded. 'Commander,' he began hesitantly. 'I wondered if . . .'

'I can't make promises,' Kretschmer interrupted. Then his expression softened. 'But I'll give evidence for your defence.'

He held out his hand.

'Good luck, Anders. And write to us from Ireland.'

'I'd like you to have this,' Shulke said holding out a tiny, silver St Christopher medallion.

'Thank you, Conrad,' Anders said gratefully. 'You've been a good friend.' Then: 'Right. I'm ready.'

Five minutes later Anders lay suspended in the harness underneath the station wagon feeling like a trussed turkey. His cheek was pressed against the gasoline tank, one leg was hooked over the vehicle's propeller shaft, and the other was a few inches above the muffler. The lowest part of his body, his back, was less than nine inches from the ground. Already the harness straps were beginning to cut into his limbs and slow his circulation. He prayed that Lillian would not keep him waiting long.

'What are his chances?' Shulke asked as he, Faulk, and Kretschmer walked away from the stable.

'Of blowing up the U-boat?' Kretschmer said, drawing deeply on the last half-inch of his cheroot. 'About fifty-fifty.'

'Of reaching Ireland,' Shulke said.

'Zero,' Kretschmer said. He dropped the cigar butt and ground it into the cobbles with his heel.

Lillian closed the sickbay's sash window, pulled down the heavy blackout blind, and locked her door. She took off her uniform and looked sadly at her stockings. They would never do. Her last pair too. Slacks would solve the problem, but David detested them. The day was approaching when she would be forced to wear the army issue horrors – when she could get them. She sighed and rolled them off. On her desk was one of Oliver Lyttelton's 'make do and mend' pamphlets, issued by the Board of Trade, containing advice to young ladies dressing up for that 'important evening out'. Its tips on 'the amazing things that can be achieved with the circumspect application of an eyebrow pencil' were just short of hilarious. Giggling to herself, she positioned her mirror, and with infinite care, began drawing a stocking-seam black line up the back of her leg with an eyebrow pencil.

It was five minutes since Anders had heard the worm-cast remover strolling through the stableyard whistling the current hit tune *I Yi-Yi-Yi-Yi-I Like You Very Much*.

The strap was cutting cruelly into his legs, and his arms were numb. Of all the men throughout the country at that time who were waiting for women to get changed, his vigil was the most painful.

Lillian critically examined her false seams. Not bad. She pulled on the pair of hated panties that her mother had made for her from parachute silk. She always felt uncomfortable in them and the vivid display of blue sparks they produced when she took them off was unnerving.

Kretschmer looked at his watch in irritation. There was another hour of daylight left. The later the girl left, the better, but he was worrying about the effect the long wait would be having on Anders.

Sweat trickled into Anders' eyes, but there was nothing he could do about it. He tried to rub the side of his face against the petrol tank, but that only made matters worse. Perhaps she had decided not to go out after all – even if it was a fine evening. There was a faint sound. He stopped breathing and listened. It was the unmistakable clip-clop of high heels on cobblestones. They got louder and then stopped. There was the sound of a key being inserted in a lock. Anders' heart stood still. My God! The doors! They'd forgotten to lock them! There was a faint exclamation of surprise from Lillian when she discovered that turning the key had locked the double doors. She unlocked them and pulled the doors open. Anders had a glimpse of her ankles as she walked down the side of the car and got in. Even with her slight weight, he was surprised at the amount the leaf springs settled.

The starter motor churned, then whined harshly as the engine fired once and kicked the Bendix pinion out of mesh. The engine started on the third attempt. There was a crunch from the gearbox. Anders had to move his right hand quickly to prevent his fingers from being caught in the handbreak linkage as it moved to release the rear brakeshoes. His body jerked suddenly as the car reversed out of the stable. A sharp pain in his calf reminded him to keep his leg off the propeller shaft's exposed universal joint. There were more crunching noises as Lillian tormented the gearbox into providing her with first gear. She revved up and released the clutch. The station wagon left rubber on the cobblestones as it shot out of the stableyard, narrowly missing a prisoner with slow reflexes.

The rapid acceleration threw a tremendous load on the shackles that supported Anders' weight. Horrified, he watched helplessly as the one that held the left side of his body slowly began to open. He desperately heaved his body to one side in an attempt to ease the burden on the shackle, but Lillian's hard cornering on the gravel drive leading to the main gate made the manoeuvre impossible. He was oblivious to the sharp stones that flew up from the tyres and peppered his face – all that concerned him was the terrifying thought that it was only a matter of seconds before the shackle gave way completely and dropped his tortured body onto the road.

Leymann and Shulke were pretending to be busy sweeping up leaves near the main gate when they heard the long-awaited sound of Lillian's station wagon. They continued working as the vehicle drew up in front of the steel gate. A soldier emerged from the guardhouse. Shulke bent down to gather up an armful of leaves and saw, to his horror, that one of the straps was trailing on the road behind the vehicle. And even worse – Anders had his hand on the ground and was struggling to push himself up.

'Evening, sweetheart,' said the soldier affably to Lillian, propping himself against the driver's door. Three times he'd asked Lillian out, and three times she had refused. But he wasn't one to give up that easily. 'He's done the brakes, then? All right now, are they?'

'Absolutely super,' said Lillian. 'Just a bit of a squeal from the back.'

The soldier looked concerned. 'Could be the shoes binding,' he said. 'Can make the drums overheat.' The soldier moved to the rear of the station wagon and started to kneel down by the rear wheel.

'I'm dreadfully late,' said Lillian impatiently.

'Won't take a minute.'

'Look, I haven't come a hundred yards. I'm terribly late, so if you don't mind opening the gate . . .'

The soldier decided he was wasting his time. After a cursory inspection of the car's interior, he signalled the corporal to open the gate.

Lillian stirred up some aggravation in the gearbox with the gear lever and hurtled through the gate, accelerating hard toward the 400-yard stretch of rough track that led to the main road. She loved fast driving – especially the weaving drive along the unmade road, swerving from side to side to avoid rocks and potholes without easing her foot off the throttle pedal. There was one particular jagged rock that jutted up at least nine inches. Since the expensive time when she had hit it, she had learned to position her hurtling car so that the rock passed between the offside wheels and the bulging centre of the rear axle.

60

The late afternoon sun sparkled on the Junkers' wings as the gang of mechanics wheeled it out of its hangar at Lorient. The aircraft was moved to a dispersal point where two gasoline tankers were waiting.

Goder and Hartz checked the flowmeters that measured the fuel as it was pumped into the Junkers; it was essential that they knew exactly how much gasoline they had aboard when the refuelling was complete.

With fuel gurgling into the aircraft's tanks, the two men completed their inspection of the cabin. The extra tanks that had been fixed to the floor looked satisfactory, and the stopcocks turned easily. There hadn't been time to install solenoid-operated fuel valves that could be controlled from the flight-deck; thus it would be necessary during the long flight to enter the cabin periodically to replenish the Junkers' ordinary tanks from the additional tanks by opening and closing valves manually.

Goder left the cabin and jumped down on to the concrete. The sun was still surprisingly warm as it had been all day. He walked into the shade of one of the gasoline tankers and looked up at a mechanic standing on a wing holding a gasoline hose steady.

Something was worrying Goder. There was a tiny but vital detail he was certain he had overlooked. It had been worrying him all afternoon, and he had been confident it would eventually come to him. But now, with less than two hours to take-off, he still could not think what it was.

61

Dusk was falling on the Cumberland fells by the time Gallagher was satisfied with the arrangement he had rigged so that he could transmit the homing signals to the Junkers without having to dismount from his motorcycle. He had lashed one of his fishing rods to a small haversack so that the rod with the antenna wire attached would be upright when he was wearing the haversack on his back. Such a short antenna would effectively reduce the range of the transmitter, but the Junkers ought to be in range from three hours before dawn when he was due to make his first homing transmission.

Homing, thought Gallagher wryly. That was a joke. Not only would his signals guide the Junkers to him, but also every bloody British soldier in north-west England. Holy Mother of God – riding around Barrow in the small hours of the morning! He wouldn't have to use his radio to arouse suspicions.

He checked the specific gravity of the motorcycle's battery with a hydrometer. He didn't want the battery to let him down at the last minute so that he would be forced to operate the transmitter with the motorcycle's engine running; he knew that he would need his ears more than any other sense in the back streets of Barrow.

He quickly packed his tent and cooking equipment and hid them in a foxhole. Tonight he would dine in Barrow and find himself a girl with a warm heart and a warm bed to rent.

62

Fleming recognized the station wagon that pulled out of the turning 200 yards ahead of his Bentley: it belonged to the crazy nurse who had tried to pass him when he and Brice had arrived in Cumberland.

Fleming's foot went to the floor. The Bentley's pistons increased their pounding and sent a great surge of power through the gearbox to the Brooklands thoroughbred's rear wheels.

Lillian heard the approaching howl of the Amherst Villiers supercharger and looked in her mirror. She smiled. It was the conceited naval commander. She accelerated and swung into the middle of the road. She wasn't going to let the arrogant oaf get past that easily.

63

It was dusk in Lorient when Kneller's phone rang.

Doenitz was standing some yards away looking out of a window, but he could plainly hear that the caller sounded extremely agitated.

'*What!*' Kneller said disbelievingly.

Kneller clapped his hand over the mouthpiece. 'It's Goder, admiral,' he said in a strained voice.

'Well?'

'He wants all the electric fans in the headquarters building to be put on a truck and sent to the airfield immediately.'

Doenitz lifted the electric fan off Kneller's filing cabinet and coiled the wire around the base. 'Tell him that he'll have every fan we can find in twenty minutes.'

Kneller swallowed. 'Shall I ask him why?'

'There'll be time for that later,' Doenitz said, moving quickly to the door. With that simple statement he demonstrated why he was an admiral and Kneller was not.

64

Lillian waved to Fleming as the Bentley swept past. Fleming gave her a languid salute, and Lillian watched the coupé receding along the coast road before she turned off the main road and drove up the deserted track that led to the secret spot on the cliffs.

She could see the roof of David's Austin 7 above the gorse bushes. He got out when he heard her car approaching.

65

At six o'clock, Doenitz's Mercedes arrived at the airfield and parked near the floodlit Junkers. Kneller gaped in astonishment at the aircraft, too stunned to move. Doenitz was already striding across the concrete, stepping over heavy electric cables that snaked toward the aircraft from a roaring generator truck parked nearby.

There were electric fans everywhere, trained on the

gasoline tankers standing by the Junkers. Some were positioned under the wings, blasting air upward at the wing fuel tanks, and several were actually on the wings training streams of cool air into open inspection panels.

'What the devil's going on?' Kneller muttered.

'I think I can guess, John.'

A mechanic passed the word to Goder that Doenitz had arrived. The pilot appeared in the Junkers' doorway. He jumped down and gave Doenitz an embarrassed salute. 'Thank you for sending the fans so quickly, admiral.'

Doenitz carefully moved around a dangerous looking tangle of electric wires and leaned into the aircraft's cabin. As he expected, there were more fans clustered around the fuel tanks. One mechanic was even placing wet towels on top of the tanks.

'Will someone tell me what is going on?' Kneller pleaded.

Goder was crestfallen. 'It was my fault. The gasoline tankers have been standing in the sun all day, and it's been exceptionally warm. The fuel warmed up in the tankers and expanded so that, although we'd filled Iron Annie's tanks to the brim, we couldn't pump the full weight aboard.'

Kneller immediately understood. Had the Junkers taken off loaded with warm fuel, it would have contracted rapidly as it cooled, depriving the aircraft of gasoline as effectively as if there had been a leak in every tank.

'How much longer will all this take?' Doenitz asked.

'We should be all right now,' Goder said. He signalled the generator truck to cut electric power.

A mechanic unscrewed one of the Junkers' gasoline filler caps and inserted a refuelling hose. Other mechanics did the same with the wing tanks. The gasoline tanker's pumps were switched on. Fuel could be plainly heard gushing into the Junkers' tanks.

'Ten minutes ago we filled the tanks up to the brim for the second time,' Goder said.

Five minutes passed before Goder announced that the Junkers had now received its full weight of gasoline. The portable floodlights and the electric fans were loaded on to a truck and driven away, followed by the gasoline tankers and the generator truck. The runway landing lights came on as Goder and Hartz shook hands with Doenitz.

A solitary fire engine drove across the airfield and waited expectantly halfway down the runway to one side. Doenitz and Kneller moved clear and watched Goder and Hartz walk around the big transport aircraft for a final visual inspection. Goder paid particular attention to the giant clamps that gripped the 21-inch torpedo between the undercarriage legs.

'We should have chalked a suitable message on the torpedo,' Goder commented as he followed Hartz aboard and closed the door.

The two men settled themselves in their seats. Goder checked that the three central throttle levers were back in the closed position so that the brakes were firmly on. He checked the magneto switches and turned the port engine over on the starter to prime the fuel injectors.

Goder smiled at Hartz as they went through the prestart procedure. 'Nervous?' Goder asked.

'Terrified,' the younger pilot admitted.

'You won't be now that you've got something to do.'

The port engine coughed, and within a few seconds all nine cylinders of the BMW engine were firing smoothly.

'Sweet as honey,' Goder said, repeating the procedure with the starboard and nose engines.

Once all three engines were checked and running correctly Goder, not wishing to waste fuel, immediately teased all three throttles forward to get the Junkers moving. The brakes came off but nothing happened. Only when all three counters were showing six thousand revolutions per minute did the grossly overloaded aircraft begin to roll.

There was an ominous creak from the undercarriage when the wheels passed over the first of the seams in the runway concrete.

'My God,' Hartz muttered to himself. He knew the feel of the Junkers well enough to be certain that it would never make it. Its normal take-off speed was around 55 knots. He and Goder had calculated that it would take at least 70 knots to generate enough lift to get the Junkers air-borne. Goder had placed a marker two-thirds of the way along the runway. If they weren't air-borne when they reached it, there was just enough runway left to shut down the engines and apply the brakes.

They passed the 400-metre marker with the air speed indicator showing a miserable 25 knots.

At 500 metres the Junkers was up to 35 knots.

There was another heart-stopping jolt as the Junkers hit an extra wide seam.

Forty knots. Just enough speed for Goder to bring the tail up to reduce drag. It also reduced lift by decreasing the wings' angle of attack, but speed was the all important factor.

Fifty knots. The fire engine was pacing the Junkers. The entire airframe shook as the wheels pounded over the seams.

Sixty knots. The throttles were wide open. All three engines were delivering their maximum 675 horsepower output. Goder's hand went to the trim wheel. He edged the flaps down and felt the familiar pressure in the seat of his pants that tells a pilot when his wings are developing lift.

Seventy knots. The seams were now punishing the aircraft with shuddering, sledgehammer blows at three-second intervals. More flap. Seventy knots. Tail too high. Bring it down a trifle. Eighty knots. That was the last marker that flashed by. Too late to stop now. Takeoff or bust. More flap . . .

The pounding stopped. The Junkers was air-borne. Goder held her level to build up more air speed and then gently pulled the big transport's nose up for a slow, fuel-conserving climb to eight thousand feet.

66

It was dark when Anders crawled slowly out from under Lillian's station wagon and sprawled exhausted on the grass. It had taken him fifteen minutes to disentangle his aching limbs from the harness – fifteen minutes of unremitting torture. As he lay on the grass, the events of the past hour were a confused whirl of images. There was the moment when he had just managed to drag the trailing strap out of sight before the soldier from the guardhouse saw it; the hideous charge along the unmade track where a boulder imbedded in the ground had missed him by centimetres; and lastly, the deadly chase along the road with his helpless body hanging precariously in the path of a thundering Bentley that was sitting on the station wagon's tail.

Anders listened carefully for some seconds. Lillian and David had disappeared over a small hillock.

He squeezed back under the station wagon, released the clips that secured the kitbag and the greatcoat, and dragged them behind him into the undergrowth.

He felt better after a short rest and was even able to obtain a bearing on the Pole star through a break in the clouds. He unrolled the greatcoat and pulled it on. It was of a similar colour and cut to the British navy's overcoat. It fitted reasonably well and at least it concealed his lacerated uniform.

He cleaned his face on handfuls of grass, swung the kitbag over his shoulder, and stumbled off in the dark toward the main road.

67

While Anders was trying to find his bearings on Cumberland Fells, Alan Brice was repositioning an inspection cover on the magnetic torpedo on *U700*'s bow torpedo room. Petty Officer Evans stepped through the watertight door holding a steaming mug.

'Coffee, Mr Brice.'

Brice gratefully accepted the drink, sipped cautiously and tried hard not to grimace.

'I made it just like you said, Mr Brice,' Evans said proudly. 'It *is* all right, isn't it?'

Brice put the mug down. 'Let's say that we've both made progress this week, Evans – me with my torpedo and you with your coffee.'

Evans grinned. 'Are you staying aboard for the test dive, Mr Brice?'

'I wouldn't miss it for the world.'

'Do you reckon she can go as deep as them gauges say?'

'No reason why not. It's an all-welded pressure hull so that there are no rivets to be forced in by water pressure – and it's made of the best Krupp steel.'

Evans looked doubtful. 'Ours creak and groan something horrible at two hundred and fifty feet.'

Brice smiled. 'So do ours. Don't worry, you'll be boasting about this to your grandchildren. What time do we leave?'

'Oh seven hundred,' Evans said.

68

Gallagher woke and was seized with panic. He groped in the darkness for his watch. A book fell off the bedside table, but the sleeping girl at his side didn't stir. Gallagher found the light switch. It was 2:30. He sank thankfully back onto the bed. He had never expected to fall asleep. He pushed back the covers and looked at the girl. He had found her in a pub near the docks. Her husband was in the army, she had said, and she didn't fancy the idea of joining the Land Army or working in a factory to find the money for the rent. Gallagher wondered how much rent she had to find each week for the dingy room with its worn linoleum floor covering and brown leaves wallpaper that had long gone out of fashion.

He rolled a five pound note into a cylinder and pulled back the covers. He gently teased the girl awake with the tip of the paper tube. She opened her eyes and tried to push Gallagher's hand away. He unrolled the banknote and held it up for her to see.

She groaned.

'Haven't you had enough for one night?' But she took the money. 'Shopkeepers can't stand fivers. Haven't you got anything smaller?'

Gallagher grinned and made a coarse reply. The girl sighed and braced herself.

69

Hartz walked his dividers across the chart and fixed the Junkers' position as 300 kilometres west of Ireland at fifty degrees twenty minutes north. He double-checked the position by means of the *Console* radio navigation beacon receiver that collected the signals through the direction-finding loop on the top of the Junkers' fuselage. He had a good fix. He wrote the position down, returned to his seat, and handed the slip of paper to Goder.

'Okay,' the senior pilot said. 'Time for a course alteration.'

Goder brought the Junkers' nose around until it was heading due north.

They were halfway to their destination.

70

The streets of the grey, granite town were deserted. Anders stepped into a shop doorway and looked carefully around before unfolding the map and striking a match. The road map was of no use in identifying the town. And yet it had to be Ulverston – there was no other town of a comparable size in the area. Anders hastily dropped the match when he heard a vehicle approaching. It was a baker's van with slitted black-out cowls over its headlights. The name on the side of the van had been painted over. It was the same with the shops. Place names and telephone numbers had been obliterated, and he hadn't seen one signpost that night. The British were very efficient.

He walked for another ten minutes, pausing now and then to search shop windows for clues. He saw a house with a plaque screwed to the wall near the front door. He crossed over, but the plaque, put up by a proud owner of the house, merely informed him that it was where Stan Laurel of the Laurel and Hardy partnership had been born.

He passed a telephone box. A hundred yards farther on he stopped, raced back to the box, and pulled the door open. He nearly dropped the matches in his excitement. The label in the centre of the dial had been removed and then unofficially restored by means of a strip of gummed paper. It proclaimed: ULVERSTON 234.

He was halfway to Barrow.

71

Gallagher sat on the edge of the bed smoking a cigarette. The girl had fallen asleep again clutching the five pound note. He looked at his watch – 3:30. Thirty minutes to his first scheduled transmission. He stood and pulled on his clothes, taking care not to wake the girl. He looked down at her and felt in his jacket pocket for his wallet. It contained one hundred pounds in assorted used notes. He hesitated. Why should he? What had the British ever done for him except kill his father? And yet the girl had done everything he had asked of her without complaint. He pulled the money out of the wallet and dropped it onto the pillow. She didn't stir when he drew the bedclothes over her shoulders and gently kissed her on the cheek.

He went quietly down the stairs and let himself out the backdoor. His motorcycle was leaning against the outside toilet. It took him ten minutes to connect the fishing rod and strap it to the haversack. He wheeled the machine down the passageway between the houses and pushed it a hundred yards along the street before swinging his leg over the saddle and kicking the starter.

Anders knew he was on the outskirts of Barrow because he had been able to identify a number of features from the map, and the advertisements in a newsagent's window had given mostly Barrow addresses. A truck was parked at the side of the road some twenty yards ahead. Anders thought it was deserted, but suddenly a door opened and the figure of a man was framed against the red glow of the softly illuminated interior. Anders was familiar with red lighting because it was used in U-boat control rooms at night to preserve the night vision of those going on lookout duty. The vehicle would be military. It was, in fact, an army wireless truck. Anders could see the direction-finding loop mounted on the roof, but it was too late to turn back. The soldier had sat down on the truck steps and was nursing a hot drink. He had seen Anders and was watching his approach with interest.

Hartz moved aft into the Junkers' cabin and opened the fuel cock on the main tank. The level in the sight glass sank as the fuel drained into the underfloor tanks. He yawned and rubbed his eyes. They had been flying for nine hours.

'Lucky swine,' muttered Corporal Anderson, eyeing Anders walking past the radio truck. 'Skulking back to his ship for breakfast. Navy types have all the luck.'

The captain slipped one of the headphones off his ear. 'Did you say something, corporal?'

'How much longer are we going to keep this up for, sir? Maybe he's gone home or changed his frequency?'

'Charlie One will hear him if he has, corporal,' was the captain's unsympathetic reply.

A motorcyclist rode by with a fishing rod and a haversack strapped to his back.

My God, thought the corporal. Bloody all-night anglers as well.

The corporal was now convinced that he was the only soldier in the north of England who wasn't getting time off.

Gallagher had spotted the direction-finding loop on the top of the truck. 'Holy Mother of God,' he muttered to himself. He prayed that the British weren't monitoring on the forty-eight metre band that night, but knowing his luck, they probably were. He held his watch in the meager beam of the hooded headlight: 3:45. Fifteen minutes to get to the docks and start work. He had plenty of time.

Hartz sat at the radio set, put the headphones on, and tuned the receiver to 48.1 metres. He wondered who the mysterious radio operator in Barrow was who would be guiding them toward their target.

The chart under his hand showed that the Junkers had flown virtually all the way around Ireland. In a few minutes Goder would make another eastward course correction. Hartz looked out of the window, but there was nothing to see but cloud. It had been like that all the way from France.

Gallagher coasted his machine to a standstill and listened. It was a typical dockland street with depressing rows of slate-roofed houses and warehouses that had been built nearly two centuries before during the Industrial Revolution. The entire area was the same – a maze of gloomy streets and grimy tenements with only gleaming brass door knockers and holystoned front steps to challenge the pervading air of squalor and deprivation.

Gallagher had spent two days getting to know the district – memorizing the names of every street and discovering where the back alleyways went to and which ones he could get the motorcycle through if he had to.

He looked at his watch. One minute to transmission. He sat upright on the saddle so that the antenna was perpendicular and reached for the horn button.

Hartz heard the soft bleeps in his headphones and quickly reached up to rotate the direction-finding loop. The operator transmitted five pulses at two second intervals. The broadcast lasted just long enough to get a bearing. He checked the angle of the loop and converted it to a true bearing. The Junkers was a mere two degrees off course.

'He's back!' yelled Corporal Anderson, almost knocking his headphones off as his arm shot up to crank the handwheel that turned the direction-finding loop.

The captain grabbed the radio-telephone handset and spoke quickly to the other wireless truck.

'Bloody hell – he's stopped,' Anderson complained.

The captain looked surprised. 'So soon?'

'It wasn't a message, sir. Just blips, five of them. I got the last two at field strength eight from the docks area.'

'Field strength eight, corporal?'

Anderson grinned. 'That's right, sir. Sounds like we're right on top of the bastard.'

The captain stared at the corporal. 'Are you sure, corporal?'

'Positive, sir. I could even make out his morse key. Mushy make-and-break. Homemade or something.'

The captain tapped his teeth with a pencil. 'Charlie One didn't get his bearing,' he said thoughtfully. 'And if he didn't send a message, it's possible that he'll be talking again.' The captain reached for his radio-telephone. 'I think I'll notify General Bowen.'

Twelve minutes later two Bedford army trucks, each one carrying a small company of armed commandos, moved through the sleeping streets of Barrow.

Anders was hopelessly lost. Every street looked alike: endless rows of tenements, bow-fronted Victorian houses, and crumbling warehouses. He could hear heavy trucks moving in a nearby street and decided he had better hide until they had gone. The particular street he was in was about 300 metres long with a junction at each end. The road was curved so that by hiding in a doorway half way down the block, he would be able to keep both junctions under observation in case the trucks appeared.

He found an entrance to a narrow alleyway between two warehouses and crouched down, listening intently for the sound of the diesel engines. The trucks had either gone or stopped.

He was about to emerge from his hiding place when a motorcycle suddenly turned into the street. He pressed himself back into the alleyway as the machine roared past and stopped at the opposite end of the street.

Gallagher, unaware that he was being watched by an escaped German prisoner-of-war, cut his engine and listened. He felt a prickling sensation at the back of his neck as he watched the second hand of his watch – his finger poised on the horn button. He sensed that something was wrong and was tempted to abandon the next beacon or move to another street. But it had to be this street because it was near the German U-boat and there was an alleyway that he could use as an escape route if both ends of the street were sealed off. Exactly fifteen minutes after his last transmission, Gallagher tapped out another five pulses.

He listened again. Silence. Then a starter motor churned a diesel engine into life. It was a long way off. There was no wind so it could be as much as a mile. It might be a coincidence that it had started so soon after he had finished transmitting, but it was the sort of coincidence that made Gallagher uneasy. He decided to make his next transmission from the opposite end of the street in case that wireless truck had obtained a good fix.

Corporal Anderson frowned at the map of Barrow. 'That's odd, sir. That last transmission came from a different area.'

'Sure you didn't make a mistake the first time, corporal?'

'Positive, sir.' The corporal stared at the map. 'Maybe he's mobile. That must be it! You ought to tell those commandos to be on the lookout for some kind of vehicle.'

By now Anders was convinced the motorcyclist was a policeman who was looking for him or knew that he was hiding in the alleyway and was playing a game with him. Anders got a grip on himself: the man was simply having trouble with his motorcycle. Or was he? Anders braced himself when the motorcyclist started his engine.

Gallagher swung his machine around and rode to the opposite end of the street. He stopped the engine and strained his ears into the night. Nothing. He checked his watch. A minute to the next beacon. Dawn in a couple of hours. A mist was rolling in from the sea. He blew on his hands. At least it didn't matter if they were cold because he wasn't transmitting messages – just this accursed five pulse beacon every fifteen minutes.

He reached for the horn button. He got no further than transmitting two of the pulses because the diesel engines that burst into life sounded as though they were in the next street.

At first Hartz thought that the receiver had failed. He had picked up two of Gallagher's bleeps and no more. He rotated the loop antenna. Nothing. He tuned the receiver to Oslo, picked up a concert, and retuned back to the forty-eight metre band. There was nothing wrong with the radio receiver.

Gallagher kicked his machine into life and roared back to the opposite end of the street. He stopped, undecided what to do. He hadn't completed the transmission and was certain that the aircraft heading toward Barrow would continue to listen. By now the British were certain to know that he was mobile; so continuing to transmit from the same street might confuse them.

Anders heard a faint sound from the opposite end of the street to where the motorcyclist was waiting. He peered around the corner of the alleyway in time to see the darkened army truck coast to a standstill, its engine switched off. Soldiers armed with rifles jumped down from the vehicle's tailboard. They must have been wearing soft shoes, for their movements were soundless as they formed a line across the road.

Anders seized the kitbag and doubled back down the alleyway. He froze when he heard faint voices from the darkness at the far end of the passageway. They had the entire area sealed off. There was no chance of escape. He made his way back to the alleyway's entrance.

* * *

Gallagher started his machine and swung it in the direction of the waiting commandos. He didn't see the line of soldiers across the road until he was level with the entrance to the alleyway. Suddenly the street was filled with light from the truck's uncowled headlights.

'Halt!'

Gallagher slewed the machine around, kicked it into second gear, and roared back down the street in the opposite direction. A second army truck screeched across the road in front of him, its headlights adding their blazing beams to illuminate the trapped motorcyclist.

'Halt, or we fire!'

The alleyway was Gallagher's only hope of escape. He tore the blackout off his headlight and turned it full on. He spun the machine around in a skidding U-turn, dropped into first gear, and lay himself on the tank as he aimed for the entrance to the alleyway.

The sound of the motorcycle thundering toward Anders was deafening in the narrow passageway. Was the motorcyclist bent on killing him? He was too blinded by the headlight to climb the walls that lined each side of the alley. Suddenly there was the reverberating crash of sustained rifle fire. Bullets whined into the masonry above Anders' head. He dropped the kitbag and flattened himself against the wall just as the motorcyclist screamed and threw up his hands. His body seemed to be lifted from the saddle by the force of the bullets that ripped into him. His arms and legs flailed in the air. Then his body hit the ground, rolled over, and stopped within two yards of Anders. The riderless motorcycle produced a shower of sparks as its handlebars gouged along the brickwork, before falling on to its side, its back wheel spinning as the engine continued to race, and the headlight still burning.

Anders kept perfectly still, hardly daring to breathe.

The motorcyclist was motionless. But his eyes were open, and they were staring straight at Anders.

The motorcycle engine suddenly died, and a strange stillness descended. The cordite fumes from the soldiers' rifles mingled with the night mist that seemed to glow with ethereal light from the motorcycle's rear lamp.

Then there was a movement of khaki as four soldiers, led by a sergeant, moved quickly toward Gallagher's body. They were crouched low. Alert. Rifles at the ready. The sergeant dropped onto one knee by the still form, but there was no need for him to examine the body closely. He straightened up and saw Anders watching him with wide, frightened eyes. The sergeant stiffened, quickly brought his rifle up until it was pointing at Anders' chest, and jerked his head down the alleyway toward the trucks. Anders obediently moved off.

'Hey, you!'

Anders stopped and looked back. The sergeant was pointing at the kitbag that Anders had dropped.

Goder swore loudly when Hartz told him the signals from Barrow had ceased. Since picking up the first two beacons, they hadn't worried about maintaining a running fix on their position. Hartz returned aft and obtained a rough fix from three BBC stations. It couldn't be relied on because the BBC had erected small sub-transmitters near their main stations to prevent them from being used as navigation aids by the Luftwaffe.

Goder toyed with the idea of abandoning the mission and turning back. Without the homing signals they stood little chance of locating the U-boat. It was the thought of Doenitz's hard, grey eyes that made him decide to press on.

Anders stood by the truck while the commandos loaded the motorcyclist's body aboard. He was puzzled – the soldiers had caught him but weren't taking any notice of him. They seemed to be more interested in the dead man's motorcycle.

'You still here, mate?' It was the sergeant.

Anders blinked at him, not understanding.

'Submarines?' the sergeant asked.

Anders nodded.

The sergeant put a friendly arm around Anders' shoulder and steered him away from the truck. 'I expect you've seen worse. Best get back to your sub and forget it, eh?'

Stunned, Anders walked away from the scene. The sergeant watched the receding figure and shook his head sadly before turning back to his commandos and bellowing orders.

The two army trucks swept past Anders as he walked along the street. An arm waved from the leading vehicle. Anders kept walking blindly, wondering if they would suddenly return to arrest him. He had no idea where he was, but there was the unmistakable tang of salt water in the air. The trucks reached the end of the street and turned off. As they did so, their headlights swept across the large noticeboard outside a factory. To Anders, the three words on the noticeboard were the most important words in the world: VICKERS SUBMARINE WORKS.

Only the plant's main gate was guarded. Whistling a tune, Anders walked past the two dockyard policemen and reached the end of the road where a passageway led down the side of the plant. He climbed the chain link fence in the safety of the shadows and dropped behind a pile of marine gearbox castings. It was then that he heard the sound of lapping water. He dodged between piles of dockyard supplies and made his way toward the magic sound. He was crossing the railway track of a dockyard crane when a door opened nearby. He stepped back against a large crate. There were voices. Laughter. Footsteps on concrete. Anders carefully raised his head. The eastern sky was paling with the first tinge of dawn. Less than twenty yards away, the men were boarding a submarine. There was something hauntingly familiar about the dark outline of the conning tower.

And then Anders knew his search was over.

Moving silently, Anders found a flight of slippery steps cut into the quayside that led down to the water. He suppressed an involuntary shudder as the cold water rose around his body. The kitbag floated as it was supposed to do. He pushed it in front of him with his chin as he began the short swim toward *U700*.

Petty Officer Evans poked his cheerful face into the bow torpedo room where Brice was working.

'Morning, Mr Brice. Skeleton crew coming aboard. We're casting off in a couple of shakes.'

'How long before we reach the trials position?'

'Not for another four hours,' Evans said.

'In that case,' Brice said, hoisting himself on to a bunk, 'I think I'll get me a little sleep.'

Evans grinned. 'You do that, Mr Brice. We won't need to disturb you.'

Anders flattened himself against the conning tower under the overhanging wintergarten deck as two seamen untied the mooring ropes and cast off. They called to an unseen man on the bridge. The electric motors started, and the U-boat's stern began swinging away from the quay. Anders reached into the kitbag and groped beside the shoebox for the revolver. The two seamen were walking back along the deck casing to the bridge. Anders darted forward and crouched behind the main gun as they climbed on to the bridge. Had the officer on the bridge seen him, Anders was ready to hold him at gunpoint while winding the key that primed the bomb. But he wasn't seen. Thankfully Anders returned to the safety of the hiding place under the wintergarten deck to consider his course of action. The easiest way would be to prime the bomb and place it under the casing against the pressure hull. But if the British were taking the U-boat out to sea, it would be better to sink it in deep water where salvaging the boat would be difficult.

The early light revealed that *U700*'s course was westward – away from the dockyards, toward the open sea.

He decided to wait.

'So what do we do?' Hartz asked dejectedly.

'We'll have to carry on,' Goder replied. 'If we're on course, we'll be there in an hour. It's too late to think of turning back.'

Hartz looked down through his window at the mist rolling across the sea. The Junkers was flying east – toward the dawn.

'We won't find the U-boat in that fog,' Hartz said.

Goder smiled and gestured to the torpedo release lever between their seats. 'We're not going to waste that little beauty. We'll find a target.'

U700 was nearing the mouth of the estuary when Anders decided it was time to act.

The young officer hunched over the bridge coaming was about to give the order to switch the U-boat's electric motors over to the diesel engines, but his hand never reached the voicepipe cover. The cold muzzle of a revolver was suddenly thrust from behind into the side of his neck.

'Make no sound,' said a harsh, heavily accented voice. The officer looked down at the revolver and could see the gleaming noses of the bullets in their chambers. 'You understand?' The officer nodded.

Anders stepped back from the officer and kept the gun pointing at his chest. There was a fleeting recollection of the time he had pointed a gun at Weiner on this same bridge a lifetime ago. This time there would be no indecisiveness.

'You can swim?'

The officer hesitated then nodded. He climbed reluctantly down the ladder to the deck in response to Anders' gesture with the revolver.

'You give me cap and jacket.'

The officer removed his jacket and cap and dropped them at Anders' feet.

'Now swim.' Anders waved the revolver at the shore. 'Swim!' he repeated and pulled back the revolver's hammer.

The officer looked at the water creaming past the saddle tank and jumped.

Anders watched until the man had struck out for the shore before taking off his greatcoat and pulling on the officer's jacket and cap. He climbed down into the attack kiosk that was immediately above the control room and opened the locker that contained the Dräger submarine escape breathing sets. He lifted one up and looked at it critically. It consisted of an oxygen rebreathing bag that was connected by a short length of hose to a rubber mask that completely covered the wearer's face. The mask also distorted the wearer's voice.

Provided there were still smoke canisters in the deck ammunition lockers, Anders decided that it would suit his purpose admirably.

The two scientists and Petty Officer Evans spun around in astonishment as the young officer, wearing a breathing set, tumbled down into the control room.

'Fire! Quick!' Anders squawked. 'All on deck!'

'Where?' Evans demanded.

'On deck. Everyone! Quick! Quick!'

It sounded serious, and Evans wasted no time rounding the crew up and herding them to the ladder. 'There's just Mr Brice in the bow . . .' he began.

'On deck!' Anders interrupted, not understanding. Evans followed the crew up the ladder leaving Anders alone in the control room. Anders pulled off the breathing set and lowered the periscope so that it could be used in the control room instead of the attack kiosk. He grasped the handles and swung it around so that he could see the clouds of black smoke pouring out of the drainage holes from the canister. He had hidden the smoke canister under the extreme aft end of the tapered casing where the deck raked down to the foaming waterline. He smiled as he watched the men struggle to maintain a foothold on the narrow, slippery steel plate while they fought to connect an unwilling fire hose to a deck outlet.

The rest was easy. He stepped across the control room, spun the large helm wheel as quickly as he could, and grabbed a safety strap to keep his balance as the boat heeled violently. For the skeleton crew, there was nothing to grab but each other. When Anders returned to the periscope, the aft deck was deserted. Heads bobbed in the U-boat's wake. He hoped they could all swim.

He flipped the periscope to maximum magnification and studied the coastline. Five miles ahead, on the boat's starboard quarter, were heavily wooded slopes leading to low cliffs guarding a rocky headland. To the left of the headland was a small, sandy cove. Anders reasoned that if he exploded the bomb near the headland, not only would the proximity of the rocks make a salvage operation difficult, if not impossible, but he would stand a very good chance of swimming ashore at the cove.

He read off the course required to take the U-boat toward the headland and returned to the helm.

The captain of the coastguard station lowered his binoculars and stared out to sea. 'You'd better get on to Barrow,' he told his colleague. 'See if they've got a fast vessel with fire-fighting gear – their precious captured U-boat is on fire.'

There was slack water near the rocks. Anders went into the motor room and closed the sliding speed controls that shut down the electric motors. *U700* lost way and stopped.

The sudden silence in the U-boat woke Alan Brice. He sat up and yawned.

Anders went down on his knees in the control room and opened the hatch that gave access to the midships battery compartment. It was undoubtably the best place to position the bomb in order to blow the U-boat in two. He placed the revolver on the floor beside him and opened the shoebox. The six hand grenades were still neatly in place. He wound the alarm clock, which started ticking immediately, and set the mechanism to withdraw the pin from the priming grenade in two minutes. He was about to lower the bomb down the hatch when a shadow fell across him. He looked up.

'Now who in hell are you? Brice asked in surprise.

Anders went for the gun, but the American was too quick, kicking it out of reach. In desperation, Anders jumped to his feet and swung, but Brice ducked to avoid the blow and Anders' clenched fist collided with the hand-wheel. The sudden pain made him cry out. Before he could recover, Brice delivered a powerful blow that sank into Anders' stomach, and he collapsed to the floor, gasping for breath.

The alarm clock suddenly started buzzing. Puzzled, Brice picked up the shoebox. One glance as the turning alarm clock key pulled a pin out of a grenade was enough. He knew there were only seconds left. He raced up the ladder to the bridge and heaved the bomb overboard. The explosion from the priming grenade as the bomb hit the water threw Brice backward against the periscope standards. He struck his head on the torpedo aimer as he went down.

Hartz pointed excitedly at the distant plume of water that was rising into the air near the cliffs. Goder focussed his binoculars in time to see a second much larger explosion. The water settled enabling Goder to see that the explosions had taken place beside the stationary submarine that was close in to the cliffs. The submarine's profile was unmistakably that of a Type 7C U-boat.

With a whoop of triumph, Goder dropped the binoculars and put the Junkers into a dive. Hartz snatched up the binoculars. Not only did he pick out *U700*, but speeding toward it was a motor torpedo boat. It was some thirty kilometres from the U-boat but was moving fast enough to reach it in fifteen minutes.

'We've got it!' Goder yelled.

The three BMW engines screamed in protest as Goder hauled the Junkers out of the dive at 200 feet and slammed the throttles open to maintain the same air speed in level flight.

Anders ignored Brice groaning at his feet and stared at the nose-on profile of the airplane that was charging toward him at wave-top height. He was not going to let this Britisher stop him from destroying the U-boat. Not after he had got this far.

Anders pushed past Brice, jumped down to the wintergarten deck, and swung the multiple-barrelled gun down, centring the Junkers in the sights. He began to fire a continuous burst, shaking from the vibration of the yammering gun, half-blinded by the acrid fumes and deafened by the roaring of the murderously spewing barrels. Burning shell cases danced a staccato rattle on the deck plates and ricocheted off the safety rails. He could see the 20 millimetre tracer shells burning a path of light towards the Junkers. More elevation. Left. Too much. Right!

The Junkers was 300 yards from the U-boat when it flew into Anders' wall of flying lead and nickel. Bullets tore into the port wing's leading edge and chewed into the propeller blades, ripping the engine from the wing. The flight deck windows shattered and the instrument panel dissolved into shards of metal and flying splinters of glass.

Hartz was killed instantly by a tracer that lanced through his chest like a comet. Goder outlived his copilot by only seconds – but it was long enough to operate the torpedo release control before his body slumped forward.

Brice climbed to his feet, suddenly riveted by the spectacle of the Junkers cartwheeling into the sea, throwing up huge clouds of spray. The starboard wing climbed lazily into the sky, twisting and pirouetting like a sycamore seed, its black crosses flashing mockingly at Anders.

'No!' Anders said in German, his face white with shock. *'It's not possible!'*

Brice pointed at the water. 'Torpedo!' A corner of his mind noted that it was an old-fashioned 'heater' torpedo that left a track of compressed air bubbles, and the track was speeding straight for *U700*.

Brice braced himself for the explosion, but it never came. He swung around and saw that the torpedo had passed underneath the U-boat and was now streaking toward the cove 200 yards away. As he watched the wake of bubbles, the torpedo suddenly porpoised to the surface. Brice guessed that its momentum, when it hit the water, had carried it too deep and that it had only now picked up its correct running depth. The torpedo reached the shore, plowing through the surf, and several yards up the steep beach, its contra-rotating propellers whirring impotently.

A dud, Brice reasoned. Had the torpedo been equipped with a magnetic warhead, it would have exploded as it passed beneath the U-boat.

In the silence that followed, Brice heard the muted roar of the approaching MTB and suddenly remembered the other man on deck. He spun around, but it was too late. He felt himself falling back to the deck as Anders pushed by and scrambled down the hatch, pulling it shut behind him.

After a minute's destruction with a heavy wrench in the control room, Anders realized the futility of what he was doing. He sank to his knees in despair amid the wreckage of smashed gauges and valves. A small engraved identification plate caught his eye: TORPEDO DIREKTOR.

Anders stared at it for some moments. 'The spare warhead,' he whispered to himself.

Brice gave up trying to open the hatch and turned his attention to the MTB. The high-speed vessel marked by two clouds of spray on either side of its flared bows was now about four miles from *U700*.

Anders stopped hauling the hoist in the bow torpedo room when the nose of the warhead hanging from the rope was high enough above the floor to be certain of detonating when it fell. Next he piled virtually every flammable item he could find beneath the swaying warhead; curtains, mattresses, blankets, papers – anything that would burn was added to the mounting pyramid. He worked at feverish speed, aware that the MTB would be closing fast. The cheroot given to him by Kretschmer at *U700*'s commissioning party fell off his bunk as he dragged the mattress away. He spared it a cursory glance before thrusting it into a pocket. He found a large can of cleaning fluid and sprinkled the contents over the pyre and the interior of the torpedo room. He checked to make sure he had a box of matches and reached up to release the clips that secured the torpedo loading hatch.

When Brice saw Anders emerge through the hatch near the bow and fumble with a box of matches, he vaulted over the wintergarten rail and raced along the deck casing. Anders was about to strike the match when Brice was upon him, scattering the matches on the spray-drenched deck. Exploding with fury and frustration, Anders yanked the Webley out of his belt and squeezed off a shot. Brice dived sideways but the bullet hit his arm below the elbow. He gave a cry of pain and just managed to keep himself from tumbling into the water by grabbing the jumping wire with his free hand.

The MTB was less than quarter of a mile away, with a boarding party mustered on deck, together with the crew of the U-boat that the MTB had stopped to pick up.

Half crying, half cursing, Anders found the box of matches. There was one match left. Please be dry, he prayed. Please God make it dry and stop my stupid fingers from shaking!

He struck the match, dropped it down the hatch, and threw himself clear of the opening in time to avoid the huge tongue of flame that blasted into the air. It would be a matter of minutes before the fire burned through the rope causing the warhead to fall.

Brice stared at the blazing hatch, unable to credit his senses. The pain in his arm and the blood soaking into his shirtsleeve were forgotten. 'My notes!' he cried. He started forward as if by some miracle he hoped to extinguish the inferno.

Anders grabbed him by the shoulders and pointed to the cove. 'Ashore!'

Brice shook his head as if he didn't understand. Anders pushed the revolver more firmly into his waistband, hooked his arm around the American's waist, and jumped, dragging Brice into the water with him. The two men came spluttering to the surface.

'My arm,' Brice choked, fighting for air. 'I can't swim!'

Anders grasped Brice by the shirt collar and struck out for the cove.

The MTB cautiously approached the blazing U-boat. A firefighting party broke out a hose and directed the water jet at the flames leaping from the U-boat's forward hatch.

Another fire hose was brought into use, and together they succeeded in turning the flames to smoke and then to hissing steam. The MTB moved alongside the U-boat but was taking no chances – the hoses continued to blast water through the open hatch.

Anders stopped swimming and discovered he could stand. He helped Brice to his feet, and they staggered through the surf, finally collapsing on to the beach. Brice clutched at his arm in an attempt to stanch the flow of blood, and Anders saw the stain spreading into the sand. 'I'm sorry,' he said. He stood up and dejectedly watched the U-boat. There was only a wisp of smoke coming from the hatch. A seaman from the MTB scrambled down on to the U-boat's deck and approached the open hatch.

Brice called to Anders and pointed to the top of the low cliff above the cove. The two army trucks that Anders had encountered that morning in Barrow had emerged from the trees. Armed soldiers led by the sergeant were jumping down on to the grass. Anders was certain they would kill him just as they had killed the motorcyclist. Forgetting Brice, he raced to the foot of the cliff and started to climb the debris of stones and boulders that an old rock fall had piled against the bottom end of the cliff. 'Stop!' a voice yelled from above, but Anders kept climbing toward an overhang. A bullet chipped splinters from a nearby boulder, and Anders dived behind an outcrop, pulling out the revolver. He had five shots with which to give a good account of himself. He saw a flash of khaki near the top of the cliff and fired at it. Two more shots ricocheted off the boulder he was crouching behind. He didn't hear the sergeant drop down on to a nearby rock.

'Drop it, sonny!'

Anders swung the revolver around to the voice. The sergeant fired. The bullet slammed through Anders' stomach and sprayed the rocks behind him with bone and tissue.

The seaman dropped down into *U700*'s bow torpedo room and stared numbly at the blackened warhead hanging nose down from the charred remains of a rope. One by one the few remaining strands of rope were parting under their half ton load. The seaman senselessly threw his arms around the torpedo warhead and held it in a futile bear hug. But the torpedo fell.

Anders lived just long enough to see the explosion that blew the bows off the U-boat and tossed the MTB on to its beams ends as if it had been a toy. *U700* lifted its propellers high into the air. The conning tower disappeared as the boat rolled on to its sides. Then there was nothing but a swirl of sluggish bubbles erupting in the middle of the spreading oil slick that marked the spot where *U700* had submerged for the last time.

72

The soldiers were dismantling the cliff rescue winch when Lillian and Major Veitch arrived. The sergeant escorted them to the back of the truck and pulled back the blanket covering a stretcher.

Lillian nodded, her face pale. 'Yes,' she said quietly. 'That's him.'

'He had a gun,' the sergeant said. 'I didn't have no choice. It was him or me.'

'I understand,' Veitch said.

The sergeant held out a manilla envelope. 'Things we found on him. Personal things. There was a map, but that's got to be sent to GHQ.'

Lillian took the envelope. 'I'll see that they're sent to his people.'

73

Major James Veitch hated having to lie. He looked fixedly down at his blotter so that he wouldn't have to meet the expressionless eyes that were staring at him.

'He was found hiding in a shepherd's hut,' Veitch said

awkwardly, 'not three miles from the camp, by two Home Guard . . .'

'*Armed* Home Guard?' Kretschmer queried.

'Yes. But he broke away from them. They called out several times for him to stop, but he took no notice. One of them fired with the intention of wounding him but the shot went high.' Veitch paused. 'He died before the doctor arrived on the scene. The funeral is to be held in Hawkshead village. I'm prepared to grant parole to those officers who wish to attend on condition that they agree to wear British navy greatcoats over their uniforms to avoid annoying the villagers.'

'Thank you, major,' Kretschmer said tonelessly.

'Nurse Baxter will let you have his things to send to his family,' Veitch said and then paused. 'I don't expect you to tell me how he escaped, so I won't insult you by asking.'

The two men stood and exchanged salutes. Kretschmer was about to open the door to leave when Veitch spoke.

'Commander . . .'

Kretschmer turned.

'It was a courageous attempt,' Veitch said. 'He was a brave officer.'

Lillian sat down in her sickbay and tipped Anders' few possessions onto her desk. There was a silver St Christopher medal and a wallet containing limp, seawater-stained photographs of his parents. The remains of an unsmoked cheroot puzzled her, for she had never seen Anders smoke. She looked up and saw the lean figure of Kretschmer walking across the lawn toward the hall. She guessed that he was coming to collect Anders' things and quickly swept them into her drawer rather than let the German officer see that she had been looking at Anders' photographs.

She heard his footsteps outside in the corridor and

braced herself. She was frightened of the U-boat commander, and she suspected that Kretschmer was aware of her fear.

There was a tap on her door. It opened.

'I've come for Lieutenant Anders' belongings,' Kretschmer said.

Without looking up, Lillian said, 'I'll have them sent to your office, commander.'

Lillian took a deep breath as Kretschmer was about to close the door. 'I'm terribly sorry about what happened to Bernard – I mean – Lieutenant Anders,' she stammered. She looked up and met the unblinking eyes. Her courage ebbed away. To cover her embarrassment she blurted out what was on her mind: 'I suppose as you're a sailor – a fighting man – one more death doesn't . . . doesn't . . .' She groped for the right word, but Kretschmer interrupted her.

'One more death is always one more too many. Whether it's a man, or woman, or children – or a nurse in a lifeboat.'

Lillian looked up sharply into the piercing eyes, searching for a clue to the thoughts that lay behind them.

'You mean you've known all along?'

Kretschmer nodded slowly. 'She was your sister?'

'Yes,' Lillian said. 'How did you know?'

'There's a likeness. Also we picked up a list that gave the names of the passengers aboard the *Walvis Bay*. There was an army nurse. Elaine Baxter.'

'She died of exposure,' Lillian said dully.

'I'm sorry,' Kretschmer said.

'And you've known all along,' Lillian repeated disbelievingly.

'Her face was among the living,' Kretschmer said. 'They're the ones I always try to remember.' He paused.

'You must excuse me – I have to see about the details for the funeral.'

Lillian listened to his footsteps receding down the corridor. She opened the drawer and stared down at the small, sad collection of Anders' possessions. For five minutes she was undecided. She picked up the cheroot and studied it before finally making up her mind. There was an envelope and notepad in her drawer. She wrote 'Lieutenant-Commander Otto Kretschmer' on the envelope and placed the notepad in front of her.

It took her ten minutes to write a full account of what she knew about the destruction of *U700*.

74

Stein's face went white. He rose to his feet and stared contemptuously at Kretschmer, Leymann, Faulk and Shulke.

'Sit down, Stein,' Kretschmer said quietly.

Stein pushed his chair under the table. 'You ask me to be a pallbearer for a coward. The answer is no.'

'I said, sit down.' Kretschmer's voice was very quiet and very dangerous.

'Let the British carry his coffin. He's done more for them than he has for Germany.'

'We all share the responsibility for his death, Stein.'

'Not me,' Stein said. 'He lived like a coward and he died like one – running away. Don't go blaming me for his death, commander.'

'I don't want the British guessing the reason for Anders' escape,' Kretschmer said. 'Which they might do unless we show respect for a brother officer.'

Stein sneered. 'Suspect what? Anders buried that bomb as soon as he was out of the camp. He was a coward, and I don't go to the funerals of cowards.'

Kretschmer stood and faced Stein. 'If you don't do exactly as I say, Stein, I shall have no hesitation in notifying Major Veitch that your political views are such that you would be happier at one of the camps run by the Poles.'

'What political views?' Stein asked politely.

'The ones I saw you sharing with some of your SS friends at *U700*'s commissioning party.'

Stein stared at Kretschmer with sudden understanding. 'I was to have joined your boat . . .'

'That's right,' Kretschmer agreed. 'Except that I asked the admiral to find someone else. I didn't want you then. Just as I don't want you in this camp now unless you obey my orders without question.'

75

As Anders' coffin was lowered into the open grave, Major Veitch glanced around the churchyard and signalled to the bandmaster who was stationed with his musicians some thirty yards from the graveside. Two pipers detached themselves from the bank and took up positions beside the grave. The band started playing a piece of music that it was hard to imagine would ever be played in an English country churchyard during those dark days of October 1941 when Britain stood alone.

It was the German national anthem.

Major Veitch stepped forward and carefully lifted the White Ensign from the coffin. Underneath lay the German navy's battle ensign. Kretschmer was deeply moved by the simple gesture. He stood by the grave, bareheaded, holding his cap. Like his fellow officers gathered in the churchyard, he was disturbed and puzzled as to why the British had gone to such pains to provide Anders with full military honours.

The canon intoned a simple prayer and threw a handful of earth onto the coffin.

Kretschmer picked up a spade and helped shovel the earth into the grave. Then there was another surprise as six commandos led by a sergeant formed two lines near the graveside. They presented arms in response to the sergeant's orders and fired a three volley salute into the air over the grave.

Kretschmer turned to Major Veitch. He had difficulty in speaking. 'On behalf of all the officers at Grizedale Hall, major, I would like to thank you for all you have done for Lieutenant Anders.' He put his cap on and saluted.

The funeral was over.

A grey Bentley coupé pulled up outside the churchyard. Commander Ian Fleming got out and opened the passenger door for Alan Brice. The American scientist's right arm was in a sling. Fleming removed a large wreath from the car's trunk and gave it to Brice. The two men stood near the lych-gate and waited for the funeral party to leave the churchyard.

Kretschmer was the last man to climb aboard the army truck. The guard slammed the tailboard and latched it. Lillian crossed the road to the vehicle as the driver started the engine.

She was holding a manilla envelope, which she held up to the German officer.

'They're Bernard's things, commander. They were found on him.'

The truck started to move off. 'Thank you, nurse,' Kretschmer said politely. He was puzzled by her concerned expression.

Lillian kept pace with the truck. Her face was worried and drawn. 'I should have given them to you earlier, commander,' she said anxiously. 'Please don't tell anyone that I left it so late.'

'Of course not,' said Kretschmer, not looking at the envelope.

Lillian had to break into a trot as the truck gathered speed. 'You won't tell anyone,' she begged. *'Please, commander*. I could get into serious trouble.'

Lillian stopped running and watched the receding vehicle. Kretschmer gazed back at her with a bewildered expression on his normally impassive face.

Brice carefully laid his wreath on the grave beside the posy of flowers that Lillian had placed there moments before. He stepped back and saluted with his left hand while Fleming looked on.

The two men didn't speak until they were back in the car.

'The U-boat's lying in shallow water,' Fleming said. 'They'll have a good look at her today. It's possible that she'll be raised. Nothing left of the torpedo though. Or your notes.'

'I can remember the important details,' Brice said.

The army truck ground slowly up the steep fell that overlooked the village and its tiny graveyard.

Kretschmer opened the envelope and looked inside. He took out the remains of the cheroot and recognized it as one of his. He shook the contents of the envelope onto his lap – some photographs, ruined by seawater as the cheroot was, a wallet, and a letter. It was addressed to him in a woman's handwriting.

He opened the envelope and unfolded the single sheet of notepaper. The letter was unsigned. Leymann, sitting opposite Kretschmer, noticed that the colour was draining from Kretschmer's face. Kretschmer looked up from the letter and stared at the dwindling graveyard. For a moment it seemed to Leymann that Kretschmer was unable to speak. Then: 'Stop the truck!'

The driver braked. Ignoring the guards, Kretschmer jumped down to the road and stared down at the distant graveyard. He could see the splash of colour of a wreath. Slowly, he brought his right hand up to his forehead.

The chill October wind sweeping across the desolate fells caught at his greatcoat. Kretschmer stood motionless for a long moment. For the first time in his life, he wished he were a weaker man so that he might weep.

Postscript

On June 8, 1962, Lieutenant Bernard Anders' body was removed from the churchyard at Hawkshead in the presence of his family and re-interred in the German War Cemetery at Cannock Chase in England.

Ian Fleming died two years later; he was James Bond's only flesh and blood victim.

Otto Kretschmer married after the war and retired from the West German navy in 1957, having reached the rank of rear admiral.

Karl Doenitz succeeded Hitler to become head of state for twenty days before the final collapse of the Third Reich. He and his cherished U-boat arm were cleared of accusations of war crimes, but he was tried at Nuremburg for training men for war in peacetime and, perhaps unjustly, found guilty. He served a ten-year sentence at Spandau.

Alan Brice is retired and lives with his wife on Long Island. His three grandsons think that he's the best baseball pitcher in the world, although his performance does suffer on those days when his right arm troubles him.

CHURCHILL'S GOLD

Foreword

All the facts concerning Churchill's gold during 1940 and 1941 may never be revealed. The reason for this is that the Bank of England did not become a public concern until after the Second World War and therefore are under no obligation to transfer their wartime archives to the Public Record Office. All attempts to obtain information through official channels have been met with a polite but nevertheless very cold stone wall. For this reason I am grateful to those individuals in the United States, England, South Africa and Germany who told me what little they could, and I'm especially grateful to the very few who told me more than they should.

James Follett
February 1980

For Christine
who got frightened in the African Bush
in the search for informants.

Part One

KILLING

1

It had been sixteen months since the female sperm whale had copulated briefly with the old bull amid an excited welter of near-freezing foam in the lonely, icy wastes of the Southern Ocean. Now the moment of birth of her first calf was at hand.

It was a difficult birth; the tail of her firstborn was protruding from her body but the repeated muscular spasms that could crush a man to pulp were failing to complete the expulsion of the fourteen-foot calf.

The female rolled on to her side and thrashed the water white with her great tail flukes in a frantic attempt to dislodge the infant that was in danger of suffocation. Her herd sisters sensed the cow's distress. They abandoned their meal of squid and drove upwards through the warm layers of the Indian Ocean towards the sparkling sunlight.

'There! There! She blows – five sperm!'

Robert Gerrard pushed his mop of dark, curly hair out of his eyes and squinted up at the spotters' platform to get a bearing on the Malay boy's outstretched arm. He quickly focussed his binoculars on the sea and picked out the arching backs of the great beasts and the silvery plumes of their blows shining like fountains of pearls in the setting sun. The blows burst into the air at an angle ahead of the mighty creatures. They were definitely sperms – only sperms blew like that. And in December 1940 sperm whales were the only reason for the *Tulsar*'s presence in the Indian Ocean for the brief whaling season off South Africa's Natal coast.

Piet van Kleef, Gerrard's first officer, was leaning over the bridge rail, bellowing and cursing in Afrikaans at the men manning the derricks that held one of the *Tulsar*'s two high-speed whale-catcher launches.

'Hold it, Piet,' said Gerrard crisply, not taking his eyes away from his binoculars. 'Don't launch the catchers.'

The giant Afrikaner gaped at his captain in amazement. 'There's a hundred barrel of sperm out there, cap'n,' he protested, having already calculated his share of the bonus that the whales represented.

'I don't give a damn if there's a thousand barrels of sperm oil out there,' Gerrard growled. He jerked his finger at the reddening sun. 'It's too late. Sundown in two hours.'

Piet scratched his beard with a grimy thumbnail. 'Okay. So we barrel-line the bastards and pick 'em up in the morning.'

'And give every Goddamn shark around a free overnight dinner?'

Piet had served with Gerrard for ten years – long enough to learn the uselessness of trying to win an argument with the quick-tempered whaling captain from Boston. Despite his slight build Robert Gerrard possessed a wiry strength, was incredibly fast on his feet, and was accustomed to winning disputes either by use of his deadly fists or his quick thinking – two characteristics he had inherited from his Huguenot grandparents on his father's side. The American rested a sinewy arm on Piet's shoulder and gave the Afrikaner a friendly push.

'They'll feed tonight when the squid rise, Piet. They won't be far away in the morning.'

As Piet started shouting orders, Gerrard returned his attention to the small group of whales. They were cows. He guessed that the bull would be some miles seaward protectively quartering his wives. One of the cows appeared to be in difficulty for she was rolling on to her side, presenting her underbelly to her companions. It was then that Gerrard realized that she was giving birth. The huge waters thrown up by the majestic creatures suddenly cleared as the struggling cow rolled virtually on to her back, exposing the eight feet of her half-born offspring's body protruding from her belly. For a moment the fascinating scene was obscured by foam and broken water, then Gerrard, to his astonishment, saw one of the cows gently grasp the infant's passive tail and draw the creature from its mother's body.

In the twenty-five of his forty years that Gerrard had been hunting whales this was an event that he had never witnessed before, and he knew it was something that he was unlikely to see again. He suddenly felt miserably alone: the birth of the whale was something that Cathy would have loved to have seen.

Some marauding seabirds, sensing the unusual, altered course and circled the scene speculatively. Two of the cows carefully eased their massive, blunt heads under the one-ton newborn sperm whale and held its head above water to enable it to suck down its first lungfuls of air. The movement snapped the duct-like umbilical cord that was as thick as a man's arm.

More seagulls joined in the lazy circling above the whales – their harsh, uneven cries plainly audible above the suck and hiss of the Indian Ocean's swell against the *Tulsar*'s steel hull. The whale calf's tail gave an uncertain flick. Immediately it was swimming, nosing its sensitive lips along its mother's curving flanks seeking the life-giving nipples.

Gerrard tried to forget Cathy as he watched the whales resume their northward migration, their backs arching black and grey in the ochre sunlight, wind-whipped blows scattering into the air like clouds of steam from strange locomotives of the deep. For once Gerrard was glad that he wouldn't have to kill them.

There was a reddening in the water in the whales' wake. The seabirds traded height for speed and spiralled down to investigate. Gerrard adjusted the focus of his binoculars and could distinguish the purple half-ton of placenta meat on the surface, expelled from the mother whale's body a few seconds after she had given birth. The seabirds were undecided – they cautiously circled the feast at wave-top height. One albatross had no reservations; it dropped straight down, its wings flogging the air to brake its descent. But the giant seabird never reached the water; it suddenly changed its mind and wheeled sharply into the air. The other seagulls did the same while uttering shrill cries of alarm.

Puzzled, Gerrard kept his binoculars trained on the mass of meat. The dorsal fin of a Mako shark closed on the meal like a miniature Genoa sail and abruptly sheered away.

At that moment Gerrard saw the reason for the birds' uncertainty: a long, low, menacing shape moving northwards at about two knots. There was no mistaking that half-submerged profile. To Robert Gerrard it was the most despised shape in the world: the shape of one of the obscene things that had taken Cathy from him.

He lowered his binoculars. The shape was impossible to see with the naked eye. He guessed it to be about six miles distant, and checked the position of the late sun hanging blood-red above the horizon like a bloated, over-ripe fruit. The *Tulsar* was between the shape and the sun. There was a chance; a faint, impossible chance. He dived into the wheelhouse and pushed Brody away from the helm.

'What the hell?' the New Yorker protested. As a former middleweight prizefighter, and now the *Tulsar*'s coxswain, Brody was not an easy man to push.

'Sorry, Sam,' said Gerrard, spinning the chromium wheel and watching the rudder indicator slide round the scale.

'I thought we weren't going after them whales until morning?'

'We're not.'

There was a tense, dangerous note in Gerrard's voice that dissuaded Brody from pressing further questions. The coxswain watched Gerrard press the key that sounded the engine-room interphone. The *Tulsar* was the most advanced whaling factory-ship in the world – there were no voice-pipes.

'Bridge,' said Gerrard curtly. 'Listen, you guys, when I sound the telegraph for full ahead on both, I want just that and not a lot of dispute about your Goddamn turbines or I'll kick your asses all round the engine-room. Okay?' Gerrard listened to the brief reply and returned the receiver to its hook.

'Anything I can do, boss?' Brody inquired.

Gerrard felt in the top pocket of his grimy sweat-shirt for a crumpled Havana and lit it. The acrid bite of the stale cigar steadied his thoughts and nerves. The raw hatred that had erupted in his guts was replaced by the low cunning of a hardened hunter.

'Sure, Sam,' he murmured in answer to Brody's question. 'Follow my helm orders and signal for full speed ahead on both the instant I say.'

With that, Gerrard handed the wheel back to Brody and left

the wheelhouse. He leaned on the bridge rail and trained his binoculars straight ahead. The shape was nearer and still moving north at the same speed. He studied it casually without a flicker of emotion on his weathered face to betray the brute savagery he felt towards the thing out there – the thing that had killed Cathy the year before on the first day of the war against Hitler. America was not at war with Germany, but that changed nothing.

'Left a bit, Sam,' Gerrard called through the open door. He was surprised with himself at how calm he knew his voice sounded.

Brody eased the gleaming wheel through his stubby fingers, correctly interpreting Gerrard's helm order as 'port ten degrees'.

'Fine, Sam. Hold her there.' Gerrard kept his quarry in focus through the binoculars. He sensed Piet's presence at his side even before the mahogany rail creaked as the huge Afrikaner leaned his bulk against it. Piet was built like the door of a bank vault: large, round, heavy and dependable. The six-inch wide elephant-hide belt that encircled his huge gut, supporting his shapeless denims, was in perfect proportion to his floppy *Voortrekker* hat. It took little imagination to picture Piet van Kleef riding a stinkwood wagon, driving an ox team across the jagged teeth of the Drakensberg Mountains as his Boer forebears had when they had pushed north from the Cape to escape British rule.

'So what are we chasing, cap'n?' Piet inquired.

Gerrard handed the binoculars to the Afrikaner and pointed. The giant scanned them back and forth for a moment before freezing their action. His outsize thumb moved delicately on the knurled focussing wheel. He stiffened. 'Jesus Christ,' he breathed. 'A submarine.'

'A German U-boat,' Gerrard murmured under his breath, taking the binoculars from Piet, ignoring the Afrikaner's worried expression.

'Are you planning what I think you're planning?' Piet demanded.

'Yep.'

'You're crazy.'

'That's right.'

'Jesus Christ,' Piet muttered. He rested his great paw of a hand on Gerrard's sinewy wrist. 'Listen, man – how in hell do you know it's German? Here? In the Indian Ocean?'

Gerrard pulled his hand free of Piet's friendly grip. He gave a crooked smile. 'An anti-aircraft gundeck aft of the conning-tower, Piet. Only the Germans build subs like that.' He turned to the wheelhouse. 'Left a notch, Sam!'

The *Tulsar* turned one degree to port.

'What good will it do, cap'n?' Piet pleaded. 'It won't change anything – it won't bring her back.'

Gerrard stared through the binoculars. Piet noticed that his fingers were white from the tightness of their grip.

'You touch that sub and you'll be strung up so high, we'll need them binoculars to see who you are.'

Gerrard continued to ignore Piet. The Afrikaner became desperate. 'You'll be in big trouble with your government, and your government will be in one whole heap of shit with the Germans.'

The American lowered the binoculars. His grey eyes were glazed as he stared across the water but his voice was devoid of emotion when he spoke. 'Thank you, Piet. Those yellow bellies in Washington are ten thousand miles away, and that U-boat is less than four. I'm going to sink the bastard.' He suddenly wheeled round. 'Sam! Full speed ahead on both now!'

The engine-room telegraph clanged. The two languid bow-waves began climbing the hull as the whaling-ship's finely-balanced Parsons turbines poured ten thousand horsepower into the twin propellers. There was a ripple of excited commotion among the whalemen gathering along the bulwarks. Darting Malay boys were pointing and shouting; lithe, naked bodies swarmed on to the seaplane derrick for a better view. The deck began to shudder beneath Gerrard's feet as the *Tulsar*'s speed crept up to her maximum twenty-six knots. The boy who had spotted the whales was dancing up and down on the spotter's platform and yelling, 'There! There!' while pointing frantically with a skinny, outstretched arm.

The U-boat was now less than three miles away and was obviously unaware of the charging apparition bearing down on it from out of the rapidly-setting sub-tropical sun. Gerrard could even discern the outline of two men on the submarine's bridge.

'They must hear us if they've got hydrophones,' breathed Piet.

Gerrard clutched the rail in silence while staring straight ahead at the hated U-boat. The random knotted lines of blue veins on his muscular forearms pulsed visibly against a tattoo that depicted a Boston whaler harpooning a blue whale. There was a sudden flurry of movement on the submarine's bridge. The two men ducked out of sight. A Klaxon wailed faintly and the water astern of the U-boat was suddenly whipped to foam. Geysers spouted from the U-boat's deck casing vents as the craft began submerging at speed.

'Four left!' Gerrard bellowed.

The whalemen and Malays were whooping with delight. They had no idea what it was all about except that it was great fun. The U-boat captain tried a desperate move by turning his bows towards the charging ship – a move which Gerrard guessed was intended to reduce the size of the target. It was a mistake; the ill-conceived manoeuvre cost the U-boat vital speed at the crucial moment. By the time the error was realized and the U-boat had regained lost way, the *Tulsar* was less than two hundred yards away and closing the gap at nearly fifty feet per second.

'Close the watertight bow doors, Sam,' Gerrard called to Brody.

Water was creaming past the conning-tower which was now the only part of the U-boat above water. Even Piet, normally the phlegmatic Afrikaner, was beating the wooden rail with a ham-like fist and roaring excitedly.

Only Gerrard was silent as he watched the stricken U-boat disappear from view beneath the *Tulsar*'s bow. 'Hard astern both!' he rapped out at Brody.

There was a shuddering blow that caused the whaling-ship to lose way abruptly. The *Tulsar* lifted her head as her terrible juggernaut momentum carried her over the U-boat. The scream of metal on metal set Piet's teeth on edge. 'Jesus Christ,' he whispered to himself. 'Jesus Goddamn Christ.'

The hideous shriek of twisting steel plates became a dull grating sound as the whaling-ship stopped and began going astern.

'Stop engines,' Gerrard ordered.

Brody's hand groped for the telegraph lever while staring ahead through the wheelhouse window. Gerrard leaned over the rail and gazed down at the sea where wreckage was surfacing the centre of a spreading, evil-smelling oil slick. There was no sign of the U-boat. The Malay boys stopped their excited chatter.

Piet met Gerrard's eyes. The American was silent for a moment. He relit his cigar and flipped the match over the rail. Piet knew Gerrard well enough to recognize contrived casualness.

'Say whatever you want to say now,' said Gerrard. 'And then we forget it. Okay?'

But Piet could think of nothing to say.

Jack Colby, the *Tulsar*'s lanky, easy-going Canadian radio operator, appeared on the bridge and moved to Gerrard's side. He was holding a slip of paper which he studied for a moment before passing to Gerrard.

'It managed to transmit some sort of message,' said the Canadian. 'In code, I guess, because I couldn't make no sense of it – all except one word.'

Gerrard glanced at the confused jumble of letters scrawled on the paper in Colby's sloping hand. There was one clear word that virtually jumped off the paper: TULSAR.

Piet looked over Gerrard's shoulder and swore softly.

Colby grinned. Canada was at war with Germany; he had no objection to Gerrard sinking U-boats. 'Reckon there's going to be trouble, skipper?'

Gerrard returned his attention to the rainbow hues caused by the oil slick that were dancing on the water. He nodded. 'Yeah – I reckon so, Jack. Big trouble I guess.'

Two miles to the north the baby whale, with its toothless gums firmly fastened to a rubbery nipple, was greedily drinking its first meal of fifty gallons of its mother's rich, warm milk.

2

Josephine ignored the impatiently-flashing light on the Benjamin D'Urban Hotel's switchboard and disbelievingly read through the telegram for a second time. The cable from her mother in New York had been written like a letter with no attempt at word economy:

DEAR JO I DONT KNOW HOW TO BEGIN THIS TO SOFTEN THE BLOW BUT PA HAD ANOTHER STROKE LAST WEEK STOP I GUESS I OUGHT TO HAVE TOLD YOU ABOUT HIS FIRST STROKE IN MY LAST LETTER BUT HE SAID I WASNT TO AND YOU KNOW HOW MAD HE CAN GET IF HE DOESNT GET HIS OWN WAY STOP THIS TIME HE IS IN A BAD WAY STOP HE CANT MOVE ON ONE SIDE STOP HE ASKED AFTER YOU LAST NIGHT STOP I KNOW HES SORRY OVER WHAT HAPPENED BUT HE WONT SAY IT STOP IF YOU COULD WRITE HIM AND SEND THE LETTER TO ME SO THAT I CAN READ IT TO HIM I KNOW HE WOULD BE PLEASED STOP YOUR LOVING MOTHER

'Is there a reply, mem?'

Josephine looked up. The Indian telegraph boy, hot and uncomfortable in his tight uniform, was watching her with dark, anxious eyes – sensing that this was one telegram that was unlikely to produce the customary sixpenny tip. 'Is there a reply, mem?' he repeated.

Josephine shook her head. The boy was half-way across the hotel's lavish rococo lobby when she suddenly decided on a course of action and called out: 'Yes! Wait!'

The boy returned to the reception desk. Josephine reached for a pad and pencil. Without hesitation she wrote:

GIVE PA ALL MY LOVE AND TELL HIM IM COMING HOME ON THE FIRST SHIP STOP LETTER FOLLOWS LOVE JO

She ripped the note off the pad and gave it to the telegraph boy.

'Will it go today?'

'Yes, mem.'

Josephine opened the hotel's petty cash tin and realized that the tip should come out of her own pocket. She was always scrupulously correct where money was concerned. She watched the boy disappear through the revolving doors and wryly reflected that despite her resolution, her impulsive nature still ruled her life: an impulse had led to her storming out of her parents' home three years previously, ending up in South Africa, and now exactly the same sort of impulse was going to take her home again. Not even the grim news about her father's illness succeeded in overshadowing the sudden feeling of exaltation that she experienced.

She picked up the telephone and answered the flashing light.

3

At 9.30 am the black, chauffeur-driven Cadillac drew up outside the imposing Foreign Office building at the Brandenburg Gate end of the Wilhelmstrasse in Berlin. Ten minutes later, Douglas Napier, an assistant military attaché at the United States embassy, was shown into Joachim von Ribbentrop's ornate office. The Reich foreign minister was standing behind his absurdly large desk. His face tightened with anger when he saw who his visitor was and he curtly brushed aside Napier's opening pleasantries.

'I sent for the chargé. Where is he?'

'The chargé d'affaires regrets that he is indisposed, sir,' Napier replied, refusing to address the arrogant former champagne salesman as 'your excellency'. Relations between the United States and Germany had been decidedly sour since the brutal anti-Jewish Kristallnacht pogrom of November 1938 when SA rowdies throughout Germany had smashed and looted Jewish shops and businesses, and murdered their owners. Such was the outcry in America against the atrocities of that notorious night that the American government had recalled its Berlin ambassador and handed the German ambassador in

Washington his passport. Relations between the two countries had further deteriorated with the torpedoing of the ocean liner *Athenia* which had caused the death of nearly thirty United States citizens.

Von Ribbentrop glowered at Napier for some seconds before picking up a paper from his desk. 'I have yet to receive an answer to my note concerning the deliberate sinking of one of our U-boats by the *Tulsar* in the Indian Ocean. Why?'

Napier stared straight back at von Ribbentrop without flinching. 'I understand that the chargé has made it clear that a reply will be forthcoming when my government is in full possession of the facts, sir.'

'You've had forty-eight hours,' Ribbentrop icily pointed out.

'The *Tulsar* is still at sea, sir. It is impossible for my government to reply to your note until we have talked to its captain.'

Ribbentrop's face paled as he listened to Napier's reasoned objection. He smashed his fist down on his massive oak desk. 'You've received a copy of the signal broadcast by the U-boat!' he shouted. 'The ramming by the *Tulsar* was a deliberate, unprovoked act of piracy! If the United States government feels that it is unable to deal with *Tulsar*'s captain, the Führer has stated that it may be necessary for him to reconsider his attitude to American warships escorting enemy merchantships carrying strategic war material! Good day to you!'

Napier stood his ground despite the dismissal; he had been given a specific instruction not to leave with his 'tail between his legs'.

'Minister,' he said politely, 'the secretary of state has made clear that *any* country may avail itself of the cash and carry scheme to purchase arms from the United States, and that any merchantship calling at United States ports to collect such arms is entitled to protection by our warships while in United States waters.'

'Rubbish!' Ribbentrop screamed. 'The cash and carry scheme is a cheap trick by Roosevelt to help Britain and her Allies! He knows only too well that Germany does not have the merchantships to take advantage of the scheme. And what if we did, eh? Supposing we sent ships into New York to buy arms? Would the American navy defend our ships against the Canadian navy? Would American warships fight Canadian warships? I think not.'

'I doubt if Britain and her Allies would think of the cash and carry scheme as a cheap trick,' Napier observed quietly, surprised how easy it had been to side-track the pompous Reich foreign minister from the central issue. 'They're paying a fair price in dollars and gold for all the armaments supplied by the United States.'

Ribbentrop snorted. 'By its total disregard of the laws of neutrality the United States is needlessly prolonging a futile war and adding to the misery and suffering! How can the Führer seek peace while America insists on feeding the flames? Destroyers! Tanks! Field guns! Bombs! Ammunition!' Ribbentrop seemed to realize that he was in danger of losing complete control. He sat abruptly and pressed a button on his intercom. 'It is obvious that Roosevelt, like the captain of the *Tulsar*, has scant respect for human life. Your government has another twenty-four hours in which to compose a reply to our note. Good day.'

Napier gave a slight bow. 'There will be no reply until we have heard the captain's version of what happened, minister.'

Napier left the Reich Foreign Office building at 10 am. As he climbed into the back seat of his car he reflected with some satisfaction that at least he hadn't left with his 'tail between his legs'.

4

Gerrard and Piet watched the approaching launch with well-founded anxiety; the *Tulsar* was fifty miles from Durban and it was unheard of for the pilot's vessel of any port to travel such a distance to meet an inward-bound ship.

'Piet,' said Gerrard slowly, keeping his binoculars trained on the fast-moving craft, 'have you ever known a British pilot's boat to fly a Stars and Stripes courtesy pennant?'

'No.'

'Nor have I.'

'Trouble, cap'n?'

'I guess. Something tells me that that guy sitting in the cockpit hasn't come out to wish us a merry Christmas.'

That guy turned out to be Ian Boult – the austere and humourless acting United States consul in Durban – a man with a profound dislike of the sea and an even deeper dislike of those sailors among his fellow countrymen whose exploits occasionally obliged him to venture out on it. He climbed awkwardly up the *Tulsar*'s Jacob's ladder and looked about him suspiciously while wrinkling his nose at the pervading smell of whalemeat. His temper and his lightweight tropical suit had not travelled well. He glared at Piet and Gerrard, introduced himself and demanded to be taken to Captain Gerrard.

'I'm Gerrard,' said Gerrard shortly.

Boult's gaze took in Gerrard's ragged denims and stained sweat-shirt. 'Is there somewhere we can talk in private, captain?'

'I saw the damage to your bow, Captain Gerrard,' Boult stated when he and Gerrard were alone. 'Therefore we can take it the German claims that you collided with one of their U-boats are correct?'

'Yep.' Gerrard was leaning back on the chair in his day-cabin with his feet on his desk and his hands thrust into his pockets.

'Were there survivors?'

'Nope.'

Boult tried not to show his irritation at the sailor's casual attitude. He produced a notebook and pencil. 'How did the accident happen, Captain Gerrard?'

'It didn't.'

Boult was puzzled. 'But you said –'

'It wasn't an accident,' said Gerrard. 'I rammed it deliberately.'

Boult's notebook nearly slipped from his fingers. He stared at Gerrard aghast. 'You what!'

Gerrard repeated his statement. The gaunt consul strived to contain his temper.

'Why, for God's sake?'

'I don't like German U-boats.'

Boult closed his notebook. This was one meeting that wasn't going to be recorded. He sat forward in his chair and regarded Gerrard with undisguised hostility. 'Listen, captain, it may have escaped your notice, but it just so happens that we're not at war with Germany.'

Gerrard gave a sudden smile. 'Don't blame me, Mr Boult – I'm doing my damnedest.'

Boult was not amused. 'Did you know that the U-boat got a radio message out before it went down saying that it had been deliberately attacked and that it named this ship?'

Gerrard shrugged. He felt in his sweat-shirt pocket for the frayed remains of a Havana and lit it.

'Did you also know that the government have issued a statement discounting the German claim as hysterical propaganda?'

Gerrard inhaled boredly on his cigar.

'Do you have to put into Durban?' Boult inquired.

'Well I sure as hell ain't going no place else the state my bow's in,' Gerrard observed.

'The place is crawling with journalists waiting to interview you.'

'So?'

'So you tell them it was an accident.'

'That wouldn't be truthful, Mr Boult.'

'Goddamn it – we're concerned with diplomacy – not truth!' Boult exploded. 'You'll brief your crew: you were chasing after whales and you didn't see the U-boat because it was half submerged! If you don't agree to that, Captain Gerrard, you will, in the crude parlance that you sailors indulge in, find yourself up shit creek. At the least, you'll lose your ticket; at the worst, the German government could kick your ass through the Massachusetts maritime courts and pin a bill on you for several million marks for the loss of their Goddamn U-boat.'

Gerrard gazed levelly at Boult through a haze of cigar smoke. The diplomat was virtually trembling with rage and clearly wasn't bluffing. It didn't take much imagination to visualize the flurry that the U-boat's signal had created in the Berlin and Washington dovecots.

'Okay,' Gerrard agreed after a face-saving pause.

Boult relaxed. 'How will you pay for the repairs to your ship?'

The question puzzled Gerrard. 'She's insured.'

'Like hell it is,' Boult growled. 'The New Bedford Whaling Corporation are in trouble, captain – big trouble. It seems that their attempt to revive commercial whaling in the United States hasn't worked out. Hardly surprising if the skipper of their largest whaling-ship goes charging about sinking U-boats.'

The information Boult had was sketchy but he was able to tell Gerrard that the NBWC was in the process of being wound up. The news confirmed Gerrard's suspicions and accounted for the cryptic replies he had recently received from the owners in response to his radioed progress reports.

'Cheer up, captain,' said Boult five minutes later as he steadied himself on the Jacob's ladder. 'She's a fine, modern ship. Your owners won't have trouble finding a buyer. Whether or not they'd be prepared to keep you on as her captain is another matter.'

Gerrard watched the pilot's boat draw away from the *Tulsar*. He flipped the cigar butt into water and muttered one, heartfelt word to express his feelings. But he had no regrets for his action in destroying the U-boat. That was something that would never change.

5

Simon Gooding stared out of his office window at the haze-shrouded hills that separated Durban's Port Natal from the Indian Ocean before turning to Josephine.

'It's difficult, Miss Britten – very difficult.' He mopped his forehead with a spotted handkerchief. Thirty years in Durban and still he wasn't accustomed to the temper-sapping humidity. 'All shipping has to be convoyed from Cape Town, and the departure times of the convoys are kept secret. I could easily sell you a ticket and send you down to the Cape, but you might have to wait anything up to three months for a United States bound ship, and even then there's no guarantee that you'd get a passage.'

The shipping agent loosened his tie. The slow-turning fan in the centre of the ceiling made no impression on the suffocating heat in the office. He wondered how the American girl managed to look so cool and composed. She was sitting on the edge of her chair and regarding Gooding with a half amused expression.

'My country isn't at war with Germany,' Josephine gently pointed out, well aware that the sarcastic edge in her voice was causing the shipping agent some embarrassment.

'Two US-registered ships have already been sunk on the Cape route, Miss Britten.' Gooding toyed with Josephine's passport to avoid having to meet her disturbing almond eyes and found those same eyes regarding him from her photograph. He snapped the passport shut and pushed it across his desk. A tug siren wailed across the harbour and the tentative quickening of the late afternoon breeze flooded the office with the thick, heavy scent of the sugar terminal. He shut his window; it was something to do while he thought of something to say. 'I'll make some inquiries among my contacts at the Cape, Miss Britten, but I can't make any promises.' He realized that his visitor wasn't listening – she was staring past his shoulder out of the window. Her eyes refocussed on him and she gave him an acid smile.

'A United States ship is just entering the harbour, Mr Gooding.'

The shipping agent spun round. Two tugs were nudging a whaling factory-ship across the harbour. There was no doubt about the new arrival's nationality: an enormous Stars and Stripes banner that extended down to the waterline was painted amidships on the side of the hull. The lower half of the ship's bow was a mass of torn and twisted plates.

'A male driver,' Josephine drily observed.

'It's the *Tulsar*,' said Gooding hastily.

Josephine smiled. 'If it's an American ship, am I wrong in thinking that it might eventually be sailing for America?'

Gooding mopped his brow again. 'It's a whaling-ship, Miss Britten – they never carry passengers.'

Josephine stood and pulled on her white gloves. 'Are you the owners' Durban agent, Mr Gooding?'

'Yes. But –'

'That's marvellous.' Josephine dropped her passport in her

handbag and snapped it shut. 'You can make the arrangements.'

'You don't understand, Miss Britten. The *Tulsar*'s been involved in collision – she has to undergo repairs and –'

'Call me occasionally at the hotel to tell me how the repairs are progressing, Mr Gooding.' Josephine paused in the doorway and gave the hapless shipping agent a disarming smile. 'It will save me having to pester you night and day with phone calls. A merry Christmas to you, Mr Gooding.'

The scent of her perfume lingered in the office and was more noticeable than the usual smell of sugar. Gooding opened his window and watched Josephine thread her way with a determined step through the throng of chattering Indian women crowded round the market stalls. He sighed wistfully and reflected that Josephine Britten was a very remarkable young woman.

6

Of all the intelligence organizations operating in Berlin towards the close of 1940 the Institute for Market Analysis occupying all six floors of a large, drab building on the Fasanenstrasse was the least prepossessing. Unlike the modern headquarters of RSHA VI Foreign Intelligence on Berkaerstrasse or the RSHA VIF Technical Group on Delbruckstrasse, there were no armed guards at attention either side of the main entrance and, more surprisingly, no blood-red Nazi party banner to relieve the dreary monotony of its bleak granite façade. The IMA was an anonymous organization that made up for its deliberate lack of grandeur with a quiet and deadly efficiency.

It had started operating ten years earlier as a study group within the Reich Statistical Office issuing economic and military reports and forecasts based on information culled from the most abundant sources of intelligence in the world: newspapers, technical press reports and specialist journals. Under the direction of Professor Ernst Strick, lecturer in economics at Kiel

University, it had grown steadily in size and influence and now had a team of two hundred researchers, translators and collators, a fourteen thousand volume library that was expanding each day, and an annual budget approaching one million Reich marks. If Strick's powerful agency was hated by its rival intelligence units it was at least held in high regard; time and again the IMA had demonstrated its ability to produce accurate, well-formulated forecasts and surveys. It had, for example, submitted reports to the OKW the previous February that detailed the level of arms, men and time that would be required to overrun the Low Countries. It had turned out to be an astonishingly accurate forecast.

Consequently, when Dr Strick was shown into the office of Walter Funk, the effeminate economics minister, he was confident that his latest report would be taken seriously.

'Dr Strick,' said Funk warmly, shaking his visitor's hand and indicating a chair. 'A rare pleasure. A drink? I have some excellent cognac.'

Strick sat and unfastened his briefcase. 'Thank you, no, Herr Minister.' It was eleven in the morning; the economics minister's passion for drink was equalled by his passion for men. Preferably young men. 'My secretary told you why I wished to see you?'

Funk poured himself a generous slug of brandy from an incredibly ugly cocktail cabinet. 'A matter of the utmost importance, doctor? An exaggeration surely?'

Strick placed his ten-page report before Funk and said calmly: 'This document is the result of a thousand hours' work by myself and my foreign economics monitoring unit. I personally have tested all the forecasts and found them conclusive. Provided we act swiftly now, Allied resistance will collapse by mid-February and the British will be forced to sue for peace by the end of February: the war against Britain and her empire will be over within the next eight weeks.'

For some seconds the only sound in the office was the slow tick of the bronze wall clock. Strick rested both arms on Funk's desk and leaned forward confidingly. 'As I'm sure your own intelligence agency has discovered, Herr Minister, this war will be won on the balance-sheet and not the battle-ground.'

Funk's minions had told him nothing of the sort but he had no intention of letting Strick know that. He gave a faint smile and said: 'I presume you're referring to the supposed drain on Britain's gold and dollar reserves as a result of their so-called cash and carry scheme with Roosevelt?'

'It's hardly a supposed drain, Minister,' said Strick politely. He had to be careful; Funk was one of the most powerful men in Germany and was vainly proud of his own over-staffed economic intelligence unit.

'It is if the British can get fifty destroyers out of the Americans in exchange for a vague promise to allow the US navy the use of Caribbean bases that it doesn't need,' Funk replied pointedly. 'Hardly a drain on Britain's gold and dollar reserves.'

'That was an isolated instance that Roosevelt dare not repeat,' said Strick. 'My information is that the Allies are having to pay in dollars or gold before they can take away a single round of ammunition. I have exact figures from the US Treasury. An isolationist official has revealed that the British Crown Agents are quietly selling off large tracts of Crown-owned land in New York and the mid-West. The sale of Courtaulds investments in the US is well known, of course.'

Funk looked at his watch. 'I don't wish to hurry you, doctor, but I have an appointment in ten minutes. If you could get to the point –'

'The point,' Strick cut in, 'is that Britain will have exhausted all her gold and dollar reserves by the end of this month, with the exception of her emergency reserve in South Africa. Britain's $4,500 million she had at the beginning of the war is now down to less than $600 million and most of that is earmarked for Canada to pay for supplies now being freighted across the US border to Montreal.'

Funk turned over the pages of the report and came to a column of figures which he studied intently for some seconds before pressing a key on his intercom and asking for the analysis figures on Britain's gold reserves to be sent in to him.

'It will be interesting to see how your figures compare with ours,' said Funk, giving his visitor a frosty smile.

There was a tap on the door. A secretary entered and placed a single typewritten sheet before Funk. He glanced at it and smiled. 'There appears to be a wide discrepancy, doctor,' he said when the secretary had withdrawn. 'You say Britain has $600 million dollars – we say nearer $1,000 million.'

Strick frowned. 'May I see please, Minister?'

Funk pushed the sheet of paper across his desk and gazed boredly up at the ceiling while mentally preparing a case to have Strick's budget slashed for the new financial year.

'Ah yes,' said Strick, unable to conceal the relief he felt. 'I've found the error. You've assumed that the French bullion that fell into American hands when the Vichy aircraft carrier *Béarn* fled to Martinique was credited to the British by the US Treasury. In fact that has not happened. We have established that the Americans intend holding the gold in trust for the French.'

Funk's gaze dropped from the ceiling to regard the slightly-built doctor. 'Then what is the true figure according to you?'

'That Britain will be absolutely broke by mid-April. The Lend-Lease bill that Roosevelt has laid before Congress is unlikely to become law before mid-June – and only then if Colonel Lindbergh's isolationist lobby does not manage to sway Congress against Roosevelt, as seems likely.'

Funk was no fool and could see immediately what Strick was driving at. He knew that Britain was conducting the war on a desperate hand to mouth basis. She had blood and steel in plenty but that was no good without the gold to pay for oil imports, food and munitions. Assuming that the Lend-Lease bill before Congress – enabling the president to hand over to the British all the arms they wanted without payment – became law, there would still be a period of two months in which Britain would be penniless. A few well-placed rumours in those neutral countries still trading with the British would be enough to exhaust her overseas credit. There would be a month when the Führer would be able to force the British to sue for peace. But Funk could see a snag.

'You mentioned the emergency gold reserves in South Africa,' he reminded.

Strick nodded emphatically. 'Allowing for a fifteen per cent increase in gold production at Johannesburg's Germiston refinery since the last figures were published in 1939, we have estimated that gold stocks in South Africa are in the region of $200 million. Strick paused. 'Four dollars each for every man, woman and child – that's all that's left of Great Britain's wealth . . . Herr Reichminister – the British are defeated now as we sit here talking. Those figures prove it. But for Churchill to recognize that they are defeated it is absolutely imperative that we stop at nothing to ensure that the last of Britain's gold does not leave South Africa.'

7

Gooding brought his fly-swat smartly down on his desk in the South African shipping agency and scraped the remains of the insect into his wastepaper basket. The diversion gave him time to think. He had learned from previous visits by the *Tulsar* that Gerrard required careful handling; the tough, leathery-skinned American had a mercurial temper that could erupt without warning when things were not going his way.

'Well?' Gerrard demanded.

Gooding fingered the marine architect's report on the damage to the *Tulsar*'s bow. 'It's not an unreasonable estimate, captain.'

'Like hell it is.'

'It includes the hire of the floating crane to lift the bow clear of the water while repairs are carried out,' Gooding pointed out. 'Look at the welding and riveting involved – the entire bow has to be rebuilt from forefoot to waterline.'

'Six thousand dollars,' Gerrard muttered. 'Jesus Christ.' He brooded for a moment. 'Have you worked out how much I need to get the *Tulsar* home?'

Gooding had the information in front of him. 'You'll need four and a half thousand dollars to cover a skeleton crew's pay, bunkering, victualling, freshwater and harbour dues.'

There was a brief silence apart from the hum of the fan. Gooding mopped his face with a handkerchief.

'Harbour dues,' Gerrard muttered 'Jesus Christ – I sink a

U-boat and the ungrateful bastards hit me with harbour dues.'

'I'll have a word with the port captain,' Gooding promised. 'Maybe we can get a waiver.'

'Listen, Gooding, cable the owners again and tell them straight – if they want the *Tulsar* back in New Bedford then they've got to wire the money.'

The shipping agent shook his head. 'There's no money to wire, captain. The creditors want to get their hands on the *Tulsar* but none of them are prepared to put up the money.'

Gerrard ran his fingers through his unruly mop of hair. 'Jesus Christ – what a fucking mess.'

'We could try the United States consul,' Gooding suggested. 'A loan from their contingency fund.'

'Not a chance – I'd sooner take the *Tulsar* out and scuttle her.'

'So we have an impasse. Unless . . .' Gooding smiled and left the sentence unfinished.

Gerrard gave Gooding a sharp look. 'Unless what?'

'I don't think you'd be interested.'

'If you have an idea, then for Chrissake let's hear it.'

It was the capitulation that Gooding had been waiting for but a tactful opening was called for. 'If you sail home with a skeleton crew, you'll have about twenty empty process workers' cabins.'

'Yeah – I guess.' Gerrard's tone was pregnant with suspicion.

'There are American citizens scattered all over South Africa who want passages home. There are hardly any passenger services operating, and the US government won't take them out because they say their citizens are safer here than on the high seas.'

Gerrard stared at the shipping agent. 'The *Tulsar*? Carrying passengers? Jesus Christ – she's a whaling factory-ship!'

'She's modern,' said Gooding, talking quickly. 'She could easily be cleaned out – smartened up. A US ship sailing with US passengers – the Board of Trade can't object provided your lifeboats are up to scratch, which they are. And there's something else: the longer the *Tulsar*'s hanging about here, the greater the chance that the authorities might take it into their heads to commandeer it.'

Gerrard opened his mouth and shut it. 'Well . . . I guess it's an idea,' he grudgingly admitted after a moment's thought.

'How many passengers could we carry and how much could we charge them?'

Gooding made a note on his pad. 'I'll contact Hutchins at Cape Town. He's got about twenty Americans waiting to go home and there's one I know of right here in Durban. Allowing for two cooks, three stewards and a purser, I'd say that a thousand dollars per head would be a reasonable fare to New York.'

Gerrard stared at Gooding and shook his head slowly. 'Jesus Christ,' he muttered. 'Passengers!'

8

'You asked to see me, Mr Thorne?'

The manager of the Benjamin D'Urban Hotel half rose from his desk and gestured to a chair. 'Come in, Miss Britten. Please take a seat.'

Josephine perched on the edge of the chair and regarded Thorne with an icy expression. She had guessed the reason for the summons to his office.

'We were sorry not to see you at the guests' new year's eve party last night, Miss Britten.'

'I was very tired. I've been working double duties for a week.'

Thorne nodded sympathetically. 'Yes, of course. Actually, that wasn't the reason why I called you in. I was glancing through the telephone log-book this morning and I noticed that you've been making a considerable number of long distance personal calls during the past –' He never completed the sentence because Josephine jumped to her feet, her eyes blazing with unbridled anger.

'I've entered every call on my time sheet, Mr Thorne. You can check; I haven't been cheating you and don't you say I have.'

Thorne held up a consoling hand. 'Please, Miss Britten – you're the last person in the world I would ever dream of accusing of cheating the hotel. It's not that at all.'

Josephine remained standing, staring down at the hotel manager with open hostility. 'What then?'

Thorne gave an embarrassed smile and opened a ledger. 'Calls to East London, Cape Town, Port Elizabeth. I thought you were trying to find another job until I discovered all these numbers are for shipping and travel agents.' He closed the ledger. 'Why do you want to go home? And don't say it's none of my business, because I think it is if I stand to lose the best receptionist this hotel has ever known.'

'I've been here long enough for you to realize that I'm immune to flattery,' said Josephine coldly.

Thorne nodded, 'I know that only too well. I was merely stating a fact – we'd be sorry to lose you. If it's a question of more money . . .'

'It's not that.'

'No. I didn't think it was.' Thorne hesitated and said encouragingly: 'There's a stupid saying – you must've heard it – a trouble shared is a trouble halved.'

Josephine met Thorne's eyes. The hotel manager appeared to be genuinely concerned. But then she had known men before who had pretended to be worried about her. It meant nothing. Perhaps Thorne was concerned. To his credit he had never made a pass at her. She sat down and watched the hotel manager carefully to gauge the effect of her words.

'Two weeks ago I received a cable from my mother telling me that my father had been taken ill. Last week she wrote to me saying that the specialists have categorically stated that he has less than six months to live. Mid-June at the latest.' Josephine stopped abruptly and toyed self-consciously with her handbag strap. 'I've not been able to find a ship sailing home. What few ships there are are fully booked until August. I've tried everywhere – even Lorenzo Marques. There's nothing . . . nothing . . .'

Thorne suddenly realized that Josephine was on the verge of tears. He was embarrassed – certain that to offer comfort involving physical contact, such as putting an arm round her shoulders, would be vehemently rejected. The American girl solved this dilemma by moving quickly to the door and pulling it open.

'You're right, Mr Thorne,' she said, not looking at him. 'It is a stupid saying. Damned stupid.'

9

Kurt Milland guessed the impending disaster when he saw that the small training U-boat was running on its diesel engines instead of its electric motors. His warning shout was too late; there was a sickening crunch as the U-boat's bows ploughed into the massive timber pile that was designed to protect the stone jetty at Wilhelmshaven from such assaults. The timber was ripped from its mountings by the force of the impact and was brutally rolled between the U-boat's buckling outer hull and the unyielding granite of the jetty. Rivets chewed deep into the waterlogged outer layers of the pile, exposing the pale elm flesh below. The two men who had been standing on the U-boat's forward deck casing ready to heave a line to Milland jumped back in alarm and waved frantically to the men on the bridge. A group of children, well wrapped against the bitterly cold wind sweeping in across the North Sea, gave a lusty cheer of approval and were immediately silenced by Milland's withering glare as he took a threatening step towards them.

The U-boat came to rest with its battered bow gently nudging the stone steps. Milland caught the line thrown to him and dropped a clove-hitch over one of the stubby mooring bollards before stumping along the quay until he was level with the U-boat's conning-tower. The young officer on the bridge goggled at Milland in white-faced terror and followed his pointed gaze to the offending bow.

'Excellent, Herr Fischer. Excellent. If I were the enemy I'd be sinking now, would I not?'

Leutnant zur See Hans Fischer nodded miserably.

'But I'm not the enemy, am I?'

'No, Herr Kapitänleutnant.'

'I'm a friend, aren't I?'

'Yes, Herr Kapitänleutnant.'

'We shall have another discussion about what I am and what I think you are in my office at fifteen hundred hours.' Milland glanced at his watch. 'In three hours. It will be in addition to a general chat on our chances of winning the war if you partake in it.'

Milland swung his artificial leg round by pivoting his body on his sound left leg, and stumped away from the quay with a curious, rolling gait that gave him the appearance of being slightly drunk. He climbed behind the wheel of his elderly DKW and watched the trainee crew making the damaged U-boat secure in response to Fischer's orders.

A two-week-old copy of the daily newspaper the *Völkische Beobachter* was lying on the passenger seat beside him. He pulled off his mittens and reread the main story that had led to him keeping the newspaper for so long. It was beneath a banner headline:

US TREACHERY IN INDIAN OCEAN. AMERICAN SHIP RAMS U-BOAT.

Milland pushed the newspaper to one side and stared through the windscreen at the grey, windswept North Sea. His thoughts were with the forty men who had perished ten thousand kilometres from home and the man who had killed them. There was no doubt that the rest of the story would emerge in time. It was time to stop dithering and go straight to the Flotilla Commander.

Konteradmiral Hugo Staus, commanding officer of the 2nd U-boat Training Flotilla (Wilhelmshaven), was a gaunt, somewhat forbidding Prussian in his late fifties who had commanded a U-boat with distinction during the Great War. He was sitting at his desk signing defect reports when he heard the familiar squeak of Milland's artificial leg in the corridor outside his office. There was a firm rap on the door. Staus called out for Milland to enter and laid down his gold fountain pen, for he considered it the height of rudeness to continue writing when a visitor entered his office. He noticed that Milland was carrying a copy of the party newspaper.

'Good afternoon, Kurt,' said Staus. 'I hear that you've just had a little mishap with one of my precious Type II's?'

'Nothing serious, admiral,' said Milland, not for the first time marvelling at Staus' reliable intelligence – the crusty old bastard had his spies everywhere. 'One of my fledglings forgot that there's no reversing gearbox on a U-boat's diesel engines. The damage isn't too bad. I think a verbal reprimand will be enough unless you say otherwise.'

Staus nodded. The stocky officer standing before him was one of his best instructors and he had no intention of interfering in the way he ran things. Nor did Admiral Staus offer Milland a chair because he knew it would be politely refused. Milland was both courageous and stubborn. He made no concessions to the fact that he had an artificial leg and would allow no one else to make concessions for him. He knew that he would never be given his own command and yet he had thrown all his energies into the training of youngsters for their commands. Kurt Milland lived for U-boats to the exclusion of all else. Nor was he interested in women, although Staus knew from gossip that circulated around the headquarters building as freely as its draughts that there were a number of secretaries who found Milland attractive despite his disability.

'So what brings you to see me, Kurt?'

Milland unfolded the newspaper and gave it to Staus. 'It's about that story two weeks ago, admiral, when an American ship rammed and sank *U-497* in the Indian Ocean.'

'Yes indeed. A disgraceful incident. As I recall, the Americans claimed that it was an accident?'

'I don't think it was an accident, admiral.'

Staus raised his aristocratic eyebrows. 'Really?'

'I know the captain of the ship that sank the U-boat and I know why he did it.'

Staus' expression hardened. He looked down at the newspaper. 'You mean that you know this . . . Robert Gerrard?'

'Yes, admiral.'

Staus thought for a moment and nodded to a chair. 'I think you ought to sit down, Kurt.'

Milland gratefully lowered himself into a chair and released the knee lock on his artificial leg so that he could bend the joint and sit without the leg thrust out. Staus waited patiently while Milland marshalled his thoughts.

'I used to be Gerrard's first officer on the *Tulsar* – that's the ship that sank the U-boat; I signed on with him at Spitzbergen after quitting a Norwegian whaler – the *Kraken* – in 1933.' A warm light entered Milland's eyes as he recalled his whaling days. 'She was brand, spanking new, admiral. The most modern factory-ship afloat and she still is. Parsons turbines, her own high-speed catchers, a spotter seaplane – everything. She was completely self-contained, a new concept in whaling.'

'Who does she belong to?' Staus prodded when Milland broke off and groped for words.

'The New Bedford Whaling Corporation. They were a Detroit consortium who wanted a guaranteed supply of sperm oil for car automatic transmissions that they were about to go in for in a big way. They financed the *Tulsar* because the American whaling industry was virtually finished and they didn't want to rely on Japanese supplies.'

'It was a success?'

Suddenly the warmth was no longer in Milland's voice. 'Gerrard was the sort of man to make sure it was a success.' He lapsed into silence. Staus noticed that Milland's hand had dropped to his right leg and seemed to be unconsciously tracing the outline of where Staus guessed Milland's stump was.

'Tell me about him,' the older man prompted.

'Nothing else mattered to him but catching sperm. Twenty – thirty – sometimes even forty a day if the hunting was good. He'd drive men to the point of suicide to fill the *Tulsar*'s tanks. If a flenser was careless and got cut badly when splicing up a carcass, then that was too bad. Flensing-knife cuts always turn septic but we never turned back to port.'

'But you carried a doctor?'

Milland gave a mirthless smile. 'We were supposed to. But Gerrard said that they did nothing but sit around earning other men's bonuses. Gerrard was the *Tulsar*'s doctor. No one ever complained because your bonuses were three times what they were on any other ship.'

Milland's knuckles were now white from where his fingers were digging into his thigh. He seemed to be forcing himself to speak; the memories were no longer sweet.

'I was with him for four years,' Milland continued. 'I returned to Germany in 1936 and joined the navy.'

Staus recollected Milland's medical card. The naval doctors at Kiel had passed Milland as 'one hundred per cent fit and one hundred per cent disabled'. His acceptance into the navy was the result of a tenacious battle by Milland with the officer selection board until, impressed by his courage and indomitable spirit, they had finally relented.

'He hardly ever wrote,' said Milland. 'Once in 1938 to tell me he was marrying a New Bedford girl. He sent me a wedding photograph. Then there was another letter that came on the day England declared war on us. It was postmarked Liverpool. He said that Cathy was going to have a baby and that he was sending her home via Montreal on the *Athenia*.'

The silence in the room was total.

'Cathy Gerrard was one of the twenty-eight Americans killed when *U-30* sank the *Athenia*,' said Milland. 'That's why I think Gerrard deliberately rammed that U-boat in the Indian Ocean.'

Staus remained deep in thought for some minutes after Milland had stumped out of his office, then he summoned a secretary and dictated a full report on the matter to the OKM – the naval high command in Berlin.

He imagined that his account would cause a brief stir in the higher echelons of the Kriegsmarine and then be forgotten. For once his normally sound judgement was seriously at fault.

10

Gooding disentangled himself from the hotel's revolving door and crossed the mosaic floor to the reception desk where Josephine was making up the bill for an elderly couple from Ladysmith. She smilingly bid the couple goodbye and signalled to a porter to help them with their luggage before turning to Gooding and treating him to a modified version of her smile that was normally reserved for the hotel's guests.

'Good morning, Mr Gooding.'

'Air-conditioning,' said the shipping agent enviously. 'What it is to be in a place with air-conditioning.'

'It always gives trouble in mid-February when the holiday season is in full swing. Did you really come here to admire our air-conditioning or do you wish to make a reservation?'

'Neither,' said Gooding, wondering if Josephine used her talent for making one feel uncomfortable on the guests. 'You remember that United States ship that entered the harbour while you were in my office the other day?'

A look of interest flickered briefly in Josephine's eyes. 'The *Tulsar* – yes – I remember.'

'She'll be sailing for New York just as soon as we can get her bow repaired and she'll be taking up to twenty passengers.'

Josephine regarded Gooding expressionlessly. 'That's very good news, Mr Gooding.'

'I thought you'd be interested.'

'I am. How long will it take to get the bow repaired?'

'We're not sure. The Dock Priorities Committee are insisting that repairs to Allied shipping come first.'

'It's important that I'm home before the end of May at the latest – much earlier if possible.'

Gooding chuckled. 'I think we can say that the *Tulsar* will be in New York long before then.'

The vagueness irritated Josephine. It offended those qualities of preciseness and efficiency that made her such a valued hotel receptionist. 'Can't you be more exact, please?'

'The only thing I can be exact about is the cost of the passage.'

'Which is?'

'Three hundred and ten pounds.'

Josephine's aloof composure deserted her. She stared at Gooding first in dismay and then in anger. 'But that's crazy – that's over a thousand dollars!'

'There's a war on, Miss Britten,' was Gooding's smooth reply. 'Things are different now. Oil, food, pay – everything's gone up.'

'Not that much they haven't. In two years working here I've had raises amounting to no more than one pound fifteen shillings a week.'

'Look, Miss Britten – we advertised for the first time yesterday in the morning papers and by ten this morning we'd sold nineteen of the twenty passages. We've one single cabin left so three hundred quid can't be that bad. I came to pick up my car from the garage and I thought I'd drop in to see if you were still interested in going home.' Gooding moved away from the reception desk. 'I'm sorry I wasted your time.'

'I *am* interested,' said Josephine sharply, resenting being forced to capitulate so quickly.

Gooding took a notebook from his pocket and scribbled briefly. 'Thank you, Miss Britten. I shall require your fare within forty-eight hours.'

'The full amount?'

'The full amount,' Gooding affirmed.

'But I haven't got three hundred in the bank,' Josephine snapped. 'Isn't it normal to pay a deposit first?'

'In peacetime it is,' Gooding replied, glancing in his notebook. The money he had collected so far was enough to buy steel plate for the repairs to the *Tulsar*'s bow but not enough to enable the shipwrights to start work. 'I'll keep the cabin in your name until the end of next week. If you can't pay by then I'm afraid that I'll have to let it go.'

He snapped the notebook shut and walked out of the hotel lobby without looking back at Josephine.

11

The landing area in Table Bay, marked by two lines of orange buoys, was clear of floating débris. The harbour boat that had carried out the inspection moved clear of the lane and fired a green signal flare into the cloudless blue sky.

As the huge, four-engine Empire flying-boat banked and began losing height, Ralph Holden had his first glimpse of the breathtaking splendour of Table Mountain rising like a mighty black bulwark out of the South Atlantic and dwarfing the sprawling lion shape of Signal Hill. There was a layer of perfectly white cloud spread over the top of the mountain like icing and spilling over the edge of the great escarpment like a vast avalanche that threatened Cape Town and yet failed to reach its target because the cloud was dissolved by the lower layers of warm air defending the city.

'The mountain's got a tablecloth on it today,' observed a cultured voice at Holden's side. It was the elderly admiral. He was peering out of Holden's window. 'Going to seem dashed odd being pitchforked into midsummer in a matter of a couple of days. Never have got used to it.'

Holden gave the sailor his customary charming smile and said nothing. He was well aware that his presence aboard the flying-boat had been the subject of endless speculation among the other fifteen passengers during the three-day flight from Falmouth in Cornwall. Their attempts to engage the fair-haired young man in conversation in the hope of learning something about him had been thwarted by his ability to side-track questions disarmingly and replace them with questions of his own, skilfully put, so that he had ended up knowing more about his inquisitors than they about him. After the first day of the flight they had learned to leave him alone. Most of the time he sat quietly in his seat nursing a leather, GVIR-crested briefcase that was handcuffed to his wrist.

The water became a blur beneath the flying-boat as its hull lost height. Then there was a tremendous bump followed by a deafening roar beneath the passengers' feet. After six refuelling stops since leaving Falmouth they were used to the unnerving business of a flying-boat's landing and few even bothered to look at the spectacular curtains of spray thrown up on each side of the hull. Even the ghastly sinking sensation when the flying-boat stopped planing and dug its wing-floats into the water no longer caused concern.

'Smooth landing' the admiral commented, eyeing the steel chain that linked Holden's wrist to the briefcase and wondering if Holden was one of His Majesty's couriers.

'Very smooth, sir,' Holden agreed.

The admiral grunted. At least the wretched fellow was polite, which was something these days.

Holden looked out of his window. The flying-boat was taxiing to meet the harbour patrol boat that would tow it to the safety of the inner basin.

•

'Mr Holden?'

A tall, distinguished-looking man in his late fifties approached Holden the moment he emerged from the passenger terminal and stood blinking in the bright sunlight. The porter, still smarting from Holden's refusal to allow him to take the briefcase, appeared to know the tall man for in response to a nod he carried Holden's suitcase to a waiting Rover and placed it in the car's boot. Holden realized that the Cape Coloured porter who had accosted him in the terminal was in fact the car's driver. Holden disliked other people taking the initiative; there was little warmth in his handshake.

'Plum,' said the tall man breezily, oblivious of Holden's coolness. 'Sir Max Plum. I expect your people gave you a photograph of me before you left. Prepared you for the worst.' He gave a booming laugh and steered Holden to the rear door of the car that the porter was holding open.

'Good flight was it?' Plum inquired, settling himself beside Holden in the back seat as the Rover drove through the dock gates and into Cape Town's waterfront sprawl of warehouses and seafood stalls surrounded by shouting women of every conceivable nationality.

'Very pleasant,' Holden murmured.

'No point in going to the bank. You must be pretty tired so I thought we'd go straight home. Mary will rustle up something to eat.' Plum looked quizzically at his visitor. 'Is that okay with you?'

'Certainly – provided I can get down to work right away.'

Sir Max Plum, president of the Reserve Bank, gave a faint smile. A permanent under-secretary at the Treasury in London had tipped him off about Holden: 'Fellow's a glutton for work. For God's sake don't get in his way.'

The car sped through the Malay quarter and headed southwest into the pleasant Tuine Gardens suburb with whitewashed bungalows overlooking terraced gardens with neat, Protea-filled flowerbeds.

Gradually the smaller bungalows abandoned the climb up Table Mountain's lower slopes and handed over the struggle to larger, more imposing residences.

Plum's house was a spacious, timber-framed chalet with a

broad stoep – a veranda – overlooking Table Bay. The pincer-like arms of Cape Town's artificial harbour reaching out into the Atlantic resembled a series of taut silken threads laid on a flawless sheet of blue glass.

'Some view, what?' said Plum with a proud wave of his hand.

Plum's wife, an erect, greying woman, came down the steps of the stoep to greet Holden. She was a little surprised by his smart, lightweight tropical suit; visitors from England on the flying-boat usually turned up in heavy, unsuitable clothing. Obviously the fair-haired young man with the disturbing blue eyes was a careful planner.

'Mr Holden – how nice to meet you. Your room's ready and I'm sure you must be dying for a bath and a change. I know that you and Max have a lot of business to talk over, but I'd love to hear about London when you've got the time. It must be absolutely frightful with all that bombing. Some tea in thirty minutes.'

She bustled away to harangue hidden servants lurking in the depths of the house.

'How much does your wife know?' Holden asked the bank president two hours later. The two men were sitting on the stoep.

Plum put down his whisky glass and stared at Holden in surprise. 'Nothing, of course. Only three people in South Africa know the reason for your visit: you and me, and Villiers at the Reserve Bank in Pretoria – he has to know because he has to authorize the release of the gold.'

Holden nodded and sipped his orange juice, then set his glass down on the table. 'You're aware that the gold has to be shipped immediately?' His tone was deceptively mild.

'Are things so bad?'

'If we don't get that gold to London within the next four months, the war will be as good as over for us.'

'The naval intelligence office in Simonstown have scoured every port in South Africa,' said Plum irritably. 'Everything that can float and move has been sent to Liverpool. There isn't a ship in South Africa capable of twelve knots, never mind twenty-five. Why the devil does it have to be so fast?'

'Our experiences so far with the *Queen Mary* and *Queen Elizabeth* have shown that a fast, unescorted ship can avoid U-boats and surface raiders.'

'Then send one of the *Queens* here to pick up the gold, damn it,' Plum muttered.

Holden nodded to the distant harbour. 'You can't move a ship in or out of Cape Town without the whole of South Africa knowing about it. The same applies to every other port. It only needs one of our pro-German Boer friends in the Ossewa-Brandwag to squawk on his radio-transmitter that one of the *Queens* has turned up here and we'd have every U-boat that Doenitz can muster lying in wait off Cape Town.'

'Smuts has had all the Ossewa-Brandwag fanatics interned,' Plum pointed out.

'The director of naval intelligence in London thinks otherwise,' said Holden. 'He's convinced that Ossewa agents are still helping surface raiders – possibly transmitting shipping movements to U-boats who relay them to Berlin. Only last month an American ship accidentally rammed and sank a U-boat off Durban. So what was the U-boat doing there if it wasn't relaying intelligence? There hadn't been reports of incidents between merchantships and U-boats.'

Plum remained silent. Holden had been well briefed.

'If we sent a warship to Cape Town or Simonstown,' Holden continued, 'the Germans, knowing that all warships are desperately needed on the North Atlantic convoys, would guess what it's for and throw everything they've got at it.'

'Not if the gold was moved under the cover of a Cape convoy,' Plum pointed out.

Holden shook his head. 'We can't risk shifting the last of our gold a quarter of the way round the world in a convoy. We need a ship that is both fast and nondescript.'

'Well there isn't one.' Plum felt in his pocket and produced a sheaf of papers which he handed to Holden. 'That's a list of every ship lying in South African ports. There's nothing that fits the bill.'

Holden studied the list intently, slowly turning the pages as he finished scanning the columns that listed names, class of vessel, tonnage and performance, and where lying. He came to the last page.

'They're no good,' said Plum shortly. 'That's the appendix – ships belonging to neutral countries that are awaiting repairs.'

Holden's quick eye spotted a figure – twenty-six knots. 'There's a whaling factory-ship here that's more than fast enough,' he observed. 'Lying at Durban.'

Plum peered at where Holden's finger was pointing. 'But she's no use – she's American owned and registered.'

'So?'

Plum stared hard at his fair-haired visitor who was regarding him with an amused half-smile. 'Damn it, man!' he protested. 'We can't move the last of our gold on an American!'

'Why not?'

'Because it's unheard of, that's why not!'

'Which sounds like an extremely good reason for doing it,' Holden murmured. 'The *Tulsar*.' He frowned. 'The name sounds familiar.'

'She was the American that collided with the U-boat off Durban,' Plum replied stiffly.

Holden unhurriedly drained his orange juice and stood. 'I shall require a seat on the first flight to Durban, Sir Max. I'd be grateful if you would kindly make the necessary arrangements and book me into an hotel there.'

'Now?'

Holden smiled. 'I think so. It never ceases to amaze me just how quickly the present can become the past.'

12

A room key dropped without warning on the desk. Josephine quickly looked up and smiled at the Englishman – not flinching from the dispassionate blue eyes.

'Hallo, Mr Holden. Is your room okay?'

'I expect it will be adequate,' Holden replied. 'I shall be gone for a little over an hour. I've left two shirts on my bed. I'd be grateful if they could be washed and ironed please.'

Josephine promised that they would be ready the following day and watched the Englishman move across the lobby to the revolving doors. He moved silently, with cat-like grace. The discreet steel chain that she had noticed an hour before when he had first checked in was still in place, linking his briefcase to his wrist.

A girl entered the lobby through the revolving doors as Holden went out. She gaped after the departing figure for a moment before crossing to the reception desk.

'Wow,' she breathed. 'Who's that?'

Josephine stood and reached for her white gloves. 'A new guest,' she said coldly.

'He looks like Leslie Howard. Did he bring a wife?'

'You're three minutes late, Jenny,' said Josephine tartly. 'I made it clear that I had an important appointment.'

The Zulu looked old enough to have fought in one of Cetshwayo's *impis* at the Battle of Rorke's Drift. His magnificent ostrich feather head-dress almost fell off as he gathered up the shafts of his gaudily painted ricksha. He gave Holden a broad grin.

'Where to, baas?'

'The docks, please.' Holden replied. He settled in the cushions and repositioned the ricksha's straw sunshade.

The Zulu eased the ricksha out of the hotel forecourt and broke into an effortless, loping jog along the crowded seafront.

Holden glanced back. Another ricksha was following a hundred yards behind. The passenger was the American girl from his hotel.

'Look, Mr Gooding,' said Josephine in what she hoped was a reasoning tone. 'I worked my passage from New York to Cape Town as a stewardess and I've worked as a receptionist in several large hotels since I arrived in South Africa, so I don't see what the problem is.'

Simon Gooding thoughtfully scratched his nose. 'Being a ship's purser isn't quite the same thing, Miss Britten.'

'It's not so very different from running a hotel,' Josephine retorted. 'And besides – most of the *Tulsar*'s passengers will be Americans – right?'

Gooding nodded.

'Okay then. It's going to seem pretty strange to them sailing on a whaling-ship – maybe they'd be glad to have a fellow American to turn to with their problems. Believe me, I know from running the Ben D'Urban Hotel that Americans seem to have more problems than most.'

'Why are you so keen to get home, Miss Britten?'

'That, Mr Gooding, if you'll forgive me for saying, is none of your damn business.'

The shipping agent thought for a moment and shrewdly said: 'Okay – I'll sign you on as the *Tulsar*'s purser for half the fare.'

'No,' said Josephine emphatically. 'That wouldn't be fair. If I'm worth employing as a purser, then I'm worth paying.'

Gooding conceded defeat. He knew from experience that a good purser was vital. 'Okay, Miss Britten We'll pay you ten dollars a week as the *Tulsar*'s purser.'

'Twelve,' Josephine countered, 'and I'll look after the menus as well.'

'Twelve then,' Gooding agreed, wondering if his business might do better if he took Josephine on as a partner.

Holden stopped at the end of the quay to run his eye over every detail of the *Tulsar*. He knew little about ships but was able to appreciate her fine lines. She was obviously of an advanced design and had represented a considerable act of faith by her now bankrupt owners in their chances of reviving New Bedford's whaling industry.

According to the specification that Holden had studied at length during the flight from Cape Town, the *Tulsar* had an overall length of 530 feet, a displacement of 7,000 tons, and her 27,000 shaft horsepower gave her a respectable top speed of twenty-six knots. The raised superstructure aft that housed the crew's quarters was divided by the canyon of the whale slipway that sloped down to the waterline at the stern. Forward of the crew's quarters was the open expanse of the flensing deck where the blubber was stripped from the whales. After that the carcasses were hauled under the seaplane platform to the lemming deck where the whalemeat was hacked from the creature's skeleton. At intervals around both decks were circular, hinged covers over the bone and blubber chutes. Immediately aft of the bridge were two high-speed whale-catcher launches slung from derricks. Mounted on the bow platform of each catcher was the ugly, business-like shape of a Svend Foyn explosive head harpoon-gun.

Holden moved to the crumpled bow and gazed at the damage. It seemed incredible that the ship could have sustained such a blow and remain afloat. He assumed that there was a watertight bulkhead in the bow. From what Holden had learned during the previous twenty-four hours about Captain Robert Gerrard, he wondered just how accidental the collision with the German U-boat had been.

He became aware that his presence on the quayside was attracting attention from the ship; a giant Afrikaner wearing a *Voortrekker* hat was watching him suspiciously from the top of the gangplank. Holden sauntered on, one hand thrust casually in his trouser pocket and the other holding the briefcase.

A shunting engine clanked across his path wearily pushing a long train of wagons loaded with beef. Through the intermittent gaps between each wagon and the next, Holden caught a glimpse of the hotel receptionist. She was near the administrative buildings but had vanished by the time the train had cleared from his field of view.

As far as Holden was concerned, the girl was following him, and it worried him.

When Holden was worried, he could be extremely dangerous.

Josephine returned to her room an hour after her successful visit to Simon Gooding and took a quick shower to cool off. She rarely ventured out of the hotel's air-conditioned interior on summer afternoons but the brief trip had been more than worth the effort.

She was half-way through a letter to her father when there was a tap on the bed-sitting-room door. It would be the pageboy with the cold drink she had asked him for.

'Come in.'

The door opened. Josephine turned to the door and immediately pulled her dressing-gown tightly closed – the fair-haired Englishman was standing on the threshold.

'Mr Holden,' said Josephine, quickly adopting the inane smile she reserved for hotel guests. 'You must've taken a wrong turning – you're in the staff quarters.'

Holden closed the door and leaned against it. He pushed his hands deep into his pockets and smiled lazily.

'I didn't take a wrong turning,' he said. 'I followed directions most carefully.'

It was a situation that Josephine had handled before, although this was the first time that a male guest had tracked her down to her room.

'Please, Mr Holden – I'll have to ask you to leave right now otherwise I could get into trouble and you could be thrown out of the hotel on your pink little ear.'

'We'd better keep our voices down then, Jo. Do you mind if I call you Jo or do you prefer Josephine?'

'Right now,' said Josephine, 'what I'd prefer is for you to beat it – or do I have to put it more crudely?'

Holden crossed his hands over his heart. 'I swear to go when you tell me what colour you're going to wear tonight.'

'Colour? Tonight? Just what the hell are you talking about?'

'We're dining together at the King Edward's Chart Room. I understand that it's the best restaurant in Durban.' Holden paused and added: 'I'm accustomed to the best.'

Josephine tried to pull the door open. 'So am I, Mr Holden – which is one reason why I won't be dining with you tonight. Another is that I'll be on duty.'

Holden's smile became a grin. 'No you won't, my lovely. The girl who's on duty at the moment has agreed to work some overtime.'

Josephine was confused. 'Joyce? Why should she do that?'

'She's susceptible to either my smile or my money' said Holden. 'Or both, maybe? Who knows?' He opened the door. 'I've hired a car for a few days, and I'll be ready at eight o'clock sharp. White would go well with your dark hair, I fancy.'

Josephine opened her mouth to protest vehemently at Holden's cavalier attitude but was too late.

Holden held his brandy glass up to the candle for a critical examination before tasting appreciatively. 'Brandy has suddenly become unaccountably scarce in London,' he commented.

'That's why you came to South Africa?' Josephine suggested.

'Can you think of a better reason?'

'What business are you in, Mr Holden?'

'Ralph,' Holden corrected. 'You have my permission to use my first name. Permission to use my second name is denied to everyone – even my mother. Have I told you about my mother? A remarkable woman.'

Josephine gave an acid smile. 'I suppose she taught you the art of dodging direct questions? Oh, please don't look surprised, Mr Holden – every time I've asked you a question about yourself, all I've received in reply is a compliment. You liked my dress during the soup; my hair during the fish; and my perfume during the main dish. It's fortunate that this isn't one of those twenty-course meals otherwise I might end up thinking I'm Jean Harlow.'

The eight-piece band finished their tuning up and proceeded to torment a Glen Miller slow number with an aplomb that tempted few couples to move on to the dance floor; the majority to remain seated.

'We shall dance,' Holden commanded, rising to his feet.

'Saved by the orchestra,' Josephine commented, also rising. 'And how could any girl refuse such a polite request?'

'My leg doesn't take kindly to being pulled,' Holden warned as he steered Josephine round the dance floor.

'And my foot doesn't take kindly to being trodden on.'

'Blame the band,' said Holden with cheerful arrogance.

The band standardized their music and improved rapidly. More couples crowded on to the tiny dance floor. To Josephine's relief Holden didn't take advantage of the waltz to press himself against her. Emboldened by their success, the band tackled a foxtrot. Josephine realized that Holden was an accomplished dancer, and, to her surprise, she made the unexpected discovery that she was actually enjoying herself.

'Why the smile?' Holden inquired.

'A friend of mine once said that there is no such thing as an Englishman who can dance.'

'Why did you leave home?' Holden asked abruptly.

It was a question that Josephine would have normally taken offence at, but the meal, the luxurious surroundings and the Englishman's not wholly unpleasant company had mellowed her defences. 'I wanted to see the world,' she replied. 'Does that sound corny?'

'Not unless you think it does. Did your parents mind?'

Josephine laughed. 'It was the second war of independence.'

'Which you won?'

'By default, I guess – I walked out.'

'Never to return?' Holden queried as he skilfully guided Josephine round a swaying couple who appeared more than a little drunk.

'That's what I said at the time,' said Josephine, avoiding the Englishman's eyes by gazing over his shoulder.

The band came to the end of their number. There was some desultory clapping. Holden led Josephine back to her table and poured her the last of the wine.

'Where was home?' Holden asked a minute later as they watched the couples.

'New York. Greenwich Village. My folks have a hardware store there.' Josephine regarded the Englishman thoughtfully. 'Why are you so interested in me, Mr Holden?'

Holden gave an easy laugh. 'You don't often find unattached American girls so far from home. How did you manage it?'

'By working, Mr Holden. By working hard. I joined a steamship company in New York, which was why I had the bust-up with my father – he didn't like his daughter working as a stewardess. That's what he said at the time.'

Holden was watching her carefully and noticed the sadness in her eyes at the mention of her father.

Josephine shrugged. 'I guess the truth was that he didn't like the idea of losing someone who was working for next to nothing in his run-down store.' She focussed her eyes on the glass of wine she was holding and wondered why she was telling everything to this stranger. It wasn't the wine. Wine was something she had learned to cope with, and she hadn't even approached the four-glass ceiling that she had decided on at the beginning of the evening.

'I was pretty good at running the hardware store, Mr Holden.'

'I'm sure you were, Josephine,' Holden murmured, sensing that the time was approaching when he would be able to manipulate the conversation round to the reason why he had taken Josephine out for the evening.

'While I did the buying, the store showed a profit. Not that that did much good because that meant more money for Pa to spend on liquor. I was worth more than Pa was prepared to pay me, so come 1936 when I turned twenty-one I took myself off to The General Navigation Steamship Company and got myself a job at four times what Pa was paying me. A year later I found myself in Durban and fell for the crazy Englishness of the place.'

'Even the docks?' said Holden casually.

Josephine stared at him. 'Hell, no. I never go near them unless I can help it.'

'A rough place for a woman,' Holden observed, his eyes fixed on Josephine.

'I can look after myself. What I can't stand is the stink of sugar. I was there today. It's getting worse.'

Holden was surprised by the unexpected admission. 'You went to the docks today?'

It was Josephine's turn to look surprised. 'Sure. I want to go home. I don't see what business it is of yours, Mr Holden, but I've fixed myself up with a working passage back to New York.' She broke off and frowned at the Englishman. 'So what's so funny?'

Holden poured himself some more brandy. 'Forgive me, Josephine. I was smiling with relief. I too went to the docks today on business. In fact your ricksha followed me.'

'You thought *I* was following you?'

'At the time – yes.'

'Why should I do that, Mr Holden?'

Holden smiled disarmingly. 'My apologies, Jo – I jumped to the wrong conclusion.'

'My name is Josephine or Miss Britten. You haven't answered my question.'

Holden smiled disarmingly. 'My apologies, Jo – I jumped

candour. 'To be honest, I thought you might be spying on me for my company's business rivals. So I thought I'd invite you out tonight in the hope that half a bottle of wine would make you confess. Instead I discover that you're looking for a passage.' He smiled ruefully. 'This evening's going to cost me a fortune. Serve me right.'

Josephine stared levelly at the impudent Englishman for some seconds before she allowed her icy expression to relax into a faint smile. 'I've enjoyed this evening, Mr Holden. It's the first time for a long time that I've been out with a man and not had to spend the entire evening fighting him off. . . .'

'There's still time,' said Holden mischievously.

'. . . but there's something you ought to know,' Josephine continued, ignoring the interruption. 'One thing I've learnt since leaving home is not to expect favours, return them, or grant them.'

'Quite so, Jo,' Holden agreed.

'Just so long as we understand each other.'

Holden raised his glass. 'Let's drink to our understanding, Jo.'

13

'Telegram for you, sir,' said the pageboy, dropping the morning papers on the end of Holden's bed and holding out the buff envelope to the Englishman.

Holden pushed himself up on to his elbows and added a sixpence tip to his thanks. A sharp pain behind his eyes was a reminder that South African wine and brandy made unhappy companions.

'Breakfast in thirty minutes,' said the pageboy cheerfully before he left the bedroom.

Holden opened the telegram and spread it out on the coverlet. He removed a slim, black codebook from the briefcase that he kept under his pillow and proceeded to transcribe the meaningless jumble of code groups into plain text.

PURCHASING COMMISSION IN NEW YORK REPORT THAT TULSAR NOW ACQUIRED STOP HAVE CONFIRMED THAT OWNERSHIP SECURED THROUGH USA HOLDING COMPANY THEREFORE TULSAR CAN REMAIN US REGISTERED SHIP AS INSTRUCTED STOP VILLIERS AWAITING YOUR INSTRUCTIONS REGARDING SHIPMENT STOP CONTACT YOU REQUESTED IS INSPECTOR HUGO MARGENT STOP PRIVATE ADDRESS GOLF LINKS HOUSE MITCHELL ROAD DURBAN STOP GOOD LUCK SEE YOU SOON LONDON STOP LACY

Holden leaned back on the pillows. He was pleased with the information; Lacy was a colleague of his in London – an efficient but unimaginative civil servant who had dealt with everything and hadn't questioned why Holden should want the name of the officer in the Natal police who was responsible for tracking down members of the fanatical Ossewa-Brandwag. Even more important to Holden was that he now had absolute control of the *Tulsar*.

He composed a reply to London on the back of the telegram and encoded it.

THANKS FOR GOOD NEWS RE TULSAR STOP URGENT YOU GET USA HOLDING COMPANY TO TELEGRAPH THEIR AGENT HERE ADVISING HIM THAT I AM NOW ACTING FOR NEW OWNERS STOP AGENT IS SIMON GOODING STOP TELEGRAPHIC ADDRESS GOODSHIP DURBAN STOP HOLDEN

It would take at least six hours for Gooding to receive the message from New York, Holden reasoned, therefore there was little point in seeing him until the following morning.

The midday temperature edged over the hundred mark and brought games of beach cricket to a standstill. There was little movement among the holidaymakers on the crowded beach and the only sounds were the thin cries of the sea's hemline of children trying to encourage drowsy parents into the tepid water.

Holden opened all four doors of his hired car to allow the

interior to cool and spread a street map of Durban out on the burning roof.

'Mr Holden.'

It was Josephine. She came down the hotel's front steps and approached the car. Holden folded the map and dropped it on the car's front seat.

'Good afternoon, Jo. I'd be encouraged if you told me that this is as hot as it ever gets here.'

Josephine glanced up at the clear January sky. 'It's the God-damn humidity. New York can get like this. You should've got the houseboys to put a mat over the car.'

'I'll remember in future,' Holden promised. He looked expectantly at the American girl, waiting for her to speak.

'I enjoyed last night,' said Josephine awkwardly.

'Same here.'

'I vaguely remember talking about my plans to return home.'

Holden felt in his pocket for his car keys. 'That's right, Jo. To patch things up with your parents.'

'I don't normally talk about my plans with anyone, Mr Holden. Perhaps it was the wine. I don't know. The trouble is that the ship I'm returning home on isn't sailing for two or three weeks. Perhaps even a month. In the meantime I still need my job here, so I'd appreciate it if you told no one what I told you.'

Holden slammed the car's passenger doors and sat behind the wheel. He ran his fingers through his fair hair and smiled up at Josephine. 'I usually stick to orange juice so the chances are that I might forget whatever it was you said. You're free tomorrow evening, so let's go for a swim and talk it over then. Okay?'

Holden started the engine and drove out of the hotel forecourt leaving Josephine smouldering with suppressed anger.

'I've heard of you, Mr Holden,' said Margent, folding the letter and returning it to his visitor. He was too much the experienced policeman to have missed Holden's slight start of surprise. He smiled and rested his chin on a set of knuckles that a prizefighter would have been proud of. 'Please don't worry. I know nothing of your business in South Africa – only that you've been given clearance to send and receive coded telegrams.'

Holden relaxed and sipped his orange juice. It was late afternoon but the midday heat still hovered persistently among the lengthening shadows of the acacia trees in Margent's garden. He set his glass down on the stinkwood table and came straight to the point:

'I want to know about the Ossewa-Brandwag.'

Margent absently drummed his powerful fingers while he considered his answer. 'Translated literally it means the "Ox Wagon Torch Watch" – a term which has little meaning to outsiders unless they understand the almost sacred esteem in which the ox wagon is held in Afrikaner folklore. To the *Voortrekker* families pushing up country into the unknown interior, the ox wagon was their home, their transport, their place of worship, and at night – when they inspanned their oxen and formed a laager – the ox wagon became their castle.' Margent paused to fill a briar pipe. 'Origins of the term Ossewa-Brandwag vary but the one I like was told to me by an old Boer when I was a lad. At night in the laager one small lamp would be kept burning by the night watch so that in the event of an attack the women would be able to light torches quickly and so provide light for them to see as they reloaded their menfolk's rifles.' Margent struck a match and lit his pipe. 'It's the story I prefer because it fits the concept of the Ossewa-Brandwag story today – a torch kept burning by the night watch in readiness.'

'They're Nazis?' Holden queried.

'That's the label we give them for propaganda purposes. In reality, they're a group of extremist Afrikaners who aren't necessarily pro-Hitler but totally opposed to South Africa being a British ally. To them it's a betrayal of everything that they and their parents fought for and died for during the Anglo-Boer War.' Margent examined the bowl of his pipe. 'I've arrested about twenty Ossewa-Brandwag kommandos so far – fellow countrymen whose parents, wives, children died in British concentration camps. Did you know that the British invented concentration camps and that sixty thousand men, women and children died in them?'

Holden countered the question with one of his own. 'How strong is the Ossewa-Brandwag now?'

Margent smiled. 'We've got about fifty in Internment Camp One at Koffiefontein.'

'In England they'd be hanged,' said Holden sourly.

Margent shook his head. 'Smuts has insisted on internment. He'll have to govern when the war is over and sees no point in providing the Nationalists with a load of ready-made martyrs. Anyway, the few we have interned so far seems to have deprived them of effective leadership – they were the really fanatical members of the *Broederbond*. Some of them were undoubtedly Nazis.'

'Are there any big fish that you've not caught?'

'Not on my manor, there's not. They're mostly in the Cape Province. The Cape police operate differently – they prefer to keep the bastards under observation. They won't know what hit them if they start their blowing up power line stunts in Natal.'

'Who are they, inspector?'

'There must be hundreds of them.'

'The big ones – the organisers.'

Margent looked curiously at his visitor. 'Why is it so important, Mr Holden?'

Holden gave a slow smile. 'I'll be signing on a crew within the next few days to take a ship to England. And it's vital – absolutely vital – that we don't find ourselves turning an Ossewa-Brandwag fish over to the fifth columnists in England.'

Margent sucked on his pipe for a moment. 'There are two that I know of. One is a Port Elizabeth lawyer named John Voster. Son of a Karoo sheepfarmer in the north-eastern Cape. He went to Stellenbosch University, which is an absolute hotbed of Nationalism. He was the registrar to the Judge President of the Cape and before that chairman of the student branch of the Stellenbosch Nationalist Party. Right now he's a "general" in the Ossewa but I'd say his ambitions are more political than military. If the Nationalists should ever grab power in South Africa, then Balthazar Johannes Voster is the sort of man to climb to the top of the antheap. It's certain that the internment order against him will be signed before 1941 is out.'

'And the other one?' Holden prompted.

'Paulus Jan Kramer. A killer, and the most dangerous man not behind wire in South Africa today. He's German by birth.

His parents were Prussians who settled in what was German South-West Africa before the League of Nations mandate took the colony away from Germany. In 1933, fired by the appointment of his hero Hitler as chancellor, he tried to organize a number of settlers into an armed uprising. He received a ten-year jail sentence at Windhoek but served less than two years and scooted off to Germany for a year once he was freed. We don't know what he did there but as soon as he turned up in Cape Town he started printing an anti-semitic newspaper that folded after its first edition. In 1938 he was accused of murdering a Jewish girl at Bantry Bay just outside Cape Town but the case was never proved. Now he owns a restaurant in Cape Town and has the outward appearance of being a respectable businessman. My guess is that he spent his year in Germany learning how to handle explosives, how to use a knife, a radio-transmitter, and so on.'

'Can you let me have the addresses of these two?'

'John Voster is in the Port Elizabeth phone-book, and Paulus Kramer is in the Cape Town book. You pay your money and you take your choice.'

Holden left Inspector Margent an hour later. He sat back in the car and considered the two names the policeman had given him. There was no hard evidence to suggest that the politically ambitious John Voster was a Nazi, but there was no doubt that Paulus Jan Kramer most certainly was.

His choice was Kramer.

14

Robert Gerrard leaned on the bridge rail and moodily watched the first sperm whales of the season being hauled up the whale slipway on the far side of Durban's harbour.

'I'll tell you something, Mr Gooding,' he said to the perspiring agent. 'As I see it, new owners means that they'll want this ship at sea working. And if they want it working – they'll have to pay to have her repaired. And if they can't afford to have it repaired then why the hell did they buy it in the first place?'

Gooding wiped his forehead. It was nine o'clock and already the cool of the morning was in retreat. He unfolded the telegram that had arrived from New York an hour earlier and read it through for the tenth time. 'I don't understand it,' he muttered. 'I just don't understand it.'

Gerrard took the telegram from him. 'So who's this guy Holden?'

'How the hell should I know, for God's sake?'

'Captain!' a voice bellowed from the flensing deck. It was Piet; he was gesturing to the gangplank. 'Guy here to see you, captain! The one who was nosing around yesterday!'

Gerrard told the Afrikaner to show the visitor up.

'Well now,' breathed Gerrard, watching Holden wearing a crisp white suit and holding a briefcase pick his way carefully along the lemming deck in Piet's footsteps. 'What in the world is that?'

'I have a suspicion that *that* is our Mr Holden,' said Gooding.

Holden dismissed Piet with a wave and raced nimbly up the companion-way two steps at a time.

Gerrard guessed that he was English before he spoke.

'Good morning, gentlemen,' said Holden, giving Gooding and Gerrard a perfunctory handshake. 'My name is Ralph Holden. I represent the new owners of this ship. I would be grateful if you would kindly show me to your day-cabin, captain, and order me some chilled orange juice. I have a great deal of talking to do.'

'First things first,' said Holden, spreading papers from his briefcase on Gerrard's desk. 'How much will the repairs to the *Tulsar*'s bow cost?'

'About one thousand five hundred pounds,' Gooding replied.

'And what about the total to get her ready for sea loaded with provisions and fuel?'

'Repairs, victualling and bunkering bring it to around two thousand five hundred pounds.' Gooding reached into a pocket. 'I've got the figures here.'

'I'll take your word for it, Mr Gooding. How soon can the *Tulsar* be made ready if work starts now?'

Holden's unblinking blue eyes made Gooding feel nervous. 'Five weeks.'

Holden opened a cheque-book, wrote briefly, tore out the cheque and handed it to Gooding. 'Five thousand pounds which you can draw from the Standard Bank here in Durban,' said Holden crisply. 'That ought to cover bonus payments to the shipwrights to have the *Tulsar* ready in three weeks. I've already squared the priorities committee.'

Gooding goggled at the cheque. 'Three weeks?' he said faintly. 'I don't think that's possible.'

'You may use the money to make any necessary incentive payments as you see fit. I shall expect a detailed account when the *Tulsar* is ready to sail and will make out a separate cheque for your commission. Right now I'd like a receipt, please.'

Gooding realized that he was dismissed. He pushed the cheque into his pocket and left the cabin mopping his forehead and muttering that he would be gone ten minutes.

Gerrard lifted his feet on to his desk, hooked his hands together behind his neck and regarded Holden almost sleepily. 'Now you're not going to tell me that you're interested in the *Tulsar* catching whales, are you, Mr Holden?'

'What's the *Tulsar*'s cruising range, captain?'

Without moving or taking his eyes off the Englishman, Gerrard replied: 'Eleven thousand miles at ten knots; eight thousand at twelve knots; five thousand at fifteen knots.'

'How about at twenty-six knots? The *Tulsar*'s maximum speed?'

'It would be a pretty crazy thing to do unless we'd caught a lotta whale early in the season and wanted to be first in to get the highest prices.'

'But how far?' Holden pressed.

'Maybe two thousand miles if the turbines didn't blow up first.'

'Supposing you used your whale oil tanks for fuel oil?'

'Now I know you're not interested in whales.'

'Captain,' Holden's tone was icy. 'I'd appreciate it if you would answer my question.'

Gerrard was unmoved. 'And I'd appreciate it if you told me what all this is about. Why have you bought the *Tulsar*? She ain't much good for anything except catching and processing whales.'

Holden drummed his fingers on Gerrard's desk before replying. 'I have permission to tell you because of the U-boat you sank and because it is considered essential that you should know. The consequence of knowing is that your life is in constant danger should you show the slightest inclination to divulge the information.'

Gerrard's lazy eyes opened a little. 'Danger from whom?'

'From me.'

'That's interesting.' Gerrard observed. 'Back home I have a reputation for being what is known as a tough cookie.'

'I haven't killed enough people to have acquired a reputation,' said Holden mildly. 'But I'm willing to make a start.'

Gerrard suddenly sensed that there was more to the smartly-dressed Englishman than he had at first supposed. He met Holden's unwavering gaze and shrugged. 'Okay. I guess you'd best tell me.'

'The *Tulsar* is required to ship a large quantity of gold bullion to England as quickly and as discreetly as possible. Speed is of paramount importance, not only to avoid interception by surface raiders and U-boats, but because the gold is needed to maintain the flow of arms and food from the United States to Great Britain. Without it we're finished.'

Gerrard lifted his feet off his desk and lowered them to the floor. 'We?'

'The Allies. I represent the British government. The bullion held in Pretoria is worth us $240 million and it's the last of our gold reserves. Our holdings in London and Ottawa are now completely exhausted.' Holden watched the American dispassionately and noted that he appeared shaken.

'Jesus Christ,' Gerrard breathed after a pause. 'Two hundred and forty million bucks.' He whistled. 'Just how much gold is that?'

Holden smiled thinly. 'The gold refinery at Johannesburg mint it into 995-fine bars weighing twenty-five pounds each. We have to ship eighteen thousand bars. That amounts to a little over two hundred tons.'

Gerrard shook his head disbelievingly. 'Jesus Christ,' he repeated. 'Jesus bloody Christ. Two hundred tons of gold . . .' His voice trailed into silence.

'Normally the bars are packed two to a box,' Holden continued. 'But because your cargo manifest will say that you are carrying lead, we will be using wooden crates normally used for pigs of lead. Each crate can hold ten gold bars making a total of eighteen hundred crates. Do you have plans of the *Tulsar*?'

Gerrard opened a drawer and pushed three sheets of paper across to Holden. 'Some rough sketches I did before our last refit. You can keep them.'

Holden studied the dimension drawing of the *Tulsar*'s below-deck layout. 'Each crate measures a foot high by a foot wide by five feet long – there's plenty of room. We can get the repair gang to insert two bulkheads here and here to create a hold.'

'There's something you've overlooked,' said Gerrard drily.

Holden raised his eyebrows. 'And what might that be?'

'We sold passages home to raise money.'

'Why should you think that that is something I've overlooked?'

Gerrard decided that he didn't like the self-assured Englishman. 'Because, if we're no longer sailing for the States –'

'How many passages have you sold?' Holden interrupted.

'Eighteen.'

'And they're all Americans?'

'Except for a Canadian couple.'

Holden gave a thin smile. 'Excellent. All of them will provide first-class, ready-made cover.'

'The trouble as I see it,' said Gerrard deliberately, 'is that they've purchased tickets to go to New York on the not unreasonable assumption that this ship is going to New York.'

'I'll have to announce a change of destination in mid-Atlantic,' was Holden's smooth reply. 'And I'll also arrange their passage from the UK to America on a neutral ship. Any more problems, captain?'

Gerrard shook his head reluctantly. 'I guess you've covered just about everything, but it's the craziest scheme I've ever heard of.'

Holden's answering smile was bleak. 'Of course it's crazy. Who in their right mind would think the British stupid enough to ship the last of their precious gold a quarter of the way round the world on a whaling factory-ship under a foreign flag?'

'No one,' Gerrard agreed. 'I guess you'll be coming along on this crazy trip?'

Holden nodded. 'I'm sure you can find an extra cabin, captain.'

'Sure,' said Gerrard dismissively. 'But there's one thing we must get straight first if you're coming along. You may own the *Tulsar*, Mr Holden, but *I'm* her captain and *I* give the orders. Okay?'

Holden shrugged. 'I don't see any problems there provided you follow my orders, captain. I know nothing about the day-to-day running of a ship.'

Gerrard didn't like the Englishman's answer. 'The smooth day-to-day running of the ship may mean that I'll be giving *you* orders, Mr Holden. I just want to satisfy myself that you'll obey them.'

Holden returned Gerrard's dispassionate smile. 'Let's deal with that problem when it arises, Mr Gerrard,' he suggested amiably.

15

As the Lockheed Electra airliner passed over Durban Harbour, Holden could see that repair work was well under way on the *Tulsar*'s bows; the floating crane was alongside the whaler and two repair barges were in position. To his right the brutal escarpments of the Drakensburg Mountains rose sheer and forbidding out of the red soil of Africa.

The note of the two engines changed as the airliner levelled out at the top of its climb. Holden ordered an orange juice from the steward and glanced at his watch. It was 8.05 am. The Electra was capable of covering the thousand-mile flight to Cape Town in just under five hours and was scheduled to return to Durban the following day. Holden hoped that there would be no hitches to delay the aircraft's return because he had told no one of this trip and his absence from Durban for much more than twenty-four hours would hardly pass unnoticed. He had even purchased the ticket out of his own money and taken a seat at the front of the aircraft to avoid being seen by the constant procession of passengers visiting the aft toilet.

The Ford taxi bumped along Tafelberg Road high above Cape Town and deposited Holden outside the lower station of the Table Mountain cableway. The vast north-facing edifice of Table Mountain acted as a giant sun-trap, warming the air to an intolerable level so that after five minutes waiting for the cable-car Holden was sweating profusely,

The cable-car glided smoothly into its concrete niche. The attendant opened the door and held the gently bobbing car steady for the five passengers to disembark. A minute later, with only the attendant for company, Holden was aboard the car as it began its awesome one-mile climb up the precipitous sandstone slopes of Table Mountain.

'Bloody cold up there,' said the attendant, nodding to the thick layer of white cloud that covered the summit. 'Always happens when the sou'easter gets up. You won't be able to see anything.'

'I could hardly visit Cape Town without visiting Table Mountain,' said Holden.

The wind strengthened as the car maintained its steady climb like a money spider hauling itself up a cobweb. Holden instinctively braced himself as they neared the mighty avalanche of cloud spilling over the edge of the mountain. And then the car was into the 'tablecloth' and the temperature plummeted.

'Told you,' said the attendant as Holden turned up his collar.

Holden made no reply but stared upwards at the tower-like upper cable station that was looming out of the fog. It seemed that the car was stationary – that the broad lip of the mountain was sinking down to meet them. There was an almost imperceptible bump as the car came to a standstill.

'Don't go too far from the station,' warned the attendant, holding the car firmly against the platform for Holden. 'Come back if you hear the hooter. Stay on the paths otherwise you'll surprise yourself with how easy it is to fall off the edge.'

There was nothing to see on the mountain but the squares of

yellow light that marked the windows of the small tea-room. Holden's footsteps sounded curiously dead as he moved along a narrow track that threaded its way through beds of wild belladonna lilies and crassulas. The path was so narrow in places that clumps of wet grass brushed against his trousers. He stopped and listened. There was no sound – not even the birdsong for which Table Mountain was famous – just a dead silence. Holden began to appreciate the cunning of the man who had selected this place for the rendezvous, for he had all the advantages – especially if he was familiar with the plateau's rocky terrain. He was probably watching him now – satisfying himself that Holden was alone.

A rock hydrax suddenly broke cover near Holden's feet and gave an angry cry as it scampered into the fog. There was a sound some yards behind Holden. He quickly followed the small rodent and crouched behind a rock, peering back along the path. A figure of a man materialized out of the mist and walked past the rock where Holden was hiding. The man muttered a curse under his breath and quickened his step when he realized that his quarry had disappeared. That was enough for Holden: keeping his feet on the muffling clumps of grass, he darted behind the man and sent him sprawling on his stomach. The man tried to roll on to his back but Holden seized both his arms and doubled them up into the small of his back. It was a painful hold but the man made no sound.

'Mr Kramer, I presume?' said Holden pleasantly.

The man's face was pressed into the grass. He twisted his head sideways, swore in Afrikaans, and tried to throw his adversary off his back by bucking his powerful body. There was a sudden vice-like grip either side of his neck that sent a lance of pain stabbing into his head. He groaned.

'Please keep very still, Mr Kramer, and I won't hurt you.'

Kramer stopped struggling and the terrible pain mercifully eased. He felt the unseen fingers moving under his coat.

'I'm not armed.'

'Just making sure.' Holden stood. 'Okay – get up.'

Kramer climbed to his feet and sullenly regarded his smiling attacker while rubbing his neck.

'There won't be bruises,' said Holden. 'I didn't use enough

pressure. Even so, you were as near to death just then as you are ever likely to be.'

'You're Holden?'

'How do you do, Mr Kramer? You're a disappointment to me. I imagined that the commander of the Ossewa Cape cell would be much too astute to allow himself to be ambushed so easily.'

'Who gave you my name and phone number?'

'Our mutual friends in Berlin,' said Holden. 'A long time ago. I've lost touch now which is why I've contacted you. I understand that you have a wireless transmitter. Now that would be useful because the authorities in Cairo are making difficulties for anyone who wishes to send cables to Germany.'

'I don't know what you're talking about,' Kramer growled.

'I have some useful information concerning the shipment to England of the last of the Allied gold from South Africa,' said Holden. 'Information that I'm prepared to part with in exchange for two million Swiss francs paid into my account at the Bank of Montreux. Tell Berlin that the deal would be most profitable because the gold amounts to something like two hundred tons' worth or sixty million pounds, and its capture should not pose too many problems for the Kriegsmarine.'

Kramer pushed his hands into his pockets. 'I know nothing about you. I don't know who you are and I don't know if you can be trusted.'

'Of course you don't,' Holden agreed. 'But you must admit that we have enough information on each other to get ourselves hanged should one of us go to the police.'

Kramer noticed the quality of Holden's clothes. 'You're English?'

'With a higher esteem for money than my country.'

'Who do you work for, Mr Holden?'

'The Treasury.'

'Your address?'

Holden gave him his Kensington address.

'Tell me about this ship,' said Kramer.

'Not until I hear from my bank that half the money has been credited to my account.'

'Where are you staying?'

'The Benjamin D'Urban Hotel, Durban.'

Kramer asked disinterestedly: 'This ship . . . it sails from Durban?'

'Full information when I've had half the money.'

Kramer considered. 'It is not for me to make decisions, you understand. I pass the information. Nothing else.'

Holden said that he understood. Kramer pointed into the fog. 'The cable-car station is that way, Mr Holden.'

Five minutes later, when he had made certain that the Englishman had gone, Kramer picked his way across the fog-shrouded plateau to the massive overhanging rock of the Silverstream Buttress near Platteklip Gorge where a party of Portuguese navigators had first climbed Table Mountain in 1503. He went down on his knees and cleared away some heather from immediately under the overhang, exposing a large, flat rock about two feet across. He strained briefly to push the rock to one side and lifted a small suitcase out of the hollow which he placed carefully beside him before releasing the two catches and opening the lid to reveal the neatly stowed headphones and the coil of antenna wire. The suitcase was a Telefunken Mark III 'Afu' *Agentenfunk* – or agent's transmitter-receiver.

He flipped the toggle switch to the 'T' position, pulled on the headphones and uncoiled the antenna wire. Being over three thousand feet above sea-level and with no obstructions, it was sufficient merely to toss the antenna wire over the edge of the gorge so that it hung straight down. Table Mountain made an excellent site for a low-power ten-watt radio such as the Afu. The faint hum in the headphones told Kramer that the set had warmed up. He watched the meter in the centre of the set and operated the Morse key in a random manner. The needle dipped which meant that the set was working satisfactorily despite the damp conditions it was stored under. The main advantage of the set was that its frequency was kept in tune by a quartz crystal and consequently required little skill other than a knowledge of Morse code to operate it.

Kramer's Morse had been hurriedly acquired during a crash course on his last visit to Berlin. It was poor, but that was an advantage for it enabled radio-operators on U-boats to identify his 'fist' quickly. He calmly transmitted a stream of Vs and waited for the U-boat's acknowledgement. The answering bleeps were sharp and clear, indicating that the U-boat had tuned in to him. He carefully keyed out:

ARE YOU READY FOR MY MESSAGE

Back came:

STANDING BY

Kramer's shaggy eyebrows knitted in concentration as he began keying his message for it would be necessary for him to make a deliberate error in the eleventh and twenty-second position of the text as a security check before the U-boat would accept the signal as genuine. An error in the thirty-second position would tell the U-boat that he had been caught and 'turned' and was being made to send false information.

Slowly, with painstaking care, he laboriously broadcast a full account of his meeting with Holden, remembering to make the deliberate keying errors in the right places.

16

'What puzzles me,' said Strick, 'is how he managed to open a bank account in Switzerland.'

'Difficult, but not impossible,' said Admiral Canaris. 'He works in the Treasury. The chances are that he has access to the London–Geneva radio-telephone link and has used it for his own purposes.'

Strick considered it likely that the British would keep a tight control on such a link but didn't contradict Admiral Canaris. As head of the Abwehr – OKW's vast intelligence and counter espionage organization with ten times the budget and resources of Strick's own IMI – the prematurely white-haired admiral with his preference for scruffy civilian dress and his air of good-humoured indecisiveness, although not highly thought of in party circles, had nevertheless won for himself considerable power and influence by his uncanny ability to be in the right place at the right time.

'What have you been able to find out about him, admiral?' Strick politely inquired.

Canaris rifled vaguely through some papers in his filing basket and pulled out a document. 'Nothing much. There are several R. Holdens listed in the 1938 Treasury directory ranging from a clerical assistant to a principal officer.'

This was nothing new to Strick who had a copy of the same publication in his library. 'Have you found out anything by more direct investigatory methods, admiral?' Strick tried to sound tactful.

'Our South African contact arranged to have his hotel room in Durban checked. They didn't find much. A few unpaid bills that amounted to about two hundred pounds.'

The vagueness irritated Strick. 'I suppose the significance of that sum depends on whether he's a clerical assistant or a principal officer,' he commented sourly.

Canaris smiled. 'Either way, I think debts of two hundred pounds are significant. The British don't overpay their civil servants. Whatever his rank, such a sum would not be easy to pay off, and it does indicate that our Mr Holden is acquiring a taste for living beyond his means.'

'Perhaps,' said Strick unconvincingly. 'But do you really think we know enough about him to risk handing over a million Swiss francs? For all we know the whole thing could be a clever fabrication by your South African contact.'

Canaris shook his head emphatically. 'No. I know him. He's our most reliable man in South Africa. I'll see Funk in the morning and recommend that the first payment is made.' He chuckled and regarded his austere visitor with twinkling eyes. 'Cheer up, doctor. We'll be getting two hundred tons of gold at a bargain price.'

17

One of Simon Gooding's basic philosophies was that energy was something to be expended as sparingly as possible, especially during the humid months of Natal's summer. The daily presence of Ralph Holden in his outer office therefore made him feel decidedly uncomfortable. Every problem that arose in making the *Tulsar* ready for sea was dealt with by the young Englishman with a speed and efficiency that made the rotund shipping agent nervous and aware of his middle age. Whether it was a shortage of steel plate one day for the repairs to the hull, or difficulty in obtaining welding materials the next, all the problems were briskly steamrollered by a combination of Holden's short telephone-calls and long cheques. Another of Holden's characteristics that Gooding envied was his ability to maintain his almost icy detachment when things were not going his way.

Gooding was gazing out of his office window watching the dockside traffic while eating a sandwich when he noticed a neat, tropical-suited figure making his way quickly through the fish market. It was Holden. Gooding had never seen the fair-haired young man hurrying before. The shipping agent returned to his desk and was pretending to be industrious when Holden burst in. He looked up – hoping that his benign, welcoming smile cloaked his alarm.

'Good afternoon, Mr Holden. How's everything going?'

'I spotted an American girl on the *Tulsar*,' said Holden curtly. 'A Miss Josephine Britten. She works as a receptionist in my hotel and I'd like to know what she's doing on the *Tulsar*.'

Gooding mopped the back of his neck. 'She's our purser, Mr Holden.'

'Since when?'

'Since I gave her the job,' Gooding replied irritably.

Holden recalled that Josephine had told him that she had obtained a working passage back to New York although she had not told him which ship she was due to sail on.

'Her name wasn't on the passenger list you gave me,' said Holden.

'Because she's not a passenger. You told me to look after the crew, Mr Holden.'

'Why does she want to go home?'

'She's not the sort of girl one asks too many questions. Anyway, it's none of my business.' Gooding met Holden's blue eyes. 'Besides, she's been damned useful. She's fixed up the cabins – supervised the repainting and even scrounged some carpeting from a hotel that's being demolished. And she's got the carpenters to fix up a bar in the restaurant. That girl knows what she's doing. She's worked every minute of her spare time.'

Holden said nothing. Gooding's statement explained why he had hardly seen Josephine during the previous three weeks. 'I need her home address,' Holden said after a moment's thought. 'All I know is that it's somewhere in Greenwich Village.'

Gooding nodded and fingered through a number of papers impaled on a spike. 'How's everything with the ship?' He removed a slip from the spike and handed it to Holden.

Holden glanced briefly at the paper and thrust it into an inside pocket. 'The hull's finished,' he said in reply to the shipping agent's question. 'Gerrard says that the riveting and welding is not the best he's seen but it will have to do. The floating crane will be lowering the *Tulsar*'s bow tomorrow.'

Gooding was surprised. 'So she'll be ready to sail by next week?'

Holden smiled coldly. 'There are a few alterations to be made. I'm having some of the forward oil separator tanks removed so that a hold can be created.'

'A hold?' Gooding echoed. 'What do you want a hold for, for God's sake?'

'We might as well earn some money on the New York trip,' said Holden. 'In addition to the passengers the *Tulsar* will be carrying a cargo of lead. The necessary papers will be with you by the end of next week.'

Gooding was about to point out that the cost of converting the *Tulsar* would hardly justify the return on the freight rate but decided that it would be wiser to remain silent.

18

The lobby of the Hotel Benjamin D'Urban was filling with the *Tulsar*'s passengers and their luggage when Holden entered after breakfast on 17 February. He watched with an amused smile while Josephine tried to placate an aggressive sugar magnate and his querulous wife.

'Mr Vanson,' Josephine was saying desperately, 'I'm very sorry but I can't give you a sailing date because I don't know it yet.'

'Know how long we've been stuck in this country?' Eli Vanson demanded. 'Over a year – that's how long. And now you say we're to be stuck in this crummy hotel.'

All the passengers had identified Josephine as having something to do with the mysterious shipping line that was supposed to be taking them home and were, with the exception of two smiling Ursuline nuns, all talking at the top of their voices. The most popular topic was the apparently far from ideal conditions aboard the train that had brought them from Cape Town.

Holden pushed his way through the crowd and leaned on Josephine's desk until she noticed him.

'I understand you're to be the purser on this ship, Jo. No wonder I've hardly seen you. I thought you were deliberately avoiding me.'

'I wouldn't dream of trying to avoid you, not unless you've caught something unpleasant that is. Is there something I can do for you?'

'You can fix me a comfortable cabin on the *Tulsar*, Jo.' Holden grinned at her look of surprise and added. 'You obviously haven't checked the passenger list that carefully, my love.'

'You're going to New York on the *Tulsar*?' said Josephine incredulously.

'That's right. I shall expect the best cabin you have.'

'Mr Holden,' said Josephine carefully. 'There are no classes on the *Tulsar*. All I can promise you is that your cabin will be adequate. I'm sorry but I can't make exceptions.'

'Not even for the owner?'

The mocking blue eyes annoyed Josephine. She looked suspiciously at Holden. 'I get the impression that you are trying to tell me something.'

'That's right, my angel – as the owner's representative I believe I'm entitled to a decent cabin. Check with Simon Gooding if you don't believe me.'

Josephine stared at Holden and nodded. 'I'll see what I can do, Mr Holden.' She turned to the honeycomb of pigeon-holes behind the desk and gave Holden a telegram. 'This arrived ten minutes ago for you, Mr Holden.'

Holden returned to his room and quickly decoded the London telegram.

JOSEPHINE BRITTEN SUBSTANCE OF YOUR 41 STROKE 3 CONFIRMED STOP NO CONNECTION WITH ISOLATIONIST OR PRO-NAZI MOVEMENTS IN USA THEREFORE NO OBJECTION TO ALLOWING HER AS PASSENGER STOP FATHER SUFFERING FROM KIDNEY DISEASE STOP HAS LESS THAN FOUR MONTHS

Holden watched the flames curl the telegram into black flakes. He stirred the remains to dust and emptied the contents of the ashtray into the waste bin. For some seconds he sat perfectly still, gazing out of the window at the rash of sunshades on the beach. When he had informed the Treasury that the *Tulsar* would be carrying passengers they had insisted on being supplied with their names and addresses to enable them to carry out security checks. Josephine's name and address had been the last. His immediate problem was Josephine's reason for wishing to return home which was obviously to see her father. He had no intention of getting involved in the personal problems of the *Tulsar*'s passengers but he liked the American girl well enough not to want her to embark on a voyage in the belief that she was going to New York when in fact the *Tulsar* was bound for England.

There was only one course of action.

Gooding had a certain strength of character that Holden hadn't bargained for. The shipping agent swept an armful of papers off his desk, crammed them into a box file and thrust it into Holden's hands.

'I can't stop you sacking Miss Britten,' said Gooding, glancing across his office at Gerrard in the hope of support. 'But I won't be party to it. I'll refund the commission you've paid me and you can find yourself another agent.'

The two men glared at each other across the desk. 'All I'm asking,' said Holden calmly, 'is for you to book the girl's passage home on another ship and I'll pay her fare.'

'There are no other ships,' said Gooding. 'That kid's worked damned hard getting everything fixed up – she's taken a big load off my shoulders and Captain Gerrard's, and I'm damned if I'm going to fire her without good cause.' Gooding pulled on a fedora and moved to the door. 'I have to go to the customs office about the cargo of lead. See if you can make him see sense, Captain Gerrard.'

'So what's the big trouble?' Gerrard asked Holden when Gooding had left.

'I had to clear all the passengers' names through London,' said Holden. 'They told me that Josephine Britten's father has less than four months to live. As I see it, that must be the reason why she wants to return home.'

Gerrard gave the Englishman a lazy grin. 'So you're going to tell her that the *Tulsar* isn't going to New York?'

'Don't be so damned stupid.'

'Seems that it's not me who's being stupid. I didn't figure you to be the sort of guy to lose his head over a girl.'

Holden ignored the American captain's familiarity. 'I just don't want to see her hurt if her father dies before she gets home.'

Gerrard shrugged. 'I don't want passengers on my back. I've only spoken to the kid a couple of times but I got the idea that she could handle them.' He grinned again. 'They're going to kick up a helluva stink when they find out they're not going to New York, so I say she stays.'

19

Holden drove eighty miles down the coast from Durban and arrived at the nondescript, depressing little town of Port Shepstone at 1 pm. He parked outside the Duke of Bedford Inn, a small single-storey hotel, and entered the restaurant where Kramer was waiting impatiently for him at a corner table.

'You're an hour late,' complained the Afrikaner. 'You had a three-hour drive and I had a three-day drive from Cape Town, and I managed to be on time.'

'How safe is this place?' Holden demanded curtly.

Kramer shrugged. 'As safe as anywhere.'

The two men ordered a light lunch and waited for the waiter to withdraw.

'Your bank will have received the money by now,' Kramer began.

'I heard from them this morning,' said Holden guardedly.

'I thought the Swiss banks were difficult about sending out information?' Kramer inquired casually, as though he wasn't particularly interested in Holden's answer.

Holden realized that for all his faults, the rugged Afrikaner was no fool. 'There are ways.'

Kramer sank his teeth into a stick of celery and chewed noisily. He was very interested in means of sending communications outside South Africa. 'What ways, my friend?'

The waiter brought their order and departed. 'I have some information for you,' said Holden coldly.

Kramer grunted. 'About time. So what about the ship? What's its name?'

'The *Tulsar*. She's an American-registered whaling factory-ship.'

Kramer lowered his knife and fork and gaped at Holden. 'The *Tulsar*? Christ, man, isn't she the Yankee that rammed and sank a U-boat just before Christmas?'

'So I believe,' said Holden noncommittally. 'Which ought to

make her that much more of an attractive target for your superiors.' Holden signalled the waiter and ordered a carafe of orange juice. 'She leaves Durban on 25 February – a week's time.'

Kramer nodded.

'There's one thing that I must insist on,' said Holden, watching the Afrikaner with hard, dangerous eyes. 'She's to be captured and not sunk. That must be clearly understood.'

Kramer grinned wolfishly. 'No one's planning to send sixty million pounds' worth of bullion to the bottom so what's the big problem?'

'*I* shall be on the *Tulsar*,' said Holden acidly. 'I shall expect to be taken off as a prisoner and sent to Switzerland.'

'You'll be interned.'

'I've made arrangements.'

'With the Swiss?' Kramer sounded disbelieving.

'It's none of your business, Kramer. Your job is to pass on the information I give you.'

The two men regarded each other with mutual distrust.

'There's the question of the passengers,' said Holden. 'They're all American citizens apart from two Canadians –'

'Passengers?' Kramer queried, his bushy eyebrows going up. 'What passengers, my friend?'

'They're the *Tulsar*'s cover. They think they're going to New York.'

Kramer bared his yellow teeth in a grin. 'Clever.'

'More by accident than design. They're to be repatriated as quickly as possible, you understand?'

Kramer nodded. 'Okay. How many of them?'

'Eighteen. Under no circumstances must they come to harm.'

'I can't see any problems, but of course the Canadians are British Allies. They'll have to be interned or imprisoned.'

'Which leaves one final question,' said Holden. 'The position of the capture. I suggest leaving it as late as possible – off the coast of France within range of air cover for the prize crew. If it's grabbed in the South Atlantic, the British will throw everything into getting it back or sinking it.' Holden hesitated before coming to the most crucial point of all – one that he had deliberately left until the end. 'You must tell your friends that the only chance they have of capturing the *Tulsar* is if they use one of their capital ships . . . such as the *Tirpitz*.'

Kramer's eyes narrowed. 'Why, my friend?'

'The *Tulsar*'s fast – damned fast. Twenty-six knots. They won't catch her with anything else.'

Kramer stared hard at the fair-haired Englishman for some seconds before nodding his agreement. 'I will pass the information today. They will require the name of the *Tulsar*'s captain.'

'Her original captain – Robert Gerrard – the man who sank the U-boat.'

'And you have the drawings of the *Tulsar*'s layout?'

'You won't need them,' Holden replied. 'I'll show the prize crew where the gold is stowed when they come aboard.'

'In case anything happens to you,' Kramer murmured.

An icy tone crept into Holden's voice. 'What could possibly happen to me, Mr Kramer?'

'We have to cover ourselves, my friend. Insurance.'

The two men were silent – each convinced that one was double-crossing the other. Holden shrugged, reached into his breast pocket, and handed Gerrard's plans of the *Tulsar* to the Afrikaner. Kramer glanced briefly at the freehand drawings before thrusting them out of sight. They were exactly what he wanted.

After the meal, the two men drank a discreet toast to the success of the venture: Kramer with a glass of beer and Holden with an orange juice.

20

Kramer's 'Cuckoo to Alice' radio signal was picked up by his colleague 'General' Rudolf Messener of Ossewa-Brandwag Kommando VI Gruppe, Windhoek, South-West Africa, at field strength three. Messener screened the signal for the deliberate keying errors to ensure that Kramer hadn't been 'turned' and rebroadcast the message on the 15,460 kilocycles wavelength using the powerful 500-watt RCA transmitter that Kramer had brought back from Berlin in 1937 in shipping crates labelled 'electrical spares'.

U-395 of the 2nd U-boat Flotilla was charging her batteries three hundred miles east of Montevideo on the far side of the Atlantic when her radio-operator intercepted Messener's signal. The keying error screen proved satisfactory so he re-encoded the message into Kriegsmarine 'Purple' on his Enigma cypher machine and relayed it on the 4,995 kilocycles wavelength – the standard frequency allocated to U-boats.

Quarter of the way round the world, at Treuenbrietzen, just south of Berlin, the antennae on the roof of a graceful, stucco country mansion that belonged to the OKW's Chieffrierabteilung listening-post, picked up *U-395*'s relay. The signal was quickly verified for authenticity in the listening-room and passed, still in its coded text form, to the dissemination-room where only the first four codegroups were decoded to establish the message's intended recipient. The suffix 'Alice' alerted the duty officer who immediately abandoned standard procedure and decoded the remainder of the signal himself without sending it to the appropriate room where it would have to await its turn.

Five minutes later, the red machine in the bank of Geheimschreiber teleprinters in Admiral Canaris' Berlin headquarters started clattering. It was the only machine that printed its text without a carbon copy.

The message's long and devious route did not substantially delay its journey; an hour after Kramer had stowed his Afu radio suitcase under the bed in his Port Shepstone hotel room, a pink flimsy was laid before Admiral Canaris in Berlin. Nor had the accuracy of the message suffered apart from the spelling of 'Durban' which had changed to 'Durbin'.

By 5.30 pm Canaris and Reichminister Walter Funk had completed their urgent briefing of Hitler that provided him with a detailed account of British plans. The real purpose of their visit was to persuade the Führer to agree to a capital ship such as the *Bismarck* or the *Scharnhorst* being sent into the Atlantic to intercept and capture the *Tulsar*. But Hitler would have none of it, for fear of another humiliating defeat similar to the loss of the pocket battleship *Graf Spee* in December 1939. His neurosis concerning Germany's capital ships had even led to the *Graf Spee*'s sister ship, *Deutschland*, being renamed because the Führer had ruled that no ship bearing such a name could be allowed to sink. *Deutschland*'s new name, *Lutzow*, had not brought the pocket battleship much luck – her stern had been blown off after Operation Weserübung in Norway.

'There are our surface raiders,' Hitler pointed out. 'We can send them into the Indian Ocean.'

'With respect, *mein Führer*,' said Canaris. 'Such a concentration will serve to alert the British and would be certain to lead to an alteration of their sailing plan for the gold. We think it best not to show our hand until the *Tulsar* is in mid-Atlantic with no friendly port to hand where she can off-load the gold. Also, even with a radio-observer on board, our surface raiders do not have the speed and radar to seek out a specific ship on the high seas – they are designed to engage and destroy enemy shipping that they come upon by chance.'

It was an argument that Hitler wasn't interested in. Once again he refused to allow the release of a capital ship, then launched into a long tirade about the uselessness of battleships and cruisers.

'Do you know how many extra U-boats we could have had if Raeder hadn't been allowed his Z-plan white elephants such as the *Tirpitz*?' he bellowed. Four hundred! And with four hundred extra U-boats at sea the war against Britain would be over now!'

Funk was tempted to point out that the war would be over within a few weeks if the *Tulsar*'s gold was prevented from reaching England, but decided that silence was more prudent when Hitler started raging about naval matters.

Hitler's voice rose to a shout as he harangued his visitors. Funk quailed before the onslaught while Canaris remained impassively silent.

'Those ships are more useful sitting at their anchorages where the British can't get at them than they would be at sea – their presence and the fear that they'll suddenly break out are tying down thousands of men and countless ships on convoy escorts that aren't preventing my U-boats from sinking merchantmen.

The U-boats are our only effective naval force – ask one of them to capture Churchill's gold.'

An hour later Canaris and Funk were sitting in Strick's office gloomily outlining the gist of the interview to Strick. The economist listened attentively and asked Funk to repeat Hitler's final words.

'He said to ask a U-boat to capture Churchill's gold,' said Funk.

'Which is exactly what we'll have to do,' said Strick. 'It was an order, was it not?'

'It didn't sound like an order,' said Canaris doubtfully.

'You can be certain that Hess can make it sound like one if he wishes,' observed Strick. 'I presume the meeting was minuted?'

Canaris nodded.

'In that case I suggest we get Hess to ratify Hitler's statement as an order; setting a U-boat on to the *Tulsar* is better than doing nothing. Maybe they'll be glad of the opportunity. After all, it was the *Tulsar* that sank that U-boat last December. What was the captain's name?'

'Robert Gerrard,' said Canaris. 'An American.'

'I wonder if we have information on him?' Strick mused. 'If the British are crazy enough to use a neutral ship commanded by a citizen of a neutral country, it would be silly if we did not exploit their stupidity by at least checking to find out if this Gerrard can be either bribed or blackmailed.' Strick picked up one of his telephones and asked a collator in the central document library to check the indexes to see if Gerrard's name appeared.

'It's a faint possibility,' said Strick, replacing the receiver and pressing his intercom button to order coffee.

A few minutes later a clerk entered his office and placed a folder on his desk. Strick opened it and quickly read through the brief report it contained while Funk and Canaris looked on.

'Well,' said Strick, pushing the document across his desk to Canaris. 'We can rule out blackmail: Gerrard's wife was drowned when the *Athenia* was torpedoed.'

Canaris read carefully through the brief report and frowned. He turned to the front page to see who had originated it. He stiffened. 'But this is amazing! Your information on Gerrard has come from a former colleague of his who is now a U-boat instructor.'

'What is so surprising about that?' inquired Strick. 'Whaling, like the Foreign Legion, has always attracted men from every nationality under the sun.'

Canaris nodded his white head. 'You miss my point entirely, doctor. It occurred to me that if we're to hunt for Churchill's gold with a U-boat, what better choice to lead the hunt than a man who knows Gerrard, knows how his mind works, and who also knows the *Tulsar*?'

21

The giant 23 Class Henshel locomotive wreathed itself in clouds of hissing steam as it grated to a standstill beside the *Tulsar*. Robert Gerrard leaned over the rail and looked down with interest at the forty flat-top wagons that the 111-ton locomotive had hauled across the highveld from Pretoria. Each wagon was stacked with coffin-sized wooden crates – fifty to a wagon – each of which bore the stencilled inscription of the lead mining corporation at Broken Hill near Lusaka in Northern Rhodesia.

'No guards?' Gerrard queried.

Holden joined him at the rail. 'Why invite awkward questions by mounting guards on what is supposed to be a cargo of lead?' he countered.

A tide of black stevedores swept over the crates to unfasten the ropes while a mobile dock crane trundled into position. Five minutes later the first sling-load of crates was guided down through the gaping hole in the *Tulsar*'s deck. Holden preferred not to think of the consequences should one of the crates fall and break open, revealing the true nature of its contents.

Holden followed Gerrard down the steel ladder into the *Tulsar*'s sweltering hold. The two men moved along the narrow passage-way between the rows of crates that were stacked eight high and secured with skilfully-tied lashing. The sun burned down with furnace intensity through the open hold on to the gleaming, oil-black backs of a team of sweating Zulus who were packing heavy bales of coir wadding between the crates and *Tulsar*'s hull.

'They're to protect the outer skin,' said Gerrard in answer to Holden's question. 'The *Tulsar*'s not designed to carry cargo. If those crates were to break loose in heavy weather they'd smash through the side like dogs going through a paper hoop in a circus act.'

They completed their tour of inspection and climbed back on to the deck. Josephine saw them emerge and closed purposefully in on them clutching a clipboard that had become an indispensable part of her accoutrement as the *Tulsar*'s purser.

'Captain Gerrard,' she said briskly. 'I have worked out the restaurant seating plan for week one of the voyage which requires your approval.'

Gerrard gaped at her in alarm. 'Why me, honey?'

Josephine was nonplussed by his reply. 'Well – it's usual for the captain to approve the seating at the captain's table unless you're happy to let me –'

'I'll eat with the crew like I always do,' Gerrard declared, glaring at Josephine as if he was daring her to contradict him.

Josephine promptly accepted the challenge. 'You can't,' she retorted. 'Having a proper captain's table is part of the social niceties of shipboard life.'

Holden smiled thinly at Gerrard's discomfort. 'I doubt if Captain Gerrard has got any social niceties.'

'That's right,' Gerrard growled, grateful for Holden's perceptive observation. 'I ain't got no social niceties.'

'Or a tuxedo to go with them,' Holden added drily.

'That's right,' Gerrard affirmed, aware that Holden was grinning at him. 'I'll tell you what, honey. As Mr Holden's the owner, how about him doing the honours?'

Holden's smile vanished. Josephine turned to the Englishman and looked at him critically. She nodded to Gerrard. 'Okay, captain, that's fine – if you don't mind the passengers coping with second best.'

22

Gerrard stood on the bridge on the afternoon of 25 February and glowered down at the excited passengers and well-wishers who were crowding round the foot of the *Tulsar*'s gangway. Those who weren't clamorously seeking Josephine's attention were either buying last-minute souvenirs from the hordes of Zulu women peddling strings of brightly-coloured beads or tripping over the luggage that the porters were unloading from the coach. Two customs officers had set up a trestle table and were proceeding to chalk mysterious runes on the passengers' trunks – a process that could apparently be carried out without examining the contents of the trunks. The two Ursuline nuns created a black oasis of tranquillity by sitting quietly on a packing-case and saying their rosaries while the newly-wed couple who had arrived from Cape Town the previous night were content to sit in a cocoon of happiness, arms tightly around each other, ignoring the chaos around them. Josephine envied them as she tried to placate Mrs Rose Lewis without losing her temper.

'Please, Mrs Lewis – I promise you – you won't have to share a cabin and the cabin will be big enough.'

Mrs Rose Lewis was a stern Canadian woman who owned several large chins and one small, embarrassed husband who was at her side and wishing he wasn't.

'And it must have an opening porthole. Herbie and I suffer with our chests at night – we must have air. Mustn't we, Herbie?'

'Yes, Rose,' said Mr Lewis obediently. He didn't suffer with his chest, but his wife took the view that her ailments, like the debts for expensive clothes that she tended to acquire, were transferable to her husband.

Josephine pacified Mrs Lewis with vague promises and was immediately involved in a dispute between Mr Eli Vanson and one of the customs officers over a fifty-dollar gold piece that Mrs Eli Vanson was wearing round her neck.

'The regulations are clear, sir,' said the customs officer politely. 'The export of gold from Britain and the dominions of the Empire is forbidden under the emergency regulations.'

'It was one of my wedding-presents to her, for Chrissake,' Eli Vanson snarled angrily. The sugar magnate had discovered when he and his wife had first visited South Africa that British customs officers were the most cussed breed on the planet. He turned to Josephine. 'Will you explain that to this creep, Miss Britten?'

'The rules are very clear,' said the customs officer, unruffled. 'Personal jewellery is allowed but not bullion or gold coins.'

The argument was ended by the second customs officer, the more senior of the two. He produced a set of goldsmith's scales and weights and said that His Majesty's Customs and Excise were empowered to purchase the gold coin at the market rate, and added very apologetically that it was his job to ensure that the only gold that sailed that evening on the *Tulsar* was in the form of tooth fillings.

Josephine unlocked the cabin door and pushed it open. 'Number six, Mr Holden,' she announced cheerfully. 'Your home for the next few weeks.'

Holden surveyed the cramped cabin without enthusiasm. The cot berth fixed to one bulkhead took up most of the floor space. The opposite bulkhead consisted of a range of lockers surrounding a wash-basin and mirror. There was a chair and a small writing desk below the only porthole.

'It's not my idea of an owner's stateroom,' said Holden.

'It's the largest cabin on the ship by six inches each way. I measured it personally.'

'That's very considerate of you, Jo.'

'As you're used to the best, it's only right that you should have the best. Of course, if you don't like it, you can only blame yourself for not buying a bigger boat. The air-conditioning controls are beside the bunk, and there's a call buzzer beside the desk. One buzz for the cabin steward, two buzzes for the bar steward.'

'How many for you?'

'My cabin-cum-office will be open eight till eight each day. There'll be a pad for messages if I'm not there.'

'I'll make frequent use of it,' Holden promised.

Josephine dropped the cabin key on the bunk. 'There's a card in the drawer which gives the times of meals.' She moved to the door. 'I hope you have a pleasant voyage, Mr Holden.'

Kramer was able to slip unnoticed aboard the *Tulsar* simply by walking up the gangway holding his Afu suitcase transmitter-receiver in one hand and a travelling-bag in the other. He chose a moment when there was a general mêlée of passengers, porters, ricksha boys and well-wishers clustered on the quayside by the ship and crowded on to the flensing deck. He strolled casually around the ship, pausing now and then to examine details that interested him, and nodding to passengers who were doing the same thing. A small group were staring up at the Northrop seaplane and arguing among themselves as to its purpose. They took no notice of Kramer as he pushed past them and made his way aft to the port lifeboat that was nearest the stern and not visible from the bridge or the quay. The lifeboat was high above the deck, hoisted hard against the curved davit heads. Kramer prayed that it would not be used for lifeboat drill. He made sure no one was looking and reached up to slacken the ropes that held the lifeboat's canvas cover in place. He pushed the radio set and the travelling-bag into the lifeboat, grasped the gunwale, and hauled himself up. He rolled into the lifeboat and quickly pushed the cover back into position. He crouched in the darkness for some minutes, listening intently for sounds suggesting that his entry into the lifeboat had been noticed. Once satisfied that all was well, he pulled a torch out of his travelling-bag and examined the interior of his new home. The lifeboat was thirty feet long and equipped with five pairs of oars. The lockers at both ends under the short decks were well provisioned with tinned food and there was a full fifty-gallon freshwater tank under each of the five thwarts. There were even blankets provided in waterproof bags. He hid the plan of the *Tulsar*'s layout under the duckboards and set about making himself comfortable.

Josephine had said her goodbyes at the hotel and had deliberately kept them unsentimental. She therefore gave a brief frown of annoyance when Jenny tapped hesitantly on her open door and entered the cabin.

'A telegram came for you just after you left,' said the girl. She opened her handbag and gave Josephine the envelope. 'Mr Thorne sent me. He said that it might be very important.'

'Thank you, Jenny. It was very kind of you to come.'

'I'll miss you. It won't seem the same without you. I'm sure to get into a horrible mess and double-book all the rooms, or something.'

'You'll manage. Remember never to lose your temper with the guests. If you always remain polite when they get rude, they'll end up feeling stupid. It always works.'

'I'll remember it,' Jenny promised.

Josephine tore the telegram open the moment she was alone.

PA OVER THE MOON WHEN I TOLD HIM YOU WERE COMING HOME STOP DOCTORS SAY ITS BEST THAT HE STAYS IN HOSPITAL BE-CAUSE I CANT MANAGE WITH HIM ALONE STOP HES STILL WEAK BUT HE HAS BEEN THINKING ABOUT YOU ALL THE TIME NOW STOP HE IS VERY SORRY ABOUT ALL THE MISTAKES STOP YOUR LOVING MOTHER

Josephine was prevented from re-reading the telegram by the sudden appearance of the newly-married husband in her doorway. He made some embarrassed small-talk before blurting out his unhappiness about the tiered bunks that he and his bride were required to come to terms with. It was one of those problems that never arose in a hotel or large ship. Josephine realized that being the purser of a ship like the *Tulsar*, while not easy, certainly wasn't going to be dull.

Kramer pushed his knife into the taut canvas of the lifeboat cover above his head and worked the blade back and forth until the slit was wide enough to give him air and provide enough light during the daylight hours to conserve his torch batteries. He unpacked his travelling-bag and placed a Walther P-38 pistol on one of the lifeboat's thwarts within easy reach of his sleeping-bag. If discovered, he intended to sell his life dearly.

•

At one minute to midnight the pilot ordered the *Tulsar*'s mooring lines to be singled up. Two dockers unhitched the fore and aft mooring springs and a small harbour tug gently nudged the *Tulsar* away from the quay. The pilot stood shirt-sleeved and motionless in the soft glow from the binnacle and called for slow astern port – slow ahead starboard. The *Tulsar* came about, pivoting on her keel until her head was bearing on the centre of Port Natal's natural basin.

There was only Gooding to wish her farewell at that hour. To the sweating blacks, labouring through the humid night to load ice into the ponds of the darkly-clustered deep sea fishing-boats, the *Tulsar* was merely another white man's ship off to the seas that they traditionally feared.

'Slow ahead both,' the pilot called to Brody at the helm.

'Slow ahead both,' Brody repeated, obeying the order.

'Saw your new bow today,' commented the pilot, feeling in the pockets of his peajacket for a packet of cigarettes. 'Looks smart, I must say, but a ship that's caught a clout like that is never the same again I say.'

' 'T'aint right, leavin' like this,' Mrs Eli Vanson said to her husband who was standing beside her on the weatherdeck.

'There should be a band, an' streamers, an' sirens instead of this sneakin' off in the night like a thief.'

'Sugar – just so we're heading for home, I don't give a damn just how we leave.'

Gerrard leaned against the bridge rail, smoking a tattered Havana, and watched the harbour lights slip by while allowing his senses to harmonize with the feel of the *Tulsar*. For once there was the muted hum of the turbines and the soft tinkle of the engine-room telegraph instead of the shuddering uproar of riveting-guns and welders' hammers. The *Tulsar* was a ship again – a living entity around him instead of a helpless mass of ironmongery at the mercy of indifferent shipwrights and equally indifferent landsmen who knew and understood nothing about ships.

Josephine awoke and realized that the ship was moving. She grimaced as she sat up in bed – the wine at the welcome aboard reception she had organized for the passengers had been a mistake. She drew the curtain back from the porthole and watched the dark, humped outline of The Bluff sliding silently past. The lighthouse swept the horizon with spokes of light. She gazed for some minutes at the departing land that had given her independence and taught her hard but gratefully-received lessons in survival. All she wanted now was for the *Tulsar* to speed her to New York so that she could make everything up with her father before it was too late; but she knew that she would return to South Africa again.

Hidden in the lifeboat, Kramer stirred and opened his eyes in the darkness. For a second the strange noises and the unfamiliar motion nearly caused him to panic before he realized that the *Tulsar* was moving. His hand reached out and touched the cold steel comfort of his pistol and knife. Reassured, he drifted back to sleep.

The *Tulsar* cleared The Bluff and lifted to the first rolling swell of the tepid Indian Ocean as if giving a sigh of relief at finally being freed from the imprisoning embrace of the brooding escarpment hills that guarded the sullen African continent.

Part Two

FIGHTING

1

The stump of Kurt Milland's right leg ached abominably and he was certain that blood was beginning to break through the chaffed skin. Another five minutes of this infernal walking, he thought, and the leather socket of the artificial leg would be too wet to hold his stump firmly in place. He tried to tighten the shoulder harness through his shirt by pushing a hand under his greatcoat but that meant letting go of the handrail of the narrow boardwalk. His right foot caught on a coil of rope, causing him to stumble against the two men he was so desperately trying to keep up with as they made their way towards the four giant sheds of Krupp's Germania Werft U-boat construction yard. Admiral Staus steadied Milland with one hand and looked at him in concern.

'Are you all right, Kurt?'

Milland clenched his teeth and nodded, aware that the construction yard manager was regarding him with contempt.

'How much further?' Staus demanded.

The civilian pointed to a completed U-boat that was receiving its final coat of grey paint. It was less than fifty yards away, moored against the concrete quay and boxed in by the rust-streaked hulls of two unfinished U-boats that looked old before they were completed. The uproar of hammering and bursts of intense blue fire from arc-welders' torches in the open-sided sheds suggested that Krupp's were tearing U-boats apart instead of building them.

The three men moved slowly along the quay, stopped beside the U-boat and stared down at it. For the hundredth time that freezing morning Milland wondered why an important training programme had been interrupted to drag him to Kiel to look at U-boats under construction; he wasn't interested in the building

– his job was the building of the fighting men who would have to take them to war.

'Some boat, eh, Kurt?' said Staus.

Milland tried to forget the pain in his right stump and ran an experienced, if disinterested, eye over the new boat. It was an ocean-going Type IXD with a surface displacement of 1,600 tons – double that of the current operational boats. Milland had read about the new boats and had doubted the wisdom behind their creation; the surface night attack technique by U-boats was proving effective. It was the method being taught by the training flotillas that depended on small U-boats with small conning-towers that were difficult for the convoy lookouts to spot. Milland decided that if the top brass had invited him to look at the new ocean-going cruiser submarines, to ask his opinion of them, then he would say exactly what he thought of them.

'Some boat,' he said to Admiral Staus. 'But too big to take part in massed attacks on convoys at night.'

Staus chuckled. Milland could always be relied on to speak his mind with candour. 'Actually, Kurt, that's not what they're intended for.'

'With respect, admiral, we should not be building boats for any other purpose other than for sinking enemy shipping. The fighting power of a submarine does not increase in proportion to its size as it does in the case of other warships.'

The manager glared at Milland. 'These boats are intended to carry the offensive into distant waters – the Pacific and the Far East.'

'I think we ought to go aboard,' Staus quickly intervened.

The manager led the way along the gangplank to the U-boat's forward deck casing. Milland was appalled at the expanse of deck and guessed that such a length of boat would pose particular problems in preventing its bow breaking the surface when at periscope depth. Maintaining correct trim was a U-boat chief engineer's biggest headache. They passed the business-like mass of an 88-millimetre gun mounted on the forward casing and climbed the steel rungs set into the side of the conning-tower. Ladders presented no difficulties to Milland for he had developed his arm and shoulder muscles so that he could climb any ladder by going up it hand over hand.

He swung his right leg stiffly over the rail that guarded the multiple-barrelled anti-aircraft guns and followed the manager and Admiral Staus down the bridge ladder into the new U-boat's softly-illuminated control-room.

'Welcome aboard *U-330*,' said the manager cryptically.

A thought occurred to Milland as he looked round the spacious control-room: 'Are the training flotillas to be issued with these boats, admiral?'

Staus smiled. 'I think not, Kurt. Especially not this boat. The aft tubes have been removed, so it wouldn't be much use for providing torpedomen with a full training programme.'

Milland was puzzled. 'Why take out the tubes?'

'To make room for the Maybach diesels,' said the manager. 'Big bastards – four thousand horsepower each. Twenty-five knots on the surface – the fastest U-boat ever built. Had thirty men working fifteen hours a day to get her ready. Radar, extra tanks to give her a twenty-thousand-mile cruising range, everything. And we haven't finished yet. We're unshipping that 88-millimetre later today and mounting a 104-millimetre quick-firing gun instead, and quadruple 20-millimetre anti-aircraft guns on the wintergarten deck.' The manager paused. 'This boat will have more hitting power than the *Tirpitz* by the time we're through, and be nearly as fast.'

Milland frowned at Staus. 'I don't understand, admiral. What has all this to do with me?'

Staus nodded to the manager. 'Leave us now, thank you.'

The manager accepted the dismissal and climbed out of the control-room. Staus indicated Milland to sit. The officer gratefully sat on the settee-berth and stretched his leg to ease the pressure on his aching stump. He looked questioningly at his superior officer.

Staus reached into an inside pocket and produced a sealed Kriegsmarine envelope which he toyed with while collecting his thoughts. 'Kurt,' he began. 'You remember telling me about your past association with Robert Gerrard – the man who sank *U-497* in the Indian Ocean last December?'

'Yes admiral,' Milland replied cautiously, sensing trouble looming.

'I reported our conversation as a matter of routine. There was nothing that reflected on you, you understand. Naturally, I thought the whole business would be a seven-day wonder and then be forgotten. But it wasn't.' Staus paused and tapped the envelope. 'What I have to tell you now, Kurt, is most secret and can be divulged only under the conditions given in these orders. On 25 February the *Tulsar* sailed from Durban bound for England with a cargo that consisted of two hundred tons of gold – the last of the Allied reserves. Without it they cannot continue with this senseless war. The Führer has issued a directive that a U-boat is to intercept the *Tulsar* and to capture it if possible or sink it if not. This U-boat.'

Milland suddenly realized why he had been hauled away from Wilhelmshaven. 'I'm wanted to brief the new captain of this boat, admiral?'

Staus shook his head. 'No, Kurt – you *are* the captain of this boat.'

Milland stared at the older man, the pain in his stump forgotten. 'I'm *what*!'

Staus repeated his statement and held out the envelope to Milland who accepted it with lifeless fingers. 'Despite your handicap, the OKM have decided that you should have command of this boat. I'll have your things sent from Wilhelmshaven. Your crew will be arriving just as soon as I can get one together at such short notice. There isn't time for a shake-down cruise which means that you'll have to carry out training *en route* to intercept the *Tulsar*.'

Milland stared at Staus, hardly taking in what the admiral was telling him.

'There's one thing I must know,' said Staus. 'You told me that Robert Gerrard was a determined man.'

'Ruthless,' said Milland, holding the envelope as if he was expecting it to explode.

'If that's the case, capturing the *Tulsar* won't be easy. You'll probably have to pump shells into her –'

'I think I know what you're trying to say, admiral,' Milland suddenly interrupted. 'If it's necessary for me to kill Robert Gerrard I won't hesitate.'

2

Milland stumped along the quayside on 5 March, his greatcoat collar turned up against the snow flurries and bitingly-cold north-easterly wind driving across the Baltic. He drew level with *U-330*'s bow and resisted the temptation to gaze at his first command. He spun his weight round on his left heel and walked back the length of the U-boat. The two men fitting a cluster of fixed radar antennae round the rim of the U-boat's conning-tower guiltily resumed work when they saw Milland scowl at them.

Milland tugged his peaked cap down more firmly on his head and looked at his watch. They were late. After three days of frustrating delays during which time the construction yard had run through their entire repertoire of excuses – sometimes inventing new ones – Milland had had enough. All he wanted to do now was to take his boat through the Kiel Canal and into the North Sea to the war – away from the stupefying morass of stores requisitions, equipment defect reports, acceptance certificates and chart amendments. It was unbelievable how much paperwork had to be got through before a U-boat could be declared operational. Only one formality had been deliberately omitted: the commissioning ceremony. *U-330* was a ghost boat. Such was the importance of her secret mission that officially according to Kriegsmarine records, *U-330* did not exist.

A bus appeared at the far end of the quay near the entrance to the harbour and rumbled towards Milland over the puddle-splattered tarmac. The vehicle stopped. Twenty men in civilian dress disembarked and dragged their travelling-bags and suitcases from the vehicle's stowage bay. Milland noted that someone had had the sense to see that the men did not use service-issue kitbags. He recognized some of them as men who had passed through his hands at the training flotilla. There was Munt – the chief engineer he had specifically requested from the

1st Flotilla, and Hans Fischer – the unfortunate officer who had bent a U-boat at Wilhelmshaven.

One of the new arrivals spotted the white cover on Milland's cap that was the emblem of a U-boat captain and cautiously approached him. Milland eyed him warily. He looked too young to be his new first officer. He returned the young officer's salute.

'Captain Milland?'

'Yes?'

The young man smiled. 'Good morning, captain. I'm Lieutenant Peter Sarne. I've brought you your crew.'

'Very good, Mr Sarne. Two lines please. Officers and petty officers to the fore.'

'Yes, captain,' said Sarne crisply. He produced an envelope. 'A letter from Admiral Staus. He asked me to pass on his best wishes for the success of your new command.' Sarne hesitated. 'And I would like to add my best wishes, captain.'

'You're a Bavarian, Mr Sarne?'

'That's right, captain,' was Sarne's cheerful reply. 'Munich – pearl of the South. They were always telling me on my officer-training course that my accent would be a blight on my career.'

Milland resisted an impulse to smile. 'Just make sure that I don't become a bigger one,' he warned.

'I'll be very careful, captain,' said Sarne solemnly.

This time Milland smiled. Sarne's easy-going good humour would prove an invaluable asset on the long mission that lay ahead.

3

Gerrard flipped his cigar butt into the water and turned to face Holden. The two men were standing on the *Tulsar*'s bridge.

'Mr Holden,' said Gerrard slowly, 'I thought I made myself plain – I'm the captain and if I say we zig-zag all over the Indian Ocean then we zig-zag all over the Indian Ocean.'

'Which we've now been doing for ten days,' Holden observed.

Gerrard shrugged. 'It's not my fault that there are two German surface raiders around the Cape. As soon as Simonstown give the all-clear we head for the Cape, and not before.'

'When was the last signal from Simonstown?'

'Two days ago.'

Holden regarded the American seaman dispassionately. 'In future I'd like to see all incoming signals.'

'They're routine warnings to all ships. You want weather forecasts as well?'

'I want to see everything please, captain.'

Gerrard shrugged again and pulled a battered cigar from his sweat-shirt pocket. 'Okay. I'll tell Jack Colby.'

'There's something else,' said Holden. 'Every morning you and I will agree a sailing plan for the following twenty-four hours.'

'Nope,' said Gerrard, lighting the cigar.

'That's an order, Mr Gerrard.'

Gerrard grinned. 'If you want to know in advance what I don't even know myself, then I guess the best thing is for you to take over the *Tulsar*.'

Holden remained unruffled. 'All I'm saying, captain, is –'

'And all *I'm* saying, Mr Holden, is that if you want to get this ship safely to its destination, then you leave the running of the ship to me. You worry about the cargo – I'll worry about the ship. Okay?'

'All I want is a measure of co-operation.'

Gerrard laughed. 'I'll tell you something, Mr Holden. You go into any waterfront bar from Sydney to Boston and ask them what Robert Gerrard knows about co-operation. They'll tell you – he doesn't even know what the word means. Maybe I'm not running a whaler now, but nothing's changed. I'm a loner, Mr Holden. I always have been and I always will be.'

4

Milland was massaging surgical spirit into his stump to harden the skin made tender by the endless walking at the construction yard when there was a tap on his door. An advantage of the ocean-going cruiser submarines was that there was sufficient room for the commander to have his own cabin.

'Come!'

It was Sarne. His eyes widened in quickly-concealed surprise when he saw Milland's truncated leg. 'Heligoland's on our quarter, captain. You left word to be told.'

Milland grunted and rolled on a new stump sock and motioned for Sarne to sit down. 'What do you think of our crew, Mr Sarne?'

'I'd rather answer that in two weeks, captain.'

'You'll answer it now,' said Milland mildly.

'We need a shakedown cruise. We need diving drill; silent running drill; gun drill –'

'We'll have plenty of time for that,' Milland interrupted.

'But we'll be in the middle of the convoy routes in a couple of days.'

'Aa we've cleared Heligoland I can now tell you the purpose of our patrol. We're not interested in shipping – what we're going after is one particular ship.'

As Milland quickly outlined *U-330*'s mission, Sarne's pale young face seemed to get even paler, but when Milland had finished, he demonstrated his ability to turn his mind quickly to the practical problems.

'The *Tulsar* is unescorted, captain?'

'Yes – because she's fast.'

'Then how can we possibly hope to find one ship in the whole of the Atlantic?'

'We have the DT apparatus – radar, and the latest hydrophone equipment which can detect propeller noises at a range of fifty miles.'

'Under the right conditions,' Sarne pointed out.

'There are two agents aboard the ship,' said Milland. 'One has a radio-transmitter which he will use to transmit the *Tulsar*'s position every twenty-four hours, and the other is one of the passengers.' Milland smiled at Sarne's expression of astonishment. 'I think we have an excellent chance of capturing the *Tulsar*, Mr Sarne.'

Sarne returned to the control-room and climbed into oilskins and pulled on a sou'wester. He joined the four lookouts on the bridge who were quartering the horizon with binoculars, watching for the sudden appearance of a U-boat's deadliest enemy – aircraft.

U-330 was making six knots to conserve fuel-oil but heavy seas were surging across the deck casing as if she was driving into them at fifteen knots. The leaden cloudbase extended like a shroud from horizon to horizon. The wind whitened the driving spray into ice that grew on the big 104-millimetre gun in a steadily thickening layer. One of the lookouts was obviously suffering from seasickness but Sarne did nothing; the best cure was to keep the man occupied.

He braced himself against the U-boat's rolling motion by holding on to the attack periscope standard. As he turned Milland's words over in his mind, a thought occurred to him: if their mission was so important, why had Milland been chosen to lead it? Why select a man who was virtually a cripple?

5

The only respite from the heat for Kramer came at night when he could risk folding back the flap of the lifeboat cover and gulp down cool, refreshing draughts of night air. He had endured two weeks in the lifeboat with the sun beating down unmercifully on the dark blue canvas above his head; two weeks of lying in his own sweat, hardly daring to move for even the slightest exertion made him giddy with heat sickness; two weeks of nagging worry, wondering why his compass was saying that the *Tulsar* was zig-zagging east when its course ought to be south-east to take it down to the Cape.

The luminous hands of his watch were showing 3.30 am when he unlaced the cover and stood up. The night air tasted like champagne. His most pressing need was to visit the toilet.

He listened carefully. The only sound was the faint hum of the turbines and the steady surge of the Indian Ocean creaming past the *Tulsar*'s hull. Satisfied that all was clear, he swung his leg over the side of the lifeboat and dropped silently to the steel deck plating.

Mrs Rose Lewis prodded the bulge that sagged down from the upper bunk. The bulge stirred. 'I can't sleep, Herbie.'

Herbie made a distinct snoring sound suggesting that he could sleep and, furthermore, was sleeping.

Mrs Rose Lewis sighed and pushed her sheet down to the end of the berth. It was unbearably hot in the tiny cabin and her bunk had run out of cool corners for her feet to explore. She had lost count of the number of times she had turned her pillow over. 'I'm thirsty,' she complained to the bulge.

'Call the steward for a drink,' Herbie muttered.

'They never answer the bell at night. It's a disgrace. Everything's a disgrace.' She swung her feet to the floor and stood. 'I'm going on deck for some air. I can't breathe in here.' She groped for her dressing-gown and pulled it on. A minute later she was climbing the companion-way that led to the port deck. The cold steel made welcome contact with her feet.

Kramer crouched in the shadow of a ventilator and listened for some seconds before making the fifteen-yard dash across the open expanse of the flensing deck. At that precise moment, with impeccable timing, Mrs Rose Lewis appeared in the crew entrance and gaped in surprise at Kramer's doubled-up figure racing towards her.

'Why, hello,' she said. 'I guess you can't sleep either, huh?'

Kramer's reactions were fast for his nerves were keyed for action. He swerved towards Mrs Rose Lewis and seized her by the throat before she could cry out. His fingers sank deep into her yielding flesh and closed hard round her windpipe. She struggled feebly as he dragged her backwards towards the galley. He pushed the door open and quickly pinned her to the floor with his knee across her throat while he fumbled for his knife. She made choking noises and then began fighting with amazing strength.

Kramer ripped her nightdress open and probed below her left breast, feeling with his fingertips for the gap between her lower ribs. The woman brought her knees up suddenly and struck him in the small of the back, nearly causing him to lose his hold.

Human ribs are arranged like the overlapping slats of a slightly-closed venetian blind, thus making a downward stab difficult; the tip of the knife is liable to be deflected from rib to rib. To succeed, as Kramer knew, the blow has to be upwards – delivered with considerable force to penetrate the tough tissue between each rib and the next.

Kramer positioned the knife against Mrs Rose Lewis's chest and thrust, quickly shifting his grip to drive the nine-inch blade home with the palm of his hand. He felt a sudden spasm shudder through the knife which told him that the blade had penetrated the heart. He held the knife steady so that the pulsating organ would destroy itself on the razor-sharp steel. The woman's body went limp. Kramer released the knife. The handle twitched for a moment and then was still. There was little bleeding from the wound after he withdrew the knife – most of the bleeding from the severed heart ventricle would be filling the chest cavity.

Kramer peered to the left and right and satisfied himself that the deck was still deserted. Terrified in case he was discovered, he quicky dragged the women by her ankles towards the scuppers, taking care to keep the body on its back to avoid tell-tale blood streaks on the deck. He breathed easier once he had the body and himself concealed in the shadow of one of the towering ventilators. He debated what to do with the body. Obviously the simplest solution was to tip it over the side, but there was a snag: when the alarm was raised later that morning and it was established that the missing woman wasn't on the ship, there was a possibility that Gerrard would retrace the *Tulsar*'s course. He was a skilled seaman and would be able to make an accurate allowance for the effect of the Mozambique Current. The whaler was crewed by men with keen eyesight who were trained to study the sea. There was a chance that the woman's body might be found. Admittedly, it was an extremely faint chance, but one that Kramer felt he couldn't afford to take. It would be necessary to ensure that sharks found the body attractive. And with their ability to smell blood in the water, it was a task that shouldn't be too difficult.

He sliced the woman's nightdress right open and tore it from her body. He then made two deep, diagonal knife-slashes across her torso starting at her collar-bones and traversing down to the opposite thigh. To make doubly certain, he pushed her legs apart and stabbed upwards, twisting the blade viciously in her body before pulling it out. Blood oozed from the savage incisions. He rolled the body through the scupper with his foot. One final push and it tumbled out of sight into the white foam. The splash was inaudible.

Kramer used the nightdress to wipe his knife and the deck clean before tossing it over the side after Mrs Rose Lewis.

At 4 am Gerrard went on to the bridge to relieve Piet.

'New course for you before you sign off, Piet,' said Gerrard looking up from the gyro-compass. 'Two-two-zero. Time we headed south-west. Our Mr Holden is complaining. Who's on engine-room watch?'

'Midge,' Piet answered.

Gerrard grinned, crossed to the engine-room telegraph, and signalled for full speed ahead on both turbines. The interphone bell rang almost immediately. Gerrard lifted the handset off its hook and said: 'No arguments please, Midge. Time we got a move on.'

The *Tulsar* heeled gently as Piet spun the helm. Gerrard watched the twin hands of the turbine bridge repeaters gradually edging up to the maximum revolutions reading. The movement of the two pointers was matched by an increased hum from the turbines. The *Tulsar* began building up speed.

6

'What's the matter, Mr Lewis? You'll be late for breakfast.' Josephine discovered the little, bespectacled Canadian in the corridor outside her cabin. He was still in his pyjamas and dressing-gown, and looking very distraught.

'It's Rose, Miss Britten. I haven't seen her since I woke up. She got up in the night to go on deck for air.' Herbie watched Josephine appealingly as if the question of his missing wife was one that he hoped she would shoulder.

'What's the trouble?' Holden inquired as he stepped out of his cabin.

'Mr Lewis has lost his wife,' Josephine explained.

'She's bound to be somewhere. Mr Holden and I will look – you go on up to breakfast,' Josephine suggested.

Gerrard listened patiently to Lewis' account of the previous night and looked up at Josephine and Holden who were standing either side of the unhappy Canadian.

'Did you check the empty cabins?'

'We searched the entire ship,' said Josephine. 'Everywhere but the hold.'

Gerrard stood and glanced questioningly at Holden. 'Well, if it's okay with Mr Holden, he and I will check the hold but I don't see how she could have gotten herself in there.'

Holden shone his torch along the last of the aisles between the stacked wooden crates that were surrounded by bales of coconut matting. 'Nothing here,' he called out to Gerrard.

The American joined him and surveyed the narrow passageway. 'Maybe we ought to shift some of those bales.'

'We're wasting our time,' said Holden. He wrinkled his nose in distaste. 'And these overalls stink.'

A shadow fell across the two men. They looked up at Piet's

head and shoulders framed in the open circular hatch against the sky. 'We've found something, cap'n,' said the Afrikaner grimly. 'But we've got to stop.'

The cessation of the turbine hum woke Kramer. There were excited voices near the lifeboat he was hiding in. He knew that the disappearance of the woman was bound to create a disturbance, but there was no good reason why it should be created so close to his lifeboat. Perhaps there was something he had overlooked? A smear of blood on the deck or perhaps there was something wrong with the lifeboat? But it was unlikely because he had taken such great care to leave no trace, and the lifeboat cover was in place. A cold wedge of fear suddenly thickened in his throat: stopped engines! A crowd round the lifeboat! It could only mean one thing: this lifeboat had been selected for lifeboat drill.

He reached for his gun and waited.

Less than four yards from where Kramer lay sweating in fear, the chattering Malay seamen helped their compatriot climb back on to the *Tulsar*'s deck where Piet relieved him of his trophy.

Gerrard spread the bloodstained nightdress on the chart table and stared coldly at Lewis. The Canadian fingered the garment for a moment and nodded.

'Where did you find it, captain?' His spectacles were misting up. He removed them and nervously polished the lenses with a handkerchief.

'Not far from where you threw it,' Gerrard replied. 'Except that you didn't throw it hard enough. It was caught on the port turbine condenser outlet.'

Lewis blinked and glanced at Holden. The fair-haired Englishman was regarding him thoughtfully and saying nothing. 'I don't understand, captain.'

'It's a short length of pipe sticking out of the hull.'

'No – I mean what you said about me throwing this.' Lewis' hand trembled as he touched the nightdress. 'And what are these marks?'

'Blood,' was Gerrard's cryptic reply.

'You can't be certain of that,' Holden observed.

'I know what bloodstains look like. Why the blood, Mr Lewis?

Why not just give her a push? Or were you frightened that she might scream?'

The Canadian's eyes filmed with tears. 'I didn't kill her. If you accuse me, you'd be letting the real killer escape.'

Gerrard rested his chin on his hands. 'Mr Holden – what in hell are we going to do with him?'

'There's nothing we can do until we reach port,' murmured Holden. His mind was racing over the problem of why Mrs Rose Lewis had been killed and who her murderer was. He was certain that her husband wasn't responsible otherwise why had he identified her nightdress?

'I'm not having a killer loose on my ship,' Gerrard stated. 'Piet!'

Piet van Kleef appeared in the wheelhouse doorway. 'Cap'n?'

Gerrard jabbed a finger at Lewis. 'Have him locked in the bow compartment.'

Holden looked up boredly at the deckhead. 'I don't think you should do that, captain.'

'Dealing with murderers may not be part of the normal day-to-day problems aboard a ship,' said Gerrard, 'but it's still my responsibility.' The American turned to Piet. 'See that he has ten minutes exercise each watch.'

'But you can't do this to me!' Lewis protested as Piet gripped his arm. 'I swear before God that I've done nothing!' He tried to break free and realized that argument was useless. There was a slience in the wheelhouse after Piet had taken Lewis below. Holden decided not to intervene; there were more important battles ahead with Robert Gerrard that he was determined to win.

'You have anything to say, Mr Holden?' Gerrard inquired.

Holden pursed his lips and nodded. 'About agreeing a daily sailing plan, captain . . .'

7

Five days after leaving the Kiel Canal and heading north, *U-330* reached the Arctic Circle and steered westwards on a course that would take her round Iceland to the north before entering the Denmark Strait and the North Atlantic proper. It was a long, tedious route but it reduced the risk of the U-boat encountering the numerous RAF Coastal Command Hudsons and Sunderland flying-boats on anti-submarine patrols.

As Milland had expected, the weather had ruled out opportunities for Sarne to meet the stringent training schedule of crash dives, gunnery practice, damage control drill and escape drill. Nevertheless, the crew were efficient and morale was high. Otto Munt, the U-boat's chief engineer, had submitted meticulous daily reports on the general state of the U-boat's machinery; and his fuel-oil consumption figures were scrupulously accurate. More important – he got on well with his petty officers, and his mechanics had familiarized themselves with the two non-standard Maybach diesel engines.

U-330's radio-operator was Dieter Venner – a quick-tempered petty officer and a native of Cologne. He was also responsible for the ratings who operated the hydrophones and radar equipment.

Leutnant zur See Hans Fischer, *U-330*'s second watch officer, had admitted to once working in a top Frankfurt restaurant, a confession that led to his appointment as the ship's *maître d'hotel*. As such he was responsible for drawing up the daily menu. The responsibility had gone to his head and his ambitious ideas on what could be achieved with the limited variety of the U-boat's supplies led to bad blood between him and the cook.

The main off-duty preoccupation of the watches was speculation about the purpose of *U-330*'s mission. From the secrecy surrounding their posting to the U-boat the members of the crew knew that it was something of extreme importance. An enterprising torpedo mechanic had opened betting on the possibility that *U-330* was destined to carry out a series of spectacular raids on Allied shipping in distant waters to emulate the successes of the surface raider *Atlantis*. When Sarne and Milland were together in the control-room their conversational exchanges were listened to with studied disinterest by the control-room watch in the hope of overhearing a hint as to the purpose of their voyage.

When Milland was told that *U-330* was an hour from the Denmark Strait, he decided that it was time to end the gossip and speculation. He entered the control-room and watched Fischer writing up the log at the chart table – a task made virtually impossible by the U-boat's rolling that even her present surface speed of eight knots did little to alleviate.

'Everything in order, Mr Fischer?'

Fischer looked up from the log. 'Yes, captain. Obermaschinist Koenig managed to trap his fingers in the inspection hatch to number four battery compartment. Sanitätsobermatt Steiner has stitched him up and given him a shot of morphine.'

Milland made a mental note to pay the unfortunate mechanic a visit. He had lectured often enough on the need for senior officers to show concern for their crewmen; now was the time to put this into practice. But first there was something else to attend to.

'Mr Venner!'

Dieter Venner leaned out of his radio-operator's compartment. 'Yes, captain?'

'Switch off the bridge loudspeaker. I don't want the lookout duty watch distracted.' Milland reached up and unhooked the crew address microphone. 'Men of *U-330*,' he began, his voice echoing back at him through the open watertight door from the various loudspeakers throughout the U-boat. 'You've all been wondering about the purpose of our mission for long enough. Now is the time to put you out of your misery. Our task is the greatest that the Fatherland has ever asked of its fighting men: we are to bring about a swift end to this senseless war!'

Milland spoke for five minutes, making no apologies for repeatedly stressing the Allied dependence on gold to finance their war effort. 'The British Empire is made up largely of under-developed countries with little or no industry; the factories of Europe are now denied to them therefore only America can supply their needs in tanks, ships and aeroplanes. And America is insisting on payment in gold. Stop the flow of gold and their war effort will collapse overnight. . . . Gentlemen, I have given an undertaking the *U-330* will not fail in her objective of capturing the *Tulsar*'s gold! That is all.'

There was the sound of a muffled cheer from the engine-room followed by applause from the men in the control-room. Fischer was gaping at Milland in astonishment while Munt and his helmsman and hydroplane-operator were laughing and clapping each other on the back.

Milland thoughtfully returned the microphone to its hook and caught Fischer's eye. Milland knew enough about the serious-minded junior officer to guess what he was thinking: the Atlantic Ocean covered thirty-two million square miles. As a place to play a deadly game of hide-and-seek, the odds were stacked in favour of the hider.

8

Kramer listened carefully, sweat coursing down his face into his two-week beard, making absolutely certain that no one was near the lifeboat before cautiously lifting a corner of the canvas cover and peering out. It was mid-afternoon and the sun was beating down with unbridled ferocity.

As he expected, the deck was deserted. He slipped his binoculars round his neck and dropped to the deck. He leaned casually against the rail for some seconds, waiting and listening to ensure that he hadn't been seen. The weatherdeck where his lifeboat was situated came to a dead end at the stern where the whale slipway, guarded by safety rails, sloped down to the waterline.

For Kramer to see across to the starboard side meant walking forward to the flensing deck. There was no alternative. He moved openly – to be seen behaving furtively would be suicidal. He leaned forward against a ventilator to steady his grip and trained his binoculars on the lazy headland.

There was no mistaking the razor-ridged finger of rock reaching out into the sea with the squat lighthouse at its seaward extremity: it was Cape Point. After a huge zig-zagging sweep round the Indian Ocean, presumably to avoid the usual shipping routes, the *Tulsar* had finally rounded the saw-edged reef of Cape Agulhas – the southernmost point of the mighty African continent – and was now entering the Atlantic Ocean.

Over seven thousand miles to the north, *U-330* was also entering the Atlantic Ocean.

Hunter and hunted were now on the same hunting ground.

9

The Purchasing Commission agent from London watched the steel grab drop into the hold of the British freighter. It emerged clutching a huge load of rubble in its massive fingers. Bricks and masonry escaped the grab's hold and fell into the East River but the bulk of the load remained intact. The operator swung the jib and pulled the lever that opened the grab. The falling masonry added to the great cloud of dust that was hovering over the New York waterfront between East 59th Street and 42nd Street.

There were twenty Allied-registered merchantships at anchor in line-astern waiting patiently for attention from the grabs. The cargo they had borne as ballast across the grey North Atlantic was thousands of tons of London rubble created by the Luftwaffe's blitzkrieg. The remains of pubs, warehouses, shops, factories and churches – many of which had been built when Broadway was still an Indian trail – were providing the foundations of what was to become reclaimed land in Manhattan. When their holds were emptied and cleaned, the ships were due to be loaded with aero-engines and spares, anti-aircraft guns, rifles and millions of rounds of ammunition, bomb-sights, machine tools, and all the innumerable accoutrements of industrialized warfare.

'So what's the latest?' the Purchasing Commission agent asked his companion.

The State Department official thrust his hands into his pockets and stared out at the ships. 'We can't release a single round of ammunition – even against a post-dated cheque – until the gold is in Fort Knox and fully accounted for.' He kept his gaze on the ships so that he didn't have to look at the British civil servant at his side. 'Our lawers say that "cash and carry" means just that.'

The agent remained silent. During a visit to Washington he had seen a demonstration outside the White House by women bearing placards that urged Congressmen and Senators to vote against 'Roosevelt's War Bill 1776'. There were other banners such as 'Lend-Lease is a lease on our freedom!' and 'Another Boston Tea Party – Kill HR 1776'.

But there was a gleam of hope: the isolationists were not having it all their own way; the Committee to Defend America by Aiding the Allies was waging an effective counter-campaign with emotive posters and full-page advertisements in newspapers. But despite the encouraging signs, it seemed to the agent that there was a very real chance that the only part of London not to end up under the jackboots of the Nazis would be beneath the feet of New Yorkers.

10

At 0.02 am on 17 March, Kramer completed his observation of the moon and the Southern Cross with his sextant and took one final lower-limb and upper-limb reading of the moon to double-check.

He pulled the lifeboat cover back into place and settled down with a notepad, torch and nautical almanac to calculate the *Tulsar*'s position as best he could despite his inexperience in handling a sextant. There were two additional factors that prevented him from obtaining an accurate fix. Firstly, he wasn't a hundred per cent certain after three weeks at sea if his watch was still giving the right time. Astronomical navigation – the measuring of the relationship between the moon and the stars, and their angle above the horizon – is dependent on an accurate timekeeper. Secondly, he was uncertain of his own height above the horizon in the lifeboat in order to make reliable angle of dip corrections.

Fifteen minutes later he had a position worked out, albeit a somewhat dubious one. The latitude fix ought to be within five degrees, which meant that the *Tulsar* was due west of Walvis Bay on the Atlantic coast of the former German colony of South-West Africa. His thoughts turned to his fellow Ossewa-Brandwag 'officer' in Windhoek. Every night General Rudolf Messener would be listening for messages broadcast by Kramer which he would relay on his powerful short-wave transmitter.

Kramer returned the sextant to its case and reached for his Afu suitcase radio-transmitter/receiver.

11

Milland hauled himself on to *U-330*'s bridge and gratefully inhaled draughts of air that weren't poisoned with the stench of sweat and diesel-oil. He pulled up the collar of his leather coat and rubbed his hands briskly together. Dawn was beginning its assault on the eastern horizon.

'Good morning, captain,' said Sarne, sensing that Milland was in good humour.

'Good morning, Mr Sarne,' Milland responded. 'Some good news to end your watch. HQ have relayed the *Tulsar*'s position to us. Their agent aboard the *Tulsar* is earning his keep.' He handed Sarne a blue signal flimsy. The junior officer examined it.

'Twenty-three degrees south – ten degrees east?'

'So?' Milland demanded.

'It's a bit vague for a position, don't you think, captain? Degrees in round figures – no minutes of arc?'

Milland chuckled. 'It's better than nothing, Mr Sarne.'

Sarne said nothing. He could well understand his captain's elation. The message was long overdue – the unspoken fear had been that the agent on the *Tulsar* had been discovered.

'Still a long way to go, Mr Sarne,' said Milland affably. 'But the great thing is that we know where the *Tulsar* is and they know nothing about us. She's as good as ours, Mr Sarne.'

12

Josephine nodded a good morning to the two Ursuline nuns who were leaning against the rail like a pair of benign crows. The newly-weds – not so newly wed now – were sitting at opposite ends of the flensing deck and pointedly ignoring each other while other passengers were sitting in small groups discussing in hushed tones the murder of Mrs Rose Lewis – an issue which for almost a month had proved a durable topic of conversation. Mr and Mrs Vanson were noisily conducting one of their frequent acrimonious disputes over Mr Vanson's long hours spent propped against the bar in the restaurant trying to forget Mrs Vanson.

Josephine could still hear the sugar magnate's wife's shrill voice as she made her way down the companion-way that led to the oil separator deck. The temperature rose noticeably below deck and she felt the covers of the two magazines she was carrying stick to her hands. The sides of the cavernous gallery closed in as she neared the bow. It was a trip she made a point of making twice a day. She rapped on the steel watertight door that sealed the bow compartment from the rest of the ship.

'Mr Lewis? Are you awake?'

There was a movement on the far side of the door.

'Miss Britten?' answered a hopeful voice.

'Good morning, Mr Lewis. I've found you two more magazines. I'll leave them outside. The seamen will let you have them after your morning exercise.'

'Thank you, Miss Britten. You're very kind.'

'Did you sleep well?'

The voice that answered was apologetic. 'Not very well, Miss Britten . . . I could hear the noises. They're getting louder, I think.'

Josephine frowned. 'What noises, Mr Lewis?'

'I haven't liked to say anything before in case you thought I was being silly.'

'What noises?' Josephine asked again with some irritation.

'Well . . . a sort of metallic, grating sound.'

Josephine listened. 'I can't hear anything.'

'It comes and goes.' Lewis paused. 'It's either me or maybe there's something wrong with the ship.'

'Mr Lewis, I'm going to speak to Mr Holden about having you moved out of here.'

'You mustn't make a fuss on my account. You promised that you wouldn't.'

'I promised that I wouldn't with the captain. Unlike the captain, Mr Holden isn't an unreasonable man.'

Holden closed his book when Josephine sat in the vacant deckchair beside him.

'You've got to do something about that poor man shut up in the bow compartment,' Josephine said without preamble.

'Me?'

'You're the owner.'

'I represent the owners,' Holden corrected.

'Which right now amounts to the same thing. It's inhuman shutting him up down there. He didn't kill his wife and you know he didn't.'

'Do I?' Holden asked blandly.

Josephine sensed that the fair-haired Englishman was mocking her. She broke her own rule and allowed the anger welling up to control her behaviour.

'Listen – if you were any judge of character you would know

that Mr Lewis could not have possibly murdered his wife. My God, you've only got to look at him.'

'You mean his mild expression?'

'Yes.'

'Crippen had a mild, butter-wouldn't-melt-in-my-mouth expression, Jo. And I'll tell you something else – not one of the passengers or crew has a motive for killing Mrs Lewis.'

'How do you know?'

'Because I know all your backgrounds – even the backgrounds of those two nuns.'

Josephine stared at Holden. He was regarding her with a half smile that she found infuriating. 'Even me?'

Holden hooked his hands together behind his neck and gazed up into the clear sky. 'Even you, Jo. I know about your father's illness, and that he's not expected to live much longer which is why you're so anxious to return home. You must be as worried as everyone else about the time this voyage is taking and yet you've said nothing. I admire you for that.' He stood. 'I'll do my best with the captain.'

13

It was three hours after midnight on 8 April when Kramer edged back the lifeboat cover and gazed up at the arching splendour of the Milky Way vaulting across the clear tropical sky.

He swung his binoculars to the north in the direction the *Tulsar* was heading and quickly picked out the visible portion of the Plough in Ursa Major. Two of the stars were known to mariners as the Pointers. Kramer located them and followed the direction they indicated to the horizon. He found the point of light almost immediately. He had seen it before on his visit to Germany in 1936. It was a star never seen by those who spent all their lives in the southern hemisphere. Poised several light years above the North Pole to an accuracy of one degree, it was the star that had guided mariners through the ages from the first tentative wanderings of the Phoenicians and the Vikings. It was a star whose reliable presence had triggered the explosive spread of civilization, exploration and trade in the northern hemisphere, while culture in the southern hemisphere, with no equivalent accurate star, had stagnated.

It was Polaris – the Pole Star.

Its appearance told Kramer that the *Tulsar* had either crossed the Equator or was very near to crossing it, a surmise that was confirmed twenty minutes later when he completed the calculations based on his sextant observations.

At one minute before his scheduled transmission time, he switched on his Afu and waited for it to warm up. He wondered how far away the U-boat was and whether it would hear him.

14

'Captain to control-room! Captain to control-room!'

Milland was wide awake and strapping on his leg before the loudspeaker on the bulkhead clicked into silence.

'This had better be good, Mr Sarne,' he growled when he stumped into the control-room.

The first officer held out a signal flimsy. 'The best news since we left Kiel, captain.'

CUCKOO TO EAGLE
TULSAR 2N 30W HEADING DUE NORTH 25 KNOTS

'The first signal we've managed to pick up direct from the *Tulsar*,' said Sarne. 'The keying errors were in the right places so there's no doubt that it's genuine.'

'Two degrees *north*!' Milland exclaimed jubilantly. He moved to the chart-table and examined *U-330*'s position. The U-boat was just below the Tropic of Cancer, six hundred miles northwest of the Cape Verde islands. He plotted the *Tulsar*'s position on the chart and measured the angle between it and the U-boat with a pair of dividers.

'Twenty degrees,' Sarne commented, hoping his voice didn't reveal his mounting excitement. 'One thousand two hundred miles between him and us. We're on the same longitude – so if he maintains his maximum speed on a northern heading and we hold our maximum speed on a southern heading, we'll be converging at fifty knots . . .'

'And intercepting in twenty-four hours,' Milland finished.

'With luck. And if this weather holds.'

The two men studied the chart to confirm their deductions.

'Chief!' said Milland abruptly. 'Steer one-seven-five!'

U-330 heeled gently as her bows came up to her corrected course.

Milland watched the gyro-compass with satisfaction. 'Okay, chief. Full speed ahead both!'

In the engine-room the diesel-mechanics stuffed cottonwool in their ears and slid the throttles wide open.

15

Gerrard regarded the large black box with some suspicion. It was unlike any piece of equipment he had ever seen before and had been installed in the *Tulsar*'s radio-room by naval electronics experts from Simonstown during the whaler's Durban refit. Jack Colby, the *Tulsar*'s amiable Canadian radio-operator, had been given a brief training on the equipment's operation and maintenance.

'For Chrissake, Jack,' Gerrard muttered. 'Who in hell could be shadowing us at the speed we've been keeping up?'

Colby shrugged. 'Search me, cap'n. All I'm saying is that I've picked up his signals two nights running. Always on the same bearing – astern of us – and at the same strength. Whatever it is, it's keeping up with us.'

Gerrard spun a chair round and sat astride it, resting his chin on the chair back while he stared at the black box. It was a recent British invention – High Frequency Direction Finding apparatus – known officially as H/F D/F and unofficially as 'Huff Duff'. It was a remarkable piece of equipment because it enabled the direction of radio signals to be pinpointed at sea without the need of shore receiving stations equipped with steerable antennae. Jack Colby had demonstrated to Gerrard how the apparatus worked. It was amazingly simple; in the centre of the black box was a tiny screen less than six inches in diameter. When signals were picked up by the Huff Duff's antenna, they appeared on the screen as a glowing ellipse. All the operator had to do was spin a wheel to tune the ellipse into a hard line, and the angle of the line across the screen gave the bearing of the source of the signals. Even short bursts could be quickly located. The British had developed the equipment to locate the position of talkative U-boats shadowing convoys. Hitherto, rapid radio direction-finding at sea had been impossible.

While Gerrard was prepared to accept that the equipment worked, he was not prepared to accept that it was possible for a ship to shadow the *Tulsar* without being seen during the clear weather they were enjoying, *and* for the ship to cling doggedly to the same position astern of the *Tulsar* irrespective of the *Tulsar*'s frequent course changes. It just wasn't physically possible and he told Colby so. The lanky Canadian gave another of his indifferent shrugs.

'Suit yourself, cap'n. But there ain't nothing wrong with that piece of fancy gear. It can pinpoint Rio a treat. Someone is following us, sure enough – sitting right on our tail.'

Gerrard woke Holden an hour before dawn. Despite the hour, the Englishman was alert and relaxed as he sat on his bunk listening to what Gerrard had to say.

'Colby is convinced that we're being shadowed,' said the American.

Holden raised his eyebrows. 'By what?'

'Search me. But Colby's certain from that Huff Duff thing that there's something sitting on our tail.'

Even Holden looked surprised. 'I would've thought it impossible.'

'That's exactly what I said.'

'So what do you plan on doing?'

'Nothing.'

'Is that wise?' Holden inquired.

'Okay – so maybe we start zig-zagging again.'

The suggestion pained Holden. 'Why not do the obvious?'

'And what's that?' Gerrard demanded suspiciously.

'Take a look.'

Gerrard levelled the Northrop seaplane out at fifteen thousand feet and circled to enable Holden to sweep the horizon with binoculars. In the clear, golden light of the early morning it was possible to see over a hundred miles at that altitude and yet the only movement Holden could see on the glittering blue expanse of the tropical Atlantic was the constantly-spreading V of the toy-like *Tulsar*'s shining white wake.

'Can you go higher?' Holden yelled above the roar of the engine.

Gerrard opened the Wright Cyclone's throttle and eased the tiny monoplane into a gentle climb. The horizon stretched further and further away and began hazing into a subtle blend with the flawless blue sky.

'Clearest I've ever know it!' Gerrard yelled to his companion.

And still there was nothing.

Gerrard levelled the Northrop out at twenty thousand feet. Holden became aware of the tightness in his chest caused by oxygen-depleted air. He kept searching with the binoculars. Visibility was excellent in all directions. The *Tulsar* was completely alone in the centre of a circle of ocean three hundred miles in diameter – an insignificant speck in the middle of a vast blue nothingness.

Holden lowered the binoculars and shook his head. Gerrard cut power and lost height in a series of wide, sweeping circles round the *Tulsar* while Holden kept searching. Gerrard was about to call Colby on the radio to tell him that he was coming in but returned the microphone to its hook when he saw the whaler losing way and stopping. He flew over the *Tulsar* at five hundred feet with the intention of landing the seaplane on the leeward side of the ship. It was then that he spotted something wrong with the cover on one of the port lifeboats. He opened up the engine, pulled the seaplane round in a tight turn, and flew back over the *Tulsar* for a closer look.

'Torn lifeboat cover,' he shouted in response to Holden's query.

'Serious?'

'Yeah – a lifeboat can fill with several tons of water from heavy seas and squalls. One crashed down on a deck damn near killing two men on my first trip.'

Gerrard carefully gauged a long trough in the ocean's lazy swell and quickly cut power when the seaplane's floats touched the surface. The tremendous water drag on the speeding floats hauled the seaplane to a stop in less than a hundred yards. He taxied the wildly bucking aircraft into the relative calm afforded by the *Tulsar*'s drifting bulk and anxiously watched the ship heaving ponderously towards them. The derrick was swung out with a Malay boy clinging precariously to the hoist. Gerrard cut the engine so that the boy would not be mangled by the seaplane's spinning propeller. For crucial seconds Gerrard and Holden were wholly dependent on the boy's agility, unable to taxi clear of the *Tulsar*'s looming bulk if trouble threatened.

The boy's feet landed on the wing. There was the sound of the hoist being shackled to the seaplane's lifting-point. A second later a pair of large intelligent eyes looked down through the clear canopy. The lad gave Gerrard the thumbs-up sign and repeated the gesture to the ship for the benefit of Piet who was manning the donkey engine.

The big Afrikaner engaged the donkey engine's clutch and lifted the seaplane clear of the water. Willing hands guided the floats down on to the seaplane's platform and held the canopy open for Gerrard and Holden.

'Nothing,' Gerrard announced to Colby who was watching quizzically from the circle of chattering Malays and Lascars. 'Absolutely nothing. Not even porpoises. You might as well toss that Huff Duff gizmo over the side.'

Gerrard jumped down to the deck followed by Holden. Colby looked at Holden for confirmation. The Englishman gave an expressionless nod.

'Piet!' Gerrard yelled. 'The cover on lifeboat six has got a rip in it you can drive a bus through. Have it fixed right now.'

Piet climbed down from the derrick operator's saddle and barked an order to the Malay boy who had secured the hoist to the seaplane.

The passengers had watched the seaplane's launching and recovery with great interest because it made a welcome break in the ship's monotonous routine. Josephine pushed through the small crowd towards Holden.

'Enjoy your trip?'

'Fine,' said Holden, brushing his lightweight suit with his hands and looking in concern at an oil stain. 'Whale steaks for dinner had we spotted anything.'

Josephine was not amused. 'Have you spoken to him about poor Mr Lewis?'

'Have you got anything that will get this stain out?'

'What about Mr Lewis!' Her almond eyes went round with anger. 'Well?'

'There are other problems to deal with at the moment,' was Holden's unhelpful reply.

Josephine saw Gerrard moving towards the bridge steps. On an impulse she suddenly pushed forward and grabbed hold of his arm.

'Captain Gerrard –' But she got no further for there was a loud report from aft followed by a blood-chilling scream. Josephine followed Gerrard and Holden as the two men raced down the port deck towards the stern. There was a rush of passengers' feet behind her and then loud gasps of dismay. Josephine was dimly aware of Mrs Eli Vanson's screams as she was dragged away from the scene by her husband.

Gerrard's arm was round the shoulders of the half-naked Malay boy who had jumped down on to the seaplane. For a second Josephine thought she was going to faint when she saw his terrible injury. Blood was pumping from the boy's neck and coursing across the deck.

'My God,' she whispered. 'Oh, my God.' Despite her shock, she had the presence of mind to rip a panel out of her dress. With a fleeting, grateful glance, Gerrard tore the cloth from her fingers and rolled it into a ball which he pressed against the deep wound that traversed the boy's chest and ended in his neck.

Josephine was dimly aware of Piet's booming voice behind her bellowing at everyone to get back.

'Hold it in place,' Gerrard commanded Holden.

Without hesitation, the Englishman pressed his hand against the sodden cloth while Gerrard tried to staunch the flow of blood by digging his fingers hard into the boy's carotid artery.

'Baas . . . boat . . .' the boy moaned. 'Boat . . . boat. . .'

Blood and spittle frothed between the boy's lips and flecked Gerrard's arms.

'Okay, sonny,' said Gerrard gently, sliding his free hand under the lad's body. 'Don't try to say anything.' He glanced up at Josephine and Holden. 'We've got to get him down to the sick bay and we've got to carry him level. Okay – lift when I say.'

Holden supported the boy's back while Josephine carefully slid her arms under his knees. They lifted the boy when Gerrard gave the word and carried him through the silent crowd while Gerrard kept his grip on the carotid artery. A sailmaker's awl fell from the boy's fingers as he was lifted on to the stainless steel table in the sick bay.

Gerrard took his fingers away. The blood didn't resume pumping from the ghastly wound. He held the boy's wrist for half a minute before carefully placing the tiny brown hand across the still chest. He avoided looking at Josephine and Holden, and she knew that it was unnecessary for him to say anything.

One of the two Ursuline nuns appeared in the doorway. She looked anxiously from face to face and then at the still form on the table. 'Is there anything we can do?' she asked.

16

U-330's speed was pushed up to an incredible twenty-seven knots in the ideal weather conditions that were prevailing in mid-Atlantic.

Chief engineer Otto Munt's calculations showed that the two

roaring Maybach diesels were consuming fuel at the rate of quarter of a ton per hour. But Milland wasn't concerned; the *Tulsar* would have ample oil to enable *U-330* to replenish her tanks.

Despite the appalling bucking motion of the charging U-boat, Milland had plenty of work for the crew. Ready-use ammunition lockers by the 104-millimetre and 37-millimetre guns were filled and the guns themselves cleaned of saltwater deposits and greased. Even the quadruple 20-millimetre anti-aircraft guns were checked and loaded with long, snaking belts of tracer. Once Milland was in range of the *Tulsar*, he was determined to bring all the U-boat's considerable firepower to bear immediately – especially on the bridge and wheelhouse. With Gerrard dead there was a chance that the whaler could be persuaded to surrender. With Gerrard alive, there was no chance. Although Milland knew nothing of how Gerrard would behave under conditions of war, he knew enough about his adversary's character to make a shrewd guess that Gerrard would sooner scuttle the *Tulsar* than allow it to be captured – especially by a U-boat.

Milland thought of the times he and Gerrard had spent together: the long voyages down to the desolate, frozen wastes of the Southern Ocean – hunting amid the grinding nightmares of fog-shrouded icebergs in their relentless pursuit of the immensely profitable schools of mighty blue whales. On one occasion their bonuses had amounted to a thousand dollars each which they had blown in a memorable two weeks of warm Australian beer, hot-blooded Sydney waterfront prostitutes in dingy bedrooms who knew how to separate a man from his money painlessly, and chilly magistrates in austere courtrooms who knew how to do it painfully.

But that had been before his leg had been crushed by a blue whale breaking loose on the *Tulsar*'s slipway and Gerrard's greed had made him into a cripple.

17

It was thirty minutes since the murder of the Malay boy.

Holden reached the corner of the superstructure and dropped flat on his stomach, holding the *Tulsar*'s Lee Enfield rifle across his forearms, army fashion. He crawled behind a rearing ventilator shaft and peered cautiously down the weatherdeck to where the Malay boy had been shot. He heard Gerrard move behind him.

'You see anything?'

'He must be in the lifeboat,' Holden replied calmly and aimed the rifle at the lifeboat.

'Whoever it is we, want him alive,' Gerrard reminded Holden.

Holden said nothing. He had no doubt that the man in the lifeboat was Kramer. If Kramer was taken alive the chances were that with the ugly mood Gerrard was in over the recent killing, Kramer might talk to save his skin. Holden didn't know why Kramer had stowed away on the *Tulsar* but he did know that it would be dangerous to let Kramer live.

'You in there!' Holden shouted. 'I'm giving you five seconds to come out! You hear me!'

Silence.

Holden fired. The Lee Enfield kicked like a mule against his shoulder and the shot chewed into the heavy pulley block that secured the bow end of the lifeboat to the davit. He worked the bolt and sent two more rounds crashing into the ash block. The lifeboat swayed dangerously.

'Neat,' Gerrard commented admiringly. He raised his voice. 'Are you coming out or do we shoot you out?'

Holden fired again. The ropes holding the lifeboat parted. The bow crashed on to the deck and twisted sideways, spilling folding oars and water tanks across the steel plating. There was a movement under the tangle of ropes and canvas. Kramer had lost his pistol when the lifeboat crashed down. He cursed and thrust his hands high above his head.

'Don't shoot! Don't shoot!'

He stood up. A wild, unkempt, filthy man with a savage look of defiance in his eye.

Gerrard lunged forward and knocked the Lee Enfield down just as Holden pulled the trigger. The bullet smacked against the deck near Kramer's feet and zinged skywards, causing Kramer to hold his hands even higher.

'Don't shoot, you bastards!' he snarled.

'I thought we wanted him alive, Mr Holden?' Gerrard observed caustically.

Holden assumed a sheepish smile. 'I thought he was holding a gun.'

Holden completed his examination of Kramer's suitcase Afu and closed the lid. 'Ingenious. Ten watts' power – about three-hundred miles' range – possibly ten times that at night.'

'For Chrissake,' Gerrard muttered, taking the set from Holden and turning it over in his powerful fingers. 'All we've got to do now is find out who the bastard's been talking to.'

'You think he'll talk?'

'He'll talk,' said Gerrard grimly.

The determined note in the American's voice worried Holden. 'He's a spy and a murderer,' he pointed out. 'The British authorities are the right people to deal with him.'

Gerrard angrily stubbed out his cigar. 'Listen, Mr Holden your government may own the *Tulsar* but she's still a US-registered ship and subject to US law. And under the law, I have the power to carry out any investigation I please. Right now I aim to find out from that murdering bastard who he is, who he's been talking to and why.'

Holden wrestled with his inner dilemma: to raise too many objections to the interrogation of Kramer might arouse the American's suspicions. On the other hand there was the danger that Kramer might talk and tell everything. If Kramer did confess, Holden wondered whether he would be able to talk himself out of trouble by saying that Kramer was lying. Everything depended on Kramer and the lengths Gerrard was prepared to go to in his questioning. He looked up into the American's grey eyes and guessed that the pressure Gerrard was prepared to put on Kramer would be considerable.

Holden nodded. 'Okay, captain. We question him.'

'Piet!' Gerrard yelled out.

'Cap'n?' the Afrikaner inquired, poking his head round the day-cabin door.

'You can release Lewis from the bow compartment. Tell him we've got the guy that killed his wife, and get Miss Britten to fix him up with a meal. We'll have our prisoner in now.'

Kramer was frogmarched into the cabin between two Lascar greasers who were none too gentle thrusting him into a chair. His hard eyes glared at the two men sitting opposite him but he gave no hint to suggest that he had recognized Holden.

'Name?' Gerrard fired.

Kramer's eyes flicked to Gerrard and blazed hatred from the depths of his straggling hair and beard.

'Name?' Gerrard repeated.

Kramer hollowed his cheeks and spat. The glob struck Gerrard in the face. The American lifted his wiry forearm to wipe the mess away and completed the movement by bringing the back of his hand hard across Kramer's face. Blood trickled from the corner of the German's mouth. His lips curled into a contemptuous smile.

'Name!'

Kramer's smile broadened but he kept his eyes firmly on Gerrard. At no time did he look at Holden.

'Piet,' Gerrard said to the Afrikaner who had just entered the cabin. 'Go fetch me a two-inch chisel and a heavy hammer.'

Gerrard sat back in his chair and watched the German carefully. The blood soaking into his whiskers gave his face the appearance of a grotesque, grinning mask.

Piet entered a minute later and placed a hammer and chisel on the desk.

'Thanks, Piet.' Gerrard picked up the chisel and ran the ball of his thumb along the gleaming edge, producing a thin line of blood. He nodded to the Lascars. 'Spread his left hand out.'

Kramer tried to struggle but the days he had spent in the lifeboat had weakened him considerably. The two sailors had little difficulty in forcing his hand down on to the desk.

'Hold his little finger out,' Gerrard commanded, holding the chisel in one hand and the hammer in the other.

The atmosphere in the cabin suddenly became very tense. Gerrard matched Kramer's smile with one of his own and rested the edge of the chisel across Kramer's little finger just below the knuckle.

'Well, fella,' said Gerrard cheerfully. 'I guess you don't have to be told what I'm planning. I'm going to chop your fingers off one by one until you decide to answer my questions.' He held the hammer poised two feet above the chisel's handle. 'Name?'

Kramer's mask-like smile became a glare of defiance.

There was a sharp crack as Gerrard brought the hammer down.

Holden muttered an involuntary, 'Christ.'

Kramer made not a sound but his arrogant expression changed to bewilderment when he saw the severed end of his little finger lying on the desk several inches from his mutilated hand. Blood was springing from around the shattered bone protruding from his knuckle.

'Now his thumb.'

The Lascars spread Kramer's thumb out on the desk.

'Name?'

Kramer stared down at the desk in silence. Holden's hopes that the German-born Afrikaner would be able to hold out began to rise.

'Cap'n –' Piet began.

'Shut up!'

The prisoner looked up at Gerrard with lustreless eyes. He suddenly shrank from the touch of cold steel as Gerrard rested the chisel's cutting-edge on his thumb.

'Paulus Kramer,' he croaked.

'Who were you transmitting to?'

Kramer didn't answer. Gerrard yanked Kramer's head up by his beard and repeated the question.

'A U-boat. For shit's sake do something about my finger!'

Gerrard caught Piet's eye and inclined his head to the door. 'And you,' he said to the Lascars. The three men left the cabin leaving Holden and Gerrard alone with Kramer who was desperately pressing his finger into his left wrist to stem the flow of blood.

'Let it bleed,' said Gerrard. 'It'll help keep it clean.'

Kramer relaxed his grip. Blood flowed afresh from the gory mess where his little finger had been. The finger itself lay palely in its own macabre pool of blood.

'What's the U-boat supposed to do?'

'Capture this ship,' said Kramer.

Holden decided to take part in the questioning in the hope that he would be able to lead Kramer off dangerous ground. 'Do you know what our cargo is, Kramer?'

'Yes.' The answer was spat out. The prisoner's spirit was returning. 'Gold. You've got to do something about my finger!'

'How did the Germans find out about the gold? Have they got spies in the Reserve Bank?'

Kramer saw the lead offered in Holden's question and seized upon it. 'Yes. Several.'

'Have you broadcast our position to this U-boat?' Gerrard asked.

Kramer nodded. 'But I swear to God that I don't know where the U-boat is. Please – my finger . . .'

'How often do you talk to them?'

'Every night between midnight and three.'

Gerrard grinned. 'You're right-handed, Kramer? You wanna know why I was so considerate and worked on your left hand?'

Kramer made no reply.

'Because you'll need your right hand to talk to your U-boat friends at the usual time. You agree to that and I'll consider trying to sew your finger back on.'

18

CUCKOO TO EAGLE

TULSAR STOPPED WITH FOULED PROPELLER 9N 35W PLEASE GIVE YOUR POSITION AND ESTIMATED TIME OF INTERCEPT

Milland read through the signal again and gave it back to Sarne. He turned to Venner. 'And there definitely was no keying error in the fifth character of the text?'

'It's dificult to say, captain,' said the radio operator. 'He sent three times as he usually does. The error was there in the second transmission but not in the others. The trouble is that his Morse is so bad that it's hard to tell which are genuine errors and which are not. I needed all three of his transmissions to get the whole message down.'

'And it's the first time he's asked us for information on our position,' Sarne added.

Milland looked down at the chart. 'If Cuckoo's signal is genuine, we could intercept the *Tulsar* just before dawn.'

'*If* it's genuine,' Sarne commented.

Milland was undecided. Until *U-330* was within hydrophone range in order to get a fix on the *Tulsar*'s bearing, he was wholly dependent on the signals from the agent aboard the whaler for even the slightest chance of intercepting her. He carefully weighed the various considerations and came to a compromise decision:

'We'll treat Cuckoo's position of the *Tulsar* as genuine but we won't supply him with ours. We'll merely send him a brief acknowledgement of his signal.'

'Yes, captain.' Venner returned to his radio compartment.

Milland gazed impassively at Sarne for a moment before allowing his face to relax into a grin. 'Set course to intercept, Mr Sarne.'

The news that *U-330* was closing with her quarry swept through the boat in minutes. Bottles of beer, which Milland had strictly forbidden to be brought aboard, mysteriously appeared and were passed around by a jubilant off-watch crew.

Milland smiled thinly to himself as he hauled himself hand over hand up to the bridge. The lookouts were singing in perfect unison in the darkness, not allowing their song to interfere with their vigilance.

What the hell, Milland thought, deciding not to castigate them, they've earned it.

19

Jack Colby straightened up from the *Tulsar*'s Huff Duff set. 'Due north,' he announced. 'Range between a hundred and three hundred miles.'

Gerrard groaned. 'For Chrissake, Jack, can't you be more accurate than that?'

'That's pretty good,' said Holden. 'The Huff Duff is only accurate at providing a U-boat's bearing – not its range.'

'And it was a bloody short transmission,' Colby added.

'Jesus Christ!' Gerrard exploded. 'The bastard could be on top of us before dawn!'

Holden rose to his feet. 'Which means we had better set about putting my plan into operation right now.'

Gerrard gaped at the Englishman. 'You're not serious?'

'Why not?'

'It's a crazy idea, that's why.'

'Only if it doesn't work,' Holden murmured, moving to the door.

Josephine picked her way through the feverishly busy carpenters working under floodlights on the flensing deck. She had to shout at Holden to make herself heard above the sounds of nails being hammered into timber. Holden had his sleeves rolled up and was busily sawing through a plank. The industrious Englishman's shirt was clinging to his sweat-drenched body. The sight was even more surprising than all the unexplained activity because she imagined that Holden was not the sort of man to exert himself if it could possibly be avoided. Then she noticed Gerrard armed with a claw-hammer tearing the nails out of packing-cases. Holden stopped work when he finally noticed Josephine.

'Mr Holden. Would you mind telling me what's going on? I'm gettng complaints from the passengers about the noise.'

'They'd be complaining even more if German U-boats start firing torpedoes into us,' was Holden's unhelpful reply.

'The noise is designed to frighten them away?'

Holden mopped his face with a silk handkerchief. 'How's Mr Lewis, Jo?'

'If he could get some sleep, maybe his temper will improve so that I can talk him out of his plans to sue the lot of you for wrongful arrest. Just what the hell is it you're building? A stage?'

'Something like that, Jo.' Holden resumed sawing and refused to be drawn further on the subject of the curious structure.

20

The cloud spreading from the west trapped the warmth rising from the ocean and layered the sluggish swell with a fine, warm mist. The night was unbelievably hot. Milland leaned on the U-boat's bridge coaming and wished that he could emulate the lookouts by stripping to the waist.

There was the sound of muted laughter from the foredeck where the off-watch crew had gathered to take advantage of the breeze generated by the speeding U-boat. The sensation of speed was heightened by the rolling clouds of mist that hurled themselves at the bridge, parting at the last second to avoid Milland and reuniting in the aft turbulence. There was a curiously dead atmosphere about the U-boat which Milland attributed to the cloying mist. Even the roar of diesel exhaust from the vent and the hiss and surge of water through the deck casing drains sounded muted and unreal.

'Control-room – bridge,' said Hans Fischer's voice.

Milland flipped the voice-pipe open. 'Bridge.'

'Time for another hydrophone sweep, captain.'

'Very good, Mr Fischer. Tell the chief to stop engines. I'm coming down.'

A minute later Venner settled his hydrophone headphones comfortably over his ears and switched on the first transducer. There were several of the sensitive underwater microphones grouped around the U-boat's hull which could be selected individually to pinpoint the direction of underwater noises.

Several minutes passed as Venner made minute adjustments to the knob that controlled the underwater microphone switches. Suddenly he tensed and pressed the headphones hard against his ears. 'I'm getting something. Very faint machinery or engine noises bearing one-eight-one.'

Milland's pulse accelerated. Virtually due south! The right direction! 'Range?' he fired at Venner.

'Can't say,' the radio-operator replied. 'It could be small engine thirty miles off or a large engine sixty miles off.'

Milland weighed up the problem. 'Well at least we've got a bearing on something. We'll run at maximum speed on the surface for another hour and stop for another hydrophone sweep.'

'Definitely a small diesel engine,' Venner announced an hour later.

Milland frowned. 'The *Tulsar*'s got a number of small diesels for her derricks and winches, but would the sound from one of those carry into the water? They're mounted up on deck.'

'How about an air-pump?' Sarne suggested. 'If they've got divers over the side working to clear a fouled propeller, the chances are that they're having to run an air-pump.'

Milland clapped his first officer on the shoulder. 'Of course! It's a damned air-pump!'

Venner checked the sound-level of the throbbing engine. 'In that case, I'd put its range at between ten and fifteen miles.'

'It's *got* to be the *Tulsar*,' Milland declared. 'Goddamn it, it's got to be!' He snatched down the crew address microphone and called Munt in the engine-room. 'Chief! Full speed ahead both!' He swung round to Fischer. 'Stand by with your gun crews, Mr Fischer.'

'Gun crews standing by, captain.'

'Boarding-party standing by,' Sarne called, not waiting to be prompted.

Milland rejoined the lookouts on the bridge. The gun crews emerged through the forward hatch and hurried to their respective weapons. Sarne and the twelve men that comprised his armed boarding-party were next to appear. All the men moved silently in their soft-soled shoes. They were well drilled in their various tasks – not a word was exchanged between them. After the boarding-party had inflated the U-boat's two dinghies, they sat down on the spray-drenched deck to be out of the gunners' line of sight once the shooting started.

'Control-room – bridge!' It was Venner's voice.

Milland acknowledged.

'Radar echo,' Venner stated. 'One-eight-four. Range six miles.'

'Chief!' Milland called. 'Stop engines! Half ahead on both electrics!'

There was a sudden silence from the diesel vent that was replaced by the soft purr of *U-330*'s electric motors.

'Range five miles,' Venner reported.

The grey U-boat ran on through the warm mist at a steady but silent eight knots.

'Have the searchlight sent up,' Milland requested.

Two ratings manhandled the heavy lamp through the bridge hatch and mounted it on the swivel bracket in front of the attack periscope. It was a cumbersome thing, rarely used because it had to be unshipped before the boat could dive, and the supply cable, which had to pass through the hatch, inevitably got in the way.

'Range three miles,' Venner informed. 'What's the tonnage of the *Tulsar*, captain?'

'Seven thousand. Why?'

There was a pause at the other end of the voice-pipe. 'These DT radar sets are pretty good on range,' Venner commented, 'but they're not so good on size indication. It seems a small echo for seven thousand tons.'

Milland chuckled. 'Be even smaller by the time we've shot away its radio mast and bridge.' Despite the bantering reply, there was no humour in his expression as he peered into the darkness. The mist was beginning to lift.

It's all been too easy so far. Something's wrong!

At that moment Milland heard the sound of the engine. Fischer heard it too and glanced expectantly up at the bridge.

'I heard it, Mr Fischer. You'll hold your fire until we're within five hundred metres as planned.'

Venner reported the range as one mile. Sweat trickled into the socket of Milland's artificial leg. He felt the leg shift out of position, moving the heel so that he felt off-balance and insecure.

Dear God – not that. Not now.

The engine was much louder. Thudding away in the thinning mist. It was the only sound in the night.

There should be other sounds!

Milland realized that he was letting his imagination take over his reason.

'Six hundred metres, captain.'

Milland's heart was hammering in unison with the unseen diesel engine. His lips moved nearer the voice-pipe as he gauged *U-330*'s approach.

'Bridge – control-room! Now!'

The helmsman spun his wheel to port and at the same time Munt shut down the electric motors. Milland snapped the searchlight on just as the U-boat went about. He aimed the beam of light in the direction of the throbbing diesel engine.

'Fire!'

The big 104-millimetre was the first to open up. There was a flash and a boom followed by the whine of the shell arching through the night. Then the 20-millimetre added its quadruple yammer, spitting streaks of white tracer at the target.

Except that there wasn't a target.

Milland stared through the smoke – ignoring the fumes stinging his eyes. There was nothing there! Dazed, he heard Sarne call for decreased elevation. The main gun boomed another shell across the water. The 37-millimetre quick-firing gun joined in the racket. Fischer was yelling at the men passing heavy shells in a human chain from the ready-use lockers. Confused and bewildered, Milland swung the searchlight beam backwards and forwards. And then he saw it: instead of a 7,000 ton whaling-ship, illuminated by the beam was a makeshift raft fabricated from planks and oil drums. In the centre of the deserted raft was a puffing donkey engine. There was a banner strung the length of the raft that bore a hand-painted query made famous by Walt Disney:

WHO'S AFRAID OF THE BIG BAD WOLF?

The gunner manning the 20-millimetre followed the searchlight beam. Splinters flew from the raft a second before the main gun scored a direct hit, blasting the raft to matchwood.

'Cease firing, you idiots!'

'Light to port!' yelled a lookout.

Milland spun round and stared in the opposite direction at the blinding light bearing down on the U-boat from less than fifty metres. The charging light separated. Frantically Milland swung the searchlight round, ignoring his displaced artificial leg. He caught a fleeting glimpse of what he thought at first was an E-boat. There were two of them.

'Open fire to port!' Milland screamed. 'Open fire!'

But the confused gunners were too late. There was a bright powder flash from the leading boat when it was within twenty metres of the U-boat. The distinctive sharp crack that followed the flash was a sound that Milland knew well – it was the sound of a harpoon-gun being fired. In that instant he realized with despair that the two craft were the *Tulsar*'s high-speed whale-catchers. The bulging warhead of the Svend Foyn harpoon struck *U-330* near the bow. The ensuing blast shredded the inflatable dinghies and swept Sarne and his boarding-party into the sea. The first whale-catcher sheered away, chased by tracer flashes from the 20-millimetre gun. But the gunner mis-judged the craft's speed and sprayed a seam of miniature waterspouts impotently into its wake.

The second boat came charging in. Milland saw what was

coming – a shadowy figure was crouched over the harpoon-gun and aiming it straight at the conning-tower. Milland jabbed the Klaxon button and threw himself flat. The blinding flash and numbing concussion deprived him of sight and hearing for precious seconds. He struggled on to his good leg in time to see the last of the gunners diving down the hatch. He saw Fischer struggling in the water but was unable to make himself heard above the Klaxon's strident blaring.

The U-boat's diesels burst into life. *U-330* gathered way, rapidly building up the necessary momentum for the crash dive that the Klaxon had initiated. Already water was flooding into the ballast tanks. In the chaos it seemed certain that Munt was going to take the boat down without waiting for confirmation that the bridge hatch was closed.

Another explosion shook the U-boat. There was the sound of a high-powered petrol engine howling past the boat, but Milland wasn't interested; his immediate concern was to get down the hatch and close it before the boat was swampled. He crawled to the opening and dangled his legs into the void while hanging on with one hand and groping for the hatch cover with the other.

The hatch refused to close.

The cable! The bloody searchlight cable!

'Hold it chief!' Milland yelled. 'For God's sake someone disconnect the searchlight! I can't close the hatch!'

He could hear a commotion from the control-room. Someone was shouting about flood water. Grimly, he doubled the cable round his wrist and heaved in the desperate hope that he could tear the cable out of the searchlight. It broke free on his third attempt and fell about his shoulders. Thankfully he slammed the hatch shut and turned the locking handwheel a second before the bridge was flooded.

Without warning, *U-330* suddenly canted down by the bow nearly causing Milland to lose grip on the ladder. He could hear Munt below bellowing something about getting the door closed. Then there were noises that chilled his blood: the surging roar of water flooding into the boat, and the terrible metallic crash that could only be an engine breaking away from its mountings.

By the time he had dropped into the control-room and steadied himself on the crazily-tilting floor, *U-330* had dived past the 150-metre mark and was plunging out of control towards the ocean floor, three miles below.

21

Dawn was probing the eastern horizon when Gerrard throttled back alongside Holden's boat and grinned broadly across at the Englishman. 'Some sport, eh, Mr Holden?'

Piet, who was manning the harpoon-gun on Holden's boat, gave a booming laught. 'Beats whales, cap'n.'

'How many hits did you manage, Mr Gerrard?' asked Holden. Brody centred the harpoon-gun on Gerrard's boat and called out: 'Three on the bow – all in the same place, like you said, Mr Holden.'

'Listen!' said Piet sharply. Holden shone the helm searchlight in the direction where Piet was pointing and picked out heads bobbing in the swell. There were seven men swimming with feeble strokes towards the two whale-catchers. Gerrard opened his throttle and eased his catcher alongside the struggling men. One by one Brody hauled them over the cockpit coaming. The seventh man was in a bad way; he gave a low moan when Brody grabbed his wrist. The man's hands were coated in oil causing Brody to lose his grip. The seaman made a grab at the man's collar and succeeded in tearing away his identity disc. Brody swore, tossed the disc in the cockpit and dived into the sea. He spent five minutes in a fruitless search for the missing German and climbed back into the whale-catcher, shaken and dispirited.

Holden manoeuvred his craft and shone the light on each of the pinched, miserable faces in turn. 'An uninspiring collection,' he observed.

'Reckon they understand that throat-disease language of yours, Piet?' Gerrard asked.

Piet leaned across and addressed the survivors in Afrikaans.

They replied with blank stares. Holden's excellent French produced the same result. Gerrard regarded them in contempt.

'How about English? Who speaks English?'

The men remained silent.

'They don't look much use,' said Gerrard, turning back to helm. 'Toss 'em over the side, Sam.'

'No!' said one of the Germans. 'That is forbidden. You cannot do that.'

Gerrard jerked the speaker to his feet by the lapels of his jacket. He noticed the single gold stripe below the five-pointed star on the man's sleeve. 'Can you speak English?'

'A little'.

Gerrard was surprised to see that the junior officer was scared of him. It was something he had not expected in a German.

'Name?'

Leutnant zur See Hans Fischer.'

'Well, Leutnant zur See Hans Fischer, next time I ask a question and you remain silent, I'll kick your fucking Kraut ass all over the Atlantic Ocean. Do you understand?'

'Jawohl, Herr Kapitan.'

'Yes fucking sir!' Gerrard roared.

'Yes fucking sir,' Fischer repeated miserably.

Holden jumped down into the cockpit of Gerrard's boat and picked up the missing man's identity disc. 'Was Peter Sarne your commanding officer?' he asked Fischer after examining the disc.

'Cap'n! Piet shouted.

The Afrikaner was pointing at the sea. Thirty yards from the two whale-catchers the surface was beginning to boil white.

'Air escaping from the U-boat, I guess,' Brody observed laconically.

The erupting bubbles spread rapidly until a sizable patch of the ocean was seething with life-giving air geysering from the unseen U-boat. The six survivors exchanged glances but remained silent as they watched the phenomenon. After a few minutes the bubbles gradually diminished and finally stopped, allowing the surface of the Atlantic to revert to its rolling black swell.

A picture formed unbidden in Holden's mind of the U-boat's

remains, its crew and hull crushed by the inexorable pressure, gliding down to the ocean's abyssal floor. Gerrard appeared to be thinking the same thing as he stared down at the sea. Then he looked up and caught Holden's eye. He gave a crooked smile.

'Well done, Mr Holden. A crazy idea. But it worked like a dream, huh?'

'A measure of insanity has no countermeasures,' said Holden before climbing on to the coaming and jumping back into his own boat.

22

Milland ignored the pain in his stump from his heavy landing on the control-room floor. He clung to the back of the helmsman's chair and demanded to know what had happened.

'Pressure hull holed!' the helmsman answered.

The impact of the man's words cleared Milland's veil of pain. Before he could speak men were stumbling through the control-room. 'Everyone aft!' Munt's voice could be heard bellowing. 'Come on, you dozy bastards! Move! Move! Move!'

'Port engine off its mountings!' shouted a distorted voice from the loudspeaker.

Milland snatched down the crew address microphone. 'Motor-room! Group up and full astern both motors!'

The downward tilt of the boat steepened. Milland grabbed hold of Munt and hauled him up the sloping floor into the control-room.

'Fist-sized hole in the bow torpedo compartment,' the chief engineer panted. 'I've got the door shut and blown compressed air in which is stopping further flooding.'

'All ballast tanks blown,' a petty officer reported.

Milland glanced at the large depth-gauge above the planesman's head. The needle was steady at a hundred and sixty metres; the reversing propellers were arresting *U-330*'s slide into the depths.

'The batteries won't hold for much longer,' said Munt, reading Milland's thoughts.

'How about plugging the hole?'

'It works in theory,' said Munt cautiously, 'but never in practice.'

'As it's our only hope, we'll try it,' said Milland cryptically.

'Now!' yelled Munt. He spun the locking-wheel and the bow torpedo compartment door burst open as though a bomb had gone off behind it, releasing a miniature tidal wave of seawater that nearly swept Munt's legs from under him.

Machin and Hoffman, two engine-room mechanics who had been selected for the task because of their considerable build, dived through the open door and were immediately up to their waists in water. The water gushing through the hole in the pressure hull appeared to possess the rigidity of an iron bar – twice it blasted the wad of cotton waste out of their hands as they struggled to wedge it into the hole. They succeeded in pinioning it in place on their third attempt but with water spraying around the edge of the plug like a giant watering-can rose.

Munt offered a silent, heartfelt prayer; Milland's improbable idea had worked because, by the grace of God, the hull had been holed in one of the few places where it wasn't obstructed by pipes and electric cables. He waded into the torpedo compartment and lifted the microphone off its hook.

'Okay, captain,' he informed Milland. 'You can start the pumps.'

At dawn *U-330*'s grey conning-tower lifted slowly above the surface of the Atlantic in time to greet the sun.

Part Three

WINNING

1

It was 11 April, two days after the attack on the U-boat; Milland was taking the loss of Sarne and Fischer badly and was in no mood for Munt's reasoned arguments. He ignored the chief engineer and concentrated on transferring *U-330*'s position on to the chart. Munt waited patiently. Finally Milland looked up.

'We're seven hundred miles west of Dakar on the west coast of Africa, Munt,' said Milland calmly. 'If we hold our present course we'll pass west of the Azores, and west of the Azores is the course the *Tulsar* will take to stay out of range of the long-range bomber squadron at Bordeaux. I think you should return to the control-room now.'

Munt stood his ground. 'With respect, captain. With the port diesel smashed we can't make any more than this twelve knots. We can't dive with that plug in the pressure hull *and* we've lost twelve men *and* we've lost the element of surprise. If stopping the *Tulsar* is that important then we must signal the OKM.'

Milland's patience was dangerously near breaking-point. He controlled himself with considerable effort because Munt was now his acting first officer and was entitled to express his side of the argument. He stood and pulled on his cap.

'We maintain radio silence, Munt.' He paused and stared hard at the chief engineer. 'I will tell you this much. So long as I have a boat, a crew, and guns, I shall continue to obey my orders. Obedience to orders is expected of me just as I demand it of you.'

Munt donned his cap, returned Milland's curt salute and left the cabin nursing the growing suspicion that Milland's hard stare had been that of a man who was in danger of losing his sanity.

2

Josephine fell into step beside Holden as he was taking his customary early morning walk around the weatherdeck.

'Good morning, Mr Holden.'

Holden returned the greeting without altering his measured pace.

'As I've made clear to you, Mr Holden, I never ask for or expect favours.'

Holden leaned against the rail and inclined his head, listening to the two Ursuline nuns who were singing a hymn near the stern. Their soft notes perfumed the clear morning air. 'But you're going to ask one now?' he inquired.

'I've talked Mr Lewis out of suing you and Captain Gerrard for wrongful arrest even though you both deserve it, *and* I've spent hours heading off complaints from the other passengers over the time this voyage is taking. We should've docked in New York a week ago.'

'Don't blame me for our zig-zagging, Jo. For all we know that U-boat we sank may have been just one out of an entire pack of them.'

'I've explained all that. Even so, Mr Vanson is demanding to know why we're doing about ten knots when we could be doing fifteen or more.'

Holden resumed walking. 'U-boats have hydrophones – underwater microphones. The faster we go the easier we make it for them to hear us. So what's the favour?'

'I want to find out about my father. Mr Colby said it would be possible to send a short-wave signal to Western Union in Panama for forwarding to New York. When I asked him how much it would cost he said that the sending of messages required the captain's permission. I asked the captain yesterday and he said that it was up to you. As this is still a US registered ship – a neutral ship, Mr Holden – and I'm prepared to pay out of my own pocket to send the cable, I don't see –'

'I'll tell Mr Colby that I've no objection to your message being sent, Jo,' Holden interrupted. He pointed to Piet who was standing on the bridge, signalling to him. 'Excuse me, but I'm wanted.'

Holden entered Gerrard's day-cabin and was mildly surprised to see Fischer standing stiffly to attention before Gerrard's desk. The young German officer had his cap tucked under his arm and was staring straight ahead at the bulkhead. He had obviously taken pains to ensure that his once-sodden uniform looked reasonably presentable.

Gerrard waved a battered, glowing cigar in Holden's direction and said to Fischer, 'He's the boss. Tell him your problems.'

Fischer's eyes flickered sideways to the blond Englishman. 'We are war prisoners, you understand. It is right that we should be treated so. The man Kramer is a spy. We should not be shut in with a spy.'

Gerrard snorted. 'Kramer is nothing but a cold-blooded murderer.'

'You are too, captain,' Fischer retorted, gaining confidence. 'You sank a U-boat last year and now you sink my boat. You are American. Neutral. Is that not so?'

Holden began to feel uneasy; he wondered what Kramer had been saying to his fellow captives in the bow compartment and cursed himself for not foreseeing the situation earlier. 'Leutnant Fischer is right, of course,' said Holden, smiling at the German. 'Prisoners of war should not be locked up with civilians. It's against the Geneva Convention.'

Gerrard was not listening but was staring thoughtfully at Fischer. 'Who told you about the sub I sank last year?'

Fischer drew himself up. 'My commanding officer,' he said proudly. 'Kapitänleutnant Milland.'

Gerrard's chair fell forward. Hot cigar ash dropped on to the back of his hand but he ignored it. *'Who?'* he choked.

The American's reactions startled the German officer. 'Kapitänleutnant Milland,' he repeated nervously.

Holden had raised his eyebrows and was regarding Gerrard with interest.

'Kurt Milland?' Gerrard almost shouted.

Fischer nodded.

'You mean Kurt Milland was the captain of your U-boat?'

Fischer was confused. 'But you knew of course? He told us that he had been selected for the command because he knew you.'

Gerrard absently brushed the ash off his hand. It was some seconds before he spoke. 'Kurt was my first officer on this ship. We were old buddies. In his last letter he said that he was a naval instructor. He never said anything about U-boats . . .'

Gerrard's voice trailed into silence. Holden seized the chance to put a question that was foremost in his mind. 'Why send a U-boat to intercept us? Why not send something faster? Or was there something special about your boat?'

'It is not permitted for me to answer,' said Fischer sullenly.

'How did he manage with his leg?' Gerrard asked abruptly. 'Christ – you can answer that.'

'Never trouble,' Fischer admitted, wondering how to bring the conversation back to the question of Kramer. 'After time we never thought about it.'

Gerrard shook his head. 'Christ – he had guts. I saw his stump once after he'd stood a rough watch off the Falklands. It was a mass of blood and blisters. No complaints. Nothing.' The American lapsed into a brooding silence.

Fischer remained at attention, hardly understanding what Gerrard had said.

Holden beckoned to Piet who was hovering in the doorway and said to Fischer: 'You'll have to remain with Kramer in the bow. We have no alternative accommodation. I'm sorry.'

Fischer was about to complain about the strange metallic grating noises that he and his men had often heard in the bow but decided that the two men would not be interested. He allowed Piet to lead him away.

'Odd that the Germans should send a U-boat against us,' Holden observed when he and Gerrard were alone.

But Gerrard made no reply; his thoughts were with Kurt Milland and the hauntingly vivid image of his crippled U-boat sliding helplessly into the silent depths.

3

'Stop engine,' Milland commanded down the voice-pipe.

The exhaust vent was silenced and *U-330* lost way. Milland had judged the order well, for the U-boat came to a wallowing stop in the middle of the widely-distributed patch of garbage floating on the surface.

Two men armed with long-handled boathooks went down on their knees on the deck casing and began fishing the débris aboard. 'Careful with the paper!' Milland shouted. 'I don't want it shredded!'

The men carefully unwrapped the sodden fragments from round the ends of their boathooks and spread them on the deck.

'Mueller!' Milland shouted at a man who was watching his colleagues curiously. 'You can swim. Round up all you can!' He pointed to the remains of a carton floating some hundred metres from the U-boat. 'I want that.'

Mueller reluctantly removed his grey naval-issue U-boat overalls and dived naked into the sea. He surfaced and struck out for the carton.

Milland swung down the ladder from the bridge and stumped along the deck, holding on to the jumping wire. He stopped when he reached the two men and stared down at the items of garbage they had gathered. Most of the pieces of paper were in such a state of disintegration that it was not possible to determine their original purpose. A greaseproof wrapper for a five-pound block of South African margarine had survived well but there was no reliable way of determining how long it had been in the water.

The water all round the U-boat was dotted with vegetable peelings. Milland realized that trying to estimate how much time had elapsed since the garbage was dumped would give a very hit-or-miss result. Nor could he be certain that the garbage had come from the *Tulsar* on the basis of the margarine wrapper, because South Africa was one of the Allies' principal food suppliers.

He studied the bits of waste bobbing on the rolling swell. The stuff was spread over an area roughly two hundred metres in diameter. He felt reasonably certain that had the garbage been in the water much longer than two days it would have been completely dispersed by the wind and current.

Mueller reached the side of the U-boat pushing the sodden remains of a large cardboard box. His colleagues helped him aboard and carefully laid his trophy out on the casing for Milland's inspection.

'Turn it over,' Milland ordered. 'Carefully, you idiots!'

One of the men gingerly peeled the limp cardboard from the casing and turned it over. The faded remains of a coloured label indicated that the carton had contained two dozen tins of South African peaches. Something had been pencilled on one of the carton's blank sides. Milland went awkwardly down on his good knee to peer closely at the pencilled characters. It was a scribbled delivery note. Judging by the hastily-formed letters, Milland guessed that the writer had been obliged to write the same thing on dozens of similar cartons. The delivery note said: TULSAR P/T NATAL D/BAN.

Without saying a word but his face set into hard lines, Milland gripped the jumping wire and pulled himself to his feet.

The three men watched his stocky frame stump back to the conning-tower.

He hauled himself back on to the bridge and flipped open the voice-pipe cover.

'Chief! Same course. Full speed ahead. Everything you've got.'

The rolling eased as *U-330* got under way again. Milland stared straight ahead where the U-boat's bow was aiming at the northern horizon.

Forty-eight hours, he thought. A thousand miles.

But his determination to catch and destroy his prey would not have been weakened had the distance between them been ten thousand miles.

4

Holden entered the *Tulsar*'s restaurant when tea and coffee were being served after lunch. He nodded to Herbie Lewis and placed an envelope before Josephine. 'Jack Colby's just received a reply to your message, Jo.'

Josephine tore the envelope open and read the signal. She crumpled the slip of paper and dropped it in the ashtray. 'I suppose you know what it says?' she remarked coldly.

'That your father has less than three weeks. I'm very sorry, Jo.'

'I don't want pity, Mr Holden. All I want is for this God-damn boat to get to New York.'

'There've been a lot of complaints, Mr Holden,' Herbie Lewis underlined for Josephine.

'Complaints I can deal with,' said Holden. 'Torpedoes are more troublesome.' He moved to the middle of the restaurant. 'May I have your attention please, ladies and gentlemen.'

The low buzz of conversation and the clink of china stopped as the passengers turned expectantly to the speaker. 'As you know, of course,' Holden began when he had everyone's attention, 'the *Tulsar* was bound for New York. But we've just received instructions from the owners that we're to dock at Falmouth in Cornwall.' Holden paused. A number of passengers, Josephine included, were gaping at him in frozen bewilderment. 'To get you home as speedily as possible, the company has booked first-class passages for you on an American liner sailing from Liverpool on –'

'Hold it. Hold it. Now just hold everything, Mr Holden.' It was Eli Vanson, cigar jammed in the corner of his mouth like a facial talisman, who had pushed himself forward. He was a man with a turn of phrase that was in no way inhibited or modified by the presence of nuns. 'Just what is this shit about us going to England?'

Holden wasn't given a chance to reply. In that instant the *Tulsar* gave a sudden, convulsive shudder and stopped, transferring its ten-knot momentum to its passengers and everything that wasn't fixed to the floor. There was screaming pandemonium as passengers, tables and chairs were hurled forward against the bulkhead in a panic-stricken, struggling mass of waving arms and legs. Someone cried out:

'We've hit a mine! We're sinking!'

Holden was badly winded by a crippling blow in the solar plexus. For a few seconds his consciousness was dominated by the need to suck air into his lungs. He rose to his knees and was nearly knocked sprawling by someone crashing past to get to the door. People were screaming as they struggled to disentangle themselves from tables and chairs and each other. Flesh was ground into the broken china that was everywhere. The well-ordered world of after-lunch coffee and conversation was snuffed out in less than two seconds and replaced by confusion and terror.

Holden climbed to his feet and pulled Josephine and Lewis clear of the blindly-stampeding mass of people trying to fight their way through the door. A minute passed and they suddenly realized that they were alone in the restaurant, apart from the two Ursuline nuns who were attending to a steward with a broken collar-bone.

'Are you all right?' the elder sister inquired.

The three appeared to have suffered nothing worse than minor cuts and bruises.

'What happened?' asked Lewis when he had recovered his spectacles from amid broken glass and china on the floor.

'Well, one thing's for sure,' Holden replied, leading the way to the door. 'It doesn't feel as if the ship's sinking.'

The *Tulsar* was lying stopped and rolling abominably in the heavy swell. Piet left the anxious knots of passengers and crew who were gathering round the lifeboats on the leeward side and hurried across to Gerrard.

'Bow compartment flooded, cap'n,' he said in answer to Gerrard's query. 'I guess maybe we've hit something pretty big.'

'Lucky you got the watertight door shut so quickly, Piet.'

Piet stared at Gerrard. 'It was shut already, cap'n, the prisoners –'

Before Piet could finish the sentence, Gerrard was racing down the side deck towards the bow. He leaned over the bulwark but the flare of the bow prevented him from obtaining a clear view of the bow's pointed stem where it met the waterline. The sluggish manner in which the *Tulsar* lifted to the swell felt exactly the same as the last time they had a flooded bow compartment after the ramming of the U-boat in the Indian Ocean. There was a dull grating from torn plates moving against each other every time the whaling-ship sank into a trough.

'No sign of a log or baulk of timber,' said Piet, joining Gerrard at the rail. 'So what did we hit?'

'Let's get this opened up, Piet,' Gerrard ordered.

The two men opened the hatch that gave access to the anchor-chain compartment that was located above the flooded bow compartment where Kramer and the six U-boatmen were trapped – possibly drowned.

Daylight fell on the great mass of galvanized anchor-chain and cable. There were two hundred fathoms of it – a little over twice the *Tulsar*'s length.

Gerrard signalled to the bridge to release the anchor. There was a loud clunk from the hydraulically-operated latches followed by a splash when the stockless anchor hit the water. It plunged down, its weight dragging the anchor-chain and cable through the hawsehole with a deafening roar.

The instant all the cable had been paid out, Gerrard jumped down. He dropped to his knees and pressed his ear to the steel floor. He could hear water surging back and forth in the flooded compartment. That meant that there was an air-pocket. He banged his fist down several times. A metallic tapping answered him. It was faint, barely audible above the noise of the grating plates and the sea, and yet it was too regular to be anything but man-made.

Gerrard secured the bowline around his waist while Piet passed the rope twice around the windlass.

Josephine and Holden looked on with the other passengers as Gerrard disappeared over the side of the bulwarks. Josephine leaned out and saw him fending his body away from the *Tulsar*'s stem with his feet. He mistimed one kick and sent himself spinning dizzily round. Piet kept the windlass turning slowly, gradually lowering Gerrard until the heaving green swell was reaching for his feet before falling away. One particularly heavy swell immersed him to his waist. When it bellied down, lifting him clear of the water, he had a brief glimpse of torn metal plates splayed outwards. He signalled to Piet to stop lowering him and stared at the point where the seething maelstrom met the bow's pointed stem. He cursed the foam that rendered the otherwise clear water opaque.

For a second the maddened foam was swept away by a clean, unbroken wave enabling him to see below the waterline and to appreciate the full extent of the disaster that had overtaken the *Tulsar*.

He made a circling motion with his finger for Piet to haul him up.

'It's the shit welding and riveting carried out by those clowns in Durban,' said Gerrard savagely when he was back on the foredeck. 'The plates have split right down the stem from waterline to forefoot and she's gaping open like a hippo on heat.'

Piet swore roundly in Afrikaans. 'Could we get them out through the split?'

'Not a chance. It's too small and they'd be cut to ribbons on the plates. The only way to get them out is through the floor of the anchor-chain compartment.'

'How, cap'n?'

'We cut a hole! How do you think?'

'As soon as we make even a small hole – whoosh! And their air-pocket is gone,' Piet pointed out.

Gerrard hadn't thought of that. 'Shit,' he muttered. He brooded for a moment. 'Shit,' he repeated. He looked up. Holden was regarding him thoughtfully.

'Any chance of carrying out the rescue operation while we're under way, captain?'

Gerrard gave a bitter scowl. 'At anything above two knots that plating is going to tear away from the frames. If the plates rip past the watertight bulkhead we're right up shit creek – the pumps could never cope. Sorry Mr Holden – looks like we're going to be stuck here awhile.'

*

An hour later Gerrard spread the plans of the *Tulsar* out on his desk for the benefit of Colby and Brody who were not as familiar with the whaler's design as Piet. Holden looked at them with interest and guessed that the freehand sketches Gerrard had given him in Durban were copied from these plans.

'We know two things,' said Gerrard. 'First, that at least one of them is alive, and second, to get them out and to repair the bow we're going to have to lift the *Tulsar*'s bow clear of the water.'

'Right out of the water, boss?' Brody's expression of surprise was the best his prizefighter's features could manage.

'High and dry,' Gerrard confirmed.

'Crazy,' Colby muttered. 'You're crazy – you know that?'

Gerrard gazed levelly at his radio-operator. 'Apart from rescuing those men, we've got to lift the bow somehow to repair it. If we try to move in our present state, the chances are that water pressure will break down the watertight bulkhead or split the hull open past the bulkhead. Either way, our chances of remaining afloat are slim to the point of vanishing.'

'How about moving our cargo aft?' Piet suggested. 'Two hundred tons of lead on the slipway will lift our bow marks a good way out of the water.'

Gerrard had an uninspiring vision of the *Tulsar*'s gold sliding down the whale slipway and splashing crate by crate into the Atlantic. He caught Holden's eye and grinned. The Englishman didn't respond – he seemed preoccupied with other problems. Gerrard turned to Piet.

'How do you stop the crates sliding into the sea?'

'Easy,' said Piet. 'Wedge the first row. No problem.'

'One helluva lot of trouble shifting two hundred tons of lead, boss,' said Brody.

'Why don't we dump it?' asked Colby. 'Christ – what's two hundred tons of lead worth compared with this ship?'

'A lot if it'll help lift our bow out of the water,' said Piet.

Gerrard gazed speculatively at Holden. 'Do you have any ideas, Mr Holden?'

The Englishman smiled. 'I was thinking that two hundred tons of lead moved aft will make the rolling that much worse and there will be a danger of the ship rolling right over.'

Gerrard stared at Holden and relaxed into a grin. 'You know

something, Mr Holden? For once you and me are thinking on the same wavelength. We're going to have to think of a sure-fire way of keeping the *Tulsar* stable.'

'How about flotation bags lashed around the bow?' Holden inquired.

'A great idea. The trouble with owners is that they're full of brilliant but impractical ideas. It just so happens, Mr Holden, that we're short on supplies of flotation bags.'

Holden was unmoved by Gerrard's sarcasm. 'The trouble with whalemen,' he observed boredly, 'is that they're usually short on imagination.'

For a moment Gerrard was sorely tempted to modify Holden's patronizing smile with his fists but the Englishman was no fool and ideas cost nothing to listen to.

'Okay,' said Gerrard wearily. 'Let's hear what's stewing under those golden locks.'

5

Five days later the long search was over.

Gerrard suddenly saw the silvery fountains of the whales' blow. He waggled his wings and climbed hard. The two catcher boats, following a routine that had always worked well, peeled away from each other and reduced speed to fifteen knots in order to make life reasonably tolerable for the harpoonists.

Gerrard positioned the seaplane above the sperm whales at a thousand feet and circled. He looked down. The catchers were sweeping in wide circles round the whales, closing into positions that kept them astern of the unsuspecting creatures. Piet's harpoonist was crouched behind his weapon – swivelling it towards the tail of the nearest whale. His left hand suddenly went up in the universal gesture of forward. Piet's catcher accelerated and swung to one side. As he overhauled the outside whale, the harpoonist's sights moved the length of its blue-grey back until they reached the massive, rounded prow of the head.

Gerrard saw the harpoon flash across the intervening distance and bury itself deep in the whale's brain. The explosive head erupted silently beneath the creature's spine resulting in what whalers call a 'clean' kill. One second the whale was an intelligent, living breathing, warm-blooded being. The next second it was a wallowing mass of profitable bone and tissue of which, the whalers said, everything could be turned into dollars except its blow. So sudden had been the whale's death that there had been no communication between it and its herd sisters; they continued their leisurely pace, not noticing that one of their number was being left further and further behind.

Piet's catcher veered away to allow his harpoonist to reload. Brody closed his launch in on the opposite side of the group. There was a brief puff of white smoke from the harpoon-gun that was snatched away by the wind. Another clean kill. The rope attached to the six-foot harpoon was paid out from a safety grill beneath the gunner's feet to reduce the danger of him becoming entangled and dragged down into the depths by a sounding whale. The Malay boys in the catcher's cockpit attached the end of the line to a large, bright orange buoy and heaved it into the water.

Piet's second kill was clumsy; the harpoon exploded against the bull's head, blasting an ugly crater in the blubber. In panic, the beast blew twice and sounded, its wildly thrashing tail beating the sea into a welter of foam before it disappeared. The three remaining sperm whales, a young bull and two cows, also sounded.

Gerrard guessed that the injured whale had dived too quickly to have charged its bloodstream with oxygen effectively; it was unlikely to remain submerged longer than ten minutes. Piet appeared to have thought the same for he steered his catcher to a point half a mile ahead of the spot where the whales had sounded. He swung his craft round in a wide circle while the harpoonist reloaded. But the gunner's second weapon was not needed; the dying whale appeared on the surface in the exact centre of Piet's circle and managed one feeble blow. Gerrard could see the sea turning red from the blood voiding from the terrible wound. Then the stricken creature went into its 'flurry' – the apt name by which whalers describe the death throes of an adult sperm whale.

Gerrard called Piet on the radio and congratulated him on the clean kills.

The *Tulsar* lay nearly an hour's flying time to the south. For several days it had been lying stopped – wallowing helplessly in the swell, at the mercy of the wind and any passing U-boat. Luckily they were well away from the convoy routes where U-boats were likely to be found. Now, at last, they had the means of carrying out the repairs to *Tulsar* to enable them to continue the seriously-delayed voyage to England.

6

The strain of having to run *U-330* without his two executive officers was beginning to tell on Milland. He glowered, unshaven and red-eyed, at Dieter Venner as though he suspected that his radio-operator was playing a practical joke on him.

'You expect me to believe such nonsense? You really think you can tell me that Robert Gerrard is catching whales? You think I'm stupid? You think he's stupid?'

'I'm merely telling you what I heard, captain,' said Venner evenly. 'I'm not saying that it was even the *Tulsar* I heard, but it was definitely someone radioing directions in English to a whale-catcher.'

'In the middle of the Atlantic – in the middle of a war?'

Venner wasn't prepared to argue. As an old hand, he recognized that Milland was suffering from end-of-patrol nerves in addition to the extra burden imposed on him.

'Well, Mr Venner?'

'Isn't there a whaling industry in the Azores, captain?'

'There is.' Milland glared forbiddingly at Venner. 'What of it, may I ask?'

'Perhaps it's one of their catchers?' Venner fervently wished that he hadn't heard the transmission.

'Have you ever been to Horta in the Azores?'

'No, captain.'

'The whalemen there are poor – very poor. They can barely

afford fuel for their catchers.' Milland's voice suddenly rose to shout. 'They certainly can't afford radio and they don't speak English!'

Venner capitulated. 'Maybe I was mistaken,' he muttered. He pulled his headphones on and turned back to his switches and tuners.

'The mistake was mine in accepting you as my radio-operator,' said Milland harshly.

Munt picked that moment to enter the control-room from the engine room.

'May I have a word with you please, captain?' The chief engineer's usually amiable expression was absent. Even during the anxious moments when *U-330* had so narrowly avoided disaster, his good humour had never deserted him.

'Well?' Milland demanded.

Munt glanced at the helmsman and petty officer engineer sitting at their controls. 'In your cabin or the wardroom please, captain.'

Milland stood his ground. 'What is wrong with the control-room?'

Munt read and correctly interpreted the danger signals. His heart sank but there was no alternative; he had to keep Milland fully informed. It was his duty; Munt had a highly-developed sense of duty. He licked his lips and tried not to meet Milland's eyes, glaring with menace and lack of sleep.

'The diesel's running hot, captain.' Munt paused, but Milland said nothing, forcing him to press on. 'The oil pressure is down ten per cent which is causing the camshafts and valve gear to overheat. I've increased the water flow to the heat exchangers, which helped, but the temperature's still creeping up.'

Milland regarded his chief engineer coldly. 'So?'

'I want us to stop so that I can look at the oil-pump.'

Milland's face was devoid of expression. 'For how long?' He omitted Munt's courtesy title of 'chief'.

'Two hours, captain.'

'That is out of the question. We must continue at full speed.'

The curt rejection of his request justifiably angered Munt. The commanding officer of a U-boat had a duty to listen to and to accede to the reasonable requests of the chief engineer. Munt stared levelly at Milland. 'I'm not questioning your order, captain, but I would strongly recommend that the oil-pump is examined as quickly as possible to prevent damage to the engine.'

Milland took a step nearer Munt. The two men's faces were inches apart. Munt noticed the beads of sweat standing out on Milland's forehead. 'That's exactly what you *are* doing!' Milland barked. 'You're questioning my orders. Why? Do you know what is at stake?'

'I know what's at stake, captain,' said Munt quietly.

His calm attitude seemed to enrage Milland even more. 'You think you can run this boat better, Munt? Mm? If you do, tell me how you expect this boat to carry out its duties when rolling about on the surface while you tinker with your engine. You know what we have to do, don't you? We have to capture the *Tulsar* and its gold. Or sink it. Something we can't do with our one engine stopped while you waste time tinkering – ' Milland realized that he was repeating himself and stopped in mid-sentence.

'We don't stand much of a chance of overhauling the *Tulsar* on one engine,' said Munt, trying to make his voice sound respectful. 'And none at all if the engine seizes up.'

Milland glared at Munt, suspecting insubordination. The chief engineer met his gaze without flinching.

'We press on at full speed,' said Milland stubbornly. Without waiting for a reply, he turned his back on Munt and swung his leg through the circular door that led to his cabin.

Munt caught Venner's eye. The radio-operator pointed a forefinger at his own temple and made a twisting motion, cunningly converting the suggestive gesture into a movement to brush a strand of hair away from his eyes.

7

By three in the morning the racket from the seamen working on deck was so intolerable that Josephine abandoned further attempts to sleep. She dressed and climbed the companion-way to the flensing deck. Mr and Mrs Eli Vanson were also on deck, well wrapped against the near freezing wind and spray, and morosely watching a gang hoisting the cargo crates out of the hold and manhandling them down the whale slipway where a stout timber barricade prevented the crates from sliding into the sea. Josephine's eyes adjusted to the glare from the portable floodlights and she saw that the *Tulsar* was so low by the stern that half the slipway was flooded. Seamen working near the stern were up to their waists in the black, surging water as they struggled with ropes to make the crates secure.

'Have they got the men out yet?' Josephine inquired.

'Christ knows,' Eli Vanson muttered. 'Christ – what a crummy ship – not even the Goddamn crew know what the hell's going on.'

'It's not her fault, Eli,' said Mrs Vanson reprovingly.

Josephine left them arguing and picked her way forward, carefully judging each roll and noting the positions of handholds in advance.

Holden was leaning over the bow bulwark beneath a cluster of floodlights that had been swung out on booms to direct their light down at the water. Josephine joined him and looked down. The sight of the whales came as a shock: the huge carcasses, lashed around the bow, were grotesquely swollen to almost double their normal girth. As she watched, the bloated beasts dipped in the swell, and the ropes around the bodies tightened, cutting deep into thick, resilient blubber.

'Why are they such a size?' she asked.

Holden appeared to notice her for the first time. She was shocked by the fatigue that was showing in the Englishman's face.

'They've been blown full of compressed air,' said Holden.

'Why?'

'To provide enough buoyancy to lift the bows clear of the water.'

A man jumped out from below the bow's overhang and landed on the back of one of the whales, steadying himself with a flenser's pick. It was Gerrard.

'So they haven't got them out yet?' she asked, guessing what the answer would be.

'Not yet. Another two hours. Maybe three. I don't know.'

Suddenly Josephine's problems seemed of little importance and her smouldering anger with Holden over the change of the *Tulsar*'s destination was gone.

'Look,' she said in a reasoning tone. 'There's no point in you staying here for the next three hours and freezing to death. I'll unlock the passengers' galley and make us some coffee. Come on.' She took Holden's arm and was surprised by his acceptance of her authority. She led the way down to the restaurant and pushed Holden into an armchair. He sat unresisting and uncomplaining – his eyes ringed with exhaustion.

'Stay there. I won't be five minutes fixing the coffee. And I guess you'd like an orange juice as well?'

Holden smiled faintly. 'Just the coffee, Jo.'

She returned a few minutes later bearing a jug of coffee only to discover that Holden had slumped forward and was sound asleep.

There was nothing to do but make him as comfortable as possible, and sit sipping coffee, waiting for the dawn.

Two hours later the men working on the rescue operation were ready to cut through the floor of the anchor-chain compartments to reach the trapped men. Piet and Gerrard passed cold chisels and sledgehammers down to the men who were working in the confined space. A minute later, those passengers who had managed to sleep that night were woken by the resounding clamour of steel upon steel

8

The rasp of the saw slicing into his shattered tibia brought Milland back to screaming consciousness; his spine arched like a bow with the agony.

'For Chrissake keep the chloroform drip going,' said a voice. The voice belonged to a pair of grey eyes between an unkempt mop of dark hair and a gauze mask.

Milland felt heavy hands on his chest that forced his shoulders on to the stainless steel table. Something was pushed over his nose and mouth. He tried to fight but the sickly sweet vapour filling his tortured lungs drained the pitiful reserves of strength left in his mutilated body. The pain, like molten lead being injected into his spinal column, began to fade although the sound of sawing seemed to get steadily louder.

'Christ, the bastard must have a casehardened steel shinbone.'

'How the hell should I know? I've never cut through one before. You let go of that artery and I'll start on you.'

Milland giggled to himself before drifting off to sleep. A minute passed and then they were shaking him.

'Captain . . .'

'Jesus Christ, what a mess.'

'I've seen worse.'

'Do I keep the drip going?'

'Captain!'

For God's sake let me sleep.

'Captain!'

Milland opened his eyes. The grey eyes and the gauze mask had gone. The man shaking him was wearing the grey shapeless tunic and baggy trousers of U-boat overalls. His shoulder mark bore the lightning flash insignia of a third-class radio-operator. He was one of Venner's men.

'I'm sorry, captain, but Mr Venner said to wake you. You didn't hear his call on the loudspeaker.' The U-boatman's eyes flickered nervously to the bulkhead-mounted loudspeaker above Milland's bunk.

Milland swore and sat up. He had taken to sleeping with his artificial leg strapped in place. For a sickening moment as he stood he experienced the sensation of phantom toes. And then the familiar pain returned to his stump as it took his weight, causing the sensation to vanish abruptly. He ignored the radio-operator and ducked through the watertight door into the control-room.

'You sent for me, Venner?' The sharpness in Milland's voice was not due to his having just woken, it was now a permanent feature of his character.

The petty officer was wearing his hydrophone headphones. He swung round on his swivel stool when Milland addressed him. 'Yes captain. I'm picking up a faint HE on the keel microphones which I can't account for. If we could stop –

'Our own propeller noises? You woke me because you can hear our own propeller noises?'

Venner kept his voice respectful. 'Noises I *can't* account for, captain. If we stop our engine I could –'

'Out of the question,' Milland interrupted.

Venner spun his stool round to his console without saying a word. The helmsman looked quickly round at Milland and hurriedly returned his attention to the gyro-compass. There was an embarrassed silence in the U-boat's control-room that was disturbed only by the labouring beat of the partnerless starboard diesel.

'What sort of noise?' Milland asked at length.

'An irregular clanging. I don't think it can be machinery.'

'Bearing?'

'Dead ahead but I can't be certain, captain. There's too much cavitation noise around the microphones.'

Milland lifted the interphone off its hook. 'Munt,' he said, not bothering to identify himself, 'stop your engine.'

In the engine-room Munt recognized Milland's voice and mistakenly thought that his captain had at last seen sense. He thankfully shut down the diesel engine that he had been anxiously watching and two mechanics immediately set to work to remove the suspect oil-pump.

Venner carefully adjusted the hydrophone bearing indicator. 'It's definitely dead ahead. It's not machinery and it's not fish.'

He removed his headphones and handed them to Milland who listened intently for a moment before returning them.

'You're right: a clanking noise. Man-made I'd say. How far?'

Venner didn't wish to appear indecisive but the truth was that he didn't know. To say that to Milland in his present mood would be inviting trouble. It was better to guess.

'Fifty miles, captain.'

Milland nodded. In a reasonable voice he said: 'Give me an accurate bearing.'

Venner settled the headphones over his ears and made a number of fine adjustments to the bearing indicator. It took him less than five minutes to establish that the curious noise was on a bearing due north of *U-330*'s position.

'Munt!' Milland barked into the interphone. 'Start your engine please. I want maximum revolutions.'

In the engine-room, Munt gaped at his two mechanics and shifted the interphone handset to his left ear. 'I'm sorry, captain, but you just gave the order to stop.'

'And now I'm telling you to start!'

'But I've got the starboard engine oil-pump stripped down.'

There was a pause, then: 'Did I say you could do that?'

'No, captain. But I thought –'

You thought wrong, Munt!' The two mechanics could hear Milland's voice coming from the control-room without the aid of the telephone. 'I want that engine started within two minutes!'

'But, captain,' Munt protested. He broke off when he heard the click of the receiver being returned to its hook. Five seconds later Milland's powerful frame filled the watertight door opening. His eyes took in the dismantled oil-pump lying on the engine-room's tiny work-bench.

'I'm sorry, captain,' said Munt quickly. 'But another five minutes' running and the pump impellers would be completely chewed up. It'll take at least two hours to fit new ones.' He picked up the damaged components and held them out for Milland's inspection. Suddenly he felt very angry; he shouldn't have to justify himself or his actions – it was the captain's duty to accept the word of his chief engineer.

Milland stumped forward and knocked the impellers from

Munt's hands. 'You disobeyed my orders when I specifically said that you were to keep the engine running!'

'But I thought when you ordered me to stop –'

'I'm not interested in what you *thought*!' Milland screamed, his face inches from Munt's. 'What concerns me is that you disobeyed orders!'

Munt fell silent. Milland suddenly regretted his boorish behaviour; he would need Munt's co-operation – but he wasn't going to apologize. 'We'll run on the electric motors,' he said, turning back to the control-room.

The order astonished Munt. Sustained surface running on the electric motors was strictly forbidden – there was the attendant risk of a U-boat finding itself with exhausted batteries and unable to dive should an emergency arise.

'Yes, captain,' said Munt respectfully. 'But such an order will require your signature in the engine-room log.'

The two men glared at each other in mutual dislike.

'Give me the log,' said Milland coldly.

Munt opened a locker and handed a hide-bound book to his captain.

Milland opened the log and scrawled his signature in the last column. 'You will also group up the batteries,' he said, snapping the log shut and returning it to Munt. 'I want every knot this boat can muster.'

The chief engineer replaced the book and shut the locker without speaking. Milland's order meant that both electric motors were required to drain the batteries at full load. Being a Type IXD, *U-330* had a range of a hundred and fifteen miles on her batteries at a top speed of only four knots. Which meant that after twenty-nine hours' running, unless he could repair the diesel, *U-330* would finish up wallowing helplessly on the surface like a dying whale – unless he did the unthinkable and deliberately disobeyed Milland's orders.

9

At noon, under a leaden sky that reflected the sombreness of the moment, the last of the bodies of the six drowned U-boatmen was hoisted out of the *Tulsar*'s bow compartment and laid out on the foredeck. The seventh and final body removed was Kramer's.

Gerrard and Piet started down in silence at the row of still forms and removed their caps. Kramer was easily recognizable by his bandaged finger and his straggling beard. Leutnant Fischer could be identified by the gold stripe on the tattered, blood-soaked remains of his jacket. Gerrard realized that he couldn't even remember the names of the other five. The sleeves of all the men's clothing were torn to shreds, and their hands and forearms were badly mutilated. An image formed in Gerrard's mind of the seven men tearing at the torn metal plating in their desperate but futile attempt to escape from the steel tomb of the flooded compartment.

The only sound from the passengers lined against the rope barrier across the foredeck was from the two nuns reading in muted tones from their missals.

'So what do we do with them, cap'n?' asked Piet at length.

Gerrard appeared not to have heard. Piet repeated the question.

'For Chrissake, Piet, I shouldn't have to tell you. We sew them up in canvas, weight them with lead, and bury them.'

Gerrard crossed to the bulwark and gazed down at the bloated sperm whales lashed around the *Tulsar*'s bow.

'We're going to have to be pretty damn quick fixing the bow,' Piet remarked practically. He pointed to a dorsal fin creating a V-wake as it homed in on one of the whales carcases. 'Mako,' he added, his tone expressing the sailor's traditional hatred and fear of sharks.

The primeval fish rolled over, exposing its pale belly, and drove its crescent jaws deep into the yielding blubber. Its sleek body gave a convulsive shudder and a mouthful of blubber was spooned neatly down the creature's gullet. The killing-machine shape of a hammerhead shark nosed cautiously at the smallest whale before withdrawing and then lunging, twisting its awkwardly-shaped head to one side. The triple rows of teeth sliced deep into the whale's flesh and clamped shut. From the state of all three whales, Gerrard could see that the sharks had been gorging themselves for some time.

'They'll be through the blubber soon,' said Piet phlegmatically, 'then whoosh. We lose air and the bow goes down.'

Gerrard cursed himself for forgetting the possibility of sharks deciding to feed on their buoyancy aids.

'There won't be time to fix the bow unless we catch more whales,' Piet observed.

'Christ, no – we wasted enough time looking for those three.' Gerrard thought for a moment. 'Supposing we cram those bales of coir into the bow compartment and shore them up against the split and then fother canvas round the bow on the outside?'

Piet nodded. Fothering was the ancient technique of stopping a major leak or repairing serious underwater damage by spreading a sail over the affected part of the hull and relying on water pressure and lashings to hold the canvas in place. 'Be okay if we jettison those crates, cap'n.'

'Hell, no. They go back in the hold.'

Piet's normally unruffled expression changed to one of disbelief. 'Are you serious, cap'n? The *Tulsar*'s not built for that sort of cargo. If we hit weather and the crates get lively without those bales of coir round them . . .'

'That's a chance we have to take, Piet. The crates go back just as soon as the bow's patched up.'

Piet knew Gerrard well enough to realize the futility of attempting to dissuade him from such a seemingly lunatic course. He merely shrugged and said: 'We'll need timber to shore the bales in position.'

'We've plenty of lumber.'

'We used it to make the barricade across the slipway.'

The mounting problems and the stolid Afrikaner's lack of imagination to solve them annoyed Gerrard. 'For Chrissake, Piet, chop up lifeboat six – the one that was damaged when we smoked Kramer out.'

10

'You've lost them!' Milland shouted, his red-rimmed eyes inches from Venner's face. 'Don't make bloody excuses – you've lost the bastards. Admit it.'

For an insane moment, Venner was sorely tempted to pull the hydrophone headphones back over his ears and shut out the ranting voice. Instead he kept his eyes averted from Milland by gazing fixedly at his console. The hardest part was maintaining a respectful tone.

'I can't hear something that's not making a noise, captain. And we don't know for certain that the noise we heard earlier was the *Tulsar*.'

'We've heard no convoy reports, Venner, or maybe you haven't been listening to the radio either?'

'The radio is switched on all the time, captain.'

Milland glared at his radio-operator. He was about to add a biting rejoinder when he became aware that the electric motors did not sound as if they were running at maximum speed. He glanced up at one of the main ammeters that indicated power consumption and immediately stumped aft.

In the motor-room, Munt heard his approach and quickly pushed the sliding control against the stops. The hum of the electric motors increased.

'Munt!'

The chief engineer turned from the control panel.

'Captain?'

'Why the hell aren't we running at full output?'

'We are, captain.' Munt was appalled by the dramatic change in Milland's appearance; it seemed that the staring, bloodshot eyes were those of a madman.

'Then why the hell are the ammeters in the control-room saying we're not?' Milland raged.

'I've just tried switching the battery banks around, captain. Some are more discharged than others.' He returned Milland's gaze, confident that he could not be proved a liar.

'You had better not be messing me about, Munt. By God, if you are I'll have you court-martialled.'

Munt waved his hands at the controls. 'See for yourself, captain. The controls are fully open.' He half expected Milland to take his word for it, but the senior officer moved to the control panel and studied the settings with an air of suspicion that Munt considered unforgivable. The chief engineer had taken enough. He pushed the watertight door to with his foot so that the mechanics in the adjoining engine-room would not overhear what he had to say.

'Would you have me court-martialled for offering some well-meant advice, captain? I don't think you're getting enough sleep and I think it's likely to impair your judgement.'

Milland wheeled round and glowered at Munt like a bull facing an impudent picador. He took a step towards the chief engineer. There was an anxious moment when Munt thought that Milland was going to strike him. He stood his ground and stared right back at the senior officer. Quite unexpectedly, Milland suddenly relaxed and nodded.

'You're right, Munt. Thank you for having the guts to tell me.'

A minute later, when he was alone, Munt decreased power. It was a hollow victory, he decided as he watched the flagging voltmeters – the instruments that indicated the condition of the U-boat's batteries. The simple story they told was that *U-330* was dying.

11

That evening a layer of cloud plundered the sun of the last of its warmth. There was an hour of daylight left. Gerrard glanced up at the whale-spotters' platform to satisfy himself that the Malay boys armed with binoculars were doing their job. Only three ships had been sighted since they had left Durban, which was hardly surprising because the war had swept most shipping into convoys and the *Tulsar* had deliberately kept clear of the convoy routes.

Jack Colby joined him at the rail. 'I see the fother's in place, captain. When do we get under way?'

'Just as soon as we ship those crates back into the hold, Jack.'

Colby unwrapped a stick of chewing gum. 'When do we make Falmouth?'

Gerrard considered. 'We won't be able to make much more than three knots with that fother in place otherwise it rips away. We're twelve hundred miles from Falmouth so I guess we'll be docking around 22 or 23 May. Why the sudden interest?'

'Just picked up a signal from New York for our purser,' said Colby laconically. 'Her pa's in a pretty bad way. Won't last two weeks. Doesn't look like she's gonna get to see him, does it, captain?'

Gerrar swore softly. 'Christ, Jack. What the hell can I do about it?' He leaned on the bridge rail and stared down at the carpenters who had dragged the damaged number six lifeboat on to the flensing deck. They were preparing to attack it with pry-bars as soon as Piet had removed the emergency rations and useful fittings.

'You want me to tell her?' Colby suggested.

Piet emerged from the lifeboat holding a scrap of paper and looking baffled. He climbed the steps up to the bridge where Gerrard and Colby were talking.

'Hell,' Gerrard muttered. 'I guess I'd best tell her.'

'Sorry to trouble you, cap'n,' said Piet, holding out the piece of paper. 'But I found this hidden under the lifeboat's duck-boards. Maybe it belonged to Kramer but I think maybe not.'

Gerrard took the offered sheet and glanced at it. He stiffened with shock. 'Jesus bloody Christ.'

It was a sketched layout of the *Tulsar* with pencilled notes in his own handwriting.

Gerrard found Holden in the restaurant talking to Josephine.

'Good evening, captain,' said Josephine. 'A rare visitor. How much longer will we have to endure this God-awful rolling?'

Gerrard sat down and felt in his sweat-shirt pocket for a cigar.

'We'll be through reloading the cargo about nine, then we'll be on the move again.'

'Delighted to hear it, captain,' said Holden, wondering at what could be amiss to drag Gerrard into the restaurant.

'Miss Britten,' said Gerrard. 'I guess your job must keep you pretty busy, huh?'

'Well – yes.'

'I think he means now,' Holden commented.

Josephine rose. 'Direct requests in plain English save time and prevent misunderstandings,' she said frostily, and left the restaurant.

Holden watched Gerrard carefully. 'You have a problem?' he prompted.

Gerrard made no reply but produced the sketch which he unfolded and placed on the table in front of Holden. Nothing in the Englishman's expression betrayed the fact that he had recognized the drawing immediately and that his brain had started working fast.

'So Kramer had it all along?' Holden observed mildly – it was a desperate gamble. 'Obviously you didn't search him that thoroughly when he was captured.'

The gamble paid off because Gerrard was taken aback by Holden's cool reaction to the sketch's appearance.

'It's the sketch I gave you in Durban,' Gerrard stated.

'That's right, captain.'

'Kramer had hidden it in the lifeboat.'

'That explains everything,' Holden murmured. 'Would you care for a cup of tea?'

Gerrard felt that the interview wasn't going according to plan. 'Explains what?' he demanded suspiciously.

'Why, it's only just turned up, of course. I would've thought that was obvious.'

'Now wait a minute. Just wait a minute. Are you trying to tell me that you can explain how Kramer got his hands on this?'

'I don't have to explain anything.' Holden's mind was still racing but he felt that he was gaining command of the situation.

'Goddamn it, you do, Holden,' Gerrard growled.

'My hotel room in Durban was robbed. Some money and a few papers disappeared. Nothing important because the useful stuff was always with me in my briefcase. A robbery carried out by Kramer or one of his minions no doubt.'

'So how in hell did he manage to find out about the gold?'

Holden shrugged. 'Kramer mentioned agents in the Reserve Bank.'

'*You* mentioned them – not Kramer.'

The atmosphere suddenly became icy. Holden regarded Gerrard with an expression of profound contempt. 'If you're thinking what I think you're thinking, captain, you would do well to remember whose idea it was to destroy that U-boat.'

Gerrard realized that the smooth-talking Englishman had a valid point. He lit his cigar to give himself time to think. There seemed little point in antagonizing Holden with unfounded accusations when it was likely that a good word from Holden would lead to him remaining the *Tulsar*'s captain after they had docked at Falmouth. Then he remembered something else.

'What about the time when Kramer was captured, Holden? If I hadn't knocked the rifle down, you would've killed him.'

Holden gave a mirthless smile. 'If you hadn't knocked the rifle down, it would not have gone off. That was a remarkably stupid thing to do.'

Gerrard flipped some cigar ash into an ashtray. 'I guess I'd better get back to the bridge.'

'I guess you'd better.'

Gerrard returned to the wheelhouse. He was still suspicious and resentful of Holden. It would be best if he ensured that the Englishman was kept away from the radio shack.

At 9.15 pm Piet inspected the completed jury repairs to the *Tulsar*'s bow. The bales of coarse coconut matting were shored up against the torn plating in the bow compartment with planking cannibalized from the lifeboat, and the lifeboat's canvas cover was fothered in place over the outside of the damaged hull. It was time to start loading the crates back into the hold – an operation that could be carried out with the ship under way, provided the speed was kept down to less than three knots.

The remains of the three sperm whales were cut adrift for the sharks to finish off, and the *Tulsar*'s engine-room telegraph clanged for dead slow ahead both engines.

Gerrard thrust his hands into the pockets of his peajacket and stared through the wheelhouse glass into the darkness. 'Thank God we're moving again,' he muttered to Brody.

The coxswain grinned. 'Been a long day, boss.'

12

U-330 was creeping along on the surface at four knots, the maximum speed that Munt dared wring from the virtually exhausted batteries, when Venner picked up machinery noises on his hydrophones.

'Hydrophone effects bearing one-seven-zero, captain,' he reported. 'Dead ahead.'

Milland took the headphones and listened without speaking. 'Range?' he requested at length.

'Twenty miles,' Venner replied promptly to disguise what was a wild guess. 'It sounds like the same sort of engine noises that caught us before.'

Milland angrily banged the headphones down on Venner's table. 'Gerrard won't try the same stupid trick twice.'

'Some stupid trick,' Venner muttered to himself when Milland's back was turned.

Milland suddenly spun round. 'Did you say something, Venner?'

'No, captain.'

'If you have a contribution to make, then I'd like to hear it please, Venner.'

What the hell, thought Venner. He said: 'If it is the *Tulsar*, captain, she's not moving very fast but we don't stand a chance of catching her in our present state. So why not stop and let the chief repair the diesel if he can and give the batteries the chance to recover?'

Venner did not flinch from Milland's hard stare. 'You think you can run this boat better than me?'

'I didn't say or imply that, captain.'

'But you thought it, Venner. Very well – we will try your method.'

Milland picked up the interphone and called Munt.

At 3 am, after five hours' work making new oil-pump impellers, Munt surprised himself and the rest of the boat when he managed to coax the diesel engine into life.

A minute later, Milland tumbled into the engine-room still tightening the harness of his artificial leg. He stared at the throbbing engine and clapped Munt on the back.

'My God, chief, that's the sweetest sound in the whole world.'

'But I don't know how long it will hold out for, captain – the oil pressure is only half what it should be.'

'Never mind, chief. Never mind. It'll give us six knots.' Milland paused with one leg through the watertight door and gave his chief engineer a delighted grin. 'By the way, chief, I'll be recommending you for a Knight's Cross when this mission is over.'

Venner was woken two hours later by one of his ratings. 'Those hydrophone effects are much nearer, Mr Venner, but there's something odd about them.'

Venner swung out of his bunk and made his way forward to the control-room, yawning and rubbing sleep from his eyes. He flopped into the swivel chair with a muttered 'this had better be good' and pulled on the headphones. Suddenly he was wide awake and listening intently while the rating eyed him nervously.

'See what I mean, Mr Venner? It's not steam engines and it's not diesels.'

Venner listened carefully for a few more seconds. He smiled. The rating was entitled to be puzzled because ninety per cent of the world's merchantships were driven by some form of reciprocating engine whereas the sound in the hydrophone headphones was a curious humming.

'Steam turbines,' said Venner, laying the headphones on the table.

The rating goggled at him. 'Then it *must* be the *Tulsar*! Shall I wake the captain?'

'For God's sake no,' Venner replied with feeling. 'Let the poor bastard sleep.'

13

The whale-spotter's platform was over a hundred feet above sea-level. Gerrard lowered his binoculars and eyed the Malay boy in scornful disbelief. 'So where is this smoke now, Tommy?'

'Boss – I see smoke there. I swear, boss.'

The platform was swaying through a gut-churning thirty-degree arc, forcing Gerrard and the lookouts to hang on to the safety rail.

'Smoke, boss,' said the Malay boy glumly, seeing a one-dollar bonus slipping away. 'Black smoke. Not cloud.'

Gerrard sat down, hooked his legs around a stanchion, and used both hands to hold the binoculars steady. It was then that he saw it – a faint strand of black against the grey, heavily overcast sky. It lasted for less than a second and was shredded by the wind. Then there was another wisp of rapidly-thinning black. Cloud didn't behave like that.

'You see it, boss?' the Malay boy asked hopefully.

'Yeah, Tommy. I see it now. I'll tell Mr van Kleef to add a dollar to your pay.'

The boy's eyes mirrored his delight and relief. 'A ship below horizon I guess, yes, boss?'

Gerrard nodded. 'I guess, Tommy.' He opened the box that housed the interphone and called Piet in the wheelhouse. 'The boy's right, Piet – it's a ship. We'd better make some distance between it and us. Hard left. Ten knots.'

'You're crazy, cap'n!' Piet's voice rasped in Gerrard's ear. 'The fother will rip away at anything above four knots!'

'Just do as I say, you Goddamn obstinate Dutchman!'

14

'Munt! We're making too much smoke!'

'I'm sorry, captain,' the chief engineer's voice answered from the voice-pipe. 'Cylinder two injector's not working properly – we're blowing unburnt fuel.'

More thick, black smoke spewed from the U-boat's exhaust vent and was carried into Milland's face, momentarily obscuring his view of the ship's masthead that had edged up above the horizon. The smoke cleared and he could discern a whale-spotters' platform. It was the *Tulsar*! It had to be the *Tulsar*!

'Bridge – radar!' he shouted down the voice-pipe.

Venner's voice answered immediately. 'Radar – bridge.'

'State your target.'

Venner reeled off the course, range and angle on bow figures concluding with 'speed three knots'.

Milland strived not to show his wild excitement to the look-outs. Three knots! They'd have the *Tulsar* in range within the hour!

The grey U-boat ploughed towards its victim at a steady six knots, driven by its labouring diesel. Milland's ear was tuned to the engine's uneven beat, willing the sick diesel to keep going with an intensity that drained the saliva from his mouth.

He lifted the binoculars to his eyes. The upper decks were now visible. He could even see the seaplane. The Northrop monoplane was the one thing that removed any lingering doubts as to the ship's identity.

Curiously, the elation and excitement that had whitened his knuckles with the intensity of his grip on the binoculars was no longer there. He found himself gazing at the *Tulsar*'s familiar lines with a calculating objectivity that surprised him, for he had convinced himself that the sight of the whaling-ship was sure to arouse long-banished emotions – a yearning for the past, when he had been a whole man and not a cripple.

In the confused pattern of his thoughts, one objective stood sharp and clear: he would have to kill the American. It had been

Gerrard's eyes that had stared down at him as he lay half drugged on the stainless steel table. It had been Gerrard's hands that had held the saw that had removed his leg. Gerrard had been good on first-aid but how could he have been certain that it had been necessary to amputate his leg? And then there was the gravest doubt of all, one that only haunted Milland during moments of the blackest depression: could a surgeon have saved the leg if Gerrard had sacrificed seven days of that lucrative season by turning back to port?

Venner's voice broke in on his thoughts.

'Radar – bridge. Target's range six miles. Course steady. Speed steady.'

Milland acknowledged. At that moment the diesel engine stopped and *U-330* began losing way.

'There's nothing I can do about it,' Munt snapped in response to Milland's bellowed demands. 'The cylinders are nearly at melting-point and the pistons have seized and that's that!'

'What speed can we make on the batteries, damn you!' Milland shouted back.

'They're down to forty volts. Three knots for another hour if we're lucky.' Munt's terse reply omitted the customary 'captain'.

'Very well. Keep the electrics grouped up,' said Milland curtly and snapped the voice-pipe cover shut.

The electric motors cut in and *U-330*'s speed crept up to a little over three knots. A watery morning sun broke through the cloud and fanned wedge-shaped beams across the swell. Milland cursed his U-boat's torturously slow progress. Through the open hatch by his feet he could hear the sluggish whine of the electric motors draining the pitiful reserves of the batteries.

'Eleven thousand metres,' Venner reported.

Milland lifted his binoculars. There was something odd about the *Tulsar*'s bow. For a few seconds the splash of blue around the whaler's forefoot puzzled him. And then he realized that it was one of the lifeboat covers. The *Tulsar* had hit a mine or had been damaged by a torpedo from another U-boat and had been obliged to fother her bow! No wonder she was moving so slowly. He snapped the voice-pipe cover open.

'Bridge – radar! Gun crew on the double!'

The forward hatch clanged open. The steel-helmeted crew led by Machin climbed on to the deck casing and moved to the main gun. The men were well drilled. Within fifteen seconds they had removed the tampon and locking pins, cleaned the thick, corrosion-inhibiting grease from round the breech and loaded it with a 104-millimetre shell from a ready-use ammunition locker. More shells were passed on to the casing by a human chain.

Machin looked expectantly up at Milland hunched over the conning-tower's spray lip. 'Standing by, captain.'

'Thank you, Machin. Target should be in range in thirty minutes. I shall want you to try for that aerial array above the bridge.'

Munt's head appeared in the bridge hatch. 'Permission to come on bridge, captain?'

Milland assented and growled: 'Why aren't you nursing those damned motors?'

'There's nothing more I can do now, captain – they will run until the batteries are exhausted and then we're finished.'

Milland nodded to the *Tulsar*. 'Once we've captured her, we can transfer the crew and scuttle the boat. It will have served its purpose.'

Munt looked with interest at the whaling-ship that had eluded them for so long. 'I thought it would be bigger, captain,'

Milland handed Munt his binoculars. The chief engineer examined their target for a few moments. 'What about that seaplane, captain?'

'Gerrard won't be able to fly it off from this swell.'

'Looks like she's picking up speed.'

Milland snatched the binoculars back and frantically refocussed them. The *Tulsar* had suddenly acquired a bow-wave.

'Radar – bridge!' shouted Venner. 'Target has altered course ninety degrees to port! Speed ten knots!'

Milland stood transfixed as he slowly lowered the binoculars. His expression was suddenly haggard with the realization that he had had victory within his grasp and it was now being snatched away. There was no longer the slightest hope of catching the *Tulsar*.

15

Holden studied *U-330* for a minute and returned the binoculars to Gerrard. 'So we didn't sink the damned thing after all,' he observed.

'If it's the same sub,' Piet pointed out.

'It's the same,' said Gerrard laconically.

'Cap'n,' said Piet earnestly. 'That sub's hardly moving. Couldn't we reduce speed to five knots? That fother won't hold at this speed.'

'We maintain this speed,' said Gerrard flatly.

Holden cleared his throat. 'I've just looked at that fother, captain. Mr van Kleef is right – it won't hold.'

Gerrard ignored the Englishman and turned to the radio shack. 'Jack!'

Colby poked his head out of a window. 'Captain?'

'There's a sub out there, Jack.'

The Canadian's eyes went round with alarm. 'Friendly?'

'Not unless it's changed sides. If it starts shooting, no distress calls with our position until the water's up to your waist. Okay?'

Colby paled. He acknowledged and withdrew his head quickly as if he expected the U-boat to start firing immediately.

Gerrard turned to Holden. 'Are you prepared to obey my orders?'

Holden gave a disarming smile. 'That depends.'

'Find Miss Britten and tell her to get all the passengers below and to keep them occupied. I don't want anyone on deck. Understood?'

'Understood,' said Holden with an acquiescence that took Gerrard by surprise.

'You know something, Piet,' said Gerrard sourly, watching Holden join Josephine on the flensing deck where she was talking to a group of passengers. 'I don't trust that Limey bastard an inch.'

16

U-330's batteries finally expired. Munt quickly cut the starboard electric motor so that the tiny trickle of current was available to the port motor. It kept turning for another minute. The volt-meter pointers were resting on the zero stops. He threw the main lighting switch, plunging the entire U-boat into darkness. Faint shouts of protest reached the motor-room.

The starved electric motor picked up a few revolutions for a second and then stopped. Munt angrily shut the motor down and restored the enfeebled lighting. Thanks to his crazy captain, *U-330* was now at the mercy of the wind and the waves and would be easy meat for even the RAF's lumbering Sunderland flying-boats should one chance upon them.

On the bridge, Milland swore when the motors stopped. He was about to bawl down the voice-pipe when he suddenly realized that haranguing Munt would serve no useful purpose. The *Tulsar* was dwindling towards the horizon; all he could do was gaze after it in despair and frustration – emotions that the years had made familiar companions.

Piet leaned far out over the bulwark and gazed down in mounting alarm at the fother. The hopelessly over-stressed canvas was splitting. He could even hear the loud cracks of the parting fabric above the sound of the *Tulsar*'s bow crashing into the swell. He turned and waved frantically to the bridge. At that moment the fother parted; the wind tore the two halves of canvas away from the hull and sent them flapping and straining at their lashings. One of the coconut bales inside the bow compartment must have collapsed under the sudden load because Piet could hear the dull roar of water flooding through the gaping hole. There was the faint clang of telegraph bells and then the *Tulsar* was losing way.

'Just say "I told you so" and I'll wring your Goddamn thick neck,' Gerrard warned when he joined Piet at the bulwark. 'How long to fix another fother?'

'Forty minutes, cap'n.' Piet was staring out to sea.

'Jesus Christ! Those gunners will be punching their initials in our hull with that four-incher before then!'

'I don't think so cap'n,' said Piet stiffly. 'The sub's stopped as well. What do you make of that?'

Gerrard raced up the steps to the wheelhouse and snatched up a pair of binoculars. Piet was right. The U-boat had stopped. It was not showing a bow-wave.

Both vessels were warily eyeing each other across an intervening six miles of grey, neutral Atlantic; both were unable to move.

Josephine politely disentangled herself from Eli Vanson. The sugar magnate was lecturing her and anyone else who cared to listen on his ambitious plans to turn an army of lawyers loose on the *Tulsar*'s owners just as soon as he got back to New York. She was about to suggest to Holden that she ordered the cooks to prepare an early lunch when the *Tulsar*'s engines stopped and the ship began to slow.

'What's happened?' she asked.

'The damned fother's split,' Holden replied with an uncharacteristic flash of irritation.

Josephine followed him to the door. 'Those bales they crammed into the bow will hold, won't they?'

'God knows, Jo, but you've got to keep everyone in the restaurant in case that U-boat gets within range.'

The American girl regarded him with large, serious eyes. Her conscientious attitude to her job meant that she felt personally responsible for the safety of the passengers. 'For God's sake – it's day-time – they must be able to see the Stars and Stripes on our hull. Surely they won't torpedo us?'

'No – they won't risk torpedoing us,' said Holden. 'That might sink us. They want to capture us. You see to the passengers. I won't be long.'

'Their fother's ripped in half!' Milland cried jubilantly to Munt. 'They've had to stop!'

Munt studied the *Tulsar* through a pair of binoculars. He could see men working around the whaling-ship's bow, cutting the damaged canvas away. 'But they're two miles out of extreme range, captain,' he pointed out. 'It might just as well be ten miles.'

Milland laughed. 'She's got a hundred times our top hamper, Munt.' He grinned delightedly at his chief engineer's baffled expression. 'The wind, Munt! You're forgetting the wind!'

'Jesus Christ! The bloody wind!' Gerrard suddenly shouted. He leaned over the bridge rail. 'Piet! Can we go astern?'

'No! I've got men in the water!' the Afrikaner yelled back. He returned his attention to the Malays, who were struggling to keep their heads above water and fend their bodies away from the *Tulsar*'s jagged hull plates while at the same time battling with a perverse lifeboat cover that refused to sink so that it could be drawn under the whaling ship's forefoot.

Holden emerged on deck and gazed thoughtfully out to sea at the U-boat. The gap between the two vessels was closing, he decided. He thrust his hands into his pockets and moved slowly aft, bracing his weight alternately to the left and right as the heavy swell shifted the deck like a living thing beneath his feet. He paused and looked up at the seaplane that was lashed by the floats to its platform.

'Radar – bridge!' Venner's voice announced over the bridge voice-pipe. 'Target's range eleven thousand five hundred metres.'

Five and a half miles, thought Milland. The gap was inexorably narrowing. Nothing could save the *Tulsar* now, *nothing*! He leaned over the spray lip.

'Machin! If the wind holds, she'll be in range in about forty minutes!'

'Piet! For Chrissake get those clowns out of the water!' Gerrard's voice boomed over the crew address system. 'I'm going astern in five minutes!'

Piet left the bulwark and mounted the steps to the bridge with an ability that belied his bulk. He burst into the wheelhouse and glared at Gerrard.

'Listen, cap'n. Those boys damn near drowned getting that fother under. We need another twenty minutes.'

In all their years together Gerrard had never seen Piet so angry. The usually stoic Afrikaner's eyes were bloodshot with exhaustion and yet alive with defiance.

'For Chrissake, Piet – in fifteen minutes we'll be in range of the four-incher if we keep drifting like this. We've got to go astern.'

'May I make a suggestion, captain?'

Gerrard spun round. Holden was smiling at him. The Englishman had entered the wheelhouse from the day-cabin.

'What in hell do you want, Holden?' Gerrard demanded belligerently.

Holden kept smiling. 'I'm anxious to share your problems, captain. I have a suggestion to make. A somewhat bright idea, I fancy.'

Gerrard was scathing. 'Oh yeah? Like the last one that was supposed to have sunk that U-boat?'

'An even more brilliant idea,' Holden replied lightly. 'I'm sure you'll be fascinated by it.'

The wind blowing from the south-west where the *Tulsar* lay seemed to carry the taint of whalemeat. Milland dismissed the smell as the product of his imagination – like the sensation of phantom toes that tortured his senses when he was tired.

'*Tulsar*'s lowering a boat,' one of the lookouts called.

Milland raised his binoculars. One of the whale-catchers was being lowered down the backdrop of the huge Stars and Stripes painted on the side of the *Tulsar*'s hull. The small craft cast off and the wind unfurled what appeared to be a white sheet. There was a vaguely familiar figure at the helm.

Gerrard!

'Looks like a flag of truce, captain,' said Machin.

This time Milland was not going to be caught out by Gerrard's treachery. 'Man the AA gun!' he barked at the lookouts. 'Quickly, you idiots! Bring it to bear on that launch!'

Two lookouts jumped down on to the wintergarten deck. One dragged a snaking belt of 20-millimetre ammunition from a ready-use locker and fed the end into the breech of the anti-aircraft gun while the other swung the quadruple barrels down and aimed them at the whale-catcher now speeding towards the U-boat.

*

Gerrard saw the multiple barrels tilt towards him and swung the launch round in a wide circle so that the white flag fixed to the transom staff would be clearly seen. He spun the wheel through his fingers until the catcher was back on course for the U-boat.

Milland sourly misconstrued the circling manoeuvre as a typical piece of Robert Gerrard bravura. The American's casual stance at the helm – one hand resting on the wheel and one foot planted nonchalantly on the coaming – very nearly brought Milland's pent-up rage from weeks of frustration to the boil. For an insane, blinding instant, he was possessed of an overpowering urge to push away the men manning the anti-aircraft gun and to open fire on the one man who had been the sole cause of his misery and repeated failures. It was the white sheet that held his reason together, thus restraining him from taking the fateful action.

He watched in silence as Gerrard steered the launch round to the U-boat's leeward side and approached the stern where *U-330*'s deck casing raked down to water-level. The lookout swung the anti-aircraft gun down, keeping the launch centred in his sights.

Milland was surprised to see how much Gerrard had changed during the years since he had last seen him; the denim trousers and faded sweat-shirt were exactly the same but the weathered face beneath the same unkempt mop of hair had aged noticeably. The grey eyes were as alert and cunning as ever, quickly absorbing every detail of the U-boat but ignoring the flared multiple barrels of the gun that were pointing straight at him.

Two ratings tossed a line to Gerrard which he deftly caught and made fast while they fended the launch away from the U-boat's vulnerable saddle tanks. The two craft rolled in harmony in the same swells.

'Permission to come aboard, captain?'

Milland signalled to the ratings who then steadied the whale-catcher to enable Gerrard to jump neatly on to the deck casing. He looked up at Milland who was leaning on the wintergarten rail beside the anti-aircraft gun and gave a perfunctory salute.

'Good morning, Kurt.'

Milland's slight hesitation was because he hadn't spoken

English for a number of years – even though the acknowledgement was virtually identical to German.

'Good morning.'

'May I join you or do I crick my neck?'

Milland stepped back from the rail. Gerrard grasped one of the stanchions and vaulted up beside Milland as though he were deliberately demonstrating a prowess he knew Milland could never emulate. He even leaned back on the rails, his hands resting on them as if the U-boat was his personal property.

'What's wrong with your engines, Kurt? You've got us all baffled on the *Tulsar*.'

'State your business,' Milland growled.

Gerrard noticed that everyone was watching him; no one was paying attention to the *Tulsar*; all was going according to plan. He gestured to the whale-catcher. 'We picked up some of your crew after you went down. We put them in the bow compartment which later flooded. I figured the decent thing to do was to turn them over to you for burial.' Gerrard saw little point into going into the exact details of how the U-boatmen lost their lives.

Milland looked down at the launch. A number of shapeless forms laced up in canvas were lying in the cockpit. Gerrard didn't understand what Milland said to his crew but they immediately set about transferring the bodies to the U-boat and laying them carefully on the deck casing. Milland leaned against the rail and gave a curt order. A rating unlaced the end of one of the canvas sleeves and drew the material down. Milland stared at Leutnant Hans Fischer's face for a moment without speaking and told the rating to close the bag. He turned to Gerrard.

'I suppose I should thank you, but there seems little point as you were responsible for their death in the first place.'

Gerrard gave a faint smile. 'You've not changed, Kurt. You're still the autocratic bastard we all used to know and love.'

Gerrard's irony was lost on Milland. 'Perhaps you have changed,' said the U-boat captain stiffly.

'In what way, Kurt?'

'I didn't think Robert Gerrard was a man to deliberately ram and sink a U-boat killing forty men.'

The American's half smile and relaxed attitude abruptly vanished. His grey eyes hardened. 'That was after U-boats started torpedoing unarmed passenger liners, Kurt.' Gerrard didn't wait for a reply but ducked through the railing and jumped lightly on to the deck casing. He brushed past the ratings who were fending off the launch and dropped behind the helm.

'Gerrard!' Milland called down as the American cast off and operated the whale-catcher's self-starter. 'As you have done the decent thing, I will also do the decent thing: I won't open fire until you have returned to your ship.'

Gerrard's reply was drowned by the roar from the whale-catcher's exhaust. Milland watched the receding figure hunched over the launch's helm and wondered why he suddenly no longer seemed to hate Robert Gerrard.

'Captain!'

Milland turned.

'Message from the chief, captain,' said Machin. 'The diesel has cooled and is no longer seized. He thinks he might be able to start it.'

Milland did not reply. He was staring at the *Tulsar*. Something was wrong – there was something different about it. And then he realized what it was: the seaplane was missing from its customary perch above the whaling-ship's deck.

Gerrard swept the whale-catcher around the *Tulsar*'s stern and stopped beside the seaplane that was bobbing on the surface with its engine warmed up and running smoothly. Piet was balanced precariously on one of the aircraft's floats. He caught the rope that Gerrard tossed to him and drew the two craft as close together as the swell permitted. The two men quickly changed positions: Piet dropped his bulk behind the whale-catcher's helm while Gerrard scrambled into the seaplane's cockpit and pulled the canopy shut. He spared one glance down at the cluster of explosive-head harpoons that had been lashed to each float and pointing ahead. Satisfied that all was well, he opened the throttle.

The machine dipped a wingtip into the rolling swell as it began taxi-ing towards the *Tulsar*'s bow. Piet followed at a distance in the whale-catcher like a dog following its master into battle.

Gerrard rounded the bow and had a brief glimpse of *U-330*'s low profile before the seaplane plunged like an ungainly duck into a trough. He opened up to maximum power. The propeller became a spinning disc of light, sucking spray off the broken water and creating a whirling cloud of mist in the wildly bucking machine's wake. But the experienced whale-men on the *Tulsar* knew that the seaplane stood no chance of getting airborne under those conditions.

There was a grating of damaged metal when Munt operated the diesel engine's compressed air starter. The engine turned over several times but refused to fire. The two mechanics watched in silence as he checked the fuel-level in the filter. There was another explosive hiss of compressed air that was smothered by the shriek of damaged crankshaft bearings. Munt closed his eyes and kept the starter turning. It didn't require much imagination to visualize shattered piston rings scoring deep into the engine's cylinder walls. Quite suddenly the engine started.

Milland allowed himself a second's elation at the sight of water boiling past the hull before calling down a course to the helmsman that swung the U-boat's bow round until it was heading towards the *Tulsar* at a steady three knots.

'Watch the sky for that damned seaplane!' Milland raged at the lookouts. He guessed that Gerrard would be attempting a take-off away from the *Tulsar* – using the whaling-ship's bulk as a screen. He cursed himself for not seeing Gerrard's visit for what it was: a cunning ploy to distract attention while the seaplane was launched.

'Range four miles, captain!' called Machin who was peering through the main gun's range-finder.

'Open fire when you're ready,' Milland ordered.

One of the gunners quickly spun a handwheel. The barrel of the big gun slewed smoothly round on its well-greased bearings until Machin had the *Tulsar*'s image square in his sights.

The seaplane's whirling propeller racked into the water and gunned spray over the canopy. Gerrard lost sight of the U-boat for the third time and then caught a glimpse of white smoke belching from the U-boat's main gun when the next wave nearly stood the seaplane on its tail. He had no idea how far Piet was behind in the whale-catcher; the important thing was to keep his eyes fixed on the U-boat, now less than a mile away. He risked a quick inspection of the floats to ensure that the harpoons were still securely in place. The rivet-breaking roller-coaster motion meant that the air-speed indicator was useless, but he estimated his speed at around forty knots.

He was one minute from the U-boat.

Milland spotted the seaplane leaping from a crest like a hooked marlin when it was half a mile off the U-boat's quarter. The anti-aircraft gun was brought into action and the sustained roaring of its belt-fed barrels was added to the intermittent boom of the main gun pounding the *Tulsar*.

'Higher! Higher, you idiots!' Milland screamed, seeing miniature waterspouts lacerate the water in the charging seaplane's path. At that moment, the machine dipped below the swell and was lost to sight. It re-emerged seconds later in a cloud of propeller-driven spray having closed the distance between it and the U-boat by two hundred metres. The man operating the multiple-barrel gun over-corrected his aim and sent lightning darts of tracer spraying into the sea to the seaplane's left.

'Idiot! Idiot!' Milland raged. He lurched forward to the wintergarten rail and screamed abuse at the gunner.

Confused by the noise and smoke, and the burning hot shell cases dancing out of the breech, the gunner stopped firing in order to take a fresh aim at the madly-twisting target. He resumed firing a continuous burst and succeeded in chewing the seaplane's wing-tip to splinters.

'Hit the fuselage!' bellowed Milland.

The seaplane was within a hundred metres and seemed unstoppable. Suddenly its engine was plainly audible above the gun's staccato racket. In fury, Milland jumped down on to the wintergarten deck. He ignored the sharp snap of pain in his stump from the jolt and pushed the gunner away. A spent shell case rolled under his artificial leg causing him to lose his balance temporarily. By the time he was in position behind the gun, the seaplane was a roaring nightmare within fifty metres and coming straight at him. He took careful aim and pulled the trigger.

At the precise moment that Milland started firing, Gerrard judged that the seaplane was near enough. He lifted his legs over the edge of the cockpit and levered his body out on to a wing root. The water, inches beneath his feet, was a blur. If he miscalculated his jump, he would be decapitated by the tail-plane. At that moment the aircraft suddenly seemed to start falling to pieces around him. He tried to shift his weight on to the float. A searing pain stabbed savagely into his shoulder. The shock caused him to lose his handhold. He retained consciousness just long enough to thrust away with his feet from the disintegrating seaplane.

At twenty metres, Milland's careful firing could do nothing to destroy the seaplane's hundred feet per second momentum. One float broke away from the wing, causing the entire machine to slew round so that it struck *U-330* amidships instead of near the bow. Ten harpoons exploded simultaneously. It wasn't a large explosion but it was enough to blast a footwide hole in the U-boat's pressure hull just below the waterline. The harpoon-laden float that Milland had shot away drifted against the side of *U-330* and the force of that explosion lifted Milland bodily over the bridge coaming and tossed him into the sea.

The sudden inrush of water swept Venner from his stool. Even before he had climbed to his feet there was a foot of black water in the control-room. He ignored the mad scramble of bodies trying to climb the bridge ladder and the roar of water erupting thrugh the hole. Instead he pulled on his headphones, encoded a succinct distress call on the cipher machine and set his radio to transmit.

17

Admiral Wilhelm Fritz Canaris, head of the Abwehr, left the Reich Chancellory building at 10 pm and hurried to his car. The driver jumped out and opened the rear door. Canaris climbed in beside Strick, settled back in the seat and tossed his high-peaked cap on the floor.

'Well?' inquired Strick as the car moved off.

'Naturally he was disappointed that *U-330* had failed in its mission.'

'Failed?' echoed Strick. 'But we've got the *Tulsar*'s position! I don't call that failure. Surely you didn't tell the Führer that we've failed?'

The tyres of the Mercedes hissed wetly through the darkened streets. Canaris reached into an inside pocket and spread a copy of *U-330*'s signal on his lap. He switched on the reading-lamp and passed the fateful slip of paper to his companion. 'Read it again,' he said.

The words had been printed on Strick's memory since he had first been shown the signal an hour earlier, but he reread the terse message.

U330 TO BDU
POSITION GRID SQUARE AH2867. UNDER ATTACK. SINKING

'You see?' said Canaris. 'There's nothing in that to suggest that *U-330* was sunk by the *Tulsar*. And even if it was, with her top speed of twenty-six knots, she would be miles away by now.'

Strick began to get angry. 'But that's why it is imperative that we despatch a radar-equipped ship to search for the *Tulsar* now! The purpose of your audience was to persuade the Führer –'

'I learned something just now,' Canaris interrupted, giving Strick an impish grin. 'I suppose that must sound odd coming from the head of the intelligence service, but Grand Admiral Raeder is remarkably adept at keeping his conniving schemes to himself. It appears that for some time the Grand Admiral has been nursing an ambition to send a heavy surface force into the Atlantic to challenge the Royal Navy. Quite insane, of course, and the Führer has rightly refused to allow such nonsense. But to placate Raeder, the Führer has allowed him to dream and scheme.'

'What does that mean?' asked Strick.

'All the operational planning required to send a significant naval force into the North Atlantic is complete and has been for some while. Codes, lines of command, supplies – all the thousand and one tasks have been carried out. It's even got a code name – Operation Rheinübung.'

Strick made a despairing gesture with his hands. 'Then why, in the name of God, didn't you persuade the Führer to give Raeder the go-ahead?'

Canaris looked at his watch. 'The Führer will be speaking to Raeder about now. He will be telling the Grand Admiral to order Admiral Lütjens to put to sea as soon as possible. Naturally, Raeder won't be given the real reason why Rheinübung is receiving his assent until Lütjens' task force has broken through into the Atlantic – perhaps not even then. I have a feeling that the Führer may communicate with Lütjens direct.' Canaris paused. He had enjoyed his little game with the coldblooded economics professor. He smiled at Strick's expression of astonishment and added: 'Did you know that the Führer paid Lütjens a visit two days ago?'

'Lütjens is putting to sea?' Strick managed to blurt out.

Canaris nodded. 'His entire task force will move to Korsfjord when they're ready and wait for the right moment to break out into the Atlantic.'

Strick could think of nothing to say. Admiral Lütjens flew his pennant from a very special warship. With its 41,700 tons displacement, massive 'Wotan' armour-plating and eight 15-inch guns, it was one of the most powerful warships in the world. Its lurking presence at Gotenhafen on the Baltic where it was beyond the reach of the RAF was a constant, nagging threat to the British, who dreaded the terrible damage it could inflict on the Atlantic convoys if it broke out. It was well known that they would do anything and resort to any subterfuge to tempt it out into the North Sea where they would be able to hurl several battleships and cruisers against it. Even its name symbolized Germany's might and prestige.

It was called the *Bismarck*.

18

Milland opened his eyes and stared up at the deckhead in the *Tulsar*'s sick bay. He knew every light, every girder – every detail of that deckhead was permanently etched on his consciousness. Even the lines of rivets were part of the pattern. In terror, his hands went to his sides and felt the cold smoothness of stainless steel beneath the mattress. He started up on his elbows.

'No!' he croaked. 'No!'

'Easy there,' said a voice.

Milland turned his head and saw Gerrard. The American grinned.

'Hi there. How are you feeling, Kurt?'

'My leg . . . my leg . . .' Milland babbled. 'Is it –? Is it –?'

Gerrard thought his former colleague was referring to his artificial leg. He said reassuringly: 'Your leg's fine, Kurt. Can't say the same about your U-boat or my seaplane.'

'U-boat?' The German stared up in bewilderment. 'U-boat?' he repeated. And then the fog cleared from his mind. He allowed his aching head to drop back on to the pillow. '*U-330*,' he muttered.

Milland closed his eyes for a minute and opened them again. 'Tell me what happened.'

Gerrard removed the bandage from Milland's head and examined the ugly bruise on the German's temple. 'Guess you had yourself a spot of concussion, Kurt.'

'What happened!' Milland suddenly shouted. He pushed himself up on his elbows again and grimaced in pain.

'I charged you with the seaplane. There were harpoons –'

'After that.'

'We both ended up in the sea. I'd stopped a splinter in the shoulder but the water brought me round. Next thing I found myself hanging on to your collar until Piet picked us up in the catcher. Remember Piet? He wants to look by later.'

'How about my men?'

Gerrard remained silent.

'Well?'

'I'm sorry, Kurt.'

Milland stared up at Gerrard. 'Not even one?'

Gerrard placed a fresh lint over Milland's temple and unrolled a clean bandage. 'I guess they were as lousy swimmers as they were gunners. Piet searched around for three hours.'

Milland's eyes were fixed on the deckhead lights. 'You won't get the *Tulsar* to England,' he said in a flat, detached tone. 'I've failed but there will be others. They'll throw everything at you.'

Gerrard eased Milland into a sitting position and started tying the bandage around the German's head. 'Done pretty well so far, Kurt.'

Milland made no reply.

'How did your people find out about our cargo?' Gerrard asked, making the inquiry sound like a chance, conversational remark. He continued winding the bandage around Milland's head. 'Well, I don't blame you for not talking, Kurt. But we caught your guy Kramer.'

'I guessed,' said Milland sourly. He suddenly remembered that Admiral Staus had told him that there were *two* agents aboard the *Tulsar*. From what Gerrard had said, it was certain that the second agent hadn't been caught. The first agent was Kramer. What was the name of the second agent – the passenger? It had been typed on his sealed orders which had gone down with *U-330*. An English name. He cursed the blow on his head. For Christ's sake what had his name been? The name! The name!

Gerrard finished tying the bandage. The door of the sick bay opened and a slightly-built, fair-haired man wearing a well-cut suit entered. His aristocratic features reminded Milland of the British actor Leslie Howard. Milland tried to remember if Leslie Howard had such intense blue eyes.

'How is he?' the man inquired.

'He's tough,' said Gerrard. 'Just like all whalers.'

The man offered his hand to Milland. 'How do you do, Captain Milland. My name is Ralph Holden.'

Milland met the stranger's unsettling eyes. He gave a slow smile and shook the offered hand.

'I'm pleased to meet you, Mr Holden.'

19

The hours of daylight lengthened as the *Tulsar* pushed northwards at two knots. The sub-tropics had been left far behind, and blustery winds alternating with driving squalls forced the bored passengers to remain below decks where Josephine did her best to keep them entertained.

Occasionally the two Ursuline nuns ventured out on deck, their black habits flapping like the cloaks of demented witches in the biting wind that held the promise of worse to come. Mr and Mrs Eli Vanson waged an acrimonious truce against each other over endless card games in the restaurant because the bar had run dry. Herbie Lewis thought about Rose, and the former newly-weds were sustaining the electric aftermath of a bitter row.

Kurt Milland sat in the guarded cabin that had been assigned to him and wondered when Holden would attempt to contact him. He spent hours on his bunk brooding about his failure. After an exercise walk that had included the flensing deck, he had noticed the new cargo hatch, and his brooding changed to scheming.

On the afternoon of 17 May the *Tulsar* was sighted five hundred miles south-west of Lisbon by a long-range Focke-Wulf belonging to the Aufklärungsstaffeln (reconnaissance) squadron. The big four-engine machine was scouring far out into the Atlantic in search of a Gibraltar convoy that was believed to be taking an extreme westward route.

The FW 200's crew studied the *Tulsar* through binoculars and noted the giant Stars and Stripes banner on each side of the hull. Lone sailings by whaling-ships belonging to neutral countries were not their concern but there had been nothing else to report so they plotted the *Tulsar*'s position, course and surprisingly low speed, and radioed the information to their base at Bordeaux.

By one of those coincidences that was to have far-reaching consequences, their signal was received at Bordeaux at the same time as a general alert from Oberkomando der Luftwaffe requiring all lone sailings to be reported to the naval high command. The order was immediately obeyed, with the result that the intelligence on the *Tulsar* was radioed to Admiral Lütjens on the *Bismarck* within the hour.

Such were the intricate preliminaries that were ultimately to decide the fate of the mighty leviathan and exhaust the meagre balance of the *Tulsar*'s luck.

20

Shortly after 10 am on 18 May a flight of four snub-nosed, single-engine FW 190 fighters under the command of their renowned *gruppenadjutant*, Oberleutnant Paul Kassel, landed at Bordeaux after a long flight from the Luftwaffe test establishment at Rechlin.

Once the pale blue aircraft were under cover the admiring ground crews were able to take a close look at the new machines and bombard Kassel with demands for autographs which he laughingly supplied with a series of exuberant flourishes from a gold fountain pen presented to him by Reichmarschall Hermann Goering.

The debonair Kassel's four machines were pre-production FW 190 A-4's and were the creation of Focke-Wulf's brilliant designer, Kurt Tank. They were each fitted with four 110-pound bombs on a fuselage bomb-rack together with wing-mounted cannons and external long-range fuel tanks. Goering had proudly described the new aircraft as having 'the speed of a fighter and the punch of a bomber'. His purpose in despatching Paul Kassel's flight to Bordeaux was to steal a march on the despised Kriegsmarine. Kassel's Wurgergruppe – 'Butcher Bird Squadron' – were required to find and destroy the *Tulsar*.

On that same day, a thousand miles to the north-east, the mighty *Bismarck* quietly slipped away from her Baltic anchorage.

From both ends of the continent of Europe, inexorable forces were closing on the diminutive whaling ship.

21

The weather deteriorated rapidly over the following week. The low-pressure fronts overhauled the *Tulsar* and slowed her to a virtual halt with mountainous seas that reared up and burst over the jury-repaired bow with a force that made Piet uneasy. He had just returned from an inspection of the fother and was standing on the bridge with Holden when the two men heard the faint drone of aircraft engines.

'They sound like the same ones we heard yesterday,' Holden commented. He searched the leaden cloudbase but there was nothing. The wheelhouse door opened and Gerrard stepped on to the bridge. He listened for a few seconds.

'You reckon they're looking for us?' Piet inquired.

'Christ knows,' Gerrard answered. 'Maybe that big four-engine job did spot us after all the other day.'

'A certainty,' said Holden.

'Okay,' said Gerrard with finality. 'We increase our speed and alter course – just in case those bastards plotted us.'

'Cap'n,' said Piet anxiously, 'I'm telling you that fother won't take any more speed.'

'Another three knots, Piet.'

'No, cap'n.'

'For Chrissake, Piet. We're asking to be bombed out of the sea if we stick to this speed.'

The Afrikaner's voice suddenly was hard. 'Cap'n Gerrard. Why are the Germans busting themselves to stop us?'

'I have a suggestion to make,' said Holden abruptly. 'A slight increase in speed will help, but do we have any paint?'

Piet gaped at Holden. 'Paint?'

'Paint.'

Piet forced his uncooperative mind to dwell on the subject. 'Maybe three hundred gallons of red primer but no top coat.'

'And brushes?'

'Plenty of brushes,' Piet replied, bewildered.

Gerrard suddenly realized what Holden was thinking and started laughing.

Ten miles to the east, Paul Kassel decided that there was little point in continuing the search that day in the worsening visibility. He switched on his throat microphone and spoke to his three comrades.

As one, the four hungry Butcher Birds turned for home.

Josephine burst out laughing. 'You're kidding? No – you're not kidding.'

'They've been complaining that they're bored,' said Holden. 'Now's their chance to do something useful.' He prised the lid off a five-gallon can of paint and stirred the contents.

'It's primer,' said Josephine.

'So?'

'One thing I do know from my father's hardware store is that you're not supposed to paint primer on top of top coat.'

'Have you had any more news about him, Jo?'

'No.'

Holden decided that her emphatic tone indicated that the subject was not to be pursued. He straightened up. 'Will you tell the passengers or shall I?'

'I'll tell them,' said Josephine. 'But I have this theory that Mr Eli Vanson will blow his stack.'

Eli Vanson blew his stack.

'I'm to what!' he bellowed at Josephine.

'Help with the repainting of the ship,' Josephine said for the second time while counting slowly up to ten to contain her temper. Eli Vanson had been nothing but trouble since Durban. She turned to the other passengers. 'It doesn't have to be done carefully. All we have to do is slap it on as quick as possible. There's more than enough brushes for all of us and the crew, and the crew will do the more difficult work of painting the hull.'

Eli Vanson's vehement protests were interrupted by the elder of the two Ursuline nuns. She took two brushes from Josephine, gave one to her companion, and told Josephine that they were ready to start work.

Persuading the rest of the passengers to help was easy after that.

By mid-afternoon, not only had the *Tulsar* changed her colour from pale grey to dark red, but she had also changed her appearance: several lifeboat covers had been stitched together and stretched tightly across the open divide of the whale slipway – the one feature that unmistakably identified the ship as a whaler.

22

The following morning, 20 May, Paul Kassel held a brief conference with his three fellow Butcher Bird pilots.

'Our only fix of the *Tulsar*'s position is now three days old,' he told his men. He placed a finger on the chart of the North Atlantic off France. 'We know that she was moving north at two knots – fifty miles a day she's making – therefore she cannot be more than two hundred miles from that position unless she has increased her speed.'

'She must have done so,' said one of the pilots. 'We've covered every square mile ahead of her last position. Either that or she's now heading west.'

The four men spent another ten minutes discussing their search tactics before walking out to their waiting fighters.

Kassel was worried because he had promised Goering that

the Butcher Birds would be tasting the *Tulsar*'s blood before the week was out.

He was even more worried that afternoon when they landed back at Bordeaux after a fruitless five-hour sortie. They had seen and photographed two ships and neither of them had resembled the *Tulsar*.

Two hours later, the refuelled Butcher Birds took off again and headed north to the tiny grass airfield at La Rochelle.

The new base brought a disastrous change of luck during the next few days. On 23 May Paul Kassel's number two aircraft hit a pothole dug in the field by Breton saboteurs and smashed an undercarriage leg, and on 25 May number four's BMW engine was beset by the usual BMW problem of overheating that led to the seizure of the motor's lower cylinders.

On 26 May, after having flown some twenty sorties over the Atlantic, he and his remaining fighter transferred to Guernsey Airport in the occupied British Channel Islands where they were obliged to share the limited facilities with sympathetic Luftflotte 3 personnel who were secretly delighted that one of Goering's blue-eyed glamour boys was having a rough time.

But the setbacks merely served to strengthen the indomitable Kassel's resolve to find and sink the *Tulsar*.

23

At 9.10 am on 27 May, when the *Tulsar* was approximately five hundred miles south-west of Brest, a low irregular rumble was heard from the north.

Gerrard spun round in his chair in the wheelhouse. 'Hey, Sam,' he called to Brody at the helm. 'Did that sound like thunder to you?'

'Queerest thunder I've ever heard, boss.'

Gerrard pulled on his oilskins and sou'wester. 'That's what I thought.'

Piet too had heard the noise and was climbing on to the bridge when Gerrard stepped out of the wheelhouse into the driving rain.

The low, menacing noise was repeated. It seemed to roll right round the horizon so that the two men had some difficulty in locating the direction of the sound.

'What do you make of it, cap'n?'

Gerrard peered into the squall-laden spray. Visibility was less than two miles. 'Well, it sure as hell isn't thunder, Piet.'

'The weather's getting very English,' Josephine observed while she and Holden were eating breakfast.

Holden frowned and held up a finger for silence.

'What's the matter?' Josephine was puzzled by Holden's sudden tense expression. The normally dispassionate face was alive with anticipation. He uttered one word:

'Guns.' And then three more: 'By God! Guns!'

'Guns,' said Piet. 'Big bastards.'

Gerrard had already reached the same conclusion. 'How far?'

'Could be fifty–sixty miles if they're 15-inchers. You could hear 15-inch guns being fired at Simonstown from off Cape Aghulas.' Piet listened for a few moments. 'Battleships or heavy cruisers maybe.'

'Or both.'

Piet nodded. Despite the appalling conditions on deck, men were gathering along the bulwarks and were staring in the direction of the ominous thunder.

The unseen battle was still raging an hour later.

'Christ, it must be one helluva dispute,' Gerrard muttered.

By 10.10 am the interval between each crashing salvo and the next was noticeably longer. By 10.20 am there was only the occasional roll of cordite thunder. There was renewed spate ten minutes later that lasted for less than two minutes and then there was silence.

Piet and Gerrard remained at the rail for a long time, saying nothing. There seemed little doubt that many fellow sailors had been killed or were dying beyond the horizon.

Just how many was not revealed until shortly before nightfall when the *Tulsar* found herself steaming through a vast area of oil, wreckage and floating bodies wearing Kriegsmarine uniforms. There were hundreds of them and more were languidly reaching the surface around the *Tulsar* when she stopped.

Nothing was said by the men and women lining the rail and gazing down at the ghastly spectacle. There was nothing that could be said; it was a scene that made the mechanical business of assembling words into sentences impossible.

A lifebelt was fished aboard by a Lascar on Holden's orders. Gerrard joined the group at the rail and watched as Holden went down on one knee and turned the lifebelt over. Through the layer of wartime grey paint, it was possible to discern the single, unequivocal word that the lifebelt had borne in peacetime: *Bismarck*.

'What's the matter, Mr Holden?' Gerrard inquired amiably.

Holden stood. 'Why should anything be the matter?'

'Oh, nothing. It's just that I though your hands were trembling a shade when you turned the lifebelt over.'

'She was a capital ship – one of the largest in the world,' Holden replied.

Gerrard grinned. 'Sure. Makes you wonder how many ships she took down with her.'

24

Oberleutnant Paul Kassel's luck changed when a U-boat returning to Lorient after a two-month patrol that had exhausted its torpedoes reported sighting a ship that fitted the description of the *Tulsar*. The only thing that was wrong was the colour. The *Tulsar* was not red but Kassel attributed this to a decoding error.

At 3.20 pm on 28 May, an hour after receiving the report, the two Butcher Birds took off from Guernsey and headed west out into the Atlantic.

After a quarter of an hour the two fighters dipped down through the cloudbase and were surprised to discover a British

Flower class corvette four miles dead ahead. The sudden appearance of the two Luftwaffe fighters upset the sensibilities of the small warship – HMS *Shepherd's Purse* – for it immediately let fly at the intruders with its anti-aircraft guns. Kassel flew so low over the ship that he could actually see the gunners frantically swing their weapons round to keep him in their sights as he roared over their heads. He chuckled to himself and guessed that there would be baffled exchanges on the corvette as to why the plainly-visible bombs under the Focke-Wulf's wings hadn't been released. He glanced back and realized with a cold shock that he was alone. He turned the other way in his seat and saw his companion Butcher Bird hit the water and break up. His attention was drawn to the port wing of his own aircraft and the five regularly-spaced holes that should not have been there. The corvette's firing had been more accurate than he had supposed – a fact that was confirmed ten minutes later by his instruments indicating low oil pressure.

The visibility improved as he flew west. The cloud lifted and enabled him to climb to a thousand feet. He spotted the *Tulsar* heading north-east and immediately put the Butcher Bird's nose down towards it. The ship was red, but it was definitely a whaling-ship – not even the clumsy attempt to camouflage the slipway could disguise that fact. He came in low. He could see men frantically running and pointing. Some had the good sense to throw themselves flat.

Only one bomb of the four released by Kassel hit the *Tulsar*. It burst through the deckhead aft of the wheelhouse and exploded, blowing out the sides of the wheelhouse and every pane of glass. Brody threw himself flat at the moment of impact and was protected from the blast by the heavy pedestal of the gyro-compass. Piet van Kleef actually saw the bomb pierce the wheelhouse roof from his vantage point on the spotters' platform and immediately assumed that Sam Brody had been killed. He saw Gerrard run along the weatherdeck and climb the twisted steel steps to the bridge.

Kassel cursed the three bombs that plunged harmlessly into the water beside the *Tulsar* without exploding. He wheeled his aircraft round to examine the whaler and was surprised and infuriated to discover that the ship was still moving.

His engine began labouring, which was hardly surprising since his oil pressure reading was a little above zero. There was no time to even consider strafing the ship with his cannons. The important thing now was to nurse his Butcher Bird back to Guernsey. He circled round on to an easterly course and listened anxiously to the note of his faltering engine.

Five minutes later his anxiety changed to bitter anger when he found out that his radio was not working. Goddamn that corvette and the chance that had found it for him! He could not even radio the *Tulsar*'s position. At that moment his engine stopped.

There was nothing left for him to do but to check his parachute harness and slide back the Focke-Wulf's bubble cockpit canopy.

He wondered what his chances were of being picked up by an E-boat.

Gerrard and Holden stood amid the wreckage and gloomily surveyed the devastated remains of the wheelhouse.

'Jesus Christ,' Gerrard breathed. He picked up a small tangle of metal that had been his sextant and dropped it in disgust. 'We haven't even got a Goddamn sextant now.'

'What about Kramer's sextant?' Holden asked.

'It was in the chart-table drawer. You tell me where the chart-table is and I'll tell you where Kramer's sextant is. Gyro-compass knocked out, telegraph out, not one chart left – Jesus, what a God-awful mess.'

'Helm's still answering,' said Brody cheerfully. 'Trouble is, boss, I don't know what course I'm steering. Could be heading back to Africa.'

'I'll get Piet to get a compass out of a lifeboat,' said Gerrard.

Josephine appeared in the entrance that had once led to the day-cabin. She was trying to balance a tray of steaming mugs of coffee in one hand and cling to the door frame with the other. Holden quickly took the tray from her and held her steady.

'Are you okay, Jo?'

Josephine's face was ashen. 'Just fine,' she said with forced good humour. 'I guess the excitement is getting a little out of hand, huh?'

'Is everything still okay below?' asked Gerrard.

Josephine nodded. 'Those two nuns are real angels. They're pacifying everyone including Mr Vanson and he's not sure how to take it.'

25

The day after the bomb attack consisted of an unremitting battle against the gale-force winds and huge seas like malevolent mountains that reared up in the *Tulsar*'s path and hurled themselves down on the canvas-shrouded bow in a welter of foam and fury. One sea had barely roared through the scuppers before the next thundered down on the battered foredeck.

Gerrard's worries were remorselessly added to with each heavy sea. Would the fother hold? How in the world could canvas take such punishment? Would the lashings securing the crates stand up? But the worst of all – something that really frightened him – was not knowing where he was except that he was close to land. The behaviour of the seas, coming at the *Tulsar* from all directions, told him that he was near land. It was land that destroyed ships, rarely the sea. For the first time in his seafaring life he was lost. He had no charts – all had been swept into the sea by the bomb blast – and no navigating instruments apart from a hand-bearing compass removed from a lifeboat. Desperately he tried to recall details from the charts of the Cornish coastal areas, but they were a part of the world he had never sailed before and no snippets of information were permanently stored in his mind. He knew that the north and south coasts of Cornwall were wild and rocky, and that there were precious few coves or inlets that were not exposed to the full fury of the Atlantic. Reduced to crude basics, the sailing directions for entering the English Channel from the south were turn right a hundred miles after Ushant. Choosing the moment to turn right was going to be the most momentous decision of his life.

Nightfall brought stronger winds that howled through the gaps in the canvas lashed down over the smashed wheelhouse. The material dementedly flapped and banged, making helm orders impossible to convey without yelling in the helmsman's ear.

By 2 am the rolling was worse and the sea more broken and unpredictable. Gerrard lay exhausted on his bunk, unable to sleep as he listened for the sound of crashing crates in the hold that would mean the end.

26

Milland brought his artificial leg down with all his strength on the back of the Lascar's head. The seaman collapsed unconscious over the tray of food he was setting down on the table.

Certain that someone must have heard the crash of cutlery and metal dishes, Milland dragged himself across the floor to the cabin door and pushed it shut. He waited in silence, sitting on the floor with the empty leg of his trousers tucked underneath him. He risked a quick glimpse outside. The darkened corridor was deserted. He picked up his leg and saw that he had hit the seaman too hard; the ankle joint was broken – a jagged mess of torn metal and sheared rivets. He cursed his stupidity and flung the useless limb across the cabin in bitter frustration. Without the leg he was helpless – the only way he could get about was by crawling.

There was an ivory-handled knife in a sheath on the Lascar's belt. Milland unfastened the buckle and withdrew it. The blade was six inches long and honed to razor-sharpness.

He sat brooding for a quarter of an hour, wondering what to do. It was the vicious rolling of the ship that gave him the idea. The leg didn't matter. If he had to crawl, then that was exactly what he would do.

He pushed the knife into his belt, searched through the

Lascar's pockets, and found what he was looking for: a box of matches.

Milland waited for two minutes in the shadow of a ventilator inlet while his eyes adjusted to the darkness. He was constantly drenched by breaking seas but didn't care; the important thing was to keep a tight grip on the matches so that they remained dry and to study his objective carefully, one of the circular blubber hatches that were located around the edge of the flensing deck. He wondered how they were locked. But wondering was no use – there was only one way to find out . . .

The hinged hatch was secured by a simple pin and eye latch. He pulled the pin out with some difficulty and opened the hatch. It was heavy and the task was not made easier by the appalling motion. The sustained booming of seas crashing against the hull effectively masked the creak of rusty metal.

Milland's arms were called upon to do much more than a man with both his legs. As a result, they were exceptionally powerful. It required no great effort on his part to hang down into the chasm, gripping a rung with one hand while lowering the hatch with the other. He felt about in black space with his leg. There were no more rungs. He pulled some coins from his pocket and dropped them. The sharp clatter beneath his feet told him that he had about four feet to fall. He released his grip and fell sprawling on to what felt like a timber crate. The next roll sent him tumbling off the crate. He managed to break his fall by grabbing the ropes that lashed the crates to the hold's floor.

He was too dazzled by the flare from the first match to see anything clearly. The second match revealed that he was exactly where he hoped he was – in the bullion hold, surrounded by crates stacked ten high and stretching along the narrow passage-way for as far as the feeble light from the match could reach. It was a sobering moment. He was completely surrounded by gold; billions of marks' worth of gold: the entire wealth of the mighty British Empire.

And one sharp knife could send the lot to the bottom. In the ponderous rolling, a dozen crates cut loose would crash into other crates and break them loose, which would in turn smash and splinter into each other until the entire cargo was a sliding, living mass that would eventually burst through the side of the hull or cause the *Tulsar* to develop such a list that she would inevitably broach to.

One sharp knife . . .

He jerked the Lascar's knife from his belt and set to work sawing at the straining lashings. First one rope parted, then another. He didn't need matches to see – just slash and hack at every rope within reach. Never in history would such a simple-performed act of sabotage have such far-reaching consequences.

He heard the upper crates sliding and felt an entire column tilt as the ship rolled. He intensified his already demented activity. The creaking and groaning from above his head was louder. Another rope parted, this time with a loud twang.

He heard the column of crates begin to topple and desperately crawled clear along the passage-way just as they came crashing down. The pool of light from a match showed that the crates had jammed themselves together into a solid, unyielding mass. He pulled himself upright and tried to dislodge the crates by pushing them, but to no avail. Sweat streaming down his face, he sank to the floor and rested. The *Tulsar* suddenly hit a particularly heavy sea. Before he could move, the crates came to life. They were breaking free and crashing all around him.

27

It was getting light when Piet hauled his glistening, oil-skinned bulk up the pitching remains of the steps that led to the bridge. He clung to the temporary safety rail with both hands. 'Pumps not holding!' he bellowed above the shrieking wind at Gerrard. 'Thirty-nine inches of water!'

Gerrard looked at the big Afrikaner in dismay. That amount of water in the bilge sump was serious. 'For Chrissake, Piet – get a party on the hand-pumps!'

'What in hell do you think I've been doing!' Piet yelled back. 'It doesn't make any difference!'

He got no further for Gerrard saw the charging green mountain and screamed out. Piet spun round in time to see the mighty sea hurl itself against the *Tulsar*'s side with stupendous force. The whaling-ship heeled violently and Gerrard had to hang on to Piet to save himself from being tossed into the seething maelstrom below. The foredeck was completely buried under countless tons of raging water. Piet thrust Gerrard against the rail and held him there until the American grabbed a handhold. Gerrard knew this time was going to be different; this time the *Tulsar* was not going to recover – she was going right over.

For endless seconds the two men clung with fear-induced strength to the rail – oblivious of each other in their fierce determination not to be swept to certain death.

Miraculously, the *Tulsar* began to right herself but the motion was too slow – too uneven. Gerrard's feet, finely tuned to the feel of his ship, sensed tremors coursing through the deck plating as though the ship was being pounded by a mighty sledgehammer.

'Cargo's broken loose,' Piet croaked.

There was a momentary lull in the deafening, mind-numbing roar of water through the scuppers. Then Gerrard heard a new sound – heavy crashes from within the ship that could only be caused by the crates breaking loose in the hold. The crashes were perfectly synchronized with the reverberating booms of the massive rolling seas pounding against the hull.

The *Tulsar* did not complete her self-righting but remained listing heavily to port as if she was cowering from the seas that were seeking to destroy her.

Holden grabbed hold of Josephine's arm to prevent her losing her balance on the resturant's sloping floor.

'Listen!' he said. 'Gerrard's going to have to give the order to abandon ship. You've got to get all the passengers on deck now. Get the crew to help. Check every cabin – but get them all out!'

'We can't!' Josephine snapped in anger rather than fear. 'He's got to give the order first. Maybe we'll be okay.'

'Don't be such a crazy bitch! Look at it! Gerrard's got to give the order!'

'What about you?' Josephine demanded.

'I've got something to do, now for God's sake stop arguing and get those passengers out of their cabins!'

Holden left Josephine and made his way to his cabin – steadying himself against the bulkhead as he walked on the sloping floor. He entered his cabin and dragged Kramer's Afu radio-transmitter out from under his bunk. He glanced round the inside of the cabin and guessed that the surrounding steel would screen the signal. He decided that he would have to operate the transmitter in the open.

'Steering's gone!' Brody screamed at Gerrard through the glassless wheelhouse window. The *Tulsar*'s head fell away and a sea rolled up the ramp provided by the hull's starboard flank. The list to port became more pronounced. Jack Cobly appeared below. With the engine-room telegraph and interphone out of action, the radio-operator was relaying messages between the engine-room and the bridge.

'Cooling pipes are bust!' he yelled. 'They've shut down the turbines!'

Brody licked his lips and let the useless wheel spin through his fingers. 'That's it then, boss?'

Gerrard stared straight ahead into the eye of the storm for a few seconds and then roused himself. 'That's it, Sam . . .' He reached for the crew address microphone and remembered that it was no longer there. 'Piet! Pass the word! We're abandoning ship!'

Holden scrambled up the steep slope of the starboard weather-deck and crouched under a lifeboat. He could hear the calls of the crew and passengers as they mustered on the port deck. He released the catches on Kramer's radio-transmitter, opened the lid and tossed the coil of antenna wire over a davit before switching the set on and waiting for it to warm up.

A weak morning sun broke briefly through the cloudbase. It needed only one person to climb to the starboard deck and he would be seen.

A minute passed. The headphone began to hum. Holden's

frozen fingers slipped on the Morse key. He blew on them and grasped the ebonite knob firmly, and started transmitting.

A sea suddenly swept up the port deck and knocked Herbie Lewis off his feet. 'Hang on to the ropes!' Piet yelled at the passengers through a megaphone. 'You all hang on and you'll be okay!'

Josephine helped Herbie Lewis to his feet, then went to the aid of Eli Vanson who was in danger of losing his footing. For once the sugar magnate was not complaining. He, like the rest of the passengers, was cold, wet, and frightened. His wife was hanging on his arm and upsetting his balance.

'It would be easier for Mr Vanson if you held on to the safety line,' Josephine shouted above the wind. But the terrified woman merely stared blankly and tightened her grip on her husband's sleeve. She hardly acknowledged Josephine's presence as Josephine checked that her Mae West lifejacket was properly tied in place.

Piet shambled along the deck holding a clipboard containing sodden papers. 'Have you all the passengers, Miss Britten?'

'All except Mr Holden,' Josephine answered. 'I've no idea where he is.'

'I want all the passengers in the whale-catcher!' shouted Gerrard. 'All passengers to the whale-catcher! Come on! Move! Move!.'

The high-speed launch was luffed out on its davits and lowered until it was level with the listing deck. Two Indian seamen stationed themselves against the bulwark and helped each passenger in turn to scramble off the treacherously-sloping deck and jump down into the launch's open cockpit.

'All passengers except Holden accounted for!' Piet yelled in Gerrard's ear.

'How about the crew?'

'One deckhand and the German prisoner. I'm just going to fetch them.'

Gerrard had forgotten Milland. 'I'll get them, Piet. You stay with the passengers. Tell Colby to start loading the crew into lifeboats.'

•

The Lascar Milland had knocked unconscious was recovering when Gerrard found him. He confessed that he had no idea where Milland was. Gerrard roundly cursed the man and half dragged, half pushed him out of the cabin before going in search of Milland.

Mrs Eli Vanson screamed in terror as the first wave threatened to tip the whale-catcher on to its beam ends. Piet started the launch's engine and swung it away from the stricken *Tulsar*. For the first time Josephine was able to appreciate the magnitude of the disaster that had overtaken the whaling-ship; the *Tulsar* was listing at an angle of more than thirty degrees and was settling deeper in the water by the bow.

Josephine stood up in the cockpit. She had to hold on to the coaming with one hand and shield her eyes from the spray with the other. She pointed at the lifeboat that Jack Colby was loading with crewmen.

'Where's Mr Holden!' she yelled at Piet.

'Cap'n's looking for him. There's nothing to worry about,' the Afrikaner replied, concentrating on keeping the launch's bow aimed into the seas.

Gerrard dropped down the rope into the hold and shone the torch around. He was deafened by the splintering crashes of crates charging into each other and cannoning against the inside of the hull. He leapt clear of a crate that came hurtling straight at him. There was blood on the floor.

'Kurt!'

The *Tulsar* heaved – a movement that provoked a tangle of crates to detach themselves from where they had piled up against the inside of the hull and to go sliding and grating into the middle of the hold. It was then that the beam of light from Gerrard's torch picked out an arm protruding from beneath a mass of crates that had jammed themselves into a corner. Keeping a wary eye on a crate that was threatening to break loose, Gerrard hooked his fingers under the crate that was lying across the trapped man. He waited for the right moment and managed to tip the crate to one side. The trapped man was Milland. The lower half of his body was pinioned under crates and Gerrard knew there was no chance of shifting them. He went down on one knee beside the German.

'Kurt!'

Milland was still breathing. He opened his eyes and stared up at Gerrard. There was no expression in his lustreless eyes. His lips moved. Gerrard bent over him to hear what he was saying.

'She's finished?'

'She's finished, Kurt. You've won.'

Milland turned his head, trying to see the chaos he had caused. What he couldn't see, he could hear. He gave a satisfied smile.

'Funny,' he muttered.

'What is, Kurt?'

The German coughed and grimaced in pain. 'Having . . . having your ship smashed up by gold.'

The *Tulsar* pitched sharply and increased its list. Two crates hurled themselves against the hull within six feet of Gerrard and Milland. A plate burst open and seawater roared through the fissure. In desperation Gerrard again tried to dislodge the crates on top of Milland. After two minutes of frantic effort he gave up and slid to the floor beside Milland to get his breath back.

'Robert . . .'

'Yeah?'

Milland struggled to form a sentence. 'I'm sorry about Cathy.'

'Yeah.'

The crates withdrew from the side of hull in harmony with the *Tulsar*'s motion and hurled themselves back at the fractured steel. More plates buckled outwards, unleashing fresh cascades of water. One side of the hold was now flooded and was a mass of jostling boards from shattered crates. The crates above Milland moved slightly, forcing a cry of pain from his punctured lungs. He moved his hand and caught feebly at Gerrard's pea-jacket, drawing him close.

'Ask him something for me,' Milland croaked.

'Ask who?'

'Holden. Ask him why he didn't contact me . . . why he didn't help.' Milland's voice trailed away. He closed his eyes. His breathing was suddenly more laboured.

'Why should Holden help?' Gerrard cupped some seawater

in his hand and splashed it on Milland's face. 'Kurt! *Why should Holden help you?*'

Milland's lips moved. Gerrard bent right over until his ear was a few inches from Milland's mouth. He heard the dying man say, 'Holden was our second agent . . .'

Holden felt the *Tulsar* give another tremor. The deck was angled at nearly forty degrees as far as he could judge in the driving, blinding spray. He decided that it was time to stop transmitting. He switched the radio off and jerked the antenna wire down from the davit.

'*Holden!*' a voice bellowed behind him.

He turned. Gerrard had an arm hooked round a stanchion and was aiming the Lee Enfield rifle straight at him.

'Just give me one opportunity to blow your head off, Holden, and my God I'll take it.'

'What do you want me to do?' Holden inquired calmly.

The coolness in the Englishman's voice infuriated Gerrard to the point where he was tempted to pull the trigger and kill Holden out of hand. 'Close that case.'

A sea burst over the *Tulsar*'s side and nearly swept the suitcase-radio from Holden's grasp. He closed the lid and watched Gerrard carefully.

'Now what, captain?'

Gerrard gestured with his rifle. 'This way.'

Holden stumbled along the sloping deck towards Gerrard.

'Okay. Now down the deck.'

The flensing deck had become a steep ramp that led straight down into the maddened sea that was raging white against the bulwarks. The whale-catcher with Piet at the helm was dangerously close to the *Tulsar*'s leaning hulk.

'On your ass!' Gerrard shouted.

Holden sat and slithered down the drenched deck. He reached the bulwark and felt Gerrard's weight crash into him. The two men were up to their waists in water. Gerrard was still holding the rifle. He signalled to Piet who then nosed the whale-catcher's wildly pitching bow in as close as he dare to the *Tulsar*.

'Throw the radio first!' Gerrard ordered.

Herbie Lewis was clinging to the whale-catcher's harpoon-gun. He indicated that he was ready to catch the suitcase. Holden tossed it to him. The Canadian caught it neatly and passed it aft.

'Now you!' Gerrard shouted.

Piet edged the whale-catcher nearer while Holden crouched on the bulwark. He judged the narrowing gap and jumped, landing clumsily on the whale-catcher's small foredeck. Herbie Lewis grabbed him by the shirt and the other passengers reached out and dragged him unceremoniously into the cock-pit. As soon as Gerrard was also safely aboard, Piet put the launch hard astern and pulled away from the *Tulsar*.

Josephine knelt beside Holden and helped him into a sitting position.

'Get away from him!' Gerrard yelled. 'No one is to speak to him!'

'Don't be so silly, and don't point that gun at me!' Josephine retorted.

Gerrard hauled Josephine away from Holden and thrust her beside the two Ursuline nuns. 'He's a spy, Miss Britten. And I say that no one is to speak to him.'

'Do as he says, Jo,' said Holden wearily.

Piet steered the whale-catcher towards Jack Colby's lifeboat which was a hundred yards clear of the *Tulsar*. Josephine was about to defy Gerrard but decided against it. Also, the unfam-iliar motion of the smaller boat was beginning to make her seasick.

A tow-line was thrown from Jack Colby's lifeboat and secured to the whale-catcher's Samson post. There was a loud crash from the *Tulsar* and Josephine was astonished to see the side of her hull burst open along a line of rivets. The second crash split the hull plates sideways. It was as if there was a crazed bulldozer inside the ship trying to smash its way out through the hull. She saw Gerrard standing in the stern staring back at his ship's death throes. Two more crashes followed in quick succession. The hull suddenly burst open. A wooden crate fell out of the wound and plunged into the sea. Several more followed and suddenly there was a cascade of splintering crates raining down into the water in one sustained splash.

The stream stopped and it seemed that the *Tulsar* was trying to right itself. But the end came very quickly: two heavy seas battered the ship on to her beam ends. One of her propellers appeared momentarily above the foam and was then lost to sight as the stern slipped under. The bow, still with the fother in place, lifted high above the broken water as if the ship was attempting to climb out of the seas that were trying to engulf her. The bow paused, undecided, and finally abandoned the unequal struggle.

The *Tulsar* sank at 2.55 pm on 30 May 1941.

Piet kicked the gear lever into neutral. Passengers and crew on both craft gazed in silence at the patch of bubbling white water that marked the spot where the *Tulsar* had disappeared.

'What course, cap'n?' Piet asked. He had to repeat the question.

Gerrard shrugged. 'East. North-east. South-east. Christ only knows where we are.'

The Afrikaner spun the wheel until the compass was indicating due east.

The weather began to moderate by 3.30 pm. The wind veered round to the south-west and dropped. By 5 pm the sun was shining and the spirits of the survivors rose as a patch of blue sky expanded from the west.

At 5.10 pm the *Shepherd's Purse* found them.

28

Lieutenant-Commander James Keron, Royal Navy Volunteer Reserve, commanding officer of His Majesty's corvette *Shepherd's Purse*, looked up and smiled warmly as Gerrard was shown into the cramped wardroom. The American's appearance after a night's sleep and a bath and shave had improved decidedly since he had been picked up the previous afternoon.

'Good morning, captain,' said Keron affably, standing and shaking Gerrard's hand. 'Please sit down.' 'My steward's been looking after you, I trust?'

'Fine,' said Gerrard, sitting at the table. He glanced quickly around. Sunlight was streaming into the wardroom. Outside was the hammer and clatter of a shipyard working under wartime pressures.

'Eleven's a little early for pink gins don't you think?' said Keron cheerfully, pouring two cups of coffee from a jug. 'Actually I can't stand anything except beer but I have to keep quiet about it otherwise they'd make me resign my commission.'

'Is this Falmouth, commander?' Gerrard's tone was brusque. He was in no mood for the naval officer's pleasantries.

'But of course. We docked at oh-four-hundred.'

'Why wasn't I woken up earlier?'

'Because you were sleeping like the proverbial top, old boy.'

'Where is everyone?'

'In a local hotel. They're all being well looked after – but no one's allowed to talk to them.'

'And Holden?' Gerrard inquired, sipping his coffee.

'Under arrest, of course, in view of what you told me.'

'What will happen to him?'

'If he is what you say he is, he'll most likely be hanged.' Keron looked up at the door. 'Ah – come in, captain.'

A thin, distinguished-looking man wearing a charcoal-grey suit entered the wardroom. He was carrying a GVIR-crested briefcase.

'Captain Steven Houseman,' said Keron, introducing the stranger to Gerrard.

'If you would kindly leave us for a while, I'd be most grateful,' Houseman said crisply when the introductions were over.

'I'll see that you're not disturbed, sir,' Keron promised, and left Houseman and Gerrard alone.

Houseman sat down and lit a cigarette from a gold lighter. He stared hard at Gerrard for some seconds before speaking. I've just flown down from London, Mr Gerrard, since speaking to Lieutenant-Commander Keron on the phone this morning.'

He opened his briefcase and removed some papers. 'Tell me about the *Tulsar*'s cargo, Mr Gerrard.'

'Two hundred tons of gold,' Gerrard replied, matching Houseman's brusqueness.

Houseman sighed. 'I had hoped that sleep might have modified your imagination, Mr Gerrard.'
Gerrard began to get angry. 'What the hell's that supposed to mean?'
'It's a polite way of calling you a liar, Mr Gerrard. Do you honestly expect anyone to believe such a crazy cock and bull story as the one you told Commander Keron? Do you really think we're such idiots as to fall for it?'
It took all Gerrard's self-control to keep his temper in check. 'If you talk to your Treasury –'
'I have,' Houseman interrupted. 'While I'm not prepared to discuss our gold movements with you, I can tell you that we never have moved gold out of Durban, we don't plan to, and if we did, we most certainly would not move our bullion on a US-registered ship.'
'For Chrissake, why do you suppose the Germans planted two agents on my ship? To count the whales they thought I might catch?'
Houseman smiled thinly. 'Ah, yes. Your two spies. Kramer and Holden.'
'You've seen Kramer's radio, haven't you?'
'Oh yes. Very interesting. Obviously he learned of your plans to sail for England and decided to stowaway. A professional agent. But he's dead.'
Gerrard clenched his fists and unclenched them. He realized that Houseman was deliberately goading him and decided not to give the arrogant Englishman the advantage by losing his temper. 'And there's Holden! A professional if ever there was! I even caught him using Kramer's radio and Kurt Milland himself said that Holden was an agent. What have I got to say to you people to convince you that I'm telling the truth, for Chrissake!'
Houseman closed his briefcase and stood. 'I've a number of inquiries to make, Mr Gerrard. You will be moved to a police cell until I'm ready to talk to you again.'
'I want to see a lawyer,' said Gerrard dully.
'That won't be possible.'
'I've a right, for Chrissake!'
Houseman moved to the door. 'Under the Defence Regulations all the rights are ours. We can hold you indefinitely with-

out trial. And if we do decide to take action, we have the right to hold trials in camera, to pass sentences in camera, and to carry out executions in camera at Exeter Prison or anywhere we choose.'

Gerrard stared back at the cold eyes and suddenly realized that he was scared.

'There's something else I'd like you to think about,' Houseman continued. 'You say the bomb dropped by the German fighter knocked out your radio shack? You were picked up a hundred miles south-west of Land's End after being in lifeboats for just over two hours. Did it not occur to you that you were rescued remarkably quickly? The truth is that two shore-based radio stations were able to pinpoint your position by radio direction-finding from the SOS signals transmitted by Mr Holden.'

Two civilian policemen from the Cornwall Constabulary called for Gerrard an hour later and drove him to Falmouth police station in a black Wolseley. He was escorted to a bare, ten-foot square cell and given a wartime prison-issue meal of fish pie and boiled cabbage.

The coach stopped inside the wired compound and a smartly turned-out corporal in khaki battledress hauled the coach's door open.

'Everyone out, please, ladies.'

Josephine followed the two Ursuline nuns down the steps and turned to help Mrs Eli Vanson.

'Where are we?' Josephine asked the corporal.

'Somewhere in England, miss,' the NCO replied as he signed the WRNS driver's clipboard. 'If you'd all follow me please.'

The bride who had been separated from her husband in Falmouth burst into tears for what Josephine estimated was the twentieth time since the long drive had begun.

'For God's sake someone else look after her before she sets Mrs Vanson off,' said Josephine irritably to no one in particular.

The nuns gathered protectively around the girl and managed to calm her.

'This way please, ladies,' said the corporal impatiently,

mounting the steps leading to a long, wooden hut.

Josephine was the last to enter the depressing building. As she did so, she glanced back. There was something familiar about the outline of the magnificent building that rose above the trees to dominate the skyline. It was a building she had seen in books and movies. And then she realized what it was: Windsor Castle.

'My God,' she said to herself. 'We must be in Windsor Great Park.'

Houseman didn't see Gerrard again until 6.30 pm. His manner was even more frosty than it had been in the morning. He sat at the table opposite Gerrard in the police station interview-room and opened his briefcase. He came straight to the point.

'We've been in touch with your agent in Durban, Mr Gerrard. According to him the *Tulsar* was loaded with two hundred tons of lead on 23 February last in Durban. We've also checked with the mining corporation at Broken Hill in Northern Rhodesia and they have confirmed that they despatched a trainload of lead ingots to Durban on 21 February.'

Gerrard looked bored. 'That was the cover for the gold that Holden fixed. No one else but he and I knew about it.'

'And the Germans you say he told about it,' Houseman pointed out, his voice tinged with sarcasm.

'Have you talked to him?' Gerrard asked.

'Oh yes. His references are impeccable. He even had an identity card on him.' Houseman's smile was icy. 'In fact, of all of you, he was the only one entitled to enter the country.'

The interview dragged on for two hours, going over the same questions with Houseman dissecting the same answers. At 8.30 pm Houseman stood up and returned his papers to his briefcase. 'The issues are quite simple as far as I'm concerned, Mr Gerrard. On two occasions you used your vessel to conduct a personal vendetta against U-boats – highly commendable as far as His Majesty's Government is concerned. What is not commendable is that you should claim that you were carrying gold belonging to this country in what we can only construe as an attempt to pressurize the government into underwriting the loss of your ship as a result of your foolhardy ventures.'

'For Chrissake, will you listen!' Gerrard suddenly shouted. 'If you do nothing about Holden you're turning a German spy loose in this country! And if all the English are as stupid as you, then I guess you're getting no more than you deserve.'

Houseman regarded Gerrard with contempt. 'I'm sorry, Mr Gerrard, but it hasn't worked. We've checked Mr Holden's credentials most carefully. He's a top civil servant at the Treasury. He's never been to Germany nor has he ever had contact with Germans or pro-German sympathizers during his frequent visits to the United States.'

Gerrard realized the uselessness of further argument with the arrogant Englishman. Houseman had made up his mind and nothing would make him change it. 'Okay,' he said tiredly. 'So what's going to happen to me?'

'You're to be deported back to the United States on the first available ship, Mr Gerrard. In view of the fact that you have disposed of two U-boats, it has been decided not to bring charges against you.' Houseman chuckled. 'You see, Mr Gerrard? We're not ungrateful.'

The interviewing officer smiled at Josephine. 'No, Miss Britten, I promise there are no more forms to fill in but I would be grateful if you would kindly answer a few questions about your background.'

The next ten minutes seemed totally unreal to Josephine; the interviewing officer politely asked the most unbelievable yet searching questions. He wanted to know what her father's nickname had been for her when she was a little girl; he wanted to know the colour of the outside of the hardware store and even the name of the nearest delicatessen. Each time Josephine answered a question, the interviewing officer made a pencil mark that was neither a tick or a cross on a long, typed list. The next question was in complete contrast to the preceeding questions.

'Thank you, Miss Britten. Could you tell me what cargo the *Tulsar* was carrying?'

'Lead.'

'Thank you. How was it carried?'

'In large crates.'

'I see. Did you see the crates being loaded aboard?'

'No.'

'Did you ever see the crates?'

'No. Yes! When they burst out of the ship's side before it went down.'

'But you never saw the contents of the crates?'

'No.'

Josephine was about to ask the purpose of the unusual questions but the interviewing officer suddenly closed his file.

'Thank you, Miss Britten.' He opened the drawer of his desk and placed a buff envelope in front of Josephine. 'I presume you're anxious to return to New York?'

'That is a classic understatement,' said Josephine icily.

The interviewing officer looked sympathetic. 'A passage has been booked to New York for you, Miss Britten, and all the other passengers on the *Tulsar*. I'm afraid that we can't say when because sailing dates are confidential. You've all been booked into a London hotel in the meantime.

'You mean that I'm free to go? To leave here?'

'Yes, of course.' The interviewing officer handed Josephine another envelope. 'Don't forget this. There are some temporary identity papers in here. A bus is due soon to take you all to your hotel, although I understand that there's a young man waiting for you outside.'

The young man turned out to be Ralph Holden.

29

All the passengers from the *Tulsar* were gathered at Euston station waiting for the announcement that heralded which platform the Liverpool train would be leaving from. Josephine sat on a station seat next to Holden. They had been waiting an hour, saying little and watching the endless streams of men and women in uniform passing to and fro. Mrs Eli Vanson arrived with her husband in tow and gathered about her a knot of passengers anxious to hear the latest gossip.

'My dears,' she was saying. 'You know how difficult it is

trying to find anything out? Well, I heard that it's an American ship – a proper ocean liner with restaurants and bars and a swimming-pool and a hairdresser's salon . . .'

'Is it a proper liner, Ralph?' Josephine asked.

'So I understand.'

'Do you think you'll ever be able to give me straight answers to straight questions?'

'I don't suppose so. But I might.'

'There you go again. No wonder London is a hotbed of rumours.'

Holden laughed and then became serious. 'Jo . . .'

She sensed his hesitancy and looked sharply at him. 'What's the matter?'

'A message came through this morning about your father.'

'From my mother?'

'Yes.'

Josephine closed her eyes for a few seconds. 'He's dead, isn't he?'

'Two days ago . . . I'm very sorry, Jo.'

'I did my best to get to him in time.'

Holden covered her hand with his. 'He'd understand.'

'Mr Holden?' said a cold, impersonal voice.

Holden looked up at the stranger. 'Yes?'

'Houseman,' said the stranger stiffly. 'Captain Steven Houseman. I've been instructed to deliver a certain gentleman into your charge.'

The two men inspected each other's identity cards and shook hands. 'I've been expecting you, captain,' said Holden. 'Where is he?'

Houseman beckoned to three men who were standing some fifty yards away. They came forward. Josephine gave a gasp of surprise when she saw them.

The man in the middle was Gerrard.

It was when Josephine left the reserved compartment on the train to see if the restaurant car was emptying that Holden hooked his hands together at the back of his neck and grinned at Gerrard.

'I suppose I owe you some sort of explanation. The trouble

was that you were so eager to shop me to anyone who would listen after we were picked up. It was something I hadn't quite bargained for. Not that I blame you, of course.'

'Just who the hell are you working for, Holden?'

'The winning side.'

'For Chrissake, can't you ever give a straight answer?'

'You're the second person to make that complaint today.'

'Will you answer me one thing? Just what did we carry in the *Tulsar*'s hold?'

'What did Houseman tell you?'

'He said it was lead.'

'He was right.'

Gerrard stared at the Englishman. 'Then for Chrissake why did you tell me that it was gold?'

'And I told the Germans we would be carrying the gold. I met Kramer in Cape Town before we sailed and convinced him that we'd be shipping it on the *Tulsar*. The Germans didn't need much convincing that someone would be carrying it because they knew it was in South Africa and they knew that we had to get it out somehow.'

'So it's still in South Africa?'

'No. It was collected from Cape Town on 10 January by a United States cruiser. The USS *Louisville* was the real transporter of Churchill's gold. It went direct to America to pay our cash and carry debts. All $42 millions' worth of the stuff – the last of our reserves. There's not so much as a single gold bar in the Bank of England vaults now. It's all gone.' Holden paused and gazed out of the window at the passing scenery. 'Not that we need it any more,' he continued. 'Roosevelt has pushed his Lend-Lease bill through Congress and now we're getting all the munitions we need for nothing. Roosevelt has done exactly what he said he would do – he's eliminated the dollar sign from the conduct of the war.'

Gerrard's face was white with anger. 'So I was the sucker who was the decoy, huh?'

'No. You were more than that. We thought that if we deliberately fed the Germans with the story that the *Tulsar* – a fast ship – was carrying the gold, then there was a chance that we might be able to lure out some of their big ships to hunt you down. God knows why they initially sent a U-boat out. That's why I was anxious to knock it out of the hunt. Of course, we never dreamed that we would winkle the *Bismarck* out of her hidey-hole.'

There was a long silence.

'Jesus bloody Christ,' Gerrard muttered at length.

'Kramer turning up on board the *Tulsar* was something else I hadn't bargained for,' Holden admitted. He smiled. 'It just goes to show – the best-laid plans and all that . . .'

Gerrard nodded slowly. The pieces dropped into place. Suddenly everything made sense. 'How many knew about the plan?'

'Less than six including myself.'

'But not Captain Houseman?'

'Especially not Captain Houseman,' said Holden with feeling. 'No imagination.'

Josephine entered the compartment. 'I managed to book a table for three in ten minutes,' she said triumphantly. She frowned and looked at Holden and Gerrard in turn. 'Hey – you two. Have I missed out on something?'

It seemed to Josephine that there were as many people crowded on to the pier to say farewell to the ocean liner as there were passengers gathering round the gangways to go aboard. Already the streamers were spooling down from the towering decks into dozens of eager, outstretched hands.

'Where's your baggage, Ralph?' Josephine inquired.

'I haven't got any, Jo.'

'But you must have something. You can't go like that.'

'I'm not going to New York.'

Josephine stared blankly at Holden. 'But I thought . . .'

Holden shook his head. 'I came along to say goodbye, Jo. Why? What did you expect?'

A porter seized Josephine's two small bags that she had purchased in London and piled them on to a trolley.

'I don't know,' said Josephine slowly 'I thought . . . hell, it doesn't matter what I thought.'

Holden took her arm and guided her to the gangway that was boarding first-class passengers. 'I've got your address in New

York,' he pointed out. 'So if I do ever go . . .' He left the sentence unfinished.

'Is that likely?'

'It all depends on President Roosevelt.'

'Why?'

'The Crown agents have an office in Manhattan. If America enters the war I'll be posted there.' He smiled down at Josephine and took her hands in his. 'I made them promise me that much.'

The gap between the pier and the liner slowly widened and the thousands of paper streamers linking the great ship to the land tightened, and then snapped. The wind scattered the broken strands and send them tangling among the cheering crowds lining the quay and the ship's rails.

Josephine waved frantically but Holden was no longer looking up at her. The last she saw of the Englishman in his own country was his fair hair as he pushed through the crowds, making his way back to the terminal building.